Cycles of
Norse Mythology

Tales of the Æsir Gods

ACORN BOOKS

GLENN SEARFOSS

First published in 2019 by
Acorn Books
www.acornbooks.co.uk

Acorn Books is an imprint of
Andrews UK Limited
www.andrewsuk.com

ISBN of Hardback edition: 9781789820829
ISBN of Paperback edition: 9781789820713
ISBN of ePub edition: 9781789820690
ISBN of PDF edition: 9781789820706

I dedicate this book to my wife, Cynthia, whose constructive criticisms helped drive its scope, and to all our dogs, past and present (Hermes, Bear, Shenoah, Portia, Orchid, Puck, Cruiser, Little Bit, and Buri), whose patient companionship saw me through the project.

Contents

Acknowledgements

I gratefully acknowledge the translators, scholars, authors, and artists whose many and varied contributions over the centuries and into the modern day have made the subject of Norse Mythology accessible. Without their efforts and critical interpretations in this field, this book would not have been possible.

A special acknowledgement of the works:

- *The Agricola and the Germainia* by Publis Cornelius Tacitus. Translated by H. Mattingly.

- *The Danish History* by Saxo Grammaticus. Translated by Oliver Elton.

- *The Heimskringla: A History of Norse Kings* by Snorri Sturleson. Translations by Erling Monsen and Samuel Laing.

- *The Poetic Edda / The Elder Edda* by Saemund Sigfusson. Translations by Benjamin Thorpe, Lee M. Hollander, and Carloyne Larrington.

- *The Prose Edda / The Younger Edda* by Snorri Sturleson. Translations by Rasmus B. Anderson, Jesse L. Byock, Jean I. Young, and I. A. Blackwell.

- *Teutonic Mythology* by Jacob Grimm. Translated by James Steven Stallybrass.

- *Teutonic Mythology – Gods and Goddesses of the Northland* by Victor Rydberg. Translation by Rasmus B. Anderson.

- *Ibn Fadlān's Journey to Russia: A Tenth-Century Traveler from Baghdad to the Volga River*. Translated by Richard Frye.

Cycles of
Norse Mythology

Cycle 1: Prophecy

In Pursuit of Wisdom

Many paths I traveled, made my road go forth. How the world will be? How the days will be? How to triumph over others? These things I desired to know.

Young I was, fair haired, with smooth cheeks, when first I wandered the long weary ways, eagerly seeking understanding; for wisdom is seldom bound inside four walls. Kin, I visited—those dwelling in far-off lands—that I might profit from their knowledge. The famous son of Bolthor honored my request. He taught me nine spells for free, but I hungered for more.

Now he posited a charge for his wisdom. For the mere price of an eye he offered me a draught from his well that I might see farther, become wiser. Cool was the drink poured from Odrerir that fired my mind with color, inspired my thoughts. Then I began to bloom, to thrive, and to be wise. Word came to me from word, deed came to me from deed; much I came to understand. For a second drink, I found the price he asked too great.

And my wisdom grew.

To test my endurance of mind and body, I hung nine days from the ancient tree. Deprived of food, parched in thirst, I gave myself over to me. With screams on my lips, I drew runes from the depths. Brought to the Æsir the sacred knowledge of how to carve them, how to stain them, and how to work with them.

And my wisdom grew.

Widely I traveled. Much I experienced. Eager to test my power, I challenged wise foes in ancient knowledge, wagered my head in contests of wisdom, and so learned the company kept in far-off halls. The one who knows nothing yet speaks loudly becomes a point of ridicule, a laughing stock when seated among the wise. Cautious, I spoke my knowledge only when needful; otherwise, I remained silent. By such prudence, I preserved my head while others lost theirs.

And my wisdom grew.

In my wanderings, I learned the languages of birds: the wren, the starling, the hawk, the eagle. But the cleverest of all, ravens, the black birds that range across the lands, calling to each other as they wing through the sky, from them I learned the most.

Like men they stand sentries to warn of impending danger. Like men they share knowledge of what they have seen, what they have heard. Like men they feast in the field after a hard-fought battle.

Two I called from the dark flocks circling high above that I might more easily learn from them what happens across the nine worlds. Munin, I called one for the clarity of mind. Hugin, I called the other for the swiftness of thought. Each day they wing across the wide world. Each evening they return to perch on my shoulders and whisper into my ears all they have seen.

And my wisdom grew.

Faring along beaten paths, for fun I hung my clothes on a signpost beside the road. It was reckoned a man by travelers, who dared not approach for fear of the stranger. So, I learned the power of disguise through the wary perceptions of others. Naked, a man is considered naught. The clothes he wears, the actions he takes, the honor he bears, and his conduct among others, are the trappings by which he is perceived, the name by which he becomes known.

And my wisdom grew.

Many roads I traveled into countless lands. Numerous roles I played that I might learn. I became known by various names, some only the winds can pronounce.

Among the gods, I am called Vifud, the wayfarer. Vak is ever alert. Hroptatyr rules as the god over all other gods. Omi heralds the crashing sound of shouted commands. On a whim, Oski grants wishes. Gondlir bears the wand of power. Hâr tells of my one eye. Harbard marks my graybeard. Ud notes my rank.

In assembly, they call me Gagnráth for sage advice given free of guile. Fjolsvith recognizes the wisdom that is mine to share. Thrôr enjoys inciting strife among advisers. At council table, Havi holds the highest seat.

Some Jotun know me as Bolverk, the bale worker, while for others I am Bölverkr, the evildoer.

Mariners, farmers too—for produce must be shipped, call me Ialk, lord of boatloads; Farma-God, the god of cargoes; Kialar, guider of keels; and Farmatýr, the burden god.

Prisoners call me Hapta-God, Hanga-God, and Gallows Lord.

Men know me as Odin, the Alfodur, and Ygg, the terrible one. Ofnir delights in entangling others in a web of words. Sidhott draws attention to my wide-brimmed hat. Sidskegg tells of my broad beard, Bileyg the far sight of my one good eye. Gangleri travels the wide worlds. As Thekk I find welcome in all homes.

In war, I clear the field as Heriar, the leader; Herian, the fighter; and Vidur, the tree of battle. Grímnir, I am called for my battle mask. Hialmberi, the helmet wearer, is found on any field where men contest with weapons. Fimblultyr accounts for my mighty strength that drives foes to their knees.

My delight in battle earned me the names Sigfodur, the war father; Herteit, the war merry; Glapsvid, the maddener; and Báleyg for the flame that burns bright in my eye when the fight is joined—for defeat in battle starts always with the eyes. Hnikar, I hold for my skill with a spear. As Atríth, I charge the field on horseback. Valorous warriors call me, Herfodur, the father of hosts, and Valfodur, father of the slain.

As a seeker of truth, I am Sanngetal. As a speaker of truth, I am Sath. Vegtam clears the way. Fiolnir notes my skill at concealment. Skilfing marks my ability to shake some men awake, while Svafnir lulls others into timeless sleep.

By these and many other names, I accomplished great deeds.

And my wisdom grew.

I listened carefully to the talk of runes, heeded the candid speech of others; good counsel they offer to an open mind capable of discernment. I became careful with words and thoughts, for each have their own power; one long suffers the consequences when either is ill-chosen. So, I learned not to reproach another for what is common among all. Many are made foolish by that mighty desire.

And my wisdom grew.

In my youth, I was quick to give and to forget affronts. As dry straw kindled on a fire flares hot, then dies to a dust of white ash that is carried away by a breath of wind, so, too, flashed my anger. As I grew older I became deliberate in both, measured as red-short iron in the forge: slow to heat, slow to cool, intense in between.

And my wisdom grew.

I sought power that I might direct my fate, to protect my kin and everything we had created. Harsh were the lessons learned. Now my heart is seldom happy. For pain that teaches, falls drop-by-drop on the heart. Endless, remorseless, it erodes shields, eating away reserve until, despite our will, comes the awful grace of wisdom.

To know one's fate begs caution. The cost of wisdom is more than an eye. Wisdom feeds on that which is within. Innocence falls before its relentless hunger, as does integrity and honor, until all that remains is purpose.

Hlebard's Hall

"But you just returned," Frigg sniffed, folding her robes about her legs. With a quick flip of an edge she jerked the pleats straight over her knees. "Must you leave again so soon?"

One eye flared bright over the goblet rim as Odin drained the cup of wine at his side. "I must be certain." He upended the cup on the table. "She is the only one who can tell me." His tongue flicked to clear wine droplets from his mustache as a sly grin crinkled his brow. "And, too, from such a venerable fount, I may gain information to expand my wisdom."

Pouting lips became a hard line as Frigg struggled to conceal the flush of anger that twisted her features. "Sometimes, I think you care more for your precious wisdom than you do for me."

Odin fumbled the straps of his boots crisscross about his legs, binding them tight for hard travel. "I take advantage of the situation, that is all."

He paused, chewing at the corner of his mustache. Her anger faded as she caught the worry reflected in his eye. "I learned much from the straying mind of Hlebard. Vast knowledge he held, but time and isolation had scattered his wits. Alone, I followed an overgrown trail choked with fir trees that wound to his dim hall huddled beneath a towering shelf of rock. Concealed in deep shadow, I would have passed it by unseen save for a single light wavering through the doorway.

Exhausted from trekking all day, I called out asking for a place to rest. Three times I called out before the etin's face, lined with the weight of years and nearly the color of the rock beneath which he lived, poked around the doorpost. It was my first glimpse of Hlebard, the ages-old giant in whose mind resides the cluttered history of his race, fragmented memories spanning eons.

I sought to befriend him, but barely had time to give my name as Thekk before he crowed out his own name and beckoned me into his hall. I trudged up the hill, cautiously gauging the entry and the nature of my host. All the while his bird eyes, bright with the madness of seclusion, followed my every step. When I neared, his face split with a wide, snaggletooth grin. I find no shame in admitting that I jumped a bit when he nearly yanked the door off its moorings for me to enter.

I stepped into the gloom of a once-great hall. Wavering flames from the hearth fire struggled against darkness that crowded in from all sides, but it offered enough light to see. Tattered remnants of grand tapestries drooped from the walls, while others, torn from their moorings by the weight of ages, huddled in piles on the floor. Shelves littered with tarnished pots, platters, and intricately wrought cups peeped from dim recesses. A thick layer of dust coated everything except the bench on which he sat and the narrow paths he paced across the floor.

You could see how his world had collapsed by the depth of dust layering the paths within his home. The oldest were only noticeable as light swales amid the centuries of fallen dust. The layers became thinner, the courses deeper along those most often used. There were far too few paths showing the regular shuffle of footprints.

With a sweep of his arm, he cleared a space on the table, shoving unwashed dishes and an assortment of old clothing to the floor. Coughing from the dust that rose to cloud the air, he beckoned me to sit. As I gingerly took a seat, he thrust a mug of ale into my hands, then settled himself on the bench across from me and began talking. We spent the entire evening deep in conversation. There was no contest of knowledge or danger of losing my head. The old giant simply wanted to talk, to revel in the company of a guest.

Starved for companionship, the ancient paid no heed to what he said. The course of our discussions drifted as a river in flood that leaves its channel to flow unchecked in all directions. At times, we followed the same track, at other times, well... I could not tell. Still I gleaned much of worth.

There were moments when his voice raged with angry squeals. It was then I learned from him an uncomfortable truth: the cold, enduring hate of etins who would forever deny our rights, an entire race dedicated to destroying all we have created. Steeped in the wisdom of his people, he recounted the intent of frost to regain the nine worlds and recover the body of Ymir at all costs." Odin hunched over to finish knotting the bindings of his boots. "Though garbled amid the ramblings of his mind, his words held dire warnings for our clan. I travel now to assure myself of their truth."

Frigg snatched a thick staff from beside the high seat, its length contorted with serpents and gripping beasts. Runes of power used by giants when the world was young circled it from tip to knob. "Then take the staff he gave you. Its carvings offer support for one on a difficult trail. With it in hand, you are certain to return unharmed."

Shaking his grizzled head side to side, Odin gently took the staff from Frigg. "The mind of an old man is like the apple tree. Fruit, bud, blossom, and dead leaves of all the years of the past flourish together. Old and new and that gone out of remembrance, all three are there." He ran his fingers along its length, tracing the intricate forms covering its surface. They lingered a moment on the image of Fan, the serpent of eternity whose head formed the knob.

"From the doddering old fool, I gained this staff of great power, a parting gift of his ailing mind. It was easy to guide his wandering thoughts to the proprieties of hospitality. As I prepared to leave I reminded him of his duty as host. At my suggestion, we traded staffs. I gave him a limb hacked from a willing yew. He gave me this cherished possession. I consider it a good bargain."

Odin propped the staff against the seat, stood up stretching his back so the joints popped. "A staff is only useful to the walking traveler. This trip I ride; it would only get in my way. My sturdy mount, a warm cloak, a trusted blade at my waist, and ready wits are all I need for this journey."

He glanced around. Spying his cloak draped across a nearby bench, he picked it up, swung it around his shoulders, and then knotted the cowl beneath his chin. "I take a dark and dangerous road; one I traveled long ago as a mourner to her burial. Planted in the frozen earth, she will not have moved. I will call her from her rest and make her speak. She will tell me what I want to know."

Journey to Niflhel

Whirls of drifting snow scattered before driving hooves as a powerful man with thick shoulders and scar-gnarled hands, hunched atop a cloud-gray stallion, dodged across a landscape of jagged boulders nestled amid mottled humps of ancient ice. Alone on his mount, he followed the path of the dead far into the depths of darkness, where fires of dwarf-built forges glinted as specks of light and the warmth of the sun was a distant memory.

Already the pair had passed through Helgrind—the great golden gate of the dead. As they thundered across the Gjoll Bridge, Modgud, ward of the bridge, raised a hand to halt their advance. They brushed by her without slowing, their passage rattling the overpass built for the tread of spirits lighter than air.

With agile step, they paralleled the course of a raging river choked with blocks of blade-sharp ice that tumbled from high in the Nidaveller Mountains. The river's hungry current ate away at the ice gripping the banks. Across its wide expanse there were air holes, fissures, and much open water.

Horse and rider scrambled along the crests of desolate ridges where screaming winds trailed the rumble of collapsing cornices of snow. The ghosts of what will be, haunted the air as the pair crashed their way through the white drifts, straining for each length, while the rider's breath puffed a stream of soft curses.

The rider drew back on the reins, slowing his mount as the path narrowed to a gash in the face of a rock wall. Glaring into the hollow darkness, he clapped the horse twice on the shoulder. The stallion snorted back at the familiarity. "Take it slow my friend. There is no way around. We must go through. The dead may not care about bruised limbs, but I do."

They wound through the corridor of towering rock, each step carefully placed amid rubble clogging the path. Dark skeletons of firs frowned down from the ridges above. The trees, long stripped of their needles by cold incessant winds, seemed to reach out to each other for support, their bare branches clawing the air.

Winds bayed, hunting in packs rushing through the cleft, their steady pressure from behind driving the pair onward. At times, the rider dismounted that they might squeeze around boulders blocking the way. At others, he rode high in the saddle with rock walls nearly brushing his legs. As the pass broadened, they broke into the open, glad to be free of the confining walls.

"We've made it." Thumping the horse on the neck, he turned a weather eye skyward. "Now if this just holds..." As he spoke, the low ceiling cracked wide, shaking curtains of sleet from black, overlapped clouds. The mix, caught by driving winds, spattered across the ground, freezing wherever it touched.

Drawing his hood to shield his face from the stinging spray, the traveler leaned forward, shouting into the ear of his mount. "We are on a fool's quest perhaps, but we will finish it. The sooner we are done, the sooner we return to the warmth of home." Nudging the stallion to speed with his heels, the great horse whinnied his agreement. Stretching out into a ground-eating stride, he swept along a wide track to a massive gate of webbed iron that blocked the mountain pass.

At Nagrind, the gate to Niflhel, the rider stood up in his saddle. "Open the gate!" His harsh command rang along the frosted iron. "I, Odin, Alfodur of the Æsir, son of Bor, son of Burl, he born of the rime of Ymir, demand you let me pass." Ice-crusted hinges squealed in protest as the Na-Gates swung wide, allowing horse and rider to cross into the bitter realms of the niflgódur, the twice dead damned by the namaeli.

The weight of darkness grew with each step as the pair turned their steps north along a cold-blighted path that twisted through the ancient funeral grounds of the etin. The horse's eight hooves thrummed across a plain scattered with burial mounds wreathed in white, their caps blasted clear by fierce winds. Thick as stars in the sky, they covered the steppe, the furthest mounds fading into darkness behind a curtain of swirling snow.

The rider directed his mount toward a fortress hall whose dim walls rose out of the plain. Along the east wall of Eljudnir—the shadowy hall of the dead—where bare ground peeped through thin patches of gray snow, the traveler dismounted at a narrow mound crusted with frost and unmarked, save by time.

Prying a stone loose from the frozen earth, he scratched runes into the hard soil of the mound, mal runes to loosen a lifeless tongue. Using a sharp blade, he drew blood from his forearm, a shallow cut to bleed, but not damage. Fumbling the knife back into its sheath, he used two fingers to daub blood into the shallow grooves.

About the spot, he poured drink offerings: mare's milk mixed with the labor of bees, a drought of strong ale brewed in the land of summer sun, and cool water drawn from Urd's well. Over the mound, he sprinkled a handful of barley grown in the sunlit fields of Idavoll. Then three times he called the wise woman from her grave, shouting his commands into the frosty air. "Arise you, who know the stories, those ancient and those yet unlived. Arise you, whose wise counsel once guided the lives of etins and gods. Arise you, for whom the past and future are but sides of the same coin, and the present a passing moment."

A misty form crawled from the frozen earth as smoke from a smudged fire struggles into the air. It turned lazily upon itself, became thicker, took on shape, until an old woman, bent and frail, little more than the weight of her bones, wavered before the thick-robed visitor.

She was frightful to look upon. After so many years, little remained of her once full form. Her cheekbones were massed with knots of blackened skin that had dried under the intense frost. Her eyes had receded until only dark sockets remained, empty pits that swallowed all they turned to.

Spectral hands lifted to examine both cheeks, trembled as they caressed a withered brow, and lightly fingered tufts of grizzled gray hair that clung to a skull wrapped with shrunken, ice-burned skin. Tenderly, they stroked a long nose, twisted from the cold.

The hands raised before lightless pits, turned front to back, their blue veins popped, the skin wrinkled as dry wood whose grain rises when left too long in the wind. Bit-by-bit, they wandered down shoulders to pat the wasted body concealed beneath the funeral cloak, its once-full flesh now hollowed by the dry ravaging of cold. A soft sigh escaped parched lips, the sound snatched away by a chill breeze that swirled snow across the frozen ground.

Deep, dark pits, scoured of life, turned to face the cloaked visitor, holding his gaze while withered lips cracked in voice. "Who calls me to stand here, a shadow of my former self? Who dares disturb my rest?"

The traveler spoke, his gravelly voice pitched for dead ears. "I, Odin, Alfodur of the Æsir, have restored your tongue and given form to your litr that I might partake of your wisdom. In life, you knew past and future. In death, you took your knowledge to the grave. I desire this knowledge."

The aged spirit stared back, her hollow eyes echoing the emptiness of the land. "I know you Odin, the ancient sacrifice. You seek wisdom, but, as you well know, wisdom exacts a toll that takes many forms.

The present is a crust of harsh realities, familiar and easy to accept until the crust is shattered, exposing them for all to see. While dredging up the buried past in search of knowledge exposes candid, uncomfortable truths that are often difficult to admit.

Future knowledge is a terrible twin-edged blade. The front stroke is certain, a strong forward thrust that brings relief in knowing what is to come. But the backstroke, that terrifying rebound, brings fear of changing what has become known.

This is the price of my knowledge. Are you willing to pay?"

Odin raised himself to his full height until he towered over the ancient shade. "Never have I run from a challenge," he slapped a hand against his chest, "or failed to pay a debt once incurred. I have always sought the priceless wisdom of knowledge, regardless the cost to myself. I demand that you declare the stories of gods and etins, those you remember from the first to the last."

The gray head tottered on a thin neck. "Very well, you have called me." Wasted arms folded back into long-familiar positions about the spare form. "This time I obey your summons.

I was born the daughter of honorable Jotun in the early days of Ymir's settlement. Well I remember those who raised me from infant to adult. My gift became apparent at an early age, was nurtured, flowered, and grew strong: to know the past that was, the present that is, to see far ahead events that will be. Much I came to know, a powerful seeress with clear sight. So much swam before my vision that I often wished I were blind.

To know the last, the first cannot be hidden. To look into the seeds of time and say which will grow and which will not, requires a shrewd eye and sharp ear. Listen closely to the memories I recount; I will not speak of them again. For ages past and ages yet to come their weave holds much that is important."

The seeress turned into the blustery winds and stretched out her arms to embrace the world. "Attention I ask from all the sacred children of Rig, those living and those not yet born. Hear me as I sing of time and the price of purpose!"

At the Dawn of Time

"At the dawn of time the sun was nowhere seen. No stars marked the heavens. No sky stretched above. No earth spread below to give support. There were no ocean waters to foam or rush. No air to breathe. No heat or cold. No form to grasp. There were no directions to mark the way, only a vast emptiness swelling with promise.

Seeds of purpose filled this void, innumerable in number, bottomless in sum. In eternal motion, carried along by their own weight, they diffused through the vacant space. Quickened by intent, they sped through the emptiness, a strange storm of primal seeds that collided, fell apart, then drew together again in continuous conflict. But as like attracts like so, too, the primal seeds united into large masses. Those drew into greater masses, grew dense enough to separate their members while settling out their weightier parts.

Hot grew one region where the seeds clustered together, moving faster as they drew close. The space filled with raging flames as heat in a forge beats out fire. Muspellsheim was born from this furnace. In this world of blistering red sands, the stench of sulfur fills the heated air, rocks burn, and waters steam.

Cold grew opposite the flame where the seeds clustered together, moving slower as they drew close. In heavy gloom without light, the space chilled from the lack of warmth. Niflheim was born, a dark world of intense cold, seething snow-fed rivers, its sky choked with sleet. A wintry realm devoid of life.

Between the two lay Ginnungagap, where the seeds of purpose traveled wide paths. Here lay the remains of the once-great void, a chaos of empty thought filled with the promise of intent.

The great rivers of Niflheim poured their strength into this silent, vacant realm. Eleven in number, they share a name these venom cold rivers: Elivagar they are called. Here the chill waters of Svol kept pace with the trembling flow of Gunnthra and outran the steady pull of Sylg, whose deep channel swallows all. The noisy waters of Fimbulthul roared challenge against the turbulent stream of Gjoll and muted the ceaseless din of Hrid's raging snowstorm of cold, white water. As the broad waters of Vid ambled along their way, the waters of Fjorm tumbled in their eager rush to destination, while Ylg swelled from its bed to spread its depth across the void. The flashing waters of Leitpr danced along frozen banks, as the fearsome crush of Slid, choked with sharp-edged blocks of ice, gouged out banks, scouring new channels.

The ragged waves of the Elivagar Rivers broke far from their source, spread their courses deep into the void, freezing to their beds in the bitter cold. Slowly, the great emptiness filled with ice, built up layer-on-layer, as snow fallen on a mountain glacier deposits new beds that increase its thickness.

In Muspellsheim, sparks escaped from deep fissures in the rocks. The radiant embers leapt into the air, spreading their heat to warm the hoarfrost of Ginnungagap and adorn the heavens with stars. In the center of the void swirled mist and hard, whipped rain. Where ice from the frozen rivers met the glowing embers cast out from the fiery world, it was mild as a windless day."

The Start of Life

"Where warm ember-laden winds met swirling frost, droplets condensed into a thick sludge that settled into the likeness of a man. Born was Ymir, the roarer, the wise giant, ancestor to all giants. Aurgelmir, his descendants call him, the mud bellower.

Young were the years when Ymir made his settlement among the cold tongues of the Elivagar. With outspread arms and booming voice, he named it Utgarda, the outer enclosure. Stretching himself to his full length in the void, the great giant sought to make himself at home. But blistering flames plagued his head, while congealing frosts chilled his bare feet. In sleep, he sweat.

Great beings emerged from his body. From under his left arm grew a male and female; Mimir and Bestla they were called. His feet begot a six-headed son, one foot with the other; Rimgrimner, he was called. From these sprang the clans of giants: one of high birth, one of low, one of life, the other of killing frost and fire. In Utgarda, they spread wide their seed.

The icy rime continued to drip, the liquid congealing until it formed the great cow, Audhumla. She stood in the gentle breeze, lowing out across the great void. From her udders ran four rivers of milk, the seed of life, vital sustenance for the giant and his offspring.

To eat, each day the great cow licked salt from the rough surface of the frozen rivers. She worked her tongue leisurely across the ice, melting it with each pass. On the evening of the first day a man's hair appeared in the frost. On the evening of the second day the man's head cleared the surface. On the evening of the third day his body lay free of the ice. Burl was this man: huge, strong, and beautiful to look upon.

He fathered a son, Bor, he called him, who took as wife, Bestla, a daughter of Ymir. Three sons she birthed. The first they named Odin, for as he grew he seemed to be everywhere; Uth others called him. The second they named Vili, tall, white, with a lanky build; Hoenir others called him, the long-legged one. The third they named Ve, for the cleverness of his hands; Lodur others called him, the Flame of the hearth. From these three grew the clan of the Æsir."

As a branch weighted by the season's frost dips to touch the ground, the seeress bent to trail her fingers through the snow. The mist of their passage made no mark. She seemed to sag, ready to disappear back into the earth, before pushing herself erect and returning her attention to Odin.

Snow spiraling about the ancient specter lifted a dusting of ice crystals that sparkled in the darkness of her hollow eyes. "This is my home. Mani, who counts the years for men, hands me this faded flower, this empty hall of memories recurring from the past and future, laments from long centuries of vigil. In the wanderings of the night, I hear the names of ancestors and descendants recounted in the darkness, great noble warriors sounding the trumpet of battle, the thunder of charging horses grinding enemies underfoot, the cheers of the victorious, the screams of the dying."

Odin scuffed his feet clear of a small drift of snow that had begun to build up against his boots. "You say little," he snorted, "but allude to much more known, like a river whose eddy currents indicate boulders and deep pools concealed in its depth. How can I come to know these things? Or are there secret keys to understanding of which I know nothing?"

The seeress let the emptiness of her gaze settle over Odin until he began to restlessly shift his stance. "These are not things to understand. In your eagerness, you think to control. To think is to forget a difference, to control impossible, and so you fail."

Gritting his teeth, Odin fingered the bright-edged blade strapped at his waist in whose burnished edges lived the violence of battle. With effort, he lifted his hand from the pommel. "Continue your tales, old woman!"

The Killing of Ymir

"Early in the primal dawn, the sons of Bor sought to direct their fate. With skill, they contested against giants whose numbers outreached their own. Each day, they struggled to control their realm.

It was long ago that the raven of war first shrieked among the three brothers. Harsh words were uttered when fierce-spirited Odin barked grim talk with his kin. 'Must we forever remain in the shadow of giants? Did not our father's father emerge from the same rime? Are we not heir to the same temperament as the sons of Frost? Smolder with the same passions as their fiery kin? Hold the same lofty thoughts as their high-browed cousins?

Their numbers swell even as we speak. We must stop this arrogance! If they live, their race will overwhelm all. With nowhere to live, our line will be as nothing. We must strike now or never know the bold conquests of worthy foes. A warm bath we will draw for Ymir's offspring and bid them sleep forever in its embrace. Let us wash his feet in blood!'

As one, the sons of Bor crowed out their lust for victory. Snatching up axe and blade, the brothers rushed from their hall, goading each other with daring pledges of brave actions to come. Together, they charged the great giant from three sides, the head helping the foot and hand.

Wielding strong, sharp-edged weapons, they sliced into the wall of living flesh, feeling with each blow the tremors wracking Ymir's great frame. A loud groan escaped Ymir's lips, rattling the void with its agony, a mournful blast that sounded across the worlds, announcing his end. The giant called out once to his attackers before life parted from his body. 'Bold you act, impetuous and arrogant. By the deeds of your own hands you color the skein of fate with blood. Know this, if you learn nothing else, your oaths will destroy you, you warlike men.'

The sons of Bor killed the great giant. As he fell, his life's blood gushed from his body, drowning all the giant race of Frost, save one, Bergelmir. From high atop his gristmill, the wise, mountain-old giant spied the deluge as it rushed down on his settlement. With blood lapping about their knees, Bergelmir snatched up his wife and children, tossed them into the wooden mill box, then dove in behind as the surge swept it free of the mill. In safety, the family spun along the raging red floodtide. Rattled about in their wooden shell, they watched helplessly as the flood rose to drown the land.

Long they drifted amid the crimson waves, huddled together, faces pressed into each other's shoulders, their rough-hewn vessel battered by pulsing currents, until the floodwaters subsided, and their rude craft came to rest on a high mountain plain.

Staring out across the lands, Bergelmir saw the end of all things and wept. His jaw clenched. Three times he pounded a fist into his palm to quell the tears. Three times he cried out in anguish. Resolved, he turned to his family, giving stern encouragement. 'Our ending is not yet. We will continue to live. From this vantage, we will make due until our line once more fills the valleys.'

Wasting no time, they settled in as best they could. Tearing apart the mill box, they used its wood to build a shelter. With unbroken kernels, still fresh from the mill box floor they planted a crop that sprouted—grain heads bursting—in the rich blood of Ymir. With each season, they prospered.

Many giants sprouted from the seed of Bergelmir. Spreading out across the lands they gathered their strength under Jotuns, clan leaders eager to exercise their power. Hlér, the listening sea; Fornjótr, the old giant; Geitir; Kári; and Bolthorn, the terrible thorn; Hrimner, the frost; Rimner, the rime maker; Hrimgrimner, the frost mask;

Vafthrudner, the way strong; and Thrudgelmer, the strange-headed. These, the first were called.

From them sprang warriors of great renown. There was Rimgrimner, rime helmet, the mighty three-headed clan chief. Utgarda-Loki safeguards the lands of Jotunheim with powerful magics. Hrungnir, the champion with a three-cornered heart of stone, stands defiant against all contenders. The air rings with Skrymer's proud boasts while Thrymheimr's deafening challenges echo among the hills. Sokkmimir, the deep thinker, offers strategies that never fail. These and many more were born over the cycle of years to raise up their shields of war.

Giantesses too made their mark. There was Aurboda, whose stormy anger churns the ground to mud. Angrboda, born of misery, delights in creating anguish. Thokk huddles alone in her cave, her gratitude difficult to earn. Fenia and Menia work the mondul of prosperity. For them, the increase of fortune is grist for the mill. Hyrrokkin, the Smokey one shrunk in fire, wise in the ways of seid. Two who rose to prominence among the Æsir: Jarnsaxa, the iron chopper, and Gunnlod, the inviter of war. All mothers of champions. All heroines in their own right.

In snowy reaches spread the hearty Rimethurs, inured to bitter cold. Fimkaldr is the grandfather; Very-Cold he is called. Vinkaldr is the father; Wind-Cold he is called. Vákaldr is his son; Spring-Cold he is called. In the deep reaches of winter dwell Jökull, the ice sickle, and Snær, the snow. With them resides Vindsvaler, the father of winter. Beside him stand Vindloni and Vindsval, brothers whose sharp breeze increases the cold. Hunkering behind them is their father, Vasad, whose bitter damp creeps into already aching bones.

At world's end perches Hraesvelg, the Corpse Swallower. The huge, eagle-shaped etin sits with arms spread wide. The wind from his beating wings drives storms across the sea.

But as fire rejects cold, so, too, did the cousins of Frost reject the kin of Bergelmir. Safe from the deluge in their burning land where the red tide never reached, the fire giants scoffed at the fate of frost. No aide was given. No succor offered to survivors. The children of Muspell turned back to their hearths, indifferent to the lot of their icy kin.

Amid the fires of Muspellsheim, Surt, the Black One, and the sons of Muspell raised up their flames to ward their land. Here, amid the embers of a continuously dying and reborn world, they bide their time, ready to defend all they consider their own."

————·————

The seeress paused, tilting her head to stare out at the burial mounds swaddled in frost that disappeared into the distance, then turned her sightless pits to the dark sky empty of stars. "These, now, are the line of my people."

Odin glanced out at the wind-blasted knolls, nodding his head at the sheer number visible from fleeting glimpses as the curtain of falling snow parted then closed. "Most perhaps, but not all. Your kind still haunt the high places where winter snow never fades."

The seeress returned her gaze to the ground. She stood silent as a thick current of snow, pushed by hissing winds, slithered blindly across the ground. Dark sockets tracked the stream of snow as it meandered into the darkness beyond. Bobbing her head with the rhythm of its movement, she again took up the tale.

————·————

"Those born of Ymir's armpit won free of the deluge. They traveled north along treacherous paths stained by the crimson flood line to settle in Nidaveller, near the navel of the world. Behind the wall rock of Mount Hvergelmir they made their home in a golden hall northeast of the roaring fountain that bears its name.

In this protected silence, Mimir watches over the well of knowledge. On its surface floats the price paid by seekers of wisdom that spices the drink he takes each day. At his side stands his sister, Bestla, who joined with Bor to birth three fair-haired sons, the foundation of the Æsir clan.

Mimir's seven sons share the hall. Clever, with the skills of their wise father, they control the seven changes of weather which make up the economical year. Gormánudr controls the first month of winter. His hand marks the season change when the first breath of cold races across the lands. Frermánudr manages the second month of winter. He greets the arrival of the first freeze; Frost month, he is called.

Hrútmánudr oversees the third month of winter when deep snow settles into the valleys and rivers freeze bank to bank. Enmánudr ushers in the final month of winter when cold loosens its grip and snow begins its retreat from the land.

Sólmánudr governs the start of summer when the lands warm, rousing plants to life; Sun month, he is called. Selmánudr guides the husbanding of livestock when the high mountain fields, freed from their burden of snow, sprout lush grasses to fill the meadows; Pasture month, he is called. Kornskurdarmánudr, the seventh son, directs the harvesting of grain, hay, and slaughtered meat, provisions stored away in preparation for the coming winter; Harvest month, he is called.

Joining them in their golden hall is Svasud, the delightful one, father of summer. Delling, the dayspring, greets his son Dagr, the day, to flood the hall with sunlight. Billing, the twilight, together with Nott, the dark night, shade the close of a grateful day. Naglfari, the fingernail; Fjorgyn, the earth; Narfi, the binder; and the prosperous Aud lend their stability in counsel. Nidjar, Annar, Nat, Norve, and Mane also call this hall home."

———————

Frowning, Odin raised a hand to wipe the sleet from his eye. "You relate names and places as a farmer tallies his geese and goats." He shook the water from his fingers before blotting them dry on his cloak. "Of what need is there to know the name of each blade of grass in a field? It is enough to know the field."

Her death mask brightened with a broken smile as the seeress rustled her robe, swirling streams of gray vapor about the frozen mound. "In folly, many seek to know of the end of the journey," her voice sighed across the distance, "but not the events of the journey itself. Ever hungry for the outcome, their impatience leads them into endless troubles. You ask for knowledge; this I provide. Wisdom is knowing what to do with the knowledge."

She turned her empty sockets from the Alfodur to stare at the grave beneath her feet. She shifted a foot, watching it slide over the frozen earth without making a mark, before tucking it back beneath her misty pall. "Events often wrap themselves about places, lending meaning to their names. Their character infuses the rocks, the soil, the trees, even the grasses, everything you would so callously ignore. Such events hold the form for things to come. Without their foundation to build upon, that which is known would be lost, and that which will be, forever unknowable."

Odin scowled, his brow twisting into a dark shelf at the correction. He would gladly have throttled the seeress' thin neck, were she not but tenuous vapors. Instead, he swallowed hard, gritted his teeth, and bowed his head in acceptance.

The shrouded figure turned to gaze out across the frozen landscape, her dark pits staring at a distant point lost in the gusts of falling snow. "For those newly born, everything happens for the first time—a breath, a sight, a joy, a love, a hate. Even ancient stories take on new life when grasped by young ears. For those in whose breast the fire of life burns bright, the glorious stories of past events are an inspiring call to perform great feats of their own ere their day fades into twilight. For those whose song has cracked through disuse, deeds of the past are often forgotten, their memories fading away, as runes carved into batua stones are worn away by the endless passage of wind and rain."

Odin snorted, started to speak, then stopped and jerked his chin at the seeress, a silent command that she continue her recollections. The aged shade drew into herself, then lifted her gaze to the gray sky. "I sing now the memory of days when the sons of Bor wove with joy and sorrow a universe that was their own."

A Time of Creation

"With cheers and curses, the sons of Bor dragged the body of Ymir into the center of Ginnungagap. Using long blades and heavy axes, they dismembered the giant. The air whistled with lusty blows that sent his arms flying off to the sides, his head tumbling to his feet, his legs toppling backwards as his torso crashed down. With the pieces of his body, they filled the void.

From Ymir's flesh, they formed the earth. Flayed from his corpse, they spread it out beneath their feet to make solid ground over which green plants would grow.

From his blood, they made the sea, cinching it tight around the earth. Its rolling waters, racked with tides and stirred to froth by storms, are dangerous to navigate.

From his backbone, they created mountains, great rocky summits rising high into the sky. The lofty peaks form the natural divide of streams that flow down the slopes to irrigate the plains.

From his broken bones, they raised up sharp crags and steep, rocky cliffs. They made hills of his knuckles. His teeth they fashioned into stones. The remaining, smaller chips they worked into gravel.

Ymir's skull they raised high over the earth using its great dome to form the sky. They set four sturdy pillars at the corners to ensure its stability: Nordi supports the north; Sudri balances the south; Austri stabilizes the east; Vestri fixes the west.

His brains they tossed into the air to float free amid the home of stars. From them, they crafted the clouds, charged with thoughts of hail and snow, the hope-of-showers that drift endlessly about the world.

When warm rays of the sun shone brightly from the south, Ymir's dismembered remains, choked with the seed of Adhumbla's milk, erupted with life. The ground sprouted a living carpet of tangled green herbs. Vines spread over the land, climbing cliffs, their twining greenery shrouding hillsides. Tall grasses stretched their wide blades to embrace the breadth of meadows. Huge firs thrust up from the giant's chest, their limbs spreading to cloak the mountain slopes.

Wind rushed in from the sea across the land. The air shivered with the rustle of green leaves. Flowing waters gurgled among the new shoots. Warm sunlight streaked the ground, exalting flowers in the meadows, while cool shadows cloaked heather-grown glades sheltered from the wind."

A chill breeze nipped with special venom at any exposed skin. The harsh crunch of his boots against flinty snow granules whispered in the air as Odin inched forward, ignoring the icy wind that chafed his cheeks. At each word from the seeress, he eagerly nodded his head, a delighted smile crooking his lips.

————·————

"In Nidaveller, they created the World Mill to balance the earth. Amid to roots of Mount Hvergelmir, they built a solid foundation, then anchored the millstones, Eylúdr and Lúdr, fast to the bedrock. Hvergelmir fountain, the roaring kettle, a maelstrom dangerous to ships and death to whales, draws all into the navel of the nine worlds through the eye of the millstones.

Out near the far edge of the nine worlds where the vapors hang thinnest and stars graze the horizon, they pressed nine maidens from the west into hard service to drive the mondul of the World Mill. On the Grotte of Skerry the bodies of giants who had drowned in the great deluge of blood, and others felled later by the sons of Bor, are ground into limb-grist—the loam layered across the world to keep it fertile.

Forever the great mill turns beneath the world spike—the central star. Steadily, inexorably, it rotates the heavens, and regulates the ocean currents that cause the ebb and flood tides. The constant motion stirs up storms that lash the sides of mountains, crumbling cliffs into the sea. Breakers of the ocean attack rocks on the strand. The constant assault grinds them down, depositing meal from the mill along the coastlines."

————·————

The seeress swept her left arm to encompass the mounds shrouded in darkness behind her. "And my kin? What of them? What to do with a foe who once hotly contested your dominance?"

————·————

"The edge of the frozen sea, where broken sheets of wind-driven ice pile up in serried ranks along the shoreline and heavy snow blankets the headlands, the sons of Bor set aside for the clans of giants to live, the kin of Bergelmir who rebuilt their numbers after the bloody flood.

Jotunheim the brothers called it, but the etins preferred Utgard, in honor of Ymir's first settlement. It is a chill land wrapped in dark, brooding firs, iron-cold wolf trees that rake stark fingers skyward, ragged mountain valleys where the Yurkul dwell, and wind-swept tundra dusted white with hoar frost. Here, the giants are hemmed in, their land encircled by the great outer sea. Their voices boom across the expanse in a low, grinding howl of frustration."

———————

The seeress swept her right arm in the opposite direction, back the way Odin had traveled. "The dross given away, what to do with the prime?"

———————

"With Ymir's eyelashes, the sons of Bor built a garth far inland from Jotunheim; a stronghold called Midgard—a fertile land of verdant meadows; fresh, winding streams, meandering rivers; thick stands of beech, fir, and towering oak.

A wall of close-set pillars, sunk deep in pits, arcs across to enclose this lush green land. The formidable colonnade of heavy pointed timbers reaches high into the sky. Hard to climb, impossible to breach, it bars entry to giants.

The river Ifing separates the lands, its wide course is a second, more daunting obstacle set in place by the far-thinking brothers. The deep channels are difficult to ford; the treacherous currents remain free of ice year-round and form a ready snare for war-eager Jotuns bent on conquest."

———————

Odin puffed out his chest. He thumped it three times with his gloved fist, the booming echoes mixing with the hollow cry of the wind. "Together we led great ventures and measured ourselves against the accomplishments of other clans. It is proper that our actions hold a place of prominence in your memories, for ours are the actions that shaped the world. Great were our deeds when we slew the ages-old giant and by our hands created the earth. Great were... were..."

The emptiness of the seeress' gaze bore down, freezing Odin's boast in his throat, turning his words into a strangled cough.

"You bray as one who delights in hearing the sound of your own voice over the counsels of others." She hunched the fog close about her shoulders. "You came to hear my words." A wizened finger tapped the side of her head. "To grasp their meaning, you must listen."

Odin growled in reply, but before his tongue could form words the seeress raised a hand, palm out, silencing his interruption. Frowning, he settled back on his heels as her voice cut across the winds. "Listen."

"From Ymir's heart sprang a mighty ash tree that climbed through the center of the worlds. Its branches spread out to brush the vault of the great giant's skull. Always green, it straddles the nine worlds, its lofty branches embracing the heavens. It is called Yggdrasil for its ancient rider; Mimamirth for its lower branches that spread out over the well of wisdom, while Lorad marks its upper canopy of leaves.

Three roots sustain the tree—spanned far apart across the lands to support its height and burrowed deep into the earth to bear its weight. Beside each root lies a spring that rises from a different world. Their waters offer sustenance to the mighty tree. Beneath the southern root, swans flourish in the well of Urd. Strength and vitality are drawn from warm saps that rise to heal its wounds and shield the tree against bitter cold. Deep in the cold land of Niflheim, the eastern root draws nourishment from the well Mimir guards. Here, Hoddmimir's wood lies protected beneath the tree, a haven for the first life. On the high plains of the Nadr Mountains, the northern root tree draws raw strength from the Hvergelmir fountain, the swirling torrent that each day spews forth its contents to drench the land.

Yggdrasil, the great ash tree, a living pillar reaching through the center of all, stands unbowed before the ravages of time, solid against the splitting of the earth. Dew runs from branches high in the tree to fall as mist in the valleys below. Its roasted berries give aide to women with difficult births. Such is its power.

Its foliage succors many creatures. Its leaves are fodder for Heidrun, the goat from whose turgid udders flow endless streams of nourishing mead. The great hart, Eikthyrnir, wanders among the limbs nibbling its buds and flowers. The stags Dain, Dvalin, Duneyr, and Durathror browse on leaves from the highest boughs. Are, the mighty eagle perched amid the top-most limbs, scans the horizon for movement. Vedrfolnir, the wind-bleached hawk, sits watchful between his eyes. Ratatosk, the sharp-toothed squirrel races around its trunk, chattering ceaselessly as he carries antagonizing messages between the proud eagle perched above and the tangle of serpents nestled below.

In Niflhel lies Nidhogg, the dark serpent who gnaws at the tree's northern root. Gravitnir's sons, Moin and Goin, help with the savage assault. Grafvollud and Grabak huddling between, join Svafnir and Ofnir in biting the roots.

Yggdrasil suffers agonies incomprehensible to men. Bitten from above by stags that nibble its leaves, decayed at the sides by the ravages of time, its roots worried from beneath by the clutch of Nidhogg, each day is a trial of suffering. Always it endures."

———————

Fighting a growing urge to yawn, Odin sucked a deep breath of frigid air. Gasping at the sudden pain of cold spiking his lungs, he doubled forward, gripping his knees, eyes bulging, as ragged coughs ripped from his chest. Plumes of steam burst from his lips and a ribbon of drool ran from the corner of his mouth to freeze in the chill air.

The seeress paused, waiting patiently amid the buffeting winds, until Odin suppressed the coughing spell and could stand up straight, his breath once more his own. As he dragged a gloved hand across his mouth to wipe away the rime caked on his lips, she took up her story.

———————

"From the horns of Eikthyrnir, the great hart that paces the branches of the great ash tree, drip the endless tears of Lorad. The precious dew wends its way to the Hvergelmir fountain, the roaring kettle of turbulent waters. With a breath, it inhales, a thunderous maelstrom drawing all waters into the navel of the worlds. With a breath, it expels, a seething cauldron that is the source of all the rivers of the worlds. With steady purpose, the discharge of waters pours across the lands as the rivers wind their tortuous return to the sea.

The calm, cool waters of Svol brace Saekin's advancing rush. Síth takes the long route home, while the broad, slow-moving flow of

Sid meanders its way from the source. The loud roar of Fimbulthul accompanies the placid flow of Fjorm's chill waters. Gunnthorin trembles within its banks beside the wild rage of Eikin as they wind their way downhill to rejoin the sea. Rin follows Rennandi's one true course. The wise waters of Víth hold deafening converse with the low growl of Gomul's ancient flow. Grad eagerly chases the gaping rush of Gopul, Gipul, and the spear-teaming waters of Gervimul as they flow past the lands of the gods.

Vimur joins the snaking flows of Ormpt, Kormpt and the two Kerlaugs that hold Thrudvanger in their watery grip. Treacherous to ford, they wind their way across the plains of strength.

Thyn beats itself to a froth racing Tholl and Holl. Vegsvinn hurries along its long familiar course. Vina offers friendly converse to those who will listen, while the rapids of Thund devour all speech. The milk-white waters of Nyt run stark beside the dark waters of Not. Together these rivers quench the fields of Midgard.

Ylg swells over its banks, washing away the natural levees, to drown the lands with muddy water. The chuckling waters of Leiptr bring delight to those who seek rest on its banks. Van springs ever hopeful from its wolfish source. Gjoll dazzles the ear with its noisy flow. Vid spreads along its generous plain, while the wide waters of Ifing protect the land of men. These rivers flow through Midgard down into Niflheim.

Nonn's currents eat away its earthen banks, ripping heavy stones from its bed. Hronn crests with waves to challenge the sea. Gunnthra spreads out, ready for battle. Vond bundles its streams into a mighty flow. Sylg swallows any who would dare cross its expanse. Hrid's raging snowstorm of white water, Strond, Odur, and the venom-cold waters of Slid grind their way through Niflheim."

———·———

A crystal mist drifted through the air, caressing, wrapping everything in a clinging robe of white. Gusting wind drove the frost in needles of fire through heavy woolen weaves to torment the flesh. Snorting a jet of steam, Sleipnir shook himself in discomfort so his mane slapped, and bridle rattled. Odin glanced over his shoulder at the sounds. Catching the discomfort flickering in Sleipnir's eyes, he briefly chafed his own shoulders in commiseration, before returning his attention to the seeress as her voice rose on the keening winds.

———————

"The flood tide of Ymir's blood had long ebbed away when the three brothers stalked the lands that they might better see the power they now held. Along the shores of the Midgard Sea, its strands lashed by the storm blood of Ymir, two trees struggled from the sandy banks. Ash and elm, capable of little, lacking in fate, they had life, but not breath, spirit, or vital spark.

Eager to fill a vacant land, the sons of Bor plucked the trees from the ground where they clung tenaciously to life. Exercising their abilities to the utmost, from them they created people.

Lodur, eager to display the greatness of his skill, gave them lá, the warmth of blood, and laeti, the power of conscious movement. He also bequeathed speech, hearing, sight, and the essence of family type. Finally, he imparted litr goda, an inner body made in the image of the gods.

Seeking to complement the gifts of his brother, Hoenir gave them ódr—intelligence, personality, and ego. As the essential kernel quickened, from this gift grew understanding, memory, imagination, and resolve.

After weighing the gifts of his brothers, Odin decided they were lacking an essential state. Summoning his abilities, he bestowed önd—spirit, breath, and conscious life. These nurtured the power of thought, courage, honesty, sincerity, mercy, and the humility of bearing misfortune.

They adorned these first people with clothes, draping the wooden pair in finery stripped from their own shoulders. They bestowed names on the couple to reflect their original nature. The male they called Ask for his supple strength. The female they called Embla for her tenacity.

Innocent in the ways of the world, the young couple needed time to adjust to the sudden onslaught of experiences. To protect them from the depredation of giants while their gifts matured; the brothers endowed the pair with a homeland behind the lashes of Ymir, deep in the fortress land of Midgard."

A sharp gust caught the corner of the seeress' shroud, lifting it to expose a bare ankle of white bone. Odin's eyes shifted momentarily to the sight, which on a fleshed woman would have been cause for arousal, but here drew only disgust. He jerked his attention back to the lightless pits of her eyes as another blast of icy air billowed the hem, raising it higher up the thigh, exposing tatters of dry, blackened skin. The ancient paid no attention, and continued her recital, indifferent to the winds.

"Branches of Yggdrasil hang heavy with fruit, seeds of life that ripen quickly, then, tumbling from their purchase, splash into the saga pond that forms a shallow pool near its roots. A gracile, white-feathered bird stalks the muddy water using its long bill to scoop up the ready fruit from the warm waters of the pond.

In this guise, Hoenir carries the ripened fruit of the great tree to the waiting homes of Midgard. The manna mjötudr, these little fruits of man, are born to the maternal lap, seeds that germinate into children. Each seed is bestowed with the gifts given to Ask and Embla that the generations of men may prosper.

As a spark rouses and spreads into raging fires, so, too, the children of men multiplied from this seed. Like swarms of bees building hives in favorable locals, they spread across the land of Midgard. To all corners reached the many houses of men.

The Svehans are skilled hunters, superior to all others in stature. The Skritobinians, also called Skridfinns, are foremost on skis. In snow or on dry land, they are swift and unequaled in pursuit. The Gepidae, though brave, are sluggish by nature. The Thuringians are celebrated for their mounted skill and excellent horses.

The warlike Herulians offer challenge to all their neighbors. The Goths scatter opponents by the strength of their battle cry. The Lombards' braided beards wave beneath their chins, while the Suebi's topknot brings terror to their foes.

Along the banks of mighty rivers live the Vangiones, Triboci, Usipi, Tencteri, and Nemetes. While the Frisii make their home beside the shore of the great ocean.

In forestlands dwell the stern-faced Chatti, deliberate in their every action. Surrounded by enemies, the haughty Bructeri stand forever defiant. The Chauci keep their reputation dear, held up in peace as high as it is in war.

In the north live Scani, Geats, Rutosi, and Vannen. Farther still, in lands gripped by endless snow, the Lapps range free. To the south, across a stormy sea, the war-Skyldings are pressed from below by the Franks. From the east, the Wends sound their challenging call. Farther east, where sharp winds rule, the Varangian, Sabir, and Wisu live shoulder to shoulder with Pechenges, Ugrians, and Balamjar.

The Maju, Suwaz, and Khazar occupy the rolling plains of tall grass extending southeast from foothills of the high mountains. These and many more grew to mark the world with their presence."

———— . ————

The great gray horse whinnied with impatience at the cold. He stamped forward to nuzzle Odin's shoulder. Reaching around, the Alfodur drew a hand across Sleipnir's broad nose, passing a bit of unused rye to the eager lips. "You draw out events I already know. My mount grows impatient with your tale."

The seeress turned her cold stare onto the horse, nodded her head at the light of understanding that twinkled in its eyes. "Animals are wise, often wiser than those who claim their loyalty. You would do well to heed the urging of your mount. He knows you do not belong in this land. To idle in this region is to forever remain, worried by the cold, the return path obscured by relentless snowstorms."

Odin tugged his cloak about to shut out the wind that scrabbled at its edges like living fingers. "I am not a tree," he grunted, "born to remain always in one place. I am made to journey unafraid across the nine worlds. The path I followed here is the path I know to return. You say to trust my mount. That I do, for he knows the way better than I. Were I dead in my saddle, still he would return my body to the light."

The seeress bowed her head. "You think well of your mount," a smile cracked her lips creating small fissures that radiated down her chin, "and the wisdom that is his to hold."

Odin clapped a hand against the neck of Sleipnir. The horse snorted and tossed his head at the familiarity. "Always," he laughed. "Never do I doubt him. His judgment I trust above all others."

Black pits bore down on the Alfodur who glared back unbowed. "Acknowledging superior abilities in others is the mark of true wisdom, though it can hold one up to ridicule."

Odin puffed his chest. "None would dare such an affront," his breath spilled from his lips in a great cloud, "for I stand ever ready to challenge all assaults against my honor!"

A dry chuckle whispered from the ancient shade. "Face honor must bend to purpose."

Odin bristled at the words. The seeress interrupted his anger by lifting her voice to carry over the racing winds. "Listen now. My vision rings clear, as I tell of how, with hard won knowledge, the sons of Bor crafted life from the random embers that flashed outward from Muspellsheim, arranged the heavens, determined the times of day, and set the course of years."

"In Utgard lived Nott, the dark night, daughter of Narfi, the binder. Three times she married. Three times she was bedded. Three children she birthed.

First, she married Naglfari, the jagged nail. To him she bore a powerful son named Aud, endowed with wealth. Second, she married Annar, the rushing water. His issue was a daughter, lovely and lush; Fjorgyn they called her, the Earth. Third, she married Delling, the shining one. Their son was Dagr, the bright day, beautiful to look upon.

Their first encounter with the mother and her youngest son dazzled the sons of Bor. Enthralled by their contrast, the three brothers convinced Night and Day to join their efforts in building the world. To make use of their nature, they assigned them a place in the heavens. To carry out their duties, they were provided carts drawn by strong horses.

As light is driven by gleam, and darkness is spurred by gathering shadows, so, too, they follow each other on their journey across the worlds. Night passes first, shrouding the lands with her black cloak. Hrimfaxi, the frost-maned steed, pulls her wain. Each morning as she passes to rest, the foam from his bitted-mouth sprinkles the land with frozen dew. Day follows close behind his mother, scattering her dark raiment with his light. The horse Skinfaxi, whose shining mane illuminates the sky, draws his wain."

Odin flexed his arms, releasing a small avalanche from the drifts of snow that filled the long creases of his robe. His hands sang with needles of pain as he beat back spurs of frost that crusted the cuffs. His fingertips, white from the cold, alternated between numbness and an agonizing ache. He tucked them protectively beneath his armpits in hopes of regaining some feeling. The seeress watched his struggle against the cold, her features impassive as stone, but never paused her speech.

"To the west lived the proud chieftain of a great clan, Mundilfari, the moving hand that creates fire. This stern-minded sovereign dwelled in a bright hall cradled between the mounds of well-watered hills. Alone, he raised his two children, their mother having passed away years before. A handsome son named Mani, whose face shone silver-white to illuminate the darkness, and a striking daughter named Sol, who blushed a lustrous yellow-gold to brighten the day.

The gods were astonished at their light, for no beauty could be brighter. Taking the father aside, they stated their claim that children of such splendor belonged among the Æsir. They demanded he give them over for a life of duty greater than farm labor.

Mundilfari, outraged at their command, ignored their desires. Instead, he arranged for his daughter to marry a nearby farmer called Glaur, for the striking glow of his cheeks. By directing his son to wed the farmer's daughter, he ensured both children were bound to the area. Together, the couples would take up residence in his hall, for he could not bear that his children might leave his sight.

Infuriated at the father's decision, the gods forbade the unions.

'This is my family,' Mundilfari snarled. 'You have no say in this matter. My children will marry whom I choose.' He turned his back on the fuming gods. 'Go find another to direct. My will is my own.'

32

Angered by the sharp rebuke, the gods rose in indignation. Storming the farm, they forcibly took the children from their loudly protesting father. 'No! No! You cannot!' he screamed as they bundled his wailing children off to the wonders of Asgard, coaxing, cajoling, and flattering the two until they calmed down enough not to fear their abductors.

'You were brought here,' Hoenir winked, 'for a life greater than living on a farm.' The two children stared blankly at him.

'More like, we saved them from a life of tedium,' snorted Lodur, 'though from their dull gaze perhaps they would have been better off there.'

'Don't listen to him,' Hoenir shot his brother an annoyed look. 'He dislikes anything that doesn't reflect from him.'

'Your appearance,' Odin waved his brothers aside, 'is brighter than anything we have seen before. Its brilliance is of use to us.' The two children stared back, uncomprehending. 'We have positions of great responsibility for you,' he waved a hand at the sky, 'high amid the heavens.'

Adrift in the void, Sol threw her hands over the edge of the world. Mani huddled close behind his sister, unaware of the power he wielded. With winged lightness, their brilliance spread through the sky and up-gleamed from shining waters. The Earth sighed with delight. Men turned their faces skyward to bask in their passing. Their piercing luster struck the eyes, awakening stinging sight as icy water from Elivagar chills the skin, raising bumps across the body.

They make their rounds, Sol by day, Mani by night, never stopping. No sleep gets their father nor has his anger abated. Alone, he ponders his fury while struggling to remain awake that he might gaze upon the beauty of his children as they journey across the heavens.

Each day Sol brightens the sky, her gentle rays warming the earth. Through Delling's eastern gate she drives the chariot of the Sun, a wain created by the powerful gods. Two mighty steeds draw the wain, Arvak, early awake, and Alsvinn, the all wise. The chariot grows hot on its course. The belly shield, Svalin, crafted of finely worked metals, protects the steeds from the intense heat. The bellows, Isarnkol, mounted beneath their shoulders, maintains the flow of air that keeps them cool.

Sol travels across the sky marking the course of the day. Dipping below the far horizon, she returns through Billing's western gate, passing into the dark forest of the Varinians as Night rises over the eastern horizon to begin her journey across the land.

Mani guides the moon along its route, his deft control reckoning up the passing years. He follows his sister's arcing path through the sunrise gate in the east, returning to his needed rest through the twilight gate braced in the west. But the effort is difficult.

To assist his labors, he seized Hyuki and Bil, the children of Vidfinn, a bold sentry on the Hvergelmir wall. From his lofty height, the moon plucked them from a hillside path as they drew from Byrgir—a hidden spring of precious song mead—an errant rivulet escaped from Mimer's well that their father had found seeping from the wall rock.

Bringing them into his home, he adopted them as his own and taught them the skills needed to assist with his nightly work. The boy, Hyuki, aids the waxing moon. The girl, Bil, aids the waning moon. Long in service, they follow Mani still."

———.———

The seeress waved her arms above her head, lifting the surrounding vapor as a fountain from a geyser. The plume cascaded down enveloping her in its white shroud as the timbre of her voice dropped with the falling mist. Odin fought the urge to breathe deep as the swirling vapor enveloped his face, stinging his eyes and pricking his cheeks. It lingered a moment, carrying the steady beat of the seeress' words, before slipping away.

———.———

"Maggots soon found life in the decaying portions of Ymir's flesh that formed the dark, rich soil blanketing the Earth. They worked their way through the loam, digging a labyrinth of tunnels amid the hills. At night, they crept to the surface to venture forth under the stars, but daylight found them concealed once more underground, avoiding the rays of the sun.

All the Æsir gathered in council to decide the fate of this new life. Using their skills, they changed the maggots into a troop of dwarves endowed with great understanding and the physical likeness of men. Three clans were created from the maggots that fed on Ymir's congealed blood. The foremost was led by the clever Motsognir. The second was guided by the silent wisdom of Durun. The third anointed the steadfast Lofar as their chief.

Motsognir's legacy they directed to dwell within the living rocks, hunkered beside veins of precious metals, wedged amid the crevasses. Clever artisans, skilled in the ways of the forge, they use the bounty that surrounds them to craft works of great wonder. Deadly weapons to ward their lands. Beautiful ornaments to adorn their homes. Useful items for trading.

At the four corners of the world stands Nordri, the north; Sudri, the south; Austri, the east; and Vestri, the west—living pillars that support the sky.

Three gifted in the practice of gand and seid hold positions of prominence in Motsognir's clan: Althiôf is the master-thief; Gandâlf bears the enchanted staff; while Vindâlf rides the wind.

Others, too, were born. There was Nidi, the dark-of-moon; Nýi, the new-moon; Vitr, the color of life; Nâr, pale as his brother Nûr, their clammy skin cold as a corpse; Bavör; Bivör; and Bömbur. Veig, the maker of strong liquor; Miodvitnir, the mead-wolf; Dain, the sleepy; Dvalin, the delayer; Nori; An; and Anar.

Thrain, the insistent; Thekk, the known; Thrôr whose voice carries across the distance; Thorin; Nâin; and Niping. Ai, the great-grandfather; Litr, the wise; Nýrâd, who proffers new advice; Râdsvid, giver of sharp counsel; and Regin, broad as the sea.

Durun's kin they assigned to dwell in the earth, secreted away in deep, hollow caverns, to keep company with shadows. Here, amid the gloom, they commune with the gentle chuckle of rivulets and the slow drip... drip... drip of groundwater into brackish pools that know only darkness. Theirs is the wisdom of solitude.

Dancing amid the darkness was Nali, the needle; Fundin, the foundling; Fili; Kili; and Iari. Vili, the chooser; Hepti, the haft; Hornbori, the horn borer; Hanar; Sviur; and Frâr. Aurvang, the loam field; Lôni, the sea pool; Bûri, the one born; Billing; Bild; and Fræg.

Lofar's clan they cast across the dank, pebble plains of Joruvellir. There, on the mud fields of Aurvangar, they dug in and spread wide their seed. With firm purpose, they ward their land, resisting all attempts at encroachment with a hail of stones cast by their ready slings.

Wrestling about this marshy scape was Draupnir, the dripper; Hâr, the gray-haired; and Hliôdôlf, the genius of sound. Haugspori, the mound-river; Hlævang, the lee-plain; Moin, the moor dweller; Skirvir; Virvir; and Yngvi.

Glôi, the afterglow; Höggstari, the striking light; Fjalar, the many; Skafid, the scraper; Alf; Finn; and Frosti. Heri, the leader; Eikinskialdi, the red oak shield; Dolgthraisir, the contentious warrior; and Ginnar, the betrayer."

Gusting snow drove a cloud of stinging ice crystals into Odin's unprotected eye. For a moment, the world dropped away and the voice of the seeress faded into the winds. Odin cursed, wiping his one eye free of tears. "The winds of this land are treacherous; their painful chill freezes your words so that I must strain to catch their meaning. Let us move to beside the wall of Eljudnir; its expanse will break the force of the winds that I might more clearly grasp the wisdom you convey."

The ancient shade drew her gauzy wrap close about her wizened neck and refused to move. "Neither the winds nor the cold bother me; I am long past any discomfort they might impart. You called me from my grave, compelled me by your spell to relate the stories that I know, but I choose where I stand."

Grumbling, Odin tugged his robe tight, then crossed his arms about his chest as protection against the warmth-stealing wind. Biting his lips, he puffed his displeasure through his teeth. "I have come far to hear your words, though the tedium of endless listings tires the grasp of my ear hands. I must fight to stifle the yawns that threaten to set my jaws agape. Get on with your tales that I might learn something of worth."

A light twitch cracked the lips of the seeress as her lightless pits bored deep into the unflinching eye of Odin. "Very well. Listen as I tell of greater works of the Æsir and their first humbling."

"Hot winds from Muspellsheim blew over the lands, carrying a rain of glowing embers that settled across the hills, leaving behind a black crust that choked out life. The Æsir gathered in an emergency council to decide what to do with the burning elements showering down from Muspellsheim and the dull slag that darkened their worlds, when the heat of the embers died away. With shrewd calculation, they decided to fashion clever beings from the material, ones that could carry out tasks at the whim of the Æsir and demand of the Jotun.

Catching the blazing embers flying from Muspellsheim, they stretched their skills to create white spirits, fair as children, more beautiful than the sun. They are called, Light Elves; difficult to look upon so bright is their glow.

In Alfheim they dwell, frolicking in misty meadows and along the foggy seashore. Clad in delicate, transparent garments, from closest rise to nearest fall they wink like jewels darting amid rocks that clutter the ground. From the wide blue expanse of Vidblain to the long stretches of Andlang, fog embraces the land, diffusing their light into the phosphorescence of the sea. This haze is a boon for travelers, for if viewed square before the eye, their brightness would blind.

Some sparks settled, coating the ground with dull embers as they died out. From this slag they created beings blacker than pitch, the Dark Elves, with a nature to match their color. Long nosed, with wiry hair bristling over their entire body, they avoid the sun, for in the Wheel's light they turn to stone. To compensate for an ungainly appearance, the gods endowed them with a deep understanding of nature and how to use this mysterious knowledge to manipulate its course.

In Svartalfaheim dwell the Dark Elves. Amid grottos deep in the body of the Earth, their echoing laughter mixes with the rush of unseen rivers. Theirs is the language of solitude."

———————·———————

Head bowed, the seeress rubbed her finger tips together, nodding as if in deep contemplation. Her head bobbed in time with her fingers, and Odin could almost hear the rasp of frozen skin across the distance. He shuddered, waiting until her face turned up and she started to speak.

"Three women of Mogthrasir's race came to the halls of the Æsir: a youth bright with life, another of practical middle-age, the third old with the wisdom of years. Powerful, skilled in the mysteries of fate, they had traveled far from the land of high-browed Jotun to better exercise the skills that were theirs. Tall, stately, their eyes shining calm assurance, they challenged the ability of the Æsir gods, those who held the responsibility of fortune—a cherished burden they trusted to no other—to direct fate with integrity.

With delicate skeins of thread, unbreakable save by them, they set down laws, wove lives for the children of men, and defined for each the intricate patterns of their fate. The gods remained silent, arms crossed before their chests. Appreciative glances flashed among the crowd. Many excitedly confided in low whispers to their neighbors as they watched the skeins unfold. Unimpressed, the Alfodur dared them to weave the lot of one who worked his own fate.

The three maidens turned to face each other. Gathering up the threads, they carefully drew them out between them. The young one laughed as she twisted her ends. The middle one frowned as she concentrated on weaving the threads in her hands. The old one squinted her eyes and grumbled to herself as she knotted the lines with flying fingers.

For Odin, they wove a skein of complex design that exposed his destiny to his stony gaze. When they finished, the Alfodur let his eyes slowly rove over the fabric of his life, sighing heavily at the windings of certain knots, laughing with delight at the flow of others.

Raising his hand, he acknowledged their superior skill, a decision agreed to by the vigorously nodding heads of all the gods. With the relief of knowing fate resided in capable hands, the gods passed to them the responsibility of managing destiny.

They are called, Norns, these three who shape the course of lives. Their subtle, intricate weave decides the fate of men and gods. On the day of a person's birth, they work out the skein of their life. For some they shape a good life, for others misfortune. Their fate lies in the weaving.

Urd is young—the past, the acceptance of understanding. Her features are free of worry. Verdandi is middle-aged—the present, the becoming of understanding. The mature lines of fated knowledge score her features. Skuld is old—the future, the responsibility of understanding. The obligation of life experience vividly etches her brow.

They dwell in a handsome hall beside the root of Yggdrasil, alongside the clear waters of Urd's well that pool beneath the tree. Resolute, the Norns succor the mighty ash tree. Each day they scoop water from the well, sprinkling it among the branches of the great tree. Verdandi answers the constant need to stem the hurt from above and below. With loving care Urd plasters the wounds that mar its trunk with a layer of white, shining clay thinned with water drawn from the well of fate. Skuld soothes the ache of its sides, her obligation clear."

———·———

The dim shade paused in her oration, watching with infinite, empty patience as Odin restlessly scuffed his feet. "Your efforts are useless." She inclined her head as he chafed his arms to ward off the penetrating cold. "Already the fingers of this land tighten their grip. Each moment you remain, endangers your life and that of your mount."

Coughing puffs of defiance, Odin drew his hood tighter about his neck. "I've braved many storms wearing less. I think nothing of this weather. I will leave when I am ready. Not before."

Black lips cracked into a grim smile. "Some bodies are willful and slow to learn. Stay or go as you please. I could not ask for a greater batua stone than the frozen hulk of Sanngetal perched forever above my grave." Sweeping her hands overhead, the seeress stirred the silent rivers of air as she turned back to her tale.

———·———

"Having given over Midgard, the mighty gods made a stronghold for the protection of their clan, balanced far above the land they had bestowed on mankind. Asgard they called it, fortress of the Æsir.

Gastrofnir encircles the gard. This massive wall of rock offers protection against the uninvited. They surrounded the lofty wall with a moat filled with rushing waters. Its great, roiling surface forever glitters with raging foam. Over its surface hovers a Black Terror

Gleam, a dark bank of kindling mist that emits wise vaferflames whose sudden bolts strike down intruders.

A mighty gate is set in the wall to allow entrance. Through Valgrind, also called Thrymgjoll, the loud, grating gate of the battle slain, only those may enter who know its secret. The gate, designed with hinges close to the ground, opens out or down at the wont of the Æsir to trap those who would force entry. Gripped tight beneath the weight of the dwarf-built gate, they perish there, unless released by the word of the Alfodur.

In the center of Asgard lies Idavoll—the eternally renewing field of great activity—a lush, many-stepped field full-flowered with produce. Three seasons of harvest keep it green. The lower level has its crop of fruits and grains. Once gathered, the middle level is ready to harvest. Once that is secured, the upper reaches are ready to store. In this way, the pantries of the Æsir remain full.

Gladsheim was built on the field of Idavoll, a hall of joy for all who dwell within its walls. Here the twelve high with the Most-High, seated on their benches of staggered height, oversee the business of gods.

The elegant sanctuary of Vingolf was raised for the goddesses of the Æsir, a comfortable hall where all dwell in welcome companionship. They gather here, free from interference, to share thoughts, unburden their troubles, and lend each other support.

Alongside Gastrofnir, Odin erected Hlidskialf, a watchtower roofed with pure silver. From its lofty height, the Alfodur keeps watch, peers into the depths of all the worlds, and carefully notes all the doings of men.

The Æsir raised a bridge of colored light to ease their passage to other worlds. Constructed with great skill, it is called Bifrost, Asbrau, and the Quivering Way. The shimmering arch reaches from Asgard to Midgard. Too light for the ponderous tread of etins, its flaming colors offer fair warning that those who would dare cross must do so swiftly. At the base of the bridge, waters boil where its delicate bridgehead meets the land of men.

In stone forges, they worked metals in quantity to ornament furnishings. With hammer, tongs, and anvil, they added household goods and deftly-crafted art to the many works of which they were rightly proud.

There at the dawn of their Golden age, they gathered together, the airy gods, in the first Husthing of their world to enjoy all that lay before them, the great works they had produced, and to honor their many deeds. On the eternally renewing fields of Idavoll each of the Æsir stood, feet planted on a broad, flat stone, and freely gave an unbreakable oath, a solemn pledge to protect all they had created."

Odin puffed his chest, nose tilted high. "My clan stands above all. None other can compare."

The seeress drew her shroud over her head. "When I was a child, I heard the same boast uttered by the great Ymir himself." She shook her head, pulling a tattered corner of the shroud across her face. "At our height, we think ourselves alone; the only ones who have ever scaled so high. It is easy to forget that the path we followed to our height has often been scaled by others."

"Far to the west along the shores of the rolling one, groves of rowan trees cling to life. Wind weaver is their roof. The all-shining warms their days. This is a land of blue lakes, rivers, sharp inlets, bays, and deep-cut sounds. Here the Vanir live in stilted homes connected by well-roped pylon paths. With steeds of wood, they ply the waterways, indomitable and proud.

Ægir and Ran rule this watery land, driving the sea winds that churn the ocean waters. The empyrean pair live in harmony, reconciled to their realms. Their nine daughters tumble across the sea. Now in frenzy, now in calm, they bend their strength to the sweep of the World Mill.

Ægir directs the winds that tear down mountain flanks before rushing headlong out to sea. They build their speed across the ocean face, then turn to rip across the headlands before hurling their strength deep inland. His forceful hand drives ships amid breaking billows. He presides over stormy seas and soothes the deep currents of his wife.

In Hlesey he takes his well-earned rest, the island home far west of the mainland breakers, protected by a wall of mountain cliffs that jut out into space. Its roof is capped with thick white clouds. The floor is lighted with gold that flickers like fire. He greets all guests with a hearty reception, gladly sharing refreshments that are his to offer. Weary travelers find welcome rest in his abode.

Ran rules over the ocean waters. In calm, she soothes the fury of the wave-lashed sea. In anger, she can shatter the strongest hull. In humor, she routes the storm-force gales, driving voyagers off course to unknown ports. It is not wise to trust her crafty enticements nor be deceived by her placid face. Be ever watchful of her mood and wary of her guile.

Snared in her fury, many call on Ægir to intercede on their behalf. For stirred to tempest, she can churn the sea to raging froth. Then, high raise the timber-cracking waves. Sails are ripped from the yards, hulls splintered, oars shattered, the till wrenched from desperate hands. Ships caught in the wilding sea are dashed to pieces, their fragments scattered across the turbulent waters.

All aboard perish, their feet set along the western path. The flesh-pounding waves swallow some, while dashing others senseless against floating timbers. Some forget how to swim and in panic breathe the water. While others, their limbs numbed by the cold surges, wallow and sink beneath the surface.

About Ran's hall whispers the constant hiss of ocean currents that scour the coastlines and swirl together to trap unwary mariners. Each day Ran spreads her net beneath the ocean waves. In its mesh, she drags the drowned into her spacious cavern to serve her in the twilight of this underwater Valhalla."

———— . ————

Coughing into his fist, Odin made to disturb the chronicle of the seeress' memories. The crone waved his disruption aside. "You have traveled far to hear these words. I would rather have stayed at rest than heed your unwelcome summons, but you compelled me, so I must answer."

The trembling mist thickened around her, for a moment obscuring all but the dark pits of her eyes. "So, do not interrupt my flow Biflindi, though you believe you already know that which is related. In your world of warmth and light everything happens, yet nothing is remembered. Recollections are banished to an underworld of dust, chance, and nothingness.

In this land where lies the time that dreams squander away, I hold the memories of all things locked within my breast and keep their understanding sealed behind my lips. Here, astride this frozen bench of shadows as the ancient stars slide across the sky, I wonder at the passing of years: how many times, across how many generations have I watched these events play out?

Events carry us the way a leaf, fallen in a river, is borne off by relentless currents to its end. It is the same for everyone, even the Æsir. Now listen as I recount your line, those known and those yet to be.

Yggdrasil spreads its branches across the nine worlds. Asgard lies protected beneath its limbs. The Æsir dwell here, the offspring of Bor's stalwart sons, in halls distributed across the gard.

Odin joined with many women. From them the Æsir derive. With Frigg, he fathered Baldur, the innocent god of light, and Hodd, the blinded god of war, rudely educated in the secrets of darkness. In passion's embrace, with Hlodyn, Frigg's mother, he fathered Asa-Thor, the god of storm. With heated runes, Odin melted Rind's shield to father Vali, the avenging god. Embraced by the strong arms of Grid, he fathered Vidar, the silent god.

Thor joined with Jarnsaxa, the Iron-chopper, an etin woman of like nature, one willing and able to accept the brunt of his forceful love. From their pairing, she bore Magni and Modi that strength and courage endure. With Sif, the golden haired, who cherished the sanctity of wedlock, he fathered Thrud, a daughter whose bravery leads her among the Valkyrie. He adopts as stepson, Ull, the archer, who like his father Orvandel, never misses his mark.

Baldur joined with Nanna, Nepp's daughter. To them was born a son, Forseti, destined to become a renowned arbitrator of legal matters. This child, when grown to adulthood, takes the delicate Roskva as wife in a failed attempt to end a feud between houses that once were close.

Joined Idun with Bragi, a skald of unsurpassed skill. Happy in each other's company, they delighted in conversation, laughter was their second nature, but no child was birthed from that union.

Joined Tyr with a woman used to the life of campaign. A son she bore for the one-handed god of oaths, but what need has 'Just war' with a child when the offspring of others perpetuate his existence by rushing to join his ranks.

Joined Hodd with no one. Darkness became the companion of this blinded god. For light, he hovered near his brother, Baldur, whose brilliance illuminated the deepest shadows.

Joined Njord—an enemy made kin—with his sisters to birth Freyr, the god of summer sunlight and Freyja, the goddess of love and war. In later life, his smooth feet win him Skadi, the warrior daughter of Thjasse, but their dissimilar natures—she the mountains, he the sea—made issue impossible.

Joined Freyr with the giantess Gerd, a stunning beauty glimpsed longingly from afar. His payment to Gymir for her hand was the bane of the gods.

Joined Freyja with Svipdag—a valiant warrior of men—for the terror of the gods he delivered into their hands. Among the Æsir, he was called Hermod, Od, and Skirnir for his many positions within the clan. From them sprang Hnoss and Gersemi, Freyja's precious jewels.

To wait on the goddesses many maidens came from the land of men, others from the frozen wastes of Jotunheim. Each were assigned duties to match their nature.

Stern-faced, Syn guards the hall doors in Asgard, refusing entrance to the uninvited. A zealous defender of court cases she does not want refuted, those in legal trouble call on her for aid.

Fulla, with loose-flowing hair held back by a gold band about her head, is the virgin handmaiden of Frigg. Trusted confidant of the goddess, hers is the plenitude of ripened fields.

Gna, astride the great horse Hofvarpnir, delivers messages across the nine worlds and runs errands for Odin's wife.

Hlin, appointed by Frigg, stands guard over those Fjorgyn's daughter desires to protect from danger. She uses her abilities to safeguard lives.

Eir is a handmaiden of Freyja. She is the most skillful in the healing arts. Those who practice the craft call on her for aide.

Gefjon protects those in life who die a virgin. In death, they serve her—an entourage of chaste retainers. Well-versed in the ways of the world, her wisdom rivals that of Odin.

Sjofin and Lofn manage the love affairs of men. Sjofin turns their thoughts to love, while Lofn arranges their unions.

Var listens to the oaths of lovers, those whispered in the silence of an embrace or shouted out from atop a mountain. She rewards those who keep their pledges. Any who break a trust, face her harsh punishment.

Vor is a careful inquirer from whom nothing is hidden. Those who call on her become able to use what they learn.

Snotra is courtly and wise. Skilled in tactful good humor, she offers clever counsel to those who call on her good graces.

Saga lives in Sokkvabekk, the deep stream of memory. There she keeps the history of the gods. Odin often visits the hall to refresh himself at her pool.

These mark the clan of the Æsir, those gods who strive to protect and preserve the nine worlds from dissolution."

———————

A sharp clang of metal-on-metal echoed through the thin air. Odin jumped at the sound and glanced over his shoulder. Gray forms shuffled through the mist of driven snow that scrabbled at the edges of his robe, hungrily seeking out the warmth of his body.

The ancient seeress cackled at the Alfodur's discomfort. "What bothers you, Hâr? Is it the shades of your own making that shamble about, those dregs of man that Urd has inflicted upon us? This was our land, a hallowed place for our honored dead, long before it became a dumping ground for those you judge as unfit and of evil disposition."

Odin bristled at the words but was impotent to take any action against the spirit he had raised. "I fear nothing, be it alive or dead! Now continue with your tales though you have told me little that I don't already know."

Winds moaned with the pain of living, giving voice to the fear and mystery of the frozen dark. The ancient shade flickered in the chill breeze, a guttering candle offering little light and no warmth. "We are the river of time whose intangible course carries lives and empires to dust. Being born has an ending. So, too, the tally of a life lived."

Staring at her feet, she gathered the mist into herself. Her voice crackled with the cold as she lifted her chin to the sky. "I speak now of the responsibility of judgment."

Judgment at the Thing of Urd

"From Eikthyrnir's horns run endless rivers that fill the cauldron well of Hvergelmir there on the high plains of the Nadr Mountains, deep in the domain of Urd. North of the fountain lies Niflhel, a dark, misty land of harsh cold, a realm of unhappiness and torment that accepts the turbulent waters of the river Slid. South of the fountain, beyond the Hel gate stretch the glittering plains of Niflheim, a bright realm of warmth and bliss that accepts the clear waters of Gjoll and Leiptr. Tethered before Gnipa Cave, the entrance to this gated land, Garm of the bloody breast keeps watch. The greatest of all hounds gives bold voice to warn off those who do not belong.

To this place the dead march day-on-day; those taken by sickness or old age, fallen by accident or to intent, or bravely toppled by the winds of war. Traveling westward from the lands of men through the green realms of the gods far beneath the world, they pass a mighty linden tree where Hel-shoes hang like fruit for those in need. The deserving can pluck freely from its branches. For the unworthy, a strong wind races through its limbs, lifting the leather fruit from their reach and they must continue the journey unshod.

The dead cross the treacherous currents of the river Slid, wading through waters choked with scythe-sharp blocks of ice. Those of clean spirit ford the torrent unscathed, their flesh unmarred by the brittle edges, the cold of the water unnoticed. Those guilty of dark deeds in life suffer in the crossing, their limbs chilled to pain by the frigid waters, their bodies slashed, bones broken, as they fall prey to the blocks of ice that tumble in the current.

On the opposite shore the dead scramble up hard, clay banks, their bodies unmarked as they drag themselves from the icy waters, the memory of the crossing held clear. Line-on-line they shuffle in silent procession across a stony plain of low, grown shrubs whose thorns tear at their feet. Glad now are those with feet shod in leather.

A gold-roofed bridge spans the clear waters of the Gjoll River, whose raucous course runs past Helgrind. The gate rings with the boisterous voice of the raging current. The dead cross over this raised path and take the long southern road. At Helgrind they wait, menaced by Garm, the tethered hound that guards the way, until the key, Gillingr, is turned in the lock. The gate swings wide as the dead pass through to reach the final judgment.

A thingstead is held beside the well of Urd where, in high-backed seats, the Gods join with Fate in judgment of the silent shades who have passed from life that their final destiny be known.

Each day the gods travel the Rainbow Bridge, the hooves of their mighty steeds striking sparks from its surface. Asbrau quivers, its colors shimmering as they cross, but it does not collapse beneath their weight. The steeds of the Æsir fly swiftly to Urd's Thing. There is Silfrintoppr with the silver tuft, Gulltoppr with the golden tuft, and Sinir, the thick-sinewed. Gisl, the sunbeam; Gladr, the bright; Gullfaxi of the golden mane; and Gyllir, the golden one. Hofvarpnir, the hoof kicker; Skiedbrimir, ever eager to race; and Lettfeti, the light of foot.

Wave on wave of silent, shambling shades arrive at the thingstead of Urd. The dead crowd benches around the rostrum where the gods preside from their high seats. Mute, they receive their Udr ord, the final judgment of fate. Each stand before the dais to face the inquest. Odin rules over death by combat while Urd rules over all other death.

From the sage's high seat, the gods stay watchful, waiting, as they contemplate the speech of the silent dead. Wisely, they consider the advice of others to ensure unbiased judgment.

Those few who in life learned the secrets of mal-runes can restore the power of speech to their tongue that was silenced by death and speak as witness on their own behalf. The remaining stand mute before the court, relying on evidence given by others.

The ravens, Hugin and Munin, offer what they know, what their eyes have seen as they passed over the worlds.

The person's hamingje is called, the most critical witness in the proceedings, one whose integrity is never doubted. With them since they first drew breath, the hamingje know their person's actions, their every intention from birth to death.

A person's appearance, their clothes, their hair, the trim of their fingernails, the condition of their feet—reflections of the esteem others held for them in life—are all considered before a final judgment is given to each as determined by the course of their lives. These irrevocable verdicts never die and cannot be protested.

It is rare for children to stand before the judgment thing. Only those whose actions were evil in nature, exceeding that of one past their majority, face the stern gaze of the silent tribunal. All others fall under the protection of Frigg, who cares for them in the realm of memory, where honeydew is their food, and joy is forever.

With final judgment, each are handed a goblet risted with runes stained red, an uncut sheaf of grain sprouts along its side, the serpent of eternity encircles stem and bowl, its rim is struck with gripping beasts that watch the entrances to the lower world. Each must drink—none can refuse this hoard of Fánn's brewing augmented with fateful power, a cool-bitter draught to seal the judgment.

Those whose actions in life were of good or laudatory reputation, receive Urd's judgment, the bana ord—ords tirr. They drink of three draughts well mixed: the waters of Urd's strength, the cold sea brine of Hvergelmir, Son's liquid drawn from Mimir's well. The warmth of Mang flows through their litr. They receive tangible form and their physical strength returns. Like the great tree, their bodies are healed. Their tongues are loosened, and speech restored. Sorrows lift as the painful memories of life are wrapped in a comforting haze of forgetfulness.

The chosen of Odin and Freyja, the Einherjar in bloodstained byrnies, travel in the company of Valkyrie. They march across the bridgehead of Bifrost along the arc of the multicolored way to the great halls of Valhalla and Sessrumnir. There they take their seats among honored warriors, the valiant fallen in battle.

All others travel to the glittering plains where their hamingje has arranged a home, a bright land where the lines of life run smooth and the blessed dead live in bliss. They travel through shadows along a path worn deep from an eternity of use. Darkness fades as they pass into a sunlit garden flourishing with fresh green herbs. Clear minded, hearts brimming with joy, they trek the warm, green world of the gods. In this land of light, they hold converse with friends long past and ancestors from the dawn of time.

Those whose deeds in life were evil in nature receive Urd's judgment of a Dauda ord, the namaeli—the second death. They drink deeply of a cup spiked with venom; a brew that forebodes misery. It returns form and sensation to their litr, but that is all. Regrets, cruel memories, and the longings of life are held close, while their tongues remain locked so that they suffer in silence.

To die this second time means entering Niflhel, the cold silent realm of misery, with no hope of absolution. The fetters of the Norns hold them prisoner as they silently travel the weary northern road, a treacherous path of sharp stones blanketed by icy mists. From their former hamingjes flow endless tears as they watch them fade away.

The doomed are driven before ranks of heipter, the callous guards of the damned, armed with limar, scourges of thorns, and nagaikas, rawhide leather thongs twined with bits of lead that hiss through the air to open wounds on backs and legs. Beat without mercy, chided as cattle before an angry farmer, they are driven through Nagrinder— the great Na-Gates built into the Nida Mountains. The chill waters of Slid tumble past Nagrind to rime the dark gate with frost. Its deep waters well with the tears of ten thousand streams. On its back, it carries the pains of all men.

The gates open wide to a dismal land of murky darkness. At this dim portal, the twice dead are met by the agents of their punishment, each according to the deeds they committed in life. Some, seized by the brood of Nidhogg, are carried to their torments beneath leathery wings. Others, snatched up by birds of prey, talons sunk deep in their bodies, are wafted away, writhing in agony, through a granite-colored sky. Others are driven on through the bitter cold to face their final judgment.

On Corpse-Strand a dark hall stands far from the light of the sun. Its frosted doorway opens north to endless fields of ice. The entryway smudged with soot—residue from the fires of ages—leads into a dim gallery filled with gray inhabitants. Walls pulse of their own accord, a writhing surface woven of poisonous serpents whose heads point inward, tongues flicking, mouths agape. Their fangs drip venom onto the condemned sitting below on tiers of iron benches, silent, wrapped in their own thoughts, burdened with memories, each at the level appropriate to their deeds.

Here the children of man suffer terrible consequences for cruel actions, untrue words—when one lies about another, for dishonorable acts, false oaths sworn freely, and taking delight in twisting the minds and actions of others to their pleasure. The upper tiers are drenched in venom. Waste flows from those seated at bench. Each lower tier adds clotted grime of their making to the noxious runoff from above. The spillage forms Vadgelmir, a turgid stream of foul pestilence that meanders through the hall, a clotted morass through which all must wade.

In murky woods, the bodies of traitors are hoisted up to hang from low, twisted limbs. Below, cowards flit among the gnarled boles chased by packs of howling wolves. When caught and dragged down as a winded hart, they are torn to pieces.

Perjurers, murderers, and rapists wade through the icy grip of venom cold currents filled with crushing blocks of blade-sharp ice that freeze, batter, and slice them at every turn.

Here in the cold, dark land wolves tear at corpses, hawks pluck at soft flesh, while Nidhogg, the foremost serpent, sucks at the bodies of the dead."

Prophecy's End

Odin glared at the wraith standing unbowed before him. Shoving back his hood, he leaned forward until his skin tingled from the touch of mist that swirled about the barren grave. "Many tales you have related of events known and unknown to me. They have expanded my understanding. For this knowledge, I am grateful. But what can you tell me, not just hints, but actually tell me, of events yet to be? What can you tell me of the threat of your kin to mine? These, above all, are the things my mind is keen to know."

The seeress settled her head into her shoulders, thickening the mist about her breast. With a deep sigh, she raised her arms overhead, shook clenched fists to the gray sky. Again, her voice took on the pain of memory.

———————

"I see a future, now already dwindling, an extending corridor of passing time which wears us all away. Look! See the white-haired waves towering high as storm clouds gather to block out the sun. While about the hearts of all living things swirls a mounting fear from that which is to be!

Much I have already told you, but you insist, so I will tell you more!

Two golden children arrive from the west, visitors to the shores of men, emboldened with the intent of their purpose. One brings the benison of culture and class order, gifts that the dust of men may prosper. Such are the blessings of Sceaf. Gladdened are the Æsir. The other teaches the art of seid and inner knowledge, gifts that the dust of men might control their fate. Such is the curse of Gullveig. Angered are the sons of Bor. Together they are the catalyst, igniting the sparks that fan the flames of your future.

Much I have told you. Listen as I tell you more.

Wars the Æsir fight against implacable foes of frost and a rival clan who become your greatest ally. By enduring these you grow great, spreading peace and integrity across the worlds.

But always harmony carries a kernel of discord. Bearing the yoke of purpose over countless years exacts a terrible toll. Memories fade, honor wanes, even integrity crumbles beneath its weight. I remember

51

the many acts of the haughty gods as in pride they sought exceptions to pledges, twisted words to meet their desires, all to carry forward the burden of their oaths. So, deceit spreads across the worlds, planting the seeds for what is to come.

Inflamed with hate, etins cry out for vengeance. Their voices carry across snow-laden fields, demanding an end to the Æsir and all they have created. Three children born out of this conflict: a wolf, a serpent, a corpse, with dispositions of fire and oak like their father, will rise to mark the end of the Æsir.

Much have I told you; I will tell you more.

To know the final conflict, when great oaths break apart, their honorable words forgotten as the once-brilliant day passes into twilight, requires the rhythm of blood and breath. These actions are not of yesterday, nor of today. Time does not pass for events not lived. The unknown cannot easily be explained.

Spear Age, Mace Age, the folly of man. Goaded to action are the peace loving, they who had always held their hates to leash. Discarded are red shields of truce. Brandished are the white shields of war.

Sword Age, Axe Age, the bane of peace. Brothers battle to the death. Parents slay their children. Siblings break their kinship bonds. The wrath of neighbors turns outward. The world of men divides into camps in which no man trusts his fellow.

Wolf Age, Wind Age, the blight of winter. Air yields snow and biting winds without end. Summer sunlight dims, offering no warmth. The sun hangs bloody on the horizon. Famine visits the homes of men. Ocean stirs storms against the heavens. Flooding waters drown the land.

Metal Age, Fire Age, the raging of flames. The weapon of no man spares the other. The valiant disappear, and no seed remains. The twilight of the gods' approaches. Choked with fear, men seek to ransom their lives. The sun shrouds her face as the living huddle together for safety but find only death.

Black clouds laden with the soot of many fires fill the sky. Violent winds roar from all directions. The earth trembles, then splits wide. Mountains tumble from their lofty heights. Reddened is Gerrion with the gore of men; happily, she hides the heads of many.

Seeps, streams, and gushing rivers run dry, only brown sedge remains to mark their course. The moon, with raised horns dripping red, hangs low in the shivering dawn. The countryside lies gasping with thirst and dying from hunger.

Loud blares the Gjallarhorn, calling all to battle. Its mournful tones I have twice heard echoing across time. Always it announces an end. Always it heralds a new beginning. As a child, I heard it sung when the sons of Bor loosed the life's blood of Ymir across the lands, his final cry echoed with its call. In the wanderings of my sight of what will be, its tones announce the end of the airy gods.

Awakened are the flames of Surt's slumbering fire. The world crumbles beneath the scourge of wood. Stars fade as the raging inferno turns all to embers, its advance stalled by the gods themselves; the reserves of Muspellsheim drained that a new world may live, and men may prosper once more."

Odin stomped his feet to shake off the creeping numbness of cold, gritting his teeth against the agony of sharp prickles that flashed up his legs. "You feed me obscure dribbles, as if I could fill my pockets with sand and so know the beach. Events have happened, yes. Events are happening now, of course. Events will happen, but when? How much time must pass before I see the promise of your words?"

A soft sigh caught up amid the swirling snow whispered across the narrow gulf of the grave. "Time is measured by the faces of Mani as he sweeps across the sky, by the changing seasons of sun and snow, by the ebb and flow of tides, by sand washed clean by waves.

The tiny grains ground out by the World Mill measure out the ages of the dead. Caught up by currents, they cover beaches in a smooth, gray blanket or form mighty bars that stretch out into the sea. For a moment, they dampen the strength of waves, until a storm surge or a restless tide washes them away, only to pile up again.

The sand of every cycle is the same, its history infinite. It never stops. You ask when, I tell you to wait. Events will take care of themselves."

The seeress drew gauzy wisps of fog about her form. "I have related all that you have asked." She tucked her head low between bony shoulders. "Do with this knowledge what you will. I share no more sight. Now leave me to my rest."

Collapsing into herself, she returned to the cover of her mound. Fists clenched, Odin watched the tendrils of her litr soak into the frozen earth. When the last wisps disappeared amid the swirling snow, he stomped back to his waiting mount, his boots drawing protests from the outraged snow.

Cycle 2: The Victory Gods

Sceaf of the Scani

Sceaf coughed, rasped his tongue along dry lips, his voice cracking as he beckoned for water. Calloused, surprisingly gentle hands propped up his head, swept his long white beard aside, and pressed a bowl to his lips. The cool water trickled over his gums, some escaping from the corner of his mouth to dribble down his beard onto the heavy woolen blanket tucked around his shoulders. When he had enough, he waved the bowl away and was tenderly laid back. With a soft groan, he repositioned himself on the bed.

A hand patted his shoulder. He glanced up into the face of his son, Scyld. Bangs of golden hair framed his pale blue eyes, enhancing the sadness of impending loss that crouched within. "Is it well with you?"

Sceaf nodded, dragging a hand across his mouth. "It is well." He looked around at the circle of faces, some smooth chinned, some bearded, some as white as his own, that surrounded his bed. "My eyes have grown dim. Is everyone here?"

"All." His son gestured at those gathered, the most trusted aides of his father.

"Good." Sceaf's voice, though weak, seemed to fill the room. The gathering leaned forward that they not miss a word. "I called everyone here to arrange my affairs and to give direction on how you are to act once life has loosed its tie with my body. My command is simple and there is no room for dispute. All I have, I leave to my son, Scyld. As Domarr, he is to take the mantle of leadership on my passing."

Scyld made to protest, but Sceaf waved away his uncertainty. "You are ready for these responsibilities. Already you hold a position won by your own merits, along with the honor it entails. I have watched you dispense justice with an even hand and seen for myself your bravery on the field of valor. So, too, you have my trusted aides in whose confidence you can rely."

Scyld bowed his head. "It will be as you say father." In unison, the gathered aides inclined their heads to Scyld. "And while we would rather you remain among us for years yet to come, we resign ourselves to your passing." A tear trickled down his cheek and he made to wipe it away.

Closing his eyes, the old man exhaled a deep breath, puffing the hair about his lips. "It is well."

His son looked about the gathering, taking heart from the intensity of their returned gaze. "Father, now that your end is near there are things," he swallowed hard before plunging ahead, "there are things I would know." Scyld wrung his hands then squared his shoulders to match the set of his voice. "It is celebrated that you came to these shores as a child; at least those are the stories told around our hearths. Never have I heard you speak of this. Now I ask, what can you tell me of your people, my ancestors? I would know the worth of my line."

Glancing from the corner of his eyes, Sceaf pondered his son. He was large with broad powerful shoulders, pale hair cropped in a warrior's cut that bared the sides of his head, the calm lines of his features firm and ready for action—in all ways true to the seed of his line. The young man shifted uneasily on his feet, letting his eyes dance a moment among those gathered before snapping back to his father's face. "I see that this is important to you. You are a child of the Scani, born here, raised here; these are your people. Still you have a right to know of your forebearers."

He ran his hand along his chest. "My beard reaches my belt, a snow-white carpet covering my chest. My years have advanced until none living remain that witnessed my arrival from the sea. Listen to this, the story I recall of my beginning. I will speak it only once. This, son, is the legacy of your line, the worth of those you call kin."

Sceaf wriggled his shoulders into a more comfortable position, then turned his face to the hearth fire as a burning log collapsed into the ashes, sending a fountain of sparks up the chimney. The draw of air twisted images across the coals, winking in a constant dance of red, yellow, and black. For a moment, a face appeared to him in the blush of embers, familiar, laughing, fading as another, then another took its place.

"The picture I hold, like all impressions from youth, is still strong. My dim eyes see it all play out as vividly as in that far-off time. It was long ago... so, so long ago. Yet, I well remember those who bore me. Far to the west where the waters of the world meet the setting sun, on the outermost edges of the heavens where the mondul of the World Mill sweeps wide, I was born to nine sisters: Angeyja, Atla, Eistla, Eyrgjafa, Gjalp, Greip, Imd, Ulfrun, and Jarnsaxa brought me forth into the world.

My homeland was a place of water, floating homes, and swiftly sculled boats. Its people were proud masters of their element. Rich in the knowledge of their world, none dared challenge their rights. In these far lands warmed by the setting sun, my mothers cooed over my arrival. Holding me close, they reminded me that I was a special child of enormous power, full of greatness to come. New to the land of the living, I accepted the truth of their words.

In the years before my majority, they prepared me for a long journey, empowering me with the knowledge of what was needful. From Urd's well they gathered the earth's strength. From the Hvergelmir fountain they drew the cool sea's endurance. From Mimir's well they took inspiration and wisdom. They blended the waters in a crystal goblet, then, gathering me into their arms, pressed the cup to my lips and bid me drink.

While I sipped, they whispered words of clear counsel as to my purpose. I became drowsy, overcome by the potent draught, yet I fought sleep. Well do I recall the jouncing as they nestled me in a beautifully adorned ship, comfortably braced amid offering gifts. They drove the ship into the spray, eastward across the surface of the ocean, its hull hoisted on the shoulders of towering waves, its prow crowned by the rising sun. I remember the gentle rocking of the waves, the sight of Sol bobbing over the bow before I fell asleep."

———————

Here the old man shook his head. "I recall nothing more until I awoke, cradled in the arms of a fisherman's wife." He glanced at those surrounding him. "It is here I have to rely on the stories you have all heard, those passed down by your forbearers."

———————·———————

"It was the early days of the world, when the first generations born of Ask and Embla sought to find their place among the lands of Midgard. They lacked fire to warm their homes, the art of the smith was unknown, even the husbandry of plants was a mystery. But they lived in innocence and goodness of heart.

Like the land of my beginning, theirs, too, was a land of water. But where in my home men had prospered by mastering their surroundings, here they struggled each day for survival, sometimes feasting in plenty, more often starving in famine. Their homes stared over a shoaled portion of the sea; a sodden coastline with long stretches of mud-land archipelagoes where the surf broke limply on the sand. Here, the moan of the offshore wind vied with the cry of low-flying gulls.

It is said a well-crafted ship arrived from the west, propelled across the waters without sail or oar. It came to rest on a sea bench that checked the waves along the coast of Scani. The people rushed through the foaming surf and dragged the boat onto the beach.

Inside they found me, fast asleep, my head resting on a sheaf of grain. About me were arranged riches of many kinds. Near my head lay treasures of gold. Stacked near my feet they found tools for working the soil, others for building halls. Spears, long blades, coats of mail, and other weapons of war were set about on benches. In my dreaming hands, I held a fire auger.

None recognized the markings on the boat or the embossed images that adorned the treasures stacked about the benches, for them my origin was a mystery. Still I was greeted as if I were a long-lost kinsman and given constant tender attention. Because I had arrived resting on a sheaf of grain, they dubbed me Sceaf."

———————·———————

He chuckled, breaking into a rattling cough that shook his frame and quickly brought the comforting hands of his son. When the spasm subsided, he waved Scyld away. "I am as last year's leaf clinging to its stem. A breath of wind and I fall." He sighed, sinking back into the comfort of the straw tick. "In this hour, I find it difficult to remember that once life called on the duties of life, not the obligation of death."

The old man rubbed a hand across his face. "Where was I? What was I saying?" He pinched the bridge of his nose. "Oh, yes..."

———·———

"As a young man, I lived up to the name my adopted people had given me. I sprouted quickly to tower among men, tall as a stalk of golden grain pushed high by spring rains to ripen in the summer sun. Many years I dwelled among the Scani. Became a great benefactor of my foster kin. I passed on the knowledge that had been given me: the counsel of my mothers. I taught them many things to enhance their lives."

———·———

A smile creased his lips as his thoughts drifted inward. "By my hand, they were elevated, their society organized."

The group waited while Sceaf bobbed his head listening to words none but himself could hear. Eyes darted back and forth before settling on Scyd, who sat near the head of the bed. The young man took a deep shuddering breath, then reached out and gently prodded his father's shoulder.

Sceaf jerked at the touch. "What?" He looked about, his startled expression fading as he returned from his reverie.

"Father," Scyld gave a slight nod to the group around the bed, "you were telling us all of your arrival in this land."

"Yes, yes, I suppose I was." Sceaf fidgeted a moment with the blanket before relaxing back against the pillow. He glanced as his son. "I was speaking of the things I had brought?"

The young man nodded. "That you were, father."

———·———

"The fire auger," Sceaf began, "was the first tool men learned to use that they might know the many blessings produced by the sacred fire: warmth, light, protection, and cooked food. With fire controlled, I taught them the art of the smithy: how to build a furnace, the breath of bellows, how to roast bog ore and smelt it into iron, how to forge this resource into all they needed.

First, they learned to make tools for working the iron: tongs for securely holding hot metal, hammers for shaping, anvils for bracing, shears for cutting thin pounded sheets, and sharp-edged files for grinding sharp edges. With these, they created goods for the home, utensils made by their own hands. Rivets for fastening, clasps to hold closed their robes, forks for spitting meat, knives for cutting, pans for cooking, even ladles for scooping.

Using the smithy tools, they crafted scythes for cutting, axes for chopping, plows for working fields. With these, they learned to clear ground, till the land, plant the furrows, and reap the harvest.

Weapons, too, they learned to forge—keen-edged blades, spear tips, and barbed iron for arrows—to defend all they had built from the avarice of others. For ever-vigilant must men be who prudently gather the wealth of security about themselves.

Carefully, I instructed them in the craft of runes—how to carve, how to stain, and how to interpret—that they might understand the power of coded knowledge."

———————

A warm smile of reminiscence spread across Sceaf's face, flushing his cheeks with a soft glow. "Years ago, the Scani adopted me, brought me up to cherish life. In due course, they made me their chief. I like to think they were pleased with my counsel." A scattering of "Yeas," circled the bed.

"I made every effort to rule wisely, with honor and consideration always held close. Yet there was more I wanted to give to those who had accepted me as one of their own."

He glanced around from under bushy white brows, amused at the attention focused on his tale. The counselors leaned forward as if circling a well-laden board after a hard day's toil, the fragrance of the dishes capturing their minds, the food their sole interest.

———————

"I often journeyed along green paths, trekking across the lands. Many knew my name, Sceaf, chieftain of the Scani, but few knew my face. That I might travel unknown among my people to observe their true nature, I called myself Rig in these wanderings, and was a welcome guest in all homes. In those days, people were settled in different locals and in homes of varying condition. Yet, I found happiness even in the meanest hut.

In each home, I encountered different customs. Some wove cloth of homespun wool or flax. Others ploughed fields, harvested grains, and baked bread. Here, they crafted implements in the smithy. There, they directed the affairs of others. Wise counsel I gave that all might work together and prosper.

Along the low road, I traveled through dank flats of soggy marshlands. It was hard going with sucking mud threatening my balance at every step. Exhausted, I was glad to stop at a rough-hewn hut with mud wattle walls that sagged toward the rising sun, its poorly thatched roof gaped to let in rain, its front door propped open with a log.

Near the eldskáli, the central fire, sat an old man and an old woman. Their hair hung in long, greasy ropes. Their skin drooped in sallow folds from their cheeks. To ward off the breath of chill, damp air, they draped cloth of rough burly across their shoulders. Its sides were drawn close about their waist with a knotted thong of simple bast.

They looked up as I stumbled through their doorway and smiled warmly in greeting. With welcoming gestures, they bid me take a place beside the coals at a seat brushed clear for an unexpected visitor. They had little to entertain guests but offered the best of their home. A heavy loaf made of dried peas and pine bark was set on the bare board. A drink of cool water served in a wooden cup, crudely carved of burled fir, was set beside. I accepted the hospitality, enjoined the couple in pleasant conversation. Good counsel I gave to the home that they might prosper under the heavens.

Three nights I stayed, gathering my strength from the weary journey. Each day I ate with the family, shared their lives. At night, I slept in the middle of the reed mat between the two, the best position offered to guests. For such selfless generosity, I blessed their home.

Nine months passed from my visit before they knew fruition of the blessing I had bestowed. The old woman bore a child with dark hair thick as flax. The squalling boy was rinsed well with cold spring water, then wrapped tight in burly cloth of rough weave. They called him, Thrall.

The child grew into a strong man, thick of muscle, with a wide brow and blunt powerful fingers, his legs bowed, his back bent from heavy labor. He wove bast ropes for baskets, worked with swine, looked after goats, cleared brush, dug dirt, dunged fields, and wrested peat from slippery bogs.

The old man brought a girl to the home; bandy legged, stringy hair, ragged clothes, arms burned from hard labor in the sun. Slave-girl they called her. The son of the house sat next to Slave-girl. The two talked together, touched shoulders, stroked forearms, each night slept in the same bed.

Thrall and Slave-girl came to an agreement, made their home in the house of his parents, worked hard, lived content, and were happy. They bore many children; a noisome brood quickly put to work. From them comes the class of Thralls."

———·———

"A drink." Sceaf beckoned with his fingers. "My throat catches at the memory." Scyld passed his father the bowl of water. Sceaf took a sip before handing it back. He dropped his head and closed his eyes, chest wheezing with each breath. Those gathered about his bed stirred in unease but calmed down as Scyld raised a reassuring hand. After several moments Sceaf blinked, a gentle smile creeping across his lips. "Memories... Now, where was I? Oh, yes..."

———·———

"Along the middle road, I traveled amid fertile valleys and broad coastal plains. I passed harrowed fields where crops grew tall, and pastures where livestock grazed within tended fences. Here the path was packed hard from much use. Day had begun to wane when I stopped at a handsome, well-built home with solid, earthen walls braced by squared wooden beams, its roof thatched with thick bundles of rushes, its door latched with bands of braided leather and sinew.

Near the eldskáli, the central fire, sat a mature man and woman. The man's hair was trimmed above his brows, the woman's locks were wrapped in a headdress, their tanned skin shown where not covered.

They rose when I knocked at their doorpost. With gestures and friendly words, they bid me enter their home. They cleared a space for me near the fire. When I had taken a seat, they turned their attention back to their work. The man busily fashioned a bench for the house, leveling the wood by hand. He spoke with me between passes of an adze—its metal marked by the shaping of his own hand—of neighbors nearby, livestock, and the weather. The woman spun wool; her nimble fingers twisting the fibers into long threads as she made ready for weaving. With each turn of the distaff, she smiled at our conversation.

The pair were dressed in sturdy clothes made by their own hands. The man wore a close-fitting tunic pulled over a gray kirtle that reached his knees. He belted it tight at the waist with a narrow leather strap. As the woman labored at chores, her floor-length kirtle brushed the ground. She had brooches gilded in tin clasped at her breasts to hold a double-looped smock in place. And about her neck hung a small disk of hammered copper, symbol of the family wealth.

They offered the best of their home to entertain their guest. Heavy bread of coarse-ground barley still warm from the fire and boiled meat in bowls were set on the board. Strong ale served in a fired clay mug was set beside. Famished by my long journey, I accepted the hospitality, enjoined the couple in pleasant conversation. Good counsel I gave to the home that they might prosper under the heavens.

Three nights I stayed gathering my strength. Each day I ate with the family, shared their lives. At night, I slept in the middle of the bed between the two, the best position offered to guests. For such selfless generosity, I blessed their home.

Nine months passed from my visit before they knew fruition of the blessing I had bestowed. The woman bore a stocky child with brown hair, rosy cheeks, and lively eyes. The gurgling boy was rinsed well with warm water, then wrapped tight in a woolen cloth. They called him, Farmer.

The child grew into a strong man, broad shouldered, with a clear brow, powerful hands, his legs and back straight. Ready to work, he drove oxen, built homes, raised barns, and labored in the smithy forge. With a firm hand, he guided the plow.

The father brought a young woman to their home with keys on a belt wrapped about her waist to marry the young man. She was straight-legged, her hips strong for birthing children. Always her eyes smiled while laughter bubbled from her lips. Her tongue was not hasty but measured with careful thought.

Farmer took her aside. They spoke, touched shoulders, stroked forearms, and planned their future. Before their families, they gave ring oath to bind. Daughter-in-Law they called her.

The young couple settled together in a home built with their own hands. They spread a coverlet over their bed, worked hard, lived content, and were happy. Many children were born to their home, eager offspring that spread out to make their way in the world. From them comes the class of Freemen."

———·———

Sceaf smacked his lips as his eyes began to drift. "They did well."

The gathering stirred. One made to speak but was silenced by the harsh glares of the others. Scyld patted the elder's shoulder. "Please continue father."

The old man cleared his throat and pointed his bony finger toward the ceiling.

———·———

"Along the high road, I stalked crests of hills that offered vantage over the surrounding lands. On a rise overtopping all others I stopped at a handsome home with strong walls of well-fitted stone, a roof shingled with wood, its door latched with struck iron and opened by a large ring.

When I called from the gatepost asking shelter for the night, a servant drew open the doors. With a smile of greeting, he ushered me through the narrow entry into the main room of the hall. Near the eldskáli sat a young man and a young woman, confidence shining bright in their eyes. Their skin glowed a clear, healthy pink. Their eyelids were daubed with makeup to increase their beauty so that it might never fade. They wore bright ornaments on their clothes, braided in their hair, draped about their necks, and arrayed on their arms. Their fingers flickered with jewels. Intricate and restless in quality, the adornments seethed with masses of wild animals, storm waves, and the rushing wind.

I was made welcome with courteous words. They commanded a place be made for me at their hearth, then returned their gaze to each other eyes. My boots drew protests from rushes strewn across the floor as I crunched along the length of fresh cuttings to a comfortable seat near the fire.

The man sat at a bench in a fitted tunic stitched of bright cloth reinforced with thick leather. His beard was trimmed to follow his jaw. His hair at front and sides was cut close to fit a helmet; the long hair behind pulled back into a tail was tied off with a cord of braided sinew. With nimble fingers, he twisted gut bowstrings, fashioned arrows from lengths of ash fletched with split quills from the wings of swiftly flying geese and set barbed iron at their tips.

The lady of the home sat beside him, back straight, a cluster of silver pendants draped about her neck—symbols of the wealth of their home. Her long locks were tightly wound about her head in a fletta. Around this she bound a scarf embroidered with complex designs—the knots of sailors, the windings of serpents—and clasped in place with a silver brooch. A nut-brown cape hung from her shoulders to wrap her legs. With idle fingers, she tugged the sleeves of her pale blue blouse, its flowing edges hemmed with silver threads. She stroked the material to smooth out the wrinkles, then rose to do her duty to their company. With a silver pitcher brimming with clear ale, she saw to the needs of their visitor. As she poured a bowl of the heady drink, I spoke my gratitude. Her beaming smile warmed me more than the drink.

They offered the best of their home to entertain their guest. On a polished table, they set loaves of fine white bread, platters of boiled pork meat, roasted birds arranged on skewers, a variety of delectables served on silver plates, and wine in etched silver goblets. While we ate, the couple engaged me in clever conversation, talked of current events, entertained me with stories until the day had passed. I delighted in their hospitality. Good counsel I gave to the home that they might prosper under the heavens.

Three nights I stayed gathering my strength. Each day I ate with the family, shared their lives. At night, I slept in the middle of the bed between the two; the best position offered to guests. For such selfless generosity, I blessed their home.

Nine months passed before they knew fruition of the blessing I had bestowed. The woman bore a child with blond hair. His clear blue eyes were sharp as a wolf's. The smiling boy was rinsed well with warm water, then wrapped in a soft linen cloth. They called him, Lord.

The boy grew strong in the hall of his parents. His mind quick, feet swift, hands strong, legs and back straight, his broad shoulders unbowed from labor. Every day he practiced with shield, bent the bow, wielded the thrusting spear, attacked, and parried with keen-edged blades, learned to swing the oaken quarterstaff. On hunt his swift feet paced the steeds. At home, he trained horses for war, swam the surf to build his strength, in all ways kept himself ready for battle.

The father sent messengers over the land to seek out a young bride fit for his son, a prime match in wealth and status. From a Chieftain's hall, they brought a maiden, strong hipped, long, slender hands, her hair the light gold of the midday sun, beautiful to look upon. Keys hung from a belt wrapped about her waist. On her brow rested a bridal veil adorned with flowers. Erna, they called her for her brisk and vigorous manner.

The young couple exchanged oath rings while giving vows on the pledge stone. Settling in the hall of his father, they spread a coverlet over their bed, loved one another, enjoyed their lives, and were happy. Many children were born to their home, eager offspring that spread out to rule the lands. From them comes the class of Nobility."

———·———

Sceaf fluttered a hand. "Thus, each of you hold a piece of me." He glanced at Scyld, who frowned down from the bedside. "This is my greatest legacy. My blessing given to the three classes of men, your kin."

Reaching out, he took each of his guests by the hand and squeezed warmly, then fell back, exhausted by the effort. Crooking a finger for his son to come close, he took hold of Scyld's sleeve; his voice croaked low, and all strained to hear his last words. "My time has come. I feel the dogged pull of western paths that can no longer be denied. On the strand where I arrived those many years ago, you will find a boat ready to return me to my first home. When I have died, place me in the boat. It will know what to do."

Breath hissed from Sceaf's lips as his hand fell limply to his chest. His face seemed as one fallen into a deep, peaceful sleep.

His family gathered together to prepare his body for the journey west. With tufts of wool they silenced his ears and stopped his nose. A richly embroidered scarf bound his jaw closed. With a sharp blade, they pared his fingernails and trimmed his hair. After dressing him in his finest robes, they placed sturdy Hel-shoes on his feet. When all was ready for his final journey, they broke a hole in one wall of the death chamber, hauled his hooded body through the breach, and then carried it down to the foaming strand where he had arrived as a child.

There, in a narrow inlet sheltered from winds and strong waves, floated the same beautifully adorned boat that had borne him to their shores those many years before. Now it waited to receive the dead. Hoar frost glittered across its bow and brightened its deck. The ocean colt rocked in the waves, eager to return to sea.

Amid wails and flowing tears, the sorrowing people laid Sceaf in the boat. In gratitude, they piled treasures about him equal to those he had brought as a child. When all was done, they stepped back. The boat pulled away from shore, drove far beyond the breakers, and turned its bow toward the setting sun.

Raising Thor

In the early days of the world when green plants first crawled over the bare bones of Ymir, Odin traveled the lands with his brothers, independent, free of care, enjoying everything they encountered as they spread wide the seeds of their vision.

On one such journey Odin encountered Fjorgyn, the Earth. He first glimpsed her when he topped a hill far ahead of his brothers who were struggling up the slope in the shadows behind him. What he saw took his breath away.

As Day ushered his mother from the land, Sol lifted her hand over the edge of the heavens, bursting her golden light across a panorama of lush meadows dotted with clumps of dark-green shrubs. Stands of birch and ash rustled their leaves in a light breeze wafting among the hills. Herds of four-footed creatures grazed placidly along open hillsides. On the valley floor a stream wound its way through meadows alive with the dappled greens of long-stemmed grasses and the bright, waving colors of wild flowers.

Alone in the center of this magnificence a matron reclined on a flat rock adrift in a pool of radiant sunlight. She was of full luscious form, lovely to behold. Her soft, benevolent features peeped from behind a waterfall of dark silken hair that cascaded about sun-browned shoulders draped in the mottled green finery of the land.

From his first look, her beauty overwhelmed him. The attraction was so strong, he charged down the hill heedless of all else in his eagerness to reach her side. Bent over breathless, hands braced on knees, Odin stooped before the vision that wavered just beyond his reach. Ignoring the sharp pains that gripped his chest, he raised himself tall before the matron, boldly announced his name, and between gasps for breath, made known the weight of his mighty desire.

The matron bowed her head in greeting, a brilliant smile illuminating her face. "I am Fjorgyn, a mother of many children. I offer fruitful bounty to all who treat me with kindness and respect. Your name is known to me. I have heard it called on the winds and whispered amid the rains that water the ground. You are of a powerful line, bursting with endless vitality. My family too is powerful; it would do well were our houses joined. I have a daughter who would make you an excellent match. Taught by my hand, she is well practiced in the many skills of her mother."

Odin stared hard at Fjorgyn, his lips trembling with a stammered round of noncommittal grunts. Before he could get his speech under control, the matron raised her hand to halt his efforts. "My blessing you may have on condition that you wed my daughter before the next day sets and take full responsibility for all your actions, those past, those present... and those yet to be."

Caught up in the rut of desire, Odin readily agreed. "That which you ask, I pledge to do. I have traveled much, done great deeds, and created many wonderful things. Never have I avoided the consequences of my actions, but boldly faced them, be they pleasing or unwanted."

Hearing these words, Fjorgyn lay back, spreading her arms wide in welcome. "Then know my blessing." Odin bedded the matron to the delight of both.

The following day Odin wed Frigg, daughter of Fjorgyn on the very rock where Odin had paired with her mother. After the ceremony concluded with oaths given on the pledge rock, Frigg bundled up her few belongings, said her goodbyes, and left with the three brothers who returned to their hall in Asgard.

Endowed with her mother's strength, Frigg took her place at the head of the Æsir clan, the keys of home belted at her waist, the airy clouds draped about her shoulders, the distaff wielded as a scepter. She took to the duties of home life, using the skills taught her by her mother to keep everything in order.

Everything was well in Asgard. Abundance reigned. The new couple lived in happiness, entertaining the frequent guests who visited from across the worlds to share their bounty.

When Fjorgyn found herself expecting, she decided to hold Odin to his pledge of responsibility. Arriving full and ripe at the hall of her erstwhile lover, with a broad smile she introduced him to the duty of fatherhood. Frigg was furious on discovering her husband had impregnated her mother, and the clouds reflected the blackness of her mood. But the honorable wife swallowed her pride to the necessity of station.

As the pangs of birth roused groans from Fjorgyn, a midwife was called to assist. Fjorgyn waved her away. With the ease of a long-familiar routine, she bore a genial son of fiery temper. An unlikely child endowed with the strength of the father and the deeply rooted compassion of the mother.

Still damp from his mother's womb, the infant was presented to Frigg. His lusty squalls and thrashing limbs quieted as with stiff arms she drew the child close to her breast. Lips clenched into a thin hard line, Frigg glared down at the newborn nestled in her embrace. Fury surged in her breast and she would have gladly given him away or left him to the mercies of wild beasts in the forest, but when his clear blue eyes gazed up into hers and he beamed a delighted smile at the one who held him, her anger melted as snow before the summer sun. From then on, she happily raised him as her own.

———— . ————

On his first day, he squirmed from his mother's embrace to crawl the length of Odin's hall. Showing no fear of fire, he circled close to the eldskáli, laughing at the flames dancing among the embers.

Frigg drew a sudden breath of alarm. "Get him away from the flames!" She gestured madly at the fire glowing in the center of the hall. "He'll get burned!"

Jumping from his seat, Odin snatched up the child. Shuffling back to Frigg, he placed the boy in her arms. "He'll do it again. Mark my words, he'll do it until the first ember lands on his skin, then he'll learn to stay back. How quickly he understands the lessons of life is how we will know the wisdom of his mind. We will then know what to expect of him as he grows. For now, it is too early and too risky to trust his wits."

Frigg hugged the protesting child to her breast as he squirmed about in her arms to stare bright-eyed at the dancing flames. "You would risk your child being scarred for life, just so he gains your precious wisdom!"

Odin lifted his cup of wine, took a long pull before spraying a puff in response. "Certainly not," he sniffed, wiping a hand across his mouth. "Never will I let such harm fall to the boy. Besides, Lodur would not let anything worse than a warning sting happen to our son."

———— . ————

On his second day, he tottered about the hall, climbing benches, balancing on seats, and dashing out the open doorway, too swift for Frigg or Odin to catch.

Frigg darted around the benches, her grasping fingers just missing the squealing child who scooted among the seats. "Catch him! Catch him! He's heading for the doorway!"

With a low grunt, Odin lunged forward, snatching up the wriggling youth before he could escape the confines of the hall. "The boy is slippery as an eel!"

On the third day, the proud parents presented him to the clan. He amazed the assembled gods by playfully throwing about ten great bales of bearskins. His parents were so astounded at this feat that they named him Thor for his strength and disposition.

Odin thumped his chest, three times he thumped his chest, until the rafters echoed with their hollow drum. "Strong is the line of Bor in childhood, but none have ever shown such strength at such an early age. I predict a remarkable future, for when full-grown none will be able to resist his might!"

The gathering laughed, clapping their hands at the announcement. Many words of agreement raced around the room as the child chuckled happily in his play and continued to juggle the heavy bales of furs.

Frigg puffed her breast and beamed out across the group as she heaped praise upon her son. "He is precocious. Already he insists on accompanying his father and myself during the performance of our duties."

Odin's grin strained at the edges as he watched the antics of his son. "Yes, he is becoming quite a handful."

On the fourth day, he was larger and far stronger than any child known before. A roguish smile crinkling the corners of his eyes made it difficult not to hug him on sight. Laughter burbled from his lips as he played with those about him, his candid tongue winning him many friends. But when he felt tricked by some good-natured prank, his tantrum caused the sky to echo his protests.

Nat tousled the boy's hair and leaned back, a smile beaming across her face. "You are such a delight. Narfi, come meet this child."

A heavy warrior with a dour looking face slid down the bench. He leaned in, casting a long shadow over the boy. Glancing up at the dark looming figure, Thor nervously tucked his playthings behind him.

"You like games do you. Let me show you a favorite of mine." The dark man reached out a hand. "Hand me that piece of silver, the one I saw you tuck away in your pocket just now. Come on," he beckoned impatiently with his fingers, "be quick about it."

Thor looked at Nat who smiled back. "It's okay," she nodded encouragement. "It's a trick... just a trick." Reluctantly, he took the piece of silver from his pocket, gripped it tightly for a moment, and then gave it over to the man.

The dark man took the piece and held it up to his nose for a quick sniff before gnawing it between yellowed teeth to test its purity. Satisfied, he held the coin between two fingers. "Here it is." He waved it back and forth before the boy's eyes then brought his hands together with a sharp clap. "Now it's gone!"

Laughing at the boy's astonished gaze, he turned his hands, showing first the empty palms then the clear backs.

The child clapped his hands with delight. "Now bring it back."

Narfi chuckled, a harsh nasal snort. "Sorry lad. It is gone for good. And what doesn't come back," a leer twisted his lips as disappointment flashed across Thor's face, "I keeps for myself."

"That's not fair!" Sparks leapt across the child's thick brows. Dangerous flames flickered in his eyes. Outside the hall, the sky grew dark and lightning flashed among the black clouds roiling overhead. Deep rumblings rattled the shields covering the hall roof.

Nat clutched Narfi's arm, drawing him close. They both turned an uneasy eye to the rafters that shook with each crash of the storm. "You had better give it back to him."

———————

On the fifth day, his parents deemed it time to foster this lively child. With his growing strength and stormy nature, they found it difficult to uphold their responsibilities while raising him with the attention he required.

Odin stared into his cup watching his breath play across the surface of the wine. "He is growing at such a rate that neither of us can continue to perform our duties and watch him at the same time. I say the time has come for us to foster him out."

Frigg spastically knotted her robe in her fists. "But who can we trust to raise him in our stead? His strength is great, his temperament volatile. I would not put the charge on just anyone. They must be strong, yes, but also patient and caring. He is at an impressionable age when attitudes can be easily molded. Soon he will take his place in the clan. At that time, I would have him know the worth of his being and cherish the ideals held by his family."

Odin pursed his lips. "Your words are well spoken. That is why I have arranged for his fostering by two, such as you describe, who can handle his excessive energy and provide the necessary guidance."

———————

On the sixth day, he was placed in the foster care of Vingnir and Hlora, the heat and flashing light of the portending storm. Tall, thin, with sharp piercing gazes, their long sandy hair streaked with gray, so alike in look, so close in nature, they seemed reflections of the same person. Odin paced before the couple, waving his arms as he spoke, his voice rising and falling with the pattern of his gestures. Every few moments he stopped to punctuate his speech by smacking his right fist into the palm of his left hand.

The couple watched in silence from seats of equal height, their shoulders wrapped in the folds of dark robes adorned with silver pieces that sparkled like stars, the hems stitched with intricate weavings of gold thread. "Ten bales he tossed! Ten bales of heavy bear skins! It was a feat of strength unequaled by any so young."

The couple nodded as they eyed the petulant youth who stood beside his father, jaw set, eyes staring at the floor. Odin laughed and slapped the boy on the back, winning a sharp glare from the young man. "Don't let his stubborn silence fool you. He is quite precocious. He is just angry at coming here."

A look flashed between the couple, a bright light that momentarily illuminated the room then faded away just as quickly.

Ving raised his hand in salute. "Delighted, we accept the honor of raising a son of the Æsir. Under our tutelage, he will learn respect, the obligation of duty, and the supreme value of truth. Above all, he will learn to control his power."

Nodding her head, Hlora spread wide her arms. "Let the boy join us in this, his second home."

Grinning, Odin guided his reluctant son with a light push on his back that sent him stumbling forward. "It is with full trust that I place my son in your care to guide into his majority. For if anyone can handle his energy it is you."

As Odin turned to leave, he called out over his shoulder. "Beware of his anger. None are safe, within or without, when he throws a tantrum. The hall shakes with his fury, the sky blackens, and the clouds thunder in reply." Then before the couple could respond to his parting words of caution, Odin slipped through the doorway of their hall, leaving his son standing unbowed before the couple.

Hlora stared at the boy, taking in his firm stance, defiant glare, broad shoulders, and youthful good looks. "It is a heavy charge the Alfodur has laid upon us."

Ving nodded as he rose in stately grace from his seat and stepped down to where the boy stood in sullen silence. "True, but it is a charge we proudly bear." He paused, arranging his robes, as he looked over a child nearly his own height, smiled as he met the boy's unflinching gaze, nodded in appreciation of his proud stance. "Your name is Thor?"

The youth stared back from watchful eyes just visible beneath dark bushy brows framed by an unruly thatch of dirty blond hair. His chin jutted forward as he pushed a short reply through his gate of bright white teeth. "Yes."

Ving patted Thor's shoulder, felt his skin prickle and the hair rise on his arm. A satisfied smile lifted the corners of his lips. With a whisk of his robe, he swept around the boy careful not to brush up against him and returned to his seat. "Then know you are most welcome in our home, but you will not be allowed to sit idle waiting in pampered silence for your majority. Responsibilities you will have then, so responsibilities you will have now; a load commensurate with the strength of your broad shoulders."

Thor's eyes brightened. A broad grin stretched his lips at the prospect of doing something useful, of being permitted to take part in events other than play. "When do I start? I am ready to start now!"

The couple laughed as Ving leaned in to his wife. "Such it is with persons destined to perform great deeds. What they have already done seems hardly worth notice. What they have undertaken to do seems worth toil, danger, and life itself."

Hlora waved a hand at a nearby seat. "Come rest yourself. Patience first. Tomorrow will be soon enough. Then you will assist us in the performance of our duties. With flashing heat, we illuminate the horizon of the sky, announcing the coming storms to the homes of men. Storm rains refresh the lands, bringing the blessings of growth."

Ving's eyes glittered as he reached across to grasp Hlora's hand. "You, Thor, I think, may be the gathering storm."

On the seventh day, a bold, strong-muscled youth, with flowing hair the color of fire, full grown into his sense of self, strode purposefully into Odin's hall. He paused, his gaze flickering upwards, as he passed beneath the leaping wolf and hovering eagle.

Silence fell across those gathered about the board. Many smiled, recognizing the youth who moved among them. The young man stopped before the seat of Odin, bowed his head to the Alfodur, smiled broadly to light the room, then turned slightly and bowed his head to Frigg.

With a massive fist, he smote his chest; the hall echoed with the sound of a mighty wave crashing against the ribbed hull of a ship. Boldly, he announced himself to the clan. "I am called Thor, my name bestowed on me by my parents who rule this land. Ving-Thor, I call myself in honor of my foster parents, whose wise counsel taught me the principles of truth, duty, and how to apply both in the practice of honor. Father, I have come to take my place at your side. My strength, I pledge in the service of my kin, to protect our home, our family, and all they have created. By right of blood, I make this claim. Never will you regret my declaration."

Smiling, Frigg bid her son be seated. By her own hand, she poured him a mug of ale. "Gladly, we welcome our son now returned into the hearth of our hearts."

Odin raised his goblet in salute. "Warm greeting, I give to my son, Asa-Thor, that he knows welcome in our homes and draws strength from kinship bonds."

The joyous roar of the gathering shook the rafters. Everyone was delighted at the return of one born to their clan. Songs of welcome were sung while solemn pledges were given over mead. For his abilities and lineage, he was assigned position of importance among the clan; guardian of Asgard, protector of men, ward against the children of frost, and consecrator of his mother's blessings.

Geri and Freki Come to Dine

In the rime-cold lands where giants dwell, and frigid air steals the warmth from unprotected bodies, a heavy-cloaked figure, astride a golden mount made his way across a stretch of frozen earth scoured clear by sharp blowing winds.

A dark hump on a mound of white caught his attention, a soft movement—gone in a moment. He climbed the hillside, breaking a path through crusts of drifted snow. Near the top, he found a pair of wolf pups suckling at the cold teats of their dead mother.

She had been a large wolf, not young, not old, but worn down by the tight skin of famine that rules in difficult lands and harsh weather. Her coat was stiff with frozen blood, her lips stained red with crystals of life dew. She lay curled before the den, ribs shattered by a heavy blow, gray back turned to the frosted waste; her dying effort to shield a dark hole that angled down into the earth from biting winds that blew across the steppe. Snow and dirt scuffed around the entrance, the ground spattered with blood, the snow deeply scored by claws and stomped down by heavy tread, told of a bitter battle. A thick club of fired oak lay nearby; its length smeared with clotted gore and gray hairs.

Tracks of a giant snaked off into the far hills, the path clear to the naked eye, marked by wide breaks plowed through random drifts of snow that stretched from the hills onto the plains. Wide streaks of dark red blood marked the erratic trail.

Hunger had driven the whelps from the protection of the den, dared them to crawl into the shivering cold to seek nourishment from their fallen mother. They were so starved down that their ribs stood out, hipbones and shoulder blades jutted beneath taut skin, and each joint of the backbone lay visible.

As Odin reached down they turned as one, black lips curled back, to face the danger. Twice he reached for the pair. Twice he was met with menacing growls and sharp white teeth that nipped his fingers. A third time he caught them up by the scruff of their necks, then tucked the snarling pups securely into his travel pack.

His charges in tow, Odin returned to Asgard, driving his mount to exhaustion in his urgency. Rainbow colors shimmered the air as he thundered over the Quivering Way. Guards leapt aside as he dashed through Valgrind into the courtyard of Valhalla.

With hydromel from Heidrun's utters he nursed the whelps. Fed them meat once their skin plumped to conceal their bones. Each day he bid them grow strong. In the warmth of Valhalla, he raised them to adults, taught them the ways of hall life, how to maneuver on the battlefield, taught them friend from foe. Grim they were with the lessons. Greedy they were to learn.

The pair grew large, their massive heads gated with sharp white teeth. About their strong shoulders sprouted a thick ruff of gray fur. They greet visitors with unwavering stares from clear yellow eyes that shivered fearful hearts.

Brave and great of spirit, they took quickly to slaughter—such was their nature. Their speed no quarry could escape; neither man nor beast could resist their power. Not even in the densest thickets could they hide, so sharp their hearing, so keen their noses to scent. But it was in the home their greatest value shown. Strong watchdogs, they prowl the great halls. Sleeps one at noon, the other at night that none may enter unless invited.

Geri and Freki, foes of giants, crouch beside the seat of Odin, each to one hand, red tongues lolling as they keep watch. They gorge from the bowl of the Alfodur, feasting on all the meat served to him, while he drinks only wine.

The Ender

Harsh the bolt from dark cloud fell, striking hard the green crest of a mighty oak—scattering leaf from limb in the brilliance—a bright flash that took the tree by force. The fire penetrated the leafy arbor, the ragged tip boring deep into its heart. The mother, Laufey, a green isle, round, smooth, fertile. The father, Farbauti, a bright jagged edge. Born was a son from this tryst of parents so unalike. They called him Loki, the Ender.

With dark hair, deep, brooding brown eyes, full lips quick to laugh or hurl harsh invective, Loki took on the character of his mother and the essence of his father. Wearing a form to charm the senses, his soft, handsome features concealed a harsh spirit and housed a quick, cunning mind.

Again, the bright flash of opposites united to conceive a second son. They called him Beylist, the flame of the dwelling. Plain-featured, spirit solid, calm of nature as his mother, for him the greatest pleasure lay in the comforts of his own home and the company of his immediate clan.

The brothers were raised in the family's holding, a heavy timbered hall surrounded by patches of cleared land and thick fingers of dark green fir trees nestled deep in the eastern forest of Jarnvid just beyond the Mœotin Marsh. Together they spent many hours exploring the dark forest paths of the Ironwood.

When the surroundings became unknown, Beylist grew uneasy. Tugging at his brother's jerkin, he urged their return home, eager to be back amid the familiar. But always Loki dared to travel further, to climb higher that he might see beyond the horizon. Unlike his younger brother, Loki was not content with a settled life. His restless spirit desired adventure. Leaving home, he sought out his fate among the far-off kin of his mother.

Working the lines of fate to his own purpose, the son of Laufey came before the great gods, there in the early days of Asgard, to stake claim of kinship through the blood of his mother. "Loki, I am called, and Ariel for my lofty thoughts. My father is Farbauti, a noble Jotun. My mother, Laufey, a gentle creature of Fjorgyn's line. Born in turmoil from the collision of two worlds, I eagerly seek to find my place in both.

From the far eastern land of my birth, I have traveled to find the new, the different, the exciting. Always I seek what lies over the next hill, curious to view that which others only dream. A cunning mind is my sole burden on the road. For wits are ever needful when gauging the character of another's thoughts, distinguishing the dull minded from sharp, to discern friend from foe, the foolish from wise.

Mine is the inborn ability to change shape; an inheritance of my parent's disparity. It is a useful deception for confounding enemies. As a snake doffs its vestments to take on a shiny new frame, so, too, I can shed one form for another.

I stand here now, fearlessly before my mother's people, demanding the rights of filial recognition. Accept me and I pledge my skills to protect that which you have created. Never will you regret the decision."

All together the Æsir gathered in council, to decide what to do, those powerful gods. Harsh language flowed among them over the dark son's lineage and his bold claim of kinship.

The supplicant sneered at the unrest his entreaty had caused. When he heard the disparities passed among the gathering, a bright flame coursed up his neck to flush bright red on his cheeks. He swallowed hard to check the anger that threatened to burst from his lips. "You bawl as a herd of goats frightened by shadows in the night, letting your minds run away with thoughts of wolves when a bush stands before you, shrouded in darkness, waiting for Sol to shine her light and reveal the familiar."

Three times Odin clapped his hands for silence. When all had quieted, he glared at Loki, who stood, chin raised, unbowed before everyone. "You dare chastise those whose clan you ask to join? I would consider it a bald affront, and have you tossed from this hall did your words not carry the sting of truth." He chewed a moment on his mustache, then looked out across the gathering. "And while my kin might feel otherwise, it is a daring I admire."

Alone Odin rose and made decision for the clan. Drawing a knife from its sheath at his waist, he made a shallow cut on his palm. He passed the knife to Loki, who did the same. Blood welling from their wounds, they clasped hands. Odin's voice rang out across the gathering as he drew Loki close. "I freely mix my blood in the bond of brotherhood and pledge to never drink ale unless it is served to us both."

Knowing eye peered deep into shrewd gaze. "Warm greeting, I give to the son of Laufey that he may draw strength from our kinship. Words of caution, I offer to the son of Farbauti. Many are those who know a great deal that think others know little, and often in the practice of deceit find afterward it was they who were deceived."

The Son of Nine

It was pasture month with farmers driving their herds to the mountain meadows when a hardy traveler arrived from the west to stand before the Æsir court. He strode across Valgrind, pushing through the doors of Valhalla with the assured bearing of a confident warrior. Clad in a byrnie with rings that reflected the sun, a silver helm adorned with ram horns tucked firmly beneath his arm, he glided between the benches. A heavy sword hung at his waist, its plain leather scabbard worn from much use.

Fair featured, with white skin and teeth that glowed like gold, he dazzled the entire court. "Heimdall, I am called. My home lies far to the west in the watery lands of Vanaheim. Of nine mothers, I am the child. Of nine sisters, I am the son. My mothers' do duty on the mondul of the World Mill, assigned the task by the sons of Bor when the world was young. Never have they faltered in this charge.

In days past I trod dusty roads as Rigg, offering knowledge to the progeny of Ask and Embla. As Sceaf of the Scani, I brought culture to the lands of men. By my hand, I improved the lives of many. Four generations I lived among them as adopted kin, came to understand their nature, to cherish their lines.

My abilities are great. My knowledge of the natural world is broad. With nine skills, I challenge those who would lead. At board games,

I stand undefeated. Runes I never spoil; with a deft, steady hand, I carve and clearly stain. My skill with a warrior's blade is great; always my edge draws blood. With the bent yew, I hit all I shoot at. On skis, nothing can escape me—neither man nor beast. At sculling, few can match my speed. I can follow a track like a hound, both in thaw or hard snow, across rocks, sunbaked clay, even fresh green fields prove no challenge. I've mastered music, verse as well, and can use both to call up passions at will: pleasure and gladness, sorrow and sympathy, or all consuming, blood-boiling hate.

Wary by nature, I am silent—my counsel kept close until needful. My sight is keen, as are my ears. None can approach that I do not know it long before they present themselves. All this I offer to benefit your honor."

The shining warrior thumped his beast three times, then held out his hand to the high seat. "By the long duty of my mothers, by my many daring actions, I ask to join the Æsir. Accept my heartfelt request for kinship and I pledge myself to the honor of this clan and the protection of all you have created. Never will you regret the decision."

All together the Æsir gathered in council to decide what to do. A short time they took to discuss. Everyone remarked favorably of the young man, impressed by his bearing. After everyone had spoken their mind on the matter, Odin rose and made decision for the clan. "Warm greeting, I give to a new relation of the Æsir. Let him know welcome in our homes and draw strength from our kinship."

All Æsir were delighted at the ruling. Songs of welcome were sung while solemn pledges were given over mead. For his skills, he was assigned a position of importance among the clan, to stand guard at the bridgehead of Bifrost—the ultimate sentry whom none can surprise. For his use, they gave him Himinbjorg, the heaven-set lodging nestled among the clouds that he might rest in comfort at the end of day.

Heimdall raised his cup, turned in a circle to take in all of his new kin. "You have bestowed on me a great honor; I will never betray your trust." He took a deep drink then lifted his voice to the sky. "From across the windswept ocean waves, I came to the halls of Asgard to give the oath of kinship. Accepted, I ready myself to stand watch on

Asbrau. Never have you had such a sentinel. From the bridgehead's high arch, I will keep cycle with the birds, sighting 100 leagues out, ever watchful for the advance of enemies. My keen ears perceive all that makes noise, sprouting grass, spreading trees, the settling of eiderdown on the rocky headland, and wool growing on sheep. None will be able to approach that I cannot hear them. From this day forward, the security of my new kin is my only concern."

The Birth of Baldur and Hodd

Soon after Heimdall's arrival, Frigg bore two sons. The first child, eager to glimpse the day, was born in the morning when warm breezes rushed across the land and geese called as they winged to familiar haunts. The second son fought his mother all day. After a prolonged labor, he was born in the harshness of deep night as the clear notes of the wolf pack howled through the hills and home fires guttered from the cold.

Through the rest of the night, and well into the next morning, their lusty wails banished rest from the halls of Asgard. Handmaidens rushed about caring for the mother spent from exertions of a difficult birth. Themselves weary, they sought to comfort the squalling newborns.

Frigg's tired smile beamed from the birth bed as Odin knelt beside her. "We have two fine sons." He cocked his head and grinned. "Listen. You can hear them announcing their arrival. Let all take heed, for great things are in store."

Reaching out, he pushed back a lock of hair, still damp with sweat, from Frigg's forehead. "They will do us proud," she sighed then drifted off into sleep.

On the third day of their life Frigg held her first son up before the court, turned him round to show off his clear brow, bathing all in the glory of his bright, shining beauty. "I invite everyone to greet my son. I call him, Baldur, the warmth of my heart." Loud cheers and thunderous applause filled the room, while Odin beamed from his seat, radiating pride, as he gazed on the smile of his son.

After Frigg introduced Baldur, Odin lifted his second son up before the court, turned him round so all could see the dark fierceness of his features, his hard eyes, and the bushy black hair that already covered his head. "I invite everyone to greet my son. I call him, Hodd, a born warrior." The room rang with cheers. Frigg looked up from nuzzling Baldur, tenderness glistening in her eyes from the wondrous gaze of her son.

———

The brothers grew swiftly. Different in nature yet inseparable in friendship, there was not one without the shadow of the other. All who met them were delighted as the pair engaged in pranks to frustrate their parents, in all ways mischievous boys learning the ways of their world.

Frigg threw up her hands in exasperation, stomped across the room, and collapsed onto her seat. "What have they done now?"

Fulla smiled into her hand. "They have soured the beer again. Audhrimnir grumbles that he will need to brew another batch."

Frigg pinched the bridge of her nose. "No." She shook her head "Go tell him I will fix it. I have no stomach to hear Thor's loud complaints again. First it will be him, then the rest of the hall."

She twisted in the seat, repositioning her robe until she was comfortable. With a sharp gesture, she beckoned Fulla to attend. "I swear there are times I wish we had fostered them out."

Fulla smiled inside her cheeks as she slipped behind the seat and busied herself arranging Frigg's hair, knowing full well her mistress would sooner have cut off her arm than release her sons to the care of another.

———

Each day, the boys received instruction from their parents that they might discover their place in the Æsir clan. It was here their differences shown.

Conciliatory and joyous, Baldur shared the caring nature of his mother. He took readily to Frigg's instructions as she taught him the ways of Fjorgyn's line, the arts of growth, patience, and perseverance. Indulged in all things, he found his way into the hearts of everyone who met him, always he was greeted with delight.

Stern-minded, Hodd shared the war-like nature of his father. Each day, he trailed after Odin and in all ways emulated his every action. Eagerly, he took up the instruments of war, learned well the hard line of blade dominance. His brooding aspect was always respected but avoided.

Each night, the boys whispered from their beds words only the other could hear, sharing all they had learned that day. In the darkness of their room they pledged to always support each other in all things.

————————

Alone with Frigg in his great hall, Odin folded his arms. "You coddle the child too much," he frowned down at his wife. "It will make him weak and unable to defend himself. Of what use is peace without the strength of arm to protect it?"

Frigg, eyes stern, snapped her robe over her legs. "And what you do with Hodd makes him strong," she flared back. "You teach him to enjoy war so his only solution to all problems is the naked sword or the arrow. Mark my words, he will die by the edge of a blade. At least Baldur will know mercy. Hodd will only know the fear of others."

Odin snorted as he turned aside. "It may be as you say," his gaze passed out the doorway to rove over the hall roofs visible between the open posts, "but I wish the best for my sons. Soon they will take their place in the clan. I would have their honor always held high."

Frigg idly ran a pleat of her robe between thumb and forefinger. "Remaining true to one's nature is the surest path to honor. Though their temperaments are very different, they hold each other in the highest esteem. Let us follow their lead and trust the fates."

Grumbling beneath his breath, Odin slumped down in his seat. Snatching up his goblet, he took a long pull of wine. "I have never been good at trusting fate."

———————

On the seventh day, the brothers presented themselves before the clan in the great hall of Gladsheim. Grown to their full height, they made a proud, ungainly pair as they marched up the aisle between the benches, one slender and fair, the other stocky and dark.

Shoulder-to-shoulder, they came to a stop before the high seats of Odin and Frigg. They glanced at each other from the corner of their eyes. Light smiles twitched their lips. Odin raised a hand for silence. "Who is it that stands before me? Name yourselves. Say why you would speak with me?"

The fair brother stepped forward to make claim before the assembly. A gentle sigh ran through the crowd as the young man's lips parted into a dazzling smile. "I am called Baldur the Good, my name bestowed on me by my parents who rule this land. Skilled in the healing arts and the powers of growth, I have come to take my place at my parents' side. My abilities I pledge in the service of my kin, to protect my home, my clan, and all they have created. By right of blood I make this claim. Never will you regret my declaration."

The dark brother stepped forward to state his claim. He glared side to side, his harsh stare commanding silence. "I am called Hodd, my name bestowed on me by my parents who rule this land. Well skilled in the arts of war, the bow and blade are natural extensions of my arm. I am here to take my place at my father's side. My abilities I pledge in the service of my kin, to protect my home, my clan, and all they have created. By right of blood I make this claim. Never will you regret my declaration."

Smiling, Frigg bid her sons be seated. By her own hand, she poured them mugs of crisp ale. "Gladly, we welcome our dear sons, Baldur and Hodd, into the hearth of our hearts."

Odin raised his goblet in salute. "Warm greeting, I give to my sons, Hodd and Baldur, that they know welcome in our homes and draw strength from kinship bonds."

The joyous roar of the gathering shook the rafters. Songs of welcome were sung while solemn pledges were given over mead. For their skills and lineage, the brothers were assigned positions of importance among the clan. Hodd was given a place on the Ljónar that strength be considered in every decision. To him was assigned the duty of managing battles for the Æsir. Baldur was given a place on the Ljónar that peace be considered in every decision. To him was assigned the duty of managing reconciliation between foes.

Far Ruler

Along dark, mountain paths Odin hunched through thick, nearly impenetrable forests where deep silences echoed with the drip, drip, drip of dewdrops slipping from leaves amid the high branches. A peaceful smile crooked his lips as he took a deep breath of fragrant humus and damp moss. "I am close now. I can feel him. He should be in the open glade just beyond this thicket."

Gently parting a web of branches, Odin worked his way through the scrub, muting the sound of his passage so as not to alarm the earth-brown sentinel standing outside a squat, brushy mound raised up amid the bracken on the far side of the clearing.

The tall, well-built figure turned as Odin strode across the open space from the forest fence. Quiet, blue eyes peered from above the harvest sprouting of youth-now-a-man that flocked his cheeks and upper lip. His flaxen hair tied back with a leather thong allowed an unfettered gaze of the ancient warrior's approach.

The sentry rolled his shoulders, braced his feet wide, and jerked clear the nut-stained tunic cinched at the waist with a plain leather belt. A long, heavy blade was slung over his left shoulder. His right hand twitched beside a short hunting knife strapped at his hip.

Odin raised his hand as he stumbled through the tufts of grass dotting the clearing. "Hail Vidar. I bring greetings from your kin in

Asgard." The young man raised his left hand, silently returning the greeting.

Odin stomped forward, letting his eyes rove over a wattle hutch of intricately woven grasses that seemed to grow up from the ground behind the young man. "So, this is Landvide. Your mother spoke well of it."

Vidar cocked his head to one side as he examined the grinning, hooded figure that leaned heavily on a worn walking staff. His shrewd eye took in the scuffed leather boots that bound the traveler's feet to mid-calf. A dark gray travel cloak soaked through by rain hung limp from the shoulders. Its hem frayed from the constant snagging of brambles, its length caked with splotches of mud, told of a hard journey filled with hazardous falls.

The right hand quit its dance and fluttered to rest on the handle of the knife at his waist. "My home can be difficult to reach. How is it you found me?"

Odin winked at the young man as he drew back the gray hood from his head. White hair spilled out over his shoulders, a blizzard of snow capping a mighty mountain. "Your mother and I have... an understanding. She told me where I could find you."

Vidar snorted. "I am surprised you made it past Grídarvöll." He spat sideways onto the ground. "My mother is known for her harsh treatment of those who presume familiarity."

Odin fluffed his beard to shake it free of the forest damp. "She did not menace me in any way," he grinned at the thought. "In fact, when I told her of my mission, she gave me exact directions. She even sent me along with her blessing."

Vidar said nothing but shifted his stance until the morning sun shone over his shoulder into Odin's eyes. "What is it you want, Father?"

Faint tendrils of steam swirled from Odin's cloak as sunlight warmed the glade. He shook his travel pack from his shoulders. "Do you mind if I rest a moment?" He set the pack on the ground beside his feet. "The journey to your hall has been difficult. Last night's downpour chilled me to the bone."

Keeping his gaze focused on Odin's hands, Vidar swept an arm toward the entrance of his hut, a dark hole nested with sharpened branches pointing inward; easy to enter, difficult to exit.

Odin blinked at the rabbit warren entry that required crawling on hands and knees. "I favor the feel of the sun to the cramped shadows of your hall."

"No," he shook his head, "I've come to invite you to rejoin your kin in Asgard. I think you will find our halls somewhat finer, certainly they are a good deal more spacious than this snarl of twigs you call a home."

Blue eyes squinted over a mouth that stiffened into a firm line offering no cooperation. "I prefer it here where the quiet forests stretch wide than being closeted behind a great wall amid the incessant bickering of family."

Odin laughed, his booming voice raising a flock of ravens from the nearby trees. For a moment, their raucous calls filled the air, then faded as they winged to a new roost on a far hill. "Have no fear that you will lose being far ruler of this vast, empty domain. It will remain yours, always. You can return here whenever you like. But if you join the rest of your kin, you can share in the tributes of men and the benefits they confer."

Vidar turned his face aside, his eyes darting between the forest edge and the disheveled figure that tottered before him. A stag stepped from the wooded shadows to crop at a clump of grass near the edge of the glade. The two watched until it took notice of their presence and bolted back into the trees.

Odin dragged a hand across his face. "I worry for you," he squinted up at his son, "with only birds and harts for company. Being alone allows one time for reflection. I, too, seek solitude from time to time. But too much aloneness deprives one of the warmth companionship brings and dulls the mind from lack of conversation."

Vidar folded his arms across his chest but said nothing to interrupt Odin's speech.

Odin placed a hand on his breast as tears threatened to burst the dam of his eyes. "When you removed yourself to this remote outpost it left a hole in all our hearts... in my heart. I ask you, all your kin ask you, to return to your rightful place at our hearth."

The young man glared straight ahead, heat flushing his cheeks. He blinked suddenly to clear his eyes. His overly stiff lip and bright, watery gaze caught Odin's attention. "It pains me," the ancient gambler grinned inside his cheeks, "to see you so far from home. I prefer my family close. There is power in unity. When we stand together, none can defy us. Here. I've brought a token of my sincerity."

Odin rummaged through the pack at his feet, spilling provisions on the ground before cradling a pair of quilted leather boots from its depths. "These are a gift; a gift of special power crafted from the leather castoffs of men. Imbued with the silence you crave and the strength of sacrifice, they are an example of what can be yours."

With a low mumble of appreciation Vidar accepted the boots. He turned them over in his hands, admiring the play of sunlight across the textured surface that marked the grain. A smile twitched the corners of his lips as he untied the stiff, hard-cured leather that bound his feet and slipped the boots on over bared skin.

The soft leather gently embraced his feet and reached protectively up to his calf. He rocked back, enjoying the feel of sudden comfort, then slid forward, silent as the padding of a cat. When he ran, it was with the breath of wind.

Vidar came to a stop before Odin. Bending low, he ran a caressing hand over the boots, letting his fingers trace the seams. He grinned up at the Alfodur. "We can leave now and be drinking mead in Gladsheim by nightfall."

Odin stared at the young man, a deep frown shadowing his face. "It took me seven days to get here, slogging through bogs that threatened to suck me down into their muddy depths, climbing over deadfalls, fighting the heavy brush, and squirming my way through rank-on-rank of crowding trees. Now you say we can return by nightfall."

Vidar smirked down at his new boots. "My mother is crafty. Like I said, she takes exception to familiarity." He twitched his chin at the forest. "There is an easier route than the one she sent you along to get here. Wait here while I get my pack, then we can be off."

While Vidar left to gather his travel gear, Odin rearranged his pack, hoisted it onto his shoulders, and cinched it tight. A self-satisfied smile crept across his face as he settled himself to wait.

The First War

In the bright early days of the world, when the sons of Bor sought to forge the boundaries of their reign, a daughter of the Vanir traveled east to visit the land of Midgard. Gullveig they called her, Bright Gold, for the luster of her hair. A seeress of gratifying prophecy, skilled in the manipulation of nature, she visited the unsuspecting homes of men. With spells, she molded minds, twisted lives, and played with fates. Freely, she taught her knowledge to the offspring of Ask and Embla.

The Æsir grew angry at the meddling in the affairs of men by a member of another clan. To guard their rights and to protect the land of men, they captured the golden-haired woman, bound her limbs, and bundled her off to their halls. With much ceremony, the glorious gods convened a Husthing in the great hall of Valhalla to decide the fate of Gullveig for the malicious practice of seid. Quarrels raged among the court concerning the fate of the maiden who stood unbowed before them.

Throwing back her head, Gullveig shouted over the din of voices filling the hall. "You consider yourselves wise beyond years, but that conceit does not confer the right to judge others." As a flood of derision rolled from the gallery, she raised her voice louder, as a swimmer swamped by towering waves, gasps for breath. "I say you have no right to judge me! I say you—"

"Silence!" The Alfodur's ferocious glare choked the words in Gullveig's throat and hushed the grumblings of the crowd. "You have no voice in these proceedings. Your teachings have instigated enough misery. The world of men is in turmoil. We have every right to hold you accountable for the mayhem your teachings have caused."

A muscle twitched the maiden's cheek. "I don't deny my actions." She shrugged her bound hands in appeal. "But I have the right to defend myself before this..." a sneer curled her lips, "this council."

Odin pounded a fist on the table. Those seated nearest jumped and cringed away. "I said silence! Speak again and I'll have your tongue out." He rocked back, drumming his fingers on the armrest of his seat. "Three days we have gone without sleep, bickering over your fate. The time for talk is done; I will listen to no more. By my hand, I decide. Not only have you held us up to ridicule in the eyes of men, but you have brought dishonor to your own clan. For such affronts and the threat you pose to our rights, your life is forfeit."

He gestured to a fire pit stacked high with burning wood then clapped his hands three times. Four guards detached themselves from the walls and, with pikes lowered, advanced on the maiden. Thrusting from four sides, they skewered Gullveig and lofted her, writhing and shrieking, above the pit of ravenous flames. Curses howled from her blackened lips as the fire consumed her form. Twice while the greedy flames charred her flesh, she used her arts to survive the pyre, reborn each time, choking from the ashes. Staggering, smoke still curling from her scorched flesh, Gullveig glared across the fire pit at the high seat. "I do not die easily, old man. Besides, if you think my death will return things to the way they were, you are greatly mistaken. Knowledge, once shared, cannot be destroyed."

Odin leaned on his knee, a painful grimace twisting his lips. He called to the guards, his voice raw from the smoke clotting the hall. "Again. Add more wood. This time press her down into the flames."

The guards advanced, pikes lowered, backing the young woman toward the flames. Roughly tossing Gullveig into the pit, they pinned her deep in the coals with their pikes. Among the seated gathering, hands drifted over noses to block the stench of burning flesh. Many others clapped hands over their ears as her screams echoed through the hall, while the guards struggled to hold her down. The sputtering fire sent tendrils of flame arcing through the air. The guards cursed when struck by the wild flames but held to their grim task.

For many hours they endured a raging fire that roared as if alive, fighting to keep their footing as a thick, oily soot rose to coat everyone and everything. When the blaze subsided, they stumbled back, dropping pikes with shafts nearly burned through, the iron tips melted from the heat. Only the gentle crackle of the fire could be heard.

Everyone waited, breath held, expecting to see Gullveig scramble from the pit. When nothing happened, Odin shouted orders to the sweating guardsmen. "Quickly now, gather up her remains. Don't miss a thing."

Carefully, they scraped Gullveig's remains from the coals. In the center of the pit they found her heart, half-burnt, half raw still quivering amid the ashes. A deep growl rumbled from Odin's throat when he saw the bloody mass. "Take it, take all of it far from here. Dump it in the shadows of Jarnvid. Scatter it over the frozen loam for the wild things that haunt the forest."

Word of the brutal execution spread across the lands, finally reaching the watery inlets of Vanaheim. Angered, the Vanir sent a delegation to Asgard demanding restitution, weregild paid to the kin of Gullveig for her death. They met in joint council with the Æsir; faces stern, eyes hard, and made their unyielding claims. Harsh words were uttered, curt speech that flew as barbs from both sides.

A minister of the Vanir turned his sallow face to the Alfodur. "You brazenly cut down one of our clan, an action that strikes not only her family, but all the Vanir. What price for the life of our daughter? What price for our honor? To satisfy our loss, we demand the Æsir yield tribute by sharing the sacrifices offered by men."

Odin snorted and the rest of the Æsir followed with derisive laughter. He leaned forward, forcing his words through clenched teeth. "You dare demand payment for just treatment. Gullveig directed her craft to lessen the respect men held for the Æsir and by such deeds diminished the honor of the Vanir. Because her actions disrespected both clans, we share equally in her death. The punishment meted out was just for all concerned."

The Vanir refused this course of argument and turned their heads to face east. A leader from their group stood up to speak, a venerable god of the sea, wise in years. "I am plain of speech, preferring to let my actions speak for me. Loath am I to draw the saddening sword; little do I hide it, but a warrior fights when he must, regardless the foe." He waved a hand at the Vanir delegation. "We are honor-bound to seek revenge or to receive tribute for the death of kin. You know this. But arrogance clouds your vision. Were your eyes any more dimmed you would run full into a cliff wall for fear of the pebble glimpsed at your feet."

"Arrogant! Arrogant!" Odin thumped a fist against his chest until the hall rafters echoed with the sound. "By the strength of our arm we embrace that which is ours. All others we deny. With spear, blade, and hard-slung stone, we stand ready to resist. There is no foe we cannot defeat, no challenge we will not accept. Listen as I shout our victory cry—proud and defiant for all to hear."

With a loud yell of anger, he hurled a spear over the indomitable Vanir, sending them skittering from the hall, and so dedicated the first war of the world.

Wolf smoke crossed the land—tall columns of white smoke twisting high into the sky from wolf's dung fired along a line of sentry posts to warn of an invading force. The mighty host of Vanaheim marched onto Vigrid plain, a sea of warriors flooding the land, trampling the verdant earth to dust, and washing up against the walls of Asgard.

The air rang with the remorseless tramp of stalwart soldiery as legions swarmed the field, both sides strengthened by auxiliaries— alike equipped with arms, alike inspired. The sheen of polished byrnies and sharp glinting edges formed a landlocked sea of shimmering silver.

They attacked, hurling heavy stones that crashed against shields and crushed the stoutest limbs. Death-dealing weapons sliced through the air, their wicked edges biting deep into exposed flesh. The imposing wall of Asgard rang with the cries of bold warriors, as lines of mounted fighters thundered across the field, their charge shaking the ground. A hard day was had by all. Many were washed by showers of blood that moistened the lips of fallen combatants, clung to ringed byrnies, and turned the dust to mud.

For a time, the Æsir held within their fortress. The moat of vaferflames surrounding the walls kept their attackers at bay. But the tide of war proved too strong to resist. Through clever strategy, the wise Vanir breached the wall of Asgard.

The venerable war leader of the Vanir crouched in his tent surrounded by his field commanders and set out his plan. After tying back a lock of graying hair, he pointed a finger at the nearest warrior. "You, take the body of my servant killed in the last exchange. Dress him in my best warrior's cloak and byrnie of hard-linked gold rings that he might be marked from afar. Give me his plain gray cloak that I might blend into the twilight shadows. Two must make the leap that one may cross in safety."

He looked each of the commanders in the eye, smiling at the steady confidence that gazed back. "Have your warriors ready to advance when the gate falls. Tear down the battlements on either side as soon as you enter, lest our comrades be funneled through a narrow passage that the foe can easily defend. Tumble rock into the nasty brew surrounding the wall, fill the way that our warriors can cross in safety. With multiple breaches in their fortification the Æsir will need to flee or fight to the last."

A grim smile of necessity twisted his lips as he drew his servant's cloak, still wet with blood, about his shoulders. "Be ready. All this must happen quickly."

Under cover of twilight he charged the gate. Shoulders humped with lifeless cargo, he dodged across the moat of roiling black cloud. A flashing bolt crackled the air with eye-dazzling brightness. In the afterglow of his passage, the servant's scorched body clad in splendid garments tumbled amid the churning vafer while he clung as a spider to the wall, concealed in the shadows beside the gate.

The Æsir, convinced the foeman had perished in the attempt, jeered from their high perch at the body tumbling amid the black froth and at the enemy horde howling in impotent rage from across the flaming moat.

The bold leader of the Vanir waited until those within had settled down for the night. Once certain everyone was asleep, with sure grip, he scaled the walls of Asgard. Atop the wall he drifted among the shadows, dodging weary sentries, until he located the lynchpins of the gate. Swift blows from the flat of his heavy blade released Valgrind from its moorings. The mighty gate of Asgard shuddered and fell, its torrent-swept timbers blown loose by the winds of war. Into the breach rushed a flood of howling warriors who attacked the walls, crumbling its frame into the moat.

Shaken from their sleep, the surprised Æsir snatched up their weapons, but the tide of shrieking warriors was too great. Dodging, parrying, cursing, they were driven from the place by the wave of singing blades, escaping with great leaps over the wall into the night, as hares harried by a pack of hounds' dart to the safety of shadows.

Odin glared over his shoulder, listening to the loud cheers of victory that carried on the wind. The squelching of mud mixed with the grinding of his teeth as he turned back to working his way through the darkness.

———·———

In the gray light of morning the sons of Bor and their kin stalked the bloody mire of the battlefield, picking their way through heaps of corpses, disturbing the black-winged scavengers that squawked as they jostled for choice morsels plucked from gaping wounds and unprotected eyes.

Their hoard of life emptied, few protested the rapine of the hungry flocks. But as the birds became more ravenous, more aggressive, the stagnant air whispered with an occasional groan as beaks tore into still-living flesh. Eyes of the company sought out the source of the sounds. Some thought to offer what help they could, but with a sharp gesture Odin drew them along, ignoring the bodies scattered about the ground, his jaw set with grim determination.

In an area cleared of the carnage of battle, they came together to debate their best course of action. All were called to join the discussion. None were left out.

Odin raised himself up before the group, his one eye smoldered with a flame that refused to die as he took in the blood-spattered garments and strained faces that tracked his every move. Three times he cleared his throat, then spoke out loudly so his words carried to all. "We stand tall this day, not through success on the field of valor, for our halls have fallen to worthy foes, but through our refusal to surrender. We are at a crisis. None must hold back. Everyone must speak their minds! To hoard your thoughts now, as a miser hoards his gold, is a luxury we cannot afford."

So, they spoke—all the gods and goddesses—there on the blood-soaked plain of honor and kinship, of responsibility and sacred oaths.

Near the front of the group, the thump of a fist against chest was followed by a loud, defiant voice. "Death should not deter us from resistance. For in the eyes of the brave, life counts for less than the loss of honor."

Odin waved his hand to encompass the bloody field. Many eyes followed his gesture, taking in the mounds of dead, while others refused to look away from their feet. "Are we to die? To lay down our lives and fade from existence as names half-remembered from a fitful dream?"

From along the edge sounded a ragged voice filled with the weariness of battle. "Why seek to rush Skuld? There is no easy way to flee from one's fate. Each is destined to seek their appointed place, compelled by the imperative of necessity, with body held fast by death. Let the Vanir keep what they have gained."

Odin winced at the words, while low mumbles whispered from the group, some in agreement, others against. Stretching out his hand palm up, he let his gaze rove across the faces, looking each in the eye until they glanced away. "Are we to set aside our honor, to relinquish our rights and live as beggars, or worse yet, as slaves in our own land?"

A flock of ravens lifted from their feast, filling the air with raucous calls, as a lone voice shouted from the back of the group. "Little will be accomplished by our death. In defeat the wise know soft dealing can often achieve that which general massacre failed to gain."

Nodding, Odin pointed at the speaker. "This. This." He swallowed hard. "If we do not reconcile with our foe, be ready to gaze with sorrow upon our homes become desolate halls where only winds dwell. A silent land where there is no joy and our names are forgotten in the mists of time."

He pounded his fists against his thighs. Those closest, edged back from his rage. "No! No! No! That I am not willing to accept! For our survival, I set aside my pride, though it burns my gut and sets my teeth on edge. Let us treat with the Vanir and close this cycle."

A Hard-Won Truce

All together they gathered, Æsir and Vanir, those war-bound foes with red shields of truce raised high, beneath the protecting limbs of the great ash whose boughs stretched across the heavens to speak of ending the bloody conflict, of yielding tribute by sharing the sacrifices of men.

Odin immediately exerted his will over the proceedings. At his insistence, the two factions held council in the open air downwind from the plain where many on both sides had died. "There is no need to keep our camps separate; we both agree this must end." He gestured toward a clear meadow that sloped away from the battlefield. "We will pitch our tents along the southern edge, filling the space between the hills and plain where the winds blow strongest."

Once the camps were set up, leaders from both sides gathered on an open knoll hedged with hazel poles. They came openhanded, their weapons left behind in their tents. One after another stepped past the poles to take their seat inside the circle. All eyes turned to Odin as he lifted his hand. "Much has been said. Much more has been done. Many have lost their lives because of this. It is time we put an end to this war."

The Vanir leader placed a hand to his nose. "Faugh! The stink here is incredible. Can we not meet elsewhere? Somewhere upwind?"

Odin turned his head to look out over the plain where bloating corpses were being stacked on wooden pyres for burning. "Why? For honorable foes, the result of warfare is no mystery. The smell reminds us of the price paid. It ensures we do not forget those who have fallen."

A grimace rippled through the Vanir delegation as their leader reluctantly nodded his head in agreement. "Very well. Let its urgency direct our talks to a quick resolution. We have no wish to endure this any longer than we must."

Seven days they met, driven by the growing smell of decay while burial fires burned across the plain, choking the air with thick, greasy smoke. Sharp-tuned were the ear hands that grasped at words, cautious of glib speech that was clever at making and breaking oaths. With two capable edges, such tongues can be used for either purpose.

Seven nights by the glow of the fires they held conference until the last of the fallen warriors were consigned to ash. Gathered before the burial mound, as the final stone was set to seal the howe, both sides agreed to a workable settlement.

Odin thumped a fist to his chest; a deep sound that nearly snatched away by the steady breeze. "Then it is agreed. You will vacate the lands of Asgard. In return the Æsir will provide room for the Vanir on our high council of twelve. As council members, the Vanir will share in any tribute received from the lands of men."

The Vanir leader bent his head to listen to the advice of his delegation, then turned back and thumped a fist to his chest. "It is agreed. To end this war and as weregild for Gullveig's death, we will share power with the host of Asgard. You can have your lands back; they are too dry for our liking."

Odin's lips gave a slight twitch as he nodded and beckoned to the serving girls who stood nearby. "From this day forward, we are forever reconciled." Cups brimming with ale were passed to each within the hazel round. Once all hands were filled, Odin raised up his cup. "Today we give the oath of fraternity on the bodies of honored foes, by the side of a mighty ship, the rim of a sturdy shield, the back of a powerful horse, and the keen edge of a strong blade. Always, rightful honors will be accorded between clans. With this drink, we pledge that none should break this treaty by word or deed, for what is pledged over the drinking cup must come true."

The foes edged together around a large iron kettle, ever watchful, for easily some veer from goodwill to hate. Hard glares flashed from both sides as cups were tipped back. When all had drunk, in truce they spit into the kettle. This mark of trust became Kvasir, their finest attributes. Raised up by the powers of both clans into the form of a man, cultured and wise beyond all others, he climbed from the kettle to stand proudly between the groups, the living embodiment of their compact.

Wiping his chin, the Vanir leader stepped around Kvasir, who gazed about with clear, wondering eyes, delighted by everything. "Drinking and spitting are fine, but this has been war. Prudence demands our truce be sealed with an exchange of hostages. We will not accept persons of no consequence; they must be of merit and rank."

Odin toed the ground, scuffing up a small pile of dirt. "Agreed."

The Vanir leader's head nodded like gentle waves rolling onto a beach. "Then let each side set their demands. We ask for..."

Odin blurted out his demand before the other could finish. "I would have the one whose daring leap across the vaferflames cost us the war. I will accept no other."

The Vanir delegation ground their teeth at the interruption. Many hands strayed to the empty spaces at their waists. "Very well," the Vanir leader frowned. "But he is a great leader among our clan, easily worth two of yours. We would have your wisest counselor, also one of your brothers as hostage."

Odin started to protest but held his tongue as a black look crept over the Vanir leader's face. He forced a smile and raised a hand. "Agreed. There is one counselor that I consider wisest of all. And as you live by the sea, I happen to have a brother who enjoys water."

Exchange of Hostages

Hoenir and Mimir traveled in celebrated pomp to the courts of Vanaheim, raised up beside the sea. Braided chins bobbed, and goblets tipped back as the pair were announced in the lofty hall of Ægir. The leader of the Vanir waved his hand, directing them to seats of prominence near the head of the table. Waiting maidens stared down their noses as a great show was made of clearing room at the bench.

Once served, they whispered to the servant girls not to stray too far with the pitcher. With a flourish, they waved their cups to their hosts. When none joined the salute, they glanced meaningfully at each other, then gave a polite nod to the leader.

Setting his cup aside, Ægir daubed at his lips with a cloth drawn from his right sleeve. He glanced at the pair as he tucked it back into the cuff. "Warm welcome I give to all who visit my court. Newly arrived from the rude plenty of your home, it will take a while to accustom yourselves to the magnificence of our halls."

Mimir drained his mug in a single pass, thumped it down, and snapped his fingers at a young maiden making her way along the far benches with a large pitcher of ale balanced in her hands. A wall of pinched frowns followed his urgent demand for a refill. "If it please you, my companion and I will be direct in our speech, for that is the way in Odin's halls."

Laughing, Ægir clapped his hands for another drink. "Speak on. We enjoy lively discussions."

The captive guests raised their cups in salute, this time joined by a scattered few about the head table. Hoenir winced over the rim of his cup at the wide, toothy grin that spread across Mimir's face.

Days passed in conversation as the celebrated hostages made their presence known among the halls of the Vanir. Laughter faltered to sour silence as Mimir spoke his mind on all he saw and heard. Wise, clever beyond means, he saw through the machinations of court life, made glib comments on the actions of the leaders, cheerfully pointed out their flaws, and delighted as a child in baffling them with riddles.

"Come now, the answer is right there before you. Do you need a few reminding hints? It wanders among the mounds and herbs and has a row of downward-pointing teeth." Mimir turned about, taking in the hard stares glinting from the surrounding benches of seated Vanir. "Anyone?"

He shrugged his shoulders at Hoenir, who sat hunched at the table, covering his eyes, ignored by the stiff propriety perched along either side. "In Asgard the women would have already guessed the answer. It is a rake; a tool that farmers use to work the ground."

Mimir grinned at the silent glares. "All right, here is an easy one. One I am certain you are well-equipped to answer." He cleared this throat and raised his chin until he looked over the heads of the seated Vanir. "My mask is dark, my dress white. Silent I cross the ground and stir the waters. Spun up from my surroundings, lofted by the very air, I soar high above the homes of men. Carried free of land or water by the power of clouds, my ornaments send forth the loud, clear song of a liberated spirit wheeling across the sky."

"Well?" Mimir nodded at the gathering, making tiny beckoning gestures with his fingers. "Feel free to call on each other for help."

Uttering a deep sigh, Hoenir stood and clapped his hands for attention. Mimir glanced over his shoulder at the interruption, while the rest of the hall turned twitching eyes on the speaker. "My kinsman can get carried away when he has had too much to drink. I will take him outside to clear his head. When we return, it will be my turn to entertain you with tales of my exploits beneath the great tree, Yggdrasil."

"A swan," Mimir shouted as Hoenir lead him though the doorway into the darkened courtyard beyond. "The answer is a swan!"

"Over here!" Hoenir dragged Mimir into the shadows that cloaked the courtyard walls. He glanced at the bright shape of the doorway where the warm glow of the eldskáli could be seen flickering within the hall.

"Honestly," Mimir snorted, shaking his head, "I do not see how Asgard fell to this lot. It is only by the bold actions of a single, daring warrior that they won your hall at all, yet they act like any one of them could defeat you at a whim. They are imperious and given to rash actions. Their moral character is flexible to say the least. And," he pointed a finger to the sky, "they are incapable of answering the simplest riddles."

At a flurry of sharp gestures from Hoenir, he stopped talking and grinned at his companion. Hoenir glanced uneasily about the shadows. "Keep it down!" His voice was a low hiss escaping between gritted teeth. "You are wise in the ways of the nine worlds, but a wise man should know when to keep watch over his tongue. As you say, our hosts are imperious, as such they will brook no insult, and, mark me on this, they take all that you say as an insult."

Mimir snorted again. "Let them." He stared hard at the brightly lit doorway. "Anything is better than to be false; he is no friend who only speaks to please. If they spurn frank, honest speech, then they are both foolish and ignorant, characteristics I would never have ascribed to them."

Hunching into himself, Hoenir tugged his robe tight against a sudden chill breeze that wafted in off the sea. "We live at their suffrage. If you continue haranguing them with advice, as you have been doing since we arrived, they will have your head, I am sure." He stared off into the darkness clutching the collar of his cloak tight at his throat. "As for myself, they will find a dull-witted fellow full of tiresome stories. Such a guest becomes bothersome and is more often ignored than called upon. When asked for advice, I will always defer to your good judgment."

Mimir tapped a finger against his lips. "So," he carefully eyed the brother of Odin, "you will play the fool in wise company."

Hoenir bobbed his head. "Offending no one, but himself, a fool is often asked to leave wise company where attitudes of self-importance run deep."

Mimir clapped a hand on Hoenir's shoulder. "You hope they will send you home rather than keep you around." He gave a firm squeeze, nodding in appreciation. "A sly strategy, it is a credit to your clan. It is not the course I take. My path is set. We each must follow what we know." A sad smile tipped Mimir's lips as he issued a deep sigh. "Yes, we must each follow what we know."

He draped an arm around Hoenir's shoulders, drew him in tight and winked. "Let us return to the good graces of our hosts. I would see this plan of yours put into action."

––––––––––––

Gentle lapping waves bobbed a fleet of skiffs moored about the homes of the Vanir. As the tide drew out, they tugged at their ropes, eager to follow the call of the restless currents that swirled amid supporting pylons sunk deep in the mud and sand.

Twice, Mani had shown his full face above a massive hall crouched over the strand, its dark island encircled by a cluster of smaller dwellings that seemed to float atop the sea. The light of his passage reflected from the waters, strengthening the divide between light and shadow. On his second passage, as the scudding clouds parted to free his view of the world beneath, the chiding cadence of Mimir's voice rose from Ægir's great hall to fill the evening air.

Mimir rocked back in his seat as he sipped at his mug. "Really, you are quite wrong. Reward never comes from an ill man's mouth; but a good man will raise you up in favor and goodwill."

He took another swallow then shook his finger at the great leader of the Vanir who sat stone-faced on his high seat. "So, too, your actions define the perceptions of others. Take this penchant of yours to freely bed family. I've even seen you take kin behind those curtains of yours. Though concealed by discreet words and ceremony, it is a spectacle that outsiders find quite distasteful. If I were you, I would—"

Ægir slammed down his cup. He leaned forward, his face twisting into an ugly mask as words burst beyond the gate of his teeth. "Enough! I have had it up to here," he jabbed a hand over his head, "with your constant barrage of unrequested advice! It is arrogant and demeaning. As well I consider your jibes at our conduct insulting! It is a misery to have you in our court!"

Mimir's eyes twitched as he marked the fury on Ægir's face. He sipped slowly at his own drink, lips pursed in thought. "The miserable man knows not what he ought to know; that he has no lack of faults."

Ægir sputtered as a menacing grumble raced through the Vanir gathered in the hall. Mimir glanced around at the sounds, then raised his mug in salute. "Come. Come. A man of parts should be genial with his guests, of good manners, and ready speech at all times."

A bellow burst from Ægir's lips as he leapt from his seat. Drawing the sharp blade at his waist, with a single flickering blow he struck off Mimir's head. The trunk toppled backwards from the bench spouting blood to drench the floor and spattering those seated nearby. The head bounced across the board, rolling to a stop before Hoenir.

The brother of Odin dared not move, nor take protective notice, his every muscle tensed as Ægir stomped forward, snatched up the head by the scalp and glared into Mimir's face. The eyes seemed to focus for an instant as the lips struggled into a final light smile.

Ægir gritted his teeth, his words grinding like hard kernels beneath a millstone. "The bitter tongue works death to the head. Now our halls are blessed with freedom from your endless scold. The silence is refreshing to the ears."

He flung the bloody head into the lap of his closest retainer. "Take this away and pickle it in a keg! As his words stung like salt spray in a wound, let his tongue forever rest in brine!"

Hoenir squirmed in his seat, coughed to clear his throat as he made to speak. "You!" Ægir rounded on him. "Do not say a word! Your dull wit and incessant string of long-winded stories have bored us until we can no longer stand your presence. Our women run when you rise to speak, while our warriors drink double just to endure the repeated tales of your tedious adventures. While Mimir was over-generous with advice, when we asked for your counsel, you always deferred to his guidance. So, there was no need for asking you at all. Certainly, there is no benefit to having you in our home."

Stomping over the headless body sprawled on the floor, he returned to his seat. "I will have my hall cleared of all Æsir voices. Bundle up your belongings. You will leave our court tonight! This very night! But I would not have you travel empty-handed back to your kin. Take with you the brine-cured gift of our disdain. Present it to Odin. I can think of no more fitting gift for the Æsir."

Seated alone, everyone long since sent away from celebrating Hoenir's return to the Æsir court, Odin wrenched the lid from the keg to peer down at the slack lips and blank eyes floating beneath the brine. A single tear dropped from his cheek to ripple the liquid's surface. "So, old friend, it comes to this. Though wise beyond measure you ignored the principal rule of the captive: to defer."

The Alfodur dragged a hand over his face, his fingers lingering to tug at his beard. "Long ago I learned to endure your stark candor, to glean the intended wisdom from your jests. It brought clarity when blind to myself. I have need of such wisdom still. In the shallows of their shortsightedness the Vanir, aggravated by its frank discourse, think they have forever silenced your tongue. I have learned much during my travels and say you will speak again!"

Thumping the lid back into place, Odin tucked the keg under his arm and stalked from the hall, mumbling to himself on his way to the stables. "This is a deed best done in private."

Crouched in a shadowy niche beside Mimir's well, Odin spread his tools across the ground: a sharp awl, three large jars filled from the three wells that water the mighty ash, a shallow bowl for mixing, a cup of mare's milk, a handful of barley, a selection of worts from the wood, and a small pot of honey.

Using the awl, he carefully carved runes on a slip of hazel wood, then stained them with blood daubed from a cut made on the back of his hand. After combining the milk, worts, and honey in a bowl, he sprinkled the mixture in a ring about the keg. Pouring out the brine, he bathed the severed head in healing liquid drawn from the three wells. As the powerful waters seeped into every orifice, every pore, he chanted spells to recover Mimir's errant litr and trap it within his skull.

Dead eyes fluttered to life as a croaking voice coughed its first words. "The light is bright. It sends spears of pain through my mind. My tongue is thick with the taste of the sea. But my body..." The voice quavered with understanding. "I live again. There is only one knowledgeable enough to dare such an act. Odin, Alfodur of the Æsir, I ask you why? Why?"

Odin drew a heavy hand across his brow before collapsing onto a nearby root. He stared at the slack face swelled and wrinkled from its long immersion. His sunken eyes crinkled as a tired smile struggled to lift his lips. "I am loath to lose such a knowledgeable friend. Your trusted companionship is dear to me as are few others. It is not just the continued presence of your company that I desire. I have always relied on your wisdom. Now I can be certain it remains available to me in times of need."

The head closed its eyes, the face sagged. A weary voice whispered across the rushes surrounding the spring. "No rest then."

Odin stared at his hands while absently scraping the toe of his boot against the root. "No, I cannot afford to lose you now. There is much for you to share, and I feel... no, I know, there are events in store that require your insight."

The head puffed its cheeks but said nothing as Odin lowered it into the keg and secured the lid back in place. "But now that I have succeeded in my designs we have time," he yawned deeply, "and I must rest. I will conceal you here by your old haunt, safe from the meddling hands of others."

He wedged the keg into a dark niche formed by the root that twisted down into the earth beside the well. "Yes, I will keep you safe here amid the roots of the great tree. You will remain tucked away in this hollow until I call on you."

The Lay of Njord

Stumping along cobble paths swept free of debris, Njord followed a battle-scarred troop through Valgrind—the loud, grating gate of the battle-slain—into the mighty hall of Valhalla, where Odin sat in regal prominence. Morning sunlight chased shadows from entry doors that grumbled open to receive them. He squinted up at the crouching wolf and hovering eagle as he passed through the warrior's way, this time not in the flush of victory, but as a chosen hostage for peace.

Odin stood, cup in hand, as Njord swept down the aisle between the benches and halted before his seat. He raised his chin to stare directly into the Alfodur's eyes. Odin glared down his nose, chewing at the gray hairs of his mustache as he examined the unhappy visitor who stood unbowed before him.

Resigned to the worst, the bold son of the Vanir did not flinch when Odin suddenly lifted his cup high overhead. Three times he raised his cup in salute, each time urging all others gathered in the hall to do the same. "Today begins a new era of compromise with a valiant foe who defeated us in battle. In reconciliation, a representative from their ranks stands before us, a hostage to remind us of our oaths. They hold two of our own to remind us what will happen should we forget."

He paused while the gathering fidgeted with scattered grumbles and ready glares. "But this is no ordinary delegate, a lesser agent assigned to us out of snide arrogance while we have been forced to surrender two of our best. No, this is one I demanded from their ranks. Today, it is our honor to have a venerated warrior in our midst, one who has accomplished feats of unparalleled daring."

Spinning about, Odin thrust his face forward, letting the strength of his breath wash over the reluctant guest. Njord held his ground and stared straight ahead, feeling the eyes of the crowd burning his back. "It was you, was it not, who made that bold leap across the moat, daring the vaferflames to single-handedly breach our wall. It was you, who gave victory to the Vanir!"

Raising his chin, Njord turned about, taking in the entire room, undaunted by the stern looks pressing in from all sides. "I am a warrior for my people, bound by duty to support them in every effort, to bend my every skill to their success. It was my strategy that won your halls."

A broad grin spread across Odin's face as he stepped forward and pressed his cup into Njord's palm. "Always we stand ready to honor greatness, be it among friend or foe. I can think of no greater tribute than to welcome such craftiness, such courage, such principled action into our clan."

Swallowing hard, Njord nodded to the now-eager smiles that surrounded him. He drained the cup then raised it in salute to Odin. "Foes reconciled and honored become stalwart kin. While on occasion my features can be fierce, today my countenance is serene. I am honored to accept this gracious gift of kinship among the Æsir."

Cheers rang through the hall, accompanied by the thunder of stamping feet as Njord was assigned a high position in the clan. To honor his brave deeds in the recent war, he was given a room in the hall of the valorous. To acknowledge his gift for strategy, he was assigned a seat of prominence at the council table.

Days passed in feasting. Gaiety filled the hours. The nights were spent in learned discourse and ribald banter. No topic was off-limits to the revelers. Responses met raucous laughter or thoughtful nodding as their import was considered.

When a plan was proposed to send a contingent of warriors across the white-capped waves of the open sea, Njord coughed into his hand for attention. The gathering hushed to listen as he spoke to Odin. "May I speak candidly?"

Odin took a stiff draught from his cup, smacked the wine from his lips, and then held out the cup to a young maiden who quickly refilled it. "I have learned to value the honest speech of others. In my hall, it is expected of kin, and of true friends."

Njord frowned, slowly stroking his beard. "I have listened to your plans for daring the broad expanse of ocean. For many years, my duties have lain with the sea, and while I do not doubt the hardihood of your warriors, they are not seasoned sailors. The sea is difficult even for experienced hands. I tell you now that should you attempt such an arrogant action without respecting the course, you will fail."

Heads nodded all around the board and hushed mutterings passed between benchmates as Odin's eyes glinted over the rim of his cup. "This must happen. This will happen. You warn of failure should we ignore the power of the sea but propose nothing to support our course."

Njord stared at the ale in his mug, swirling it around until the liquid lapped at the sides and surging foam created a minor tempest that threatened to breach the rim. "I have much experience managing tides and directing winds—fair or foul. If you will trust my abilities and be guided by my counsel, I am certain this expedition will triumph."

Odin took in the approving grins that beamed from all sides, then thumped his fist three times on the table. "When the abilities of all are bent to a common goal, any endeavor is certain to succeed."

A second passing of Mani's full face found Njord perched on the edge of his bed, rocking back and forth, his face buried in his hands, moaning his anguish into the darkness. "The sea. Always the sea has existed for me. Abyss and splendor, chance and wind, both one and many oceans that girdle the world, an endless stream whose beginning is its end. And I... I who once gazed on it all with wonder distilled, who directed its course as one does his own breath, now find myself bound to dry land far from its embrace, fretting the passing days, estranged from my home."

The silence echoed his loneliness as he knuckled his eyes to drive out the tears damned behind their lids. "I have been treated well, even adopted as kin—not at all the hatred I expected when I arrived—yet still I sit among strangers. My heart aches for the faces of home. Each day I futilely strain my ears for the call of seabirds or the familiar sound of rolling surf that lulled me to sleep since I was a babe. I pray for an end to this pain. I ask that the fates allow me to hold my family close once more."

Njord took a deep breath. "Imagine," he puffed the word slowly through his lips, "I who unflinching faced the enemy's blade find myself unmanned by loneliness." A hiccup, a light chuckle shook his chest. He swallowed hard to suppress a recurrence. "It would rather have fallen in battle than endure this bitter agony of restless days and sleepless nights."

———————

When Hoenir returned in sad delight from the halls of the Vanir, Njord thought that he would be released in kind. Eagerly, he approached the high seat, but Odin shook his head as he softly thumped the keg resting beside his bench—the grim present from the Vanir. "I will not give you leave to return to your kin. The gift of Mimir's head sends too stern a warning. We need you to remain as hostage to the Vanir's good conduct."

Leaning back in his seat, Odin reached around to take up his cup. He spun it in his hands as he watched the disappointed look that blanked Njord's face. "But your distress has not gone unnoticed. The nighttime echoes of your anguish belie the brave face you wear each day. To show the high esteem in which you are held, I will allow a visit by your family. Name the members and I will send for them."

Njord stroked his beard as he considered Odin's offer. At each pass his fingers paused on the gray tufts shining amid its once-full redness. "I miss all of my kin but miss my sisters most of all. I would have them stay with me until the seasons are renewed."

Odin clapped his hands at a messenger who immediately dashed through the open doorway. The Alfodur raised his cup, joined by those around the board, while heat bloomed bright red on Njord's cheeks and tears threatened to burst from his eyes. "It will be as you ask."

———————

Sun month, when the lands warm, the ice clears from the sea, and the cloak of Snær retreats to his mountain home, found Njord, wringing his hands with excitement, awaiting a low-slung cart drawn in great pomp by two white horses that rattled across Thrymgjoll, lowered just for its arrival.

Three sisters of the Vanir stepped daintily from the cart, each dressed in high style for their visit among the Æsir. In large chests strapped with ash wattles, they brought enough finery to keep them comfortable for a course of seasons. In their arms, they bore gifts for their hosts.

Njord rushed to greet them outside the entry to Valhalla. Beckoning them to his side with open arms, he planted grinning kisses on their lips. With a flourish, he guided the three beneath the crouching wolf and hovering eagle. "These," he joyously announced to all within the hall, "are my sisters."

The hall resounded with hearty shouts of greeting. The sisters rocked back at the buffeting welcome. Njord beamed while they glanced nervously among themselves.

"It has been a long journey," the youngest demurred. "Is there somewhere we can refresh ourselves. We are so used to ocean breezes that our skin prickles from your dry air."

"Not to mention the stench," muttered the middle sister. The eldest sister nudged her to be silent.

"And rest," the eldest dragged a hand across her brow. "The overland travel has worn us out." The other two nodded agreement.

"Of course," Njord guided them from the court, "follow me."

By day, the sisters joined in the revels of the court, where the Æsir found them pleasant, though stiff and proper. At night, they remained silent while the others discussed topics of interest. No amount of questioning could elicit more than a prim smile or a slight nod in response.

Frigg leaned along the bench. "They seem nice enough," she whispered into Hoenir's ear, "but quite full of themselves."

Hoenir winked. "In that," he replied from the corner of his mouth, "they hold true to their line."

When it came time to retire, they lined up by age and followed Njord to his room. Njord stood by the post bowing to each as they passed, then trailing behind, a slight smile quirking his lips, he drew a heavy curtain across the entry.

Each night the procession was the same. Each night their moaning whispered through the hall, drawing lascivious winks from some and snorts of disgust from others.

They stayed for a full cycle of seasons, delighting in each other's company. When Sun month roused plants to life and flowers bloomed across the fields, the sisters packed their travel chests. Njord hugged each one, bid them a pleasant journey, and asked that they convey his blessings to everyone at home.

Laden with gifts the sisters returned to the halls of the Vanir leaving behind the fruits of their visit. With them Njord had begot two children of great promise that brought immense joy into his life.

Freyr, he called the boy, a lord. Handsome, strong, easy of nature with a face that beamed bright as the summer sun. Everything fertile seemed to bloom in his presence.

Freyja, he called the girl, a lady. Beautiful, proud, and independent of nature, she stood always ready to fight for her rights. A simple touch from her hand bestowed warmth and love.

On their third day of life they were grandly presented to the gathered ranks of the Æsir clan. Lifting each child over his head, Njord slowly turned about showing to all the beauty radiating from their faces. "Behold the genius of clouds, the brilliance of sunshine. Together they burst the folded buds, set the blossoms, and poured sweetness into the swelling fruit. Spring flowers drip from their golden locks. With their passage, frozen fields green with smiling splendor. These are the gifts my children offer the nine worlds."

The Æsir were delighted with the children. Songs of welcome were sung while solemn pledges were given over mead. To honor their special natures, they were assigned high places among the clan.

Freyr, they named the god of summer sunlight. For a tooth gift to match his nature, they gave him Alfheim, the bright, clear land of the light elves. Here they built him the wondrous hall of Upsala, a building to touch the summer sky.

Freyja, they dubbed the goddess of love and war. For a tooth gift to match her nature, in battle half the chosen dead belong to her. On Folkvang, the Warrior's Fields, they built her the mighty hall of

Sessrumnir, where she alone decides the choice of seats.

To Volund, a stalwart supporter of the Æsir, one pledged to sustain the gods in all things, was entrusted a solemn obligation. To him fell the honor of foster father to the children of the water god. With graceful forbearance, he accepted the duty to raise the children. "In my hall," he proudly announced, "it will be as if they were my own."

His children given to another to nurture, Njord approached Odin to ask a favor. "The land where I was born sits by the sea, its shores lapped by the steady roll of ocean waves. It is by the sea I would build a hall to spend my days. Because I am bound to this land by oath, know that I will not leave without your consent. You will find me readily available whenever I am needed."

Odin dragged his fingers through his beard, letting his eyes rove among the hall beams. He edged close to Frigg and whispered into her ear. She whispered back. Nodding, Odin sat up in his seat. "You have been honorable in all your dealings. Your every action has proven you to be a trusted member of our clan. Choose any location—so long as it falls within our domain—and you will have skilled workmen to do your bidding."

Njord pursed his lips, considering. "The homes of the Vanir are constructed differently from yours." He sucked at his teeth seeking to find the tactful words. "They are made to endure the constant assault of the sea, while yours need only brave the wind and rain of an open meadow. I fear your craftsmen may have difficulty adapting their skills to the needs of the project. It may be best if I bring in workers from Vanaheim experienced in the crafts of my people."

Odin sneered at the conceit. "You underestimate the expertise of our craftsmen. Our halls are built to withstand the fiercest weather; from the mountains to the sea and everything in between." He jerked his chin at Njord. "Tell them what you want. By my order, it will be done."

On a reedy shore of the ocean the lonely god built for himself a hall, Noatun it is called—a place of ships. Erected on a wooden platform of pylons sunk deep in the muddy sand, the whole lashed together with sturdy ropes, it floats as an island above the sea. A narrow walkway is its only approach from land. A single ladder reaches down its welcome hand to greet ship-born visitors.

Here, estranged from his home, he passes his time in the company of sea birds, seals, and the occasional visitor. At night, he rests on a bed of woven ropes strung between two stout beams, lulled to sleep by the songs of swans. Each morning, he is awakened by gulls calling along the shore and the cry of terns returning from across the wide waters.

Njord, the ocean-loving god, gray as the turbulent tides he governs, soothes the path of courageous sailors, and welcomes all who visit his home.

The Master Builder

In the spring, when flowers bloom across the high meadows and snow clears from the mountain passes, a giant astride a large well-muscled horse drew up along Asgard's great wall. A shout boomed from his barrel chest, shaking rubble from the fortress fence. "Attend the gate! I would speak with those who dwell behind this shield of crumbled stone."

A voice called down from atop a silver-capped tower that sported its roof above the ravaged wall. "Ho, stranger! Who are you? What do you seek in this land?"

The giant gazed about until he spied the sentry leaning out over the tower rail. The etin smiled, taking his time responding as he climbed off his horse to stretch his legs. "I am called the Master Builder, for I am skilled in the artifice of stone and wood. And this," he patted his horse on the neck, "is Svadilfari my mount. In all ways, he is my most trusted companion."

He raked his eyes over the battlements, taking in the jagged cracks and gaping holes that compromised its integrity. "From the damage that I see before me, you who live in this gard seem to have a problem. Perhaps, I can help. I would speak with those who order these halls. I have an offer to make that would benefit us both."

A loud shout from the sentry directed inside was followed by a harsh, muted conversation with persons behind the damaged wall. After the noise settled down, the sentry allowed the giant to approach the gateposts while a Ljónar of hastily convened Æsir crossed over to meet with him.

The giant stood before the gathered judges, one hand grasping the reins of his horse while with the other he waved at the fortifications whose blocks tumbled across the ground and choked the foaming currents in the channel surrounding the wall. "Your gard lays open to attack from without, the walls about the gate shattered by the storm winds of a previous battle. I confide it is unpleasant for me to see such a lofty edifice in ruin. What you need is a solid wall of heavy stone, high and impregnable as a mountain cliff, the faced blocks tightly joined to safeguard those within. I can build you such a wall."

He paused, letting the promise of his offer penetrate as members of the Ljónar leaned together in hasty conversion. "I ask a pittance for this service. Mine is lonely work and the long days and empty nights have taken their toll. It is a wearisome burden that can be eased by the warmth of a female companion. I have heard of a great beauty born within these walls. Though she is young, I would have the one called Freyja as wife."

At these words Njord bent close to whisper in the Alfodur's ear. Odin gently patted the sea god on the shoulder. "Do not fret over your daughter. A loyal friend fosters your children. Under his protection even we would have difficulty getting them away."

Odin turned back to face the giant, let his eyes rove over thick legs, sturdy as tree trunks, to take in a broad chest braced with powerful arms bulging beneath a sweat-stained leather tunic, rough calloused hands, thick fingers curled from heavy labor, and craggy features nut-brown from the sun that marked an honest, determined face. "You claim great abilities and promise an extraordinary feat, but what previous accomplishments can you relate? Tell me what else you have accomplished to merit our interest."

The builder shook his head, trembling the ruff of gray hair that sprouted from beneath his cap. "Let me see," he frowned, scratching his head. "I have left my mark across many lands. My kin credit me a master at my craft. Gilling found no quarrel with my work. He paid me handsomely with silver and clear-brew, as have Surt, Sokkmimir, and scores more for the staunch fortresses I have built for them. I move from job to job. Since none are near to laud my praises, I have only myself to recommend me. I need no one else to speak on my behalf. You can accept the truth of my words that I make no claim I cannot back up."

Drawing his cloak tight about his shoulders, Odin stepped forward from the Ljónar. "Your claims are bold," he looked directly into the Master Builder's eyes, "and your offer interesting, but we must discuss its merits among ourselves. Until we return, camp here and make free to graze your horse in our fields."

In Gladsheim the gods gathered together in council to decide how they might best respond to the Master Builder's offer. Mugs brimming with ale were passed around as all settled to begin the discussion.

Eager to be heard, Loki leapt up from the bench, raising his hand so none might interrupt as he spoke. "The Master Builder makes a good offer. We need the wall repaired. If he can rebuild it so that it cannot be torn down, then I say we should take him up on it."

Frigg fidgeted in her seat beside Odin, her fingers dancing between her cup and her robe. "But he is obviously a Mountain Giant! His appearance, the skills he claims, and the demands he makes; all reflect his true nature. How can we trust him? Do we dare trust him? With Thor traveling the far eastern roads, how can we protect ourselves from his wrath should he become angry?"

Loki lifted his mug to his mouth, paused, tapping its rim against his lips, and then set it down. "Not all etins are out to harm and destroy. I was raised among them and can attest to this. We simply make his conduct a condition of the deal. If we get him to give an oath, he will abide by that or die."

Baldur leaned forward and thumped his fist on the board. Though still new to giving voice in council, all bent close to hear the wisdom of his words. "He speaks of great skill, but can we trust his work? A pile of rubble ringed about our gard would suffice to meet his part of the bargain. And with no period for completion, he might never finish the wall. I say we specify that he has a single season, from start of spring to end of summer, to complete the job."

A murmur of agreement had circled the group when Heimdall

raised his hand to speak. "As it stands now, he could walk away at any time, leaving us burdened with a partial wall with no consequence to himself. I say we add a penalty if the task is incomplete. As he is an etin, it must be a bold incentive—one to capture his attention. Let his life be forfeit if he fails to complete the wall within the allotted time."

"If we make it a wager," Loki stomped his foot, laughing, "he will be doubly bound by the conditions. It is a wager we cannot lose, for no one, not even a giant with the skill this one professes, can complete such a monumental task within a single season."

Odin nodded, grinning at the council. With a sharp clap of his hands he called for the Ljónar to reconvene and give the Master Builder their reply.

Impassive, his massive arms crossed before his chest, the Master Builder stood unflinching before the Ljónar as with stern voice Odin set before him the conditions of the wager. "We have discussed the merits of your offer, but the contractor's wages you ask are high. They are not ones we will readily pay for the menial task of building a wall." He kept a shrewd eye on the builder's face, looking for any reaction. "You are daring, and honorable, if I am right, willing to gamble your skills for that which you desire else you would not have approached our hall. To one such as you, a wager is more tempting than the dull certainty of a day's pay."

Odin pressed a hand to his chest, turned to face the Ljónar, then turned back to face the steady gaze of the builder. "We, too, find this enticing. So, we propose a wager: within one season's time, from now until fall of the first frost, you will rebuild Gastrofnir by yourself or admit it cannot be done and forfeit your life. However, should the first frost find you have succeeded in completing the wall with no stone left to set, then your price, Freyja, the jewel of the Æsir, will be wed to you on the following day." Odin thrust out his jaw while the rest of the Ljónar bunched up behind him. "These are our conditions." He looked directly into the dull sheen of the Master Builder's eyes. "Do you accept?"

The giant's lips pulled into a deep frown. Slowly scraping a thumbnail against his nose, he considered the words. "Then a wager it will be! I will agree to your conditions, if you will give bound oath to mine." He ticked off his terms one by one on the fingers of a massive hand. "I will have safety from attack by all your kin while I work, and forever after I complete the task. Because you demand my life should I fail, I also add the condition that on completing my task I will be given dominion over the sun and moon to adorn my days and make pleasant my nights."

An uneasy murmur passed through the judges as they leaned close to whisper in urgent tones. After several moments of hushed conference, Odin smiled at the giant. "Agreed," he nodded. "Now, if you—"

"And," the Master Builder pointed a thick finger at his horse grazing nearby, "I will have the use of Svadilfari to haul stones. He is my trusted right hand in labor. Without him at my side I will not accept this wager, and your wall can remain open to any passersby who wish to enjoy the company of your halls within."

Again, an uneasy murmur coursed through the Ljónar. As Odin cleared his throat to balk at this addition, Loki slipped close. "Why do you hesitate?" The eagerness in his hushed tones reached to all those standing nearby. "It is a sure bet that we cannot lose! There is no way one skilled giant, even one with a horse to drag his stones, can finish the wall in the allotted time. I say we accept the wager with his conditions. Let him rebuild the bulk of the wall. When he fails, as he must, we can finish the remainder ourselves while ravens feast on his flesh."

Everyone agreed that Loki's reasoning was sound. Speaking honorable words of promise, they struck a bargain with the giant, exchanging spittle to seal the wager. Eager to win a beautiful bride, the Master Builder began at once to repair the wall.

From a cliff face across the valley, he quarried great blocks of stone and with great skill, dressed their sides to fit his needs. Grunting loudly, he lifted the stones from the ground, stacking them tier-on-tier while wriggling each course into place. The blocks were so closely set, their joints so seamless, the wall face seemed a solid cliff growing unbroken out of the earth.

Each day his mighty stallion, lathered with foam, dragged the blocks from the quarry. Sweat spilled from the builder's craggy brow as he hoisted each block into its place, framing the gate and swiftly concealing each breach. His progress was so rapid the gods became concerned that the Master Builder would easily meet his deadline, and their oath would force them to part with their most precious treasures.

Taking Loki aside, he who had encouraged them to make the bet, they urged him to find some way to void the plan. "What a pitiful bunch," Loki laughed at their fears. "I will do nothing of the sort. You freely made this wager. Live with it."

Voices turned ugly. A ring of menacing faces formed around him, squeezing close until there was no direction he could turn without encountering threats to his body and position in the clan. Sweat beading his brow, Loki agreed to intervene in the wager using whatever trickery or deceit was necessary to ensure the wager concluded in the Æsir's favor.

For several days, the clever Loki watched the Master Builder laboring at his work. He smiled at the strength of the stallion as it dragged the stones with ease and provided the craftsman with his course of daily materials. Light glinted in his eyes as he conceived a plan.

Using his dual nature, Loki turned himself into a mare. With tail raised to entice the stallion, twice he ran by the Master Builder's horse. Twice the Master Builder strained his every muscle to rein back Svadilfari's surging strength. The third time Loki approached, the stallion, eyes wild, nostrils flared with desire, reared up, breaking away from the giant's grip. His traces dragged through the stone dust as he chased the mare into the woods.

The Master Builder shouted in anger, his screams for Svadilfari to return echoed off the wall as the stallion's flank disappeared among the trees. In a fit of rage, he filled the air with harsh words and smashed stones to dust with his fists.

For seven days, the stallion and mare mated in the forest far away from the construction site. Concealed amid thick, shadowy stands of oak, Loki occupied Svadilfari well beyond the first frost that whitened the morning ground and flamed the oak leaves scarlet red.

To salvage the promise of his wager, the Master Builder exerted all his strength and applied all his considerable skill to completing the job on time. But without his horse to haul stone blocks, on the final day the wall remained unfinished, the last course scattered about the ground.

Thor arrived that morning fresh from the land of etins. He was appreciative of the skilled construction, marveled at the formidable strength of the new wall, but when he was told of the wager—made with a giant of all creatures—sparks crackled about his brow and thunder rumbled on the horizon.

Choice words he offered to everyone for daring to enter such a dangerous bargain. "You are all fools. And you—," Thor rounded on Odin. "You are my father, so I respect you, but this—," Thor slapped the palm of his hand against his forehead. "You claim wisdom, yet you wager with an etin."

Odin's eyes flashed, but Frigg placed a calming hand on his shoulder. "It was not your father's decision alone. We all agreed to the wager."

Heimdall added his voice to Frigg's. "We needed the wall rebuilt. The giant owned the skills to do it."

Baldur laughed from his bench as he took a drink of mead. "It was a wager we could not loose: to rebuild the wall in one season. Should he succeed he won the Sun, the Moon, and the hand of Freyja. Should he fail, his life was forfeit." He grinned, wiping sweat from his brow. "We never dreamed he would get this close."

Njord snorted with disgust at Thor's attitude. "If it were not for the cunning of Loki, he would have taken away my precious gem." He turned his face aside. "As it is, Loki lured away the builder's horse, slowing him down long enough to ensure the outcome of the wager fell to us."

Chewing his mustache, Vidar stared moodily into the coals glowing in the hearth. "He wagered his life against completing the wall. He lost."

Odin spoke up, his anger held in check by Frigg's commanding grip on his arm. "It is good you have arrived home in time. As the strong guarder of our clan it is your duty to collect our winnings."

Thor started, sparks leaping from his brow. With difficulty, he caught his tongue in mid-protest. Turning a baleful eye on his kin, he hunched his shoulders and stalked away, cursing under his breath, to perform the detested task.

Enraged at the responsibility, Thor confronted the Master Builder. "You there," he let fly the vehemence fuming in his breast. "You misbegotten son of an etin! How dare you show your face in Asgard? You bragged the skills of a master mason, yet all you have shown is the ability to dig ditches. You deserve the payment you get for a clumsy, half-finished job."

When his anger elicited no response, Thor's rage ebbed. He stepped back, studying the impassive face of the giant who stood silent and unbowed before him. "You do not run. That is good. I am sent to collect on the wager. This is a duty I dislike, but which I am bound to fulfill. You have acted honorably in your dealings." Thor scowled. "It is more than I can say for my kin."

The giant's lips twitched at his words, but he stood motionless, chin held high. "I had guessed that the loss of my horse was not due to the chance appearance of a rogue mare in heat. But even with the deceit played against me, I will not flinch from the wager I made nor the stakes that were agreed."

Thor nodded, then raised himself up tall before the Master Builder, letting his voice carry the sadness of his duty. "The wager is done and though your effort was mighty, you failed to achieve the boldness of your claim. You have lost and by the terms agreed upon, your life is now forfeit. I hold here your death in my hand."

The Master Builder remained impassive and stared unflinching into the eyes of his executioner as Thor lifted the stone hammer he gripped in his fist. With an anguished cry that echoed among the clouds, the god of thunder brought his weapon down in a swift arc, crushing the etin's skull with a single blow.

The Birth of Sleipnir

In a forest glade protected by maternal oaks, a cloud-gray colt was born of the union: Svadilfari with a changeling god. Blind in blood, legs folded beneath, from the grass damp with birth fluid he rose shakily on knobby knees to take his first tentative steps. On stiff legs, he began to walk. On shivering toes, he began to run. His legs blurred to eight as he began leaping through the air, each bound carrying him further, until he seemed to fly as if on wings.

Still aching from giving birth, Loki guided his son to the wall of Asgard and placed him in a pasture with the rest of the Æsir horses. No one stopped Loki nor offered words of thanks, but silently stepped aside as he hobbled off to his bed. Instead they crowded around the pasture fence examining the colt and whispering to each other behind their sleeves.

The foal grew fast, as do all kin of the gods—sturdy, strong, and larger in his sixth month than any other of the Æsir horses. Light gray with a silver mane, on a cloudy day he disappeared against the sky. Many laughed at his ungainly appearance, for few could doubt his eight legs seemed a confusion as he ambled about the pastures. But when he ran the laughter stopped and all stood in awe at his speed, as swifter than the wind, he flashed through the air.

As the seasons changed, he developed into a robust stallion, well-muscled, with a broad back. Trained to the equestrian rules of war, his clever mind quickly learned the form. On field, on path, on track he surpassed all other horses. Always Loki looked on, pride shining in his eyes at his son's every accomplishment.

In the colt's second year, Loki beckoned Odin to join him in the courtyard outside Valhalla. There he proudly presented him with the promise of his loins. "Please accept this gift; he is the best of me. Endowed with the strength of his sire and the ingenuity of his dam, he is the swiftest of all horses, the most noble of all steeds."

With delight the Alfodur accepted the gift as he gazed with gentle understanding into the bright, intelligent eyes of Loki's child. "I have watched you since you first arrived. You are magnificent! I have never seen your like."

The colt stood with calm assurance as a crowd of Æsir gathered close, talking, shouting, some laughing. Odin plumped at the audience's attention. "What shall I call you? Your sire was a powerful stallion, a slippery traveler. Your dam clever beyond words." Odin winked at Loki. "In honor of such lineage I will call you Sleipnir, the slippery one."

Applause burst from the gathering as the Alfodur ran a hand along the rippling flank. Smiling, he patted the sleek neck, then gripped the bridle to nuzzle flaring nostrils. Amid the cheering of the crowd, he whispered low so only Sleipnir could hear. "We will ride together, you and I, to places undreamed of by others. Companions until the end."

Bold and Feral from the East

Restless grew the young across the lands in the early days after the first war when tales of heroic battles were fresh and the honor of kinship pledge among reconciled adversaries was held in high esteem. Eager for adventure, one of strong will and courage donned his best armor—a forest-green byrnie of iron rings linked hard by hand. At his side, he belted a sturdy, fire-forged blade—a deadly battle needle balanced to his right fist. Leaving his home, he set off at a brisk pace to seek his fate among far-off relations.

Tyr arrived from the east to stand before the Æsir and make honorable claim of kinship. Broad shouldered, stout about the middle, double braids of dark hair framed swarthy features offset with bright, fiery eyes. Three times he thumped his chest, each beat the deep resounding echo from mountain caves.

"Tyr, I am called!" His shouted voice swelled to fill the hall. "Across rough seas and flattened fields, I come bold and feral from the east, urged by the fates to stand before you. East of the Elivagar Rivers whose rime-cold waters are death to unwary travelers, in a hollow mountain at the far end of the heavens you will find the hall of my stepfather, Hymir, a wise and brave Jotun.

It is a great distance to his home, but not so far that the Æsir have not visited; the Alfodur knows my mother well. She has told me many stories of their acquaintance before my birth that I might know my true father. By blood right, I claim relation to the Æsir."

Odin's lips twitched with a light smile. He tipped back his cup to conceal the laughter threatening to burst from his lips. A sharp glare flashed from the corner of Frigg's eyes as the young warrior slapped a hand to his chest.

"Honor and justice, I hold dear." His glittering gaze swept the entire court. "Always, I strive to protect those who struggle against unfairness. With the righteous might of my strong arm, I stand ready to support an honorable cause; I am always prepared to aid those in need. In war my arm never tires. Courageous, I am always in the forefront, for it is such daring that wins battles. In peace, I stand ready to defy, ready to defend. And while I prefer the exhilaration of war, I never excite peaceful men to wrath. Wise in the ways of the world, I use my voice sparingly, preferring to let my actions speak for me."

Spreading his stance, he lifted his chin. "Accept me," his gaze settled on the Alfodur, "and I pledge my strength to uphold the honor of this clan. The power of my hand will protect all you have created. Never will you regret the decision."

All together the Æsir came in council, to decide what to do, those powerful gods. They took a short time to discuss. Many spoke favorably of the young man, some demurred—concerned that kinship too freely given would quickly lose its meaning.

Then Njord was called on to speak that he might rightly guide their judgment. Voices hushed as the god of ships rose to his full height before the gathering. "Many have commented on the bearing of this young man; even his detractors have held praise. Such is the telling mark left on those raised with honor and responsibility."

Shaking his robe free of his legs, Njord crossed the room to stand beside Tyr. Smiling warmly, he rested a hand on the young man's shoulder. "But know too that I am well acquainted with the family of this man. Their mountain hall lies nearby an inlet frequented by trading boats from my people. They are known for their independence, integrity in all dealings, and respect for freely given oaths. There is no dishonesty in his speech. He lays a valid claim of kinship, for Blood, Pledge, and Duty form the foundation of strong familial ties."

He let his gaze rove across the gathering, looking each in the eye. "I speak as an Æsir. We would do well to have such a stalwart heart held close within our ranks."

After everyone made known their stand on the matter, Odin rose to decide for the clan. "Warm greeting, I give to a new relation of the Æsir that he will know welcome in our homes and draw strength from our kinship."

All Æsir were delighted at the ruling. Songs of welcome were sung for the beaming youth. Solemn pledges given over mead accompanied by hearty slaps on the shoulder. For his honor, character, and physical power, he was assigned a prominent position in the clan. Where a just cause needs a strong arm, there stands Tyr ready to give aide.

The Birth of Forseti

Joined Baldur with Nanna, Nepp's daughter. With her he fathered a son with golden hair, a clear broad brow, and bright eager face. Forseti they called him, the presiding one.

When Night had filled the sky with her presence, three maidens came to Breidablik, the great hall of Baldur. Three times they called for admittance, their gentle voices shivering the rafters. Baldur himself opened wide the doors that they who shape the fates might enter. Urd, Verdandi, and Skuld bowed to the master of the hall, then filed though the gleaming hall, youngest to oldest, to stand at the bedside of his beloved son.

Exercising their arcane knowledge, with skill they twisted the threads of fate. They fastened the silver warp of the web beneath the hall of the moon. The golden woof of the web they bound beneath the hall of the sun. In the south, they anchored an end beneath the edge of ocean. Northward they knotted a thread beneath the pole star and bid it hold forever.

When they had finished, the Norns turned to face the father, far vision shining in their eyes. As a snake fascinates its prey, they held his attention with their gaze while they related the fate of his newborn son.

Spoke Urd as she rustled dust from the folds of her robe. "Hear what we know. Now good seasons are come to all, for born into summer's light is a glorious flower."

Spoke Verdandi as she pinned her cloak closed at her throat with a silver broach that winked in the hearth light. "In a seat of justice sits Baldur's son, one day old. His eyes see only the truth. His ears are ever deaf to lies. His lips speak only fairness."

Spoke Skuld as she cinched her leather belt tight at the waist. "He becomes a friend to righteousness, a pillar of integrity whose justice all may call upon in times of need."

Spoke Urd as she drew a hood over her waves of flaming red hair. "A wife he is bound to take that will secure a bond between powerful houses."

Spoke Verdandi as she tucked her nest of golden ringlets beneath her cowl. "A strong, intelligent woman, well-trained in the skills of her mother."

Spoke Skuld as she tied a headscarf around her coils of dark, gray-flecked braids. "Roskva she will be called for her quick mind and lively spirit."

Then the three filed from the room, oldest to youngest. Politely declining Baldur's offer of celebratory victuals to honor their visit, they departed the twinkling hall and returned to their home beside the great ash tree that spreads its limbs wide over the nine worlds.

———————

From his earliest days, Forseti showed himself wise in judgment, resolved arguments among guests in his father's hall, reconciled squabbles between servants. As he grew to manhood, through clever actions he proved the promise of his youth, with each deed rising in standing among the Æsir.

Gathered together, the mighty gods, to decide on the position Baldur's son would hold among their clan. With unanimous voice, they appointed him a member of the Ljónar, an arbitrator of legal matters.

Dressed in the robes of his appointed position, from a high seat he dispenses justice, settles grievances, arbitrates disputes, and decides the rule between warring factions. For those who trust in his judgment, his unbiased decisions bring satisfactory resolution.

Those concerned that they will be fairly heard, anxious that their plight will be equitably considered, he counsels with candid speech. "My duties I consider sacred, with honor and justice held in highest regard. With a shrewd ear, I listen as both sides present their arguments. My judgments are impartial. I keep cloistered during a case, removed from outside influences to ensure my decisions remain free from the stain of corruption.

When tempers flare among plaintiffs and exception is taken to a decision, I offer these words to all parties: 'Those who call on me to decide their case agree to abide by my final judgment. They are bound through penalty to uphold the accord. For those who disagree with my decisions, know that your offense is more excited by a perceived legal wrong than an actual wrong. For the first looks like being cheated and the second like being compelled.'"

The Lay of Ivalde

Along sharp ridges of the Hvergelmir Mountains, the sworn watchman of Yggdrasil's root stood guard, Ivalde by name, a bold warrior of stern mind and fierce temperament. Dark hair drawn into a knot atop his head capped intense black eyes that glared from a strong face marred by a splayed nose. With broad shoulders filling out a byrnie of iron links hard-forged by his own hand, he cast a long, menacing shadow from his hilltop post.

His first wife was the giantess Greip. She bore him three sons destined for greatness. Volund was the first, an accomplished craftsman at the forge. Orvandel was the second, a champion with the bent yew. Slagfin was the third, skilled in verse, capable with the sword. Aided by these sons he guarded the borders, contended against high-minded storm-giants and children of frost that threatened the domain of Urd.

When that pairing ended, he took a second wife, Sol, she who drives the sun along its path. Two children rose from that union, a daughter called Bil for her innocent, unguarded face and a son called Hyuki for the brilliance of his eyes.

Ivalde often trudged the mountain paths, his gaze always turned to the distance, ever watchful for incursion by the frost. During a long vigil along the base of towering ridges, he sought to slake his thirst at a shaded spring. The small, trickling stream, inaudible when the wind blew, lay concealed in a deep cleft shielded from the sky where it dribbled from a crack in the mountain wall, an errant course escaped from the foot of Mimir's well. At the first draught, his eyes sparkled, his thoughts flowed as free as the wind, and the taste of knowledge filled his mind. With a second draught, he knew to keep the spring secret that he might enjoy its discovery undivided.

Night after night, he crept to the hidden cleft, glancing over his shoulder to be certain he was alone before dipping his cup into its clear waters. With each inspiring drink, each savoring thought, he considered himself wise, clever beyond means, and superior to all others.

The longer he imbibed of the waters, the more unreasonable he became. Stern before, now he became a tyrant. Where consideration for others once lived, now bloomed arrogance. Often, he quarreled with those about him and in all ways sought to impose the certainty of his will on others. His constant torrent of sharp rebuke washed away the good will of friends and family alike.

The sons of Greip rebelled at this harsh treatment. Together they confronted their father, defying his unyielding control. Volund thrust out his chin, letting his anger flow unchecked over the sharp ridges of his teeth. "Your demands of us are perverse. Always we give you our best, yet each time you toss it back in our face."

His brothers joined in chorus behind him. "We will no longer put up with this!"

Dismissively flicking his hand, Ivalde staggered across the room and threw himself onto the nearest bench. Snatching up a mug, he downed it in a single gulp, then wiped his mouth on the cuff of his jacket. "My sons, bah!" He shook a finger at the frowning faces swimming before him. "You are useless, the lot of you. Unable to wipe your own ass without me there to tell you how."

Volund slammed his fist on the table. "I say enough," he roared back at his father. "You treat us, your own blood, as you would a slave."

Ivalde raised himself up, weaving side to side. "Enough? I say when you have had enough. You are worthless, the lot of you. Only good for slopping hogs."

Volund spat at Ivalde's feet. The watchman snapped his jaws shut at the glaring hatred of his son. "You are no father to us," Volund sneered. "From this day forward, we hold nothing for you but contempt. Do not look for our forgiveness. There is no hope of reconciliation." Slagfin and Orvandel closed ranks behind their brother, grumbling their agreement with his words.

———·———

Angered by the rejection of his sons, Ivalde sulked in his home. Refusing to stand guard, he neglected the duties of his sworn oaths for the excitement offered by the waters. Voice raging, he stomped about the hall cursing everyone, slamming benches and tables, always demanding more drink. The children of Sol huddled together, cringing through the violent outbursts of their father as he kept them close that they might not escape his control.

"You!" He snapped his fingers. "You there, pissing in the corner. Come here girl. Bring me another bowl from the bucket beside the hearth."

Bil clutched her brother, slipping around to hide behind his shoulders. Ivalde kicked a bench aside. "You will do as I say!" He slammed his fist on the table, bringing squalling tears from his daughter. "Your brother cannot protect you and sniveling for your mother will not help. Both answer to me as do you."

Each night Mani passed overhead, silver tears leaving tracks across his cheeks as he took in the events below. His horns trembled at the condition of the children lashed by Ivalde's terrifying dominance.

One night, thirsting for the potent waters, a craving that had grown since the liquid first touched his lips, Ivalde ordered his children out alone to draw a fresh pail from the spring that he might imbibe in the seclusion of his home. "You there, boy!" Ivalde lurched across the room and cuffed his son, sending him stumbling into his sister. "Make yourself useful. Get your sister. The two of you take Sægr, the pail beside the hearth, and fill it fresh from the spring; the one I've sent you to before. Take Simul, the pole there in the corner, to carry it between you. I don't want to hear excuses. I want it full or so help me you will feel my boot, the both of you!"

The children scrambled along an arduous path following their father's instructions to the concealed spring. Quickly, lest they suffer the bruising wrath of his anger, they topped off the pail with the cool clear liquid and hoisted it up on the pole to ride suspended from their shoulders. In the darkness, relieved only by the glow from Mani's face, they felt their way back along the twisting mountain path, sliding on gravel, stumbling over rocks, squeaking in alarm when the precious song mead slopped over the pail rim.

Mani watched their efforts, nodded in appreciation at their diligence, took pity on their condition. Satisfied with all he had seen, Mani beamed down from the clear sky. The children stared in awe as he stretched out his hand. "Come with me. I am Mani, your mother's younger brother. I offer you a life of purpose and refuge from your ills. You have only to take my hand for it to be so."

Timid fingers reached up, then desperately grasped the shining mote of his hand. Smiling, Mani plucked the two from the mountain path, wafting them to his home in the sky. Taking the pail left upended on the trail, he drained the pool that had formed in the hollow cleft. With a light touch he collapsed the hillside to staunch the flow, forever stilling the errant song escaped from Mimer's well.

Delighted to be free from the oppression of their overbearing father, the children took up assigned duties in Mani's nightly work. Hyuki aids the waxing moon, clearing away the growth of shadow until his face shines full and bright from the sky. Bil aids the waning moon, grooming the growth of shadow as it spreads to conceal the light of Mani's face.

Ivalde was incensed at his double loss, but he mourned more for the buried spring than from the pain of his missing children. Gathering his weapons, he stormed from his hut. Raging heavenward, he attacked the moon-god, firing his cart so it glowed red in the night sky.

Blade drawn, Hyuki blocked the path of his father as he sought to protect his new home. "Come no further, Father. This is my home now." Licking his lips, he raised his sword, letting its tip dance just before his chest. "And I protect it."

Ivalde crouched low. "Like your stepbrothers, you seek to deny my rights." His red-rimmed eyes danced about as he brought them into focus. "Like them, we are now enemies. And this," Ivalde's sword smashed past his son's guard, "is how I deal with enemies." No match against the weapon skills of his irate father, Hyuki suffered a fierce wound clear to the thighbone.

Mani charged into the fray, desperate to protect his nephew. "Stand down, watchman." Tossing his dark cloak aside, Mani drew his bright striker. "You spill the blood of an innocent," he positioned himself, a wall of white light, between the raging father and his fallen son, "and so know my contempt."

Ivalde squinted his eyes at the glaring brightness of Mani's fury. "You dared to take my children and destroy my spring." He spat between his fingers at Mani's feet. "I fired this sky cart in payment and would gladly have left you to burn, but now I will much more enjoy leaving you without a head."

Sparks showered from the lusty blows of their keen-edged blades, streaking in clusters across the sky, as Mani drove the berserk back to the rocky ridges of Hvergelmir.

Howling in frustration, Ivalde called on the Æsir to intervene. A Ljónar was convened with Forseti presiding as both sides made their cases. The gods, angered at Ivalde's audacity, supported Mani, their sharp verdict condemning the watcher's actions.

Eyes starting, fury lighting his face bright red, Ivalde shook his fists and stomped his feet, outraged that the gods sided with Mani. Indignant, humiliated by their judgment, he damned them and all they had created. With curses flowing from his lips, he fled the cold ridges of the Hvergelmir Mountains, throwing off the shackles of his sworn allegiance to the Æsir. With no regret or thought of return, he sought out the warmer climes of southern lands.

In the heat of Muspellsheim's deep dales, the rogue sentry was given refuge in the hall of Suttung, son of Gilling, grandson of Surt. Suttung was delighted to have a retainer of such lofty pedigree in his home. Eager to take advantage of the unexpected opportunity, he promised the northern warrior his daughter Gunnlod as wife if he swore fealty to his hearth.

Without hesitation, Ivalde stepped forward, drew himself up to his full height before the Jotun. "Little respect I was shown by the Æsir for years of loyalty. I gladly accept your offer." His bitter voice filled the air as he swore an oath to protect his new home, to stand sentinel in the lands of Suttung as he had done for the Æsir.

The Death of Kvasir

To signify their truce and end their war, the Æsir and Vanir spit into a kettle, mingling their fluids to seal the peace. Kvasir was born from this potent broth, the honorable ideal of both races. Raised up in the likeness of a man, tall, broad shouldered, with golden hair framing a gaze free of guile, he was handsome to look upon.

Serene of nature, he consumed nothing that had life, nor did dark dreams plague his sleep. For Kvasir each day was a joy, each night a delight. Wise beyond the lofty heights reached by Odin, there was no question he could not answer, no puzzle he could not solve. Both clans were proud to call him kin.

To satisfy his curiosity of what lay beyond the high walls of Asgard and the watery inlets of Vanaheim, Kvasir traveled across the worlds, delighted to inspect the many lands spread out before him. He freely shared his knowledge with every race he encountered along the way that they might grow wise and prosper.

Passing into Nidaveller, the land of dwarves, Kvasir boldly navigated its dark paths. Coming to the hall of Fjalar and Galar, he was welcomed as an honored guest, feasted as a king, and in all ways treated well.

Galar bowed, nearly brushing the floor with his nose. "It has been such an honor having a distinguished guest of your station in our hall," he gushed to their esteemed visitor, "we scarce dare to ask a question." He glanced at his brother then back to their guest. "There is a niggling thing that has stumped us for years, which I am sure you could divine in a moment."

Kvasir laughed as he took a deep drink of mead. "You have been so considerate I would be an oaf to refuse any help that is mine to give."

Fjalar directed their guest to a side chamber. "Then please come this way. We prefer to consult your wisdom in private. That on which we seek your aid lies in here."

"As you wish." Laughing, Kvasir hoisted himself from the bench and followed Fjalar while Galar slid in to take up the rear. As they entered the chamber Kvasir was surprised by the flash of heavy clubs crashing down onto his head.

Tossing his bloody club aside, Galar stepped around the body, then jerked his chin at Fjalar. "Grab his shoulders. I'll get his feet." Together they dragged Kvasir beneath a beam that ran down the center of the room. Their victim was moaning from the ringing blows as the dwarves strung him up by his heels with a rope thrown over the low-hanging beam. Slitting his throat with a sharp knife, they set three vats beneath him to catch the blood: Son was one, Bodn another, Odrerir the third.

When Kvasir's body was drained, they spiked his blood with honey and carefully selected herbs from the forest. Using long wooden ladles, they slowly blended the mixture, then covered each vat with a wooden lid, letting them sit until the liquid fermented into a potent draught. When the time came to taste, when the first drops touched their tongues, their eyes sparkled, their minds ran free and they knew to keep the special brew secret.

Worried by Kvasir's long absence without any communication, the Æsir took up a search for their errant kin. Their quest took them across the worlds into the land of Nidaveller, eventually reaching the hall of the murderous dwarves.

An imperious crashing at their door brought Fjalar and Galar running. They stepped back in surprise at the small troop of Æsir led by the white god standing outside. Heimdall raised a hand palm up. "I give greeting from Asgard. We come in search of our cousin Kvasir. We have tracked him across the lands, exhausted every lead. His trail ends here. Beyond this point no one has seen him. We come to you in the hope you can help our search."

The dwarves coughed, sharing a quick glance. A smile snaked across Fjalar's face as he bowed to the searchers. With sweep of his arm, he invited them into their home.

"You look weary. Please come in. You might rest awhile beside our hearth. Do you thirst? Do you hunger? What little we have, we share."

Heimdall shook his head; a movement mirrored by those who stood behind him. "We cannot rest until he is found. The urgency of our errand calls us onward. We ask only if he is here or if you have seen him pass this way."

Galar frowned at his brother, who sighed heavily, tugged his collar around, and slipped timidly forward. "We have seen him. He was our honored guest for many days, then..." his voice choked as he wiped a tear from his eye, "then..."

"He died!" Galar blurted the words. "We are sorry to deliver such sad news. He perished here in our hall. There is no need for you to continue searching."

Fjalar steepled his fingers before his face, muffling the solemn words that passed his lips. "We did right by your cousin, laid him out in the finest we could afford."

Galar nodded, his long nose bobbing at each shake of his head. "Consigned to the pyre along with all his belongings, his ashes were cast into the sea, for that is the custom of our people. There is nothing left of him here."

A low murmur of sadness ran through the Æsir. Many hands raised to blot away the tears that ran down their cheeks. Heimdall took a deep breath to calm the shaking in his voice. "How did Kvasir die?"

The dwarves bowed their heads, hands covering their mouths to conceal their grins. "Constipated with boundless knowledge," Fjalar quipped to the floor, "he choked to death for lack of a questioner."

"One learned enough to challenge his intelligence." Galar forced back a snigger that threatened to burst free from the clenched gate of his teeth. "I fear our company bored him to death."

Heimdall, sputtered, made to speak, then fell silent, his hand drifting toward the blade at his side. Anger flashed in his eyes as he ground his teeth and gave a curt wave to the troop. Muttering among themselves, the Æsir stalked away from the hall. At the top of a rise they paused to cast black looks over their shoulders before disappearing behind the crest.

Fjalar and Galar slowly closed the door, peering through the narrowing crack until the Æsir disappeared over the far hill. Behind the door, they leaned against the frame posts laughing and clapping each other on the back, delighted with the cleverness of their ruse.

———————

The pair jealously guarded their hoard of mead, sipped the intoxicating elixir, and considered themselves clever beyond means. But how to turn this wisdom to their advantage? Through hospitality they saw a way.

Eager to prove to themselves the power bestowed by the drink, they decided on a deadly plan. With kind words, they invited Gilling, a neighboring Jotun who was much revered in the region, to visit for an extended stay at their hall. Smiling broadly, they bid him bring his entire household and all the comforts they would need. For while they could offer rude plenty in food, drink without end, and entertainment, their lodgings were bereft of the luxuries such a noble Jotun demanded in his own home.

In handsome carts dawn by matching white stallions, Gilling arrived with his wife and a small staff of servants. In the back of the carts, strapped down for travel, were large chests packed with enough finery to keep them comfortable for a full cycle of the Hastener. The dwarves rushed out to greet them as they drew up before the hall. The carts they ordered stored in their barn. The horses were pastured in their fields where salt grass grew in great clumps. With grand gestures and wheedling words of welcome they invited the visitors to enjoy the hospitality of their home.

Days passed in laughter, the nights with entertainments. The board was always set with fresh victuals, the cups always brimming with mead. His hosts were so companionable that, when the dwarves invited him to join them on a fishing expedition, Gilling readily agreed to the venture.

In a shallow boat, they put out to sea where swift currents turned to the far horizon, and there, with the sharp application of an oar to his head, they left their guest wrapped in Ran's embrace. The pair rowed back to shore, working out their story. Together they delivered news of the tragedy to those in their hall. With somber voices, they related how a great wave had caught them up, nearly capsized their boat.

Fjalar groaned, dragging a hand down his face. "When the sea raised its fist to strike us, Gilling was tossed from his bench into the churning waves. We last saw him thrashing about as the waters closed over his head."

Galar stared at his feet, his voice numbed with sadness. "There was nothing we could do to save him, for just then a second wave caught our craft, spinning us about. It was all we could do to stay afloat." He sighed, tossing a glance at Fjalar who nodded his head in agreement. "When we regained control of our boat, he was gone."

The servants gnashed their teeth, wailing at the news. Gilling's wife cried out three times and clapped her hands until they bled. The dwarves left the visiting household to their mourning to take stock of all the Jotun had brought. Clever they thought themselves that night as they divided Gilling's possessions between themselves.

Gilling's wife stayed on mourning the death of her mate. Each day she asked the dwarves to point out where he had died that she might know where to direct her grief. She wept so loudly and so incessantly, they quickly grew tired of her laments.

On the seventh morning, the bereaved wife, eyes red, her voice hoarse between ragged sobs, clutched at Galar's sleeve. "Show me. Show me again where he drowned."

With sympathetic words for her well-being, Galar guided the matron to a portico overhung by a high beam on which the dwarves had balanced a granite millstone. "Stand here. From this vantage, you can see the spot, there," he pointed out to the rolling sea, "just three fingers to the left of the headland." As Galar directed her gaze out to where Gilling had drowned, Fjalar tipped the millstone from its perch, crushing the keening widow in mid-wail.

Word spread of Gilling's death and the unfortunate circumstances surrounding his widow's accident. When the news reached the ears of Suttung, son of Gilling, the newly installed Jotun traveled to the dwarves' hall to demand recompense for his family's loss.

Suttung ambled across the room, ignoring the offer of a place near the hearth, instead taking the highest seat on the bench. Grumbling, Fjalar and Galar slid down to lower seats while the Jotun filled a cup from a pitcher that stood on the center of the board. He took a drink, eyeing the pair, who cast nervous glances, at the floor, at his feet, at each other. "I will be direct. My parents died while enjoying the protection of your home. By the rights of family, I demand weregild."

The dwarves rose from their seats, snorting at the claim. Strutting about with puffed chests before the visiting Jotun, they looked down their noses. "We owe you nothing," snapped Fjalar. "Their deaths were accidents," sneered Galar.

"Were they?" The dwarves quailed under Suttung's fierce glare. "I have heard reports from their servants that lead me to believe otherwise."

"Lies," shouted Fjalar.

"Nothing but lies," whined Galar.

"No matter." Suttung set his cup aside. "I'll have payment one way or another." Lunging from his seat, he seized them both by the collar. With main strength, he dragged them from the hall and down to the beach where a small boat bobbed beside a narrow dock. As the pair clung together quivering in the bow, he rowed out to sea far beyond the line of white breakers onto the rippling body of ocean. Bumping against a rock that stood dry at low tide, he beat the pair off the boat, leaving them stranded as he rowed away, stopping just beyond the first line of waves.

As the tide came in and the first waves washed over the rock splashing water around their ankles, the dwarves dropped to their knees. "Spare us!" Fjalar scooted forward until he reached the edge of the rock. "We have many goods to trade if only you will carry us back to dry land."

"Yes, many," pleaded Galar. Suttung watched from his boat, saying nothing.

As the waters rose to embrace their waists, Galar screamed and clawed up Fjalar's back, attempting to climb above the rising water. Fjalar dragged him off his shoulders and thrust him back onto the rock as the foaming water sucked at their legs, threatening to drag them from their perch. "Take our lands! Take our home! Gold, silver, take it all, just spare us!" Still Suttung watched from his boat, saying nothing.

When the water reached their necks and foam wet their nostrils, with gasping breath they offered their most valuable possession. Flailing his arms, Fjalar rose on his toes to lift his voice clear of the waves. "Song Mead! We have song mead crafted from the blood of Kvasir. The powerful liquid bestows on the drinker the tongue of a skald and the knowledge of a scholar."

Galar sputtered, spraying brine with his choking cries. "It is our most precious belonging! Take it! Take it as compensation for your parents! Just spare us!"

Suttung sat for a moment, letting the pair suffer just a little more before drawing at his oars. He nudged the boat alongside the dwarves who scrambled over the rail to flop, breathless and shivering, in the hull of the boat. Without a word Suttung bent his back to the oars until its prow bumped the beach.

With a sharp cry Fjalar and Galar leapt from the boat. Staggering through the surf, the pair collapsed, mewling onto the beach. They lay there weeping uncontrollably as their fingers spasmed, digging furrows in the damp sand.

Suttung stepped up beside the shivering pair and kicked them repeatedly until they rose on shaking legs. "I'll have my payment," he sneered, giving Fjalar a cuff behind the ear that sent him stumbling. "Now."

Heads bobbing, tears streaming down their cheeks, the dwarves scuttled up the slope to their hall. Inside, they lead the way to a locked storeroom. Sliding a key from a concealed niche beside the doorframe, Fjalar unlocked the door, pushing it open wide to reveal three vats nestled in the shadows.

Shoving both dwarves before him, Suttung slipped into the storeroom. Lifting the lid from the nearest vat, he dipped a finger and licked the brew from his fingertip. A smile crept over his face. "Bring them out." He jerked his chin at the casks. "All of them."

Under the Jotun's baleful eye, the dwarves wrestled the three vats from their wooden cradles, lugged them along the hall, and loaded them onto a cart readied outside the door. They scurried back as the Jotun hauled himself up behind the horses. With a flick of the reins the cart jolted forward.

The weregild paid, Suttung returned home. He stored the three wide-rimmed vats of song mead in a gray, rocky place called Hnitborg—a fortress hall nestled amid the basalt crags of his homeland. To ensure its security, he placed his daughter, Gunnlod, on watch over the liquid hoard.

Odin Steals the Mead of Inspiration

Long the Æsir suspected foul play in Kvasir's death. On hearing of Gilling's accident, their suspicions became certainties. Returning to the hall of Fjalar and Galar, they questioned the dwarves, this time with savage intent. Through the judicious use of fist, knife, and fire they extracted the truth of Kvasir's fate from the unwilling pair.

Planning among themselves, the Æsir stalked away from the hall, the smell of scorched hair and burnt flesh trailing after them. Behind the door, the dwarves lay stretched out on the flagstones, ragged gasping mounds, bruised, bleeding, and barely alive.

On learning of the mead crafted from Kvasir's blood, Odin knew Suttung would never give him access to the precious drink. Bringing all his craftiness to bear, he considered how he might capture the mead and so regain a bit of Kvasir for his kinsmen. After much deliberation, he decided on a course of action.

Advance orders were given to his húskarlar of how to prepare for his return. "The wait will be long," he grumbled, "but when it happens it will be swift, so everything must be ready beforehand."

Donning his travel cloak, he plopped a broad-brimmed hat on his head—its brim canted to dip low over one eye. He pondered a moment, fingering the carved staff he had won from Hlebard's hall. "Too noticeable. It would mark me before I could speak a word." Taking up a plain hazel rod, he turned his feet on the long journey to the land of Baugi, Suttung's brother.

———·———

An afternoon sun angled across the land turning drying grasses to gold flame as an ancient traveler stumped along a well-beaten dirt path. In the fields of Baugi's farm, Odin encountered nine slaves harvesting hay. He listened as they grunted with each hard swipe of their scythes, complaining of the toughness of the grass, cursing the dullness of their blades. From his place on the path, Odin whistled for attention.

When they looked up from their work, he beckoned them to join him. "I am a stranger traveling through this land, but I could not help overhearing your difficulties. In my youth, I have done the work you undertake and know the difference a well-maintained tool can make."

"You speak truly, stranger," snorted the foremost slave of the group. "A sharp edge would make our work easier, but our master is a skinflint when it comes to lifting our burdens."

"I have with me," the old man muttered, rummaging through the travel pouch slung over his shoulder, "a whetstone of uncommon properties. With just a few swipes along the edge it can hone the dullest blade to Regin-sharpness. Now where did it go? Ahh, here it is." He drew from the pouch a flat, fine-grained black stone—three fingers wide and twice the length of his hand.

Another slave stepped near and hungrily eyed the stone. "We have nothing to give in return for such service." He reached out to touch the stone, then jerked back his hand when the old man shifted his attention. "Even the clothes on our backs are not our own."

The stranger offered a kindly smile as he raised a hand to ward off further protest. "I ask for nothing in return. If you will pass me your scythes, it would give me pleasure to ease your burdens."

Eagerly, the slaves gave their tools into the stranger's hands. For free he sharpened their scythes, swiped the stone from beard to toe until the edges glittered in the sun. Easily now the blades sliced through the grass.

Each wanted the whetstone for themselves. Together they decided to take the sharpener from the one who had done them a good turn. Holding their scythes at the ready, they approached the elderly stranger. "Give us the stone old man, or we will try these carefully honed edges on your neck and pry it from your lifeless fingers."

Odin scanned the faces fanned out before him, taking in the resolution set on their lips while shrewdly noting the furtive glances that passed among them. "Since there are nine of you and only one of me, I must bow to your demands. I give the stone to the one who can catch it."

Grinning, he tossed the stone into the air. The nine slaves fought each other to get it, hacking left to right with the sharp scythes until none remained alive.

Laughing to himself, Odin retrieved the whetstone from where it lay in the grass. After wiping off the blood that stained its surface on the kjafal of a fallen slave, he continued his journey.

At Baugi's hall Odin stopped for the night. Three times his voice rang out from the darkness asking shelter for a weary traveler. His third hail brought the grumbling farmer to the door. Baugi filled the frame of the open doorway, his shoulders brushing both posts as he squinted out into the night. "Who is it that calls? Are you a friend come visiting or a reaver bent on plunder? Know that I have an open hand for one and a fire-hardened club for the other."

The gloom rippled with movement as an exhausted voice called out in reply. "I am only what I claimed, a weary traveler seeking shelter." A chuckle rang from the shadows. "Though I certainly hope to be counted a friend before I leave the comfort of your hospitality."

The farmer grunted, shaking a massive club at the shadows. "Step forward into the light. Let me see you that I might gauge your worth. Do not be shy about doing as I say or know that the next farm lies a hard day's travel over the far ridge with rocks, forests, and wild beasts between."

Hearth light spilling from between Baugi's legs illuminated a brilliant smile as Odin stumped forward from the shadows and set his travel pouch at his feet. Turning his head from side to side, Baugi examined the shadows before focusing his attention on the weary figure leaning heavily against a worn walking staff. His shrewd eye took in the dark gray travel cloak, its hem festering with thistles, its length smudged with patches of trail dust. Leather boots worn from a long journey bound the traveler's feet to mid-calf. On his head a broad brimmed hat gripped a fringe of white hair, its brim dipped low over one eye to conceal half the face leaving the rest lit by a twinkling eye and gentle smile.

Grunting acceptance, Baugi stepped aside with a welcoming wave. "You do not have the bearing of one I should fear, so enter and let my roof keep off the night damp. If you hunger, I've just set dinner. There is more than enough to fill your belly."

Odin peered around the jamb as he edged through the entry into the firelight. A rough-hewn bench and slab table filled one side of the open area inside the doorway, while the remaining length of the hall was partitioned into bays that paralleled the central fire.

He nodded appreciatively to the farmer. "You have a fine home." A warm breeze from an adjoining room at the far end carried the odor of manure with the soft lowing of cattle. He took a deep, savoring breath. "I always enjoy the smell of a well-run farm."

The farmer gestured down the hall with his club. "You may make your bed in a bower beside the eldskáli, but do not block the path to the doorway. Misfortune has visited my farm. I do not know, but there may be more to come. I might need to race from the hall to confront the danger." He jerked his chin at the board. "You'll find food and drink over there."

While they ate, Baugi regaled his visitor with stories of his recent difficulties. "The Norn's weave is always difficult on farmers. It has been doubly so for me. This morning I had nine slaves to work my farm. Now fate has decreased my wealth; all nine slaves lie dead in the field. With no men to work my farm I am bound for a pitiful harvest."

Baugi slowly dragged his fingers through his hair. "You would think being brother to Suttung, the Jotun over these lands, would buy aid, but it does not. We are all left to fend for ourselves."

His guest nodded, thoughtfully stroking his cheek as he stared off into the distance. "Yours is a sad tale."

Pushing his bowl aside he leaned in close. "Bolverk I am called in this land, a strong hand at cutting and loading hay. Your need is great, so I make you this offer. I will take on the work of nine men. As payment, all I ask is a drink, a mere sip of Suttung's fabled mead. For the story has spread across the worlds of its power to expand the mind."

Shoving a plate of curds closer to his guest, the farmer reached across the table to a clay pitcher and poured himself another cup of ale. He raised an eyebrow at Bolverk, who slid his cup forward to be refilled. "I do not control the actions of my brother and cannot speak for his generosity. I can say only this, and it offers little hope; since the mead came into his hands he has shared it with no one."

Baugi took a large bite of dark bread and followed it with a long, noisy slurp from his cup. He belched loudly, wiped his chin with the back of his hand, then held up three fingers. "He keeps three massive vats filled with the precious drink ready at hand to quench his thirst. He calls them Odrerir, Son, and Bodn. His daughter Gunnlod watches over the vats. She is loyal to a fault, so suffers her father's command. It is a lonely burden to place on such a young woman, as she is rarely allowed to leave her position to socialize with others of her age and rank."

Bolverk shook his head at the thought. "It is a shame to waste such youth."

The farmer nodded his head in agreement as he swirled the contents of his cup, watching it lap close to the rim. "But always my brother has looked to his own needs. When our father died, as the eldest son he inherited rule by right. Since then, he has freely imposed his will, leaving those about him to bear the brunt of his dictates."

Baugi drained his mug before pushing away from the table. "As for myself, I face a difficult harvest with few experienced hands to help. And while you do not seem capable of achieving all you have claimed; I have no other prospects. If you agree to undertake the work, I will go with you to speak with my brother. Perhaps together we can persuade him to part with a cup from one of his vats."

"Let it be so." Bolverk spit into his hand, Baugi spit into his own, then they shook to seal the agreement.

"The night grows late, and morning waits on no one." Baugi yawned wide, showing all his teeth, and arched his back, his massive fists fanning the air over his head as he stretched. "Tomorrow will see the truth of your claim."

The new farmhand climbed to his feet and shuffled off to a bay. Baugi called after him while clearing dishes from the table. "Remember what I said earlier. Do not block the path to the doorway."

———————

That summer Bolverk did the work of nine men: tended livestock, worked the fields, cut hay, shocked and threshed grain. The farm prospered and Baugi was pleased. When the last leaves of fall brushed the ground and the sharp nip of frost hung in the air, Bolverk went to the farmer to gather his wages. "Your harvest is in, your cattle fat, your larder well stocked. I have fulfilled my part of the bargain. I am come now to have you fulfill yours."

Baugi dragged his fingers through his hair as he looked out over the farm. "I admit I thought your brag the wanderings of a weak mind. But you have surpassed all you claimed. Let me grab my cloak and we will be on our way."

Together they visited Suttung in his mountain home where Baugi told his brother of their agreement. Suttung sat a moment in stunned silence, then leaned forward, slapping his hands hard on the arms of his seat and braying with laughter. "Bolverk, my brother calls you a capable, nay, a gifted worker. But I see before me a poor bargainer. To negotiate with a stranger for the goods of another is sheer folly. I will never part with a single drop of my precious drink."

Chuckling at the disappointment that shown clearly on Bolverk's face, the Jotun clapped his hands three times for his attendants. "I would never send a guest away thirsty. So that you have no reason to complain of my hospitality, I will share a lesser mead brewed last week from freshly threshed grain. It is ready to filter and in need of tasting.

I crafted it for the upcoming marriage of my daughter Gunnlod to a new retainer from the far north. He calls himself, Ivalde, but I have dubbed him Svigdur for his great thirst."

The visitors sat together at the great table of Suttung. Heavy mugs brimming with fine ale were set before them. They drank while chatting amiably with their host about his preparations for the upcoming nuptials.

"The celebration will be held in three days, here in this hall." Suttung waved his arms, directing their gaze to different points about the room. "A seat of honor will be set up beside my bench, the guests circled around. The bride will serve the oath drink to seal the union, as is custom."

Bolverk drained his mug, smacked his lips, licked the drops from his mustache, and then rapped the table top for more. "This is an admirable drink. Your skill at blending rivals Ægir, who, if the stories tell truth, brews mead for the gods."

Suttung looked pleased as a servant refilled his mug. "Your thirst is as great as my daughter's groom. You do justice to my efforts."

"Farm work, like battle, builds a man's thirst." Bolverk tipped back his mug, smacking his lips as he set it down. "Who will be allowed to attend?"

"The landed." The Jotun eyed his guest, noting his patched cloak and dirty, unkempt hair. "My guard will ensure only those invited will get through the gate."

"The landed." Baugi snorted. "And just when did you plan to invite me, your own brother?"

A light twitch flashed across Suttung's lips as he sipped at his mug. "Let this be your invitation... personally given."

After another round, they again praised the excellent brew. When it became apparent that no more ale was forthcoming, the party thanked their host for his generosity and left the severe hospitality of the mountain hall. A massive dwarf with broad, heavily muscled shoulders, legs like tree trunks, and a dull, lifeless stare, dragged open the gate at their approach. Angling through the gate, they skirted the watchman's ready club, then turned along the wall.

Once out of sight of the guard, Bolverk grabbed his companion's arm. "It is as you warned," he growled low. "I expected his response.

145

But that which cannot be gained through straightforward action can often be achieved through cunning. In his arrogance, your brother has given us much information with which to work."

Bolverk pulled an auger from his pocket. "This is Ratit. Its bite can drill through solid rock. Use it to bore a hole through the mountain wall while I keep watch. It will open a small entrance into Suttung's hall that I might better appraise the situation."

With much grumbling Baugi bent his back to the task. He worked the drill hard so stone chips flew as snowflakes swirling in a winter storm. After a half-day's work, Baugi rose to his feet, hands pressed against his lower back. "There." He gestured at the hole with his foot. "The drilling is complete. Tell me how this will gain the drink you crave."

Squinting at him with his one good eye, Bolverk said nothing as he bent over and blew into the hole. Stone chips flew back into his face. He turned on Baugi, his eye black with anger. "Do you think me an idiot not to expect betrayal?" Bolverk brandished a menacing fist before the farmer's face. "Get back to work! Keep at it until you have drilled completely through!"

Reluctantly, Baugi bent to the task, his labor spreading sweat across his back and soaking his tunic. When finished, he rose slowly to his feet, dragged a hand across his face, and silently gestured at the hole. This time when Bolverk blew into the hole the stone chips flew inward with his breath. Satisfied the job was complete, he shook his cloak and turned himself into a snake. As he glided into the borehole, Baugi, startled by the sudden transformation, struck at him with the auger, but Bolverk was so small and so quick that he easily avoided the attack.

On reaching the end of the tunnel the snake peeped from the hole, flicking its tongue as it peered along an empty passage—one end an open hallway, while the other end led to a closed door. Satisfied he had penetrated Suttung's hall, Bolverk returned through the hole, making it larger as he pulled himself through that he might move in comfort between the spaces.

A frightened Baugi looked on, jaw slack, wide eyes staring, as the snake slipped from the hole, shimmered a moment in the sun, and the form of Bolverk rose before him. Eye aflame, the apparition approached the trembling farmer, gripped his jerkin with both hands, and lifted him effortlessly from the ground. Bolverk held him suspended, glaring in anger, until Baugi began to whimper and sweat poured in runnels from his brow. "Though you tried to strike me dead, I will let that pass if you pledge your aide to the undertaking I will now propose."

He shook Baugi until his head lolled and his teeth clacked. "Listen carefully. You have seen that I possess extraordinary skills. You are a farmer. For your help in this endeavor know that it stands within my power to ensure your harvests for years to come. Plenty will be a constant companion in your home with bumper crops to ensure your wealth. What do you say?"

Avarice flashed in Baugi's eyes. "Tell me what you have in mind," he grinned.

Bolverk lowered the farmer until his feet firmly touched the ground, then laid out his plan. "Your brother's hall lies inside a mountain. It has a single entrance, a heavy gate guarded by a fierce dwarf. You are Suttung's brother. The guard will trust your word. As you pass him on your way to the wedding celebration tell him that you spotted the groom coming up the path behind you.

Soon after you pass I will arrive disguised as Svigdur and announce myself to the sentinel. Once I have entered the hall he will believe that any who arrive after showing the likeness of Svigdur to be a dangerous imposter bent on disrupting the wedding festivities. He is duty-bound to ensure the imposter never enters the hall. After you have made known your presence to your brother, make an excuse—a reasonable excuse—to leave the festivities and return home. I will take care of the rest."

Baugi began to mumble with unease over his part in the deception. Bolverk waved away his concerns. "Rest assured you will be held blameless in these events. If you follow my directions, you will never have spoken an untruth and will be able to claim, with all honesty, your innocence in the events that will unfold."

———————

Odin spent three days working out the details of his stratagem. On the eve of the festivities, he put his daring plan into action. Recalling the groom from his days as guard on Mount Hvergelmir, he assumed the form of Svigdur, donned his mode of dress, and adopted his mannerisms. Working his voice to a low gravel, he ensured he spoke like the ancient guard lest in an awkward moment his speech give him away. Any misstep in speech, dress, or action would expose his masquerade and he would be put to death.

In this guise, he announced himself at the front gate of the hall. The great dwarf raked him over with a penetrating stare before nodding acceptance at his appearance. The bars rattled as the gate opened to let Svigdur pass. With heavy tread, the dwarf guided the suitor along the path to the great hall. Three times he beat against the hall doors to announce the arrival of the expected groom before returning to his station at the gate.

A great noise rose as the wooer of Gunnlod strode into the hall. All the guests stood, their voices raised in welcome. With the pressure of many hands on his back, Svigdur was ushered before Suttung who hailed him with warm words. "Greetings Svigdur. Tonight, the seat of prominence is yours." He waved him to a high seat of gold that had been set out in his honor.

Svigdur grinned as he took the seat.

"I fortified myself with an early meal," he patted his stomach, "knowing the events of tonight."

Heavy mugs brimming with celebratory drink were passed, one after another, into his hands. Odin drained each with a flourish that brought cheers from the crowd. In full measure, he played the champion drinker, downing mug after mug of hearty ale until he swayed side to side in his seat.

As his mind grew thick and his vision clouded, he fought to maintain caution in speech and manner that he might not be discovered. But his tongue loosened by excessive drink slipped with occasional responses inconsistent with the honored groom.

Suttung frowned as Svigdur tipped back another mug of ale. "Your capacity for drink is great. I have seen this proved many times. But it may be unwise for a wedding night. You don't want to be useless to your bride."

The groom thumped down his mug and loosed a long, low belch that brought laughter from the gathering. He wiped the back of his hand across his lips as he struggled to focus on the face of Suttung.

"I've made fair promises to the good woman. She will not be disappointed tonight."

The Jotun pursed his lips and shook his head. "There is no poorer provisioning for the bridebed than to be drunk on ale."

"Long ago I learned the measure of my own stomach." Svigdur chuckled, patting his middle, then beckoned for another mug. "Many's the time I've come to places too early and the ale wasn't brewed, or to others too late and the ale was all drunk. But tonight, I've arrived to full casks and good company. Tonight, we celebrate by drinking this fine ale by the fire."

The gathering cheered, and calls went out for more ale. Suttung eyed him curiously, beginning to suspect there was more than just drink behind the glib words.

As Odin swayed in his seat, Gunnlod came forward carrying a pitcher in one hand. An ornate goblet that had sat empty all evening at the table end, she filled with mead. With a light smile she handed the drink to her betrothed. "By my hand, I offer you this pledge cup."

The groom smiled back before downing the drink in a single gulp. "By my hand, I accept this cup."

As the hall boomed with applause, Suttung rose and solemnly placed his daughter's hand in the gnarled fist of the grinning groom. "With your oath, I give you my daughter as wife that your lives forever be bound."

With gentle, coaxing words Suttung's daughter led her drunken wooer from his seat. Again, the hall rang loud with cheers as the pair left the room. Suttung sat hunched at the table, toying with his mug, spinning it around in the palms of his hands, as he watched the back of the groom reel from the hall.

———·———

Outside the wards of the rocky hall the true Svigdur reached the gate of Suttung's gard. From the shouts that echoed up from the great hall he knew the celebration had begun without him. Filled with rage, he banged at the gate. "Is there a gate keeper? Where is the gate keeper?"

The dwarf sentinel stumped to the gate, raking the visitor with a piercing gaze. "Yea, there is a gate keeper. I am he and may your head not be yours for asking."

Svigdur spat commands in the sentinel's face. "Open the gate!" He kicked furiously at the bars. "I demand immediate entrance!"

The dwarf drew his lips down about his chin as he frowned at the arrogant solicitor who stood, fists planted on hips, outside the gate. "That I will not do. Already knife has gone to meat and drink to horn. None may enter who have not been invited."

"Invited!" Svigdur spluttered at the dwarf's response, a strangled sound that roared from his throat.

"Invited!" With main might he grabbed the gate rings and shook them until the bars rattled.

The dwarf gripped the club at his waist. "Step away," he raised his voice to drown Svigdur's rage, "lest I strike your fingers from your hands. Who are you to make such noise and disturb those inside this hall?"

Svigdur stepped back, tugging his vest straight, and wiping spittle from the corner of his mouth. "Know creature that I am Ivalde, sworn retainer to Suttung and wooer of his daughter, Gunnlod. I am called Svigdur in this hall and have been promised the maiden's hand in marriage. I arrive tonight to claim my bride!"

Lifting his head slightly, the dwarf braced wide his feet. "But you cannot be he. For already Svigdur has passed this way."

The retainer shrieked with anger. "I demand admittance! Suttung will know me as I denounce the imposter who has taken my place!"

The dwarf's harsh glare passed over the man who stood raging before him, noting the familiar features that he had seen pass earlier that night. He shoved open the gate and waved him entrance. A thick knobby finger pointed along the path to an open door on the side of the mountain. Within showed a lighted room and a noisy throng of wedding guests celebrating around Suttung's board. Gunnlod was seated beside a male figure perched in prominence on a golden seat. With a cry of anger Svigdur leapt toward the vision and collided head-first with a wall of rock. The door winked out as the side of the mountain slipped down to bury the fallen lover.

The corners of the dwarf's lips quirked into a brief smile, pleased his illusion of an open door had worked. Satisfied he had done his duty, the dwarf returned his gaze to the distance.

Odin staggered alongside the promised bride, leaning heavily on Gunnlod's arm as she guided him along a narrow passage deep into Hnitborg where he spied the auger hole bored earlier through the mountain near the base of the wall outside a closed door. Drawing a key from her belt, the maiden unlocked the door and led him into a sparsely furnished chamber. A plush bed and hard-backed chair were crowded into one corner. Brush, basin, and such toiletries as a woman needs were arranged on a side table. A carpet of fresh rushes formed a narrow path across the floor, while along the far wall, three large vats, each covered with a wooden lid, bellied into the room.

After entering the chamber Gunnlod closed and locked the door. With a grieved smile to her astonished groom, she took up a long, broad blade and stationed herself before the vats.

"What," sputtered the groom, "what is this?"

"By my father's command," Gunnlod passed him a resigned look, then turned her gaze to the door, "I am duty bound to stand constant guard over these casks."

"Even tonight?"

She nodded sadly. "Even tonight."

Breathing deeply to clear his head, Odin sidled up beside her, his eyes crinkled with desire. Thrilling touches, he traced along her forearms, and honey-sweet words dripped from his lips as he sought to woo the lonely, young maiden away from her duty.

He pressed his lips close to her ear, letting the puff of his breath stir the strands of auburn hair that swung free alongside her cheeks. "You are lovely and fair-minded. I would be considered a poor husband were I not to consummate this marriage. Do not think me ale limp, unable to perform my function. With a ravishing beauty, such as yourself, none—if in their right mind—could turn away."

The maiden fought to keep her gaze fixed on the far wall. "My father has commanded me." She swallowed hard. "His is the rule of this house."

"And now I am your husband." A warm smile spread his lips as Odin trailed a finger down her forearm, pausing to gently caress the inside of her wrist. A soft gasp escaped the maiden's lips. "Surely, he did not mean you to forgo the delights of your wedding night for the mundane task of guard duty. There are greater pleasures to be had across the room on the bed."

Gunnlod shook her head to clear away a sudden dizziness that threatened to overcome her composure. "I cannot betray my trust."

"I've seen your ankles beneath your gown." Odin reached down to hike the hem of Gunnlod's dress a few inches. A bright flame flushed the maiden's cheeks, but she did not lower her blade. "Such a daring view of a shapely woman," he winked, "curls the hair on my forehead and sends my heart stone throbbing with desire."

The maiden slapped his hand away from her dress and Odin stepped back, frowning at the rebuff. "What is so special about these vats that they require you to sacrifice the promise of this night? How about allowing me a taste that I might judge the worth of guarding their contents."

"No drink. My father would slay us both. But," the maiden turned her shrewd gaze on her spouse, "I may be persuaded to let you have a sip provided you give a personal ring oath of marriage and swear to be faithful to our vows."

Eager now, aroused by the maiden's tenacity, Odin pressed her hand to his cheek. "A kindly glance from either of your eyes is worth more to me than five hundred ells of wadmal. There is no land I would not forgo to know the embrace of your white arms about my neck, no honor I would not relinquish to have the delightful smell of your breasts filling my every breath. Gladly, I swear to be faithful to my wedding vows."

Setting aside her blade, Gunnlod took her husband by the hand. Leading him to the bed, she lay down and spread her arms wide in invitation. "Prove to me the promise of your oath."

Three nights they spent consummating the pledge. On the third night, delighted with her groom, Gunnlod disobeyed her father's command and gave him access to the mead. Three drinks she allowed him, one for each night he had spent in her bed. With the first swallow, he drained the mind exciting drink of Odrerir. With the second swallow, he left dry the song of Son. With the third swallow, he emptied the altar of Bodn and took on its obligation.

Well satisfied, Odin patted his full belly, bowed to the bewildered young woman, pressed her hand to his lips, then changed himself into an eagle and flew from the room. Gunnlod's screams chased after as he swooped down the hall. On reaching the auger hole gnawed earlier through the stone, he drew his wings in tight to his sides and darted through the widened hole to safety.

When Suttung spied an eagle bursting free from the rock face near the chamber of Gunnlod, he guessed what had happened. Cursing wildly, he wrestled into his eagle cloak, yanked the black feathers over his shoulders, and dove from his high hall. Wings thundering, with main strength he drew close enough to snatch some feathers from Odin's tail. Startled, Odin squawked and burst forward, a spurt of mead dribbled from his rear to splatter across the land.

When the lookouts perched atop Gastrofnir spied Odin's approach, three vats were hurriedly spaced around the courtyard of Asgard. The eagle swooped low, spitting the mead into the vats as he passed, then dived to safety amid the gleaming halls.

As the black vafer about Asgard began to roil, its surface seething with fire-bright cracklings, the mighty giant banked sharply to avoid a deadly strike. From his lofty height, Suttung rained a torrent of abuse down on the halls of the Æsir. Three times he circled the shining halls before angling away, screaming for vengeance as he winged through the sky.

Bragi and Idun

In Midgard, an eloquent voice traveled across the lands, braved the currents of the great ocean, challenged ice-crusted mountain passes, found an exalted place in the halls of kings, a position of honor with chieftains, warm reception in the homes of Freemen and Thralls. He was called, Bragi, for his charm, with a wit well-steeped in the mead of Odrerir. A skald of unsurpassed skill, able to create a drapa on the moment and recall it unchanged days, months, even years later.

Knowledgeable in the ways of power, often his wisdom was called upon to help shape the course of kingdoms. He advised many leaders, assisting them in times of peace and guiding them in times of war. For his skillful poems and prudent counsel, he was given heavy arm rings of gold, wealth beyond measure. He freely gave away what he received, so knew welcome in all homes.

When his years had mounted until the dead he knew outnumbered the living, and his beard had become more flecked with the gray of age than the bold color of youth, he spent the last of his wealth on a small, well-built ship. After fitting it with a sturdy sail, stocking the hold with enough provisions for a full month, he struck out alone for the western horizon.

Over the sea brooded a restful silver mist. The soft, close cloud obscured all vision, so the ship seemed to float, untouched by anything save the air.

As Delling's gate opened wide with the dash of Sol's wain, the ship was surrounded in a soft light that blushed from white to pink to red. Sol climbed higher over the horizon, rolling back the mists, her bright rays igniting the water's surface with the fires of Ægir.

Bragi's ship sped over the gentle, heaving waves. He lay on the deck not sleeping, but dreaming, as his golden tongue gave clear voice to the secret longings of his heart: the mysteries of love and sorrow, the loneliness of life and death.

In this way, he whiled away his time with verse until the ship glided into a dim harbor where Death held sway. The shoreline was a mire of stinking, gray-black mud littered with an occasional driftwood snag. No tree was seen, no flower, no vine, no sign of life living or past.

The ancient skald sprang to his feet, threw back his head in defiance, and with a bold, radiant voice sang out a joyful poem of creation to rouse a dead world to life.

A warm wind rushed across the land. The ground erupted with green herbs. Vines spread across the rugged earth, casting their tendrils over cliffs to shroud the hills. Tall grasses stretched across open fields. Clumps of ferns shed tears over young streams. Stands of beech and oak rushed the shoreline. Huge firs thrust skyward to cloak the rocky slopes. Warm sunlight streaked the now verdant ground, lighting the flowers in the meadow so the grasses seemed to burst into flame.

Laughing with amazement at all he saw, Bragi leapt from the prow of his ship and slogged to shore through the foaming surf. Still singing out his song of life, the great skald strode along the beach, gladsome in the rustle of green leaves that filled the air.

But soon he felt someone near him, someone who watched his movements; delighting as did he in the song of the day. Eyes twinkling, he glanced about, eager to spot the presence that grew stronger with each step he took. Far ahead, he spied a lone figure slipping through the cool shadows of a heather-filled glade.

As he drew close, his heart leapt with such joy, he felt it catch in his throat, nearly stifling the flow of verse that fell as fresh dew from his lips. Before him a young maiden, lovely as the spring dawn, flit through the glade, stooping to caress the rich earth as she passed. Where her delicate fingers grazed the ground, clumps of bright flowers sprang into the light. Where her touch lingered, fruit trees stretched skyward, their blossomed branches laden with promise.

Entranced, barely noticing the words that continued to flow unchecked from his lips, he followed her through the woodland. Onward she led the skald, until, in a tranquil glade amid drooping ferns and pillow-soft moss, she stopped beside a gushing stream that rippled through the forest to the beach below.

In her white robe, girdled with green, she seated herself on the bank of the brook. From her golden brow, she lifted a crown of blossoms and set it beside the water. In pure joy, she stroked the earth with her fingertips, laughing with delight at each flower that sprang forth.

Cupping a stunning bloom between her palms, "Your handsome petals shine above all others. For such beauty, I will call you Baldur's Eyebrow."

She tapped a yellow and orange cluster that bobbed alongside the brook. "Now, you I will call Forget-Me-Not in memory of my father and sisters."

Tracing a finger along a violent splash of red erupting beside her leg, "And this little beauty... ah-h-h..."

She broke off, rising slowly to her feet as the elderly skald worked his way through the rough thicket before her. Bragi raised up his hands palms outward as he stumbled through the last of the bracken that protected the glade. "You have no need to fear me. My days of rut are long past, and I know the strength of your youthful limbs are more than a match for this ancient frame. I am called Bragi, a skald from the shores of men. And this place, this strange lovely place... I do not know where I have landed, but I suspect it is very far from my home."

The skald reached out to stroke the leaves of a low-hanging branch. He drew a blossom close to inhale its fragrance. "I knew the pleasure of your presence long before I saw you dancing through the shadows, for I felt someone as I walked along the shore. It gave me great delight to share my song with an unknown watcher in the wood."

He released the flower and smiled at the maiden who beamed back from beside the stream. Sunlight dancing through the leaves illuminated her in lustrous gold. She seemed to shine before him, brilliant as a summer's day. "When I spotted you among the heather my heart nearly burst from my breast, so great was the joy that sprang up inside. I knew then that I had to meet you. So, I followed like a bee that seeks out the unknown flower, guided by its inborn sense that such beauty is as necessary for life as the water we drink, the air we breathe, and the food we eat. In truth, I knew not what I would say when at last I caught up with you. A terrifying admission from one whose life has been the clever crafting of the spoken word."

As Bragi's speech ran down, the young maiden held out her hand to him. The skald took her fingers in his rough fist and touched them to his forehead. A thrill of joy followed by a flash of heat ran through his body, a long-forgotten memory of youth. At this, the maiden sank to her knees drawing Bragi down beside her, then folded her hands in her lap.

"My name is Idun," she smiled at the wonder showing in his eyes. "Indeed, you have traveled far from your home. You stand on the edge of Asgard. By chance you have stumbled upon an egress, one of the rare points in time and place that mark the boundary between our worlds. Few mortals have ever reached these shores. Those who have known its touch never left. Caught up in the desolation of the strand, they surrendered to its doleful embrace, their bones mixed with the grist that lines the beach."

"But you are different." She reached out and rested her palm against his chest. "Even at your advanced age the joy of life swells within your breast and you are able to bring it forth. Your song pleased me. I was thrilled to hear its musical tones roll over the brackish waters of the strand. For rare is the ability—through touch of hand or sound of voice—to melt death into sweet memory, heal sorrow, and bring life to rich fulfillment."

A tear coursed the great skald's cheek, followed to his chin the deep lines that scored his face, and dripped down to moisten the petals of a flower that nuzzled his leg. "I have received many compliments in my life, but none that have touched my heart as warmly as those that fall from your lips. Please, so that you would know the gallant truth that lies deep within my breast, let me return the praise."

And on the spot Bragi composed for Idun alone, a poem more exquisite than any she had ever heard. On hearing the melody of the woven words, she felt the spell of his love steal over her, drawing her close to the ancient skald.

"Full well I know where to bestow praise,
on the glorious maiden before me
seated amid the lush grasses and sweet-smelling flowers,
the lights of her cheeks beaming brightly;
the most beautiful bloom in the garden.

You are full worth every word of praise
that has ever dropped from my lips
or been spoken with earnest intent.
Never will I be able to close my eyes
without seeing your face aglow with the light of life,
your smile radiant as the sun.

In this blessed place, true love blossoms as young flowers in spring.
Enduring as the fir that shakes off the chill blasts of winter
and laughing greets the summer sun with new green shoots.
It gentles the nature and makes glad the heart
as the flower bole revels in the morning dew.

There you sit, a maiden in the full flower of womanhood,
sweet as the moon swelling above the horizon's edge.
Here I stand, a man bent with many winters,
whose heart has outgrown his years,
basking in the warm gaze of one beloved face.

My voice has become your voice, trembling on your every word.
My sight colored by your vision.
I have ceased to live within myself;
you have become my life,
a vast ocean to the stream of my thoughts.
At your touch, my blood pounds at my temples,
my heart races, and fire blossoms on my cheeks.

If I could remount the river of my youth
to the first fountain of my smiles
and once again greet you in this hallowed grove,
our couch a soft carpet of fragrant ferns,
then eager would I seek your lips,
though you be as high above me
as the circling hawk that out flies the sparrow,
and nestled in your arms find peaceful rest.

But wend all waters to the sea.
In the promise of my youth,
when the strength of action coursed through my limbs,
I sought to hold close the wonders about me.
Now as I face the brilliant rays of the setting sun,
I have only the strength to behold the splendor
of that which I had always hoped to find."

When he finished his recitation, Bragi bowed his head to the beautiful maiden. But when she drew him close with her outstretched arms, he found his mind spinning madly, halfway between hope and regret.

He gently pushed her away. "It has been many a long year since I have known the impetuousness of youth." A deep sadness crinkled his brow as he gazed into the questioning of her clear blue eyes. "And while age has taught me caution, the joy I have found in your presence dared me this one last time to bare my heart and speak truthfully. But it is far too late for me to do other than enjoy the feeling. For now, having found that which I always sought, I'm too old to do anything with it."

As Idun made to speak, Bragi held up a hand. "I am not so old that I have forgotten the fires that drive the young. But simple knowledge of the blaze," he sadly shook his head, "cannot ignite the urgent flames, let alone provide the fuel to keep them burning. I would never be able to keep up with you. You sit before me young, beautiful, so... so full of life," a tear trickled down his cheek, "while I sit here grown to such an age that your youth would be wasted caring for the withered and infirm."

Idun tilted her head back and laughed, a gentle tinkle that filled the glade with hope. The goddess reached out a slim hand to grasp Bragi's gnarled fingers. "Tradition has it that all things have their season— blooming flowers, fruiting vines, even the leafing trees. In spring, new shoots reach out. In summer, they spread their verdant limbs across the land. In fall, they retire behind dried husks, a memory of their once-full form. In winter, they rest.

All that is, save love. Experience tells me love has no one season. Rather, it is like the thunderclap heard echoing from the clouds year-round. And like thunder rumbling unchecked through the hills, in the heart there is nowhere to escape love's call."

She squeezed Bragi's hand. "Do not fret about your age," her smile brightened as she drew him near, "that is a point easily reckoned. For in the halls of the Æsir, I am keeper of the apples of immortal youth. Each day my kin make their way to my grove. There they select from a crystal casket bound with narrow golden straps, their share of the golden fruit that I prepare each morning.

Each haunt my doorway as fits their desire. Some bang on the door as Sol crests the horizon, eager to keep the bloom of youth always fresh on their cheeks. Some arrive after long intervals, preferring the lines of maturity to the endless blush of youth. There are always old and young among us.

By partaking of the physic that I brew from the fruit, you will once more know the stamina of youth; illness, age, even death will never again be your companions, and I would have you by my side for all time. You have only to come with me for all this to be true."

Eyes aglow, Bragi threw back his head, his laughter filling the glade. He reached out a hand to Idun as she stood up to ready herself for travel. "I left my home expecting death. Shoving off, I set my course along the western path, fully turning myself over to fate! But instead of death I have found rebirth in your arms. With a song on my lips, I gladly join you!"

Together, they passed upward, wending their happy way to the halls of Asgard and the welcome calls of joyous Æsir.

———————

A home was prepared for the couple in the center of Always Young, Idun's lush grove nestled beneath the protecting canopy of Yggdrasil. Here, the flowers were the brightest, the trees tallest, the grasses greenest. No leaf tumbled withered to the ground, no blossom dropped from its stem. In this grove time held life fresh and everlasting. Birds called gaily as they flit from tree-to-tree, their brilliant plumage winking in the sunlight. Plump, fox-colored squirrels raced among the limbs, while fish teemed in the pools of Idun's spring. In the center of the grove stood a sacred tree, lustrous with emerald foliage. From its boughs hung fruit the color of red gold, the precious apples of youth that only Idun knew how to prepare.

For the new couple, a feast was spread along tables within easy reach of all, the centers crowded with platters of roasted meat, loaves of fine white bread, bowls heaped with fruits. At each place sat a cup brimming with mead. Bragi marveled at the stature of the attending gods who graced the benches about the hall. He took pleasure in their conversations and delighted in the many gifts—wondrous creations all—laid at the couple's feet.

As mead passed about the gathering, the guests became boisterous. Shouts for entertainment grew with rounds of loud banging on the tables. From far back in the hall a story circle began winding its way through the crowd, with each guest telling a tale to entertain the gathering. When it came Bragi's turn to speak, the skald stepped down from his seat and nervously faced the crowd. He who had stood serene before the courts of great kings now found himself the intent focus of gods.

He took a deep calming breath, sipped lightly from his mug to clear his throat, then glanced at Idun, who smiled encouragement. Strongly, clearly, he began a poem of great battles that had racked the lands of Midgard. His words brought the battles to life, gave voice to bold warriors who braved the weapon's rain, fought for their honor in the storm of spears.

Tears fell, voices gasped, and cheers rang from the crowd as the skald guided them through the buffeting winds of war, the screams of the dying, and the barking calls of the victorious. When he finished, the gods sat quiet, staring hard at the man who stood silent before them. Then as one they erupted into shouts for another story to brace the day.

While the sun raced her wain across the sky Bragi entertained his guests. Never did he repeat a story but brought each fresh before the crowd. After each tale, the cheering crowd cried for more.

When Sol had begun her journey through Billing's gate and Mani had started his ascent into the heavens, Odin raised a hand for silence. Stepping down from his seat, the Alfodur slowly approached the groom of Idun, who stood stiff and unbowed before him. Placing one hand on Bragi's shoulder, with his other he amiably clasped the skald's hand.

Odin spoke then, his voice raised for all to hear. "When first I heard of Idun's choice I was wroth and would have denied her pairing. But our precious Idun had selected this man—this mortal man—for herself. So, I mounted Hlidskialf to observe the homes of men that I might gauge the true worth of her choice.

Know that I saw toiling thousands in Midgard, those for whom poetry and song are the highest, brightest points in life, repeating the stories this man created, and lamenting his passing from their world. Know that I heard the prayers of many calling on this man to teach them his skill, offering up sacrifices on private altars, praying that he aide their endeavors by bestowing on them his gift. It was a thing nearly beyond my comprehension, this worldly worship of a man— one not even a warrior. I was offended that a mere mortal should garner such tribute.

I arrived this day set in mind to withhold my blessing from this union. And well I would have done this, but then I heard him recite before us his stories of the lives of men. I speak, I believe, for all the Æsir. Never have I heard such eloquence. It beguiles the mind. Even I who am known for glibness stand pale before what we have heard this day. Now I say to all that it is good to have such a silver tongue within our clan."

He gazed out over the gathering. "Everyone knows where I stand on the matter. Now I ask each of you to speak freely your thoughts."

Bragi glanced about, noted the bright gazes that settled lightly upon him. He looked to Idun, whose broad smile lit the room, saw the tears coursing down her cheeks. With joyful cheers that shook the rafters, each guest freely made known their view.

After each had spoken, Odin raised both hands for silence and made a final decision for the clan. "I give warm greeting to a new relation of the Æsir. Let him be welcome in all our homes and draw strength from kinship bonds."

All Æsir were delighted at the ruling. They surged from their seats, shouting calls of welcome to Bragi while Idun beamed from her seat beside. Songs of greeting were sung while solemn pledges were given over mead. For his eloquence of tongue, he was assigned a high position as storyteller of the clan.

When the celebration had died down, Odin hooked an arm over Bragi's shoulders. In a quiet voice, he promised his new kin a treasure in fodder for his poems, his Bragarœdur. "In ten days, you will accompany me to Sokkvabekk, Saga's mansion ringed by cool rippling waters. There you will learn all the stories of times past, great events encompassing the long-remembered glories of the Æsir. These you will weave into tales to warm our hearths. They will remind us all of who we are, the oaths we have given, and of our solemn duties to one another."

Gathering the Einherjar

"A voice echoes through my mind, a voice I have heard or am yet to hear, I do not know, but it calls me to action." Odin wrung his hands as he paced back and forth before the knot of kin seated close by. "We lost many in the war with the Vanir, but time is not replenishing our ranks as quickly as I had hoped."

He stepped before the eldskáli, staring into the coals, reading the shifting colors that danced among the embers as one would runes carved on a batua stone. Firelight played along the length of his beard, throwing the creases of his face into sharp relief. Everyone remained silent, waiting for him to resume speaking. "The eloquent voice relates stories of valor amid the lands of men. I say we dip into these reserves, those we have protected for eons." He pressed two fingers to his forehead as a sharp pain spiked over one eye. "I fear a great need is coming, one that will require many strong arms."

Bragi's voice echoed from a table seated near the end of the fire. "Forests of stout apple trees grow across the lands of my birth. All the stories I have related of their bravery and honorable deeds are true."

"There is courage there. Courage we must gather to defend our home." Odin coughed and pointed at the skald as Bragi lifted a mug of mead to his lips. "What were your words, the ones you spoke; the beginning of the lead story you told when first we met in Idun's garden?"

Bragi cleared this throat and placed a hand to his chest as his voice filled the room. "The warrior's form is fairest when he dies, perished with his life's bloom intact. His honor lives in the regrets and tears of those he has left behind. To them he appears more sacred than in life, more beautiful because he died in battle. It is only when—"

"Yes. Yes, that was it." Odin interrupted as a low murmur rose from those seated. "Those who die in the weapon's rain are ours to judge. We can freely pick from the ranks of those fallen in war."

Tyr slipped from the shadows into the flickering light. "But how can we know whom to choose?" He waved away a servant as he poured himself another drink. "We will want only the best, not the rabble."

The Alfodur tapped a finger against the side of his nose. "I would prefer to personally choose, but I cannot be everywhere. I need the help of wholesome hands and minds."

Tyr laughed. "That is easily done." He waved an arm to encompass all in the room. Any of us can prowl the battlefields, watching as warriors' fight, then choosing the best from the slain."

Odin waved away the suggestion as he sipped his cup of wine. "We are skilled in many things, but none of us are so pure that we can perform such a task without prejudice. I want those who will follow my direction without question."

Ignoring the grumbles of disagreement his words raised, Odin tipped his cup over the fire, slopping some wine to hiss amid the flames. "So consecrated, they must be able to discern beyond the action. As a farmer husbands his crop to promote the best, and too they must help us cultivate the harvest of war."

"Only the chaste-minded can be appointed this trust." A satisfied smile spread the Alfodur's lips, as he raised his cup to the gathering. "Seated atop my tower I have searched across the nine worlds for those embodying these qualities." Tipping his head to one side, he whispered to Hugin, who bobbed his head at each word. Then he craned his neck around to whisper to Munin, who cawed loudly and swept off his shoulder, followed by the rapidly beating wings of Hugin. "With a thought, it is done; the call is sent. I have selected my choosers of the slain."

———————

Thirteen were first called to gather in Asgard, more would follow; virtuous young maidens to carry out Odin's commands on the slaughter field and bring ale to the warrior's bench in the great hall of Valhalla. From chieftain's daughters and worthy kin, he summoned those of martial quality, fair-skinned under shining helmets, ringed corselets glittering across their chests, honorable in nature, obedient in service.

Valkyrie, the war-minded maidens of Heriar, ride into battle delivering good fortune and assured fate. Ranged across the sky in attack formation, astride dark mounts that scream with anticipation, they tremble the air where they pass.

Brynhild, lady of the battle helmet, chief among the Valkyrie and Odin's favorite, leads the troop. Skogul, her eyes hard and lips stern, always rides point. Skeggjold waves her mighty axe, ready to cleave through the ranks of foemen. The cheers of Goll and Hlokk sound through the din of battle.

Herfjotur charges the foe, eager to fetter advancing armies. Thrud advances boldly in the line, the strength of her father glowing in every limb. Gerahod raises her deadly spear to glint in the rays of Sol. Rota canters beside Reginleif, she whose life is dear to the gods.

Gunn, always eager for battle, brushes shoulders with Radgrid and Randgrid, warrior sisters with shields held high, forever ready for the rough sport of Hild, but who are always willing to counsel truce.

Sent by Odin into every battle, they carry out his commands. Afterward, while bodies still steam on the field, they choose the valorous from the scattered dead, those worthy to join the Einherjar— Odin's ranks of tireless, fearless warriors in whose hearts the joy for battle is always coiled tight. On open plain, concealed amid forest trees, hunkered behind palisades, mustered in closed ranks, or scattered across a field, they stand with shields raised, swords and spears held high, as their voices, each in their own tongue, reach to the heavens.

"By the storm of my wound flame
I sweep the enemy aside.
Each must accept the end of life here in this world,
so each must earn fame before meeting death.

For warriors, it is best to live on in memory,
embraced by the early passing of life,
than to crumble before old age,
the deeds of one's life forgotten.

We fight across all lands,
holding positions close to the enemy ranks,
our weapons worn from heavy use,
our bodies scored with wounds.

At manhood, we grow our hair thick on chin and long on head
to veil our face in valor's pledge.
We weave an iron ring into our heavy locks
as a mark of servitude to honor
that kin and foe will know our oath.

Only over the body of a slain enemy
can we cut back our hair,
having proved ourselves worthy of our parents and our native land,
and with stern voice loudly proclaim to all
our debt paid for entering this world.

Our families watch as we face the foe.
Revered witnesses to our honor,
they ring the fields in solemn expectation.
The shrieks of our women mingled with the wails of our children
swelling on the winds to cheer us as we plunge into the fray.

Fear, the great brutalizer, we scorn.
With fierce thoughts, we face what comes next
and never look back to mourn what is past.
Suffering lasts but a little while. Then is gone.
With clear eyes, we face death undaunted."

Down from the sky ride the bright-helmed maidens of war. Thunder rolls from the hooves of their mounts; vaferflames shimmering across the heavens light the horizon with brilliant bolts of fire. Their ringed byrnies gleam with reflected light. Rays shine from their sun-tipped spears. Their horses tremble in eagerness; from their manes dew falls to wet the path and rattle the shields of brave warriors with hail.

The armored maidens charge headlong into the fray. The noise of spears grows loud as they pass. In the storm of battle their high hearts make swords sweat rivulets of blood. On the field filled with dead men they dispense triumph to the standing warrior. For Odin and Freyja, they cull the bravest from the serried ranks of dead; the chosen to battle beside the airy gods at Ragnarök. Across the steaming slaughter fields their call goes out:

"Rise up you fallen oaks!
You haters of cowardice!
You lovers of honor!

Now is the time for those chosen on the field
to ride the westerly path.
You are called to attend the Thing of Fate.
From there we travel in glorious company
to the sacred sanctuary of warriors!"

Along red roads the chosen ride. The gods have an appointed time of arrival. The hooves of their fallow steeds' strike sparks as they clatter across Asbrau. They come to Asgard suffering grievous wounds, raging with a dying thirst. Valgrind swings wide, doors are opened, and the deep tones of a war horn welcome them to the great hall, Valhalla. As they pass beneath the crouching wolf and hovering eagle their wounds are healed, pains relieved, their thirst quenched. They gather at board to feast on the eternal sacrifice—the boiled flesh of the great boar, Saehrímnir—and drink heady brew served by warrior maidens.

Audhrimnir, the swarthy cook of Valhalla, toils over the daily feast. Each day it becomes harder to stretch provisions for the growing host of warriors who arrive after bloody death and crowd the table in the great hall.

Heidrun browses on the tender leaves in Yggdrasil's top most branches, the tree's sap lending its strength to her milk. Each morning and evening Audhrimnir gathers the she-goat's milk. With a long-practiced hand, he blends it into hydromel, the potent mead of Asgard. Mug after brimming mug is dispensed among the Einherjar, who tip back their cups and shout for more.

In the pot called Eldhrimnir, he boils Saehrímnir, the valiant boar that in life was the death of many a brave hunter and his hounds. Grimly, Audhrimnir prepares the dish. He knows, as does the soot black boar that tomorrow will see the boar whole, ready to fight for his life. Such is the noble sacrifice of Saehrímnir.

Well-fed and well-drunk, eternity passes slowly for the doughty warriors of Heriar. Amusements are needed to pass the time. Each morn the lusty crow of Salgofnir rouses them from sleep. After breakfasting, they don their war gear, then ride out to the courtyard of Odin's home fields. With clash and shock they fight among themselves, savagely attacking each other, delivering vicious blows to maim.

When the day of war play is done, they gather up their weapons, lend a supporting arm to the wounded, and return to the healing comforts of Valhalla. Reconciled, they sit on the mail-coated benches, stretch out their legs, and in good-natured companionship eat their fill. Between mouthfuls, they drain goblets of strong mead, while recounting the day's exploits.

Fears do not plague their days, nor do black dreams disturb their nights. Their hearts and arms know neither languor nor fatigue. Fortified, they bide their time in endless feast and the joy of endless war.

The Children of Loki

Loki, bored with life in the Æsir courts, went to visit his family's holding, a heavy timbered hall surrounded by patches of cleared land and thick fingers of dark-green fir trees nestled deep in the eastern forest of Jarnvid just beyond the Mœotin Marsh. He spent many happy hours in the company of his brother, Beylist, passing the time of day relating tales of his adventures amid the Æsir.

When visiting with his closest kin became tiresome, he began wandering the dark forest paths of the Ironwood he had traveled when in his minority, chuckling to himself at a memory, noticing how little had changed. During these walks, he often felt the prying eyes of a watcher concealed amid the bracken that choked the forest floor. Sometimes he would catch fleeting glimpses of a willowy blond figure flitting amid the brush.

His curiosity piqued, Loki decided to capture this furtive observer and find out why he was being followed. With stealth to rival Vidar,

Loki snuck through the brambles lining a path he frequented in the morning hours. Beside a sharp curve in the forest lane, he spied a young maiden crouched behind the bole of a great tree. She seemed a beautiful creature, but as he crept nearer he noticed her golden hair was crinkled—as if held too close to a fire, her ragged clothes charred along the edges, and a breeze blowing from her direction that carried the tang of smoke.

When she saw the brother of Beylist slinking toward her through the brush, she made to scuttle away into the heavy wood. But Loki was too swift. He caught up with the maiden, grabbed her roughly by the arm, and dragged her back onto the open path.

"I had suspected one of Odin's Valkyrie sent to spy on my actions, but I never expected to encounter one of such a lofty pedigree hunkered amid the forest loam. Though wrapped in scorched rags, I recognize you Gullveig. You are a long way from the hearth fires of Odin's hall. I see you have miraculously healed from your last visit among the Æsir."

The young woman dragged a bit of tattered cloth over her bare shoulder. "No thanks to you and yours!" She spat, nearly striking his boot. "And I call myself Angrboda now, for the anguish that tears at my breast."

Loki hunkered down until he was eye level with the maiden. "That you suffer is apparent to the eye, but why do you follow me? I have seen you trailing my walks each day. I have enough of Heimdall's prying gaze, I do not need the scrutiny of another."

"You know enough," Angrboda sneered, tossing her frizzled hair to the side. "You were there. You saw the treatment I received at your kinsman's hands!"

A gentle breeze rustled the leaves overhead, rippling sun dappled shadows about the couple hunkered on the forest floor. Loki rocked back on his heels, anchoring himself in the loam, as he stared thoughtfully at a shadow bouncing along Angrboda's brow. "Yes, I was there. I know what the Alfodur presented at the Husthing. I know what the Vanir agreed you had done. And I certainly recall the bloody war that ensued because of the actions taken. But I do not know your side of the story. That you were not allowed to speak on your own behalf is an injustice I have never been able to reconcile with the honorable oaths often lauded among the kin of Ingvifreyr."

Angrboda's lips twitched at Loki's words. A deep satisfaction filled her breast at the disaffection with the Æsir hinted at in his speech. "Alright, I will tell you my story, though it carries grim results for lofty intent."

Bit by bit, Angrboda related her tale, spreading it out to appeal to the paternal essence of Loki's character. "Born a daughter of the wise Vanir, I was named Gullveig for the golden luster of my hair. Endowed with the inborn skills of a seeress and a penchant for the craft of seid, for years I sought the knowledge I would need to make my way in the world.

When I heard of Heimdall's journey, his selfless deeds in the land of Midgard, and his adoption into the Æsir clan, I was inspired. Hungry for adventure, I left my comfortable home, braving the elements as I traveled east to the land of men in the hope of emulating his efforts."

The maiden paused to wipe a tear from her cheek before continuing the tale. "In Midgard, I sought to bring mankind the gift of knowledge, of how to manipulate the forces of nature and mold their own fates."

Loki barked a short laugh. "You sought to give them the powers of the gods. The Æsir are lenient in many things, but toying with their creations so it diminishes the esteem of the creators," he cocked an eyebrow, "that they do not like."

Angrboda's voice fell to a low growl, bitterness dripping from her every word as she relentlessly ground out her tale. "Rather than commending me for distributing knowledge among men, I found the Æsir resented my teachings."

Loki chuckled softly, his gaze turned inward. "Odin is a powerful opponent. He is quick to repay any perceived affront—regardless its intent—with harsh dealing. You picked the wrong audience for your teachings."

Angrboda huffed, ignoring the interruption. "In the fires of Odin's great hall, they thrice tried to burn me. Each time they tossed my remains to the wind, and each time my skills raised me from the ashes. The last time they became so disgusted with their inability to kill me that instead of consigning me again to the flames, I was banished to the cold reaches of these woody wastes, here to wait in the company of howling wolves until the end of days."

Loki patted her shoulder in sympathy. "Often the path of good intention leads to an unsavory result. Your story wrings my heart with its injustice. Know that I am very familiar with the bias the Æsir show in their dealings with foe and kin alike. But regardless the tragedy you have suffered, you still have not told me why you have been following me. That, above all, I would know." Chuckling, shaking his head, Loki traced the toe of his boot through the dark forest loam. "If you are seeking vengeance against the Æsir, know that I am a poor recipient of your wrath. There are few in the halls of Asgard who would mourn my passing or seek to avenge an injury done to me."

The corners of Angrboda's lips turned down, drawing the lines of her face along with them. "I have no issue with you. As I said, I am a seeress with the gift to see ahead, though my vision is spotty with only points of clarity amid the murk. I have seen our children," her eyes flashed at Loki's smirk, "and know that their destiny is to assuage my anguish by bringing humility to the arrogant gods."

Loki looked Angrboda over. The heat of his lingering gaze flushed her cheeks with its intent. "We have children, do we? Have you seen anything else of note?"

The maiden turned her face aside, contemplating the deepening shadows of the forest. "Only that after the children have grown we go our separate ways. The remainder is fleeting glimpses and gray fog."

"Well then..." Loki rubbed his hands together in delight like a fly before it is ready to feast. "Know that I enjoy chastising the arrogance of others and will gladly offer my services in fathering offspring to further that aim. As for your teachings, you have a new student. Let us begin with the skill of rising from pyre ash. That is a trick I am very interested in learning."

———•———

There amid the tangled roots of the dark wood Loki joined with Angrboda. With each caress, each deep thrust, he took in her scorched heart and adopted her anguish as his own. Three children were birthed from that union, destined to be the bane of the gods: two sons and a daughter born to the son of Farbauti.

The eldest son was ugly as his ancestor Thrudgelmer. Strange headed, scaly skinned, and of a sinuous serpentine form; him they called Jormungand.

The daughter was half gray, half white, unpleasant to look upon. Imperious of nature, with a cruel twist to her lips, her they called Leikin.

The youngest son of wolfish disposition was prone to black moods and sudden outbursts of temper. Handsome, with thick, dark hair like his father, him they called Fenris.

Great portents heralded their birth: the night sky brightened with streaks of flame, the moon reddened, the sun dimmed, the earth shook until none could stand. The watchful eye of Odin noted their arrival into the worlds. A soft, steady stream of curses whispered through his beard as he recognized the sweating face of Gullveig and the sharp, eager features of Loki. From his seat high atop Hlidskialf he watched the children grow strong, racing together through the eastern forest of Jarnvid where dark trees stretch out their limbs to an empty sky.

Ravens kept vigil over the hall raised up in the deep wood beyond the Mœotin Marsh. Each day they returned to perch on Odin's shoulders, chattering into his ears of everything they had seen. The Alfodur frowned at the teachings delivered to the children by their parents and at the inherent power that would soon be theirs to command if left unchecked.

Uneasy, Odin watched as the youngest reached his majority and in rut spread his seed among the Jarnvidjur—the ogresses of the Ironwood. The offspring, raised alike to wolves with the disposition of their line, pursue the children of Mundilfari as they travel the heavens counting the years for man. Skoll chases the sun across the northern sky, all red tooth and fang, nipping at Sol's heels. Hati Hrodvitnisson pursues the moon, hating that which he cannot catch. To live, he satiates himself with the vital force of those marked for death, daubing the sky with the blood of each victim. The most fearful of all Managarm, the Moon Dog, gorges himself on the dead. Relentless, unforgiving, he shares Hati's unquenchable hatred of Mani.

Troubled by all he had seen, Odin buried his face in his hands as the words of the long-dead seeress burned through his mind, a prophecy foretelling the grave danger Loki's children presented to the

Æsir. To eliminate this looming threat to his clan, he sent a troop of valiant warriors deep amid the boles of the Ironwood to capture the three for ready judgment before a Husthing of the gods. "Just bring the two brothers and their sister. I've no interest in any offspring that might be theirs, nor their cousins. Do them no harm but be mindful of their strength. Keep them bound, always, and never, ever, drop your guard. You will get no second chance."

In the gold-shingled hall of the Alfodur the fearful gods gathered together to decide the fate of Farbauti's grandchildren. All squirmed uneasily in their seats as the fettered captives were dragged before them.

Jormungand

Loki's eldest son rose before his foes. Benches scraped back as he swayed side to side, swinging his head to take in those who sat in judgment. All shied away from his gaze, turning aside their faces to look at their hands, the walls, the ceiling rafters, anything except the fearsome glare of Loki's eldest. His form was like that of a serpent. His features, hideous with scaly skin and dagger sharp eyes, froze them in their seats.

"I stand before you," his proud voice boomed through the hall, "son of one you call kin. Stolen from my home along with my siblings, you hustled us here as one would criminals guilty of some heinous crime. What have we done that you might hold us captive and pass judgment on our lives?"

Odin spoke from his seat above the council. "Your births were heralded by a prophecy that your lives would mark the end of our own. We bring you before us to decide how best to handle the danger you present."

The son of Loki spat on the floor before the council seats. A sneer spread across his face, twisting his lips, as he glared about the gathering. "You dragged us here because of a possibility? You are fools to dread the future! Caught in a web of what might happen, you give yourselves over to fear of the unknowable! You call me monster because of how I look. I dare call you the same for ignorant actions."

The great hall remained silent at his words. None dared speak of him in scorn. Odin nodded from his seat on high. He placed his hands flat on the board before him, stared a moment at his fingers, then glanced around at the worried faces of the gathering. "Your words are well spoken. None doubt their truth. But know we do not take these actions lightly, though you think them cruel and unjust.

I have learned to respect true prophecy and the glimpse it gives of future events. The consequences have been harsh when I disregarded their course. It would be foolish of me to ignore your origin, those who have raised you, and the values they've imparted. We have suffered much at the hands of those who bore you."

Jormungand snorted and again spat on the ground. Odin paid no attention, though several Æsir started at the affront. "A wise man banks the coals of a fire before he goes to bed, snuffs out the light of a guttering candle, stamps out the blaze smoldering in the field, else the unwatched fire spreads unchecked to consume his property in flames." Low murmurs of "Ayes" and "Yeas" circled the hall as Odin lifted his hand for attention. "I ask now for all to speak their mind."

While the sun traveled the space of four fingers across the sky, the council spoke in hushed voices, deliberating the proper course of action. The Alfodur leaned back in his seat, listening to everything that was said. When everyone had agreed, they turned back in their seats to face the children of Loki huddled together in the center of the room, rattling their chains.

Odin clapped his hands three times to announce the final decision. He looked down, somber faced, at the son of Loki, who stared back in challenge through slit eyes. "We have given every consideration," Jormungand snorted in derision, "discussed every option in depth, all have agreed. You are the eldest of your siblings, and easily the most dangerous. It is with a heavy heart that I order you put to death." At a gesture from the Alfodur, Thor stepped forward, jaw set, to carry out the sentence.

Jormungand glared into the eyes of the god's strong guarder, staying his hand while he held him with his voice. "Though you act at the command of another, this deed brings no honor and belittles you before all—executioner of a bound captive."

Thor gave a slight nod and grasped him about the middle. With a mighty heave, he cast the victim down from the heights of Asgard, far out into the ocean that surrounds all lands, there to feed the codfish.

But he did not die. The wave-crowned waters of ocean cushioned his fall. Cradled in its bed, nourished by its abundance, he thrived, growing in form until he encircled the outer sea that surrounds the lands of Midgard and Jotunheim, a great wolf fish biting its tail.

When Jormungand recalls his treatment at the hands of the Æsir gods, a mighty shudder ripples along his length. He thrashes about churning the ocean to gray foam, raising tall waves that crash down, engulfing the surface. Few are bold enough to dare the sea when the Midgard Serpent is restless.

Leikin

The daughter of Loki was shoved forward to stand before the council. Cool and superior, she spurned their words, remaining silent at their insults and rude jests. "Ugly? Why, just look at her. She seems half corpse, half alive, but which side is which? She might make a decent cutting girl, if only to keep her away from the sight of others. Who would want that lurking about their hall?"

Aloof, she turned her face aside at their questions. "Who do you think you are, girl, to ignore the greatness arrayed before you? Speak up. Don't just stand there, mute as a post."

Blue gray and pale white, she flashed her silent response to the hounding speech that chased about the hall. Odin said nothing but sat with steepled fingers raised before his face as he contemplated Leikin's haughty pride.

While the sun traveled the space of four fingers across the sky to pass beyond the crest of midday, the council spoke in hushed voices, deliberating the proper course of action. The Alfodur leaned back in his seat, listening to everything that was said. When everyone had agreed, they turned back in their seats to face the remaining children of Loki huddled together in the center of the room, rattling their chains.

Odin nodded from his seat on high. The young woman turned up her nose, looking to the open doorway at the far end of the hall where the bright rays of Sol stretched across the floor, nearly reaching the eldskáli. "It is decided to let you live. But for your cold arrogance and the disdain you show this court, I decree for you a duty to match your nature: servitude to the goddess of life and death. From this day forward, it will be your eternal duty to administer to the twice-dead."

Odin clapped his hands. The god's strong guarder stalked forward, resolute, prepared to do his duty. The maiden sneered at her captors and spat on the ground as Thor grasped her about the middle. A light flex of his powerful muscles sent her spinning from the heights of Asgard down into the dark land of Niflhel.

She landed hard in the cold wasteland, her body broken on the rocks beside Eljudnir, the terrible dark hall of the dead, its ice-crusted walls sprayed with sleet and wrapped with drifted snow.

Half white, half blue-gray, her countenance grim, she hobbles about her hall, stooped over on badly healed legs. Called Hel for the scope of her domain, she does the bidding of the one who weaves the fates of men.

On an ugly-grown horse she rides, its three hooves thundering as she sallies forth from her hall in swift forays across the worlds to collect her due. In the turbulence of her passage, plagues rage across the lands. Those who survive pay dearly for her mercy. They give a bushel of oats at each harvest, fodder for her misshapen steed, ransom to prolong their lives. With sullen grace, she accepts their payment before returning to her hall to brood cold, brittle thoughts filled with venom for the fate of the Æsir.

Fenris

Shaking off the hands of his guards, the youngest stalked forward to stand before the Husthing of the gods. His head high, gaze direct, he held their glare. Fearlessly he dared they treat him with the same justice they had shown his siblings. "Were we in battle," his bold voice pressed them back into their seats, "I would soon turn your arrogant gaze to fear, but, bound as I am, I cannot defend myself, so must face whatever decision you deliver."

He raised his fists and shook his chains. "Even though my fate lies in your hands, I will not cower before you begging for my life any more than did my siblings. I dare you to look me in the eye and bestow on me the same mercies of your unwarranted judgment."

For the remainder of the afternoon until close of day, the council spoke in hushed voices, deliberating the proper course of action. The

Alfodur leaned back in his seat, listening to everything that was said. When everyone had agreed, they turned back in their seats to face the last child of Loki standing defiant in the center of the room, his chains clinking in cadence with his breathing.

Fenris bared his teeth in a wide, defiant grin as the Husthing reconvened. "Come then. Let me hear your pronouncement, old man. I am ready for any fate you might confer."

Odin strode forward, circling the bound captive. Geri and Freki snarled with ears laid back but would not follow. "You are fearless, even in captivity. Undaunted in the face of enmity, you remind me much of the offspring of Bor. And though prophecy warns us of what may be, I am not one to fear changing its course. You are young, with much yet to learn. In our halls, we can teach you."

Alone, Odin decided for the clan. Reaching out his hand, he took Fenris by the arm. "Warm greeting, I give to the son of Loki. Let him be welcome in our homes, loved no less than any of our sons."

Fenris' eyes shown bright as he gripped back hard and shook the Alfodur's arm. "I am hardly in any position to refuse. I accept this fostering among my father's kin. For as long as your words hold true, you will never regret this decision."

Orvandel's Toe

Asa-Thor, son of Odin, born of Earth, is the strongest of the Æsir. Forthright in action, the thunder of roiling black clouds announces his approach. From Bilskirnir, his lofty hall on the plains of strength, he often journeys into the eastern hills to confront enemies of his kin and those who would endanger the lands of men.

On this day, the son of Odin returned from an arduous adventure in the company of his steadfast companion, Orvandel, an archer of uncommon skill. They had traveled a circuitous route through the frozen land of Jotunheim, slaying giants whenever encountered. Now, on the final leg of their return, buffeted by chill winds, pricked by white arrows of frost that pierced their robes, they paused on the bank of the Ifing to take stock of their situation.

"The waters have risen since last we forded this course." Orvandel pointed with his bow up and down the river. "The current runs much swifter than before. It seems the Yurkul have offered up a part of themselves to obstruct our way. See there, the blue-white blocks of ice that bob along the surface. They are not sheets broken from a frozen pool, but hall-sized calves tossed free of their mountain grip."

Thor nodded as a massive block of ice turned slowly to bare a dark blue belly, teetered a moment on its end, then settled back with a groan into the frigid water. "Giants and their kin are always a nuisance. They rival the disir for the trouble they can cause."

The great archer leaned on his yew, studying the river from bend to bend. He took a deep breath before turning to his companion. "I fear the waters are well above my head, so I cannot tread the narrow path of the ford, let alone dodge the great blocks of ice. And too, the water is so cold my limbs would soon grow numb. I would sink in barely half a bowshot were I to attempt to swim its width. For you, this river is a challenge easily overcome. You must go on without me. I will follow as soon as the crest passes."

The son of Odin frowned deeply, his brow furrowed at Orvandel's words. He studied the waters, bent down to dip his fingers in the ice-choked currents, then stood, a low grunt slipping from his lips. "We have journeyed far along dangerous, wind-cold routes, together facing great obstacles that threatened our lives. Never have we left the other to suffer fate alone. We travel together or not at all. We are no more than a day's journey from the comforts of your hall. Food we will have then in plenty and hot ale to drive the chill from our bones."

With that, Thor heaved their provisions basket from his shoulders, upended the reed frame, shaking out the remaining food and leaving it scattered about their feet. "You can ride across," Thor thumped the basket with his hand, "in this. It is large enough to hold you, though you will need to fold yourself tight."

Orvandel hunched into his shoulders, his lips set in a hard frown. "I would sooner starve to death than suffer the indignity of being ferried across the waters, carried as a child strapped to his parent's back!"

Thor rolled his eyes to the clouds. Shaking his head in disbelief, he swept his arm at the cold-blighted landscape. "This land is empty of life; even birds forsake the sky. In our last days of travel, we have seen no game that could be taken by hand or with your skilled bow."

He toed the meager rations strewn in clumps about the ground. "These supplies would hold you for three days, seven were you thrifty with your meals. Long before the cresting waters fall, and the river becomes fordable, you would know the painful gnawing of famine who reigns across this desolate land. Starvation would most certainly be your fate were I to agree with your desire to remain behind."

Thor lifted the mouth of the basket. "Your death, I will not permit!" He gestured imperiously for his companion to get in. "Not while it is within my power to prevent it."

Yielding to Thor's insistence, Orvandel wriggled into the provisions basket. With a steady grumble of soft curses, he wedged himself against the frame as the son of Odin hoisted it onto his shoulders then knotted the support straps around his waist.

The river ran high between its banks, a mighty torrent, powerful in its course. As Thor stepped into the frigid waters the wild current tore at his legs, threatening to wash him away. Frigid waters surged around Thor's waist as he waded manfully across the river. Orvandel hunkered low in the pack, arms wrapped tight about his knees, huddling into himself to stay warm. His toe protruding from a hole in his boot jutted through the wide weave of the basket round. Alternately wetted by splashing waters and chilled by blasts of frigid air, it froze a shiny, painful blue. The brave archer silently gritted his teeth, holding his pain close to his breast lest Thor endanger his own life by stopping in mid-channel to aid his companion.

The wind's caress was a sharp scrape of frost as they emerged from the embrace of the waters, hauled to safety by arms of rowan branches that tightly hugged the riverbank. When Thor helped his companion from the basket, he saw the silent grimace of pain that flashed across Orvandel's face as the archer stepped onto the ground. Catching his arm, Thor helped him to sit down on the bank.

As Orvandel stretched out his legs, he spotted the bright blue digit winking from the archer's boot. "You cannot travel far on that. And should it remain untended, soon your foot, then your leg, will swell green and turn black."

Without another word, Thor reached down and snapped it off lest the ice spread further into the foot. The archer sucked a deep breath, blinking as he turned his suddenly ashen face aside.

Lifting the pack, Thor slapped the open basket with his hand. "Climb in. I will carry you the rest of the way."

With a long, low grunt, Orvandel tottered to his feet, supporting himself with his bow. "I can walk," he winced through the pain. "I have some healing skills taught to me by my wife that will get me through until we reach my hall. Once there, Groa can properly mend my foot. We have crossed the river. Let us quit talking and be on our way."

Thor watched, a smile turning his lips, as the archer stumped purposefully along the trail using his good yew as a walking staff. "Brave you were to endure the painful cold of the life-draining waters; braver still to sit silent and unflinching while I wrested the frozen digit from your foot. But your courage to continue on the trail, undaunted by suffering, fills my heart with pride. I will let this frozen toe show the nine worlds the esteem I hold for you."

To honor the bravery of his friend, the son of Odin tossed the toe into the heavens. From its high perch, it twinkles a fierce blue that all might know the splendor of his boon companion. There it hangs, the brightest of stars, a beam of frozen sunlight to guide travelers in need, a beacon over shining all the lights of heaven.

An Encounter in Utgarda

Frequently, Thor journeyed into the land of Jotunheim to quell the growing numbers of giants by daring his power against worthy foes. With each bold foray his fame grew, as did the tales of his brave deeds, feats of great strength, and honorable victories.

Loki grew curious at the accounts. With each new story, he grew more interested, carefully questioning each teller to gauge the tale's worth. The more he heard, the more he desired to travel with Thor and observe for himself the truth of his kinsman's pastime.

When Loki stated his request, Thor turned a skeptical eye on the would-be adventurer, taking in his slight build, his challenging stance, and the ever-present smirk that twisted his lips. "Why do you ask to join my expedition? You know I journey to the icy lands of Jotunheim. You are accustomed to ease here at the Æsir courts. I fear you will find great discomfort along the route of this frozen trail."

Loki laughed, his clear eyes guileless before the fiery gaze of the god's strong guarder. "The lips of many have recounted tales of your grand feats performed in far-off lands. The stories are so amazing, their scope so astonishing, I desire to witness such deeds firsthand, perhaps even to play some part in their plot and earn a bit of honor for myself.

And do not fear you will end up carrying me across the length of icy waste, fainthearted, because cold winds have numbed my vigor. I am quite familiar with the country's treacherous weather. Remember, I was born in the Ironwood. I spent my minority raised among the etin."

Thor smiled at Loki's words and his apparent earnest desire for honor. "Very well. You may accompany me. I leave with the passing of the next night to challenge one in that land of frozen dreams who is considered the greatest among his people. Be ready to leave then, or to stay behind."

———————

When Night retired from the land and Day advanced to illuminate the sky, Loki joined Thor at his wain. He waved as he approached, receiving a curt nod in reply. Thor hoisted a sack of provisions into the cart, cinching it down tight that the jostling ride not send it tumbling across the ground. "We travel first to Orvandel's hall. There we will rest the night before continuing our journey on foot."

Loki stepped forward, shaking his head. "Why wear down our feet on rocky paths," he slapped the nearest goat on the rump, "when you have such stalwart beasts to carry us." The animal spun about, loosing a kick that just missed Loki's face. Loki fell back, curses flowing freely from his lips.

Thor emitted a sharp bark of laughter that cut through the chill morning air. He reached out a steady hand to calm the animals, gently rubbing their ears to let them know they were safe. "You had best stand well back from my goats. They do not brook familiarity from strangers. Their horny feet can bruise the unwary; their sharp teeth can slash. It is bad to start a long journey with a limp."

Loki glared at the goat as he rubbed his jaw. Under his breath, he swore vengeance on the animal. "You should warn your traveling companions as to the treacherous nature of your beasts, lest you be blamed for their actions and be repaid in kind."

Thor stroked the horns of the nearest goat. The animal turned its head to nuzzle his arm. "Taking liberties without forethought is unwise. When traveling, a man should always carry a full store of common sense. Only the foolish approach an unknown beast without caution."

Pulling himself onto the wain, Thor gathered up the reins, making ready to drive. "Climb aboard. Tanngniost and Tanngrisnir gnash and snarl at the bit, eager to begin. We've a full day's journey to our beds. While my goats can draw us through the lands of men, they cannot navigate the waters of the Ifing, the river which separates Midgard from Jotunheim. That we must cross on our own feet."

Loki snorted at the thought. "That is well for you perhaps; you enjoy the harsh dash of the elements." He lifted his feet, pointing first to one foot then the other. "But my shoes can carry me across land, water, or through the air. I need not subject myself to the rough battering of your cart nor the freezing waters of the Ifing."

Thor pointed to Loki's feet. "Then you will leave your shoes behind. If you desire to partake of my journeys, you must experience them in full."

Reluctantly, the son of Laufey removed his shoes and struggled into a pair of leather boots. "Vidar would be angry at the expense of leather used to make these boots for fear it somehow lessened his own." Loki's face brightened. "I must remember to tell him."

Thor Gains His Servants

As Sol traveled her wind-weaver course, the pair worked their way along rough roads that rattle a traveler's bones, bringing aches to joints and soreness to muscles. With each bruising jolt of the cart, each wrenching twist of wheel in rut, Loki loudly cursed his request to join the adventure.

Toward dusk they drew up their cart before the modest hall of Orvandel, a fortress holding raised up on a hill overlooking the Ifing. Thor bellowed at the entry to make known their presence and beat his fist on the gate until the timbers shook. Roused from their duties the archer's family rushed out to greet the weary travelers; their warm, cheerful smiles welcoming both into their home.

Orvandel placed a hand on Thor's shoulder. "Welcome old friend," he took his arm in a firm grasp, "to my home again. We have missed your fellowship. I see you travel in the company of Loki. Let him be welcome as well. It is a great honor for us to have another of the Æsir visit our hall." Loki crowded around Thor, thrusting forward a hand to Orvandel who stared at it before extending his own to accept.

"For the sake of your companion let me introduce my family that he might not feel he sits among strangers." With a brisk wave, the archer beckoned each family member forward. "My wife, Groa, you well know as she has been a frequent visitor in your halls. Knowledgeable as Eir in the healing arts, she is well versed in the lore of protection and growth." He inclined his head to Thor. "My children have grown since last you visited, both have reached their majority. Thjalfi has become the fastest runner in our region; it is said he can outrun the swiftest mount. Roskva is comely, clever, and loyal. Quickly, she learns the skills of her mother."

Heads nodded, and smiles beamed among the group as the archer paused his introductions. He gestured at their bags. "I see from the packs you carry that you journey into the land of etins. At your word, I will gather my bow. I've a bundle ready for travel leaning by the door. I can be ready in a moment to join your endeavor."

A sharp glance from Groa caught Thor's eye, while Thjalfi and Roskva shifted uneasily on their feet. Thor reached around to grab his travel pack. "I thank you for your offer to join our party, but our journey is brief. We expect little trouble, so there is no need for the shield of your strong bow. All I ask is a place for us to rest the night. From here we travel on foot. I need to board my goats until our return."

Orvandel grunted, disappointment clearly showing in his eyes, as he directed Thjalfi to unharness the animals from the cart. "Put them up in the far barn away from the cattle. Prop the wain alongside the shed. Take from the stores the best hay to comfort these mighty beasts."

With a wide sweep of his open arms Orvandel bid the travelers enter his hall. "You have arrived at an awkward time. I can offer rye bread and cheese curds, and modest ale not too sharp for the tongue. We have enough to fill even your belly. But we can offer nothing else. I have not yet gone hunting. Our larder has little meat to carry us over the lean months."

Thor glanced about at Orvandel's family, smiling warmly at everyone. "We have long been comrades in arms." He clapped a hand on the archer's shoulder. "You have welcomed us into your home and freely offered us the best of all you have in store. Such warmth fills a man as no food ever could. The unexpected guest must never complain of hospitality received. Spare your stores from our visit. Tonight, I will feast this home."

Thor left their company to attend his goats. Gently stroking their necks, he bid them not to fear what was about to happen. With a swift hand, he slit their throats. After carefully flaying the hide from their bodies, he carried the carcasses to a broad-rimmed pot boiling over the hearth fire. The skins he stretched out opposite the fire, leaving their legs splayed. Speaking words of power, he daubed his fingers in the goat's blood and drew out runes on the fleshed side of the skins.

Loki watched the preparations from slaughter to pot and knew Thor had weaved the providence of Saehrímnir. The son of Farbauti smiled inside his cheeks as he saw his chance to avenge himself on animal and master alike.

Boiled flesh was scooped from the pot and mounded on platters to cool. After ladling the broth into bowls, Thor called for everyone to attend him. The smell of cooked meat made mouths water as the family gathered about the board. Tears filled Orvandel's eyes as he recognized the goatskins splayed beside the hearth.

Waving his hammer, Thor invited the household to join in the meal. "Let everyone take a seat. Before you lie the gifts of Tanngniost and Tanngrisnir. But before we enjoy the beneficence of their sacrifice, heed my words of respect. Consume the flesh. When done toss the stripped bones onto the skins." As he gestured to the skins stretched out beside his feet, his voice deepened in warning. "Keep them intact. Do not miss a single bone."

The household ravenously consumed the food, dipping hard bread in the soup broth, gnawing meat and tendons from the bones. When the bones were clean, they dutifully tossed them onto the goatskins before reaching for more.

The son of Farbauti watched as Thjalfi worried flesh from a thighbone, gnawing at all sides as he sought to strip every morsel from its mooring. When the young man seemed ready to toss the bone on the hide pile, Loki slipped a knife from his belt and slid it across the table concealed beneath his palm. "Here," he spoke softly, jerking his chin at the blade, "use its sharp point to get at the marrow."

Thjalfi mumbled a greasy thank you, and with its tip dug deep into the joint to scoop out the tasty marrow inside. The knife tip wedged in a narrow crevasse, cracking the bone as he twisted the blade free. The devious Loki smiled at the faint sound. He glanced around to be certain no one had noticed before sneaking the knife back from the young man and casually returning it to the sheath at his waist.

When the feast was finished, and the board cleared, a final mug of ale heated with a hot iron poker was shared around the table. Each took a deep swallow before passing it on to the next person. As Orvandel drained the last dregs from the mug, Thor thanked his hosts. "You have been generous with your hospitality, freely sharing all that is yours to share. We thank you for providing good company, a warm hearth, and a roof for the night."

Orvandel coughed, set the mug aside, then took his wife's hand; their children took each other by the hand. Together they bowed to the son of Odin. "No, it is we who thank you for the munificent feast. I would never have asked for the sacrifice you made of your goats, even were we starving and the wolf clawing at our door. It was an unexpected generosity; one we gratefully appreciate."

Thor laughed, winking at Loki who gazed benignly on the family. "For a true friend, no sacrifice is too great. It is my privilege to offer that which is mine to provide." Stretching his arms overhead, Thor yawned deeply, showing all his teeth. "It is time we turned in for the night." He nudged Loki with his foot. "We have a long journey ahead of us. I want to get an early start."

———————·———————

When Night retired from the sky and Day had taken her place, Thor rose before Sol had fully passed the gates of her brilliant home in the east. Returning to the outstretched skins, he raised Mjollnir high over his head, blessing the goatskins with their pile of picked bones. Tanngniost climbed at once to his feet, bright eyed and prancing. Tanngrisnir tottered beside him, breathing in short bursts, eyes clouded in pain, lame on his rear leg.

Thor bent to examine the goat's leg. Running his fingers gently along the shank, he encountered the raised edge of a cracked bone. His bushy brows collapsed to a shadowy shelf until only the icy glitter of his eyes could be seen. From overhead, a low rumble shook the hall, rattling utensils hung along the walls. The household, eyes bleary with sleep, rushed into the room at the sound to find Thor hunched over the injured goat.

The son of Odin slowly straightened himself to his full height. Lips twitching, he turned to face the quivering group that cowered silently before him. Mjollnir swayed high over his head, purposeful as a storm gale that starts off low then gradually rises in violence until the entire earth begins to shake. "I freely offered my prized goats to feed your empty stomachs! All I asked was that you honor their sacrifice! Yet one among you ignored my instructions and mistreated the leg bones of this fine animal!"

A loud wail rose from the household at the tone of his words. Groa gathered her children close, a golden goose with her brood of goslings folded protectively beneath her wings. Wrenching himself away from the knot, Orvandel prostrated himself at the thunder god's feet. "My friend, the dishonor falls on my shoulders alone! My life, all that I have, is yours. I beg only that you spare my family."

Thor towered over the archer, his body shaking with rage—a black cloud of flickering vaferflame ready to burst. His eyes sparkled at the family quaking in fear. Well he would have struck them all dead, but he glimpsed the son of Farbauti chuckling softly in the shadows. Loki noticed his glance and quickly turned his face aside.

At the sight of Loki's laughter, the storm cleared from Thor's brow. Outside, the rumbling ceased. Slowly, he lowered his arm as the tremors shaking his body subsided. He glared a moment at the hammer clutched in his fist, before tucking Mjollnir securely back into his vest.

Returning his attention to the cringing household, the son of Odin spoke gravely to Orvandel. "Come, rise up off your knees. Stand before me as the proud warrior I know you to be. We have been friends a long time. You have always placed your skills at my service, backed my every effort without reservation. Your friendship never faltered, even in the bleakest of times."

"For our long-standing camaraderie, I let this pass, but my honor demands recompense." He pointed at Thjalfi and Roskva quivering in their mother's embrace. "Your children will travel with me as servants. I will rely on them as I have always relied on you."

Thor glanced in Loki's direction, observed the sour look on his face, and was pleased. What the son of Farbauti had planned, he did not know, but it was a great satisfaction to see he had thwarted one of Loki's designs.

Thor turned to Orvandel. "Have your children ready to travel. We leave at once for Jotunheim. It will be a long journey on foot." He leaned in close, choosing his words carefully to allay the concerns of the father. "Do not fear for their safety. I will watch over them as if they were my own."

He rested a hand on Groa's shoulder and squeezed so she winced. "My goats I leave in your care," his voice was edged with warning. "Apply your healing skills to Tanngrisnir's leg. On my return, I expect to find him able to travel."

When all was ready, and the children had said their goodbyes, the party turned their faces to the northeast. The chill breath of glaciers caressed their cheeks as Thor strode briskly forward in the lead. Thjalfi followed, carrying their provisions sack. Roskva bore their camp gear on her shoulders. Loki brought up the rear, grumbling at each step.

Skrymir

They traveled swiftly along stony paths that bruised their feet to a beach where sea breakers ground against the coast. From the rocky shore, they set out on a raft of trussed linden logs, the twisting timbers creaking as it glided across the deep ocean, until they came to a land bundled in fir trees.

As they clambered off the raft, Thor grabbed one corner then gestured to Loki to grab the other. "Help me drag this to the forest line."

"Why not leave it here?" Loki balked. "We'll only have to drag it back on our return."

Thor studied him silently for a long moment until Loki began to nervously shuffle his feet. "It is my experience," he explained slowly, "that some giants are not welcoming of uninvited visitors. If we leave the raft on the beach, they might find it and hunt us down before we have traveled half a day. While I can defeat many," he patted Mjollnir, "I do not relish our chances if we are challenged by a large troop. Now grab the other corner and pull."

After covering the raft with fallen branches, they gathered in the shadows at the forest line. Thjalfi gestured to the provisions sack, but Thor shook his head. "We will eat later. For now, we had best be on our way." He pointed to the sky. "Already Sol has begun her decent. I would like to be far away from the open beach ere she goes to rest."

As Night began her journey, they hunted a place to rest. In a clear glade stood a great hall, its one end an unornamented open doorway as wide and tall as the hall itself. Thor approached the entrance. He saw no gleam of fire inside. Cupping his hands about his mouth, he shouted to any within hearing that four weary travelers sought shelter for the night. Three times he called, his voice booming through the chill night air. Three times he received the echo of his own voice in reply.

The four companions crept into the hall, astonished to find it bare of furnishings. No rushes covered the floor. No benches or hangings ornamented the room. There was no trench for an eldskáli.

Loki let his eyes rove about the empty room. He stomped the ground, tapped the walls, even laid his ear against floor to listen for movement, but there was nothing to be heard. "This is a strange construction. It is unlike anything I have seen before; the floor yields beneath my foot and the wall to the pressure of my hand. Still, it is plain this hall has been abandoned, uninhabited since first it was built. Why else the lack of a fire or a fire pit? With no one here to declare possession, none should begrudge us its protection."

Chafing his hands along his arms, Thor directed everyone to spread out. "The night grows blustery and cold. We need shelter for our heads. I think we can spend the night in safety, but it would be prudent to remain on guard."

Just inside the open doorway Roskva and Thjalfi set up camp for the night. Thjalfi unshouldered his pack of provisions, hefted it three times before setting it down. "This seems light for such a trip. I swear I kept a watchful eye and that none was lost along our trail."

"You have no need of concern; you misplaced nothing." Thor nudged the sack with his foot. "Our journey had been planned for two mouths; now there are four. That is all. We must stretch our provisions but make certain Roskva and yourself always get an equal share." As he spoke, Thor cast a warning glance toward Loki. The son of Laufey shrugged before turning away to scan the horizon outside the doorway.

In the middle of the night when darkness cloaked the land, the ground heaved beneath their bedrolls and the walls of the great hall folded inward as they rocked on their foundations. A thunderous crashing accompanied the movement, as if a great giant of the forest had fallen to the earth.

While the others cried out in alarm, Thor leapt to his feet, yanking Mjollnir from his vest. One by one, he shoved his companions deeper into the hall, his sharp commands barely audible over the uproar. "Go! Now! Hold your hand against the wall and follow it inside. Seek out a safe niche. I'll guard your retreat."

To the right, near the middle of the hall, they found a side room, sturdy, snug, and easy to defend. Thor hustled his companions inside, then blocked the entryway with his broad shoulders, his hammer held ready before him.

After several moments, the ground ceased to shake. The sudden stillness was as a breath held. Cautiously, Thor lowered his hammer and craned his head to peek around the entryway when the air was rent with a dull roar that rose and fell in steady rhythm as waves crashing onto headland cliffs.

Cursing sharply, Thor jerked back around the corner. An abrupt gesture sent the others into a low crouch. He waited, shoulders hunched, his hammer poised to strike, but when nothing happened, he took a deep breath and relaxed into a guard position with feet spread wide. Taking their cue from his shifted stance, the others settled in as best they could with the ceaseless din.

The tempest raged all night, the walls quivering with the gale. The travelers got little sleep huddled together behind the son of Odin, who stood resolute in the doorway.

When Delling threw open his gate to let Sol charge into the sky, Thor left the protection of the dimly lit hall. A short distance from the wide doorway he spied a giant stretched out asleep on the ground. Rays of the sun were just beginning to light his craggy features. The etin was broad-browed, thick-limbed with a deep barrel chest, larger by far than any Thor had met before. His snores trembled the branches of the trees, shaking flocks of birds from their roosts.

The son of Odin quickly strapped on his belt of strength, felt the divine power surge within him. Eyes agleam, he strode to the side of the giant, Mjollnir raised high over his head, eager to strike. With a snort the giant awoke, sat up yawning, and dug two massive fists into his eyes. The opportunity of a surprise strike gone, Thor tucked his hammer back into his vest.

Setting his fist on his hips, Thor shouted up at the giant now smacking his lips after a huge yawn. "Who are you that disturbs the forest with your slumber, keeping all awake throughout the night?"

The giant glanced about at the sound, searching sky to forest before climbing to his feet. When he noticed Thor standing nearby, his face broke into a broad grin that flashed a gate of snaggled teeth from between thick lips. "There you are. I thought I heard someone, but you are so small I almost missed you." Digging his fingers between his butt cheeks, the giant rose on his toes in an ecstasy of scratching. "Ah," he moaned, "that's better."

"Now," he grinned again, "you would know my name." The giant thumped his chest with a massive fist; the hollow echo of an ocean wave striking the ribs of a long ship resounded through the forest. "I call myself Skrymir, for I am not shy in letting others know my worth."

Bending low, he winked at Thor. "But I need not ask your name little man. There is only one of your stature bold enough to wander our lands with a paltry few companions. You must be the great Asa-Thor. Your strength and demeanor are well known to my people. But I must ask, of all the things to do in this world, why did you drag off my glove?"

With a grunt of satisfaction, Skrymir stepped across the open glade to retrieve his glove from the ground. A fire crept up Thor's neck to flare red on his cheeks when he saw that the empty hall where they had sought refuge the night before was nothing but Skrymir's glove; its thumb the side room he had guarded.

The son of Odin struggled to quell his temper, grinding his teeth as Skrymir pulled on his gloves. The giant frowned as he tugged them over his massive wrists. "Few travel our domain without a purpose. Where are you bound?"

Thor wrenched his vest straight then combed fingers through his beard before replying to the giant. "We travel across the wonders of Jotunheim seeking the one called Utgarda-Loki, he who is considered the greatest among your people."

Skrymir stroked his chin as he stared off into the distance. A cold breeze from the north rustled his thick black hair. "Many in our land are considered great. I am one of them. But few among my kin are as knowledgeable as the mighty Utgarda-Loki. He lives among the foothills of the snowcapped peaks. I am bound toward the northern mountains. It is the same direction your journey takes you. For the next day, we travel the same path. If you are amenable, I would enjoy company along the way."

Thor conferred with his companions, their voices hushed, their gestures sharp and silent. After agreeing on a course of action, he shouted up to the giant. "Since you are familiar with the trail before us, we agree to travel together for as long as our paths hold the same."

Skrymir's thick lips spread into a wide grin that again flashed his gate of yellow teeth. "Excellent! But first let us each eat. It is an arduous journey across uneven ground. Your troop will need all their strength to keep up."

Hunkered each to their own company, the giant squatted beside a grassy knoll, the Æsir clustered a short distance away, opened their food bags, and ate a morning meal. When all had repacked their provisions, Skrymir gestured at Thjalfi. "Your troop can travel faster if I carry your burden. It is as nothing to me, but for you less weight means lighter feet."

Thor glanced at his companions who nodded silently at the suggestion. "Agreed. You can carry our provisions."

The stout thurs relieved Thjalfi of their provisions sack and lashed it to his own. He then pointed to Roskva's pack. "That, too, I can carry with ease."

Thor shook his head as he repacked their camp into four sacks. "No! This we will spread out across our own shoulders. A person can last a long while without food, but without fire and shelter the cold can kill in a night."

Skrymir hoisted his pack onto his shoulders, rolling his arms to settle the straps comfortably into place. "A wise decision. Let us be off."

The giant took large strides across valleys, easily fording streams, stomping over deadfalls. His every step was thrice that of the others. Thor's troop struggled with the brisk pace, stumbling along at a quick trot to keep up. The thurs pushed on all day without tiring, while Thor and his companions scrambled behind. At evening, he stopped to set up camp under the canopy of an ancient oak.

Shucking the pack from off his shoulders, Skrymir called out to his exhausted companions. "It has been a long day on a difficult trail. I am too tired to eat. I will rest here. But take your food bag from my pack and prepare your evening meal." With a soft crunch the thurs settled onto the ground, wriggling his shoulders and hips to make himself comfortable in the mat of dry leaves spread out beneath the oak. At once he began to snore so loudly that the tree leaves rattled with his every breath.

Thor dragged Skrymir's rucksack to his side, but try as he might, he could not loosen any strap nor unravel any knot that secured their food bag to the giant's heavily loaded pack. His brow grew dark and his eyes flashed bright. Color spread from his neck to flower bright red on his cheeks. In a frenzy, he tore at the knots that secured the pack, scrabbled with fingers, gnawed with teeth, but despite his fury the bag remained cinched tight.

Thor's eyes glinted clear as ice as they settled on the sleeping thurs. Gripping Mjollnir firmly in both hands, he dashed to Skrymir's side and struck the giant a fearsome blow full on the head. With a soft snort the thurs rolled to his side, half awake. "Hmmm. What was that?" He swiped at his forehead. "Likely a leaf fallen from this tree brushed my head." As he spoke he noticed Thor loitering nearby. "Ah-h, I see you returned the food bag to my pack. Having eaten, you must be ready for sleep?"

Thor grunted. "We are just preparing our beds." Slouching back to his companions, he moved them to the bank of a stream, out of earshot from the giant. "Eat what you can find. We will get no food from our pack tonight." He stared blackly at Skrymir who rolled to his side scratching his rear. "At least we've water for tonight. Drink what you can hold. It will help keep hunger at bay."

They got little sleep that night, unnerved by the presence of the lofty giant. Wide-eyed, each took their turn at watch, feeding occasional branches to the campfire, their attention focused on the slumbering etin.

When night was halfway through her journey Thor heard the rumbles of deep sleep from Skrymir, snores that echoed through the forest. With stealth to rival Vidar, he crept alongside the sleeping giant, raised Mjollnir high over his head, and brought it down on the etin's temple with such force the hammer sank in up to its haft.

Skrymir gave a snort and sat up. "What was that?" He fingered the side of his head where Thor had struck. "Something woke me from a pleasant dream, perhaps an acorn fallen from some high branch. I swear this tree seems bent on disrupting my sleep." He spied Thor standing in the shadows nearby. "Oh, Thor it's you! What keeps you awake this night? Is this tree trying your slumbers as well?"

Thor quickly tucked the hammer into his vest. "I was unable to sleep," he crossed his arms before his chest, "my thoughts restless with the night. I felt a short walk to stretch my legs would do me good. I did not mean to disturb your rest." Grumbling beneath his breath, he stole back to his companions, vowing that should a third opportunity present itself to deliver a well-placed blow that would be the end of the giant.

Propping himself against a boulder Thor fixed his attention on the sleeping giant. In darkness, he waited, chewing at his mustache, fingers stroking the hammer concealed beneath his vest, eyes focused on the dim form stretched out before him.

Just before Sol was to begin her journey, the giant's breathing deepened, and his thunderous snores rocked the forest. Waiting for just this change, Thor drew Mjollnir from his vest, its handle gripped tight in both fists. Leaping to his feet, he dashed to the giant's side. Shoulders heaving, he put all his strength into the blow, striking the giant squarely on the temple. Again, the hammer sank in up to its haft.

Skrymir sat up, brushing at the side of his head. He examined his fingers then sniffed lightly at their tips, a puzzled frown crossing his face. "Huh. There must be birds roosting in this tree. It seems as I awoke some droppings struck my head." The etin noticed Thor standing by his side. "A-h-h, you are up early I see. That is good. Night is gone, and Day begins his passage. For those on a journey it is time to travel."

Skrymir rolled over, scratched his backside, then climbed, grunting, to his feet. "I have overheard the hushed conversations among your group. You marvel at my stature and are amazed at my vigor. Well, be prepared to be even more astonished. Near to here lies the hall of Utgarda-Loki. There you will encounter others of my people who surpass me in size and strength as the eagle surpasses the raven."

The thurs shrugged into his pack, yanking at the straps until it rode easier on his shoulders. "Some advice I will give you. It will be good if you take it, do you well if you accept it. Check your arrogance at the door. The worthy retainers of Utgarda-Loki are intolerant of bragging from ones they consider smaller than themselves. Your wisest course might be to return to your own lands. But if, as you claimed on our meeting, you truly seek an audience with Utgarda-Loki, then head due east into the now rising sun."

He jerked his chin at the bright hand of Sol just cresting the horizon. "When you reach a broad, open plain overlooked by a flat-topped mountain, its slope edged with three square valleys, you will have reached your destination."

"As for myself—," Skrymir pointed to a ragged, white-capped, gray line edged with the rose of dawn that peeped over the tops of the fir trees. "From here I direct my feet north to those mountain peaks you see in the distance. That way finds my journey's end."

Without uttering another word Skrymir turned to face the peaks. He took three steps, disappearing among the firs. The weary travelers huddled together, listening to the fading sounds of his footsteps crunching through the forest. None were sorry to see him leave nor eager to see him again.

Loki spat and kicked a branch across the ground. "He took our provisions with him. Now we have no choice. We must continue on in hopes the dwellers in Utgarda are generous enough with their food to provide us with rations for our return."

In Utgarda-Loki's Hall

Thor and his companions traveled a hard trail along flinty ground that scuffed their boots, through brush that snagged their clothes and drew ragged scratches across their bare limbs. When Sol had crested the sky, they emerged from the forest path onto a beautiful plain that stretched out wide before them, its far edge marked by a flat-topped mountain bordered by three square valleys. In the center of the plain stood a fortress with walls towering so high above their heads they had to crane their necks back to see its top.

Loki pointed at the distant mountain, ran a level finger to note its flat top, counting each of the valleys that marred its slope. "If the giant spoke rightly, it seems we have reached our goal. This must be the hall of Utgarda-Loki."

Thor dragged his fingers through his beard as he studied the fortress walls. "So, it appears, though I doubted the truthfulness of Skrymir's words. It seems a powerful place, more massive than anything I've seen before." He shifted his pack, set his jaw, and strode forward across the plain. "The timid stand about gawking while the bold take action. Let us make ourselves known."

They approached the fortress wall, but its gate was shut tight, the frame secured with iron bars. Thor exerted his greatest strength to pull down the gate, but it would not budge from its moorings. As Thor, his red-faced nearly bursting, began to heave, Loki stepped forward.

"This gate is reinforced with iron bars. It will be a long time before you tear it down." He calmly placed a hand on Thor's shoulder. "I suggest that if we cannot walk over an open gateway, instead we walk through the gate."

Taking off his pack, Loki threaded his way between the iron bars. Safe on the other side, he beckoned the others to follow. Thjalfi and Roskva slipped through, their narrower bodies making the passage easy. Thor followed their lead, cursing beneath his breath as he painfully squeezed his larger frame between the bars.

Beyond the gate, they spied a heavy-timbered hall, its thick walls built up in the center field of the gard. The southern door was propped wide open, letting the sunshine stretch into its depths. Inside they saw many figures gathered at table, their long legs folded beneath or stretched out before the benches. All were huge with heavy manes, the noise of their revelry deafening.

On approaching the hall, they were halted at the door by the outstretched palm of an enormous etin. He stood in their path, an unmoving wall of solid muscle and matted brown hair, feet planted wide, chest wrapped in straps of black leather. A dirty loincloth swung between naked thighs tufted with wiry fur. Horny, amber nails capped the toes of his bare, thickly calloused feet. Leaning forward, the etin thrust out his chin and let the power of his breath wash over the group. "Who are you to enter our home uninvited? Tell me quick if you seek entrance here! A silent tongue will find you hobbling through the gate, your backsides aching from the toe of my foot."

Thor stepped to the front of the group, raising himself until his head reached the giant's waist. "We come from the land of Asgard seeking audience with Utgarda-Loki, the one known as greatest among your people."

The etin tilted his head to one side, listening to the words. When Thor finished speaking, he grunted for the group to follow him inside the hall. Conversation stopped at their entrance. All eyes followed as the Æsir troop strode between the crowded benches.

At the far end of the room they halted before an etin taller than the rest. His hair pomaded with a mixture of pine resin and fragrant oils, then bound with a cord into a tall knot atop his head, added to his already considerable height. He reclined on a seat constructed of a whale's rib bones bound together with straps of braided sinew and thick bands of copper, the yellowed bone surfaces decorated with carved images of winding serpents biting their tails, all mounted on a platform overlooking the tables. His luxurious robes spilled down from his shoulders like a waterfall. Animal shapes raced across their weave, chased by twining serpents of intricate design. Interlacing patterns in silver thread traced the hem, swirled up the sides, then down the long sleeves.

Their guide bowed to the seated thurs, nearly touching his forehead to the floor. He gestured at the group of Æsir, then without a word returned to his station by the door.

Thor called out to the leader seated on the high bench, his respectful voice ringing over the din in the hall. But the giant refused to notice them.

Thor's brows grew dark and he called out a second time, raising his voice until the rafters shook. Still the giant refused to notice them.

Furious now at the slight, Thor's voice shook as he called out a third time, the clouds outside echoing his demand.

This time Utgarda-Loki looked down his nose at those who stood before him, letting his gaze flow from face to face before settling on Thor. "Our country is vast." His deep, solemn voice filled the hall. "Its snow-capped peaks reach the top of the sky. Our wide plains stretch farther than the eye can see. The massive forests of thickly grown fir trees reach to the sea edge making travel across the land difficult. News travels slowly when covering such a distance. But this day the wind brought me a rumor of exalted visitors to our land."

He shifted slightly to better view his guests. As he did, his robe parted revealing two puckered scars stained black crossed above a large bony knee. His hand floated down to flip the hem, closing the draft. "Because only the bravest would dare visit our shores, am I correct in assuming this modest fellow who stands before me is Asa-Thor? Grand stories of your prowess marvel all who listen, the tales of your strength are beyond compare. For one of your... stature, surely there must be much hidden from the eye. We gathered here are eager to see for ourselves the scope of this concealed greatness."

"Let's see." He tapped a finger against his lips as his gaze shifted restlessly around the room. "I know!" He leaned forward, bright with anticipation. "Tell me at what skills you and your companions can compete. For it is a rule in my hall that none may remain in our company who are not superior to others in some skill or application of knowledge."

197

The travelers conferred a moment, heads bent close together, pointing among themselves until all agreed. Pushing forward from the group, Loki raised his voice, so all could hear his boast. "Mine is a skill at which I have never been bested. I say no one in this hall can eat their food quicker than me."

The great giant nodded, licking his lips. "Now that would be an accomplishment worthy to see, for in this hall we have many hearty eaters whose teeth endanger their very fingers when at table. To test the strength of your claim I will pit you against the most ravenous of my retainers."

Snapping his fingers, Utgarda-Loki called out to a wild thatch of unruly red hair seated at the end of the bench. A tall, thin creature with long lanky limbs unfolded from his seat and sauntered to the front to challenge Loki's boast. As the gangly etin reached the group, the great giant swept a hand forward in introduction. "This is Logi, one of my most valued heralds. In our land, he has never been outdone when there is any food to be had."

A wooden trough filled with boiled meat was set on the floor. Loki stationed himself at one end while Logi settled himself at the other end. At a command from Utgarda-Loki they began. Each started eating with such voracious appetite, the food seemed to disappear before them. Their fingers flew. Their jaws worked in a blur. They stopped when they met in the middle of the trough. Thor and his companions were astonished, for while Loki had sucked the meat from every bone, Logi had not only consumed the meat, but the tendons, bones, and trough as well.

Utgarda-Loki turned to face his guests, his features impassive, his voice calm. "Your companion failed to uphold his claim. Perhaps another among you is capable of some great feat?"

Shouldering forward from the group, Thjalfi boldly announced his challenge to the mighty thurs. "In the hills where I grew up, there is no one on foot or mount faster than myself. It has been said that I can outrun the wind. With an equal track, I will gladly race the swiftest from among your troop."

The giant king grinned wide at the daring young man. "Foot racing!" He slapped a hand on his thigh. "Now there is a sport I admire! There are many among my court known for their speed, but there is one among them who is faster than all. You will need to be very swift to defeat him. But such a contest cannot be held indoors. Runners must be free to stretch their limbs to the utmost and so reach their greatest speed. The open field outside this hall will provide an excellent course."

Gathering up his court, Utgarda-Loki ushered everyone outside the great hall to where a long stretch of level plain, bare of grass and free of stones, offered a sure path for the contestants. From the midst of his lofty retainers, the giant king beckoned a smallish fellow no taller than Thor—a dwarf among the giants, to run the race against Thjalfi. As the retainer reached the group, the great giant clapped a hand on his shoulder by way of introduction. "This is Hugi. Do not let his stature fool you. Though small, he is swifter than he looks. I have every confidence he will give you a good race."

The start and end points for the course were marked and observers stationed along the route to ensure a fair contest. The racers positioned themselves at the ready as Utgarda-Loki shouted out his commands. "The swiftest is never decided by a single sprint, but by the outcome of three matches. Let this be the first race between worthy opponents."

At his call, they bolted from the start. Both opponents stretched their legs to the fullest, but Hugi was so far in the lead that, on crossing the finish line, he turned casually about to face his challenger who pelted along many steps behind.

Utgarda-Loki placed a hand on Thjalfi's shoulder as they paced back to the starting post. He bent close, speaking low into the runner's ear. "I have seen no visitor as fast on his feet as yourself, but Hugi was swifter still. You will need to exert yourself to your utmost if you are to have any chance at defeating him."

When the contestants had readied themselves alongside the starting post, Utgarda-Loki dropped his arm to signal the start of the second race. They ran furiously, each runner straining almost agonizingly for a longer stride. Again, Hugi quickly outpaced his opponent. When he turned about at the finish, Thjalfi trailed by the distance of a bowshot.

Leaning close, Utgarda-Loki whispered into Thor's ear. "I have no wish to alarm your man. I see he can run a good race, but skilled as he is, I doubt he can win. Now comes the true test of speed; the endurance of a third race."

Both runners lined up beside the post, eager for the challenge. At the king's shout, they sprang from the line. Heads bent forward, necks outstretched, the runner's feet slapped the ground, raising puffs of dust. Shouts of encouragement roared from the crowd as the pair sliced rapidly across the thinly grassed field. Once again, Hugi's wind-scorching stride brought him first across the finish line. When he turned to face his challenger this time Thjalfi lagged at the halfway point. Everyone agreed the contest was done.

Utgarda-Loki turned, frowning at Thor. "Your group has not fared well in these contests of skill. Perhaps you can redeem the losses of your companions." He swept his hand in a broad arc to encompass the sky. "Tales of your exploits have preceded you, some difficult— if not impossible—to believe, so impressive are the deeds related. Surely you, of all your companions, are capable of some feat which none can best."

Thunder rolled along the horizon as Thor pushed his reply through clenched teeth. "In Asgard none can outdrink me. Let me pit myself against one in your hall who is known to be a champion drinker. Their knees will wobble long before I've had my fill!"

Grinning at the boastful words, Utgarda-Loki leaned down to look directly into Thor's flashing eyes. "An honorable challenge in any hall. Worthy of a great warrior used to slaking his thirst after a hard-fought battle. Come let us return to where mead flows in plenty. There we will see if you are equal to your brag."

They returned to the hall. When everyone had taken their accustomed positions at bench, Utgarda-Loki rapped his knuckles three times on the board. He shouted for his cupbearer to bring the feasting horn topped off with his best mead. The cupbearer solemnly glided down the aisle carrying a large horn curved in upon itself with many turnings. Taking the proffered horn from the bearer, Utgarda-Loki lifted it high above his head three times so all could see.

A jeering cheer rose from the gathering as he turned to present the horn to Thor. "This is the communal horn of my hall from which all my retainers drink at blött. It is considered well drunk if drained in a single pass. Some few do it in two, preferring to breathe between swallows, but none have ever failed to empty it in three."

He passed the massive horn to the son of Odin, so his hands bobbed with its weight. "It is your boast to out drink any challenger, but before I let anyone accept your challenge you must first prove your ability to equal that which all here are able to do."

Thor eyed the vessel that weighed heavy in his hands. Wonderfully inlaid with precious metals, the rim inscribed with symbols only the etin knew, it did not appear overly large though its coiled length seemed great. Hungry from having nothing to eat in the time they traveled with Skrymir, Thor was confident he could drain it at a single pass.

He tipped the horn to his lips and began taking mighty swallows of the excellent mead. When he had drunk as much as he could, he peered into the horn. To his surprise the liquid lapped just below the rim, only marginally lower than when he had started.

Peering over Thor's shoulder, Utgarda-Loki glanced into the cup to mark the effort. He snorted, shaking his head at what he saw. "You made a decent first attempt, though from the strength of your boast I expected more than a barely lowered head. I am certain you will do better the second time."

Thor glared at the giant, then back at the cup. Without a word, he lifted the horn to his lips. Holding his breath, he sucked at the mead. With each swallow, he struggled to lift the horn higher, but could not raise it beyond his shoulders. The coiled end sagged as if weighted down. When at last he could drink no more, Thor lowered the horn and peered inside. The level seemed hardly lower than before, though now the cup could be carried without fear of slopping liquid over the rim.

Utgarda-Loki again peeped over Thor's shoulder, shaking his head. "I am greatly disappointed at this pitiful exhibition. You must be drawing it out for effect and mean your third drink to be the greatest."

Saying nothing, Thor lifted the horn to his lips. Keeping his eyes focused on Utgarda-Loki, he pulled hard at the drink, swallowing mouthful after mouthful of mead until his eyes started and face flushed bright red. A sharp look from the giant king silenced a burst of scattered mutterings among the gathered host.

When he could drink no more, Thor lowered the horn, took a deep breath, then looked inside. The liquid had dropped further below the rim, but nowhere near what he expected. He handed the horn back to the etin and turned away without a word.

Utgarda-Loki glanced into the horn before quickly passing it off to his cupbearer. "Take this away. No one need be reminded of what has been accomplished this day." Taking a deep calming breath, he tugged his robes straight, then turned sympathetic eyes on the son of Odin. "It appears you overstated your capacity for drink. You may be great among the Æsir, with feats to shock and awe friend and foe alike, but among my people you will never seem as grand unless you excel at other contests. Perhaps you can redeem yourself in our eyes with success at another feat."

Thor grumbled low in reply. "At home, such drinks would quench the greatest of thirsts. Yea, I will try my hand at another contest. What do you propose?"

A mutter rose from a giant near the head of the table. He jerked his attention back to his own drink as Utgarda-Loki waved his hand at the gathering. "There is a contest of strength our children play; they vie with each other to lift my cat from the ground, so all its feet dangle free in the air. I would never have proposed such a thing to Asa-Thor had I not seen for myself that your might is nothing like what we once thought."

At his words a massive cat, gray with dark-striped sides and orange fur beneath, slunk from around the throne. The cat leapt into the center of the hall where it crouched, belly flat to the floor, the tip of its tail twitching side to side. It stared straight at Thor with yellow eyes glittering defiance.

The cat hissed, baring sharp, white teeth as Thor approached, grasped it roughly about the middle, and lifted it high over his head. Yowling loudly, it arched its back. All four of its feet remained firmly on the ground. Thor raised himself up on his toes, stretching his burden toward the roof of the hall as he sought to hoist the cat higher, but despite his best effort only one of the cat's paws drifted from the floor.

Utgarda-Loki clucked his tongue. "Your previous exploits prepared me for this. You fared as well as I have come to expect. It is no reflection on your strength. Rather, the cat is large, and you are short compared to the children of my folk."

Angry now, Thor tossed the cat aside to land with a hard thump against the dais. As he stomped toward the etin king, it slunk away behind the throne, casting a hateful glance over its shoulder before disappearing into the shadows. Utgarda-Loki stepped back as Thor thrust forward his chin. "You dare compare me to a child! Then let one of your brave worthies step forward and wrestle me! Let them try their strength directly against mine. Then you will see the true power that rages through my frame!"

Utgarda-Loki cast an eye over the figures hunched about the benches and slouching against the walls. All of his retainers were silent. None looked up from their cups to meet his gaze nor stepped forward to accept Thor's challenge. "I see none among those gathered here who would risk their dignity wrestling you. Though, there is one who dwells in my gard who would sorely test your strength." He clapped his hands. "Let Elli, my nursemaid, be brought forward." Three giants sprang up from the table, falling over each other as they rushed from the hall to deliver the king's command.

They had not waited over long before a thin shadow tottered through the far doorway, slowly resolving itself into an ancient crone with a long, wobbly nose. Though she seemed barely able to walk, none stood to lend her their arm in aide as she shuffled to the center of the hall.

Thor glared at Utgarda-Loki, anger leaking from his every pore. "What is this," he snarled, striking his fist in a palm. "You dare pit me against an old woman! In every trial, you seek to embarrass me!"

The etin king appeared wounded at the words. "Never would I seek to embarrass the great Asa-Thor." He pressed a hand to his breast in dismay. "But everything I have witnessed today has made me reassess the extent of your strength."

"Come. Come." He beckoned to the old woman who shuffled forward along the benches. Stoop-shouldered, head bowed to her navel, her long, gray hair clumped in greasy locks dragged the floor collecting dust as she swayed before them, a fragile reed trembling in the breeze.

Beaming a conciliatory smile, Utgarda-Loki waved Thor ahead. "Do not be shy in your challenge. I am certain in Elli you will find a good match. Though she appears frail to the eye, know that she has dashed many to the floor who boasted strength equal to your own."

Distaste hissing loudly between his clenched teeth, Thor stepped forward to challenge his opponent. Loki's muffled laughter accompanied the silent, wide-eyed stares of giants at table as he took the crone's hands in his gnarled fists, carefully, that he might not break any bones. When he gave a gentle nudge, he met the resistance of stone. The old woman bared toothless gums as Thor leaned forward, exerting his strength, but the harder he pushed, the more firmly rooted she seemed to become.

As astonishment crept across Thor's face, the crone displayed her skill. With a drop of her hip, she twisted an elbow, drawing the god's strong guarder to one side until he slipped his footing. The gasp of the gathering was lost beneath Thor's growl as he lunged to keep his balance.

Heedless now of her age, he clenched her hands until his fingers ached. Heaving side to side, the contest grew fierce with neither party giving ground. Elli's smile remained lively. The dark, cavernous pits of her eyes were locked onto the bright black gems that glittered beneath Thor's brow. Still grinning, the old crone twisted her hands forward and, seemingly without effort, bent Hlodyn's son to one knee.

At that moment Utgarda-Loki clapped his hands. With a sharp command, he called for the contest to end. He stared hard at Thor, who stood shaking with heaving breaths as Elli tottered away, then passed a hand over his eyes. "Let this be the last contest in this hall. There is no need for you to challenge anyone else. Today you demonstrated for everyone the magnitude of your true strength. But since we have kept you in contest all day, we cannot very well put you out into the cold night of the world. You must stay, sharing the warmth of our hall, if only until the Everglow returns."

Utgarda-Loki motioned for his retainers to clear an area of the nearest bench for the visitors. Food and drink were set before them and they were treated well the rest of the night.

When next Sol began her climb into the sky, Thor and his companions knuckled sleep from their eyes before taking turns rinsing their faces in a wash bowl passed from hand to hand. As they gathered their travel gear, Utgarda-Loki entered the hall.

"Wait! Do not be overeager to leave our presence." He gestured for them to take seats at the front of his table. "You cannot quit our hospitality without a meal to start your journey." With a sharp clap, he ordered the board set.

While they breakfasted on cold meats and hard bread left over from the night before, he enjoined them in cordial conversation, asking after their families, speaking of the weather, in every way acting the considerate host. When all had eaten their fill, they were provided a pack stuffed with provisions enough to last many days on the trail.

The giant king accompanied them to the fortress gate of Utgarda. Once they had passed beyond the gate, Utgarda-Loki smiled confidentially to Thor. "So, how has the son of Odin fared in this excursion into Jotunheim? In all your travels, have you ever encountered challengers of equal merit?"

Thor shook his great mane of hair, while a deep frown muffled the low grinding of his teeth. "In truth, I have never seen their like. As for challenges this trip, I have been disgraced. It galls me no end to think you see me as small and insignificant."

Utgarda-Loki clapped a hand on Thor's broad shoulder, then stepped back inside the gate and hurriedly drew up the iron bars until they locked in place. Safe inside the gard, he called out to the travelers. "Now that you are outside the fortress walls of my hall, I can reveal a truth ripped from my very heart. While I decide among my people, you will never again be welcome inside these walls. I would never have allowed your presence among such a close gathering of my folk had I known the power you hold. It is so potent, you nearly brought down disaster on all of us."

He shook his head and tapped a finger against his temple. "When you were close enough to be entrapped, yet far enough from myself not to perceive the truth, I induced you to see what I wanted you to see. I deceived you with chimerical spells, as I did when first we met in the Mirkwood."

The travelers started, staring hard at Utgarda-Loki. Thor's brows grew dark and Loki began to laugh while Roskva and Thjalfi shared a meaningful glance. "I see the light of understanding grow in your eyes. Yes, I was Skrymir, your giant companion. I sought to test you long before you reached my hall."

A hash chuckle escaped his lips as he rolled his eyes to the sky. "It was such a sight; it was all I could do to pretend sleep and not break out in laughter. Your attempts to untie the food bag were stymied because it was fastened with Grésjarn, an iron wire that conceals its own ends. None can unravel it unless they know its secret."

Utgarda-Loki stepped forward, shaking a finger at Thor, whose face had begun to flush pink. "Three attempts you made on my life, three heavy blows delivered by your hammer. Had any of them connected, they would have ended my life. But each time you struck, just as your hammer began to fall, I moved a mountain in between without your knowing. That mountain you see there in the distance, the one with the flat top and the three, square valleys, those valleys mark the impact of your blows. The deepest of the three marks your last attempt."

The etin dragged a hand across his face and squeezed the bridge of his nose, before letting out a deep breath. "I did the same in each of the contests held in my hall, using spells to conceal the true nature of each challenger.

"So, it was with the first contest. Loki, ravenous though he was, could not outstrip the hunger of Logi, the wildfire whose flames consume everything in its path. Now Thjalfi, though faster afoot than anyone I have ever seen, had no chance against Hugi, my mind. For whom, no matter how swift, can outrun a thought?"

Thunder rolled over the mountains while dark clouds gathered overhead, the blackest swirling about the peaks. Utgarda-Loki glanced up as bright bolts of lightning flashed across the sky. "But you Thor, of all the challenges witnessed, yours were the greatest, the most unnerving. Your contests exhibited amazing fortitude. They brought such alarm to my people that everyone at the table quaked with fear. It was all I could do to keep them dashing from the hall in panic.

Your draughts were miracles themselves. The coiled horn that you thought small was joined to the waters of the all-encircling sea. When next you visit the ocean, you will see how far your draughts lowered it. They even increased the tides that turn the World Mill.

You performed no less a feat when you lifted my cat from the floor. A chill ran through all those present when one of its feet left the ground, for the cat was really Jormungand, the Midgard Serpent that encircles the world. Your efforts raised him from his watery bed to nearly touch the vault of Ymir.

Everyone was amazed at your stamina when you wrestled my nursemaid Elli, for in truth she is old age that comes to all things. Old age is death's day breaking. Once she beckons with crooked finger there is none who can resist her forever. But one knee you bent to her in the struggle. Only one knee! It was a deed I would have thought impossible had I not seen it with my own eyes."

The great lord of etins heaved a sigh as a great weariness slumped his shoulders and sagged the lines of his bright features into long, droopy folds. "No, we were none of us prepared to witness an exhibition of your true strength."

He rallied, drawing himself erect before turning into his fortress stronghold, shouting over his shoulder as he walked away. "Now it is best for both of us if you leave and never again seek me out. Such a meeting would fare badly for both of us. Rest assured I will use every stratagem I know, every weapon at my disposal to guarantee I never fall under your power."

At these words, the son of Odin roared out in rage. His companions cringed away as he charged forward, Mjollnir raised over his head to strike down the thurs. In the blink of an eye Utgarda-Loki and his fortress vanished, leaving the group standing alone on a broad, barren plain, a vagrant wind teasing the edges of their robes. Only the flat-topped mountain with its three, square valleys remained on the horizon to mark the day's events. With nothing to strike, Thor's anger ebbed away and the dark clouds which had swirled overhead, quickly vanished beneath the brilliant rays of the sun.

Turning away from the plain, the group began their arduous return to Orvandel's hall where Thor's goats—rested and well fed, Tanngrisnir's leg healed from Groa's ministrations—waited to take them back to Asgard. Immediately on their arrival Thor began preparations for the return home. None spoke, taking their cue from his sullen silence to all questions about the journey.

In the open courtyard, Thor barked commands to Orvandel as he lashed their travel packs to the sides of the wain. "We return at once to Asgard! Have your children ready to travel!" The great archer made to protest, but when he saw the black look on Thor's face, he snapped his teeth closed. Silently, he helped Thjalfi and Roskva pack the items they would need for their journey.

As if the bank of a river had suddenly given way, a torrent of harsh words, raged to all within hearing, flowed freely from Thor's lips as he waited for the children of Orvandel to say their goodbyes. "Our journey to Jotunheim is ended in disgrace. Through trickery they humiliated, not only myself and my companions, but also every Æsir and Vanir. And I... I was unable to land a single blow, not one strike of just recompense against the etin scourge. Be assured, I will not rest until I have paid them back!"

Thor glared directly at Loki as everyone climbed aboard his wain. "The first to feel my might will be the misshapen serpent that girdles the world! His skull I will dash to pieces!"

Thor and the Midgard Serpent

Weary after a long hunting foray, and still many miles away from their home, the victory gods sought a place to rest. The augur's cast directed them to Hlesey, Ægir's high mountain hall. A herald was sent ahead to announce their arrival while the main body followed close behind.

The herald received a cheerful greeting as the lord of winds welcomed him into his home. "I am always delighted to have company. Tell me, how I may entertain my honored guest?"

The herald cleared his throat. "I thank you for your generous offer," he raised himself tall before the bright face of Ægir, "but I come as a messenger, not yet as a guest. Your hospitality is well known, your name spoken as praise in every home. A hunting party of ás and ásynja approach. After many days on a demanding trail they ask for a place to rest in your mighty hall. Your skillful hand at brewing is famous across the nine worlds. To slake their thirst, they request your excellent mead be served to all in cups filled to the brim and heated through with a hot iron poker."

Laughing, Ægir swept his arm to encompass his hall. "What I have I gladly share. Let all make themselves comfortable."

The lord of winds busily prepared for the arrival of his visitors, eager to have a few new faces to liven up his day. But when the doors of his hall opened to the multitude that flooded across the threshold, he balked at serving so many. When all had crowded around the board clamoring, some for food, others demanding drink, Ægir shuffled to his place at the head of the table. His eyes focused on the tabletop as he raised his hands to quiet the joyous laughter barking from the jostling crowd.

"My dear friends, the generosity of your presence fills me with delight. I would happily feast you all and warm my days with your company, a host can know no greater wealth, but you arrived at a lean time. It pains me no end to admit that I do not have the resources to entertain your company. I can manage a small drink and a light meal for each, but I simply cannot host you longer without dangerously depleting what little reserves I have in stock."

Offended by the stingy hospitality offered, Thor ordered the esteemed mountain dweller to prepare a feast for the entire Æsir clan and to brew ale enough for all to last the feast. "You complain of hardship imposed by guests, when any fool can see your larders are fully stocked and your grain bins overflow. Faced with evidence of such privation, we would not want it said that our request brought starvation to your home. So, to supplement this meager plenty we offer the provisions we carry, and the game brought down by our own hand. Now you can be certain there is enough to go around without depleting your store."

The sharp rebuke delivered to him in his own home humiliated the mash blender. Set to defy, he spat his angry reply through clenched teeth. "I thank the son of Odin for his generosity. Your concern for the welfare of my home and unbounded largess are appreciated, but I am afraid I still cannot honor your request. I have enough vats to address my own modest needs and to offer refreshment for a few guests, but none massive enough to brew ale for all of you. For that I need a larger vessel," his gaze flashed among his guests, "but there is none readily at hand."

Thor leaned forward, fire sparking along his brow. "Then we will find one."

"You just do that," Ægir sneered, confident in his taunt. "And if by chance you find one, bring it here and I will gladly brew your ale. Until then I will not lift a hand."

In the courtyard outside the hall doorway the glorious gods gathered to discuss the issue. Questions were posed, and arms waved overhead, but none knew where in the nine worlds they might procure such a large vessel. Then Tyr stood before the group, his left hand raised for attention. "East of the Elivagar Rivers in a hollow mountain at the far end of the heavens near the shore of the all-encircling sea lies the hall of my stepfather, Hymir, a wise Jotun." He looked directly at Thor. "From the center beam of his hall hangs a cauldron of wrought metal a league wide and just as deep that even Ægir would find difficult to fill. The cauldron is the pride of his possessions. Know that he will not give it freely—not to stranger, son, nor adopted kin. It must be won with courage and, if need be, guile."

A low murmur of approval rumbled through the gathering as Thor clapped Tyr on the shoulder. "Then we will be sure to ask boldly to his face."

———————————

In a wain drawn steadily by his goats, Thor and Tyr traveled a full day to Orvandel's Hall, the archer's home that stands on the edge of the ice-cold waters of the Ifing. There they surrendered Tanngniost and Tanngrisnir to his care. Waving aside the archer's offer to accompany them, they continued, on foot, to Hymir's great hall.

After crossing wide plains frosted white with snow, they climbed the slope of a hollow mountain that formed the natural gard to Hymir's home. A giant woman noticed their approach and stepped forward to confront them. When Thor saw her nine hundred heads loom high above the gate set in the mountain wall, he reached for his hammer to end her days, but Tyr stretched out his hand to check the protector god's mighty arm. "Hold your weapon Veor. It is only my grandmother, Edda, who greets us."

The ancient silently looked them over, stared hard each of her nine hundred heads to gauge their intent. Wide smiles shown down as beams of sunlight as she recognized the one who in his youth had eased her burdens and made bright her days. Her heads nodded in greeting as they entered.

Tyr's mother met them at the hall door, a handsome, clear-browed woman with a fletta of long flaxen tresses wound about her head, all held in place with an ornate copper pin that peeped out from behind her head. Her flowing robes glinting gold, now silver, seemed a frozen waterfall spilling over the threshold. In each hand, she proffered a large mug of ale to quench their thirst. Smiling brightly, she bid them welcome. As they stepped through the doorway, she leaned close to offer words of caution. "My husband is renowned for being stingy to guests and ill-tempered with their company. He does not suffer the uninvited with grace; to them his deadly glare is harsh enough to shatter stone. It would not go well were he to encounter you first, unannounced visitors—one a stranger—loitering in his hall."

She pointed across the room to the kitchen galley. "Conceal yourselves behind this pillar, there inside that cauldron hanging beneath the hall gables. Stay hidden until I present you, lest his cruel gaze crumble you to dust."

Thor thanked the good woman for her hospitality, especially her advice. Finishing off their drinks, the pair climbed up to the cauldron. Gripping its lip, they pulled themselves into its spacious cavern. Their footsteps seemed to echo forever.

Thor glanced around marveling at the size. "Is this the vessel of which you spoke?" Tyr stomped his foot, so the cauldron rang with a deep, mournful tone. Grinning, Thor sat down, stretching his legs out before him. "Then let us settle here as your mother directed to wait for the lord of the hall to arrive."

Near twilight the stern-minded Hymir returned weary from the hunt, robe caked with snow, his hair rimed with blue-white frost, his cheeks coated with ice, a single icicle dangling from his chin. He laid the day's take near the door, a brace of stags strung together by their fetlocks. Shedding his heavy cloak from broad shoulders, he shook it free of crusted ice before hanging it on a peg beside the main entrance.

Shambling into the hall, the mighty Jotun headed straight to the blaze crackling in the hearth. Hovering over the fire, he wrung the cold from his hands as melting water dripped from his chin to splash hissing into the flames. He grunted thanks as a large mug of crisp nut-brown ale heated through with a hot iron poker was set beside him within easy reach.

The lady of the hall called over her shoulder as she examined the game beside the door. "A successful hunt means plenty; it comes at such a welcome time too. Our son has arrived to visit your hall, he whom we've missed on his long journeys. Hlodyn's celebrated son accompanies him, Veor, the great warrior of the Æsir. They sit over there behind the pillar."

Hymir jerked his gaze to where his wife pointed. The pillar crumbled beneath his harsh glare. The sudden loss of support split the great cross-beam overhead in two. Eight kettles tumbled from their high perch, cracking as they struck the floor. The largest one remained whole as it bounced across the stones. Tyr and Thor emerged from the unbroken vessel. Dusting themselves off, they strolled across the floor to greet their host. Delighted, Hymir's eyes followed his stepson, but his thoughts turned black as night when he spied the companion who strode alongside.

In honor of his son's visit home, he offered up fresh meat for his guests. Three oxen slaughtered in the field, their flesh boiled, cut into fist-sized chunks, and mounded on trenchers, were set on the board. Thor alone ate two of the offerings. It seemed an affront to his rock-boned host, who felt the son of Odin had consumed more than his share, leaving the rest seated at the table to go hungry.

"Your appetite is severe to a tightly run household. If you are to stay longer than a night, tomorrow I must hunt for food we can live upon. It is best if I forage in the sea. A haul of cod, and whale meat if I can get it, will more than assuage the greatest hunger."

"It grows late," Hymer pushed himself to his feet. "Such an excursion," he stretched, yawing widely, "requires an early start. Tyr is familiar with this hall and knows where best to rest. You may stay up. As for myself, I must sleep."

The guests stayed overnight on bedding of rough comfort arranged in a bay alongside the central fire. The next day, after all had breakfasted—the Jotun again annoyed with the extent of his guest's appetite—Thor asked to join Hymir's fishing expedition. The etin, not keen on companionship, questioned the strength of his visitor. "Though a champion among the Æsir, you are small. With little experience on the sea, I fear you would be more hindrance than help on a boat trip so far from land. Unable to man the oars or endure the cold, you will likely catch a chill. I would feel bad returning you to your kin with sniffles and a runny nose."

Thor checked his rage at the Jotun's ridicule. It was only with great difficulty that he kept his hammer at his side. Thrusting out his chin, he forced a reply through his teeth. "Let the trip be as far from land as you please. It will be seen who begs to row back!"

Hymir snorted as he left to ready the boat. Thor called out to Hymir's broad back as the giant slouched away. "What bait will we use? Direct me to it and I will load it up."

Hymir stopped, the grinding of his teeth sounded over the breakers of the sea. "Let each fisherman look after himself," he shouted over his shoulder. "It is enough I provide the boat and the gear. My bait I will not share. Gather your own, but do not dally. I push off before the Everglow rises beyond a finger width, with or without the strong guarder of the gods." Hymir took two steps then sneered over his shoulder. "You might try searching among my herds. One who boasts of great strength and valorous feats should find it easy to find fishing bait in a pasture."

While the giant readied the boat with sharpened hooks, coils of line, nets, gaffs, buckets for bailing, a sack of provisions, and two kegs of fresh water, all lashed down tight beneath the seats, Thor hunted about for suitable bait. A loud bellow from the fields drew his attention.

Approaching Hymir's oxen herd, he singled out the great bull that called to the sky. Boldly taking the bull by its horns, with a mighty twist he tore off the head of Himinbrjotr, Hymir's biggest ox, forever silencing his bellows against the heavens. With the bull's head gripped in his hands, he trotted back to the beach. When Thor tossed the bloody bait into the bottom of the boat to roll about their feet, Hymir said nothing, but ground his teeth as he glared into the bull's lifeless eyes.

With main muscle, they shoved the boat from shore, using an oar to poll its prow into the lapping waves. After settling themselves on the benches, Thor waved Hymir to a different seat and manned the oars alone. He dug deep into the water, pulling so hard with each stroke that the wave colt charged across the sea, its bow rising free of the brine with each surge.

When they reached a good distance from shore, Hymir called for him to halt. "You can stop now. We are at the region that is mine to fish."

Thor grunted at his words but paid them no mind and continued to bend his back to the oars. Hymir glared about him, at the shore falling farther away, at the water churning with their passage, at the dark features of the one laboring on the bench seat.

"Stop! We are far enough out! Go too far and we will find ourselves beyond the shoals where fishing is best and into the deep waters where we must battle the currents to stay within sight of land."

Thor continued rowing. "Sit down," he sneered, "or you will find yourself swimming back to land. My appetite calls for the largest fish, those who can easily fill your larder. We will not find them by staying close to shore."

Far he rowed, well beyond Hymir's fishing grounds, out into the tracks of the Midgard Serpent. His rock-boned companion sat ill at ease, the deck bench becoming increasingly uncomfortable as the shoreline dwindled to a thread.

When they had traveled far enough, Thor wasted no time on talk or explanation, but grabbed up a line from beneath his bench and baited his hook with the head of Himinbrjotr. With a mighty heave, he cast the offering into the water, letting the line slip through his fingers as it sank to the floor of the sea. Gripping the line in his clenched fists, he waited for the bottom dweller to take the bait.

Grumbling under his breath, Hymir baited his hook then cast it into the dark waters. Immediately, he received a strike and hauled into the boat a great gray whale. Laughing, he again cast his line into the sea. It only grazed the surface of the water when it pulled taught, rocking the boat to the side.

Smirking, Hymir called out to his companion as he laid his second catch in the keel. "I've caught and boated two whales while you sit limp-fisted with line slack waiting for a first strike. You will need to fish better than that to make it worth bringing you along."

Beneath the waves the bottom currents swept up the bull's head, bouncing it along the sea floor to Jormungand, who waited patiently with gaping mouth for the chance arrival of any morsel. As the head disappeared into his cavernous maw, the serpent gnashed down on the food freely delivered. At the prick of the angle hook jerked back his head. The line snapped taught, smacking Thor's fists hard on the rail. In rage, he yanked back the line, embedding the hook deep in Jormungand's jaw.

Drawing hand-over-hand on the line, Thor hoisted the serpent from the sea's embrace until Jormungand glowered from beside the boat. Runnels of salt water ran down his face back into the sea as he twisted on the line, fighting to break free. Thor returned the serpent's deadly glare. "So, wolf fish, now how many of your feet touch the ground?" Drawing his hammer from his vest, Thor raised it in his gauntleted fist, eager to dim the life of the great circumciser as the serpent's hateful head thrashed at the surface.

Hymir fell back into the boat, trembling at the sight of long teeth, sharp as scythes, gnashing at the saxboard. His quivering lips sputtered guttural pleas that he not run afoul of Loki's horrible offspring, as the serpent's melon-sized eyes, red as coals, swiveled about to focus on him with the undying hate of his line.

Terrified their boat might capsize from Thor's actions, leaving them screaming prey for a furious serpent, Hymir drew a bait knife from his belt. Leaping forward, he chopped the line against the rail. The sinister red eyes of the wolf fish flashed above the surface before sinking beneath the waves.

Angered at losing his most dangerous catch, Thor brandished his hammer over the head of the thurs, furious that, had the treacherous giant not cut his line, he would have triumphed over Loki's son. But at sight of the headland so far away, he forced his arm back to his side.

Eyes glittering, black storm clouds rumbling overhead, the son of Odin gestured at the oars then waved his hammer toward the shore. The frightened thurs scrambled onto the bench, fumbled the oars into the oarlocks, and bent his back to the dip and pull of each stroke.

Sweat dripped from Hymir's brow as the sea colt skimmed across the waves, still roiling from the serpent's breach.

They drove along the rocky headlands to beach the boat on the open strand. Leaping over the side into the surf, Hymir snatched up the bowline and, feet churning, dragged the boat higher up the shore. With sharp gestures, he directed Thor to tie off the craft to the shoreline trees. "Wait here until I return with aid to manage the boat."

Suspecting trickery from Tyr's stepfather, the son of Odin waved the etin aside. "Help will not be necessary. I will carry it to your home." Flipping the oars into the hull alongside the whales, he heaved the boat to his shoulders and began the difficult trek to Hymir's hall.

Halfway along the rocky path the etin attacked with a flurry of sharp knees and swinging fists. Enraged at the deceit, Thor tossed the boat aside, grabbed Hymir about the waist and slammed him bodily to the ground, starting his eyes from his head. With a bellow of rage to rival Himinbrjotr, Thor yanked Mjollnir from his vest, eager to strike.

Hymir cowered in the dust, hands raised to protect his head. "Spare my life Veor," he begged. "Stay your awful hand and you can take from my home that which most pleases you!"

The son of Odin found it difficult to quell his temper peaked to such a high rage. The hammer shook hard in his fist, hungry for the etin's skull. With great reluctance, the gift of Sindri sank to his side. "I stay my hand this one last time. You will provide food and drink. Once I have had my fill, then I will see what you have to offer. But there will be no more trickery, or my hammer will finish what it started!"

Hoisting the boat onto his shoulders, Thor continued climbing the rocky path to the hall entrance nestled in the high wooded ridge. Outside the door of the giant's home he set the boat on a line of fir rollers, while Hymir rushed inside to arrange for dinner.

At table, the ever-contentious etin began to demean the strength of his visitor. Hymir lifted his drinking cup, held it out so light glinted from its crystal sides. "You are a powerful rower, this I have seen, but no one would be considered strong unless he could shatter a crystal goblet such as this."

Snatching up the goblet set before him, a match to the one Hymir held, Thor struck it hard against a pillar. The pillar split in two, but the glass remained whole. Hymir's laughter boomed through the hall. "A pitiful effort for such a vaunted warrior, unable to break a simple drinking cup." He slapped his palm against the table. "Maybe you would like to try something easier. A stick of kindling, perhaps?"

Tyr's mother approached the bench and bent to pour more ale for her son's companion who sat glowering at the still chuckling Hymir. As the kindly woman leaned near, she whispered advice that only the burning ear hands of Thor could grasp. "Smash the goblet on Hymir's skull. You will find it harder than any crystal."

The son of Odin heeded her wise counsel. "I will not tolerate mocking words from the lips of an arrogant Jotun! Your head is large with conceit, your skull thick with arrogance! Let us see if it is harder than this cup!" In rage, he rose with bent knees, and brought his divine might to bear. The goblet slammed against the skull of his host, exploding into a cloud of glass shards that rained tinkling to the ground.

The stunned Jotun stared at the scattered fragments that glittered about the floor. "It is a terrible loss when I see such a treasure in pieces on the floor." His voice croaked as he looked up with unsteady eyes. "What more will you take from me?"

Rocking back in his seat, Thor gazed about the hall, taking in the ornate tapestries and well-crafted furniture; letting his eyes linger over valuables displayed to flaunt the family's wealth, until Hymir began to squirm in his seat. Finally, he nodded at an object across the room. "There! That cauldron I see leaning against the far wall. Its sturdy sides and deep bottom can brew enough ale to feast my clan all winter. That will be the payment I take for your life."

The crafty Hymir smiled at the choice, a vessel that none but he could move. The thurs waved his hand at the cauldron while he took a long slow drink from his goblet. "Certainly, you can have the kettle, provided you can carry it out of my home. Though in truth I am sore to see it leave, for never again will I be able to truly brew my ale."

Striding across the room, Thor grabbed the kettle by its rim. His might was severely tested as he heaved it from the floor and carefully settled it over his head. The handle-rings banging at his heels, he made his way out of the mountain hall, mindful of every step. Tyr followed behind, watching their back.

They had not gone far when the sky split wide with a flash of fire. The earth trembled as over the eastern cliffs flowed the many-headed army of Hymir's retainers girded for combat. Before all ran the stern-minded Hymir, bellowing in anger, a wicked blade raised overhead.

Eager for battle, Thor set the kettle down and took up his hammer. The sky grew heavy with billowing dark clouds illuminated from behind with lurid flashes of light. With a savage cry, he swung Mjollnir amid the throng. Flames leapt into the air and screams echoed from his every blow as Thor waded through the horde striking madly to all sides until he stood alone amid the rubble of lifeless bodies heaped along the mountainside.

Clouds of steam rose from the freshly slaughtered host, as Tyr tugged his stepfather's body from a tangled mound of corpses. Rejecting Thor's help, he dragged it to a flat-topped boulder overlooking the scene. There on the field of battle Tyr performed Death rights for the one who had raised him. Somberly, he wiped Hymir's face and hands clean of gore, straightened his limbs, placed his blade on his chest, then wrapped him tight in his long woolen cloak that he might journey well along the western road.

When the preparations were done, he knelt before the body of his stepfather. "Now that the number of steps you were given to walk on this earth have been taken, I say that I too have died. Though you fell in valorous struggle against a worthy foe, I would rather have you back in your hall secure in the arms of my mother, fulfilling your duty as her protector."

When the obligations of the son were complete, they gathered up their travel gear. Thor hoisted the cauldron to his shoulders and they returned to Ægir's hall to join the gods assembled there.

When Ægir saw the size of the cauldron Thor carried in on his shoulders, his eyes sprang wide and his jaw dropped to bump his chest. Setting it before the mash blender, the son of Odin waved his hand at its gaping maw. "Waste no time turning your skilled hand to the task. Your excuses have dwindled to nothing and you now have a vessel more than capable of brewing enough ale to feast us all."

The Battle with Geirrod

On a forest hill, east of the Ifing, Geirrod's high hall stood proudly amid the trees. His court was renown across the worlds for its grandeur, the Jotun recognized by all for his sharp cunning. To amuse himself, Loki borrowed Freyja's falcon cape—a cleverly-woven cloak of golden feathers that changed the wearer's form into that of a swift falcon—and winged his way to Geirrod's court. There he sought to test his craftiness against the clever thurs.

Perched on a sill high above the court, he observed the happenings in the great hall. From his high seat, Geirrod noticed the vagrant bird intently watching the movements in his home. At first, he paid little heed, but when the bird remained throughout the morning he suspected something was amiss. The Jotun subtlety gestured to a nearby retainer, who leaned close to receive his whispered command to capture the over-curious bird.

But the clever Loki would not be trapped. He waited until the creeping servant had nearly reached his lofty perch, then laughed at the grasping fingers and flew away. Still laughing, he circled the hall, once, twice, then fluttered back to the sill. Again, the servant crept toward his position, but failed to catch him before he escaped.

Understanding this was no ordinary bird, the shrewd thurs ordered the sill slathered with honey. The next time Loki returned to the sill, he chuckled to see the servant sliding along the wall, sneaking his way for a third attempt. This time, as the servant approached, he could not fly away from the perch. He frantically beat his wings, but try as he might, he could not move; his feet were stuck fast in the honey.

A sneer of triumph spread across the servant's face as he snatched the bird from the sill and bundled the terrified Loki to the seat of the eagerly waiting Jotun. Held before the shaggy brows of the rock-boned thurs, Loki quaked with fear as Geirrod glared into his eyes, shook him once, twice, a third time so his head flopped about, while demanding he speak. "Come! Out with it! Tell me who you are within this bird shape and why you baldly dare to spy on my court!"

When the bird gave no reply to his question, the thurs snorted to his retainers. "This foul creature refuses to speak! I will give it time to reconsider its silence. Lock it away in the oaken chest that rests behind my seat. There it will have a snug, secluded place to ponder."

Three months the son of Laufey endured the dark chest with no food, save the few of Idun's apples secreted in his vest pockets. He became so light-headed from hunger that he feared death if imprisoned longer. When he was taken from the chest, skin drawn tight at the cheeks until his teeth shown, ribs standing out over a belly cleft to his backbone, knobby knees, sharp elbows, barely able to stand, the starved Loki quickly admitted his name.

Geirrod frowned down from his seat, pinning the trembling captive with his glare. "I see your time in the chest bestowed the blessing of wisdom. Not only did it unlock your tongue, but it encouraged you to discard your miserable disguise. Now tell me, worthless Æsir, why you chose to spy on my home?"

Loki shivered, arms wrapped tight about his bony frame, as he teetered on his feet before Geirrod. "I meant no harm. I only thought to see for myself the elegance often told of your court. Show compassion on a foolish action. I will do whatever you ask of me, give blood oath to bind my words with my deeds, just do not return me to that dark casket."

The thurs threw back his head and burst out laughing. Retainers all around the hall joined in until the entire room thundered with their roars. Loki's eyes darted side to side as he cringed into himself.

Still laughing, Geirrod leaned close, letting the strength of his breath wash over the cowering figure. "So, the fledgling that haunted my windowsill would have me spare his life? Very well. Then know my terms! Refuse them, or in any way contest my rights in this matter, and you will again know the horrors of that closed chest. I will relax in my seat as your muffled rustlings lull me to sleep."

Loki's head bobbed so hard on his thin neck it seemed ready to fall off in a moment. "Of course! Absolutely! Whatever you ask!"

The etin stroked his chin, tapping a finger against his lips as he considered the opportunity. "I have long heard of Thor's strength; it is said to rival mine. I would test this and remove all doubt as to whose is greater. For your freedom, you will give a binding oath to bring him here, but without his complement of godly weapons, that I might prove him the weaker."

Loki readily agreed to Geirrod's conditions. "It will be as you say. As ransom for my life and freedom from imprisonment, I swear this solemn oath to bring Thor to your court without his battle gear that you might test your strength against the strong guarder of the Æsir."

Geirrod stretched, smacking his lips in a wide yawn, as he looked down his nose at the emaciated figure quivering before him. "Have you a plan?"

Tugging the folds of his robe close about his shoulders, Loki wobbled forward to a bench, then collapsed with a grunt. "I have a plan, but I cannot return like this. I must have food to regain the flesh I have lost, or I will draw the attention of Odin. I doubt he would be satisfied with my explanation. For once his interest is piqued, he will relentlessly seek out the truth."

Geirrod sniffed and leaned back in his seat. "That is no concern of mine; the oath you gave is unbreakable. How you get Thor here is up to you. But I agree that you cannot return in the wasted form you have now." With a sharp clap of his hands, he ordered the board set for Loki.

Loki feasted in Geirrod's hall for a full month, regaining the flesh he had lost during his forced confinement. Once plumped back to his normal shape, he returned to Asgard, there to find Thor sitting alone in his hall with a cup of ale, his feet propped on the hearth warmed by glowing embers.

The son of Farbauti insinuated himself onto the bench beside Hlodyn's famous son. "Hail, mighty protector. I see the god's strong guarder takes his drink at the mead bench while others are out doing manly deeds. I guess all heroes deserve a day of rest."

Thor's heavy gaze settled on the cunning Loki. "What plot are you devising, son of oak and fire, that you intrude on my company?"

Loki turned an astonished face, innocent of guile. "What intrusion? Can I not join my adopted kin in a drink and friendly banter?"

The brows of Odin's son sank to a dark shelf. He muttered into his cup before taking a long swallow. "Your words are often double-edged blades. The listener must always be cautious, lest they be cut by one edge while avoiding the other."

Loki stretched out, crossing his legs. "It is true I am crafty with words, but I hold no malice for one as great as yourself. Rather, I hold you in the highest respect and am concerned only with your honor. It is in this regard I have news that might interest you."

He bent close, speaking low for Thor's ears alone. "Far to the east lives a mighty Jotun whose shrewdness has amassed him an army. He proclaims his strength the rival of yours."

Bracing his forearm against the table, Thor leaned forward as thunder rumbled in the sky. "Name this etin who claims strength equal to mine that I might know who I send to tread along the red road."

The cunning Loki smiled inside his cheeks. "Geirrod is the name by which he is known. Even now the blight of his claim spreads. There is not an Asynjor that does not know of his boast... and that you have done nothing to challenge it."

Thor's hand clenched his cup until his knuckles shown white. "Nothing! Nothing!" The cup crumbled, its contents spilling across the table. "He will soon know the taste of Mjollnir. I will dash his skull to pieces."

Loki nudged Thor with his foot. "It is a certainty that with your hammer and belt of strength you are more than a match for Geirrod. But just think of the renown you would win were you to defeat him without your weapons. Then there would be none across the nine worlds who would dare doubt your strength."

Thor nodded his head, his breathing slowing as he considered Loki's words. "There is merit in what you say. I will leave my weapons behind. But only a fool charges into battle without gathering knowledge of his opponent, especially when such knowledge is readily available." He snatched up Loki's cup and finished off its contents. "There is someone I must visit before venturing to Geirrod's courts. Gríd, mother of Vidar, is known to be familiar with those who dwell in that region. I will confide in her counsel."

Loki laughed. "This is well and good. I, for one, have never doubted your strength or courage." He clapped a hand on Thor's shoulder. "I would accompany you on this challenge to witness for myself the humbling of this rogue Jotun."

Thor pierced the son of Laufey with a hard glare until Loki's smile faltered and his hand slipped from his shoulder. "I do not want your company on this trip, for were you to accompany me it would be forever said that it took two Æsir to defeat Geirrod instead of one. I also prefer to face my dangers from the front, rather than having to watch my back as well."

———————————

Tanngniost brayed loudly and Tanngrisnir nipped at his trace companion as Thor drew up his cart before the modest hall of Gríd. Climbing down, he bid his goats stay, then beat his fist on the gate to make known his presence.

Roused from her duties, the lady of the hall stepped from her door to warmly greet her visitor. "A son of Odin is always welcome in my home. To what do I owe this pleasure," she tilted her head, smiling at her guest, "or do you seek Vidar?"

Thor bowed lightly to the good woman as she took his arm and guided him into the hall. "I do not seek the silent one—leave him remain in the solitude of the forests—but instead have come to ask your advice on a matter of importance to me."

Gríd gestured to a cleared bench beside the fire. "Please take a seat by the hearth. Do you hunger, or is your thirst greater?"

Thor wrung his hands over the flames, squeezing the cold from his fingers, before seating himself and stretching his legs until his feet rested beside the coals. "I have eaten already, but a mug of ale would not go amiss."

The lady of the hall topped off a mug with crisp amber ale and handed it to her guest. Thor took a long swallow. He held the mug out, smacking his lips, then cradled it in his lap. "Your brew is excellent as always, but I have not come just to drink your ale. I travel to the court of Geirrod deep in the northern reaches of Jotunheim. I know you are familiar with the land. It is said you have friendly contacts among its people." He set his mug on the hearthstone, for a moment drawing aside Gríd's inquisitive gaze. "Boastful words have reached my ears, boasts that I plan to challenge without my weapons. Before I confront this arrogant Jotun, I would know more about his character and what I might expect to encounter."

A light smile twitched the corners of Gríd's lips. "You are well known for your strength." She cocked an appraising eye at her guest. "Now I know there is wisdom that guides it. For what is the value of strength without a double share of wisdom." Hugging her robe close, Gríd stood before the hearth, staring deep into the burning coals as she gathered her thoughts. "It is good you came to see me before charging into Geirrod's domain. I do know of him and none of it is good. Geirrod is a cunning Jotun. There is much danger in facing him. He maintains a large band of battle-hardened retainers. A single warrior—especially one without weapons—would be quickly defeated. He is devious and vicious; his taste for underhanded dealing is well known. Expect to encounter his plots even before you meet him. When you finally do face him, be ready for sudden, unexpected tricks."

"A moment." She walked across the room to a chest nestled against the wall. Lifting the lid, she reached inside and drew out a wrapped bundle. From a dark recess beside the chest she took a staff. Returning to the hearth she placed the items on the bench beside Thor. "You say that you plan to face him without your weapons, then I will lend you mine: my staff Grídarvöll, my iron gloves, and my belt of strength. This way you can still make the honest claim of having faced him without your weapons of battle, for a prudent warrior takes advantage of resources encountered along the way."

One by one Thor examined the gifts, hefted the staff to gauge its weight and strength, slipped on the iron gloves to ensure they fit, cinched the belt of strength tight about his waist—felt its power surge through his frame. With a broad smile, Thor accepted the gifts. "These are much welcome. Your wise counsel is appreciated. I will return them to you once I have chastised the arrogance of this etin."

———————

Eager to test his strength against the boastful giant, Thor struck out from Asgard along paths east. At Orvandel's hall he left wain and goats behind. Gathering to him the warriors of Gang, the troop headed into the frosty land of Jotunheim, halting their march at the banks of the

Ifing. Gazing across its wide waters, the column shied back from the frigid torrent as they sought a more equitable place to cross.

Thor waded into the rushing waters, while the warriors of Gang crossed further upstream, where a submerged ridge provided a natural ford for those who knew its narrow path. With each step the water grew deeper, the churning stream dragging gravel from beneath hesitant feet.

As suddenly as a wave charging the beach, the water increased in volume, engulfing Thor's thighs, then swiftly climbing to his waist. The strong current seemed too treacherous to wade. "I am Veor," he shouted to the waters boiling about his waist, "son of Hlodyn. It is my right and my intent to cross your expanse! You have no hope to defy me!" The flow gave no heed to his warning.

Foaming rapids swallowed boulders along the channel, swirled with sharp eddies that tore at the earthen banks, their increasing depth threatening to wash everything away. A deep grinding echoed over the rushing waters, the sound of boulders talking in the bed of the river, ready and eager to crush the bones of anyone attempting to cross.

"You refuse to shrink from the anger in my eyes and will not retreat from my curses." Planting his feet wide, Thor dug Grídarvöll into the stony riverbed to brace himself against the stiff current. "But my voice is louder than any river; hear its wrath and be ashamed to have barred my way!"

Upstream, the warriors of Gang struggled in vain against the rising crest. Shouts, curses, and no few screams erupted from blue lips as the unruly waters swept the band of doughty warriors into Thor. Orvandel scrambled onto Thor's shoulders while the remaining warriors clung to his belt and jerkin as fleas to an unkempt dog.

The son of Odin moved slowly, careful of his newly embarked passengers, a living raft crossing the river. The ice-cold waters rushed against the battle coat to numb fingers and stiffen limbs. Dangerous currents tugged at the desperate warriors, threatening to drag them from their purchase.

As he took another careful step, Thor chanced a glance upstream. There a massive white form hunkered in the river, a daughter of the frost squatting down over the course, feet planted securely on the river bed, her kirtle lifted high about her knees. From her gushed a mighty stream, the source of the rising waters.

"A-h-h, it is not the river which threatens my purchase. See me giantess; here stands Asa-Thor! You will not wash me away as easily as a clod of earth from a river bank!"

Reaching down into the frigid waters, Thor dug a rock the size of his head from the mud of the riverbed. Arching his back, he heaved the stone to staunch the flow at its source. The giantess screamed, bent double, and hobbled quickly away. Her thick brow of cropped white hair bobbed across the sky then disappeared over the valley rim, chased by her fading wails.

The crest passed, but the flow still threatened. The protector of men caught at a rowan sapling that bent its strong branches to the water. Its roots tangled deep into the riverbank, the supple wood held fast to the earth as hand over hand Thor hauled himself and his ragged cloak of warriors from the rushing stream. The warriors, grown weary of their ride, loosed their frozen grips to drop onto the bank as ripe fruit falls from the tree at harvest. Amid the din of groans and soft curses a headcount was taken. All the warriors were safe. None were lost.

After a short rest, the stalwart troop resumed their trek to Geirrod's hall. The rawboned thurs himself met them outside the walls of his gard. The Jotun noted their numbers outstripped his own. Confronted by a large force, and with his earlier plan at the river failed, Geirrod decided on a new strategy. That which he could not achieve with strength of numbers, he would achieve with bold cunning.

"I recognize you Veor, fearlessly stationed at the head of a large entourage. I see you arrive unburdened of your godly weapons; for such grace, how can I not be hospitable. In honor of your visit, it gives me great delight to offer pleasant lodgings equal to the esteem that I hold for you and all your kin." With a grand flourish, Geirrod directed the group to a goat's shed located at the far end of the muddy courtyard.

The visitors gathered in the open entry, noses wrinkled, taking in the cramped byre. The walls were stained black with urine, clumps of soiled straw covered the floor, and the air reeked of its recent lodgers who bleated from pens outside the shed.

Orvandel snorted. "Pleasant indeed!" He kicked a mass of dung across the floor. "The goats of my hall know better accommodations!"

Thor grunted a command to his troop, swept his arm to take in the shed. "Make yourselves as comfortable as possible but remain on guard with weapons ready. I expect a host who treats his guests in this manner has more mischief in store than squalid quarters."

A chair of simple lines, its seat brushed clear of filth, was stationed in the center of the shed floor, the sole furnishing to accommodate all the guests. Thor settled himself in the chair as the others arranged themselves about the rude lodging. Without warning the chair began rising swiftly into the air while the warriors shouted out in dismay. On approaching the roof, Thor braced himself against the rafters, thick timbers of sturdy oak that groaned as he pushed down hard, straining himself against the seat. The force of his efforts was relieved by a loud crack followed by two sharp screams that pierced the ears. The chair collapsed back to the floor with a jarring thud.

Geirrod's daughters, Gjalp and Greip, had squatted under the chair, hoisting it up on their shoulders as they attempted to crush Thor against the roof. He had broken their backs by pushing down. The warriors of Gang jeered the injured pair as they dragged themselves from the shed, wailing loudly, crawling through the mud back to the main hall.

Disappointed his third plan had failed, Geirrod decided on a direct confrontation. He sent a servant, hunched over and partially lame since birth, to summon Thor. Arriving at the byre, the servant stood outside wringing his hands as he stammered out his message. "Th-th-the lord of this gard requests the great Asa-Thor join him in his hall to compete face-to-face in feats of st-st-strength."

Thor stepped from the byre, his shoulders filling the entry. He examined the speaker cringing beside the gate, nervously tugging his robe around his spare shoulders, and noted the effort he expended keeping his feet pointed forward. "Tell him I will attend."

"My m-m-master," the servant swallowed hard, forcing out the rest of the message, "my master asks that you come alone."

"So," Thor nodded, stroking his beard, "he wants a private audience. Very well. Tell your master I will be there." The servant bowed before scuttling away to deliver the reply.

Orvandel slid up from behind as the servant disappeared into the hall. "He seeks to demean you, just look at the cripple he sent to deliver his message. You know he plans a trap. At least allow me to join you. I need not enter the hall, but can stand in the doorway, my bent yew providing a shield of arrows should the need arise."

"Yea, he may well mean mischief. But I will attend alone just the same." Shaking off the protest of his warriors, Thor took the gifts of Gríd from his pack. Their objections died away as he donned the iron gloves, strapped the belt of strength tight about his waist, and strode fearlessly into the etin's hall.

A large fire burned the length of the room cleared of benches. Thor approached until he stood opposite Geirrod, a wall of flame rising between them. Sneering, the etin stepped forward to the fire's edge. Shadows danced across his sweaty features as he spat into the flames. "Great are the tales I've heard of your deeds—bold, brash, and ruinous to my kin. The accounts of your strength, I dare say, are paltry compared to my own. Let us gauge the worth of these stories by testing your skill in dodging iron."

With that, Geirrod snatched a piece of red-hot iron from the roaring flames and hurled it at Thor. Fjorgyn's son caught the bar in his mailed fist. Twisting it in the air, he fed the glowing shaft back to the startled etin. The crafty thurs dodged behind a stone pillar, but the glowing bar pierced the column, flinging him back, impaling him against the far wall. Geirrod screamed, unable to free himself, as the heat from the bar ignited his clothes.

Thor glared at the giant pinned against the wall, shrieking, writhing in a bloody tapestry of flame. "Your arrogance reaps a bitter harvest rich in tears. By my hand, you have paid a heavy reckoning for inhospitality and over-weaning pride."

The Challenge of Hrungnir

Along frost-slicked ways, Odin journeyed astride the sure-footed Sleipnir. On the border of Jotunheim they encountered a bold thurs who kept lonely vigil atop a high hill. He stood beside a white horse with flowing, golden mane, reins gripped in hand as he scanned the horizon. The giant shouted out from his hilltop ward as the pair passed below the crest opposite his station. "Who is the intruder helmed in shining gold that rides boldly through our land on such a fine horse?"

Odin sat back on his mount, the reins clasped lightly in his hand. "Call me Vafud, for I travel far and wide. My steed is swift; his eight powerful legs carry me across the nine worlds. In all Jotunheim he has no equal."

The rock-boned thurs laughed with a voice to shake the hills. "Your horse may be fine, wayfarer, but mine takes far longer strides. He is called Gullfaxi for the bright color of his mane. Swift as the wind, your head I would have in a moment should we choose to charge from our post."

The son of Bor yelled back at the sentry, his voice barbed to taunt. "You speak bold words etin, as if you owned force enough to back them up! Who are you to challenge me?"

The giant grinned wide, bearing a gate of snaggled, yellow teeth. He thumped his chest with a gnarled fist that sent a hollow boom echoing among the ravines. "My kin call me Hrungnir, but you can call me champion, for I have never lost a contest."

Odin spun Sleipnir about on the path and spurred him into a full gallop. He laughed back over his shoulder as they dashed to the top of the nearest hill. "A winner is known by the finish, never the beginning! You may have my head if you can catch me!"

Incensed by the intruder's bold taunt, the mighty thurs leapt onto his horse. With a sharp kick of his heels, he spurred his mount into swift chase. The giant leaned forward in his saddle, chin jutted against the wind, eager to repay the stranger's arrogant brag.

The pursuit was brisk with both riders laying on the backs of their mounts. But the eight-legged horse kept ahead, his flying hooves always just over the hill. In blind fury, the giant lashed his horse to such speed its golden mane snapped in the air.

The chase was so swift, his intent so focused on closing the gap between riders, that the thurs stormed through the gates of Asgard without realizing. He stretched forward an eager hand, his fingers raking the back of Odin's cloak as they charged into the fortified courtyard.

As Valgrind slammed closed behind, the etin spun his horse about, glaring at the grinning face of Odin, who calmly approached the wary rider. With a flourish the Alfodur waved his hand to the unintentional guest. "A brisk ride and a race you nearly won."

Hrungnir growled down from his seat as his horse danced around the courtyard. "In another length, I would have had your head."

Odin rubbed a hand along the back of his neck, remembering the feel of the iron talons that raked the back of his cloak. "That you may, but now you are here and custom demands hospitality. So, be welcome. Come rest awhile in the hall of the mighty. Such a ride deserves a drink."

Inside Valhalla, the lofty giant sat down at the bench. Snatching up a nearby empty cup, he banged it on the table top. "What do you have to offer a celebrated champion of his people?"

Reluctantly, Freyja waited on the guest. Hrungnir let his eyes take in her beauty as she leaned close to fill his mug. Grinning, he let his fingers stray to touch her sleeve, then her dress. "You are a beauty that is certain." Her face pinched with a sour look as Hrungnir snaked a hand along her thigh. "What you need is a great champion to thrust himself up your skirt and show you the power of a real warrior." She slapped away his roving hands, while the giant laughed loudly and took up his cup.

"This is a dull place. Let us have more drink to liven the afternoon." With relish, he drained each bowl that was set before him. At each round, his voice grew louder, his manners more brash. His boasts echoed from the rafters and rang the golden shingles. "And that is how I alone defeated the host. Standing on the field, my doughty whetstone stained red, I shouted victory over the fallen scattered about my feet."

Odin nodded and sipped at his cup while the rest of the Æsir company sat in annoyed silence. "A mighty victory to be sure. It reminds me of an adventure of my own when I single-handedly slew—"

Hrungnir waved him silent. "The exploits of old men tire my ears.

My own deeds are greater than any I have heard or ever will hear." He slammed his mug on the board. "Another. I'll have another." When Freyja edged near with a pitcher to top off his cup, the giant reached out and tugged her robe. "When you are done filling cups, bend over and I will fill yours." Again, she slapped his hand away, then stomped off while Hrungnir's jeering laughter chased after her.

Odin's knuckles turned white on his cup as his eyes jumped between their bellicose guest and Freyja's disappearing back.

Frigg leaned in close. "Do something. This etin guest of yours insults your family and disrespects you, here, in your own home. You must get rid of him."

"Aye." Odin chewed his mustache as he studied the black looks from those about the table. Hrungnir had begun booming another brag, when Odin motioned a retainer to his side.

"Carry this message to my son at Bilskirnir." He whispered. "We have a giant at our table, whose loud, grating voice has become tiresome, and his lascivious actions obnoxious and insulting. His strength is too great for us to remove him. Tell Thor that he is needed to remove this raucous and impertinent guest from Asgard."

As the retainer rushed from the hall, Odin leaned close to Frigg. "It is done. In a short while we will no longer need to tolerate the giant's outbursts."

———————

Thor burst through the wide doors of Valhalla, brows clenched in fury, Mjollnir gripped in his mailed fist. When he saw Hrungnir leaning back with a cup in his hand, he pointed a shaking finger at the giant. "I was summoned and came as quickly as could, but I never expected to find this! Tell me, who among you allowed a lowly etin to drink at our table?"

The giant laughed as he stood to face the rising storm. "None say 'No' when a powerful visitor enters the hall. Odin invited me to drink—your very father—to diminish his near loss in our race. It is by his safe conduct I remain."

Thor hefted his hammer, eager to crush the skull of this arrogant guest. "Then it is an invitation you will soon regret, as I stand here ready to revoke its privilege."

The giant laughed in defiance of the storm, then took a deep drink from his cup. "I know you Veor. You are much talked of in my land. It is said that you hold honor and courage in high regard. Foolish to race, I left my weapons at home, else we would now be clinched in combat, testing the truth of this hearsay."

The giant puffed out his chest, then struck it three times with his fist, the dull thumps echoing back from the golden shingles. "Call me Hrungnir. I am a champion among my people. Of stone I was born, indomitable and strong. My heart is stone; its three sharp corners have never broken. My head is stone; no blow has ever marked its brow. My shield is stone; thick and wide, it repels all attacks. My weapon is a whetstone, broad and flat to crush doughty opponents."

Everyone moved back to make room for the bloody fight they knew must happen as Hrungnir stepped out around the table to approach Thor. "Though I have none of my weapons to challenge your attack, I stand before you ready to defy you barehanded. Know that you will earn little renown from killing an unarmed opponent and be rightly branded coward for such a craven act. But if you are willing to stay your hand, I can offer a greater test of courage. Face me, if you dare, on the border at Griottunagard, the rocky fields between our lands. There I will spill your blood across the courtyard of stone. Your head I will have for a wall ornament!"

Thor's eyes glittered with excitement. No one before had ever challenged him to duel. "Even stone crumbles before my hammer's blow, but today I hold back my strike that I might deliver a stronger blow. You have named the place, now name your time! There we will test the strength of your boasts."

The bold giant strode from the hall, head held high. He called back over his shoulder as he mounted his horse. "Meet me in three days at the appointed place. I look forward to our engagement for I am keen to end your reign of terror among my people."

Hrungnir returned the way he had come, lathering Gullfaxi into a heavy sweat as he raced back to Jotunheim, eager to bring his kin news of the duel. The tale rapidly spread across the frozen lands. He became famous for his daring trip; a giant who not only set foot in Asgard, but also shared drink among the Æsir.

Though delighted with their champion's notoriety, his kin grew concerned over the challenge, for Hrungnir was their strongest protector. Should fortune turn its light from his face and he lose the duel to Hlodyn's celebrated son, they would have little hope for the future. To aid him in battle they fashioned a comrade built up from the clay of Griottunagard. He stood nine leagues high above the plain and three leagues broad under the arms. In his chest beat the strong heart of a mare. Mokkurkalfi they called him, the dense cloud.

On the day appointed for the duel Thor and his servant Thjalfi arrived on the edge of the rocky grounds. From across the plain of Griottunagard the giant's towered over the rocky ground: one of solid stone, one of dense clay, their height dimming the morning sun. Hrungnir stood fast with his thick shield held to fore, whetstone perched ready on his shoulder. By his side stood Mokkurkalfi, his clay feet sunk deep into the earth. The giant's champion shouted out across the plain. "Come forward Veor! Stern foes stand ready to face your fury and diminish the heights of the Æsir!"

When they saw that two stood ready to duel one, Thjalfi drew Thor aside. "They break the rules for the dual that they themselves defined, but I have a plan to even the odds." When Thor made to protest Thjalfi placed a hand on his arm. "Trust that I hold your honor in the highest esteem. You will in no way be lessened should my plan succeed. Conceal yourself here at the edge of the field while I advance to speak with the treacherous etin. Keep a close watch. Attack the moment you see the stone-browed giant shift his battle stance."

The cunning Thjalfi sprinted ahead to where the giant's feet spread wide across the plain. He called out from deep within Hrungnir's shadow. "You who stand before me, feet planted in the mud, your shield held high to ward off attack, do you really think yourself ready to face Hlodyn's celebrated son in combat? Thor observed your battle stance and nearly fell over laughing. He travels now underneath the earth in the warm embrace of his mother to greet your pathetic preparations from below."

At the announcement of Thor's underground attack, Hrungnir hastily slipped his shield from his arm and planted his feet on its broad expanse to ward off an attack from beneath. Lightning flared across the sky. Booming thunder shook the air. Too late he learned the trick played by Thjalfi.

Thor stormed across the rocky field, hurling his mighty hammer as he rushed forward. The clouds echoed his battle cry. Starting back at the sight of his opponent charging across the plain, Hrungnir flung his whetstone in challenge. Mokkurkalfi stood quaking in fear, his feet rooted to the earth, and wet himself at the sight of the storm god. First in pieces, then all at once the clay giant crumbled before the onslaught.

Caught with a full maiming blow from the mighty Mjollnir, Hrungnir tumbled forward, collapsing onto his shield, his brow shattered into fragments that rained down across the plain. The ground shook as he crashed to the ground.

Thor tried to dodge the etin's swift response, but the heavy whetstone slammed into his forehead, sticking fast in the bone. Blood gushed into his eyes, dimming his vision to danger. Blinded with blood, Thor staggered about, then fell as the earth rolled beneath his feet. A massive leg of the fallen giant toppled over, pinning him to the flinty ground.

With the duel ended, the gods gathered on the plain forming a ring around their trapped protector. Many tried, howling in frustration, but none could move the etin's limb. Then the son of Jarnsaxa stepped forward—a boy only three years old—and flung the leg from off Thor. "I am sorry, father, to arrive late, else I would have slain the foe with my own hands."

Magni's father climbed to his feet, thankful for the aid of his son. "Powerful you are. More powerful you will become. For your help, I give you the horse Gullfaxi, won by me from the stone champion by right of duel."

Odin grumbled about the group, loudly making his displeasure known to everyone. "It is shameful to waste such a splendid gift on one so young, when all know it was my craft that made the duel possible! By all rights, the mount should go to me!"

Resting a hand on Magni's head, Thor raised his voice for all to hear. "It was my son that released me from the trap when none other could budge the limb of my flint-hearted adversary. By right of deed, to him goes the honor of my gift."

Thor returned to Thrudvang, blood dripping from his wound. Declining all offers of assistance, he demanded that Groa, the trusted wife of Orvandel, a good woman whose skill in the healing arts rivaled Eir, be brought to charm the whetstone out of his forehead.

With poultices of herbs, she stopped the blood. With chanted spells, she loosened the bloody stone. Before she could finish her work, Thor, eager to thank her for her aid, related the tale of Orvandel's toe.

The archer's wife, recalling her husband's attempts to ignore the pain as she tended his foot, shook her head at the thought of the frozen digit winking high in the heavens. "You wrenched the toe from his foot when he wasn't looking?

Thor laughed. "Exactly so. I snapped it off and he never said a word, nor uttered so much as grunt."

Groa grinned. "Then I can expect silence from you as well." With that she yanked the loose stone free from his forehead. Thor's bellow shook the walls while thunder filled the air and lightning crackled across the sky.

She stuffed a fistful of herbs into the gaping wound to staunch a sudden gush of blood, then bound the herbs in place with an ell of linen wrapped firmly about Thor's head. When the blood stopped flowing, and Thor's outburst had quieted to a low moan, Groa gripped his chin. Turning his face side to side, she examined the bandage. "It was close. You'll have a scar to remind you."

Gathering her robe about her shoulders, Groa settled herself at his knees. Tilting her head back, her keening voice filled the hall as strongly she sang, powerfully she sang, healing spells for the recovery of Odin's son.

Forseti's Marriage to Roskva

For several years Forseti worked hard to establish his position within the Ljónar. His faultless resolutions delivered accord between foes. No one disputed his judgments. Everyone praised the impartiality of his relentless sense of justice.

When his position in the clan was secure, Forseti, the great arbitrator, raised a hall near his father's home, with golden shingles to dazzle the eyes. Glitner he called it, a place of rest from the responsibilities of his official duties. Often, he sat alone propped before the hearth fire, pondering his future, until the ache of loneliness drove him back to the familiarity of his duty.

On a bright sunlit day, when the hair on his chin had thickened to full manhood, Roskva, a respected servant of Thor, caught his attention. He was entranced watching her, finding any reason to be near her, speaking with her. Her shyness delighted him in ways he could not express. "It must be," he thought. "I must, mustn't I?"

Never one to rush into a decision, Forseti weighed the longings of his heart against the counsel of his head. With solemn thought, he ticked off his criterion for decision: the desire for a close companion to ease his loneliness; the urges of his loins; the ache of his heart; the woman's bright beauty, intelligence, and adeptness in the skills of her mother; the great trust Thor placed in her; his own trust in the son of Odin's estimation. In all ways, he found it an excellent match.

With the dignity of determined purpose, he approached the Thunder god to put forth his proposition to take as wife one whom he protected.

"Asa-Thor, Oku-Thor, strong guarder of gods, protector of men, always I have held you in high esteem. When you speak, your words carry weight. Truth and honesty are your second nature."

The young suitor lightly thumped his chest then held out his hand palm up. "I, Forseti, son of Baldur, stand before you, seeking your consent to a marriage. In your household is a woman whose charm and good looks have found favor in my eyes. I appreciate the diligence she shows in performing her duties. In all ways, she commands my utmost respect. Roskva is her name. I would have her as wife. I ask for your blessing of this union."

Thor stroked his beard as he carefully examined the young man who stood before him. The steady eyes and square shoulders bespoke one who would not leave without attaining that which he came for. "This woman is under my protection. Her father is a close friend. I trust her as I trust few others. What do you offer her that I should bless this union?"

Forseti dug into the pockets of his vest, dragging out objects of great value hoarded for just this moment. "I bring these gifts for you," he carefully arranged them on the table before Thor, "that you will know the sincerity of my request."

Thor picked up a gold ring, turned it over in his hands, hefted its weight, then tossed it back on the table. "These are proper gifts meant to dazzle a parent's eyes, but I am not her parent and you are not asking to marry me. I ask again, what do you offer her?"

Forseti nodded. "Yes. Yes. You are right." He lifted his right hand. "There is much I have to offer my prospective bride. I live in a grand hall of which she alone would hold the keys. I hold a position of distinction within our clan. In every way, she would share this position and the honor it confers.

I have watched her from afar. My heart aches with longing each time she passes before my view. I would consider it a blessing, the greatest honor, were we to spend the rest of our days together. I have put the matter before her brother, Thjalfi. He accepted the matter favorably, but said you, as her protector, should have the greater say. So, I ask again for your support in bringing about this marriage."

Delighted with Forseti's request, Thor's chest swelled with pride at the thought of Roskva's house aligned with his own. He had grown fond of his charge. The proffered match met with his blessing, a match he was certain her father—a close friend and companion in arms—would readily approve. "I will certainly add my voice to bring about the match."

Calling Roskva to his side, Thor presented Forseti's proposition. "For many years, long before you were born, your father and I have been faithful friends. When you joined me on the journey to Jotunheim, I promised to watch over you and your brother as I would my own children. You have remained with me, attending to my needs, and are now of age, skilled in your mother's arts, well capable of managing a home of your own. This young man has asked for your hand in marriage. He is highly regarded among our clan. Your brother has already given his consent, as I am certain would your father. I believe it a good match for both of you. You will have my blessing, if you agree."

When the maiden did not respond and instead turned her gaze to the ground, the young judge sagged against the table. Dejected, he fumbled his best offerings back into his pockets. As he turned to leave Thor grabbed his arm. "Wait. Hold your place."

Again, he presented Forseti's proposition. "This young man has asked for your hand in marriage. He has honorably made his request, presented valuable wedding gifts to show the earnestness of his intent, asked for and received the consent of your brother, he even asked for my blessing. He deserves an answer from your own lips. Will you have this man as husband? Speak your will."

This time Roskva's shy glance signaled her agreement. "Yes. Yes, I accept." At her words, Forseti's smile brightened the room, while his booming heart threatened to burst the cage of his chest.

Laughing to fill the sky, Thor drew the couple together and placed their hands one over the other. "Choices freely made, pledges freely given, to all this I gladly give my blessing. Tomorrow I will hold Mjollnir over your heads to consecrate this union. It will not be too soon."

Cycle 3: The Sword of Vengeance

Contest of the Craftsmen

In the early days when the earth first flowered, wondrous works flowed into the hands of the gods, gifts that increased their power across the worlds. Then master smiths vied in skill to create earth-protecting weapons that the worlds might remain safe from the chill embrace of frost. From the forges of Sindri and Volund came creations of such power that no others could match their innovation. Unstinting, they supported the gods, always offering up always their best. The worlds prospered as their creative force flowered across the lands.

Loki saw this bond and grew jealous. How was he to drive a wedge between the Æsir and their greatest supporters? In vanity, he saw a way. With great cunning and subtle insinuation, he contrived a contest of artistic skill, a dispute in which both sides must lose—one their honor, the other the prize.

The Æsir women are endowed with rare beauty. Their full, shapely forms dazzle the eyes. Confidence shines from their striking features. Proud, they hold their heads high, always. Among the women of the Æsir clan, Sif's flowing locks were considered the loveliest of all. She spent long hours with a boar bristle brush, tending her hair until it glistened as polished gold in the sun, and often spoke of her tresses as one does a great treasure. Many admired its luster.

The son of Farbauti scowled each time he heard the praise of others for her hair while his deep, rich, ebony locks went ignored. One afternoon Loki vented his jealousy as Sif took her rest beneath the shade of a linden tree. With stealth to rival that of Vidar, he crept to the side of the sleeping woman, shifted himself into the guise of an ant, and worked his way through the golden windings of her hair until he reached her scalp. Using sharp pincers, he clipped off each hair at its base. He did not stop in his efforts until her head was completely denuded.

The deed done, Loki dropped to the ground and returned to his normal form. Chuckling softly to himself, he crept away, smirking at the thought of the bald woman resting peacefully beneath the tree. "Now flounce about the Æsir courts, flashing your shiny scalp among company. Let us hear the praises sung of a docked sheep."

When Sif awoke, she felt the cool breeze caress her bare scalp. As she gazed in shock at her hair spread like amber rushes about the ground, her shaking hands flew to her head, encountering the numb coolness of freshly exposed skin. She screamed and wrapped a scarf about her head. Streaming tears, Sif rushed back to Thrudvang and shut herself away, refusing to see anyone.

On hearing his wife had hidden herself from view, Thor stood outside her doorway, his pounding fist shaking the walls. "I will not be refused. Let me in and tell me what has caused you to become upset." In tears, Sif cracked open the entry. As Thor shoved through, she unwrapped her scarf from her bare head. Eyes wide with astonishment, Thor reached out a hand, but dared not touch. His voice faltered as his hand floated then fell to his side. "What? How?"

With shaking hands, Sif wrapped the scarf about her bare scalp. "This afternoon I took a walk among the nearby hills. The day was warm, so I decided to rest beneath a wide limbed linden tree on the rise just beyond the gate. I had not slept long, Sol had barely moved in her course, but when I woke I found my hair... my golden hair strewn about me like rushes spread across the floor. I covered my head in disgrace and ran home." At this she burst into tears, heavy sobs shaking her shoulders. "I am ashamed. I cannot be seen like this. I can never go out again."

Thor's brows grew black as night at the humiliation imposed on his wife. His teeth ground like the rattle of hail on stone. Heavy clouds darkened the sky while thunder boomed on the horizon. He knew there was only one who would dare such a base deed. Storming from his hall, he followed Loki's trail into the deep wood. There, concealed among the limbs of an oak tree, he found the culprit wrapped in the protective arms of his mother.

Thor dragged the dark son from the deep shadows. With one hand, gripped tight about his throat, he pinned the squirming Loki to the ground. His free fist swept high, ready to strike. He spat in fury at his captive, letting the venom of his words flow freely from his lips. "For the humiliation you brought on my wife, I will break every bone in your body and dash you along the westerly path!"

Loki begged for his life, choking his plea past Thor's crushing grip. "A prank! It was only a prank! A slight meant in jest, nothing more. Let me live and I will undo what I have done."

The god's strong guarder glared at the quivering form. "That which you have done cannot be undone! What is pruned at the root cannot grow! What you have done is... is..."

The son of Laufey launched himself into the breach, speaking quickly to fill the brief pause in Thor's speech. "But there are those of great skill who can work wonders, so grand is their understanding of nature. They work in seclusion at their smithies, forging endless treasures as they expand their knowledge. I can compel them to make hair from gold, an artifact that will grow like any other hair. This I swear to do if you free me."

Thor stayed his fist from obeying his anger, reluctantly letting his hand settle to his side. "Destroying you would not ease my wife's suffering, though I would gain much satisfaction from smashing your skull into tiny pieces. If you can do that which you claim, I will let you live. But if you fail to return to her what was maliciously taken, and she continues to weep alone in her room, know that I will take great delight in crushing the life from your miserable bones!"

Released from Thor's iron grip, Loki staggered to his feet and tottered across the glade to lean gasping against the bole of an aged oak, the dark blue bruises on his neck a painful reminder of his promise. "Trust in my oath." The words rasped painfully through Loki's swollen throat. "You will not be disappointed." Thor snarled once, before stalking away, leaving him alone in the glade.

Swiftly, Loki flew from Asgard into the dark realm of Nidaveller. With a grin spreading wide across his face, he made his way along paths long planned.

———————

First, he visited the forge of Volund, a smith of great ingenuity and skill, the eldest of Ivalde's three sons. Smiling warmly, Loki raised his hand in greeting as he was ushered into the smithy of the master craftsman. "Regin you are. Long have your gifts brought pleasure to the mighty Æsir. They ask now for three examples of your best, a challenge to your great skill."

Volund stood silent before the son of Farbauti, eyes watchful, ears tuned to telling words, as he listened to the Æsir's challenge. Loki lifted his hand with thumb and two fingers raised. Bending each one down as he ticked off the treasures designed to test Volund's ability at the forge. "Hair made from gold that grows as any other hair. It seems a grand lady of the Æsir court has misplaced her luxurious locks and requires an urgent replacement. A formidable weapon that is so finely crafted it cannot be defeated in battle. Lastly, a sturdy craft capable of swift transport across air, land, or sea at the whim of its pilot."

The master smith stoked his fire, staring into the quickening flames as he pondered his reply. He spoke slowly, choosing his words with deliberate care. "Long ago, my brothers and I pledged that we would support the Æsir in all things, bend our every skill to their needs, and together ward this border of Jotunheim against intrusion by the children of frost." He tapped a finger to his chest. "Why, I have been given the honor of foster father to the children of the water god. Always I have been ready to serve. They will not find me reluctant now."

The son of Ivalde turned to his forge and pressed himself hard to the work. His furrowed brow beaded with sweat as he stretched his skills to craft three objects of great value. At the end of day Volund passed three treasures into the hands of the devious Loki. A hank of hair fashioned of the purest gold. The spear, Gungnir, its golden tip etched with victory runes. Skidbladnir, a ship cleverly crafted to fold up and fit into a pocket.

He carefully instructed the son of Farbauti on their use. "Take these, my finest works, to the Alfodur that he will know the respect held by his most-loyal servants."

Delighted with the works, Loki gathered up the treasures. He assured Volund as he left that the Æsir would prize his gifts above all others. Once out of sight of Volund's hall, Loki burst out laughing as he sped away through the dim light to visit the forge of Sindri and his brother Brokk.

Firelight from Sindri's forge flickered across the smithy walls throwing into relief hammers and tongs strung about the beams— the working implements of a smith's life. From the entryway, Loki cleared his throat, a soft cough barely heard, then again louder, then a third time still louder. Slicked with sweat and smudged with soot from the fire, the dwarves turned from their forge at the intrusion, started when they saw who stood between the door posts.

Brokk stepped forward to greet Loki. Bowing his head, he spread his arms wide in welcome. "What brings the celebrated son of Laufey to this, our humble workshop?"

Loki heaved a travel pack from his shoulders and set it on a nearby bench. "Your skills as craftsmen are well-known across the nine worlds; all covet the objects you produce. Many consider your brother the best at smithcraft." He rested a hand on the sack, drumming his fingers against the bumps of the objects within. "But now I bring a challenge to his ability. In this sack are three priceless treasures crafted by Volund, the son of Ivalde, in a single day, each exquisite piece exhibiting superior skill. I wager your brother cannot make three treasures of equal value in the same period."

Brokk and Sindri pulled the bright works from the sack, grunting in appreciation as they carefully examined each one. Brokk looked up as they returned the items to the bag. "These are indeed the works of a gifted smith. I am certain my brother could do as well or better. But you, son of Farbauti, are known to us and your wager is suspect."

Affronted, Loki raised himself over the dwarves that he might more easily look down his nose. "Don't be so quick to spurn my challenge. To the winner falls a great honor: acknowledgment across the nine worlds of the greater skill. To decline indicates the fear of inferior ability."

The brothers grumbled together, then Brokk turned to Loki. "And who would judge between the works?" The dwarf settled his fists on his hips. "We would never agree to have you the arbiter."

"Why the gods themselves will judge," Loki laughed. Plucking at his vest, he lifted an errant speck of ash before his eyes, examined it closely before tossing it aside. "They in Asgard for whom the gifts are destined. As their impartial decisions sort the dead, so, too, they will decide the greater skill."

Loki swaggered across the room and bent over to peer into the mouth of the glowing forge. A rolling carpet of blue flame danced over the bed of coals, its light glinting in his eyes. "I am eager for this challenge. In fact, I am so confident of the works I hold that you can also have my head if you are able to surpass them."

The dwarves conferred in the whispers of a cat, now in the raging bellows of a bull, slapped each other on the shoulders, then turned as one to the son of Farbauti. Brokk stepped forward, eyes squinted, glaring up at Loki. "I speak for my brother Sindri and myself. We accept your wager, his skill against that of the son of Ivalde. The stakes—renown for superior skill and your head, or recognition as second best."

Loki bowed to the dwarves. "I'll remove myself to another room while you work." He winked at the two. "I know how jealously you makers guard your smithy secrets." His laughter faded as he stepped from the chamber while Sindri prepared to work.

The master craftsman stoked the fires of his forge as his brother Brokk worked the bellows. He slid a pig's skin into the oven's maw then bid his brother to pump steadily until he withdrew what he had put in.

Air gushed from the bellows, bursting the fire into brightness. As Brokk labored, a fly buzzed into the smithy, circled once, then landed on the back of his hand. The fly bit deep the flesh between thumb and forefinger, sending a needle-sharp pain lancing up his arm.

Brokk's muscles twitched at the sting, but the dwarf continued pumping the bellows until Sindri returned and pulled the charged work from the forge—a boar with bright, golden bristles. Sindri examined the creation, poked at different spots along its length, nodded with satisfaction at the outcome. At once he began the second work.

Next Sindri placed gold in the forge, wriggled it deep into the coals, then again bid Brokk to pump hard without stopping. Brokk bent his back to the effort. Air gushing from the bellows breathed life into the fire. The fly returned to the smithy, buzzed twice about Brokk's head before landing below his ear. This time it bit twice as hard as before, a sharp, burning flame driven deep into the dwarf's neck. Groaning in discomfort, Brokk continued to work the bellows until Sindri called for him to stop. With long tongs the smith reached deep into the flames and withdrew a golden arm ring from the fire.

When it had cooled, Sindri examined the creation. He held it up to the firelight, squinting as he sighted along its edge and turned it in his hands to check for imperfections. The dwarf grunted in satisfaction at the outcome then began the third work.

This time Sindri placed raw iron in the forge, liberally dusted it with clean, white sand, then nestled it deep amid the glowing embers. He firmly directed his brother to work the bellows without pause, for should he falter in his effort, the high heat necessary to set the form would fail and the work ruined.

Brokk gripped the bellows handles and pumped hard, keeping a steady rhythm to match his breath. With each stroke air gushed over the coals, lifting the flames to a dazzling brightness. Again, the fly returned to the smithy, buzzed three times about Brokk's head before settling itself on his brow. The fly crawled across Brokk's eyebrows, rubbed its forelegs together, then bit hard at his eyelids, opening wounds that trickled a stinging flow blood into the dwarf's eyes, clouding his sight.

Still Brokk continued to work the bellows, struggling to maintain a steady rhythm until the pain became unbearable. On a down stroke the dwarf paused to wipe away the blood. At that moment Sindri returned and with an anguished cry rushed to the forge. Using an iron hook, he dragged a hammer from the fire.

The master smith hunched over the still-glowing hammer. Using a metal awl, he carefully prodded its length, then flipped it over to examine the other side. He found its handle short, but all else free of defects. With a sharp exhale of breath, he stepped back, exclaiming the project had barely escaped ruin. "Were there more time I would recast it, but already Night chases Day from the sky and the period of the challenge closes. We will go with what we have, for although the handle is short, still it is the greatest of my works."

With many harsh instructions to his brother, he gathered the treasures into a travel pack and placed them under the care of Brokk, who went with Loki to Asgard to settle the wager.

The two traveled along roads east, Loki keeping up a steady prattle while Brokk trudged on in silence. They wound their way through the worlds along rough paths until they reached Asgard.

Immediately on their arrival, Loki called a council of the clan, informed them of the bet made with Sindri, and asked for a judgment to settle the wager. On hearing the request, the gods became angry at such a foolish bet, one certain to breed antagonism between skilled craftsmen. But with Loki's word bound by the offer of his head, they could not negate the wager.

A Ljónar was hastily convened in Gladsheim with three chosen to judge: Odin, Thor, and Freyr. Gravely, they took their places in the high seats. Brokk and Loki advanced, sacks over their shoulders, until they stood before the domars. Eager to conclude the challenge, the son of Laufey presented his case first.

Loki stepped forward to lay before the domars the glittering pleadings of Ivalde's sons. With a flourish, he held each gift aloft, turning it side to side as he described its merits. "I present to you three treasures expertly crafted in the forge of Volund. You are well acquainted with his abilities. He has often bestowed gifts from his forge on members of the Æsir clan. Know that these are his most skilled creations."

Over his head, he shook a spear, battle-bright and long. "To Odin I pass Gungnir, a weapon of superior make, a mighty battle spear to make foes tremble. Its golden tip is engraved with victory runes. Thrown it never misses its mark. When stoutly thrust, nothing can stop its penetration. Nor will it catch when removed."

In a gloved hand, he hefted a lump of twining gold. "To Thor I give a hank of golden hair, its luster equals the fire of the sea at sunset. Take care in its handling, for when touched to bare skin it roots and grows as any other hair."

He waved a small packet over his head. "To Freyr I give the great ship Skidbladnir, cleverly designed to fold up like cloth, it will fit within a pouch or a pocket. When unfolded its sails always catch a fair wind. Its spacious hold can carry all who dwell in Asgard, along with their belongings."

The judges murmured with pleasure at the wondrous works, turned them over smiling in appreciation, astonished by their complexity, delighted with their utility. Cradling the golden hair in a gauntleted hand, Thor leapt to his feet and rushed off to bestow the gift on his wife. When the sun had peaked the sky, he returned to the Ljónar, a satisfied grin spread across his face as he sauntered across the hall to take his seat.

Then Brokk stepped forward eager to present his offerings. "You have seen the works of a talented smith crafted with competence and imagination. Greater still are the works of my brother, a master craftsman at the forge."

He reached into the bag his feet. "I present to you three treasures expertly crafted in the forge of Sindri. You are well acquainted with his skill. He has often bestowed the gifts from his forge on members of the Æsir clan. Many you use each day, some you wear for decoration. Know that these are his most skilled creations."

Sweeping his hand into the air, he twirled a ring between his fingers, so its fire flashed through the room, drawing the attention of every eye. "To Odin I give the arm ring Draupnir that his treasure will always be renewed. Every ninth night be ready with cupped hands, for when suspended, this ring drips eight rings of equal weight."

From the bag, he hauled a shape familiar to any hunter. "To Freyr I give Battleboar," he patted its shoulder, "Gullinbursti he is called, a gold-bristled boar that can carry its rider over sky, sea, and land, by day or by night more swiftly than any other mount. Its bristles glow with such brilliance that neither darkness nor gloom will ever obscure the way."

He approached the judges and with two hands swung a shining hammer over his head. "To Thor I pass the mighty Mjollnir. Its handle is short, its head narrow enough to carry snugly inside your vest or hang comfortably from a belt loop. Though it may seem small, know that its power is great. With this hammer you can strike any blow without fear the weapon will break. If thrown, it never misses its mark. But be ready, as it will return to hand no matter how hard it is flung."

The dwarf gently placed the hammer in Thor's hands. "Megingjard, the belt of strength you gird about your waist will increase your godly strength tenfold and let you bring any force to your blow. Jarngreipr, the iron gauntlet your wear on your fist will ease the hammer's handling, lest the very bones of your hand be shattered by its power."

248

As Thor hefted the hammer to gauge its weight, Brokk turned slightly and spread his arms to the entire gathering. "Its authority is not only for war, but for consecration as well. When held overhead, its focused power can bring life to the most desolate land and bestow the blessing of protection on any person, place, or event."

Together the gods conferred in judgment, carefully considering the merits of each gift. After a short deliberation, they announced their decision that Sindri's hammer was the superior gift as its power offered the greatest protection against frost giants and their kin. Sindri, they declared, had won the wager.

Loki's eyes danced in alarm at the decision of the Ljónar. He shook himself and slid his features into a bright, convivial grin. Smiling benignly at Brokk, Loki raised his hand in salute. "A wager well won. Your brother is indeed Regin above all."

A deep frown drew Brokk's lips to his chin and he mumbled to himself as he shook out his sack. Coughing lightly, Loki slowly dropped his hand. "That honor is certainly a great prize to carry home. I feel my bloody head would be an ungainly burden, hardly equal to the nobility of the judgment that is now yours. I have many items of greater value than my head. They are certainly easier to carry. For instance, my shoes can flit you across land, sea, or sky. They are yours for the asking. I also have gold, silver, jewels—just name it."

Leaning close, Loki whispered confidentially behind his hand. "Perhaps knowledge is more to your liking. I have a certain arcane spell I would be willing to share... resurrection from pyre ash?" He raised his eyebrows. "What do you think? Will you take that for my head?"

Brokk set his jaw. "There is no hope for that in this or any world." He glared at Farbauti's son. "Do not think me so slow as to not recognize the vermin that stung me while I managed the bellows. Your gilded skull will make an excellent drinking cup."

Leaping to his feet, Loki sped for the door. He shouted over his shoulder as he shoved past Syn and rushed from the hall. "Then you must catch me to claim your prize."

When the dwarf realized that Loki meant to renege on his bet, he lunged forward to grab, but Loki was already far away, his shoes wafting him through the air to disappear over the far hills. "The trickster runs," Brokk stamped his feet, snorting in frustration, "and you all just stand there! You knew the wager! You decided the winner!"

Odin turned his face to one side, letting his gaze roam among the pegs on the far wall. "We know the terms. But it is not our responsibility to help you collect your winnings."

Brokk screamed, flapped his arms, and with a bull voice called on Thor to help him catch the elusive quarry. "You are the protector of your clan! It is your duty to uphold your clan's integrity and deliver to me the winnings of a wager honestly won by your decision that was made in your own hall!"

Thor ground his teeth, mindful of how the events had begun. Taking a deep breath, he reluctantly agreed to assist. "It is as you say my duty, one I have been called on many times to perform. And since I was a member of the Ljónar who delivered the verdict, it is my responsibility to see it carried out in all forms. Wait here until I return. Loki, devious as he is, will not have hidden himself where I cannot find him."

From Hlidskialf, Thor spotted Loki on a far-off hillside cowering amid a grove of ancient oaks. He expended little effort capturing the fugitive and brought him before the blood-eager dwarf.

While Thor held the unresisting captive, Brokk hefted a long blade in his hand, scraping a thumb across its edge to test its sharpness as he made ready to gather his winnings. The quick-witted Loki only grinned as the dwarf raised his blade to strike. "Truly, you have won the wager and so have a right to my head. But you have no right to the neck on which it is attached. That remains mine."

The dwarf's brow grew dark at the truth of Loki's words. "Then if I cannot separate your head from your neck," his black eyes flashed bright as he crooked an arm beneath Loki's chin, "at least no one need listen to your cunning lies." Brokk ripped a strand of leather from his jerkin. "Since your head is mine to do with as I will, with this strap, Vartari, I will still your braying voice."

Taking a sharp awl from his vest pocket, he swiftly punched holes through the struggling Loki's lips, then threaded the strap through each hole, crisscrossing the strand to bind shut his mouth. Bleeding, moaning, hands clasped to his mouth, Loki knelt on the floor rocking back and forth while Brokk's laughter echoed through the hall.

The Sons of Ivalde Rebel

When Volund heard the judgment of the gods, that Sindri's gifts were prized over the works of his own hands, he grew enraged at the perceived slight. As he brooded, his anger became a dark blot that spread to consume his spirit. In fury, he called a council of his family.

After everyone had seated themselves at bench in his hall, he wasted no time on pleasantries, but stomped about before his brothers, shouting harsh words to challenge the ear and stir the heart. "Those we once held in high esteem have shown they hold us in contempt! By choosing Sindri's works over those of our house, they demean our skills, heap humiliation on our heads, and offend our family's honor."

Volund's brothers, angry at his unforgiving words, tumbled over each other in their urgency to speak. Orvandel, the middle brother, pounded his fist on the board, three times he pounded his fist for attention, knocking over their cups and spilling ale across the wood. "The gifts were created by your hand alone! We had no part in their manufacture!"

Leaping to his feet, Slagfin, the youngest brother, jabbed an accusing finger at the Wonder Smith. "You brought this on your own head by accepting the challenge of a known trickster! We have no part of this insult!"

Volund faced his brothers, carefully choosing his words that they might securely nest their barbs. "It is true I alone accepted the challenge to my skill, stretched my abilities to their utmost that only the best be presented to those we respected above all. Since the gifts were given in all our names, all of us fell under the judgment. The humiliation of our best considered lacking, belongs to us all."

The brothers winced at the sting of the rebuke and reluctantly agreed with his words. Orvandel placed a hand on Slagfin's arm, then spoke pointedly to Volund. "As the eldest, you make decisions for the family. But do not let anger color your judgment and put a blot on all our names."

Volund stared through his brothers, a cold blackness gripping his thoughts, the agony twisting sharp in his guts. "Prepare for a journey! We leave this day! This very day!"

His jaw bunched as a mist clouded his eyes. He groaned once, twice, a third time before pushing his painful resolve through gritted teeth. "And our first task is to rid ourselves of an unwanted obligation! Gather up the children, Freyr and Freyja. You will find them playing in my hall. These children are the brightest lights in the Æsir clan. Let the mighty gods feel the humiliation of their greatest treasures treated as chattel, to be cast aside when no longer wanted. There are some enemies of the Æsir who would be delighted with their company. A gift of the children will ensure our safe passage through their lands. We can drop them off along the way."

They sped across the snow, consigned their burdens to the howlings of a sooted hall, then turned their feet along northern paths. Always they scanned the skies, cast furtive glances over their shoulders, ever watchful of pursuit.

A small troop of Æsir caught up with them far beyond the raging waters of the Ifing in the foothills of the Wolfdales, deep in the cold lands of Jotunheim. When they spied the three brothers flying over the snow, the ljóna sent by Odin rushed forward to reconcile with Ivalde's sons.

Foremost from the group hurried Njord, the first of the gods seized by fears on account of the bitter judgment. Behind him Hodd labored grim-faced through the snow, bow clenched in his hand, his head bent into the wind. Freki trotted alongside, his keen nose the reason they had found the brother's trail. From far down wind, his sharp nose had caught their scent lingering on the air, brought along a winding course before it could perish - dispersed by the constant winds.

Hodd shouted out when they came close enough that Volund's ear hands might catch his words. "Wait! Hold your flight! We want to speak with you! For the sake of ancient friendship and mutual respect, the Alfodur sends us to seek reconciliation!"

Volund called a halt of his group that he might reply to the arbiters of the gods. The brothers fanned out across the trail, taking a ready stance with hands resting on their weapons. The master smith shouted over the howling winds, his voice muffled by the heavy snow coursing between them. "Once our hearts were held by honor, our minds transfixed with esteem for those we served. We gave you our best, always. More than anything in the nine worlds we believed you held the same esteem for us, that we could always count on your support. But now where trust and respect were deepest, a spreading cancer turns all to hate. There are no words you can speak, no payment you can offer, that will change our minds."

Njord beseeched the fugitive group. "Where are my children, the bright jewels of our clan? Name your price and we will ransom them!"

Volund's bitter laughter was biting as the wind. He replied with a voice ripped raw and bloody from his throat. "Freyr and Freyja I once cherished as stepchildren. I crafted elegant jewelry to enhance their natural beauty, made clever devices to entertain their minds. Joyously, I raised them as I would my own. But such beauty left our lives forever when you snubbed our greatest gifts in your judgment court. No longer did we accept the burden imposed on our house, the weight of an obligation we no longer recognized. You can find them now among the etin, given as gifts to the Howlers, those warlike giants whose screeching deafens the ears. Their virtue is at the mercy of their new hosts."

Njord cried out, loosing his anguish to the winds. In a breath, he roundly cursed the sons of Ivalde, calling out Volund for special disgrace. Orvandel shouted to the sea god. "Who are you to throw such invectives?" His laughter cut across the blowing snow. "It is we who once held the honor of your clan higher than we held our own that by right can freely direct such words. You have no right to utter them."

Hodd choked, then bellowed out, angered at Orvandel's rejoinder. "Just who do you think you are speaking like that to one who is greater than yourself? Only an equal can speak thus! Not the sons of a sniveling watchman who abandoned his post along with his honor!"

Hodd reached to nock an arrow on his bow, but the great archer anticipated his move. A gray winged gosling flit through the air and cut Hodd's bowstring so it drooped useless across his hand.

Yanking another string from his vest, Hodd tied off one end, braced the bow against his foot, then, with a soft grunt, bent the yew into a sharp curve. He dropped the string as a second arrow whiffed through the air to slip harmlessly between his fingers. Cursing loudly, he finished restringing his bow. When he fumbled an arrow from his quiver and placed it against the taut string, a third missile launched by the great archer struck the arrow from his hand.

With a roar Hodd called on Freki to punish the sons of Ivalde for their brazen impudence. But as the wolf plowed through the deep snow, the brothers, laughing among themselves, continued their journey. Within a few strides they disappeared into the foothills, hidden behind a thick curtain of falling snow. The parallel lines of skis that marked their path were quickly buried beneath a blanket of white.

Waving his arms overhead, Hodd yelled for them to return. Njord watched, tears frozen on his cheeks, as they disappeared. Freki stopped his charge and stood chest deep in the powder. The fearless wolf howled before turning back.

Gambanteinn

Volund and his brothers traveled northward through the cold lands of Jotunheim. Skirting the dead realm of Niflheim, they headed deep into the Wolfdales where even gods journey with difficulty. There Volund poured out his anger at the Æsir. In a fit of creation, he directed his talents to visit vengeance on those who snubbed his skill by crafting a weapon superior to Sindri's hammer, something different in the field of war.

The cunning smith built a forge on a side hill in a notch where the wind always blows, curved its foundation walls to capture the bellows of the air. He fixed plates over vent holes set along the hollow to control the draw of air that drove the fires of his smithy.

With focused rage, he used all his skills to create a metal that was both strong and flexible. In a furnace of clay brick mortared to prevent leaks, he placed a terracotta crucible sealed closed with a thick layer of wet clay. Its inside he had filled with raw iron, a blend of carefully selected metal ores, charcoal ground from the burnt bones of a bear, and, to bind impurities, a handful of sky-blue sand washed clean with pure water. He filled the open spaces inside the oven with black coal dug from the ground, heaping it over the crucible until it was buried, then sealed shut the top of the furnace.

For three days and three nights he tended the fire as the harnessed wind drove the furnace to a high heat that set the metal's color, purified its essence, and infused its matter with spirit. Fighting sleep, he spent the hours adjusting the dampers, pushing himself to ensure the fire burned with an intense heat that never lagged.

On the fourth day, he wedged a pick into the bricks, working the tip through the mortar, before giving the handle a sharp twist to break open the furnace. Using metal tongs, he lifted the crucible from the furnace ash, its entire surface popping sparks. Three strikes of a hammer broke away the vessel walls. Three more, each blow raising a cloud of sparks, chipped away a sand-caked crust of impurities, to free a metal ingot of uncommon qualities; brittle yet strong, flexible yet rigid, imbued with the power of the wind, glowing bright as the sun.

In the forge fire, Volund reheated the raw metal, then worked with a hammer to drive it pure, folding the bright red-yellow metal over itself, drawing out its length with each blow. He toiled long in the smithy, the passage of time forgotten, hammering day and night without stop to shape the metal to his needs.

With each blow, he fashioned a yellow-hot blade, indented a fuller down the center of one side for strength, beveled its edges to cut, and tapered its tip to pierce. Along the blade, he etched victory runes, stained its length with a mixture of charcoal and clay. He set his mark on the metal above the hilt, an eagle with wings outstretched—the symbol of the master smith.

Driving the blade deep into the fire, he slid it about in the blushing coals until it's entire length glowed bright yellow, then in one swift motion drew it from its bed and quenched its length in a barrel of glacier water—blood from the Yurkul that hugged the hills above their hall—kept for this purpose inside the smithy door.

Ignoring the waves of heat and steam rolling from its surface, he swung the blade up beside his face and with a practiced ear listened for the telltale of success. There was silence. Volund listened intently until he was certain. The blade echoed back the low rumble of the forge fire, the whistle of the winds drawing through the flues, but there was no ping announcing the metal had cracked and that he would have to start over.

His eyes smoldered with satisfaction as he sighted down its length for straightness. The metal had not warped or twisted, but cured true to receive a sharp edge, with a form to take a blow without breaking.

The blade ready, he cleared his benches. Laying out his tools for fine work, he began the slow, arduous process of infusing spirit and delicate balance into its length. When he completed the great work, the finished weapon would move as if of its own accord. In the hands of a worthy warrior it would offer shrewd guidance in battle, giving its wielder victory over all opponents.

With grindstones, soft cloth, and fine sands, he settled in to polish the blade. Each day he worked the darkness from the surface, every pass bringing out the inborn brightness of the metal until it reflected the sun. Drawing fine-grained whetstones from hilt to point, he sharpened both sides of the blade to cut at a touch. He called it Gambanteinn, the Sword of Vengeance.

Seasons passed as the gods listened for word of the famous craftsman, heard tales from the frozen north whispered on the high winds, consulted with occasional sightings by Hugin and Munin, in all ways possible kept track of his actions. When word reached them of a new weapon being created, one that could defeat gods and Jotun alike, they acted to delay Volund's actions until trusted allies could be engaged to capture the Wonder Smith and lock away his dangerous weapon.

The Swan Maidens

High amid the cold reaches of the Wolfdales, the sons of Ivalde raised a hall of wood and stone, with a smithy built along one side where the bare hill dropped away to forest, and the wind was a constant companion. They furnished it with articles of their own making: benches, board, bowls, cooking utensils, weapons for hunting, skis for riding across snow. Here they stayed while Volund crafted his vengeance.

Nearby the hall stood the basin of Wolf Lake, its still surface reflected the sky, its clear waters icy cold even on the warmest day. Hunting early one morning, the brothers approached the lake hoping to surprise a stag come down from the hills to drink. Stealth their companion, they snuck through the undergrowth to a sheltered cove then peeped out from a break in the brush to sight along the shore.

There they spied three beautiful maidens on the bank, tall and full formed beneath their linked mail. The maidens sat chatting together, knees touching, a distaff wobbling between them, as with deft fingers they spun linen: one adding, one twisting, one wrapping. Their swan robes lay on a nearby rock. Adorned with bright white feathers that fluttered in the light breeze, the robes seemed ready to fly at an instant.

The brothers eased back through the bushes, careful to make no sound that might disturb the maidens. Hunkering out of sight behind a deadfall, they conferred in hushed voices over what they had seen.

Slagfin spoke first, hands fluttering, eyes dancing, his gushing voice filled with excitement. "I saw three long-limbed maidens, fair skinned and beautiful, taking their rest on the shore."

Orvandel cleared his throat as he thoughtfully stroked his beard. "One had braids of fiery red hair, another was crested with raven-dark ringlets, and the third sported locks the luster of yellow gold."

Squinting his eyes, Volund drew his lips into a deep frown. "Each wore a byrnie with linked rings and I saw swanskins draped on a nearby rock. They are surely Valkyrie sent to spy on us. We must kill them to silence their tongues."

Slagfin cried out, despite Volund's harsh glare. "No! We cannot! To destroy such beauty would be a crime against nature, one that could never be forgiven!"

Orvandel joined in to continue his brother's plea. "Besides, we have been in these cold reaches a long time. The warmth of a female companion would be welcome."

Slagfin eagerly nodded agreement and Volund grudgingly admitted their truth. Together the brothers decided on a strategy to keep the maidens from flying away by stealing their feathered garments from the shore.

Having the keenest interest in the women, Slagfin volunteered to retrieve the cloaks. Sneaking through the undergrowth, concealing himself behind boulders scattered along the shore, he crept up on the maidens. Silently, he slipped their swanskin robes from off the rock, then scuttled back to his brothers with the feathered bundles tucked beneath his arms.

When the maidens finished their task, and prepared to leave, they were panicked to discover their swanskins missing. As one they cried out in anger, waving their arms overhead.

Shaking an accusing finger, the one with golden hair rounded on her sisters. "Why didn't you put a rock on them," she yelled, "to keep them weighted down?"

The one with raven black hair stuck out her jaw and planted her fists on her hips. "I thought you did," she spat back. "You were the last to take off your robe. That made it your responsibility!"

The one with fiery red hair kept her voice calm and, ignoring the other two, scanned the horizon. "It matters not who should have done what! The fault lies with each of us for not paying attention! Were we in battle, the enemy would have had our lives! Let us pray they did not fly far. For without them to loft us through the sky, we will have great difficulty returning home."

Frantically, they searched behind boulders and dug through the brush that crowded the basin shore but found nothing—the robes had vanished. The young maidens gathered together on the beach to decide their next course of action.

The three were engrossed in loud argument when rustling from the bushes drew their attention. The sons of Ivalde emerged from the undergrowth, each holding a swanskin for the maiden they had chosen. The brothers waved the skins before them as the maidens looked on in alarm. Volund lifted a cloak and sniffed its edge. "Looking for these?" His lips spread into a taunting grin. "We have them as we now have you."

The maidens drew close together, heads held high, their gold byrnies shining in the northern sun. They stood relaxed, shield arms turned to the fore, hands resting on the worn pommels of the keen edged blades strapped at their waists.

The one with golden hair jerked her chin. "I am called Hladgud, the Swan White. Though I am the youngest of my sisters, you will not find me hiding in a fight, but always in the front, eager for the fray. Who are you that brazenly steal our garments?"

The one with raven-dark hair tossed her head, springing a lock of her hair free to droop over one eye. "Call me Olrun. Like my sister, you'll find me always ready for war, my arm wise to the heat of battle. Why do you detain us?"

The one with flaming red hair let her gaze linger over the three bothers before pressing a palm to her breast. "I am called Hervor, a strange creature of many moods. I am the eldest of us three, so know when to fight and when to parley. What do you want for the return of our feathered cloaks?"

Stepping forward, Volund swept his arm to take in his brothers. "We are the sons of Ivalde. Our hall lies in the next dale. I am called Volund. Along with my skill at the forge, it is said I can bind the winds. My bothers are Slagfin, a skilled bard and warrior, and Orvandel, the greatest archer ever known."

A light breeze chased a v-shape across the smooth surface of the lake to stop at the shore where Volund stood rustling the feathered cape. He turned a hard eye on the maidens. "You are Valkyrie of Odin, and act as his eyes and ears while you travel. The swanskins gave you away. But even without their brilliant white feathers, battle prowess shines from your features and your warrior garb making you easy to mark."

Hladgud flexed her fingers on the handle of her sword but stopped when Olrun gave a slight shake of her head. His attention focused on Hervor, Volund appeared not to notice the exchange. "Because we do not want the eye of the Alfodur spying into our lives, our price is simple, and one you cannot refuse." He tipped his head and cocked an eyebrow at the horizon. "That is unless you wish to brave on foot the cold, heartless terrain that stretches unbroken to the ice-cold torrents of the Ifing and experience the terrors that dwell between."

The three Valkyrie remained defiant, but now their glances swept between them in alarm. The smith gave another shake of the swan robe. "If you choose to remain, you will stay with us. For you cannot leave while we possess your cloaks."

Volund speared Hladgud with a direct glare, flustering the young warrior. "Should you remain true to your nature and try to attack, know that I have strapped at my side a weapon crafted by my own hand that is capable of defeating any adversary, be they gods, etins, or the race of men. It can bring the power of the sun to earth and direct the hand of a skilled warrior to certain victory over all opponents. It is more than a match for your weapons."

The maidens had no choice but to acquiesce. For while in flight they could safely traverse great distances, to journey on foot from the heart of the Wolfdales would be a cold, certain death. As well they knew the smith's skill in the craft of weaponry. They had seen for themselves on the field of battle the deadliness of Gungnir, Odin's celebrated spear. Any doubts of Volund's claim vanished when he drew his blade partway from its sheath. As the metal cleared the scabbard it seemed as if the sun had risen from the earth, its brilliance dazzled the eyes, and the sudden blast of its heat flushed the skin.

Bowing their heads to the inevitable, the three Valkyrie unbelted their swords and reluctantly handed them over to their captors.

Delighted with the promise of companionship, the brothers returned to their mountain hall with their sullen guests shuffling in tow.

As swans that mate for life, they paired off into couples. Volund paired with Hervor, Slagfin joined with Hladgud, and Orvandel took Olrun as companion. Volund gathered together the swanskins, wrapped them in an oil-soaked cloth bound tight with twine, and tucked them away in a darkened recess within his smithy.

With great delight Slagfin showed the maidens their lodgings, eagerly rushing about the hall pointing to the board, the fire, the bedding, running a hand along the benches. The entire hall was made open to their captive guests. Only the smithy was placed off bounds. Volund spoke to his swan maiden as he gently stroked Hervor's hair. "The smithy fires are harsh to beauty of the flesh. They scorch skin, frizzle hair, furnace fumes sting the eyes and burn the throat. It is no place for those unaccustomed to its rigors."

Seven years they embraced as lovers, the brothers' attention drawn from anger back to the pleasures of home life. Merriment filled the hall once bereft of joy. When the men left to hunt, they stacked cords of wood for the fire. They took from the larder only the provisions they would need, leaving all else for the comfort of their swan maidens.

The days they were left to their own devices, the maidens searched the hall for their swanskin cloaks. But there was always some chore to distract, some new gaiety to indulge that drew their attention away from the hunt. Seven years they enjoyed a life of peace, drawing delight from the domestic life and the comfort of a devoted companion.

On the eighth year, the maiden's thoughts returned to the excitement of battle and those they had left behind. They became discontent with their home life, chafing at even the most minor of daily chores. Soon their restlessness spilled out into the everyday. They who had once reveled in companionship now turned to vicious quarreling. Day on day their fighting raged through the hall. Though the brothers tried to avoid the arguments, they were not safe from the sharp edge of bitterness growing between the sisters.

Volund attempted to withdraw into his smithy, to drown out the bickering with the harsh clang of hammer on metal, but the shrill invectives of Hervor sought him out and drove him from the sanctuary of his forge. Readily, he joined the company of his brothers in extended hunting forays to fill the larder, exchanging the clamor of the hall for the solitude of the forest dales.

When the men were away the sisters gathered, their quarrels immediately silenced. In earnest they sought their swanskin cloaks. Together they scoured the hall from end to end. By the ninth year, they had exhausted all locations without success. Discouraged, they sat together to discuss what to do. The men had left to hunt brown bear, the great beast of the forest hills, and they had the hall to themselves.

Pounding her fists on the table, Hladgud spit her frustration through clenched teeth. "We have turned this hall on end and found nothing!"

Olrun rubbed her face, digging at the long lines of weariness that marked her brow. "We have even searched the hearth. Soot and ash are all we have found." She slumped dejectedly against the wall. "If they have destroyed them, we are stuck here for good."

Hands folded in her lap, eyes unfocused, Hervor stared at the table deep in thought. "It is true we have well searched this hall. From rafter to wattle we have left no stone unturned. Even the nearby forest we have hunted in our zeal. But you mention soot and ash. There is one place we have never looked for fear of the dangers that were raised when we were first brought to this place."

The sisters stared at one another, then leapt to their feet, and raced to the smithy of Volund. They stood in the doorway awed at the works that lay partially completed on the benches; great treasures to make the mouth drool, some were obvious in their function, others were mysteries.

Tearing their eyes away from the wonders they began their search of the smithy, careful to avoid the dangers often spoken of by Volund: the blistering hot stones of the furnace forge, the smoldering fires that made them cough, the kettles of strange steaming liquids, and pots of colored powders perched on crusted tripods.

Pausing to wipe away the tears welling from the stinging fumes, they prowled the dark corners around the furnace, prodding with their toes the strange shapes resting there. In a shadowy recess beside the forge they discovered a bundle tied tight with bast rope and caked with the collected grime of nine years. When they unwrapped the soot-stained cloth, the brilliant white feathers of a swan lit up the room.

With a cry of triumph, the three raced back to the hall, each retrieving their silver helmets, ring byrnies, and bright-edged swords from storage chests where they had lain since their capture. Once more the maidens donned their garb of war, then stretched the swanskin cloaks about their shoulders. Together they stepped from the hall into the clear bright day. First one, then another rose into the air. Only Hervor looked back at the hall, her gaze lingering a moment before she, too, spread her arms and flew away.

They soared over the broad expanse of the Wolfdales, dipped close to the ground as they crossed the Ifing, shouted with delight as they skirted the dark edge of the Mirkwood, returning to their home in the Æsir courts.

Standing before Odin, the three maidens of war reported everything they had seen and heard. They told of the hall far to the north nestled deep in the Wolfdales, of the three sons of Ivalde, and the good treatment received at their hands. When asked of what they could report regarding Volund's creations, the three glanced among themselves.

Hladgud replied to the Alfodur. "We saw many wonders in the hall of Ivalde's sons."

"Clever creations, mysterious in nature," Olrun added to the report. "But none as magnificent as the blade Volund always carries at his side."

Hervor glared at her sister before turning her eyes to Odin. "We have seen for ourselves its brilliance, the power of the sun unsheathed. He worked on it constantly the nine years we spent in his hall. Well he would have finished the work and used it to his advantage—it was nearly complete when we first arrived—had his attention not been turned to his guests."

Hladgud and Olrun nodded their heads in agreement.

"Volund claims," Hervor took a deep breath, "he claims it more than a match for any weapon in the Æsir armory. The blade is finely balanced and exhibits an intelligence of its own. When wielded by a skilled warrior, it guides the fighter's arm to victory over any foe. The one who carries it cannot be defeated in battle. When unsheathed its energy can be focused," sweat suddenly beaded her brow as she recalled the heat of their first encounter, "it can bring the fire of the sun to earth, so great is its power."

Odin's face collapsed into a heavy frown and he raised a hand to cover his eyes. A round of curses for Loki flowed freely from his lips. "The smith was always one of great passion. Quick to bestow his allegiance. Quick to react at the slightest provocation. An enthusiastic ally, he stood by our side as long as he felt we valued his family above all others. But when Loki contrived the contest of skill, he was sorely affronted that Sindri's works were more highly prized than those crafted by his own hand. Then he became a deadly foe, boundlessly and recklessly vengeful."

The Alfodur slumped back in his seat, staring up into the shadows of the hall rafters. The Valkyries shifted uneasily as he sat, lips moving as if speaking to himself, his voice a low monotone. "I know the greatness of his skill, just as I knew the goad of humiliation would drive him to surpass himself. And it has happened as I feared. In his anger, Volund has crafted a terrible weapon. One that must be acquired at all costs if we are to remain safe."

Pulling himself upright, he beckoned to a retainer, who approached from his post beside the door. "There is only one I can call upon, a trusted ally who knows the frozen region and is familiar with the hidden paths of the dales. I must speak with Nidud, King of the Njara. I have a dangerous and unpleasant task for him."

The Tragedy of Volund

Cold, weary, their limbs sore from hard travel, the sons of Ivalde returned from the hunt, their packs burdened with the butchered flesh of a brown bear brought down in the forest. They entered an empty hall, the air chill, its hearth ashes cold, quiet save for the low rumble of wind rushing outside the door. Absent were the sounds of incessant bickering. Nor were there the sounds of women busy at chores. Silence and stillness reigned through the rooms.

The brothers swiftly searched the hall but did not find the sisters. Wringing their hands, they called for the maidens, but received no answer to their cries. They searched the forest and nearby dales but found no trace of their passage.

Volund noticed his smithy door ajar. With a heavy heart, he entered the workroom to find the dim recess empty of its package, the oilskin wrapping tossed aside beneath a bench. When he gave the news to his brothers that the maidens had recovered their wings, Slagfin and Orvandel clapped their hands, their voices crying out into the night.

"Perhaps," Slagfin babbled, "they grew tired of being cooped and needed to spread their wings." He looked hopefully at his brothers. "They'll be back, yes?"

"Perhaps," Orvandel muttered as Volund turned his face aside.

As the days passed and hope for the maiden's return faded, resentments grew between the brothers. Often strong voices were uttered at table, harsh accusations tossed across the board. Volund bore the brunt of the heat.

"You! All of this is your fault! If you hadn't..." Slagfin's voice broke off and he collapsed into his seat, face cradled in his hands.

Orvandel rested a hand on his shoulder, but Slagfin shook it off. The archer turned baleful eyes onto his older brother. "He is right. We stand here today punished by your arrogance. We each have lost something precious, our heartstones cracked wide because we followed you on this worthless act of vengeance."

Volund rocked back in his seat sputtering. "We were humiliated! Our family honor trod upon! Each of us bears the shame."

Leaping to his feet, Slagfin jabbed a finger at Volund. "Don't you dare! Don't you dare throw that into our face again! Your revenge is nothing but a brutal double-edged blade. It lost us our position with the Æsir. It gave us our swan maidens. It won us some delight, a bit of happiness. Now it has taken that away, never to return." Slagfin stomped away, yelling over his shoulder as he sought out his bed. "I do not want to hear any more of your speeches! I am done with your vengeance and I am done with you!"

Volund clamped his teeth, glaring straight ahead as Slagfin's back disappeared into the shadows of the hall. Orvandel's voice cut through the uneasy silence. "We are all in agony over our loss. You and I have known this pain before, but for Slagfin... this was his first." The archer stared at a point far beyond the wall. "We all desire to have back that which we once held dear."

Days passed with few words spoken between the brothers. Finally, Slagfin, the most heartsick of the three, filled his travel pack with provisions, bound snowshoes to his feet, and left the protection of the hall. Teeth clenched against the aching pain that threatened to burst from his lips, he traveled south in search of Hladgud.

Not long after, Orvandel reached a decision. He filled a travel pack with provisions to last several weeks, then lashed long wooden skis to his boots. After hooking a bow and quiver over his shoulder, the archer glanced at the smithy where the steady ring of Volund's hammer sounded. He took a deep breath to steady his decision, before directing his feet along paths east to the home he had left years before.

Volund alone remained in the hall, certain that his swan would return. Heart aching, he created gifts to bestow on her when, again, she walked through the hall door. With delicate care, he drew red gold into a set of nested rings, then crafted a master ring graced with closely spaced jewels. The rings of gold he strung along bast ropes that hung from hooks along the wall to ensure the winds would not impede her travel.

Long were the empty days, longer still the silent, lonely nights. Often Volund found himself gazing to the south, scanning the skies for winged movement, but always he returned to his forge, there to work out his frustrations.

———————

Soon after the return of his Valkyrie, Odin visited the hall of Nidud—valiant warrior king of the Njara. In the hearth room Odin paced before the fire while Nidud peered over the rim of his cup waiting for his guest to calm down. "Who is this man you want me to capture?"

Odin snatched a cup of wine from the board, took a long pull, and then held it out, impatiently snapping his fingers, to be refilled. A young maiden crept forward with a pitcher and refilled his cup before scooting back to her post beside the hearth fire. "You have heard of him I am certain. His name is Volund, a master smith whose skill is renown across the nine worlds. He lives alone in his hall now that his brothers have left, so report my ravens, Hugin and Munin, who watch from the fir trees that surround the hall."

Nidud stroked the long dark hairs on his chin, nodding slowly as he searched his memory. "Yes, I do know of him. The tale of his loss to Sindri for a challenge in which you yourself were a judge is well known. Why concern yourself with a second-rate smith? What possible danger can he hold?"

A sour expression crossed Odin's face. "Yes, there was a contest arranged by Loki." He snorted in disgust. "Yes, Volund lost, but only just. That did not diminish his ability in any way. Oh no. In fact, it made him dangerous." In the hearth, a log collapsed amid a swirl of angry sparks that billowed outward before fleeing up the chimney. "He removed himself to the remote land of the Wolfdales. There he has bent his skill to crafting a weapon of unimaginable power. It must be captured at all costs, for should it ever be used to its full potential it will be the death of everyone and everything."

Levering himself from his seat, Nidud moved to stand before the hearth fire. He tossed a handful of kindling onto the coals, stared unblinking as they smoked a moment before bursting into flames. Several times he turned to speak, but each time stopped and returned his gaze to the hungry fire.

Finally, he turned to face Odin. "I obey you in all things, such are the oaths I have freely given. You set before me a dangerous task. Not only is the journey itself fraught with peril, but I doubt the smith will willingly give over his weapon. If he is as dangerous as you claim, it will take subtleness and craft to overcome him. I do not dare a direct confrontation."

Grinning, Nidud thumped his chest; three times he thumped his chest, so the room echoed with its sound. "This is a mission I willingly accept, but my men and, of course, my queen will expect recompense for the hazards that must be faced."

Odin turned a shrewd eye on the gold-eager king. He nodded, a slight smile twitching the corners of his lips. "Your efforts in this matter will be more than adequately rewarded by the wealth gathered in Volund's smithy, and the wondrous works crafted by his hand that are certain to be about."

Eye burning, he gave a stern warning of caution. "Take from his home whatever you want. Just remember, the blade at his side must be captured at all costs. Lock it away as soon as it is yours. I'll not remind you again of the deadly consequences to all should the weapon ever be used."

———————

Eager to plunder the wares of a master smith, Nidud gathered up his troops, and with sharp commands drove them deep into the Wolfdales. Cloaked in evening shadows, they approached the hall, voices hushed, footsteps muffled, shield edges glinting in the light of a waning moon. Dismounting beneath the eaves of Volund's hall, at Nidud's command they rushed through the doorways hoping to surprise the occupant. Warriors dashed about searching the hall, but the smith was nowhere to be found. Banked coals and warm hearthstones warned of his imminent return.

Hungry for the promise of easy spoils, Nidud's men took advantage of the Wonder Smith's absence to loot the hall. Rummaging through its side rooms, they scooped up treasures of astounding designs, tucking them away in sacks, even secreting some inside their vests. Hanging from a thick beam over the hearth, they found seven hundred gold rings strung together on a bast rope. Nidud untied them from their tether. He carefully examined each one before returning them to their moorings, all except for the bejeweled master ring; that he stashed securely in his pocket.

He barked orders to his troops to hide their horses in the nearby forest and keep them quiet. "Clamp your hands over their noses and muffle their feet with your robes. There must be no snorting, no whinnying, no stamping of hooves; no sound at all save the wind through the trees. We set a trap for a clever beast. Should he suspect anything, our quarry will bolt back into the woodland. Once in its shadows, we will never find him or his weapon. He knows this area far too well."

Armed men were concealed about the hall, some huddled inside behind entryways, some in shadowy niches along the outside walls. "We will wait until the smith returns. I'm certain he is not far."

Along twilight paths the smith puffed home through the cold; the necessity of food had driven him to hunt the forest. Stumbling over the threshold, he swung off his pack, its bottom dripping with the bloody flesh of a stag and set it inside the doorway. He dragged a heavy cloak from his broad shoulders, shook it free of snow, then pushed it onto a peg beside the entrance. The cloak dangled a moment before slipping from its support and crumpling into a heap on the floor. Volund stared at the fallen cloak, started to turn away, then turned back and picked it up. With a weary sigh, he hung it back on the peg before shuffling into the main hall.

He paused, listening to the stillness of the hall. The hiss of air drawn up the chimney followed the rumble of wind pushing against the walls that made the beams creak. Taking a deep breath, Volund crouched before the hearthstone. Using an iron poker of his own make, he dragged open the banked coals, so they flushed in the drawn air. Slowly, a handful at a time, he kindled a hot fire with branches of dry fir taken from the ready pile alongside the hearth. With each limb, the flames leapt higher, driving the shadows back into the corners of the room.

In the flickering light, he took the string of gold rings down from over the hearth. Chanting words low and barely audible, he kept cadence with the winds gusting outside the hall. One by one he counted out the rings, stacking them in neat towers on a bearskin before the fire. On finding the master ring missing, he glanced around, thinking his swan maiden had returned. Three times he called out her name but received only silence in reply.

The Wonder Smith hunched a long while before the fire staring deep into the dancing flames, his ears pricked for sounds of her footfalls. He started at a sound from the shadows, but quickly settled back into his reverie as heat from the fire soothed muscles weary from travel, lulling him into a deep sleep.

Volund awoke in great discomfort, his limbs twisted as if from a fitful dream. The fire had dwindled to a small knot of coals surrounded by gray ash. Heavy ropes bound him hand and foot, weighing down his limbs so he could not move. Tugging furiously at the ropes, Volund shouted out to the darkness. "Who are the bold warriors that would bind me in my sleep? Come, show me your daring faces that I might look upon such bravery."

Nidud slid from his hiding place, a shadow amid shadows. Stepping around the captive, he approached the hearth and tossed a handful of kindling onto the blushing embers. A blaze leapt up among the stones, throwing his features into sharp relief.

He toed the rings stacked beside Volund. "Tell me smith, how you came by this gold so far removed in the Wolfdales. You must have taken it from elsewhere for I have never heard of such treasure in these hills. Only south in the land of the Njara are there stories of such a hoard."

Volund grunted as he twisted around onto his side. He stared evenly into Nidud's eyes. "This gold is not part of Fafnir's hoard. It would be a fool's effort to carry it from the warm summers of Gnita-heath, even were Grani's broad back available to haul the load. This is wealth made by my own hand, for my own purpose. It is considered a great treasure by many, but I tell you now this hall knew greater riches when my brothers and our swans were safe within its walls."

Nidud snorted at Volund's reply. With sharp gestures, he directed his men to scour the hall for more treasure. "Collect the tools from the smith's forge," he nudged Volund with his foot, "and gather up the prisoner. We return to Saevarstadir, the great hall of the Njara."

———— · ————

The furious smith was dragged into the hall of Nidud, his hands bound before him, his ankles hobbled with a heavy rope. Driven by sharp blows, Volund staggered to a stop, unbowed before the king and his household. Nidud's daughter Bodvild sat to his left, his two young sons to his right.

Rising to his feet, with deliberate care Nidud drew a gold ring from an inside pocket of his vest; the master ring he had taken from Volund's bast rope. He spun the ornament in his hand, so its jewels caught fire in the hearth light. Holding it out at arm's length, he turned it side to side; all eyes sparkled in awe of its splendor. "Such beauty belongs on the arm of youth." The queen arrived as he made a great show of slipping the ring onto his daughter's arm.

Nidud smiled when Sinmara entered the room. The queen wrinkled her nose as she edged by the smith. Volund glared at her as she passed, then returned his attention to the ring on Bodvild's arm and the sword hanging at Nidud's waist. A heavy groan escaped the prisoner's lips. "Bodvild wears the red gold ring," he cried out, "the one I had meant for my swan bride. From Nidud's belt hangs the sword crafted by my own hands, tempered for my own ends. Now all are carried forever from me and I shall receive no compensation for their loss but what I can take by my own craft."

The queen took her seat beside Nidud, fluffed her robes for comfort, then spoke low for the king's ear. "This one has the manner of a wild forest beast. His eyes shine bright with malice. See how he rages. Even bound he threatens his betters. I fear it will be impossible to hold him unless we permanently hobble his strength. Be quick, my king. Drive the tip of a sharp knife deep into the flesh behind his knees. Cut the tendons to stop the might of his sinews."

At a nod from the king, his retainers grabbed the smith. A blade flashed, and the prisoner screamed in pain. As Volund lay gasping on the floor, Nidud leaned back regally in his seat. "Do not think we give no thought to the care or needs of our guests. We are not inhospitable in this hall." He waved an arm toward an open window, where the rumbling surf and shrieking of seabirds could be heard. "On an island near the shores of Saevarstadir we have set up a smithy for your enjoyment. The skilled hands of our best artisans built the forge. Why, we even furnished it with tools brought from your home. We spared no expense in its construction. You have all you need to continue making great works for the pleasure of your hosts."

Nidud clapped his hands. "Remove him my presence but treat him well. His new home awaits." Grabbing him beneath the arms, the retainers dragged the moaning smith out of the room. After they had exited through the entryway, Sinmara clapped her hands for a servant to wipe up the trail of blood that marked the floor.

After dressing his wounds, they took the prisoner by boat to the island. There he rested until the slashes healed. Armed men brought provisions, then left as soon as the task was done. None dared remain with the smith, even injured his presence was too powerful a force. Certainly, none dared visit alone, save the king, who often sculled the short distance to check on the comfort of his captive guest.

Volund wasted no time worrying about his legs. Quickly, he fashioned a harness of leather suspended from a pole that pivoted about the smithy. The contrivance freed him to move in any direction about the forge and among the work benches.

Taking little sleep, he quickly struck out a bitter river of clever items, intricate prizes of polished gold and silver for the delight of Nidud's household. They received high praise from all the court. There was scarce a robe or arm that did not sport some brilliant ornament of Volund's design.

The works captured the eyes of Nidud's sons, kindling a great desire in their hearts. Greedy to own such wealth, they asked to accompany their father when next he visited the smith.

On a day free of clouds, the horizon clear of haze, when the sea waves rolled smoothly before the hand of a gentle wind, the king's skiff touched down on a narrow dock that jutted out from the lonely island. Nidud and his sons marched along a rocky path that wound its way to the forge prison of Volund. The smithy squatted on a small rise perched well above the highest tidemark. Acrid yellow smoke belched from its chimney. Caught by sea breezes, the smoke spread to fill the air, stinging their eyes, and burning their throats.

Nidud stood outside the smithy door, fists planted firmly on his hips, and hollered out to the wonder worker within. His imperious voice demanded their presence be acknowledged. "Drag yourself away for the smithy fires, Volund. Open your door! You have guests! Nidud, King of the Njara demands admittance!"

Volund shouted from beside the forge, his eyes focused on the work before him. "I cannot stop you from entering. That privilege has been taken from me. But if you can wait, I will be with you in a moment. Let me bank my fires so my projects hold."

Turning to his sons, Nidud stared them evenly in the eyes to ensure they would understand his concern. "I need not remind you to touch nothing. A smithy is a dangerous place, and a devious mind can make it doubly so. Now be cautious and follow my lead."

Pushing open the heavy wooden door, Nidud crossed into the dim light of the smithy. His sons crowded close at his heels. As they jostled each other through the doorway, one reached out to stroke a golden object that lay uncovered on the nearest bench.

Volund floated before them, suspended by his harness in the thick air. He greeted his visitors with a silent nod, letting his eyes linger a moment on the two young men before turning his attention back to the king. "I see you no longer wear the blade you took from my side. Was it too sharp for one such as you to carry?"

Nidud smiled at the taunt. "I had the blade locked well away in a chest banded with hand-forged iron; the whole sealed shut with nine Njard-locks." He shook his head. "Never again will that blade see the light of day. We will speak no more of it."

Volund jigged a moment in his harness; keeping his eyes on the king but focusing his attention on the wandering hands of his sons. "Then what brings you to my prison? It is enough you pester me with your sudden visits, but now you bring children to disturb my work."

Grinning at Volund's discomfort, Nidud drew his sons around from behind to stand in front of him. "My sons are curious about what you do. Show them around your workplace, maybe display some of your skills at the forge."

A scowl twisted Volund's lips and deep furrows creased his brow. "I've too many things in the making to waste time performing for children."

The sons of Nidud shouted together, their voices shrill in the confines of the smithy. "We are not children!"

The one clutching his father's cuff poked out his head, shouting defiantly at the smith. "We have both come into our majority. Gladly we shoulder a man's responsibilities."

The other took a half-step forward to brace an arm across his brother's chest. "As men, we eagerly face dangers which any warrior might readily face."

Nidud laughed at their boldness. "My sons are of their own minds. You will find them ever eager and alert."

Volund rocked back in his harness. He cocked his head to one side, staring at the young men before him. "Then let me show you around. Touch nothing unless I say."

While Nidud examined the many works scattered about the benches, Volund led his sons around the smithy, showing them its workings, answering their questions. One of the young men reached toward a pot perched on a tripod of iron. "What's in here?"

Volund swayed around and slapped the young man's hand away before he could dip his finger into the pot. He barked a stern warning to the youth so that Nidud glanced around at the sounds. "What did I just say?" Clutching his hand as if wounded, the young man began a sniffling protest, but Volund growled over him. "That pot contains a powerful solution of lye. It is strong enough to eat the flesh from bones. Had you dipped your finger you would have quickly lost its use!"

He beckoned sharply for the two to follow as he swung around to the far side of the room. "Come over here. Mind your heads on the bellows. This is where I smelt metals."

Volund led the boys to the opposite side of the smithy, away from where Nidud stood beside the benches looking over works in progress. At the far side of the smithy they paused beside a chest. Great straps of iron wrapped its sides and a solid lock held it firmly shut. The sons of Nidud demanded the keys that they might see what lay inside.

The smith fumbled a key from around his neck, snapped it into the lock and heaved open the chest. The young men's breath hissed from between their teeth at the site of its glittering contents. Inside the chest, stacked nearly to the top, rested a cache of red gold worked into necklaces, silver brooches, jeweled arm rings, and incised buckles to charm the eye. Grinning wildly at one another, their eyes shining bright with avarice, they each dug a fistful of the precious works from the chest to shake before the other's face.

Volund watched the hunger build in their eyes. He spoke quietly to the young men as he softly closed the lid and relocked the chest. "I see by your actions you mean to have this for yourselves," he muttered. "That is well and good as I have not the means to spend it or the heart to desire it. Other than its value as a resource to draw on when creating my works, it is of little use to me."

He glanced back across the length of the smithy to ensure Nidud was otherwise occupied, then beckoned the young men nearer. With a low voice, he gave instructions. "In two days, return alone. When you arrive, I will give you the key to this wealth. It will take both your strength to carry off this treasure. Tell no one of your intent to visit—servants, parents, or siblings. Otherwise, I am certain, you will be forced to share this bounty." He leaned in, beckoning the boys closer. "It is more profitable for the strong-minded to act quickly with bold intent lest that which they most desire passes into the grasping hands of another." Volund inclined his head toward their father.

The brothers glanced at one another. Each knew the hunger that lay in the other's heart. With a sharp nod of their heads they silently agreed to the smith's plan.

Two days Volund spent in furious activity preparing the smithy for the arrival of Nidud's sons. With deft hands, he arranged everything to ensure their visit would run smoothly.

Early on the second morning, when Day had begun to lighten the sky, but before Sol crested the edge of the heavens, the brothers slipped through the hall gate whispering their plan to one another. "Let us go see the bright gold. We must collect our wealth and hide it before the hall fully awakes."

In a flat-bottomed skiff, the two sculled their way to the island where Volund waited. Ramming the boat onto the beach below the dock, they leapt ashore then rushed up to the smithy, pushing and shoving to see who would arrive first. Chests heaving, together they beat on the smithy door, loudly demanding the key to the treasure.

As Volund cracked the door, the two boys shouldered past him into the dimness of the smithy. Again, they demanded what he had promised. When the Wonder Smith fumbled the key from about his neck, they snatched it from his unresisting hand and raced to the chest behind the forge. While the two ran their hands over the treasure, Volund swung up silently behind the boys. They barely heard the whisper of a Regin-sharp blade slicing through the air before their heads tumbled from their shoulders.

Volund buried their bodies in a hole he had dug beneath the forge. Solemnly, he dipped his hands in a pool of their blood. "By my own hand," he smeared the bellows with their life dew to mark his deed, "I take recompense."

Their eyes he scooped from their sockets and set aside in a cup of seawater. Their teeth he pulled from their jaws and collected in a bowl to dry. Their heads he placed in a pot of strong lye, leaving them submerged until the flesh dissolved from the bones of the face. When the skulls were clean, he rinsed them well in seawater. With a serrated edge, he sawed off the skullcaps then scooped out the softness inside. He scrubbed them thoroughly in seawater before setting them inside the vent of his forge to dry.

Their skiff he set to sea to obscure the young men's path. With deft fingers, he strung a set of thin gold rings over the doorway. "While I can no longer bind the wind as I used to, I can still direct the sea breeze enough to push their empty skiff into the swift currents that run away from this island."

As Sol drove her wain into the sky, Volund watched search parties scour the headland shore and ships set sail to search the nearby waters. When they came to his smithy asking questions, he growled at the searchers clustered outside the doorway, eyes staring at their shuffling feet. "I have not seen the whelps of the king! It is not my duty to watch them. I have seen nothing from my perch on this rock. The horizon remained clear all day long until you intruded on its edge. Now go! Return your hound noses to the sea! I have more important things to do than labor my jaws with underlings of the king."

He slammed the door, returning to his work, as the searchers rushed back to their boats, pushed out into the strong currents, and resumed their hunt of the coastline.

———————————

Once the skulls had dried from the forge's heat, Volund removed them from their niche. Using metal hammered into thin sheets, he layered their outside with silver and leafed their inside with gold. His lips twisted into an ugly smile as he meticulously crafted a pair of goblets that the Njara king might better enjoy his wine.

The boys' teeth he set into a pair of matching brooches. Polished and arranged in tasteful patterns, they lit up the room with their brightness. The delicate ornaments of worked silver and inlaid gold he sent to decorate the flowing robes of Bodvild.

Their treasure-hungry eyes he fashioned into exotic gems. With a jeweler's sense, he fastened two of them on chains. The others he mounted in rings of gold. These he sent to Sinmara, Nidud's queen, to enhance her maternal beauty.

The missing skiff was found a week later shattered against rocks along a dangerous stretch of coastline where breakers crashed against a crumbled cliff. Belongings from Nidud's sons—coats, a shirt, a hat—were found tucked beneath a bench seat. It was believed Ran had claimed the young men for her own.

Great were the laments that flowed from Nidud's hall as the king and queen collapsed sobbing into each other's arms. Their wails carried across the waters to mix with the sound of roaring surf.

In her room Bodvild paced the floor, eyes puffed red, tears trickling down her cheeks. In a fury of grief, she dashed her belongings to the floor, wrenched off the arm ring her father had given her and threw it hard against the far wall. On retrieving it from the floor, she found the ring bent with a gaping crack along one edge.

Sobering at the sight, she tucked the ring into her pocket. "Father and mother have grief enough. I'll not bother them with this. Only one has the skill to fix this ornament, the master smith kept on the nearby island. Few dare his presence alone, but I am my father's daughter. He does not fear the smith. Nor do I."

Appropriating a skiff from the main pier, Bodvild sculled to the island. Tying off at the island dock, she made her way along the islet path to the forge nestled atop the hill. A feeble stream of smoke curled from a chimney that canted up through the center of the roof. The smithy door stood ajar to faint rustlings from within. Taking a deep breath, Bodvild marched across the threshold, loudly announcing her presence as she shoved through the door.

Her hail interrupted Volund bent over a bench, busily working on a large pile of gold leaves. The smith jumped in his harness and hastily covered the project with a cloth. Breathing hard, he turned to confront his intruder. "What? Who?" Glaring at the maiden before him, Volund spat rough language to drive her away. "My legs are crippled, so I cannot escape this cursed rock. And you think that gives you the right to impose yourself on me. I don't need some skinny little bitch interrupting my morning. Go on! Get out of my workshop! Leave a man in peace!"

Bodvild rocked back at the buffeting string of curses. Frowning, the proud daughter of Nidud stood firm and refused to leave.

When Volund saw that she would not be deterred, he softened his tongue. "Alright," he gave a short nod, "what brings the beautiful Bodvild to my prison?" The young woman jerked in surprise at her spoken name. "Yes, I know who you are. I am surprised you have no escort." The smith peered around her shoulder to the empty doorway. "Does your father know you are here?"

Bodvild lifted her chin as she looked the smith directly in the eyes. "Only my handmaiden and the dock master know I've come to visit you. Both are sworn to secrecy, by oath to me."

Reaching into her apron pocket, she withdrew the broken ring. "I've come for this. It is the most wondrous of works. I have seen nothing like it before. My father gave it to me the day you arrived at our hall. I broke it in a fit of grief over the loss of my brothers. The delight it gave me is gone now that it is damaged. It is so finely crafted I dare not have another work on it. Can you fix it?"

Volund started when he saw the ring. He held his breath and reached out to take gently it from her hand. Running his fingers around the outside of the bent metal, he felt them catch at the uneven break. The image of a white swan rose before his eyes. "I can repair the damage. It will be as if it never left your arm."

The smith swallowed hard before turning away to brace himself over the bench. "Return in two days," he called over his shoulder. "I will have it ready then. You had best come alone to retrieve the ring, or your father is certain to take back that which he freely bestowed upon you."

After two nights' sleep Bodvild returned to Volund's smithy. When Day had brightened the morning sky, but before Sol had crested the horizon, she snuck out of her father's hall and sculled the short distance to the island. The voyage, though brief, was lonely. A heavy mist swirling from the water's surface dampened her clothes and chilled her skin. When the skiff finally bumped the dock, Bodvild dropped her pole, snatched up the bow rope, and leapt briskly ashore. With a few quick turns, she hitched the skiff fast to the pier.

The plaintive call of a seabird sounded from somewhere down the beach. Bodvild squinted the length of the empty pier, ignoring the lonely cry. Drifting curtains of mist flowed along the shore, thinning a moment to show waves lapping against rocks, then thickening to obscure her feet as she made her way toward the pilings that marked the worn path to the smithy. Shivering, arms hugging her chest, Bodvild stumbled along the dirt path to the smithy on the hill. She knuckled the door but was unable to announce herself through the chattering of her teeth.

Volund swept open the door, eyes squinted at his early morning visitor. Long locks of limp, dark hair framed Bodvild's face, made pale and clammy by the mist. The robe draped about her shoulders steamed lightly and violent tremors shook her frame.

With a curt wave, he bid her enter then closed the door against the cold as she stumbled to a seat at bench alongside his table. The smith poured out two mugs of strong ale, quenched a red-hot poker in each before passing one to Bodvild. "It is a chilly morning for open travel by water. The sea fog can strip the heat from a body before the sun rises enough to ward off death. This drink will return warmth to your cheeks."

Bodvild gulped the brew, felt its heat spread out from her center and still the shivering that quaked her limbs. She downed half the drink, took a deep breath to compose herself, and then patted a sleeve against her lips before turning her attention to the smith. "It has been two nights. Have you repaired the ring?"

Pulling the red gold ring from his smock pocket, Volund placed it in Bodvild's hand. Her eyes sparkled as she held the ring to the forge light and gently ran her fingers around the edge. Nowhere could the break be seen or felt.

The smith drained his ale, cleared his throat, and slowly refilled his mug. "Do you know the history of that ring?" He reached over to table to top off Bodvild's cup.

Bodvild shook her head as she took a deep drink. "That," Volund pointed a finger at the ring, "was crafted by my own hand. Not only am I its mender, but its creator as well. I had made it to grace the arm of my beloved," a wistful smile flickered his lips, "she who I would have had as wife. Your father intervened before she returned.

I was captured, and the betrothal ring taken before I could present it to her."

The young woman started at his words, began to utter sincere apologies, but Volund waved his hand. "Do not worry that I desire its return." He topped off their mugs. "That time is long past. I doubt I will ever see my swan maiden again. Know that you are fully her equal in beauty. The ring shines as brightly on your arm as it would have from hers. It gladdens my heart to see it enhance such loveliness."

Bodvild blushed at the complement. Taking up her mug, she gulped down the bitter ale. Volund poured her another drink, offered up a toast to her beauty, then another to her family's grief. In this way they spent the time until, overcome with the strong drink, Bodvild sank into her arms and fell asleep.

Volund watched her a moment, letting his gaze roam the length of her body, then wiped his mouth on his sleeve and swung around to her side. "All injuries" he muttered gathering up the young woman, "must be repaid in full." Floating over to his pallet, he gently lay her down on the rough tick.

When the rays of Sol flared over the edge of ocean, burning away the sea mists, Bodvild awoke, her head throbbing with a dull ache, her dress hiked up about her waist. The young woman, understanding what had happened, buried her face in her hands and began to weep.

Volund sang out from across the room, his strong, cheerful voice blaring in the maiden's ears as he buckled on a cape of metal feathers. "You have no need to weep over events done. The shame does not reside with you, but with your parents, for it is by their actions this transpired."

Wrestling a leather strap around his chest, he wound it about his arms before cinching it tight at his shoulders. "And give no thought to their wrath. As I contrived revenge against those who wronged me, so, too will I protect the one who now bears my child. Return to your father's home. Wait there for his call. Know that you will not receive harsh treatment from his or anyone's hand."

"And now..." Volund waddled out the smithy door. Flexing his arms to spread wide the wings of his bronze cloak, he caught the stiff breeze that blew in from the sea and lofted into the air. He called down as he rose higher with each beat of the metal wings. "Long I labored in secret to design my escape, building this cape from remainders while I produced trinkets for Nidud. Little did he miss the bits and pieces, provided there were larger works to dazzle the eyes."

Still weeping, Bodvild watched as Volund circled into the sky. Head hanging low, hot tears coursing down her cheeks, she trudged to her skiff, climbed in, and sculled slowly for home. A soft whimper escaped her lips as she thought of facing her father's fury when he discovered the liberties the smith had taken.

———————

Volund circled the hall of Nidud, a large bird of prey flashing in the sky against the morning sun. He spotted Sinmara in the courtyard as she stood outside greeting the day. He watched as she walked along an open hallway. When she slipped into a side chamber, he settled down on a nearby wall. "Day sends his mother to rest while Sol begins her climb across the sky. Arise Nidud, lord of this hall. There is much we have to discuss."

A weak voice replied from Nidud's chamber. "That voice which calls me to rise, I recognize its tone, its timbre. Hearing it close to my chamber bodes ill. Know Volund, for I am certain it is you, these days find me always awake. I've little desire for the dreams that plague my sleep. With my sons swallowed by the great ocean, food and drink are ashes in my mouth. All joy is wrung from my heart."

Laughing delightedly from his perch, Volund called out cheerfully to the king. "Then I may have news of their fate that you will find of use."

Nidud stumbled to the doorway. Bracing himself against the frame, he squinted into the morning light at an eagle shape perched on the wall. The face of Volund grinned from amid a halo of bright golden feathers. The king cried out from beside the doorjamb, his voice forced from a raw throat, his stomach knotted with fear. "Tell me," he demanded. Tell me what you know of my sons!"

Volund fluttered a wing, filling the air with a gentle rasping as the metal feathers folded back into place. "Before I share that information," he shook his head, "you will give me your oath on ring, on cup, on shield rim, and on blade edge that you will not harm my lady. I will have your word that you will protect her life and any life she carries as you would protect your own. For my bride is well known to you, freely given to me by your hand on the day I arrived with the pledge of a betrothal ring. She bears my child within your hall."

Nidud choked, attempted to speak, failed, and then tried again. "What? Who here? Do you mean..? How dare you!"

Volund grinned, the feathers surrounding his face rattling in a light breeze that rolled over the wall. "What is done cannot be undone— the pledge or the deed. For the knowledge that I hold of your sons, I will have your binding oath."

Nidud wrung his hands, nodded once, twice, then with a deep sigh, began his vow. "For the knowledge that you hold regarding the fate of my sons, on ring, on cup, on shield rim, on blade edge, I freely pledge to protect from harm the lives of your lady and the child she bears as I protect my own life and that of my family. By the honor of my name all this I freely swear."

Satisfied, Volund lifted a wing, the long feathers gesturing to the sea. "Go to the smithy you built, the one raised on the desolate island. There under bellows stained with crusted blood you will find the bodies of your sons." The golden wing swung around to point at the hall. "For their heads, look no further than your own table at the skull mugs, gilded with silver, from which you liberally drink each day. To bask again in their youthful gaze, seek out the jewels that adorn the neck and grace the fingers of your queen. To see their bright smiles, light up the room, look to the brooches that hang from the robes of Bodvild."

A deep sob hiccupped Nidud's chest as he gripped tight to the doorjamb to keep from collapsing. "Now, know that your only daughter carries my child, a granddaughter to grace your hall. Name her Skadi, for she is born of harm and damage." With those words, Volund spread wide the golden wings of his cloak, caught the breeze that rose over the wall, and spiraled gracefully into the sky.

Nidud wailed loudly at the smith's speech. "Your words cut deep a heart that once beat with joy, but now aches only with sorrow. Never could I wish worse on another." He shook a fist at the retreating form flashing in the sunlight. "I was a fool to make you my prisoner, for in truth then I became your captive. In my hall, there is nothing strong enough to hold you, all fetters you would eventually break, even the might of muscle you would overcome. Nor is there one skillful enough in my húskarlar to strike you down with a far-flung arrow there where you hover against the clouds."

Nidud turned his weary face from the image that dwindled to a speck in the sky, his eyes puffed red from a constant flow of tears. "You there, Thakkrad, the most trusted of my slaves, tell my daughter to attend my presence."

Bodvild arrived as commanded before Nidud, dressed in a flowing robe of white lace. She kneeled at her father's feet, her head bent low to hear his judgment. Nidud stepped down from his seat, raised his daughter's chin with a gentle hand. "Is what the smith said the truth, that he lay with you on the island," he choked a moment as the muscles of his jaw began to jump, "that you now carry his child?"

The trembling maiden replied to her father, tears coursing down her cheeks as she spoke, lips quivering with each word. "Volund spoke the truth. Bold as a daughter of the Njara should be, I went alone to the island prison to retrieve an ornament repaired by the smith. Overcome by strong drink offered at his table, I could not strive against him. I do not know, but it is possible I now carry his child."

The queen began a sharp rebuke, her voice pitched to a shrill whine that was silenced by Nidud's raised hand. He glared at his daughter. As the anger of a dishonored father welled up in his breast, the taunting laughter of the smith echoed in his mind and he recalled the oaths freely given to protect child and mother. He raised a hand to cover his eyes, took a deep breath, and then dropped his clenched fist to his side.

Lifting his chin high, Nidud scanned the room, gazing deep into the eyes of those gathered there. "The moment we took Volund captive, bound him with his own ropes, relieved him of his treasures, and crippled him so he could not run, it was that very moment we fell under his power. His is the nature of vengeance crafted with as much skill as was his on the forge. Innocent of such patient cunning, how could any of us hope to stand against him?"

He reached out to his daughter, grasped her shaking fingers, and gently guided her to her feet. "The ring on your arm, the one I gave you, know that it once belonged to him. Let me have it now. I will lock it away with his terrible blade that we might hide the enticements of Volund and perhaps, in time, forget the pain he brought to our house."

The Taking of Groa

The wife of Orvandel fell on difficult times when her husband followed his brothers into the cold land of the Wolfdales. Alone, she found herself the desire of a King, a bold, impetuous man for whom desire was action. Halfdan, a king among men, favored by the Æsir gods, learned of the flight of Ivalde's sons and that Groa remained behind in the family hall under the protection of her aged father, Sigtryg. Word had come to him of Groa's timeless beauty and, in hushed tones, of her powerful skills. The more he heard, the greater grew his desire to possess that which once a great warrior held dear and by possessing raise himself in esteem.

Warm winds of an early spring blew across the hills melting snows and encouraging new growth when Halfdan called to his side a diviner skilled in seeing that which clouded the vision of others. He stated his bold plan to take for his own the woman left behind. With booming voice, he commanded the diviner to look ahead, to spy out that which he might need know to crown his endeavor with success.

Runes stained red she cast on a clean white cloth that the gray curtains of tomorrow be parted. Before her eyes rested Thurzaz—the glyph of Thor's protective hammer and the vexing thorn—to guide Halfdan along the way. The diviner cleared her throat, carefully choosing her words that the king might understand. "Success in any endeavor falls to the one prepared and willing to navigate a thorny path. To accomplish your grand desires, you must boldly defeat a valiant warrior, one fated to survive all weapons save the bright metal of Freyja. For only with gold can he be conquered."

The great king thumped his chest. "It is a challenge I readily accept."

The diviner raised a cautionary finger. "There is more. When at the brink of success, as that which you desire stands before you, be careful how you grasp the prize. For while a stem firmly pinched between fingers will avoid the thorn, the overeager hand that grasps without thought will be impaled. Such unexpected pain makes for hasty action."

Halfdan pondered the hidden secrets of the diviner's words. Inspired with boldness, he turned his warrior hand to the task. With fixed purpose, he crafted a mace of gnarled oak that had been baked to hardness over a low fire. Using a drawknife, he shaped its length to balance in his hand. To its head, he fixed a knob of gold.

In his strong right hand, he hefted the dreadful weapon. "With this I will claim victory." Across his broad shoulders, he draped tanned goatskins. His waist and legs he swathed in the hides of woodland beasts. Clothed in this bestial finery, Halfdan journeyed along wet ways where cold, damp wind chilled exposed skin. Glad he was of the hide's protection as he scraped by the thick boles of stately firs lining forest paths.

He cautiously approached a high hill. From this vantage, the hall of Orvandel overlooked the bend of a wide, untamed river. For the next two days, he watched the hall while deciding his next move. Always the low, steady roar of rushing waters sounded above the wind. In a forest glade below the hill, he hid amid bushes bordering two shallow pools scooped out of the earth, their sides and bottom lined with rocks for bathing.

When Day had sent his mother to rest, Groa emerged from the high hall. Stepping outside the gate, she scanned the countryside for any sign that Orvandel had turned back. A steady breeze, chilled by the Ifing, stirred the long, golden locks about her shoulders as she gazed out across a still landscape. The horizon empty of movement, she sighed deeply, drew her robe tight against the brisk air, and slowly made her way to the bathing pools to perform her morning ritual.

In the shadows beside the pools she spied a fur-clad warrior hunkered in the brush. She stepped forward to confront the intruder. "Who are you that darkens my path? I know you to be a man, but of what kind I am uncertain. Often rabid warriors skulk about in the skins of beasts."

Halfdan slid from the shadows into the light. "Call me Halfdan, for I am brave in battle." His massive fist thumped against his chest until the forest glade echoed with its beat. "I bend my knee to no one save the gods. Often I have drenched my greaves wading through the bright red blood of stalwart foes." He pointed his mace up the hill toward the hall. "Tell me if you can of the one called Groa, wife of the valiant archer Orvandel known by all to have left this land for the cold embrace of the Wolfdales. She is said to sit alone in this hall with only an old man to protect her. I have traveled far to make her my own."

Lifting her chin, Groa looked down her nose at the warrior who swaggered beside the pool. She replied to his arrogance with a clear calm voice. "I am Groa, wife of Orvandel. Know that I stand before you unafraid. My father is Sigtryg, a noble warrior long-familiar with the ways of battle. Many foes have fallen by his hand, his gleaming byrnie stained red with their blood. He resides in my hall as defender of my honor. His battle prowess is so great, the Norns have fated that he will never be defeated by the weapons of a lesser foe. Return to the safety of your own lands or he will leave your battered, lifeless body to the relentless beaks of greedy ravens."

Halfdan laughed and swung his mace in a wide arc. The breeze of its passage swept the hair back from Groa's face. A golden flash winked from its head as it slipped through a shaft of sunlight that pierced the canopy of overhanging trees. "Since I do not fear the bold and mighty, why should I fear the ancient and infirm? Know that long before I fall in death, your father will lead the way. When I have finished with him, you will accompany me to my hall."

Halfdan's words sent a sharp chill shooting up Groa's spine. She cried so loudly for protection that startled ravens lifted from the trees, filling the air with shrieks of alarm. At the sound, Sigtryg burst through the hall doors, casting about for his daughter. In his hand, he held a long, sharp blade. Draped over spare shoulders, the polished iron rings of a byrnie jingled loosely about his once-broad chest.

Again, Groa called out for help, bringing Sigtryg dashing down the hill, his feet flying across the heath to where his daughter stood beside the forest pools. With a practiced glance the battle-scarred warrior assessed the situation as he burst into the clearing. Without a word, he raised his blade and rushed the fur-clad menace. The two fought back and forth across the glade, splashing through the pools, churning the ground to mud. The sound of metal rang against fire-hard oak as a raging torrent of fierce blows rained from the prosperous mace of Halfdan to beat back the ready blade of Sigtryg.

Chill winds rustled through the tree limbs as the golden club flashed down onto the shoulder of Groa's aged father. The old warrior grunted in pain as his blade slipped from his now useless hand. Teeth gritted, he bent over to retrieve the blade from the muddy ground with his good hand. Sigtryg's fingers had just touched the handle, when Halfdan, crying out in triumph, brought down his mace on the crest of the warrior's head. With a dull crunch, the golden knob buried itself in the nest of gray hair. Blood gushed down to fill the lines of Sigtryg's face.

Chest heaving, Halfdan grinned up at Groa. "And so, I conquer with my mace of gold, he who the fates forbid to fall beneath any lesser substance. Now the prize is mine to take."

———— . ————

Halfdan brought the reluctant Groa to the promise of his windswept hall and there enjoyed the fruit of his victory. He was delighted with the beauty of his new consort, but much annoyed by her refusal to wield her skills for his advancement. Often, he commanded her to use her power to increase his greatness. Always she refused his order saying he was better served using the strength of his own hand to achieve the glory he desired.

Furious at each rebuff of his will, he would toss her upon his bed. "In this," his harsh voice whispered in her ear, "I will brook no refusal."

After several months, a pronounced swelling beneath her robes gave notice to the king that Groa was with child. Elated at the news and unable to contain his joy, Halfdan called for a feast in celebration. Many guests of royal blood were invited to join in the festivities. Among those who arrived was Sumbul, king of the Skridfinns, an old foe now in tenuous alliance, accompanied by his lovely daughter Sygne. When Halfdan's gaze first fell upon the young maiden, her beauty struck him, brilliant as a flash of lightning filling the evening sky. A gentle smile from the young woman quickened his heart and confused his mind. Swallowing hard, he struggled to turn his attention back to the guests celebrating in the great hall.

Gayety and laughter filled the air. Animated conversation rang from every bench. Once the revelry had reached a riotous mood, Halfdan rapped his knife handle on the tabletop for attention, then lifted his cup in toast. "I call all gathered here to raise your cups. Today we celebrate the imminent arrival of my child. Be it son or daughter, the child will share the boldness of my line and, in the fullness of time, inherit all that I hold."

He turned, cup lifted high, taking in the entire gathering. "To the future king... or queen." Halfdan winked at Sygne. He laughed as the maiden blushed and all joined in his merriment. Only Groa remained silent, staring straight ahead, knuckles white on her clenched goblet.

When everyone had drunk to his announcement, Groa stood before the gathered guests, shaking her robes straight, waiting until she had their attention. Once the sweep of their eyes settled on her, she let the tone of her voice cut through the gaiety. "It is right for the king to honor the birth of this child which grows within me. For he... yes, I know it to be a boy... is the son of an honorable warrior, undefeated in battle."

Halfdan puffed out his chest, beaming at all of his guests. Taking a large draught from his cup, he waved his hand at Groa to be seated. But the brave woman, daughter of an honorable line that never flinched in fear nor shied from the truth, remained standing and continued to speak. "Know that I bear the son of Orvandel, he who long ago took me as wife." She glared into the eyes of Halfdan, holding his gaze as a viper freezes the rodent it is ready to devour. Her every word was a barbed dart that made his heart leap in agony. "Together we lived a rich full life; not this half-life I am forced to endure with another."

Halfdan's fist crashed onto the table sending bowls and cutlery clattering to the floor. His voice boomed through the hall. All the guests drew back into their seats, their conversation silenced by his outburst. "Be silent woman! Know this, if nothing else is clear... I won you when I crushed the skull of Sigtryg in harsh battle beside the forest pools. You are mine to do with as I please. Your life and that of your unborn son I hold in my hands." He held up his hands, flexing his fingers. Groa looked down her nose unafraid. "Though your vile words shame me before this gathering, I who have often sated my thirsty blade on the blood of worthy foes will not degrade my honor by putting a pregnant woman to death. But I will never raise the son of another in this hall. Such an obligation I will never accept. For I stand as high above the father as a mountain stands above the plain— proud and indomitable. It is through this higher honor that I send you away to fend in the forest where first we met. Let the elements and beasts of the wood decide your fate."

Halfdan leaned back in his seat, beckoning the captain of his guard close. "Waste no time, take her from my hall. Discard her in the heavy wood that borders her lands."

Once the good woman was led away, he rapped his knife handle on the table and called for more drink to be brought. Lifting his goblet high in salute, he bid his guests lift theirs. "You were all invited to a celebration. Let us celebrate." As Halfdan took a draught from the depths of his cup, his eyes turned to Sygne and his heart smiled.

The Birth of Svipdag

In the land of Midgard, a child was born, one destined to challenge the gods, to become their greatest foe, and their most stalwart supporter. Groa screamed from the labor stanchion, hands clenched on the supports, sweat streaming from her golden brow, as her son emerged into the dawn light. Drawing his first breath of air, the child issued a deafening squall to announce his arrival. Svipdag, she called him, he whose face shines like the day.

Groa snuggled his bloody body close to her breast, his head tucked beneath her chin. With a soft voice, she whispered counsel to young ears that still rang from his own cries. "Always, I will hold you dear. You can forever rely on my skills to protect you in times of need."

Three maidens came from the west, the Norns carried by the winds, to visit the newborn son. Gathering around the birthing bed at the three points of being, they drew out the strands of the child's life before his young eyes. One strand they securely fastened in the north, one in the south, a third in the east. But when they sought to fasten the final strand in the west, the threads parted and slipped from their fingers. Quickly, they repaired the break then refastened the strand in the west, where it held firm to its mooring.

Together they spoke to the tired mother, their words as one thought, their voices calm.

Spoke the youngest, "You know good woman..."

Spoke the matron, "the meaning of what we do..."

Spoke the eldest, "and the significance of what you have seen?"

Groa gazed at the Norns with a steady eye, nodding lightly at their words as she cleared her throat. "I well understand what I have seen and what it portends for my son. I am glad to see the broken thread refastened."

With a sharp glance among themselves, the Norns ducked their heads through the door, leaving the exhausted mother cuddled with her son on the bed.

———————

Svipdag grew as a leak among the fresh shoots of spring grass, a sturdy reed waving high amid the rushes. Long-legged, with wide, well-muscled shoulders. A handsome, cheerful face framed by thick, black hair. Groa watched as he developed into a young man; each day pride swelling in her breast. Saw him walk, run, then master the mount. Laughed with delight at his every action and celebrated his every success. She was so pleased by her son that she wished the days would never end.

Nine years passed before Orvandel returned. Footsore from the long road, he arrived in his hall to find himself father to a son he did not know. Orvandel stared hard at the boy, tears welling in his eyes as the features of Groa and Olrun swam before his vision, blending themselves into the child's face. The brave warrior grinned wide, his booming laugh echoing through the hall. Wrapping sturdy arms about the boy, he drew him tight to his chest while tears of joy coursed down his cheeks.

Groa smiled as Orvandel struggled to make up for lost time. With bow and blade, he trained his newfound son in the ways of an honorable warrior. Through word and by deed, he instructed him in the duties of a reliable man. As they worked together, the two grew close, with admiration and mutual respect cementing a bond of love.

In the year before his majority Groa called Svipdag to her bedside. Long she had used her skills to hold close the strings of her life that she might remain in the world and see him grow to manhood. Now, in sickness, she lay weary on her bed, her once-great skills expended, her feet firmly planted on the western path.

Svipdag edged close to the sick bed, hands clenched at his sides, fighting to still the quivering of his lips. Groa took his hand and bid him join her. "You sit beside me bright as the day, as brilliant to me now as when you first arrived in my life. Know that you come from a powerful line, knowledgeable in the ways of the world, respected for their experience with the weapons of battle. Their honor you inherit. Their skills are yours to wield. You are bound for greatness far beyond that achieved by any other man, of this I am certain."

Groa gasped as a sharp pain lanced through her body. She drew a ragged breath that shook her frame. "Remember, my shining boy," her trembling hand reached out to rest against her son's chest, "to always hold your destiny close that none may take it from you. And should you ever find yourself in need, though the sleep of death weighs heavy on my eyes, you have only to call upon me and I will reply." Svipdag caught her hand as it slipped from his breast.

Loud wails rang from the hall of Orvandel as the announcement was made that the mistress had died. Heads were dusted gray with ashes scraped from the hearth. Hair was left to hang free, the unfettered locks dangling unwashed. An older mare, one past her birthing prime, was sacrificed. Throughout the night the alfar were feasted with horseflesh while the household lamented their mistress' passing. When Sol crested the horizon, the ceremony done, Groa was prepared for her journey.

Calling on the aide of servants, Orvandel and Svipdag sat beside the cherished dead while Groa's body was prepared in the traditional way: her nose stopped with plugs of wool, her ears muffled with wads of flax fibers, her jaw bound closed with a light scarf tied off atop her head. They wrapped her in her finest robe, the edges clasped at her breasts with silver brooches. Sturdy, richly ornamented Hel-shoes were placed on her feet for the good woman's journey west. They oiled and brushed her hair until it shone a bright, pale yellow before swathing it in a blue kerchief edged with silver thread. With a sharp knife, they cleaned and trimmed her fingernails.

A hole was broken through the wall beside her deathbed. Careful not to bump, they carried her body through the rent. Praises were sung in honor of the good woman, the words carrying over the soft rumble of the Ifing, as they interred Groa's remains in a howe built of thick stone perched on a high hill that overlooked her home.

As the entrance stone was set in place, Orvandel took his son in his arms, grasping him close while grief spilled from his breast and great heaving sobs shook his shoulders. Svipdag dammed up his tears, holding back their flow until he could be alone. Keeping his lips firm, his features stern, he patted his father's back, supporting him until he could hold his head high.

Mani cycles though the heavens, counting the passage of years for men. When twice the Hastener showed his face from hidden to full and the pain of loss had faded from the depths of Orvandel's breast, the archer turned his face to life.

Heart empty, eyes clear, Svipdag looked on as his father took another wife to hold dear, Sygne, a young woman of gentle nature who held close the sanctity of family and wedlock.

A year after she had joined the household, Orvandel's new wife bore him a son, vigorous with a strong, lusty wail. They called him Ull for his head of woolly hair. His lean features sharp as the shaped yew, he grew swift like the leak that sprouts in early spring. He adored his older brother and trailed after him whenever he could.

Sygne watched with unease as her son chased after Svipdag, his legs a flurry as he struggled to keep pace with the long, sure strides of his older brother. Her brow peaked with worry, she drew Orvandel aside in private conversation. "Svipdag has become a bold man grown well into his majority. The fires of youth burn strong in his breast. If undirected, they will do great harm."

Orvandel listened with grave attention to his wife's concerns. "I often consider myself blessed to have a son as strong as Svipdag. Twice he delivered me from the wretchedness of despair. Once when I returned to my home heart-weary from a long absence. Then again when his mother passed away. He holds a dear place in my home. I would not have him fall into an errant life. We must give him a focus that will challenge his mind, capture his heart, and bring him the accolades of honor."

Together they decided on a plan. Calling Svipdag to the hall, they bid him take a seat at table that they might speak candidly with him. Orvandel took care with his words, speaking clearly that he not be misunderstood. "You come from a line of strong-minded warriors. But know that lineage is not enough. Honor and bravery, not birth, are the true signs of one's greatness.

Your life to now has been void of actions that can bring honor to the brave. For far too long I have sought to keep you safe from harm. This cannot continue. To persist in protecting you from bold action will create a false sense of pride and involve you in snarls of self-deceit. You must be allowed to prove your own worth with deeds performed by your own hand, for to each of us is given a sense—if we listen—that guides our way to right action."

Sygne reached across to squeeze her husband's hand in support. "I know of a great wrong that was done," he wrung his hands as his gaze shifted away from Svipdag's face, "the delivery of innocent children into the hands of lecherous etins. It is a misdeed that will take great courage to right."

Swallowing hard, Orvandel took deep breath to steady a sudden shaking in his breast. "This is a quest for a young man, to rescue a sister and brother from the icy clutches of foul-tempered giants. They are children of the Æsir. The boy is bright as the summer sun, brave, with an honorable nature. The girl is beauty beyond anything you have ever known, with a face to quicken the heart. If you accept this quest, it will bring you great honor, heal a long-standing stain of dishonor, and restore peace between once-great allies. Their powerful kin will be grateful. You can expect a great reward for their return."

Sygne leaned forward whispering soft, compelling words to the ear hands of the young warrior. "You must go abroad to the far ends of the world in search of the Menglödum—those fond of ornaments— and return them to their rightful place. Along wet ways where snow and piercing cold slow the journey to a crawl, you will find the two children held in the power of the great fimbul-winter. In a dark hall filled with evil smells, they are guarded by giants of rude disposition, whose shrieks can weaken the limbs of even the fiercest warrior. Unwelcome visitors are greeted with foul speech and the awful stench of their kind.

Their hall lies in a far-off country, difficult to find, hard to access. You must cross a great expanse of ocean where raging storm waves challenge daring sailors with death. The kin of the Menglödum have employed every stratagem at their disposal to locate the place where the captives are held. All their attempts failed."

Svipdag shook his head. He thumbed his cheek in thought, then spoke, his eyes sharp to match his words. "I know of the Æsir. The power they are said to wield is legendary. How is it you easily perceive that which they are unable to fathom?"

Orvandel raised a calming hand to interrupt the distrust that colored Svipdag's speech. "She can speak of such because I have told her. The house to be healed is our own." He struggled to keep his eyes focused on those of his son. "It was my brothers and I who committed the terrible deed. Ours is the dishonor you must rectify. It is the responsibility of our family."

Turning from his father, Svipdag stared deep into the fire roaring in the hearth. "This is not a task I willingly accept, for the dangers are far beyond any that I have ever encountered. Nor have I ever heard stories of such hazards recited by any hardened warrior. You have made it abundantly clear that the honor of our family is at stake. It is for you, father, and the memory of my birth mother, that I reluctantly accept this quest."

He picked up a stick of kindling that lay on the floor, slipping it slowly through his fingers as he spoke to the blushing coals. "You have also told me of a great beauty, one whose hand a warrior able to achieve that which the gods cannot, may, with right and honor, ask for his own. If her splendor is all you claim, and her clan as powerful as rumored, then I will be happier with such a union than a reward of silver for efforts expended."

Turning away from the fire, he looked unflinching at his stepmother until, growing uncomfortable with his stare, she took a sudden interest in examining her fingernails. "But there are other duties of honor that I am obliged to perform first, those called on by the blood of my grandfather and the harsh treatment of my birth mother at the hands of another. For great deeds are required of me before I can know myself worthy of such a highborn woman." His lips flashed a sharp smile that just as quickly disappeared. "Her lofty kin will demand such proof before considering me an honorable equal."

Svipdag tossed the kindling into the fire. He watched as it burst into flames, letting the bright light dance in his eyes before shoving himself to his feet. "Know that it is with such thoughts that I don my ring byrnie, take weapons from their rack, strap thick-soled boots to my feet, and slip a heavy traveling cloak over my shoulders."

Orvandel drew a hand across his face then stood up to move around the table. Lips set in a firm line, he approached his son, clasped his neck, and kissed his forehead. "He who holds must first discover. He who has discovered must first seek. He who has sought must first brave all impediments." The great archer found it difficult to control the pride and fear warring in his breast, but his heart held fast, and he kept secret his desire for the young warrior to stay. "Go forth my son and do what you must."

The Spells of Groa

Mani smiled from the night sky, lighting a winding path that snaked through the darkness up the hillside. Climbing to where Groa lay,

Svipdag stood quietly before the rocky mound of her howe. The stacked blocks reached above his head, reflecting the radiance of Mani's face into a silver barrow. A narrow recess cast in deep shadow concealed the limestone slab that sealed the mound's entrance.

Using a freshly cut hazel wand, its sap still dripping, he dug speech runes into the earth before the entryway to loosen a lifeless tongue. He drew a sharp blade across his forearm—a shallow cut to do no injury—then using two fingers, daubed the deep grooves with his own blood. About the spot, he poured mare's milk mixed with the labor of bees, a draught of strong ale brewed from grain harvested in the heat of summer, and cool, fresh water drawn from a nearby spring. Lastly, he sprinkled a handful of barley over the threshold, the white grains forming a shining path in the moonlight.

He called out three times to the wise woman who slumbered peacefully within. "Awake Groa, daughter of Sigtryg. Awake Groa, wife of Orvandel. Awake Groa, mother of Svipdag. Beside your howe, your son calls you to awake. The time is now to redeem the promise you made on your deathbed, to give aide should ever I need help. I stand here today in sore need of your aid."

Groa's voice stirred from the grave, a whisper on the wind that kissed his ear. "My son, what problem so weighs your heart that you call from the damp mold one who long ago left the living behind?"

Svipdag wrung his hands as he shuffled uneasily before the howe's limestone portal. He spoke sharply, his words hissing through clenched teeth. "My stepmother, the golden-haired Sygne, the one whose white arms now embrace my father, compels me to embark on a monumental task that even the gods have failed to accomplish. A cruel play has been laid before me, to journey to a place where none may go. There I am to rescue a brother and sister from the bitter grip of vicious etins. With gentle words, she stirred my desires while capturing my sense of duty until I cannot refuse. I long for one that cannot be possessed; Menglad is her name—one glad in her necklace."

Groa's voice rippled with a breeze that stirred the curls on Svipdag's head. "She bids you reach above yourself. The one who has captured your heart, the lover of ornaments is none other than Freyja, the daughter of Njord, a god of the sea. Far ahead I see through the mists that which the fates hold in store for a bold youth, a course set down for you at birth. The path before you is long, its turnings difficult. Great honor and true love will be yours if you can complete the journey."

His forehead resting against the entry stone, he spoke to the litr of his mother, his voice a whisper in the shadows. "Give me the wards promised in my youth, those that will ease my journey and protect me from harm. For I see great dangers along the path before me."

Groa's voice whispered from the darkness of the howe, its tones caught up amid the chirrups of insects calling out in the night. "Far ahead I see into the mists of time to where the greatest perils lie in wait. Nine spells I give to ward your journey.

As an infant taking his first steps, so, too, a youth embarking on a dangerous quest may doubt his balance. The first spell I chant to strengthen your resolve and inspire confidence in your own powers.

Brutal actions and harsh words are often the ways of strangers. The second spell I sing to lift your heart, though scorn and evil you encounter along the way.

Rime-cold rivers will bar your path. With the third spell, I part these raging waters that you may ford their treacherous embrace without fear of sickness, injury, or death.

The challenge of enemies you must face, a test of your courage and resolve, for in their power your life will stand. The fourth spell I speak gently to soften the hearts of foemen, turning their malice to goodwill.

When bound as a prisoner, with the fifth spell I endow your limbs with the power of Leifnir's fires to burst fetters.

Across the hall of Ran you will journey where towering waves and strong winds threaten your life. The sixth spell will calm stormy seas that you might swiftly cross their broad expanse in safety.

Over mountains you will travel—the high forested etin's way—and through regions of terrible cold. The seventh spell I utter to harden you against piercing arrows of murder frost. It will keep your limbs supple regardless the chill.

Through the lands of the dead you must pass. The eighth spell I chant to protect you against the coercion of the niflgódur, the damned dead, that you may not be led into folly.

In contests of wit, you will engage before your heart's desire can be fulfilled. With the ninth spell, I bestow a glib tongue when with haughty foes you endure a war of words.

On bedrock stone, I offer these nine spells. Let them ease your mind and speed your journey. Remember to remain patient. Hold always the view to a good outcome and the Norns will guide events to the right course. Now go." Svipdag strained his ears, desperate to hold onto the memory of his mother, as the whisper of her voice began to fade. "Be mindful of all I have spoken and let your life be fated with luck."

The Testing of Svipdag

Radiance burst across the sky, bolts of lightning arced cloud to cloud as high-mounted Valkyries, helmets shining, byrnies spattered with gore, charged from the field of fallen oaks. In their midst followed the chaff gleaned from the field of battle.

Across the blood-drenched ground stalked the victor. Halfdan, the glory-soaked king, stretched his arms wide to embrace the steaming field of battle. "We have fought well! Here we stand at the end of a hard day, like eagles on a snag overlooking the plain, unbowed on the field of valor, the corpses of our foes mounded high, our limbs weary from the sword storm. Great glory was won this day!"

Turning to his aide, he clapped a hand on the man's shoulders. "I would see those we have captured, the ones wounded or fallen from their own exertions. Keep the cowardly from my sight, those who tossed their weapons aside and begged for mercy at their foeman's knees. Let me see only the stern faces of the brave, those averse to flight with hearts hard as acorns, whose arms feasted on the fodder of ravens."

His aide inclined his head as he directed Halfdan to a group of brave warriors crusted in blood—their own and that of their foes. They sat together bound to a log, joined in a line by a bast rope looped about their necks. For long moments Halfdan raked his gaze over those who, only hours before, had sought to drive his troops from the field. Fierce eyes he saw; eyes that blazed defiance, even among the mortally wounded. None turned away from his gaze though roughly handled by their captors.

The king spoke loudly, so his voice would carry to all ears. "Let those with mortal wounds choose between swift death at the edge of a keen blade or to be cast back onto the battlefield where the pain of mortification and the relentless attention of ravens will mark their final time among men. Those unwounded and those whose wounds will heal, I offer a place under my banner. Hang any that refuse from the trees, their flesh offered as sport for birds."

Halfdan turned to leave, letting his Jarls treat with the prisoners, when he felt the hand of his aide draw him aside. He leaned in as the man bent close. The aide spoke softly so only the ear hands of the king might clasp his words. "There is one more. We have kept him separate from the others for fear his presence would brace their resolve, so formidable is his manner.

In the battle, he fought as a dragon among men. None could stand against the fierce strength of his arm. Nine of your best fell before his blade when he attacked your position on the field. It is through the chance of a hard-hurled stone that struck him senseless on the field that he now stands in our grasp. We have kept him over here bound hand and foot to a young oak, its sturdy roots knotted deep into the earth. Two guards have kept watch over him. If it is only the brave you ask to witness, then this is one you must see."

Boldly, Halfdan strode to face the warrior bound to the trunk of a sturdy oak. The young man stood unbowed, a full head above Halfdan, with broad shoulders to block the setting sun, his dark hair braided in a warrior's knot. His byrnie, heavily stained with the dew of battle, glinted in the fading sunlight, its links marred from the blows of numerous edges.

He held his chin high, glaring at Halfdan's approach. No words passed the captive's lips as the king stopped, crossed his arms, and looked him over. "What do I make of this warrior who stands bound before me? I have heard much of your prowess in battle. I admire such valorous actions. Tell me your name that I might recognize your line. Know I hold the power to release you or to keep you tethered to this tree, left to the tender mercies of the forest beasts who stalk the field when a battle is done."

The young man snorted. "I do not fear your decision," he squared his shoulders, "nor will I grovel to win your mercy! As for who I am, you know well the line of my kin. You took my grandfather's life when you stole my mother from her home, an honorable woman you tossed away to the very forest beasts you now use to threaten me." The warrior scowled at the king. "I am Svipdag, son of Orvandel—a bold fighter and skilled archer. My mother was Groa, a good and noble woman dishonored while held captive in your hall. My grandfather was Sigtryg, a brave warrior slain by your hand."

Halfdan stepped back at the young man's words. He carefully examined the youthful face, seeing the truth of Svipdag's claim in the color of his eyes, in the firm set of his jaw, all wrapped in the haughty pride of his mother. The king held a fist to his brow, stood a moment in silence, then slowly extended his hand to the young man. "I craved a son when I took your mother, one honorable, brave, and capable in battle. I see before me the son I might have won had I been more prudent of action.

For peace between our houses, take my hand and I will spare your life. I have never known a braver foe, one I would be honored to call son, to hold from this day forward in a bond of kinship. In my hall, you will have a seat equal to that of my blood sons. Never will you lack for anything that is within my power to give."

Svipdag laughed in the king's face. "I will never join with you or be at peace with your sons! There is bad blood between us," he spat at Halfdan's feet, "first drawn by your hand. Such wounds of honor will never heal."

Halfdan dropped his hand, stared hard at the young man, and then closed his eyes. "You are brave," he waved back the guards who had stepped menacingly forward at the prisoner's belligerent words, "I will allow you that, though rash with words and shortsighted in thought. For the actions of my past I cannot put you to death. But for the danger you present to myself and to my family I cannot let you live."

Halfdan leaned toward his aide, speaking loudly enough that those nearby would hear his command. "Leave him bound to this tree. Let his life be at the mercy of the elements and the hungry beasts of the forest. The guards are to remain on watch over him. They are not to interfere with anything that happens."

With those words Halfdan spun on his heel and stalked away. As he crested the nearby hill, the guards arranged their gear against a tree, then, ripping tufts from the ground, piled up a layer of grass to lay on. Comfortable, they leaned back, yawned hugely, and made ready for a long vigil.

Svipdag saw their weariness as they stretched out, noted the heaviness that threatened to close their eyes. He began speaking in a low, steady voice, keeping its timbre soft so it seemed the gentle murmur of a brook winding through the stillness of a forest glade. With endless tales of feats, real and imagined, Svipdag clasped the ear hands of his wardens. He held his voice to a droning whisper until a deep sleep overtook the guards.

When their first snores reached his ears, he felt the heat of Leifnir's fires rise within his frame and knew with certainty the spell of Groa was acting on his behalf. With a sharp twist, he easily snapped the now smoldering fetters that had held him bound to the young oak.

Careful not to wake the sleeping guards, Svipdag slipped a long blade from the side of the nearest, then helped himself to a heavy cloak that lay bunched near the other's feet. Staring at their bare necks, he fingered the blade, considering his next action. His lips firmed into the hard line of decision. Tucking the blade into his belt, he stole away into the nearby forest.

He trekked blindly into an unknown land, pushing his legs at a punishing pace to increase the distance from his captors. His wanderings took him through mountain passes and along steep, rocky trails that bruised his feet. In the confines of a dense forest, where the trunks of the trees crowded a narrow path, he encountered a brown giant of the wood, one wont to cover the bodies of its prey with a blanket of heavy brush.

The bear rose on its hind feet, roaring out to challenge the invader of its high mountain hall. Flashing its teeth, the bear spread wide its arms to enfold its foe in a crushing hug. Svipdag planted his feet at the challenge, drew his blade, and did not give trail. Heart storming, a battle cry burst from his breast. "Rauch-Else! Come meet your iron lover! I will not suffer your rough embrace!"

The foes crashed together with a roar to shake the trees, trampling the ground as they scuffled in a narrow circle. With a stout arm Svipdag strove against the angry beast. Swinging his blade free from the deadly grasp, he buried the naked iron in the bear's heart.

The animal's dying scream still echoed among the trees as Svipdag, raging with hunger, set his lips to the wound and drank the steaming blood that coursed from the valiant beast. Straight away, strength flowed into his limbs as the stout force of the bear spread through his frame.

Svipdag camped for several days beside the carcass, sating himself on the animal's flesh. After eating all he could hold, the bold warrior gathered up his gear and continued his journey.

A Fated Meeting

Svipdag traveled along winding narrow paths, treacherous to footing. He slipped through dark forests, wary should he encounter kin of Rauch-Else. In a narrow clearing that opened amid the trees, he chanced upon a grizzled old man topped with a ragged nest of silver hair who squatted alone beside a campfire, a cloak of thick brown wool wrapped about his shoulders. As Svipdag pushed through the brush into the clearing, the ancient's head jerked up, swinging his long gray beard dangerously close to the flames.

They remained still, sharing the prudence of assessing an unexpected stranger. The moment passed, as a gentle wave from a withered hand beckoned the weary traveler into the camp. "Come," the elder waved again. "Join me in conversation for I have a pleasant fire with food and drink to share."

As Svipdag crunched across the snow, the old man roused coals to a red glow, then tossed on a knot of fir that kindled to dancing flames. A cloud of sparks swirled into the air as he drew an earthen pot from the embers beside the fire and poured steaming tea into a leather mug sealed well with pitch.

"This bitter cold is not kind to the joints of men. It will do you good to stretch your fingers over the flames." He held out the mug. "Come, let the heat drive away the hurtful chill."

Grunting thanks, Svipdag touched a finger to his forehead and slumped down beside the fire opposite the old man. As he gratefully took the mug of tea, a booted toe pushed a bowl of roasted meat around the fire circle. "Help yourself to this offering. It's plenty is more than I can finish."

When he had eaten enough of the proffered food so that hunger no longer gnawed at his belly, Svipdag gazed across the campfire into eyes the color of a stormy sea. He searched the weathered lines of the elder's face, noted the knotted brow tufted with grizzled gray, the hollow cheeks, the deep lines webbing his face. It was the weary expression of one compelled by necessity to sustain burdens that have long tried his strength.

"Such generosity is an unexpected pleasure along such a lonely route where, until now, I've encountered only wild creatures. These paths are difficult to manage. They try even my strength, and I am a young man. How is it I find one of your obvious years traveling alone in this cold, desolate land?"

The old man turned his gaze to the fire; the dancing flames reflected in the depths of his eyes. "I seek my children. Their captors were last seen along this route. For many years, I have traveled these ways, always hoping to encounter one of them." He beat a fist furiously against his knee. Words hissed through clenched teeth as bursts of steam in the cold air. "Know that should any of them fall under my power, I will rip from their screaming hides the location of my son and daughter!"

The old man stopped, gulping to catch his breath, silencing for a moment the white puffs from his lips. Slowly, he began to breathe, jutting his chin to relax the muscles of his jaws, then stretched out his hands to the fire. "But you need not listen to the rantings of an old man. Tell me something of yourself. Your bearing suggests a brave warrior."

He gestured at Svipdag's frame. "Your limbs are whole, so skill with weapons must be yours. The edge marks that score your rings are all in front. The back of your byrnie appears unmarked, and clean as the day it was made. The gore crusted on your vest, the dark splotches staining your gauntlets, speak of hard-fought battles. And the smell, rank even to my nose, though it sniffles with the cold, tells of a long, hard trail."

The old man rocked back on his heels, satisfied with his assessment. "Yes, it is a flight shy warrior that sits before me. You seem better suited driving into an enemy line at the bloody point of a hamalt fylking than trekking alone on this windy trial. Tell me, who are you? Where do you come from? Where are you bound? What circumstance drove you into this wilderness?"

Svipdag frowned into the mug clutched in his fists. "You ask a lot of questions on meeting a stranger."

The old man smiled as he dug a stick into the fire. "When else should such things be asked, but before a banked-up fire in winter, in the quiet hours of the day, while sharing food and hot drink."

The elder tapped his chest. "To put you at ease I'll go first. Call me Knorr, for I am like that stalwart workhorse of the sea carrying the freight of many years, a goodly cargo of experience and perhaps," he winked, "a bit of wisdom. I have already told what brings me to be in this place. Now stranger, what of you?"

The corners of Svipdag's lips twitched up. Quickly, he introduced himself. Then, loudly cursing his misfortune, he related the disastrous result of his recent battle with Halfdan. "You see before you a failure. I was born Svipdag, son of Orvandel. As an honorable son, I sought the life of Halfdan, a great king in this region, to avenge the mistreatment at his hands of my mother and the death of my grandfather."

He pointed at the bowl of meat. The old man nodded, nudging it closer. Svipdag stuffed several pieces into his mouth, then continued talking while chewing noisily and gulping at his mug. "You marked the scores on my byrnie. They are the tale of my failure to avenge my kin on the field of valor. I had nearly hacked my way through his guard when a chance blow knocked me senseless. At the battle's end that blood-soaked king left me to die bound to a tree. I escaped with my life into this wilderness. Now I will never have another chance to reclaim my family's honor."

Knorr chuckled and shook his head, so the gray locks swayed beside his chin. He slowly turned a steaming mug of hot tea about in his hands, letting its warmth creep into his fingers before taking a sip. "Often delays are lamented, though they later prove to be of much benefit, taking one along greater paths than would otherwise have been traveled."

As he spoke, Knorr set his mug aside and plucked a small fir branch from the snow beside the fire. "Know the carnage of battle," he casually stripped the branch of its greenery until a single bare twig remained, "is often shared equally by foes. While this time victory slipped your grasp, the next time you meet—and you will—fortunes may be reversed."

Knorr smiled, keeping his gray eyes focused on Svipdag's face, while he idly toyed with the twig of fir, letting the stick trace delicate glyphs in the snow. "I have traveled far in this world and learned much along the way that is of value. I can see your need is great, so there is a thing I will share, for I perceive grand events in store for you."

The old man glanced side to side then leaned forward, beckoning Svipdag to do the same. "I know of a blade crafted by a master smith that sends shudders of fear through the very gods, a blade whose shine no centuries can dim. A warrior skilled in the ways of battle who boldly wields this weapon will always find victory when it is carried to the fore."

Svipdag rocked back laughing and slapped his leg. A puzzled smile quirked Knorr's lips while the young warrior continued to chuckle. "Old man I have heard this tale. It is a story told to entertain children. The way my father tells it, the blade is the work of a brother now long lost; a great smith who marked his works with the stamp of an eagle, its wings outstretched to capture the wind. He cannot show me any pieces made by his hand, and, of course, the brother is nowhere to be found. That is the way with such stories—they cannot be verified."

Mumbling to himself, the old man reached into his vest and pulled out a short, magnificently crafted knife. Twined snakes stretched the length of the blade. Holding it out, he angled the blade, so the maker's mark stood out sharply from the glowing metal, an eagle with wings spread wide in flight.

Svipdag started at the sight. "This is a lesser work from the great smith of which I speak." The old man ran a finger along the blade edge, then pricked his fingertip with its tip. "It was a gift given to me in years past. A great treasure then, I have not seen its like since. Its edge does not dull, no matter the use." He twisted the blade to reflect the firelight. "In all the half years that it has been in my possession it has never needed burnishing."

Knorr watched disbelief war with belief across Svipdag's face. Satisfied his point was made and the barb set, he returned the blade to its sheath inside his vest. "The tales you have heard are true. What I offer is real. But this is not a prize as easily plucked as a dry branch from a fir tree or ripe fruit from a low-hanging limb. To own it will take bravery, cunning, and strength of purpose.

Far north of here, south of the Wolfdales, the gard of Saevarstadir rests on a hill overlooking an expanse of frozen sea. There the blade rests in the great hall of the Njara under the watchful eye of Nidud, a wise guardian of noble mien. In a chest bound with nine iron locks, the powerful blade nestles with a companion arm ring; once a key to binding the winds, its lesser power can increase the wealth of its owner.

The route is difficult, even for a hardy traveler. It winds through regions of brutal cold where terrible obstacles block the way to an icy sea that calls with a deep, grinding voice. Take my advice, travel as fast as you can. Harness a cart as the natives of that land do, drawn by powerful horned deer. Their greater speed will allow you to cross the frozen plains before the demon cold can draw the warmth of life from your limbs.

When you reach the hall, pitch your tent away from the sun, deep in the shadows of the nearby hills. Nidud is as keen of his surroundings as any night predator. He will retreat to his hall should he perceive any unaccustomed darkness, for this great warrior has the habit of seeking solace in the embrace of the night as he treks the hill paths about his hall, lamenting the loss of his sons.

Capture him, menace his life. With your blade pricking at his throat, he will give up the treasures, for nothing is more cherished than one's own breath when another threatens to take it away. With the prizes in hand you will know fortune in wealth and in war."

Nodding at the words, Svipdag stretched out his hands to flex his fingers over the flames. "What you say is interesting, but of little value. A man could spend half his life concealed in the gloomy depths of a forest and rarely, if ever, see another, let alone know if

306

he encountered the one he sought. In darkness, the faces of all men look alike, while shadows conceal the color and cut of their cloaks, be they ragged or finely made. I need to know what paths he frequents. How to tell him from a farmer or a woodcutter passing in the night, hurrying through the chill, eager to get home."

Knorr touched two fingers to his forehead. "So, you are capable of careful thought" he grinned, "as well as courage and strength. It is no less than I expected. Know that Nidud favors the north face of hills, particularly those that rise south of his hall. For there the forest stands thinnest as the land slopes west to an open plain that glitters with frost.

As for how you will know him, he is tall, far larger than most. His face is wrapped in dark black hair, a raven's cloak that conceals all but his eyes. He likes to walk the frozen paths clad in full armor, a golden byrnie of fine metal links strapped tightly about his chest. On his head, he wears a polished golden helmet that shines day or night. To conceal himself in the night he wears a heavy robe, dark as the shadows, draped about his broad shoulders. On his right hand is a ring, mounted with a gleaming, blood red stone. In the faintest light, it glows like a fiery coal that winks in the breath of air. None other in this land dresses as does he. If you mark him, helmet, byrnie, and ring, you are certain to have the right man."

Svipdag leaned forward, a finger to his lips, his eyes keen for the adventure. "These treasures of which you speak highly, how will I know the victory-blessed sword and wealth-giving arm ring from cheap imitations?"

"The Wonder Smith," Knorr winked at his guest, "etched the waved-marked iron with symbols of victory at tip and edge. Along its polished sides flow the ripples from the ebb of Ymir's blood. Above its hilt," he patted the blade inside his vest, "stands the proud mark of the smith, an eagle with wings outstretched. When the blade is unsheathed, its power can be focused to draw the strength of the sun to earth. A skilled warrior such as you will know the truth of the weapon by its feel. The ring is crafted of gold, its edge set with closely spaced red jewels. It weighs more than it should. When dangled from the hand or suspended from a rope, on the ninth night it will drop eight rings of equal weight. Know that if you have the sword, you will have the ring."

Svipdag grinned, rubbing his hands together. Snatching up his mug from beside the fire, he drained its contents, loosed a loud burp, then gripped his knees and made ready to stand. "Wait!" The old man called him back." Do not be over-eager to rush from my company. There is one more thing I can offer to aid the success of your quest."

Grumbling to himself, the ancient rummaged through a pouch at his side. From it he drew a slip of ram's horn polished clear to show the rings, its surface etched with runes stained green. "In these lands information is not easy to obtain. One must be open to all sources. Take this slip of horn. On it are carved Mal runes, very useful in loosening still tongues."

With words of thanks and eagerness shining in his eyes, Svipdag left the camp of his ancient host. Directing his feet along the northward path, he marched out of the glade and was soon embraced by the wood.

The grizzled wayfarer watched him go, delighting at the sure steps and squared shoulders that disappeared among the forest shadows. He tossed the contents of his mug to steam amid the swamped coals then scuffed a layer of snow over the remaining fire-blackened limbs. Turning himself along paths west, the ancient mariner smiled, confident his children would soon grace his hall of ships, there where the gulls cry beside the sea.

Chant of the Niflgódur

Svipdag followed the path Knorr had described—stumbling through deep drifts of powdery snow, teetering along hard-packed snow bridges that spanned yawning chasms, and sliding across ice-crusted meadows blasted clear by incessant winds. When the cold became so bitter that each intake of breath burned deep into his chest making him cough, he found the spell cast by Groa kept his extremities warm, his joints limber.

He passed through regions shrouded in cloud where sheet ice crusted his cloak in a white rime. With each step the trail glazed with ice, becoming more treacherous. Dim figures wandered amid the haze. The shuffle of massive feet accompanied by thick sounds of heavy breathing echoed through the gray vapor. When they drew too near, Svipdag slid aside to let them pass, a silent shadow in the mist.

At times, his feet became invisible to his eyes. Growing concerned with the route, the bold warrior sought a vantage point that he might spy out the trail ahead. Balancing his way along sheer cliffs cut steep by the rage of an ice-choked river that thundered in massive steps through a mountain gorge, Svipdag scaled his way out of the mist to a narrow pass whose height promised a clear view of the surrounding land.

At the base of the pass an ice-rimed gate of tightly webbed iron built into the rock of the cliffs obstructed the entire approach. There was no way through or around save for the heavy gate to open. He leaned against a dark iron rung, puffing his breath into the frigid air, while considering his next direction. Idly scratching a line along the frosted surface of the iron, he peered through small gaps where the metal did not overlap.

Behind the gate the sky was clouded with the ragged shapes of people. Numerous as flies on rotting flesh, they tumbled through stagnant air that reeked of decay. Farther below, half-seen figures shambled along frozen paths blocked by random drifts of gray snow. There was no sound of wind or water running in its course. No words or cries came from the lumbering hulks, only the doleful grind of feet on frozen earth whispered through the still air.

This was no land of sunshine, heavy with the perfume of flowers, but a cold, dreary place that smelled of death. Tearing his gaze from the tragic scene, Svipdag staggered away from the frosted metal to slump against the cold stone of the mountain pass. As he drew a sobbing breath, a troop of limar-scourged figures, held in line by watchful heipter, stumbled silently toward the gate along the path he had taken.

Flattening himself against the rock wall, Svipdag edged into a shadowy cleft alongside the path. As they shuffled by his concealed niche, one looked up. He glimpsed green eyes swollen red with tears staring dully from above dirt-caked cheeks framed by a snarl of dull, crimson hair. The young woman dressed in a tattered cloak, swayed at the back of the throng. Her bared back was striped with angry welts that oozed black blood.

Hinges squalled in protest as the gate swung wide. One by one the figures entered. Several tried to turn back down the path but were shoved forward by those behind. As the young woman stumbled alongside the shadowed cleft, the eyes of the heipter turned to watch those entering the gate. Snaking out a hand to grip the maiden's arm, Svipdag yanked her into the darkness beside him. Her lips parted in a mute scream.

She struggled, nearly breaking free of his grip, until Svipdag placed his lips against her ear. "Be still," he whispered. "Make no sound to alert the guards." At his words, her eyes grew wide and she pleaded with silent gestures so that he knew her voice had been stilled.

From a vest pocket, he drew the horn slip with its Mal runes stained green. Waving it before her face, he drew her attention to the runes. When she nodded that she understood, he slipped it beneath her tongue. Her mouth gaped wide as a high thin wail escaped her lips. Svipdag clapped a hand over her mouth and dragged her further into the cleft.

Once the gates closed behind the passing troop, he turned the woman around to face him. "Name this place," he demanded, keeping his voice low. "Tell me who you are to deserve such treatment."

The woman spoke through teeth clenched as much against the cold as the pain of her wounds. "In this land my name is unimportant, my line insignificant." Her words lisped around the horn beneath her tongue. "Here slave and king brave the same unwarranted punishments."

Her green eyes gazed sadly over Svipdag's shoulder. "To think that I, who knew power and position among men, am reduced to this deplorable state," she flicked the shredded edge of her robe, drawing Svipdag's attention to her once-shapely legs, "no better than a beggar. My robes, which once were of the finest weave and embroidered with the shapes of animals to thrill the eye, are now these tattered remnants, their length stained with my own blood and that of my trail companions."

The young woman daubed a tear from her cheek. "But you asked who I am," she rested her hand lightly on Svipdag's forearm. "For a brave warrior, one who saved me from such horrendous treatment, I will tell my story.

At an early age, long before I was old enough to know the power of the moon's flow, I learned the wiles necessary to guard myself from the unwanted attentions of men. I used what I learned to keep myself safe and to build my position in life toward one where such knowledge would no longer be needed.

In my flowering I was the desire of many and knew the pleasure of power, the enjoyment of others doing my bidding that control over such desire brings. I became the fancy of two close friends. I seemed to them steeped in the joys of being. Each day they vied for my attentions, those that men had always sought from me. When I told them that I would accept only the best, they turned against each other. Friends once, now they became bitter enemies. In a holm edged with stones, they fought and died for precedence, each falling to the weapon of the other.

I celebrated the event for many days, delighted to know the lengths I could induce others to take. Eagerly, I anticipated the next test of my skill. I had not long to wait, for there were always others. Some were challenges to my ability. Them, I worked to become pliable, as a shipwright warps boards to wrap a hull.

I enjoyed this pastime. Many were directed by my wiles, men turned against each other or themselves, even women bent to my influence. I kept a chest filled with tokens, locks of hair cut from their heads, to commemorate each conquest.

Not long after the last challenge had passed, as I celebrated my triumph, I felt the cords of death cinch themselves about my body, binding me with ropes of anguish. From the first evening the pain increased, leaving me tottering between awake and the fitful horror of dark dreams.

I do not know if days or weeks passed by as I struggled to overcome the bonds constricting my chest that made an agony of each drawn breath. Setting my teeth against the pain, I fought for every breath. Each day I willed myself to waken with the sun, to sip water, and to take what nourishment I could hold. But death proved stronger than my will.

From my bed, I peered through a window, watching as Sol retreated to her roaring hall, her blood-red rays dissolving into darkness. She appeared mightier to my fading eyes than ever she had seemed before, as I bowed to her one last time in the world of men. The sun's glow dwindled to a point as my heart skipped, beat, then skipped again. My tongue, which knew the gift of repartee, became thick as wood. My limbs, which had carried me in joyous radiance, grew weak and stiff with cold.

Then, as darkness enveloped me, I heard the roar of Gjoll's dizzying stream mingling with the low thundering of my blood. I found myself amid a silent crowd journeying the hard, western road. It was a treacherous route, my limbs sliced by shards of ice as I forded a raging torrent, my feet torn by brambles along a low, winding path.

Hobbling into the Thing of Urd, I took a seat amid tiers of benches. Nine days I sat waiting for my turn, sliding down the benches as the line before me dwindled, while the seats behind filled with new arrivals. On the ninth day, the space cleared before me. I found myself standing alone before the judges, my voice muted, unable to defend the actions I had taken in life that I might live well and prosper.

Instead, my hamingje spoke for me, one whose voice I had seldom heard since drawing my first breath in the world. It spoke only a short while before falling silent. Then, tears coursing down its cheeks, it turned away, fading back into the shadows.

Stern faces glared down from the high seats, as ever the brutish features of men. I spied several women, but they appeared as severe as the men. Then the decision for my fate was spoken. A bearer pressed the cup of fate to my lips, forcing me to swallow its bitter drink. At once, warmth coursed through my flesh. As my joints, freed from cold, became limber, I could feel the breath of air against my cheek. I started to rejoice, but my voice, my once musical voice which had thrilled so many, remained silent."

Her voice choked as she gazed down the cleft toward the iron gate. "Then I was bullied into a line with others. With wide swinging limar and nagaikas, we were driven as reluctant cattle along rocky paths and up steep slopes to this gate."

Tears rolling down her cheeks, she gripped Svipdag's sleeve. "Please help me! I do not belong with these wretches. I have done nothing save protect myself from the despicable actions of others. There is nothing I have done in my life to warrant this treatment that those who received the orrds tir had not done in theirs.

If you would speak on my behalf, talk to those who drove me here, I am certain they would listen to a brave warrior such as you. The honorable always command attention. For this service, you will know my gratitude." She let her tattered cloak slip to bare one bruised shoulder.

Svipdag gripped the woman. As he pulled her close, she leaned into him, pressing her breasts into his chest, grinding her hips against his waist. He gripped her arms and firmly pushed her back. "I had guessed where I stood when first I peered through the iron-webbed gate. Now your words have confirmed that for me." He glanced over her head then back to her face. "This is Nagrind, the Na-Gates to Niflhel, and you... you are one of the twice-dead, one who has received the namaeli.

With honeyed words, you plied your wiles in life, manipulated others into terrible actions they would otherwise avoid, all to pleasure only yourself. But before I began this journey, I was wrapped in a powerful charm that guarded me against persuasion from one such as you. With it, my eyes remain clear that I might truly see, and my ears unblocked that the truth might never be muted.

For the sake of pity and my own thoughts of right action, I might have taken you from here. But you sought to coerce me into suffering your judgment behind the gate. For I am certain that were I to have approached one of the heipter who drive forward the groups of twice-dead and attempted to speak on your behalf, it is I, not you, who would have been driven through the dark Na-Gates.

Though I feel sorrow for the harsh judgment you must face, know that I am very much alive. My living path lies to the west, far beyond this place. I will not take on your burden. That which you created for yourself in life is yours to bear in death."

As Svipdag spoke these words, the eyes of the young woman turned to flame. "Never has anyone denied my desire," she spit into his face. "You will be the last!"

As the enraged maiden parted her lips to scream, Svipdag yanked the Mal runes from beneath her tongue and shoved her back onto the mountain path where a new troop of twice-dead stumbled along the way. When she tried to dart back into the protective shadows of the cleft, the stinging flick of a limar cut her off. With a flurry of lusty blows that opened new wounds across her back, a heipter drove her up the path and through the gate.

For a long moment, the heipter eyed the shadows where Svipdag stood motionless, hand ready on his weapon. The dull gleam of its gaze chilled the air and the young warrior fought to keep a shiver from giving himself away. A sudden movement from one of the shambling wrecks drew the heipter's attention back to the group that milled soundlessly before the gate, allowing Svipdag to move deeper into the concealing shadow of the cleft. When the gate clanged shut behind the throng and their guards, Svipdag slipped from his hiding place and raced back down the path, far away from the silent screams.

With Sword in Hand

Through dark lands Svipdag traveled, along dreary paths lined with wind-cold wolf trees, his purpose held close. He stopped before a fir-wrapped mountain that stretched its shadow across the land. The steep slope offered difficult purchase, as he clawed his way along frozen ridges until the surrounding vistas opened before his gaze.

Westward, the steep terrain sloped down to an open plain that glittered like the surface of a calm lake at sunset, even in the dim light. To the north, he spied the thin lines of white breakers that marked the ice-rimmed shoreline of a gray sea. Perched on a low rise above the breakers that crashed against the headland stood the dark hall of the Njara.

Amid shadows of the southern hills, deep in the dusky rills that skirted their northern face, Svipdag pitched his tent on a flat, sheltered area. With sharp blows from his blade, he lopped off branches from nearby firs and arranged them carefully about his tent. Certain his camp was concealed from chance sighting, he settled himself to wait for the guardian to make the nightly foray from his hall.

Enfolded in shadow he waited day on day, poised as a lynx that patiently stalks its prey. By day, he hunted to feed himself. By night, he watched for Nidud while his mind battled the growing despair that he had embarked on a fool's errand.

Night after night he kept vigil, until the Mead Ship filled the sky, its naked light congealing shadows into deep, sharp pools. As he sat in watchful silence, a silhouette slid across an open patch of snow brightly lit by the risen moon. Careful to keep his movements timed with the silences of the forest, Svipdag hugged his legs into a crouch. He peered wide-eyed into the night, trying to force the shadows to reveal the nature of the intruder.

Down from the hills shuffled a dark-cloaked figure, stooped with the careful grace of one seeking sure footing along an icy path. As the figure slipped from shadows into full moonlight a helmet flared like a pale golden globe to encircle a dark featured face. The chest peeping through a split in the dark cape burned with the fire of Ægir. From a right hand—stretched out to steady the step—a bright, red coal winked to life, its flame just as quickly snuffed as the arm fell back beneath the folds.

Jumping to his feet, Svipdag roared out a challenge. The shadow stopped, turned toward the sound, and reached to its waist. The harsh rasp of metal drawn from a scabbard cut the air. Hefting his long spear, Svipdag sighted along its length and let fly. The shaft hissed through the shadows, an invisible missile, impossible to avoid. The figure lunged toward the faint sound but was driven back as the shaft struck its side.

Shouting a great whoop of victory, Svipdag drew his sword and rushed forward. Placing a boot on the figure's chest, he brought his blade to the fore, so its tip hovered over the throat of his fallen foe. "By my own hand, I have captured Nidud, he who none other has ever dared face. It is a bold day, a great day! One that assures me of honor." He ground his heel into the foeman's chest until the breath whooshed from his lips, leaving him gasping for air. "You hold in your possession a sword of great power and an arm ring that generates wealth. I hold in my hand your life. I will make you an even exchange. Your kin can ransom your life for these treasures."

Svipdag nudged aside the cloak with his sword and pressed the tip against the flesh of Nidud's throat, its point pricking deep until the captive gagged. "And do not think to pass off relics of no worth. I can readily tell real from fake. Should your kin deal me false, they can have your lifeless body, if they can find all the pieces."

Nidud blinked his eyes and nodded. He had little doubt of his foe's sincerity. When he replied, it was with a low, guttural voice measured against the pain of the wound in his side. "Take my ring," he held up his hand, "and give it to the gatekeepers. Tell them you carry an urgent message for my queen, Sinmara. They will see the token is delivered with all haste. On its strength, she will grant you an audience. Tell her I agree to your demands. She will place the ransom at your feet."

Taking the ring from Nidud's hand, Svipdag tucked it away into a vest pocket. With a wad of dirty linen, he staunched the blood that flowed from the wound his spear had inflicted, then dragged the injured warrior back to his camp.

He bound Nidud's hands and feet with a couple turns of bast chord, then propped him up sitting against a log while he started a fire. Nidud watched the young warrior, eyes keen to his every movement. As the fire caught and its flames pushed back the darkness, he could see the strong plains of his captor's face, the firm lines of his mouth, the fierce intent in his eyes. With admiration, he marked the blade-scarred rings on the bold youth's chest.

"When first I you challenged from the protection of darkness, I took you for a common thief—one who would run when challenged."

Svipdag gave a croaking laugh, harsh from disuse. "It was the daring act of a brave man to attack an assailant concealed in the shadows."

Nidud adjusted his position, wincing from the pain in his side as he squared his shoulders against the log. "Often a swift, brazen attack will unnerve a confident opponent."

Svipdag laughed again. "Had you succeeded we would not be speaking now." He tossed a pitch knot into the flames. The fire leapt with the life-giving fuel, sending a welcome wave of heat washing over the two. "One or both of us would be reddening the snowfield with the last of our life's dew."

Flashing his teeth in a wide grin, Svipdag calmly stirred the fire until the flames danced. Nidud nodded and continued. "So, your spear cast was no accident, the off strike of a startled arm. It was the intentional throw of a battle-hardened warrior used to the suddenness of attacks."

Svipdag sucked at his teeth, then stared frankly at Nidud. "I cast to stop, not to kill. A dead man is of less value to me than a live one. Few are willing to pay a high ransom for a corpse."

Nidud closed his eyes, letting himself relax against the log. "My thanes will search for me at first light, for I always return from my vigils before Sol crests the horizon." A smile twitched at the corners of his lips. "They will find my trail. Soon you will face a score of trained warriors. Little ransom will you collect then, save for a storm of sharp edges and wide wounds across your body."

Svipdag clapped a hand on Nidud's shoulder. "Who says we wait for sunlight." He grinned at the surprise that flashed on his captive's face. "Once I've broken camp we leave for your hall. You will see its walls before the sun rises."

The old king looked on in astonishment as Svipdag took down his shelter and bundled his few belongings into a pack. When the young warrior was ready for travel, he untied the bonds about Nidud's legs and hauled him to his feet. They followed the king's path back through the hills.

Once they reached the forest fence that angled in close beside the hall, Svipdag circled until they approached the heavy timbers of the north gate. In a shallow recess beside the gate, he propped the king against the wall, hidden from sight in the deep shadows. With a gag, he silenced Nidud's voice. With bast rope, he bound his legs.

"The cold will keep you here as well as in the forest. Your thanes will not think to find you so close. I have concealed our tracks to this point. A search party will trample the rest when they emerge at dawn."

Kneeling beside his trussed captive, he took Nidud's face between his hands. "But long before Night is chased from the sky, I will have the ransom in hand and be well on my way. But before I enter this dark hall, I will have your word of my safe conduct from these lands. Nod your excellent brow if I have your word, or... you can trust me in this... I will leave without the ransom and your men can find you here, a frozen buttress for the wall."

Three times Nidud nodded. "Do not worry!" Grinning, Svipdag nudged Nidud's leg. "If all within are as true to their word as I know you to be, your icy feet will soon be warming before the hearth fire."

"Here." Pulling a blanket from his pack, Svipdag wrapped it around Nidud's shoulders. "Though this spot offers a break from the warmth-stealing wind," lifting Nidud's feet he tucked the blanket beneath his legs, "you will need this if you are to remain alive. An active man can fend off the cold, while a still man exposed to the elements will freeze before many breaths have passed his lips."

Svipdag thumped his captive on the shoulder then slipped off along the wall to the front gate, erasing his tracks behind him as he went. At the front gate, he clubbed the wooden frame with his fist while shouting out to summon a sentry. Three times he announced his presence, each call punctuated by the slamming of his fist against the gatepost.

"Attend the gate! A messenger waits in the cold." The dull thud of his fist rattled the gate.

"Attend the gate! I come with urgent word for the woman who orders this hall." Once more his fist crashed against the post.

"Attend the gate! I carry a message from the king of this land." A dusting of snow fell from the timbers above, shaken free by his blows.

A figure hunched through the doorway of a dimly lit hut set inside the gate. Drawing a heavy robe about his shoulders, he shuffled his way to confront the caller. "Tell me who shouts in the night to wake the dead and disturb the rest of the living?"

Svipdag pulled Nidud's ring from a pocket and waved it before the sentry's face, turning it so the red jewel caught the moonlight and flared to life in his fingers. "I come from conference with your king. He sends me ahead with this token that those in his hall will know me. I carry a private message for the good woman who orders this place, Sinmara is her name. It is urgent that I speak with her!"

The sentry peered hard at Svipdag, let his eyes roam the full length of the young warrior who stood unflinching before him, patiently suffering the close examination. He leaned forward to better see the ring, then held out his hand. As Svipdag passed it to him, the sentry roared over his shoulder for another to come watch the entrance while he delivered a report to the queen that a messenger waited outside the walls with urgent news from the king, news that was for her ears alone.

His steps squeaked as he dashed away through the cold snow. Svipdag shifted to a more comfortable stance while another shadow slipped forward—a burly sentry with dark brows and hard eyes—to take up his position before the gate. Together they stood, facing each other. No words passed, no sound at all save the rasping of snow as the wind pushed it in light swirls across the ground.

The drumming of running feet disturbed the stillness as the first sentry returned to the post, white clouds puffing from his lips. With insistent gestures, he urged Svipdag through the gate and hurried him along to the central hall.

Sinmara looked down from her high seat. A heavy robe of blue-gray wool was draped in long folds over her shoulders. A thin band of gold circled her brow binding heavy braids of dark hair streaked with gray. Beside her left hand stood an empty seat, to her right three more. The stone hearth beside the seats crackled with a freshly stoked fire. She cut a regal figure on the dais, stark, imperious, and alone.

Svipdag bowed his head then gazed directly into her eyes. With a sharp gesture, she beckoned him forward. "You brought to me the ring of my husband as proof that you carry his word." She held up the red carbuncle between two fingers. The gem glowed ember-bright in the firelight. "Never have I known him to let another bear this ring. I fear your message will bring despair upon this hall. Already we have suffered much. We need no more pain."

Svipdag strode forward, stopping as Sinmara raised her hand, a comfortable distance from the dais. "The meaning of words often depends upon the response of the listener." He tipped his head to the queen. "So, I will tell you a simple tale of two proud warriors who faced off in a snowy glade bathed in the Mead Ship's light. From the shadows, they charged across the whiteness. A blade was drawn. A spear was cast. One fell wounded before the other." He held out his hand palm down, then turned it over palm up to Sinmara. "As ransom for his life the fallen warrior promised three things of value: a sword of great power that fights of its own accord, an arm ring crafted of red gold that generates wealth for its owner, and safe passage from this land. All these he swore would be given if I spared his life."

Squaring his shoulders, Svipdag rested a hand on the hilt of the sword strapped at his side. With his free hand, he pointed at the ring. "That ring is brought in good faith that you would know the truth of my words. Your husband still lives. Though if you refuse to deliver the ransom promised me, know with all certainty the seat beside your right hand will forever remain empty."

Frozen by Svipdag's words, Sinmara glared at the confident young warrior who stood unbowed before her. Tears coursed down her cheeks to glint as golden streams in the firelight. "The words you speak are harsh; they chill me to the bone. Gladly, I rid this place of the demon relics. Great is their power to destroy, even locked away. Since their capture those many years ago, they have brought grief to this house. I lost two cherished sons because of them, their bodies shattered beneath a forge. My daughter was dishonored and left with a bastard child to raise." She daubed at her cheek with two fingers. "Already my heart swims with grief. I can bear no more. Not the loss of him who has sat beside me these many years."

Sinmara clapped her hands. Her shrill commands iced the air as she called to a pair of retainers flanking the hearth. "Bring the chest wrapped with nine iron bands from its storage niche deep in the hall. Place it here at my feet." The two hesitated, looking uneasily at their mistress. "Now!"

They had not waited long when the retainers struggled into the room and set a heavy chest at the foot of the dais. Its surface was a polished black that reflected the flames. Nine thick bands of wrought iron, each with its own lock, wrapped its sides to bind the chest closed. Sinmara pointed her chin at the chest. "There is your ransom; the fiendish treasures of Volund. May you fare better in their ownership than my family has endured. Now where is my husband? Tell me, that I might send men to retrieve him."

Svipdag shook his head and nudged the chest with his foot. "Before I release that knowledge I would examine the items in this box to ensure they are genuine. I tell you now it was no accident that I met your husband on that lonely patch of snow. I know much of these items." He squinted shrewdly at the queen. "I can readily tell if they are real or fake."

Sinmara climbed down from her seat. Kneeling before the chest, she drew a ring of keys from a cord at her waist. One by one she unlocked the bands that held the chest closed. When the last lock sprung free, she tipped back the lid and returned to her seat.

Svipdag crouched and drew the ring from the box, hefted it in his hands to test its weight, turned it over so the red jewels set along its rim winked in the flickering light of the hearth fire. Nodding lightly in appreciation, he slipped the ring inside his vest.

Next Svipdag took from the chest a sword cased in a thick, brown leather sheath banded with gold and silver sleeves. He gripped the hilt with his right hand, feeling it tingle in his grasp as he drew the blade. Light filled the room as he turned the weapon over in his hands. Victory runes etched the tip and wave-edge of the blade. Over the hilt stood the hallmark of Volund, the incised image of a proud eagle with wings outstretched.

"The mark of the Wonder Smith, just as the old man claimed. It appears the tales my father told were true; it even casts heat as he said. I can feel its power surging up my arm, though I scarcely believed him."

He sighted along the blade's length, twisting it so light splashed about the walls. The weapon danced in his hand as he gave several practice swipes to gauge its balance. Smiling to himself, Svipdag rested the blade on his left arm. "You will find your husband trussed up outside the north gate." He glanced at Sinmara before returning his focus to the reflections playing along the blade's polished length. "I left him in a shadowed recess just to the left of the gate, covered with a thick woolen blanket to ward off the bitter cold."

Svipdag slid the sword into its sheath as Nidud hobbled into the room supported between two retainers. Glaring at the son of Orvandel, he shook off the supporting arms. As he stumbled to his seat beside the queen, Sinmara reached over to touch the wound at his side. Nidud shook his head and she withdrew her hand.

Svipdag returned the steady gaze of the hard-eyed king. Gripping the sword hilt, he drew the blade partway from its sheath. Sinmara cried out, burying her face in her hands, as brilliant light flashed through the room. Nidud turned his face aside, hand raised to shield his eyes from the brightness. As heat began to build, he waved for Svipdag to rest the blade. "I gave my word in the bloodied glade: a blade, a ring, and safe conduct from this land, all given to you as ransom for my life. Besides, little could I do now; the cursed weapon is in your hand. Where I to direct my men to attack, with it you would lay waste to my hall and still leave unchallenged."

Svipdag snapped the blade back into its sheath. "Now that I have what I came for I will tell you my line that you might know who bested you on the field of honor. My name is Svipdag. Know the blade and ring have returned to the family from which they were taken. My father is Orvandel, son of Ivalde. His brother is Volund, the Wonder Smith whose mark I see inscribed above the hilt of this blade."

A deadly flame leapt in the young warrior's eyes as an all-consuming fire rose up his neck to heighten the stern set of his features. "I have heard much of this blade's abilities. There is one whom I owe a debt of blood. When next we meet on path or field, I will learn the truth of these tales."

With these words Svipdag spun on his heel and left the hall. Silently, Nidud and Sinmara watched him go. The retainers of the Njara stepped aside as the young man strode through the gates. He was visible only a moment, his back flashing in the moonlight, before disappearing into the forest shadows.

Battle with the Gods

The story rapidly spread of Svipdag's journey and the fabulous treasures he had won in the cold northern lands. When Halfdan heard Svipdag had gained these things, he gathered his warriors about him as a warm cloak is drawn about the chest to ward against a chill wind. With sharp commands, he bid them stand ready, for he was certain the grandson of Sigtryg would seek him out, eager for vengeance.

Others, too, heard what Svipdag had gained: those eager for valor, those hungry for the wealth of battle, the bitter enemies of Halfdan. All these and more rushed to join his banner as he marched steadfast across the lands of war-eager Jotuns and disenfranchised Jarls.

The armies met on a wide plain, a forest of sturdy oaks too numerous to count. The air rang with the rattle of war gear and loud challenges screamed from both sides. The line of Halfdan's warriors advanced, eager to inflict damage on the enemy ranks.

Svipdag shouted out along the line of his followers, bidding them to stand their ground. "Hold fast, warriors, take your stand at one another's side. Root your feet like the trees of battle you are, ready to defy the brunt of the battle storm."

Loud cheers greeted his commands as he tilted his shield over his head. "Raise a howe of your sturdy shields. Wait, impervious within its walls, while the foeman's rain thunders from the sky. Endure the reception of their hurled spears until they have exhausted their stores! Our victory in this battle will be won by patience!"

The clatter of shield edges filled the air while waves of laughter washed over the walls that sprouted around Svipdag's force. Hunkered behind his shield Svipdag shouted encouragement to his warriors. "Cast off whatever fears arise from the ravening legions mustering before you. Ignore their taunts. Grin merrily at the grim specter of war so when the moment comes for stern action you won't hold back, fearful of the weapon's sting, but sprint forward to attack the enemy with your keen edged blades. Together we will make a pile their corpses to glut the wolf!"

A dark cloud of shrikes rose in flight from the wall of Halfdan's warriors, a shower of missiles cast high into the air in their eagerness to attack. The storm broke against raised shields; a harsh rain that rattled the teeth of solidly planted warriors and fell harmlessly away as hail dashed against a cliff face. The more patiently Halfdan's warriors found the reception of their spears, the greater grew their fury and the harder they flung their weapons. Wounds were inflicted where gaps stood between the shields, but the line of Svipdag's followers remained firm and unresponsive to the challenge.

Shouts of derision followed the spear flights, until Halfdan's line found themselves with only blade or mace left to hand. Their catcalls died away as Svipdag's followers picked up the spears and flung them back with lethal results. Line after line of warriors fell beneath the shower of spears, deadly shafts that hissed through the air, armaments provided by their own hand.

When the rain cleared, both sides charged. The earth trembled beneath the drumming of running feet. The weapon storm broke with a terrible crash of shield against shield, sword against sword. Everywhere, harsh sunlight glinted from the ripple of ring byrnies or winked as rare gems from the crown of metal helmets left boldly uncovered.

War swirled in a melee of bright, arcing blades and hard-thrust spears. The harsh crash of splintering shields mixed with the throaty roar of dauntless fighters forming vast rivers of deafening sound that rebounded from the field like the echoes of raging waters channeled between cliff walls. Torrents of blood gushed from wounds, turning the ground into a slick mire. Battle fodder was harvested at such a furious pace that corpses grew knee deep along the reddened battle line.

Near the center of the boiling mass where carnage was thickest, Svipdag eyed a knot of grim-faced warriors surrounding a familiar golden-helmed giant clad in a glittering byrnie that dazzled the eyes. Swinging his shield onto his back, he turned the edge of his blade to catch the sun and charged the wall of warriors, eager to find the life he had sworn to take.

His face, spattered with gore, was a bloody mask of terrible rage. Powerfully, he swung the blade. It seemed to thrust and parry of its own accord as he hewed down the protective fence that surrounded Halfdan. With shattering blows, he cleared a wide path through its depth as if it were made of kindling. Finally, the two flight-shy warriors came face to face in a small clearing free of men. They circled slowly left, then right, setting their feet carefully in the slick red mud.

"I face a child," Halfdan spit on the ground, "hardly grown since last I spanked you with my blade and left you—a snarling whelp—tethered to a tree. Little do you know of the true weight of war."

"I have learned much," Svipdag grinned, "since last we met." He circled left, carefully placing each step. "I am not a naïve warrior to fall in battle from the weight of my own arms, prostrated with heat from over-exertion."

"You have become a famous warrior," Halfdan's hissed words dripped with venom, "fearless because of the blade you wield." His eyes fixed on the glory of Svipdag's weaving blade. It took a mighty effort to tear his gaze away from its distracting brilliance. "Without it you are nothing."

Svipdag slapped the blade against his chest. "This weapon crafted by my uncle, a master smith of unsurpassed skill, was retrieved at great peril by my own effort." He held it out, flashing its length in the sun. "It offers its strength to the brave. In an unworthy hand, it would be useless, no more dangerous than a stick swung by a child. It is strong, because I am strong. It is skilled, because I am skilled in the ways of battle." A wide grin bared gritted teeth as he stepped over a dismembered arm. "Know the debt of blood between our houses will be paid in full. I will have your life for that of my grandfather's and for the humiliation you heaped upon my mother. Feel the payment of just revenge!"

With these words Svipdag brought the blade down in a swift arc his foe could not evade. Halfdan raised his sword to ward off the strike. His blade, which had withstood assaults on numerous campaigns, shattered from the blow as the sharp edge of Svipdag's blade continued on to bite deep into his side. Blood gushed from the wound as Halfdan slid groaning to the ground. First a puddle, then a thick red lake spread across the thirsty dust where he lay.

The fallen king cried out to the sky, his chest filled with his final breath. "I call upon my sons to avenge my death. I call upon my protector, Thor, he who has always stood by my side, to drive this bitch's son from my land."

Leaning over the fallen king, Svipdag stared into his eyes as the dying man forced a smile to curve his lips. "Gone are your allotted days, your time of joy among men. You bravely face death with a smile. I will soon see if this bravery holds true to the line."

The sky grew black and thunder rolled across the battle plain. A large, heavily-muscled figure, with a brow thick as a forest fence, stepped from a dark cloud that touched the ground. With a roar of challenge, he waded into the fray, a hammer gripped in his iron-wrapped fist. He swung the smith's mace with all his might, shattering shields, crushing helms, and dashing aside those who tried to oppose his advance.

"Come one, come all of you!" he shouted, waving his hammer at the buckling line. "Let's see the boldness of your hearts. I'll pile your corpses high to blot out the sun."

Behind him the warriors of Halfdan inched forward, wary should this fearsome menace turn on them. "You behind me, make yourselves useful and guard my flank while I drive home my attack."

His strength was so mighty, his blows so swift and merciless that line on line of warriors crumbled before his assault. Nothing could withstand the power of his hammer.

His ferocious attack would have routed the entire line of Svipdag's followers had Svipdag not rushed forward to meet the threat. Thor laughed at the lone foeman standing boldly in his path. With sparks dancing about his brow, he raised his hammer to dash the warrior aside as he had swept all others before him. Prosperous mace was met and parried by deadly blade. Metal sparked against metal to dazzle the eyes. The furious blows came so quickly, it seemed a new sun had risen on the field of battle.

A roar of battle anger burst from Thor's lips as he brought his hammer around to crush this troublesome enemy that defied his might. A bright arc swung up to meet the heavy blow. Keen edge met thick haft and the hammer fell useless before the blade. Thor stared blankly at the headless handle gripped in his fist. Svipdag advanced, picked up the hammerhead and tossed it to the startled Æsir.

"I know you, Veor, son of Odin. My father has told me the story of the challenge of the smiths, the judgment of your court, and the humiliation of our house. Know that by action greater than any judgment, I have vindicated the skill of my family dishonored so long ago. For this bright blade that I hold, the last greatest work of Volund, son of Ivalde, is proved the superior weapon."

The sounds of battle diminished as warrior after warrior took notice, jaws dropped in awe at the defeat. Svipdag slapped the flat of his blade against the blood-soaked rings on his chest in salute. "For the sake of the friendship you once held for my father and him for you, leave this slaughter field in peace. Take the pieces of your weapon back to the smith who created it. I'm certain he can repair the damage."

Svipdag started to turn away but stopped and turned back to a muttering Thor. "It has been my highest honor defeating the strong guarder of the Æsir in battle. But know that should we meet once more in combat you will again taste defeat. For I hold the foremost weapon. Yours will always be the second best."

With these words, Halfdan's troops abandon the field.

———

The dead burned for seven days, great heaps of tangled butchery beyond number, bodies bursting wide on flaming pyres that crowded the countryside. A fleet of ship-ringed barrows marked the plain, their earthen hulls filled with charred bone and greasy ashes. On a high hill overlooking the battle field a line of batua stones commemorated the bravery of fallen warriors.

Svipdag had the body of Halfdan placed on a pyre, clad in his war gear, and wrapped in his royal robes. On his head, he propped his helmet, its rim wound with wire held fast without, a fortress fence to protect its wearer against the rain of keen-edged blades. On the king's breast, he arranged the pieces of the battle sword he always carried at his side, wrapping the king's cold fingers about its hilt so it rested on his chest, gripped in his gauntleted fists.

The blaze of the pyre roared to life, woken from its slumber by a burning knot of pitch. Wood smoke swirled black above flames driven by a steady wind, until the heat burst wide the bone house of the dead king. Metal glowed red, sagged, and then ran in bright yellow rivulets through the charred ricks as the fire consumed everything. He placed Halfdan's ashes in a howe raised up on a nearby hill, its walls built of thick cut stones, its interior graced with the trappings due a great warrior and honored king.

With his vengeance satisfied for the death of his grandfather and the dishonor done to his mother, Svipdag—mindful of the quest placed upon him by his father—set out to recover the Menglödum.

The Rescue of Freyja

Along rocky paths Svipdag journeyed past high headlands that over thrust the sea where breakers grind against the shore and rough winds toss the white hair of the ocean. With skilled hands, he constructed a linden raft for the eagerly sought voyage. He hewed the logs by hand then bound them together using coils of hard-twined bast rope, the knots soaked with sea water to hold fast. In its center, he rigged a short sail to catch the breath of Ægir.

Trusting the promise of Groa's spells to calm the ocean's wrath, he set out across the gannet's bath, his mind held to a good outcome. With a sturdy pole Svipdag sculled the raft from shore as the currents wound round the timbers and drew it out to sea.

The sea plate skimmed over the waves, logs creaking as it rocked with the rhythm of swells rolling across the ocean surface, its journey made swift by a steady wind that plumped the sail. For two days, the wind drove him on. He kept himself lashed to the central mast lest, in a reverie or in the embrace of sleep, he tumble into the water, an offering for Ran.

On the morning of the second day he came to a dark land bundled thick with fir trees. He beached his raft on a shadowed strand that concealed a harbor cut deep into the headland. Svipdag jumped into the surf. Dragging his raft ashore, he tied it off to a large stump of driftwood that jutted up from the gray sands.

A loud crashing sounded from inland, the measured advance of a pending storm. Three etins stomped through the forest, their shoulders brushing the highest branches. As they pushed their way through the towering trees Svipdag dropped his hand cautiously onto the hilt of his sword.

The etins stopped before him, their feet planted wide on the strand. The three crossed thick arms across broad chests wrapped in leather jerkins the color and texture of a headland cliff. Rugged faces crowned by heads thatched with thick, unruly black hair gazed down at the wayward mariner.

"Ho!" called the center etin to the traveler. "What bold man are you to brave the rough waters on wooden planks? My brothers and I have long held watch over the sea so that no foe may threaten our land. With our strength, we stand ready to thwart any invasion of wave stallions bearing shield warriors to an attack. Some daring few have tried. Always we have driven them back into the brine, their numbers lessened. But never has such a dangerous foe, a raggedy castoff in rusty rings, come as boldly to our shore as have you."

The giant leaned over until his chin hovered over Svipdag's head. "I now speak plainly." He shook a warning finger thick as a branch. "Tell us who are you that arrives unannounced here at the Skerry of Syr and why you have come. Make haste with your reply or you will soon find yourself embarked on an ocean voyage without your trusty skiff!"

The seafarer, undaunted by the three etins, stepped forward from the raft. "I have nothing to hide!" His voice rang out over the steady rushing of waves against the beach. "My name is Svipdag, son of Orvandel—a noble warrior remembered by the wise ones throughout the nine worlds. He is known to your kin from years past.

I come in search of a brother and sister of the Æsir. Many years ago, in a fit of anger, my father and his brothers left them behind as payment for safe passage through your land. An obligation was laid upon my shoulders to heal wounds left festering between two houses: that of my family and that of the Æsir. I have been sent here by my father to return the children to their rightful home."

A sea breeze blew inland whipping Svipdag's long locks into his face. Gathering them behind his head, he tied them back with a piece of twine pulled from the pocket of his vest. The giants grumbled impatiently as he finished securing the knot. "I have replied truthfully to your questions and concealed nothing about my mission. Now it is my turn to ask questions of you, if you dare answer with the same strength of honesty. Who are you to question weary travelers with such open hostility? It is obvious by the state of my arrival that I pose no threat, nor mark the arrival of a great fleet bent on conquest. I find it difficult to believe you fear a brace of fleet-footed warriors arrived from across the sea astraddle driftwood."

The tallest of the three brothers stepped forward, until his shadow swallowed the son of Orvandel. He thumped his chest with a hairy fist until the skerry echoed with its sound. "We are called Grep, my brothers and I, guardians of the Skerry of Syr. Of all those among my kin who attend the Menglödum, I alone have found favor in the eyes of Menglad. Her brother is attended by another."

Svipdag slapped his hand against his chest. "Then you can direct me," he shouted to the ear hands of the giants high above, "to where I may find them."

Grep quirked his shaggy brow, winked at his brothers, then burst out laughing—the sound of boulders crashing into the sea. He bent low and blew his foul breath over the visitor. "It is said that actions define the warrior. You will not leave this strand alive unless you can give us cause to heed your words. What have you done that we should guide your way?"

Svipdag paced a narrow circle before the brothers Grep, glancing up at the giants and then out across the white-haired crests of ocean. "You ask of deeds performed by my hand. Where do I begin? Time has flown by though the years have not and the events of my life rush headlong to the sea."

Squaring his shoulders, the young warrior positioned himself, feet braced, hand on the pommel of his blade, his chin tilted until he looked the brothers Grep directly in the eyes. "I am plain of speech and little given to ornamentation," he let his fingers drift along the sword handle, then back to the pommel, "preferring to let my actions speak for themselves. Listen as I sing my own true story."

Before them Svipdag laid out the tale of his journeys through the dark worlds, the hazards faced in ice-cold lands, the many battles fought. He recounted his triumphs, owned his failures, spoke of daring actions, and, with a hint of pride, related the many adversities overcome. He left nothing out.

Grep laughed when Svipdag finished his tale. "You tell a woeful tale of hardship and adventure. But I have found that people often make their sufferings match their recollections. They tell stories of dangerous exploits when all they have done is burn their dinner."

Svipdag smiled at his feet and shrugged. "Those who have engaged in a perilous journey," he chuckled softly, "often find it difficult to convince others of the trials endured."

Grep tapped his fingers along his chin while his brothers rolled their eyes. "Your words are as gum sap on a fir tree," he stared hard down at Svipdag, "sticky and ready to trap the unwary. When chewed by your jaws, they stretch the truth no farther than it will go. You tell of lands only spoken of in stories, of events that would fill many lifetimes. It is doubtful any one man—especially an obvious youth such as yourself—could travel so far and accomplish so much."

Svipdag shook his head. "You can trust wholly in the truth of my words," he placed a hand on his breast, "though I speak of places and events you have never seen or even imagined. Those who know only the walls of their home often suspect exaggeration on hearing of actions they cannot conceive, or feel are beyond their own capabilities."

Grep thumped his chest. "There is little I have not done!" His voice bellowed as a bull calls to the heavens. "My achievements are as many as the metal rings on my byrnie! Tales of my greatness are often sung around the eldskáli! My name falls as praise among my kin! I have heard nothing in your words that should make me take notice or stand in admiration!"

Svipdag stood his ground, feet planted firmly on the sandy shore. "Many will endure words of praise," his steady voice carried the calm assurance of hard-won experience, "if they can persuade themselves of their ability to equal the recounted actions. Beyond that, they fall into envy and incredulity, turning scorn on the accomplishments of others they know they can never achieve."

The etin stomped his foot so the land trembled, and the sea rippled back from the shore. "There is nothing you can do, little man, which I cannot! I find your empty boasts not to my liking. I would find your lies more convincing if you claimed a hand at actions I know can be done and not the deeds of a wandering mind."

The son of Orvandel stepped forward until he stood directly beneath the giant. "I see you are confident in your disbelief." He looked straight up, challenging the giant to dare disagree. "That is the way it is with those who have never traveled beyond the edge of their own lands. In my journeys, I have found that ignorance more often begets confidence than does knowledge. It is those who know little, not those who know much, who positively assert this or that action cannot be accomplished. Know that I have done all I claimed. It matters little to me if it falls outside the narrow walls of your understanding."

Grep gnashed his teeth at Svipdag's response—the sound of gravel crunched underfoot. He gestured sharply with his arm as his brothers turned away. "The hall lies this way. There you will find the Menglödum seated before the great fire. Have no doubt that they will remain where they are, for the strength of your hand is as nothing compared to the combined might found in our hall. My kin will never let them go, and your body will be cast into the ocean, food for those that dwell in its depths."

The giant snorted, frustrated with this tiny invader. "Now follow us if you still have the stomach." He turned his feet along a worn trail that snaked away from the beach. "We will soon see if your words are more than bold talk."

The cobbled path guided the way to a dark-timbered hall perched high on a rocky mound that overlooked the sea. They passed through a frost-crusted entry, a high arch of stone and wood artfully constructed, set with stone pillars to bear the heavy beams that supported the expanse of roof.

As Svipdag stepped into the long hall, the powerful smell of unwashed bodies made him gasp. Great hootings and horrible grunting sounds, like the howling of wild animals in pain, assaulted his ears. Before him, the etin court marched in slow procession around two high seats placed close beside a great fire, its ravening flames raised as protection against the bitter cold that wrapped the hall. In the seats the Menglödum, Freyr and Freyja, slumped, nearly lifeless, in thrall to their etin hosts, their present a dull shadow, their past a distant memory.

Freyr perched rigid on the edge of his seat, cheeks flushed bright red, staring stony-eyed into the fire. His fingers clenched the arms of his chair so tightly, their white knuckles winked in the flickering flames. Freyja slumped in her seat with downcast eyes watching the fire. Her hair pressed into a fletta of hard, braided horns, circled each side of her head giving the impression of a wood carving that mimicked life.

Svipdag shouted over the din to get their attention. "I am Svipdag, son of Orvandel, son of Ivalde! Know that I have traveled far to rectify the wrong my father committed. Come, let us leave this place!"

The two did not react to his cry. He called once more to the pair, his voice set with determination. Again, he received no response. At his words, the Howlers stopped their circling. All faces turned to the unwelcome visitor—grim masks of shadow and flickering light. They screamed as one and, in a body, attacked.

Drawing his blade Svipdag flashed the brilliance of the sun into the eyes of the advancing etins. With sharp cries, they raised their hands to shield their sight from the burning glare. Striking lustily left to right, he hewed them down, layering the floor with their bodies, as they stumbled before the brightness. Each blow drove them farther back along the length of the hall until they huddled screaming at the far end, unable to retreat and afraid to advance.

With a sharp gesture Svipdag commanded the two to fall in behind him. "Come to me now! We must leave swiftly. I have a raft moored on the beach. Trust me that it offers a safe return to the comfort of your family's hall."

Freyja remained seated with eyes downcast. Freyr gazed full on their would-be rescuer, then turned his face aside. He replied quietly to Svipdag's urging. "There is a blot on my litr. I am no longer fit company for kin. The indignities I have endured at the hands of the Howlers has reddened my face with shame and blackened my heart."

The young man glanced at the knot of screaming Howlers that were beginning to organize themselves. "It is right I should remain behind, stained in character as I am, for if all of us leave now, the full might of this hall would fall on our necks and we would find the beach as far away as Delling's gate. But if I stay, the etins will be slow to pursue. They are a cautious lot, preferring the bird in the hand to the one in flight."

He waved a hand toward Freyja. "Go now, brave warrior. Take my sister with you that she, at least, escape this shameful treatment. Tell my father he can find me suffering in this dark hole surrounded by jabbering demons, where I endure and hate and weep."

The bloody blade of Volund gripped in one fist, with his other arm Svipdag lifted Freyja bodily from her seat. Dragging the unresisting woman from the hall, together they stumbled down the path to the beach. With the rising screams of the Howlers and the thunder of their running feet building behind, Svipdag heaved the maiden onto the raft. Hacking the mooring line free, he pushed the raft into the surf. Freyja made no move to help but lay in a daze as he hastily sculled the craft out to sea. They passed the first line of breakers as etins thronged the beach, some wading waist-deep into the surf yelling, shaking their fists, and beating the waves in frustration.

The charms of Groa again smoothed the way, speeding the sturdy raft with its precious cargo huddled about the mast over the ocean to the ice-packed headlands.

———————————

Across the frozen borderlands of Jotunheim they traveled, heavy woolen cloaks drawn tight about their shoulders, a light pack of provisions their only food. With each mile Svipdag's heart grew fonder of his charge, for he could see her beauty was as great as his father had promised.

Each morning he greeted her with cheerful words. During the grueling journey, he helped guide her feet along the rocky path. At rest, he proffered food and made sure she drank at least some water. At night, after tucking her near the fire, he stood watch while she struggled and moaned in her sleep. But though they journeyed together, shared food and the warmth of a fire, she did not respond in any way to his presence. Always she held her head high, her eyes focused on the ground ahead.

As they neared the Ifing, the ice-cold river between Jotunheim and Midgard, he began to regret his desire. For each warm word, each gesture of concern was met with complete indifference. Never once did Freyja focus her gaze on her rescuer.

Each day in Svipdag's breast desire warred with anger until, unable to bear the wretchedness any longer, he declared his love for the distraught maiden. "See me," his voice quavered in an agony of pleading. "Look at one who suffered much in his efforts to rescue you. Alone I braved the terrors of dark worlds, endured the hardships of frozen lands, and dared the open sea—on a raft of all things. I even overcame the horrors of the Howler's home."

He dropped to one knee in the dust. "Look at one who has loved you since the moment he first heard your name." He reached out a hand to touch her robe. "Even before I had seen you with my own eyes, you were beauty beyond compare. You filled me, so I could think of nothing, but your safety and the hopeful promise of love returned." Freyja turned to examine the crest of a nearby hill, seeming to ignore his action. His heart spasmed in agony, threatening to burst from his breast.

Dragging a hand across his face, Svipdag rubbed thumb and forefinger into heated eyes that threatened tears. He swallowed hard, forcing away the rasp that had been building in his voice. "Give me a look, a nod, some token, some acknowledgement that under my protection you are willing to be reunited with your kin." Hands shaking, his gaze beseeching, he knelt waiting before his heart's desire.

Freyja stared silently at the horizon, as cold and unresponsive to his entreaties as she had been to his presence since the start of their journey.

When they reached the broad waters of the Ifing, Svipdag set up a rest camp. After making certain everything was in order, he turned to his impassive companion. "Wait here while I locate the ford. It is known only to my family and unmarked so etins cannot discover the way." He craned his neck searching the nearby riverbank. "We are near, I'm certain of it. It lies at a seemingly impassible spot where a narrow ledge of submerged rocks snakes across the river." He glanced back at his companion. "The waters climb only waist deep and the current can be strong, but it is the cold you really have to watch out for."

Freyja said nothing, letting her gaze pass through Svipdag to some far point beyond his shoulders, then returning to her hands resting cupped in her lap. "Look at me. Just look at me," he begged, frustration edging into his voice. "Do you understand what I'm saying?" Svipdag ground his teeth while Freyja stared mutely at her fingertips. "Stay here; I will be back soon. This is a concealed spot. You should be safe from prying eyes. I've left you the food and water."

He held his breath, waiting for a response. Receiving none, he spun on his heel and stomped off toward the river.

While Svipdag searched for the way across, Freyja huddled alone in the spare camp. Panic flared in the maiden's eyes as the silent, empty landscape closed in. Gathering her feet beneath her, the young woman slipped away down the riverbank, concealing herself behind a scattering of boulders and sharp mounds of dirty ice that dotted the gravel shore.

When he returned from scouting, Svipdag stared in alarm at the empty camp. He scanned the ground for etin sign but spied only Freyja's footprints leading down the beach. He followed her trail until it disappeared among the rocks. Climbing atop the nearest boulder, he repeatedly shouted her name, with each call bidding her return to camp that he might deliver her to safety. "This is foolishness! Now is not the time to run away! While we remain on this side of the Ifing the etin remain a threat! Our journey nears its end. We have only to cross the river to reach the safety of my father's hall!"

He called until his voice grew hoarse, searched until weary with frustration before stumping back to camp. Harsh words tumbled from his lips as he slammed provisions into his travel pack. He left an errant few scattered on the ground as he wrenched the pack shut and tied it off. "The ungrateful bitch! Let's see her find her own way in this desolate land. If she has the wits to hide from me, then let her fare for herself and hide from the etin. I'm certain they would delight in regaining her company." He shouted over his shoulder. "Did you hear me? I said they would delight in regaining your company!"

With a great show of effort, Svipdag gathered up his pack. He glared about, frowned deeply, and kicked the ground. Bending low, he arranged pebbles in a pattern to show the direction to the ford. Giving a final glance along the shoreline, he shuffled his way across the river. On the opposite shore, he looked back once before heading to his father's hall poised high on a knoll set far back from the bank, there to admit the failure of his quest.

———·———

Cautiously, the wounded bird returned to the camp, driven by hunger and cold to the place she had fled without thought. As she gobbled up the food Svipdag had left scattered on the ground, her downcast eyes spotted the trail he had marked. She swiftly followed to the river's edge, fearful lest the etin spy her traveling alone.

Trusting the guide of her rescuer, she waded into the icy river, knees bent, bracing herself against the current. With each tentative step her feet slid on stones in the riverbed while the rime-cold waters burned her legs. The water tugged at her limbs, but never rose higher than her waist. Moving with agonizing slowness across the river, she groped for each step as feeling faded from her feet. She slipped, then again, each time flailing back onto the submerged ridge, and with main will forced her legs, now aching from the cold, to keep moving.

Time became an eternity of endless pressure accompanied by the steady rumble of rushing brown water. She fought to keep her eyes focused on a grassy knoll that rose up along the far bank. With each step, it grew steadily into a large hill that humped up well behind the embankment.

She was cold—cold and numb—barely able to stand when she craned her neck back to see the hilltop. It dawned on her then that she had finally reached the other side.

Freyja clawed from the shallowing waters, her hands and knees gouging ruts into the muddy bank. Flipping over on her back, with shaking hands she stripped off her boots. Teeth gritted against the pain, she desperately pounded her thighs and chafed her feet until the aching blue turned to burning red.

The Ifing continued to grumble by unconcerned with her frantic struggle. Freyja stared grimly across the expanse. Its wide surface seemed frozen then suddenly it began to undulate, slowly, relentlessly along its course. She shook her head to clear away the sudden vision of Howler faces screaming before a blazing hearth fire. Mud squelching under her knees, she rocked back, screaming over and over at the dusty gray shoreline floating in the distance, until the leering faces faded.

With a sobbing breath, Freyja jerked her boots back on over feet that had only just begun to regain sensation. She wasted no time in staggering along the trail Svipdag had marked, for even on this side of the Ifing his stone guide clearly pointed to a holding perched on a nearby hill.

Teeth chattering, her body shivering uncontrollably, Freyja arrived at the hall of Orvandel. In wet, ragged clothes caked with the grime of a long trail, she presented herself as a poor traveler in desperate need of warmth, food, and shelter.

Cooing kind words of welcome, they ushered the chilled vagrant into their home. "Please," they stepped aside to let her enter, "come inside. Our fire is warm and we've food to share."

Smiling gently, the young woman nodded to her hosts as she crossed the threshold into the warmth of the hall. With head held high, she moved in stately grace to the main room and seated herself in a position of accustomed prominence. Orvandel, familiar with the refined actions of one raised amid nobility, recognized the true nature of his guest.

"You are chilled to the bone." With a sharp clap of his hands, he called for attendance fitting one of her station. "Quickly, heat water to fill the large tub. Use the clean one in the back chamber."

"And clean clothes," added Sygne. "I've several warm robes she can wear."

A hot bath was prepared, and clean clothes set beside. Servants used an iron pick to loosen the stiff braids that bound her hair until the long luxurious locks fell free about her shoulders. Refreshed, the maiden took a seat at the head of the board. For the household, it was as if the sun had risen in their home.

Before her, Sygne placed a steaming bowl of hearty barley soup topped with chunks of venison. Alongside she set a mug of heated ale to warm the blood. The young woman smiled to her hostess, then turned herself to the offering, groaning with pleasure at every mouthful of the hot food, smacking her lips with each taste of the drink. After eating her fill, she pushed away from the table and huddled beside the hearth, leaning close to the fire as if seeking the memory of warmth.

Sygne started with alarm, but Orvandel held her back with a gentle pressure on her arm. "No. She has been through much. Leave her be for now. When she is ready to rest, then..."

The fire, the safety, the quiet sounds of a household going about its business... her head began to nod with exhaustion. Orvandel gestured to Sygne, who helped the young woman to her feet and guided her away to where a warm bed covered with soft furs had been plumped for her rest.

Each day, the maiden graciously accepted the hospitality of the archer's home. She smiled little as she moved about the hall, a cloth veil shadowing her face; an action taken by her helpers as modesty, but was instead, intended to disguise, for on the day after her arrival she had spied Svipdag brooding before the hearth and wished to remain hidden from his gaze.

But Svipdag was not fooled. He recognized her every movement and his heart twisted in agony each time he saw her. But whenever they passed she averted her gaze. Whenever he greeted her, she refused to respond.

Svipdag called his father and stepmother aside for a candid talk. With a rush of words, he told them the stranger's true name. "That veiled woman who haunts our home is the very one I rescued from the etins. It is Freyja," he blurted. "I'm certain of it." His eyes became misty as they followed his voice back to the Ifing and his pain on finding her gone from the camp. "She followed the trail markers I left behind."

"Do you know what that means?" His gaze snapped back to the table. Orvandel and Sygne stared uncomprehending at their son. "It means she heard me. Even through her pain, she knows me. It means she shares the great ache that has gripped my breast from the first moment I saw her."

Orvandel raised a hand to cover his eyes. "Of course," he sighed. "To have arrived so soon after you, who else could it have been? She has the inborn radiance of her line. Her features—though older and drawn—are of the giggling child I remember. It pains me to see her in such misery. There must be something we can do to ease her suffering."

Together the three conferred about what actions to take. Svipdag demanded to discover if she harbored any feelings for him. "She followed me here on the path I laid out, braved the Ifing to come to this hall when she could have taken any other route."

"Let's be reasonable." Orvandel rocked back in his seat. "She was scared and unfamiliar with the territory. Why wouldn't she follow the path you marked?" He shrugged, his shoulders nearly touching his ears. "Where else was she to go?"

Sygne added her thoughts to the old warrior's question. "The nearest holding is three days walk; its buildings concealed in a wooded valley." She slowly shook her head as if pondering her own words. "Had she taken a route other than to one you marked, she would have perished wandering the rugged forest paths. Her presence here does not mean she has feelings for you. She simply had no other choice."

Svipdag clapped his hands together. "No!" He made a defiant fist before his face. "Together we traveled a hard road. Companions who endure such hardship come to know one another without words. I know she sees me as more than a wraith. My heart speaks to her heart, but the thrall of the etin remains heavy on her mind, obscuring her true feelings. She needs a shock to bring her back and admit to the sentiment she holds for me."

Sygne spoke thoughtfully through steepled fingers, letting her words crystallize into a carefully considered truth. "The best way to shake a woman from her personal sorrow and forcibly bring her into the present is for her to see that which she most desires taken away, never to be hers."

"To know if she cares for you as a mate we must make you unavailable. We will arrange a pretend wedding between yourself and a young maiden from our household." Svipdag's eyes widened in alarm. He started to rise, but Sygne's composed gaze held him in his seat. "And to ensure she must fully face the prospect of your loss, we will press her into the duties of a bridesmaid, one who must attend the betrothed couple from the start of the ceremony to its close at the entry of the bridal chamber. If you follow this advice, I tell you that you will know soon enough the full extent of any feelings she holds for you."

The ceremony was held in the courtyard. An arbor of fir boughs marked the pledge stone on which the couple would stand and recite their vows. Freyja stood shivering beside the bride, her eyes downcast, a floral wreath clutched in her hands. During the entire ceremony, she refused to look up, even when Svipdag slipped from the stone as his turn came to state his vows.

Throughout the gaiety and feasting, it was her role as first maid to stand beside the couple as the gathering cheered each toast that was made. Inside her cheeks, Sygne smiled with satisfaction as she watched the maiden's blanched features begin to quiver.

When the time arrived to consummate the bond, Freyja guided the couple to their bridal chamber, carrying a candle before her to light the way. She kept her eyes fixed on the bright flame gripped tight in her trembling fist. Cheeks pale as moonlight framed blanched lips that quivered as a moth singed by flame. At each step, hot tallow spilled down onto her hand. Pain shown in her eyes like the fright of a caged bird caught in the grip of the flickering flame. The pain was not from the blistering tallow, but from a more burning ache kindled in her heart that grew to a raging fire as she stood aside to let the new couple pass into the chamber.

The bride passed through the door with a coy glance over her shoulder. As Svipdag came abreast of Freyja, he noticed the layer of hot tallow blistering across her white knuckles. "Take care, my good lady." He gently touched her arm. "See to your hand lest you lose its use. It would be terrible were you unable to hold onto that which is yours."

At his words, Freyja lifted her gaze from the floor. When their eyes met, the spell of the etin was broken. The tenuous curtain, which had shrouded her eyes and muffled her heart, fell away. "You are real!" Her words spilled forth in panting sobs. "Until I gazed into your eyes, I could not tell if all this was real or one of the willful imaginings that helped me endure the hollow passing of each season in the etin's hall."

She shuddered, recalling her fear. "I dreamt so often of a rescuer who would save me from the cold confines of the Howlers, one I could give all my heart for spiriting me home to my family, that when you dragged me from the clutches of the etins, I scarce believed you were real. Even as we drifted across the wide ocean, stumbled along the frozen earth of Jotunheim, and I heard the gentleness in your voice, the concerns you expressed for my welfare while ignoring the discomforts the hard trail imposed on yourself, yes, even then I thought you were another reverie. I expected at any moment that my eyes would open to find myself still seated in dimness before the Howler's hearth, the object of Grep's desires."

The maiden clasped the candle with both hands, her shaking grip threatening to choke off the taper's wavering light. "But it was a dream I did not wish to wake from." She swallowed hard, her eyes following the shadows scampering across the walls. "For as we traveled I found my empty spot no longer empty but brimming with joy and boundless love for the one who had braved so much to see me safe. When I arrived in this, your father's home, and saw you resting beside the hearth, I dared not take the chance of waking. So, I veiled my face to avoid the temptation." Freyja sobbed and drew a hand across her eyes.

"It is only when I see you now, ready to make a life with another that I know this is no dream." She sniffed back a fresh stabbing pain that shook her voice. "By my own fear, it is the loss of my true heart's desire."

When the maiden's speech had run out, Svipdag took her hand. "You have endured much and are exhausted after such an experience. Take my hand and by the promise of my heart stone be restored."

His eyes crinkled with a warm smile. "Dear one, even before I met you, when I first accepted the charge from my father to rescue you and your brother from the chill bonds of the Howlers, I knew the desire for your hand. While I struggled across wet ways, endured freezing cold, the painful hunger of a hard trail, I held an image of you close, the likeness of a vibrant woman built from my father's description of you as a child. When I saw you huddled and dejected in the hearth seat of the etin's hall, your beauty far greater than my imagination, I wanted to always protect you. As we traveled the difficult path to home, as I saw your splendor and grace rise with each glorious dawn, I came to adore you. But when I thought I had lost you at the river's edge, I felt a great wrenching in my chest, Sol dimmed in the sky, and my world ended. It was all I could do to not let the waters of the Ifing take me as I struggled home to face my failure."

Svipdag smiled into Freyja's eyes. "When I saw you again," he reached out to brush a golden lock of hair back from her face, "standing unharmed in my father's hall, risen as if from the grave, free from the treacherous waters of the Ifing, scarce could I keep my racing heart in place - it threatened to burst from my breast."

Svipdag took a deep breath, stood up straight, and plunged on with his speech. "The ceremony you saw was false." He stared at Freyja's hand still gripped in his and gripping back just as hard, then lifted his gaze to peer deep into eyes grown wide with desire. "I did not give a marriage oath. It was a contrivance necessary to sever the bonds the etin had laid upon your mind. Know that all I have, all I am or ever will be is yours, just as it was on the desolate stretches we traveled together."

With these words Svipdag let her know he was free to honor that which he had just declared. With a smile that dimmed the candle flame, Freyja let him know that she accepted and was ready to honor her desires. "My heart is like the snowfall in spring when the sun has returned to light the sky. There is a great thaw, a sound of running waters, and a sprouting of green plants. The call of geese fills the air with music, for a long winter has broken."

Reconciled, the couple returned to the courtyard where everything had remained in readiness. This time Svipdag did not slip from the pledge stone when it came his turn to speak his vows.

The Rescue of Freyr

Notice arrived in Asgard that the jewels of the Æsir had been recovered. Gathering up his cloak, Njord rushed to the hall of Orvandel eager to embrace his children after so long a time. He was furious to find only his daughter. Drawing Svipdag aside, Njord spoke at great length with the young man, querying him on his every action, challenging each of his decisions. "I gave you aide in recovering that which had been taken from me by guiding you to a power great enough to defeat etin armies and even terrify the gods! Tell me why, with this weapon in your hands, you returned with just my daughter?"

Raising himself up tall before his new kinsman, Svipdag chose his words carefully that he be understood. Before Njord, he laid out the tale of his journey: the cold, dark lands clouded with freezing mists, the seeming endless expanse of slate-gray sea, of the brothers Grep and the Howlers, of the words his son had spoken in the etin hall. He left nothing out.

On hearing of the shame his son bore, the wise god of the sea placed a hand over his eyes. His shoulders shook as a fire rose his neck to bloom bright red on his cheeks. He turned to the son of Orvandel, placed a hand on his arm and squeezed. "Much you have endured on your travels. Much honor you have gathered to yourself. No other among men and few among the gods can hold such a claim to greatness. In returning my daughter to me, you have done me a great service. In honoring the request of my son to sacrifice himself, you have done him a greater service. By choosing to remain behind, he removed any blot to his character his captors may have imposed. For your efforts on the behalf of my family, I deem it an honor to have you as kin."

He looked Svipdag candidly in the eye. "But know that though you and my daughter have made pledge in this hall, you cannot fully possess her hand until you challenge the gates of Asgard itself. The Æsir will demand a gift, one that they greatly fear and so desire the more." He pointed to the young man's waist. "The sword you carry— the one crafted by Volund—for that they would adopt a valiant warrior from the land of men as a son into their clan."

With these words Njord turned his face to the northeast, his gaze brittle as sheet ice on a frozen sea. When he spoke, it was the sound of waves crashing against a rocky headland. "Long they have kept my children from my eyes, those I thought I had lost to time. Now my daughter is returned to her home and I know where my son is held. Though the offspring of Ymir feel indomitable in their land, they will soon learn there is no place I cannot reach, no foe I cannot overcome when I flex my full might."

Without another word, he departed for the land of Jotunheim. Following the path Svipdag had marked in his mind, he sailed across the frigid waters to the dark hall of the Howlers nestled above the Skerry of Syr. Standing on the strand he boldly confronted the etins still shaken from the deeds of the warrior youth. "Hear me children of Ymir. I, Njord of the Vanir, governor of the sea, call on you to listen. You are holding my son in your hall. I will have him back alive and safe or you will know my fury."

A loud howling sounded from the cliff-top hall as a large etin stepped up to rocky edge. "I am Beli," his shout carried down from on high while braying taunts echoed from the shadows gathered at his back. "It is my strong arm that now wards this place." He glared at the figure standing undaunted on the beach, then thumped his chest with a leather-wrapped fist. "What is this that threatens us, an ancient speck of driftwood washed up from the sea to mire itself in the mud of the strand? You claim kinship to a freely given gift and demand its return. What is that to us? Leave now old man. What is ours, remains ours. You will have nothing."

Twice more Njord called for his son's release. Twice more he was answered with shouts, jeers, and the shrill screeching of animals. A third time Njord cried out, his voice rising on a gale. "This is the last time I ask! I will not ask again! Return my son to me now or I will tear down your hall along with the very ground on which it stands! I will see your lives stripped from you, even as the raging waters of the sea rip the rocky headland from the coast and drag it whole beneath the hungry waves!"

The etins continued to hoot at his words. Amid the riot of their laughter, Beli sneered down from his perch. "Your threats are feeble, scarcely worth our notice." Two shaggy heads peered out from behind his legs and made obscene noises of derision. Beli chuckled at their antics. "Even our children see you as a fool. Take your aged carcass from our shore lest we puff our breath and blow you away."

The sea god's face turned black as he lifted his hands to the sky. From his parted lips screamed the blast of tempest winds. In a headlong rush of seething waters, wall-after-wall of towering white waves ripped wide the Skerry of Syr which had long sheltered the hall. Raging surf pounded against the ragged gash in the headland. Currents ground against the open shoreline, dragging away whole sections of the hillside. Each crash of the vicious waves shook the foundations of the Howler's hall. The thunder of violent surf coupled with the shriek of rising winds drowned out the cries of the terrified etins.

They hurriedly wrapped Freyr in animal skins and hustled him from the hall. The young man offered no resistance to his captors as they bundled him along the cobble path, only smiled at the scream of the rising gale.

Dragging their burden down the ragged cliff edge that had been a gentle slope to the shore, they delivered the unresisting youth to the ancient figure waiting alone on the beach. The old man gazed warmly into the face of the son he thought he had lost. Taking the young man in an embrace, he gently guided him onto his ship. Its sails billowing with a fair wind, the sea stallion leapt into the waves. Behind them the scream of the gale dropped to a sigh as the crested waves withdrew from the ravaged shore.

The Challenge of Fjolsvith

Svipdag traveled the western route Njord had taken to his father's hall, the same road frequented by Thor on his journeys, to challenge frost-rimed giants crouched in their cold lands. After years of hard-fought battles that raised his renown until no one across the nine worlds did not know of the One who could not be defeated, whose sword was the object of legend, Svipdag stood before the multicolored stream that arced down from above to brush the land.

At the bridgehead of Asbrau where seething waters conceal its entry, he boldly stepped through a thick cloud of steam and began his long climb along the trembling way. The white sentry marked his arrival. But unwilling to challenge a warrior who wielded the terrible weapon of Volund, he stepped aside to let him pass unmolested. With the swift feet of a rested messenger, he sent urgent word ahead to the great hall.

The vaunted warrior climbed along the windheim road to where the surrounding wall of Asgard swelled up, towering before him. The massive wall was itself encircled by a torrent of roiling water shrouded in black mist. As he approached a bolt of vaferflame leapt from the dark cloud to bar his way.

On a shining tower, high above the wall stood a sentry wrapped in a heavy gray cloak. A golden spear gripped in his fist, he waited on the warrior's advance. The sentry called out in challenge as Svipdag neared the wall, his voice carrying over the low rumble of the torrent. "What manner of lowly creature is this who skulks about our wall daring the perilous flame?" He shook his spear, so its wicked tip flashed in the sunlight. "Hold, friendless wayfarer. Advance no further. I can hear you from where you stand. Tell me what it is you seek. Answer truthfully and without hesitation or don't let the wind brush your backside as you return along the way you came."

Planting his fists on his hips, Svipdag shouted to the sentry perched high above. "What grim brute is that who menaces a weary traveler stopped to admire grandeur? Come tell me your name brute, though I suspect it is one void of an honest reputation."

The burly sentry slapped the spear against his chest, then bellowed with a voice loud as thunder in the sky. "Mine is a good name, such as yours has never been. I am called, Fjolsvith, for my wise thoughts. While generous with counsel, of hospitality I am not free. Leave now, stranger. Return to whatever lands you call home. You will find no hearth for wanderers within these courts."

Svipdag flashed his teeth in a broad smile. "I feel no need to hurry from this place at yours or anyone's urging." Shifting his stance, he placed his hand on the hilt of the great sword at his side, the familiar action of an experienced warrior prepared to draw his blade should the need arise. "The sturdy gate and massive walls that protect gleaming halls roofed in gold and silver find great favor in my eyes. I would be well content to live out my days with such beauty spread out before me."

The gray-headed sentry bristled at Svipdag's words. He shook his golden spear in a gloved fist. "You speak with a brazen tongue and so jeopardize your life! Let me know why I should not strike you down where you stand." Spittle flew from his lips as he shouted down from the heights. "Come stranger, tell me your lineage. Name your father, if you know him! There may be some worth in your line that would bear notice, though I doubt you share its glory."

Svipdag tapped a hand to his chest, then brushed the ground with his fingers as he bowed. "Vindkald you may call me, the cold wind that blows discomfort among the boastful. My father and his father are colder still. Varkald the spring cold and Fjolkald the very cold who freeze the hearts of the arrogant." The sentry grumbled as Svipdag straightened and planted his fists on his hips. "Now Fjolsvith, tell me truthfully, for I have never seen a sentry astride such a gaudy mount, what is the name of that silver-roofed tower from which you spy out movement below?"

Fjolsvith stamped his foot so the tower rang as a bell. "Hlidskialf it is called. From its vantage, the nine worlds can be seen."

Svipdag pointed at what he could see behind the wall. "And this gard surrounded by flickering flame, what do you call this place? I would never have believed such majesty existed had I not seen it with my own eyes."

Fjolsvith spread his arms out wide to encompass the court that lay beneath him, pointing with his spear from one end to the other. "In the lands of men, it is known by hearsay alone. Some call it Hyr. Others name it Asgard. It has long withstood the assault of time, longer still it will stand shimmering on the horizon."

Svipdag leaned forward for a clearer view of the court when the heat from another flash of vaferflame braced the air, flushing his cheeks with a flash of heat. He dodged backwards as the sentry burst into laughter. "Nice that," Svipdag patted his face and hair to make certain nothing was burning. "Now then Fjolsvith, tell me if you can, who holds sway over that shining hall, the one just to the right of this great gate?

Still chuckling, Fjolsvith gestured with his spear toward the hall shingled with gold, its eaves trimmed with silver. "If that is the one you mean, then know it is one of the richest halls in this gard. The lover of ornaments orders it herself, Freyja the daughter of Njord.

Svipdag's heart leapt at these words, beating so fast his throat ached. "This sturdy gate I see before me seems cleverly wrought. I would know about its magnificent construction and who might be allowed to pass through."

Fjolsvith puffed out his chest. "It is a gate unique unto itself. Built by sunblind craftsmen, it fetters any who would attempt to heave it from its moorings. Trapped beneath its weight they can only be released by a command from within. None may pass through without consent."

Svipdag nodded, made as if to speak, then stopped and gestured the length of the wall that surrounded the court. "Now this is a remarkable structure. In my many travels, I have never seen its equal in height or breadth. Its blocks are so well fitted they seem to have been grown in place."

Leaning down from the tower, Fjolsvith rapped the head of his spear hard against the wall. The sharp clink of metal on stone sparked the air. "This wall is called Gastrofnir. It forms an insurmountable barrier to the uninvited who would attempt entry. Constructed of mountain stone, hard-packed earth, and fire-baked clay, its thick walls are reinforced to stand against siege. Its massive height will remain unbreached for as long as men live."

Svipdag waved his arm at the dark waters circling the wall, careful not to step forward and again rouse its ire. "Tell me, if you can, of this great ward that nearly scorched the brows from my face; this formidable roiling black mist that covers the surface of turbulent water that surrounds the mighty wall. It seems very like a storm cloud that wreaks devastation from its bright bursts as it rages across the land."

Fjolsvith grinned down from his high seat. "That is the creation of the master smith, Sindri; it is one of his many gifts to our great hall. At a command from within," he snapped his fingers, "the vafer is separated from the waters, the dark mist of the storm cloud." He rocked back on his heels, delighted with himself. "Any who attempt to pass over its surface or approach too near its edge kindles the vafer to flame, sending a bolt of fire that unerringly seeks out the intruder."

Svipdag pointed across the chasm of black cloud to a point just inside the gate. "I see two fearsome hounds prowling stiff-legged within. They look hostile to an uninvited visitor. Who are they, and how might a man pass their guard unharmed?"

Fjolsvith laughed, pointing first at Svipdag, then at the wolves crouched just inside the gate. "The uninvited would have little chance against strong watchdogs such as these. One is called Geri; the other Freki. By day one keeps watch. By night the other patrols the halls. They will guard this court until the end of days." The wolves' ears twitched as he slapped his hand down on the rail before him, but their steady gaze never left Svipdag. "The unbidden visitor can pass their sleepless watch by offering up two morsels stripped from beneath the wings of the gay cock, Vidofnir. It is a treat they cannot resist; when tossed at their feet it will allow a man to slip by while they eat."

Svipdag rubbed his hands together as an eager smile twisted his lips. "Killing a cock is no difficult thing, simply wring its neck and be done. Where can I find this bird?"

Fjolsvith gripped his sides, bellowing with laughter. His face split into a wide grin as he pointed straight above his head. "The golden cock sits high atop Mimamirth, the great ash that spreads its limbs over this gard. His perch cannot be seen from the ground and is so high among the branches it is difficult to reach, even by a skilled climber. And know," here Fjolsvith laughed harder, "he cannot be caught while alive and his life cannot be taken by the hand."

Svipdag pondered the sentry's reply, then carefully framed his next question. "If he cannot be taken alive or die by the hand, then by what weapon can Vidofnir be felled from his high perch, and how can it be obtained?"

The gray sentry turned about at his post, scanning the great court beneath him to ensure his response would not be overheard, then leaned far out over the wall. Svipdag cupped a hand to his ear as the sentry's voice whispered down from above. "The bright blade, Lævantien it is called, the malicious sword of destruction, kept by Sinmara, queen of the Njara, in a chest secured by nine strong locks that none can break, that is the only weapon that can kill Vidofnir. Only through the presentation of a gift she ardently desires will Sinmara release the blade she guards. The mortal who can fetch this sword to give to the goddess of gold within will pass this gate... and none other."

Svipdag tapped his fingers on the hilt of his sword, then after some thought called out to the sentry. "Tell me Fjolsvith, if you know, is there any treasure a mortal can obtain that would gladden the heart of Sinmara and compel her to give up the sword?"

Fjolsvith's face split into a wide grin and he gestured with his spear to the high branches of Mimamirth. "From the golden cock that sits high atop this stalwart tree, pluck the shining feathers folded beneath his wings. Only when these are presented to Sinmara will she give over the weapon which can slay the cockerel."

Svipdag glanced up from the corner of his eyes, shaking his head. "This is the same gay cock as before, Vidofnir you called him? There is no other?"

Fjolsvith snorted with laughter. Once he had caught his sputtering breath, he straightened himself to his full height before pushing his reply through a broad grin. "There is no other."

Svipdag nodded. "You present a conundrum to one eager for honor and the accomplishment of great deeds." He thoughtfully stroked his chin. "The favor of this golden goddess must be a treasure beyond all others for one to struggle against such futility. What more can you tell me of this splendid maiden? Is she here now? Can I catch a glimpse of her from where I stand? I would see for myself the worth of her for which one must so mightily strive."

Fjolsvith pointed with his spear into the court below his watch. "Pass your gaze through the gate to the golden-haired creature seated on the far mound surrounded by nine handmaidens who watch over her well-being. Her seat is Hyfiaberg, the mountain of healing; the sick that can climb its height will regain their health, the infirm recover the strength of their limbs. But know you would waste your life in her pursuit. For the sun-bright maiden has been given as wife to one called Svipdag. She will grant her warm embrace only to him."

Svipdag slapped a forearm across his chest. "Then let us waste no more time in useless banter!" His voice carried over the roar of the black waters to echo among the halls. "It is Svipdag who stands before you! Open the gate that I may enter! Go call the lustrous maiden from her seat, for I would learn if she still holds my love dear!" The bold warrior sneered at the sentry. "And as for the great quest which you cleverly presented, know there are many ways to achieve any goal." He patted the weapon at his waist. "I bring this sword, the bane of Vidofnir, as a gift to mark our marriage. Its acceptance will reconcile the discord between our houses."

With these words Svipdag drew the blade partway from its sheath so its edge caught the rays of the sun. The brilliance dazzled the eyes and its heat prickled the skin. The sudden flash lit up the silver tower, sending Fjolsvith reeling back, impaled on the tip of a beacon of white light. The sentry gave a sharp cry. "Put it away!" He raised a hand to shield his eye. "Sheath its bright light! I will tell the golden maiden of your arrival."

Fjolsvith called out from atop his silver watchtower. "Freyja, hear my call. From outside these sheltering walls comes a man clad in a warrior's mantle. He calls himself Svipdag. He would know if you still hold your love for him dear. I believe his claim and consider him a fine catch should you accept the role of peace weaver between our houses."

At the sentry's call Freyja clutched the robe at her throat. "Wise you may be Fjolsvith, perched there atop your watchtower," she put out a hand to steady herself in her seat, "but know that should you be lying, by my hand I'll see you once more astride the gallows horse, your one remaining eye a feast for fierce ravens."

Fjolsvith shouted back delightedly from his high seat, lips split in a wide grin, a throaty chuckle in his voice. "See for yourself that Geri and Freki bound about, yelping as pups, glad at his arrival. Listen as Valgrind opens wide to bid him enter."

Freyja climbed down from her mountain seat and approached the figure that boldly strode through the gate. She bid her handmaidens stand back as she stopped before the armed warrior. She carefully examined his features, noted the faded color of his hair, the sun-ravaged face marked with weary lines of a long and difficult journey. "You have traveled far, that I can see. Your worn features tell of a hard trail. Tell me from what direction you came. Tell me your name and that of your father as a token that I can be assured of our betrothal."

The brave warrior bowed before his heart's desire. "I am called Svipdag, son of Orvandel, son of Ivalde. Along wind-cold ways, I was driven to find you. Twice I plucked you from the power of the etin, once in body and once in mind. In my father's hall, we pledged our union. It took me years following the long road to reach the entrance to your hall. Now I stand before you in the gard of your kin, eager that we fulfill the oaths we shared on the pledge rock those many years past."

Freyja's eyes followed as he slid a hand onto the pommel of the sword at his waist. "This blade at my side holds power beyond measure. It has kept me safe through numberless battles; always it has brought victory. As a token of our betrothal and for the reconciliation of our houses, I freely place it in your hands."

Pushing aside the sword, Freyja opened her arms and took Svipdag into a warm embrace. Her lips trembled, and her body shook with joy. "Long I sat atop my mount waiting for you to arrive. Sweet it is to finally see your face before me shining bright as the day. Too long we have wasted yearning for the love of one another. Know that from this time forward our lives are bound together."

The Death of Orvandel

When Day had chased his mother from the sky and Sol had begun her climb over the horizon, Orvandel stole along the banks of the Ifing, his bow strung, a fletched arrow nocked, intent on replenishing his family's larder. With silent step, he approached a wide bend that slowed the river's progress into a gentle pool where waterfowl fed, and large game tracked down to the edge to drink.

Two lightly armed men slipped through the heavy undergrowth crowding the archer's path, their ring byrnies left behind that they not make noise scraping against the brush. Silent as fox in search of prey, they separated, one sneaking through the bracken to the front, the other to the rear of the stealthy hunter. They moved as he moved, their hushed footfalls drowned by the gurgle of the river and the loud calls of waterfowl that flocked the bend.

One stepped into the path ahead of Orvandel. "Ho, there," he called to the ancient archer. "I seek the father of Svipdag. He is called, Orvandel, a noble warrior and archer of renown. I am certain he lives near here. I have cause to speak with him regarding the daring deeds of his son."

Orvandel paused before the traveler, a man his son's age, dressed in motley shades of green and brown, dark hair drawn back into a warrior's knot, his auburn beard trimmed close to the jaw. Were it not for the brilliance of his broad grin, he would have disappeared into the background of brush and sedge. Lowering his bow so the arrow pointed at the ground, the archer smiled warmly in greeting. "Fortune lies with you, stranger. I am the one you seek. Tell me who is it that asks?" He twitched his bow to the side. "How do you know of my son?"

The traveler slid forward until he stood an arm's length from the celebrated archer. "I am called Hadding, son of Halfdan." Swift as the gale wind his blade swept from its scabbard, its edge flashing as it arced through the sunlight. "It is by the hand of your son that my father set his feet along the red road long before the days of his life should have ended! Know that I have come to collect the debt of blood laid down between our houses!"

Great oaths escaped from Orvandel's lips as he sought to bring his weapon to bear, eager to seek out the heart of his attacker. A sound from behind startled the archer as another figure pounced from the brush. Gudhorm, the brother of Hadding, rushed forward, sword drawn, eager for the fight.

Gudhorm whipped his bright blade high above his head, angled down to strike. The point edge plunged deep into the back of Orvandel. The deadly stroke stilled the archer's arm, stiffening his fingers on the bowstring, so the arrow sliced by Hadding's face. The whispering dart arced harmlessly through the air into the waters of the Ifing. The light splash sent a handful of geese rising from the river to circle, hollering in alarm.

In counterpoint to his brother's strike, Hadding swung his keen-edged weapon in a wide swipe across Orvandel's middle. As his guts bulged from his tunic, the great warrior collapsed backward into the mud.

Dipping their blades into the chill waters of the river, the brothers briskly rinsed away the blood of their enemy's father before swabbing the edges dry on the clean blue cloth that stuck out beneath Orvandel's tunic. The two sheathed their swords and stood a moment over the body of the archer. Gudhorm nudged Orvandel's body with the toe of his boot. "We cannot leave him sprawled in the mud. Though he is the father of our enemy, he is a great warrior known across the nine worlds. He deserves what honor we can show the dead."

Gritting his teeth, Hadding swiftly scanned the horizon. "It is as you say, but we must make it fast. Others are bound to come searching for him. It would not be wise were we found nearby."

Hadding placed the bow in the great archer's hand, while Gudhorm straightened his limbs and set right his clothes. When they were done, the brothers nodded to each other, before rushing off through the brushwood, eager to leave the scene of their bloody revenge.

———————————

Sol had nearly run her daily course when retainers from Orvandel's hall, sent in search by his wife when he failed to return, found the archer stretched out on the muddy bank. Life flickered dimly in his eyes. His lips mumbled words, a soft cadence that kept loose his tongue. Swiftly, they bound his wounds, then on a hastily constructed litter of brushwood bore him back to his hall.

Loud shrieks started from Sygne's lips as her husband's bloody body was carried through the doorway. Her shrill commands edged with panic snapped everyone to action. Shoving tables aside, she ordered him placed on a low bench. "Wrap him snug in a woolen blanket and move the bench near the eldskáli so that its flames might impart some warmth. You," she shouted at a handmaiden who rushed to her side, "bring the healer." When the woman hesitated, she screamed into her face. "Now!"

From his makeshift bed, Orvandel beckoned weakly to the nearest retainer. The man hunched low, careful to keep from bumping against the wet spot slowly spreading along the blanket. "Bring me a wooden slip," he croaked. As the man began to move away, he gripped his sleeve with bloody fingers, "and a sharp awl to mark a message."

Sygne stared on, worry crinkling her brow, as the implements were delivered. Orvandel closed his eyes for a moment, taking slow, shallow breaths. "And so," the words flowed out with his breath as his eyes flickered open to focus on the awl and wooden slip. Forcing stillness to his quivering hands, he carved runes into the wood, carefully making each mark, then staining them with blood daubed fresh from his wound.

He beckoned the retainer close. "My days are numbered. You must hurry. Take my old mare from the stables. She may not be the swiftest of mounts in this hall, but she well knows the ancient path—the concealed shortcut that winds its way through the Mirkwood. Give her, her head; you would get lost otherwise. Carry this message to the Mikligardr of the Æsir. Deliver it into the hands of Thor."

The retainer dashed through the hall doors, saddled the horse, then bolted through the holding gate. From the first the mare took control, turning, jumping, thundering along overgrown paths, pushing herself as if she understood the urgency. The mare kept to a punishing pace. With each stride her eyes started. Foam dribbled from her lips then began spraying from her blowing nostrils. Head tucked until his cheek rested against the horse's mane, the rider cursed the stinging slap of low-hanging branches and clawing fingers of thick undergrowth that threatened to drag him from the saddle.

Together they raced along the ancient Mirkwood path slowing only when they reached the foot of Asbrau. Reining up before the misty bridgehead, the rider called out breathlessly to the white sentry who guarded the way that he carried an urgent message for the son of Odin.

Heimdall glanced over the message, grunting as he read the runes. "You," he barked to one of his sentries, "waste no time. Escort this rider to Bilskirnir. He carries an urgent message for the ear hands of Thor."

———— · ————

"The master still lived when last I saw him. He ordered me to deliver this slip into your hands." Thor's brow grew heavy, his fierce eyes glaring at the floor, as he took the slip from the exhausted courier, noting the bloody fingerprints that marred its surface. Slowly, he read the entreaty of an ancient friend.

The air crackled as frightful sparks flickered across his brow. Crumbling the wooden slip in his fist, Thor leapt to his feet. Tucking Mjollnir into his vest, he stormed past the cringing messenger. "My goats," he roared to his servants. "Harness my goats!"

He spoke to no one as he climbed into his cart and drove furiously from his hall. Dark clouds roiled across the sky, their shapes illuminated from behind by booming flickers of light whenever the wheels touched the ground. Thor ignored the jolting ride as he raced his wain to the shore of the Ifing.

On arriving at Orvandel's hall, he was somberly greeted by the húskarlar of the hall. A stable man held his wain as he climbed out into the courtyard. Thor placed a heavy hand on the shoulder of the servant, stopping him as the he led his goats away to board in the closest barn. "Tell me what you know. I would learn the truth of the urgent call for my presence. How fares it with the master of this hall?"

Tears welled in the eyes of the trusty retainer. "The lord—," words caught in his throat as he spoke. "The lord of this hall lies gravely wounded inside. He nears his final time among living men. The woman who orders this hall awaits you at the door. It is best and right that you hear this from her lips."

Sygne greeted Thor at the doorway. Her hair dangled in limp, golden strings about her shoulders. Her wide blue eyes, sunken from little sleep, were set in a brow creased with worry. The smock about her waist was streaked with dried blood, her cuffs blotted with grime. The good woman bowed to the visiting Æsir and with a voice worn ragged from sobs, bid him enter. She related all she knew as she led him through the hall to a room set along one side of the main chamber. A small fire guttered in one corner to warm the air, its flames casting shadows that danced along the walls.

"He has held on these long days waiting for your arrival. I expect you have come just in time. Already his wounds mortify; making it difficult to remain in the same room, so powerful is the stench. Today, he refused even the moisture of a wetted rag on his lips."

The archer lay stretched out on a bed of furs. A hole broken through the wall provided entrance for a shaft of bright sunlight that bathed his face and vented the terrible smell of putrefaction that choked the air.

Orvandel rolled his head to one side, his dry lips cracking into a smile as Thor entered the room. "I am glad that you have come. I've not much time left. Strongly, I feel the pull of western paths. I have used spells learned from my late wife Groa, those she taught me long ago that I might always safely return from battle. With them, I have kept my steps short when the desire to run is great."

Orvandel's throat bobbed as he tried to swallow. He smiled sadly as Sygne backed from the room, wringing her hands, tears coursing down her cheeks. "My wife worries over the inevitable." He glanced at Thor who knelt at his bedside frowning and chewing on his mustache. "You as well."

He took a slow, rattling breath, rolling his gaze to search the shadowed beams overhead. Firelight reflected from the whites of eyes damp with tears. "I was a warrior once, and young. In those days, we were blessed with the true friendship of comrades in arms. I always placed my skills at your service, backed your every effort with the full might of my will. All that I had was given freely. While family honor required I support my brother, he who led our house in the division between us, never did my friendship to you falter. I have done what I could to mend the rift that split our halls, encouraged the honor of my son to reunite our houses. In this he succeeded."

Thor placed a hand on Orvandel's shoulder and squeezed gently. "It is true that we were great friends. It is also true that even when our houses were at war my friendship for you never faltered. I am glad our friendship can flourish once more."

The fire snapped, sending a lazy curl of smoke slipping along the shaft of sunlight into the open air beyond the rent in the wall. From outside came the measured plodding of feet and the occasional hushed call of a worker attending to his daily chores. Thor enfolded Orvandel's hand in his fist. "Tell me who has done this. I see you have wounds in front. I have been told there are wounds in your back as well. Because I know you for a brave warrior who would never turn in flight, I know there were two assailants. One attacking from in front while the other struck from behind, a coward's way of battle."

Orvandel sighed. "I can tell you who dealt me the wounds and why, though the knowledge will only bring you pain." He turned his head, speaking low so Thor had to lean close to hear his words. "The sons of Halfdan struck me down. The bold one who dared look me in the eye called himself Hadding. Though I never saw his face, I know the one who struck me from behind called himself Gudhorm. They sought my life for that of their father—he whose family is known to fall under your protection—killed in honorable battle by my son, Svipdag."

He clutched at Thor's fingers. Swallowing hard, Thor fought back his alarm at the limpid grip, a grip that once could draw the most powerful yew, the fingers holding rock steady until the archer decided to release. "While it is true the deeds of sons reflect on the father and stain the honor of those pledged to protect them, know that I do not hold you responsible for their craven act." Lightly shaking his head, he struggled to add assurance to his words. "The actions of cowards who attack from ambush, afraid to honorably face a foe, do not now nor ever will reflect on you."

Thor's eyes smoldered in fury and his hands flexed at the words of his friend. "Were I not under oath to protect them, I would crush the life from their bodies with my bare hands."

Orvandel fluttered his fingers, his voice the croak of a raven. "They are as nothing; give them no more of your thoughts. Let the Norns work their fate. I did not ask you to come for vengeance, but for the sake of my family. For the friendship that once stood between our houses—a friendship resurrected, for my friendship to you that never faltered—I ask this boon." Struggling to lift his head, he reached out to tug at Thor's sleeve. "I have a son, Ull, skilled as his father with the bow, and a wife, Sygne, as loyal to me as my first. These I leave behind when I pass. I ask that when life has severed its bonds with my body, you take them under your protection, watch over them, care for them as I have done."

Fighting to keep his grip, he sought out Thor's eyes. "As friends, we journeyed far across the worlds braving many dangers. Shoulder to shoulder we fed the eagle. As friends, we part this final time." Thor watched agony flee from Orvandel's gaze as a deep peace took its place. The archer's hand slipped away, his head fell back, and a light shudder wracked his frame.

Thor remained still for a moment, fighting back a painful lump that rose up in his throat. He repeated the last words of his friend, "as friends we part this final time," then silently, sadly, reached across the body and gently closed its eyes.

Jaw set, Thor rose to his feet. Pulling Mjollnir from his vest, he held the hammer over the lifeless body of his comrade. His voice, edged with the pain of loss, roared out that all might hear his words, those in the hall... and the very gods above. "By my honor, by the truth shared between warriors, by the friendship which always held us close," his voice rasped, caught, then continued with a slight quaver, "by the power that is mine to protect, your child and wife will come live with me! Your wife as an honored companion! Your son, I will adopt as my own, raised up to live as kin among the Æsir!" Thor took a deep breath, choking back the tears that threatened to burst from his eyes. "In all this you can rely on me as I have always relied on you!"

The Curse of Svipdag

Svipdag, furious at the news of his father's inglorious death, raged about the hall he shared with Freyja, his voice shaking with anger as Thor tried to wean him away from his desire for revenge. "I ask no more of you than your father asked of me as he lay dying from his wounds. Drive the sons of Halfdan from your thoughts. Let the Norns work their fate. As I reluctantly set aside my anger over the death of a true friend and stilled the desire of my hand to strike down his killers, I counsel you to do the same."

Svipdag stopped to glare at Thor then continued his pacing. Shaking his head, the god of thunder approached a shrouded figure hunched beside the fire. "I am not gifted with a persuasive tongue. Perhaps you will have better success in convincing him to put aside his vengeance."

The figure shifted to turn his one eye on the angry warrior stalking the floor. After several moments of careful thought, Odin spoke up from his seat by the hearth, letting his words flow in measured gate so their meaning might find purchase. "There are those who hold vengeance of more account than reconciliation or self-preservation. To them I say this: long ago I learned the fallacy of death. It is only through the actions of a living will that faces unafraid the darkness and endures that which cannot be borne that we show our true worth." Scraping up a pinch of gray ash from the hearthstone, he rubbed it gently between his fingers, feeling its slickness as the gray stream trickled into the palm of his other hand. "None deny your right to vengeance, just as none deny their right to strike back at you. Let honor rest there, with both houses equal in death."

Snorting at the Alfodur's speech, Svipdag rounded on the ancient, one-eyed warrior. "Death does not deter a brave man, for in his eyes life counts for less than the loss of honor. It would be a slap to my family's face, a black spot on my integrity were I not to seek vengeance against my father's slayers."

Behind Svipdag's shoulder Thor nodded his head in agreement, but quickly turned away, cheeks blooming red, as a hot glare shot from Odin's eye. The warrior continued, oblivious to the exchange. "I faced Halfdan on the field of valor. Blow for blow, we fought as honor demands. I struck him down for the shame he brought on my house. But his sons ambushed my father, the act of miserable cowards who boast of bravery, but fear to challenge a valiant foe from the front. My father deserved a nobler end, to fall full forward in honorable battle."

He thumped a fist against his chest. Three times the harsh beat of his heart sounded through the room. "No! I cannot let this rest! I gather my grief about me as a cloak, thick as the dark storm clouds that build at midday about a mountain peak. Soon its rage will burst into flame."

Odin's cheeks burned at Svipdag's words. His eye glittered black and his voice grew harsh with the demands of command. "Their family falls under the protection of the Æsir! We have given oath to protect them! By marrying Freyja, you became subject to the oaths of our clan. It is now your responsibility to close this cycle by making resolution with the sons of Halfdan. As leader of our clan, this I demand you do!"

Svipdag sneered at the ancient god who sat before him. "Do I hear the words of Gagnráth, eager to give me good counsel, or are they the speech of Fjolnir, eager to conceal the truth? By your command and for the honor of my new kin, you ask me to endure the agony of my family's humiliation. To set aside my responsibility as the eldest son to seek vengeance for my father—a duty often championed by yourself."

Slowly nodding his gray head, Odin turned his eye to the hungry flames dancing in the hearth but spoke no word.

Freyja glided to her husband's side. "None behave with self-control in prosperity who have not learned to endure adversity." She rested a comforting hand on his shoulder. "Sweet is the joy that follows the bitterness of fate. Much you have endured in your life. Much you sacrificed to be at my side. Now we are together for eternity. Do not let this go." She squeezed his shoulder and smiled gently into his eyes as he looked around. "In our new life, we live in joy. Our days are free of anguish. Our nights together are pleasure. Let the resentments from the past remain in the past."

Svipdag dropped his head as the words of his wife penetrated deep into his breast. He reached back to pat her hand. Taking a deep breath, he replied to the Alfodur, letting his carefully chosen words carry forth his pride. "I hold the honor of my family close to my breast. As I avenged the treatment of my mother and the death of my grandfather on the sire, so, too, honor demands I seek vengeance for the death of my father on the sons. But in deference to the requests of my wife's kin and for the high esteem I hold for her, I will endeavor to come to terms with my enemies that I might live in accord with my inherited clan."

———

Svipdag rode along the Quivering Way, charging through thick clouds that concealed the bridgehead and down to the lands of men. He wound his way around hills, navigated river courses, the red shield of truce carried full before him as he sought out the hall of Gudhorm. Approaching from the west, the sun at his back, he dismounted before the gate. "Hear me," he called, rapping his knuckles sharply against the shield for attention. "I am Svipdag, son of Orvandel. I raise my voice to the master of this hall. Gudhorm, son of Halfdan, hear my words."

A thin, reedy voice shouted from within the walls. "I know who you are." The crest of a head tufted with snarls of black hair peeped from behind a grove of spears clustered behind the gate. "Come no closer. What is it you want?"

Svipdag stepped forward, hefting his shield to the fore so its color could not be mistaken. The cluster of spears trembled as if caught by a cold wind but remained firmly rooted in place. High overhead a raven circled three times amid the clouds before angling away to the east.

"By the hand of your father, my grandfather lies dead. And, too, by his hand, my birth mother was dishonored. For this your father lies dead, stuck down by me on the field of honor. Now my father lies dead, killed in ambush by you and your brother. The future holds death for us all if we do not stop this now. By the honor of my name and that of my kin, I call for reconciliation between our houses."

The gate creaked open and Gudhorm slid cautiously out, his own red shield shaking on his arm. He little relished facing the One never defeated in battle. With several nervous glances over his shoulder at his spearmen, he inched forward until he stood just outside the reach of Svipdag's sword arm. "Gladly," his voice cracked on a high note. He coughed before starting again. "Gladly, I make peace with a worthy foe."

Svipdag glared silently back. Gudhorm shivered, feeling the hate rolling in waves from his eyes. "I... I... I freely swear a solemn oath on my name and that of my family to end this feud." He hugged the thick alder planks of his shield closer to his chest, effective under truce, but no real protection against the black-eyed warrior glowering before him. "As weregild, I offer one hundred healthy white horses, all free of blemish. I will fill your purse with enough silver to honor your loss and to cover my involvement in your father's death." He extended his hand, unable to still the quaking that shook his arm.

Svipdag sneered as he took Gudhorm's hand in a crushing grip that made the young man wince. "Your offer is adequate. I am duty bound to accept it. I will send for it as I do not have the means to take it with me today." Arching a bushy eyebrow, he leaned in close until the spittle spraying from his lips flecked Gudhorm's cheeks. "But when I do collect, all that you state had better be there, or I will consider our reconciliation void and crush the life from you."

His menacing stare sent a small trickle running down the inside of Gudhorm's leg. As the young man's cheeks flushed with shame, Svipdag swung his red shield over his shoulder, mounted his horse, and thundered away. The air filled with clods of earth kicked up by his horse's hooves as he charged across the open meadow. Gudhorm watched until Svipdag disappeared over a far hill, then, massaging the palm of his hand, slumped back to his hall shutting the gate softy behind him.

The hooves of his mount crashed through forested valleys and clattered along the wet ways of mountain ridges as Svipdag, carrying the red shield of truce full before him, sought out the hall of Halfdan where Hadding now held court. Approaching from the west, the sun at his back, he dismounted before the gate and called out boldly to his enemy within. "I am Svipdag, son of Orvandel. I raise my voice to the master of this hall. Hadding, son of Halfdan, hear my words."

He had not long to wait before Hadding slammed open his gate. The grim warrior stalked across the open space to stand squarely before him, feet planted wide, one hand on his hip, the other resting on the pommel of the sword belted at his side. "I know who you are. You dare come to my hall. Were you not cowered behind a truce shield, I would have your head. What is it you want?"

Settling his red shield at his side, Svipdag took a deep breath to calm the fury that flared in his breast. A raven croaked as it rose from a nearby tree and winged away to the east. "By the hand of your father, my grandfather lies dead, and my birth mother dishonored. By my hand your father lies dead, his life taken on the field of honor. By the hands of you and your brother, my father lies dead; well I know who struck him in front and who from behind. By the honor of my name and that of my kin, I call for reconciliation between our houses. The future holds death for us all if we do not stop this now."

Hadding's lips curled into an ugly sneer that bared the yellowed gate of his teeth. "I would sooner lay with a troll woman than dishonor my family line. I am not my gutless brother, quick to cave before a strong voice or a hard stare." He spat on the ground beside Svipdag's feet. "Never will I accept peace from your hand!"

Svipdag gritted his teeth and again called for settlement. "In the name of Odin, by the honor of my name and that of my family, I call for reconciliation between our houses." He extended his hand. "You have only to take my hand for this to be so."

Harsh laughter spilled from Hadding's lips. "It is a coward who sues for peace when the blood of his father is involved." He leaned forward, letting the strength of his breath wash over the bold warrior standing before him. "I feel only contempt for such a foe. I know that I need never fear one who holds his family's honor at arm's length."

Svipdag's eyes glittered with hate on hearing Hadding's scorching retort. His breast boiled, threatening to burst its bone house, as his fingers flexed eager for the grip of his sure blade. Had he not been bound by shield truce, he would have delightedly struck Hadding down.

Nostrils flaring, Svipdag pushed his response through clenched teeth, letting the sharp hiss of his breath punctuate his words. "I have done all that I promised, humbled myself in the pursuit of peace, set aside my family's honor for that of my newfound kin. Never again will the speech of peace pass between us."

"Bold words," Hadding scoffed. "They are little more than the bawling of a suckling calf."

Jutting out his chin, Svipdag spit near Hadding's feet. "Since you refuse reconciliation between our houses, be assured I will do all within my power to see your lifeless corpse on the field – a bloody feast split wide for the ravens. I will always prosecute war against you! Wherever you live, no matter how remote the land, whenever I see your despicable face I will be there to attack!"

Hadding folded his arms across his chest. "Then know when next we meet, even should you bear a red shield of truce, blood will fill the valleys and my blade will seek your heart."

At this retort Svipdag spun about and leapt into the saddle of his prancing horse. He glowered at Hadding, threw his shield onto the ground, and with a vicious kick of his heels, spurred his mount back to Asgard.

The echo of Hadding's laughter hounded him all the way to the bridgehead of Bifrost. Across the arcing span, the mocking derision continued ringing in his ears, boiling his blood, setting his teeth into a savage grin. The white god tried to halt his headlong charge, but, unheeding, blind save to his own fury, he brushed past Heimdall's proffered hand. Thundering through Valgrind, he leapt off his mount, leaving it unattended outside Sessrumnir. His feet shook the gateposts as he stormed up the entry path and shoved through the main doors. Servants dodged out of the way, fearful of the rage burning in his face. A deep sadness grew behind Freyja's eyes as she watched her husband stomp about their hall, grimly assembling his warrior gear.

He paused in the doorway, his fury softening before the anguish clouding Freyja's face. "I must." His arm reached out, gathering her close. "It is a son's duty. My duty."

A tear coursed down Freyja's cheek as the one she loved squeezed her tight then turned away from their hall.

———————————

In fury, Svipdag fell from Asgard to wage war against the son of Halfdan. He traveled across the lands of men gathering up the enemies of Hadding's house, those who had joined him in battle against the father. When all was ready, he brought the full might of his arm to bear. The lands of men rang with the storm of their battles, as frequent as the spring rains, as cutting as the winter winds.

Watching from his seat on Hlidskialf, Odin grew concerned at the damage the husband of Freyja inflicted on the house of Halfdan and the world of men. Their furious battles raged unending. Corpses littered the fields. Dead slumped before city gates. Bloated bodies choked harbors to impede the path of mighty ships. The homes of Midgard were emptied of men, leaving the cries of women and the whimpering of hungry children to carry over the rushing winds. Flames played high into the heavens. Farmsteads were swept aside in swirls of gray smoke as forest gards crumbled to choking ash. In cities, sheets of flame charred heavy timbers and scorched black the stones of their once-protective walls.

Odin's face grew dark. He stomped about the hall muttering to himself, his eye burning bright in anger. None dared approach or speak to him lest they receive a withering barrage of sharp invective. Ygg clubbed his fist on the table, three times he clubbed his fist, and called an immediate Husthing of the gods.

With raging voice, he demanded the attendance of all the Æsir, be they near or far. "I want everyone—I mean everyone—here! I do not care if they are journeying far or sitting at bench drowning themselves with mead. There are events we must discuss. Everyone, and I mean everyone, must be present to hear my decree!"

They came from the ends of Asgard, rushing back from their travels across the worlds at Odin's urgent summons. Even Svipdag set aside his bloody weapons of war to attend. When all had gathered in the great hall, Odin wasted no time on convincing words, but immediately rounded on Svipdag. "I am enraged at your actions. You breached your promise of truce by attacking the house of Hadding." Leaning far out from his seat, he belted out his demand to the unrepentant warrior. "I demand you cease this war with the son of Halfdan or suffer banishment from this clan! This is my will! As Alfodur of the Æsir, it will be as I say!"

Svipdag stood before the gathering, raised himself tall, chin held high. The proud warrior glared at the Alfodur. "A breach of promise? He snorted. "There has been no breach of promise. I pledged only to seek a truce with the sons of Halfdan. No more than that!" Svipdag pounded his fist in his palm, each sharp smack accentuating his anger. "I made peace with Gudhorm, accepted his weregild for the death of my father, though I would rather have slit his throat. With harsh words of insult, Hadding threw the offer of truce back in my face. This I could not brook, no truly honorable warrior could. I will not scrape and bow before a hairless-chinned waif. Instead, I will feed him cold iron in reply for wounding words received under truce."

"A breach of promise indeed." The valiant warrior jabbed a thick finger at the Alfodur. "And if you demand I sue for peace again, know that my patience is far exceeded. I have no time for empty truces. The spring, the plough, and the harvest must attend themselves. All my thoughts turn to battle and the death of Hadding!"

Grinning wide at Svipdag's rebuff, Odin leaned forward. "Such thoughts," his words spit cold venom across the hall, "are best pondered alone. So, since you refuse my direct command, allow me to give you room to ponder those thoughts."

Freyja cried out as she rose to stand beside her husband. Eyes aflame, cheeks flushed crimson, she bared her teeth against the anger of the Alfodur. "You will do nothing! This is my husband. He will always remain with me!"

Pressing a palm against her husband's chest, she swept the gathering with a grand gesture of her other hand. "Once this man was counted among the greatest foes of Asgard. He battled many of you in this very room, defeating no few on the field of valor!" Freyja glanced across the gathering at Thor, who shifted his gaze to the ground. "Then you sang nothing but praise for his bravery and the honor he held dear, though it clashed with your own. He was held in high regard by all, so that when he accomplished by the strength of his own hand that which none of you could achieve—winning my freedom—and for love sought my hand in marriage, you eagerly agreed to the union. You were proud then to have him as kin."

The crowd grumbled and there were a more than a few agreeing nods. The Alfodur frowned at the supporting mutters but said nothing. "And now, when he continues to hold his honor close, an action often championed by those gathered in this very hall, you threaten him."

Freyja tossed her hair to the side. Those nearest stepped back as if driven by a sudden gust of wind. "I can no longer tell if your words have lost meaning or if new values are prescribed on a whim." Squaring her shoulders, she sneered at the silent faces. "No longer do I hear the praise of honor held in high esteem, but rather clever words spoken by a two-sided tongue eager to contrive guilty ends."

"Silence!" The Alfodur rose from his seat. "Your loyalty to your husband is commendable," the gathering moved back as he stepped forward to face the pair, "but it belongs with your family, not to one adopted into our clan. It was my command that Svipdag cease his feud with the sons of Halfdan. This he has refused. My judgment stands!"

Odin turned to the defiant warrior who stood unflinching before him. "Since you deny my command and cast doubt on my leadership, in your banishment you can wear a form that is more suited to your mind."

Smoke swirled around the startled warrior, a wreath of a dragon's breath that bound his limbs. He cried out to his wife, a single mournful wail, before the serpent cloud engulfed his form. The mass of gray-white mist whirled into a column of smoke that abruptly sank into the ground. When the smoke cleared, Svipdag was gone.

The Alfodur fell back one, two, three steps before catching his balance on the edge of a table. He turned his face away from the site, climbed wearily back to his seat, and, with an anguished groan, settled into himself.

Freyja stared as wisps of smoke dispersed into the air. "You wicked, vicious old man! How dare you take away that which is mine! I demand you tell me where you have sent my husband!"

Odin raised a hand to cover his eye. His voice was that of an ancient, a whisper dry and cracked with the pain of age. "He is gone, banished to the realm of sea giants. Changed into the guise of a dragon that he might ponder my displeasure."

Shock flashed across Freyja's face at the Alfodur's words. Her lips parted in agony but uttered no sound. She glanced around, but all eyes were staring at the floor. Hanging her head, Freyja gathered her cloak tight about her shoulders and strode dry-eyed from the silent hall.

The Brising Necklace

In the golden days of the world, master smiths, steeped in the lore of earth, vied to best one another in the creation of beautiful trappings to adorn the body and decorate the home. Many works crafted with great skill were brought before the Æsir, powerful gifts to honor their station.

Freyja was present when Dvalin visited Asgard, proffering ornaments crafted by himself and his brothers—jewelers of unsurpassed skill—to honor the As and Asynjor of the Æsir. The brilliant treasures were wonderful to behold. All were impressed by their intricate designs.

Odin turned a bracelet before his eyes, watching the light play across images scored about the band and wink from bright jewels embedded along its edge. "Beauty deserves beauty, and such beauty belongs on only one arm," he handed the bangle to Frigg, "that of my beloved." Frigg smiled as she slipped it onto her wrist. Still smiling, she held it aloft for all to see, delighting in the murmurs of appreciation that issued from those gathered within the hall.

The Alfodur spoke to his guest shuffling, shoulders hunched, in the center of the hall. "We are honored to accept such gifts, for these must be the best works of your smithy."

Dvalin glanced rapidly left-to-right before bowing his head. "I am honored to bring... that which pleases the gods."

At Odin's words, Freyja had idly turned her head, noting the dwarf's lumpy body and thick tufts of wiry black hair spotted about his pale, drooping features—so like a grub ripped from its concealment within a rotted log. Her eyes caught his reaction to Odin's statement. Her keen ears picked out the hesitation as he spoke, an intimation in his voice that there were greater works held in reserve.

She sent her gaze roving among the Æsir seated on benches about the room, but the others, occupied in the examination of the many gifts Dvalin had brought, seemed not to have noticed his pause. Freyja leaned back, smiling inside her cheeks. *The dwarf brings such wondrous gifts. Imagine greater ones hoarded in his smithy, treasures that would set her above all others.* She vowed to discover the truth of her suspicions.

That evening, when Night had completed half her journey, Freyja rose, donned her travel cloak, and slipped from her hall to the nearby stables. Silently, she harnessed her cats—a matched pair of supple lynx—to her wain and guided them into the courtyard. None spied her activities save the clever Loki. He, too, had noticed the dwarf's reaction. When he saw the hunger flare in Freyja's eyes, he rightly guessed what she would do.

Loki loitered outside the gate of her hall, passing the time in idle amusement by shifting his form from one shape to another. As Freyja guided her wain through the gateposts, he changed into a flea and launched himself though the air to catch a ride on one of her cats.

She drove the wain along Bifrost, with gentle shushes commanding her cats be silent lest they rouse the white god from his slumber. The rainbow colors of the bridge shimmered from the rippling fur of the lynx as they padded down its shivering avenue. Brilliant hues of red, green, yellow, blue danced in waves across Freyja's hair, flushed her skin, and glistened along the narrow folds of her robe. Decorative metalwork on the wain glinted with the light until she seemed astride a twinkling, multicolored star arcing across the heavens.

At the bridgehead, she turned west along roads angling deep into Nidaveller, the dark world of the Dwarves. The wheels of her wain clattered as she bounced through dim grottos where the chuckle of rivulets echoed from granite walls. Yellow light tinged with red glowed from within deep fissures that marred the rock face. At a particularly bright chasm, Freyja drew back on the reins. Climbing from her wain, she stared thoughtfully at the glow while lightly stroking the ears of her nearest cat. As its dull purr vibrated in the cavern, a mote leapt from the cat's ear onto the sleeve of her travel cloak.

"This is the place," she whispered stepping away from her cart. The lynx turned questioning eyes to their mistress. "Do not worry." Freyja gently stroked their ears until they stretched out on the cave floor. "Remain here. I'll be back soon." Slipping onto a narrow path between the rocks, she followed the winding route down to where the bright glow blossomed into the raging heat of a smithy furnace.

Four dwarves hunched before the open maw of the rumbling forge. Faces smudged with soot, backs slicked with sweat, two hunched over a bench working a length of metal, one wielding a hammer while the other gripped with tongs. Another fed fuel into yellow flames tinged blue, while the fourth heaved the bellows so each pump was an exhalation of blistering heat and choking fumes.

Behind the dwarves, in a niche carved deep into the wall, hung a neck and chest ornament made of lustrous gold with intricate, silver inlaid designs that seemed to ripple in the flickering light. Beneath the necklace, where the recess formed a shelf, rested an arm ring of uncommon beauty set with a single bright-red gem that smoldered with the fire of the furnace, a ring in style to match the necklace. Among the Æsir there was no equal. Even the beloved of Odin could not boast of such ornaments. Freyja knew she had to have them, no matter the cost.

She had entered so quietly and stood enraptured by the precious jewelry that none had noticed her approach. Dvalin glanced up from his work, looked back to the tongs gripped tight in his hands, then looked up again with a start. The rock-hard dwarf grunted to his brothers, who each stared unblinking at the intruder. Never had they seen one so lovely. They glanced among themselves. Each knew what the other desired.

Pulling her attention away from the necklace, Freyja beamed a wide smile at the dwarves. It seemed to each that the rays of the deluder—always shunned by their folk—had suddenly graced their home, for never had their smithy shown so bright. Dvalin stuttered, stopped, and then started again. "To what do we owe this honor, an unannounced visit from the Æsir jewel, she who is known as the goddess of love and war?"

Freyja sauntered forward, trailing a fingertip through the dust atop a workbench. Noticing how the dwarves watched her every move, she let her travel cloak slip aside to bare the soft curve of her shoulder, the gentle edge of her breast. She watched with amusement, smiling inside her cheeks, as their eyes popped wide and their jaws slackened.

"When you brought gifts to Asgard you spoke of offering what pleases the gods. I decided to visit your smithy and observe for myself the crafting of such luxurious works." She waved an arm to encompass the room, stopping at the recess, her open hand pointing to the necklace. "And when I arrive, what do I see but this trinket on the wall. It pleases me... I would have it."

The dwarves muttered among themselves, Dvalin spoke their voice. "It is called Brisingamen, the greatest work we have yet crafted. It is the best of each of us. We will not gift it."

Freyja again dazzled the dwarves with her smile. "If you will not gift it, then sell it to me. Gold, silver, jewels, name your price and I will pay it."

Firelight winked from the unblinking eyes of the four brothers. "We've gold enough," grunted one. "And silver in quantity," piped a second. "Jewels we pluck from the rocks as we need," mumbled a third.

Dvalin stepped forward to stand before Freyja. "It belongs to each of us; we share equally its value. What one receives in payment, so must the others." He glanced over his shoulder at his brothers who nodded eagerly in unison. With sharp nudges, they urged him on. "There is only one price for which we would part with this, our greatest work. Only one price that would satisfy us all."

Freyja's eyes drew down into hard, brittle slits. She well knew the passions of men and the leering gaze of the four dwarves had become annoying. Her anger flared at their audacity, yet her desire to own the necklace was stronger. With a clear, bold voice she asked the question for which she already knew the answer. "What is your price?"

"You!" cried Dvalin. His voice, cracking with excitement, broke on a high note. The dwarves fidgeted before the furnace fire, shuffling their feet, and giggling into their fingers, their movements sending shadows frisking about the walls. "For this necklace to be yours you must lie with each of us one night. That is our price."

The daughter of Njord grimaced at the thought of their moist, pale skin. The idea of being embraced by their misshapen bodies sent a shiver of distaste running up her spine. But her desire for the magnificent ornaments was greater than her revulsion.

"Very well, I accept your terms. Now know mine! To show your good faith, I will have the arm ring that rests on the shelf beneath the necklace. At the end of the fourth day you will deliver the necklace to me. Dvalin, as the eldest you will be the first. The youngest of your brothers last. If you renege on this deal or speak of it to anyone, I will personally have each of you fed feet first into your own furnace. These are my terms. Do you accept?"

While his brothers capered about slapping each other on the back, Dvalin took the ring from off the shelf and handed it to the goddess. Freyja slipped in onto her arm. The band embraced her skin, warm and familiar. Entranced by its luster, she knew that it along with the necklace would be the envy of Asgard. She set her jaw until the muscles bunched beneath her ears, then turned to face the four brothers clustered eagerly before her. "Let us get this over with."

Four days and four nights she spent with the dwarves, first one brother, then the next, until she fulfilled her part of the bargain. At the end of the fourth day the dwarves gathered before her, bowed deeply to touch their foreheads against the hem of her cloak. In solemn ceremony, they presented the chest ornament. Dvalin lifted it over Freyja's head and fastened it about her neck.

The dwarves stood in silent awe. The necklace had never looked so becoming as it did draped about the neck of a living goddess. The luster of her skin gave the metal a fluid warmth, alive and inviting.

Freyja spoke to the dwarves, "The deal is done."

They intoned after her, "The deal is done."

Hugging her cloak about her shoulders, Freyja retraced her steps along the path back to where her cats lay waiting beside the wain. A sly smile spread across her lips as she prepared to return to

Sessrumnir. Eager to be on her way, she did not notice the flea that leapt from her cloak onto the nearest cat. Its faint chuckle was lost amid the echoes of the grotto.

———————

As Sol peeped her head over the horizon, Freyja called her handmaidens to prepare a bath. When steam rolling over the rim told her all was ready, she climbed into the wooden tub, easing herself into the hot water until it reached her shoulders. Taking up a rough cloth, she scrubbed hard to remove the stench of the smithy from her skin.

Bright pink from the scouring, she snapped her fingers at her handmaiden. "Spread out my finest robes. I'm going visiting." She carefully adorned herself in splendor, draped Brisingamen about her neck, felt its weight secure against her chest, then slipped the matching ring onto her right arm.

"Well," Freyja turned in a circle. "How do I look?" Overwhelmed by the presence of the necklace, the handmaiden could only smile and nod her head.

One by one, Freyja visited the halls of the Æsir. Everywhere she went, admiring glances followed. Many remarked on the ornaments and how they enhanced her beauty. She reveled in them all.

At Valhalla, Frigg stared hard at the necklace. "A lovely bauble," she raised an eyebrow, "and matching arm ring too. Never have I seen such fine work. How did you come by it?"

Freyja tapped her fingernails lightly on the bright metal, smiled at the wife of Odin, then winked slyly at the Alfodur. "This was left for me at my door. The gift of a secret admirer."

Frigg cast a sharp look at Odin, but he took no notice. Filled with jealousy at the news of a rival, he glared at the sister of Freyr. "Tell me," the words hissed through his teeth, "who is this grand admirer?"

Freyja turned away at the question, uncomfortable beneath the glare of Báleyg. "I do not know. This morning a secret admirer left the necklace and ring for me at my hall. Such was their beauty, I had to wear them."

Odin beckoned her close that he might examine the ornaments. His practiced eye traced the lines, the incised designs, noting the fine workmanship. "This must be a special admirer, someone who can compel the work of dwarves, for certainly this was crafted by a master smith."

Freyja shrugged, sauntering toward the door. "I neither know nor care. The gift is in excellent taste." She gave a final glance over her shoulder at the icy stares that followed her every step. "It well suits me." With that she left Valhalla and returned to Sessrumnir, her hall on the Warriors' Fields.

Odin was galled that there should be an admirer of Freyja brazen enough to extravagantly gift her and capture her attention where he had failed, but shrewd enough to hide from his gaze. The Alfodur called Loki to stand before him in council. All others he gruffly ordered to leave while he spoke privately with the son of Laufey.

Wasting no time on pleasantries, Odin demanded Loki's aid. "Freyja flaunts herself about the court adorned with a brilliant ornament. It is dwarf-made, of that I am certain." He chewed incessantly at the hair of his mustache. "She claims it the gift of an unknown admirer. You are more cunning than any I know. I charge you to discover who gave her the necklace. I would know the name of this secret gifter."

Loki smirked into his hand, then turned away doubled in laughter. Odin glared from his seat. Hugin and Munin shifted uneasily on his shoulders. Geri and Freki pricked up their ears and cast questioning glances at the Father of Armies.

"You dare laugh at me," Odin's gaze became shrewd, "or do you find mirth in knowledge I do not have?"

Loki choked back his laughter as he turned about to face the Alfodur. "In wisdom, you are unsurpassed. How can I presume to know that which you do not? Surely, your view from Hlidskialf allows you to see all?" Odin remained silent.

"Freyja's late-night journey to the world of the Dwarves." Loki's eyes twinkled. The Alfodur stared forward, quiet, and hard as stone.

"Her visit to the smithy of Dvalin and his three brothers." Loki grinned wide, exposing a gate of sharp white teeth. Odin's lips twitched, but still he said nothing.

"The bargain she made for the necklace." Loki lifted a finger into the air. Odin remained silent, but now the grinding of his teeth echoed in the hall, the sharp rattle of hail on stone.

"One night with each brother, her payment for the ornaments she now wears." Loki stabbed his finger into his palm.

Half rising from his seat, Odin swelled his chest. "Enough of your bald talk," he bellowed. "You offer lies to sully that which you can never have!"

The son of Laufey pressed a hand to his chest, astonishment clear in his eyes. "Not so! Let me tell you how I know." Delighting in Odin's discomfort, Loki related the adventures of a lowly flea. He embellished nothing; the truth was enough.

When he finished, Odin sank back into his seat. The crackle of the hearth fire was the only sound. The Alfodur stared into the dancing flames before speaking. "If even half of what you say is true, then there is dishonor enough for us all should this tale become widely known. For the honor of our clan I place this charge on you. Get me that necklace!"

Loki shook his head. "I do not lie; all I have spoken is true. Besides, it is impossible to take from Freyja that which she does not want to relinquish. You of all the gods know this best. Her hall is sealed, and every entrance barred. Her Einherjar guard it well that none may enter unannounced."

Odin pounded his fist on the board before him, making his cup dance with each blow. With low growls Geri and Freki climbed to their feet, hackles raised, their quivering black lips drawn back to bare sharp white fangs. "You will get me that necklace or I will never see your face in Asgard again. And," his voice sliced the air, sharp and cold as the ice flows of the river Slid, "you will tell no one else what you have related to me this day. No one! Are my words and their meaning clear?"

Loki heard the danger in Odin's speech and saw the clear cold flame of his one eye. From their positions beside the throne, he noted the raised hackles and frozen stance of Geri and Freki waiting on the order of the Father of Armies. Backing away from the high seat, he kept his eye on Odin's wolves until he had reached the hall doors. Then, spinning on his heels, he dashed beneath the crouching wolf and hovering eagle. Behind him came a sharp howl of pursuit, the rush of padded feet, and the scrabble of horny claws on stone.

———·———

Cloaked in the darkness of deep night, Loki approached the hall of Freyja. Creeping around the walls of Sessrumnir, he stopped at the main entrance. On the chance that someone had neglected their duty, he leaned his shoulder against the hall door, gripped the iron ring, and shoved firmly. Barred from within against unwanted entrance, it did not budge.

Next, he turned himself into a fly. Buzzing the full length of the hall, he examined it roof to ground—checked all the windows, inspected every joint, probed each crack—but found no chink or opening that permitted entrance, save for a small hole beneath the eaves, its width no larger than a flea.

On his third attempt to breach the walls, Loki changed himself into a flea. Wriggling through the hole he had found in the eaves allowed him to slip unnoticed into the hall. Once inside, Loki reverted to form. With silent cunning, he slid from room to room, making certain all the guards were away on their rounds and all other members of the household were wrapped in sleep.

Flitting from shadow to shadow, he made his way to Freyja's bed, found her stretched out on her back, snoring lightly, the golden necklace draped about her neck, its silver clasp hidden beneath her.

Again, the son of Farbauti changed himself into the guise of a flea. Crawling across the body of the sleeping goddess, he stopped on her cheek and gave her a light bite, enough to sting, but not enough to wake. Freyja twitched at the bite, moaned softly, then rolled onto her side, exposing the clasp of the necklace at her back.

Resuming his shape, Loki unclasped the necklace and gently slipped it from beneath the sleeping goddess. He held it up, so the ornament glinted in the faint light, its chain dangling from his fingers like a streamer of pure gold. A smile spread across his face. He glanced at Freyja, then tucked the necklace into his vest, careful to keep its links from rattling.

The leather soles of his boots whispered across the flagstone as Loki made his way to the hall entrance. He gently drew back the bolts that latched shut the doors and, with a laughing grin, slipped out into the night. Feet flying, he took his prize directly to Odin.

———————

When next Sol began her climb into the sky, Freyja awoke and immediately noticed the lack of weight about her neck. Fingers shaking, she felt for the necklace, but caressed only bare skin. Wailing in anger, she flung aside the mattress bedding. Her handmaiden, panicked by the cries, rushed into the room to find the goddess crawling about on her hands and knees searching in vain for her ornament.

Freyja, eyes aflame, hair tousled in an explosion of gold, crouched back on her heels, and screamed at the maiden. "Who entered my room while I slept?"

The handmaiden flinched, afraid of her fury. "None would dare enter your bed chamber uninvited, nor disturb your sleep without good cause."

Freyja glared at the woman, noting the light of innocence in her eyes. "Then a thief has visited us in the night, for no one in my own household would exhibit such dishonor as stealing from me. Have the guards search the hall."

When the main door of her hall was found ajar, the bolts slid open from within, Freyja knew at once Loki was the culprit. Only he was capable of such stealth. Only he would dare such a base deed.

Freyja stormed up the wide avenue to Valhalla. Wrenching open the doors beneath the crouching wolf and hovering eagle, she shoved aside a startled Syn. The day had just begun, so there were few seated among the benches. Those present murmured with astonishment as Freyja stomped up the space between tables to the great seat. With a shrill voice that cut everyone to silence, she demanded a private audience with the Alfodur.

Odin stared silently at the goddess of love and war raging with the full power of her position, then waved everyone away.

"Well, I won't leave," Frigg began, but a harsh glare from Odin's eye turned her attention elsewhere. "Come everyone," she rose from her seat, urgently beckoning the others to join her. "The day waits for no one. We must all be about our duties."

When the doors closed, leaving them alone, Odin leaned forward rolling his shoulders, a wild beast readying itself to pounce. "You will not mind that I keep my wolves with me. They will share what you say with no one." He reached down to scratch first Geri, then Freki between the ears. "Now speak what you have to say."

"My necklace has been stolen," Freyja's voice exploded with such force through the hall that the walls seemed barely strong enough to contain her fury. "Brisingamen, my greatest treasure, was taken in the middle of the night by a bold thief who dared invade my hall and enter my bed chamber unannounced! Only Loki is capable of such brashness! I demand that he be punished and my necklace returned!"

Odin glared down from his seat, letting his one eye linger over her furious features. "Loki acted by my command to retrieve a cheap bauble purchased through deeds that dishonor our clan."

Freyja's lips snapped shut. She stepped back, astonished that the Father of Armies knew how she had procured the necklace. Still she rallied. "Then you have debased yourself by your hand in this; stealing from one of your own family."

The Alfodur sputtered, his face flushing crimson, and gripped tight the arms of his seat so his knuckles turned white. "You dare speak of debasement!" His voice broke like thunder over the waves. "You who sold yourself for a trinket to four dwarves; maggots beneath the earth!"

Freyja nodded. "Ahh, so that is why you stole it." As she spoke her lips flattened into a tight-lipped smile, thin and sharp as a knife. "You are jealous of what I bargained and which I have always denied you."

The Alfodur, face bright red, eyes starting, shook an accusing finger at the daughter of Njord. "Your actions have brought dishonor to all the Æsir."

Freyja shouted back, her ire equal to that of Odin. "You dare accuse me of dishonor! What I bargained was mine to bargain; it belongs to me and no one else! But you... you brought dishonor through theft from kin!"

"Enough!" Odin waved his hand and sat down, chewing on his mustache as he glowered at the sister of Freyr, who stood bristling before him. "There is dishonor enough to go around. There always will be." He leaned forward speaking in a soft menacing voice.

"But I say this with all certainty, you will never see your precious Brisingamen again unless you fulfill my request."

Freyja stared coldly at the Father of Armies, guessing what he wanted in return for her necklace, but her eyes went wide in astonishment when at last he stated his desire.

Rising from his seat, Odin paced around the golden maiden. He spoke to the floor, his voice gaining volume with each step. "We are familiar, you and I, with the violent passions that drive others, so share a taste for war. Half the chosen in battle go to me; the other half resides with you in your hall. Still, you do not visit the field of valor as often as me. This will change! This must change! We need as many warriors as we can get as stockpile for our twilight years."

He stopped abruptly and turned to glare directly into Freyja's eyes. "My price for returning your ornament is simple, you will visit the lands of Midgard. There you will help me cast runes of strife among men that the boldest may have their day."

Freyja turned to stare at the far wall as Odin continued. "Begin with the Hjadnings." His voice took on a savage edge. "Ride forth, a brilliant flame in your chariot. Stir up animosity between the kings Hogni and Hedin. Let Hedin take the daughter of Hogni—men fight hardest over a woman and a perceived breach of honor. Encourage a great battle that warriors may display their worth."

He flexed his fingers, making fists before his face. Bloodlust flared in his eye. "To ensure our culling, teach charms to Hild, the daughter of Hogni, so that each night she might give new life to the fallen, that they rise fully healed of their wounds to continue the battle. Let them tear each other apart until the final day brings our need of them."

They scowled at one another, then Freyja bowed her head. "Return my necklace and I will leave this day. You will have your ceaseless wars. There will be blood enough to drench the ground."

The Theft of Thor's Hammer

Often Loki visited the land of Jotunheim to spy on the home lives of those who lived in its cold environs, reveling in using his wits to come and go as he pleased. Through wile he kept himself free from their power. But when he spied on the hall of Thrym, he was surprised by a particularly watchful guard, who captured him outright as he eavesdropped on their private conversations.

Loki was dragged before the lord of the hall, his loud protests echoing off the high timbered walls. "Take your hands from me! How dare you accost an innocent! You do not know whom you are dealing with! Release me now or you will pay with your lives!"

Thrym rocked back in his seat, grinning wide in recognition at the dark figure shouting and trembling before him. "Welcome Loptr, to my hall. We have a customary greeting for uninvited guests who take the liberty of spying on our home."

With great delight the powerful Jotun ticked off, one by one, the brave punishments he planned. "Our knives are sharp for peeling skin. We have heavy mallets for crushing bone." He raised an eyebrow. "Fingers first, I think, then toes." Loki dew a ragged breath, nearly collapsing to the floor.

"This land is known for its wintry weather. I would not have you suffer a chill." Thrym smiled benignly, his brow twisted with mock concern. Loki, frozen in a hunched ball, could only stare back, slack-jawed, in terror. "To warm your days and nights we have braziers of glowing coals, hot iron pokers, and kettles of oil heated until it smokes."

"And let it not be said we are stingy with drink." Thrym winked in good fellowship as his retainers lounging about the hall snickered at the shivering captive. "Oh no, we are liberal in my hall. How much mead do you think you can hold? Let's get a funnel and find out."

His life threatened with assured pain, Loki recalled the trials he suffered as a prisoner in Geirrod's court—the horror of starvation in a locked chest. Dropping to his knees, Loki prostrated himself before the glowering giant. Sobs choked his voice as he crawled forward begging mercy. "Please... please stay your harsh treatment! If you let me leave your hall unharmed, I will do anything you ask!"

The clever etin stroked his chin, considering this opportunity. A leer crinkled Thrym's lips as he leaned forward in his seat. "For your freedom, my price is simple. It is one you cannot refuse." His voice boomed through the hall as he made known his demand. "Deliver the hammer of Thor into my hands by the next rising of the Everglow. Agree to this with a binding oath or know the harshness of my judgment."

Fearful, shaken by Thrym's wide, unpleasant grin, Loki gave a stammering oath to deliver the ransom. "By my blood and that of my mother, I swear to bring you the hammer of Thor."

The Jotun grinned wider to bare his full gate of sharp yellow teeth. With a brisk wave, he released the quivering son of Laufey, but not before reminding him of the treatment he could expect should he break his oath. "If you fail to fulfill your pledge, expect no mercy should the fates deliver you again into my power. All the agonies I promised before will happen." He speared Loki with an icy stare. "I assure you it will be a protracted event."

———————

Loki wasted no time racing to Bilskirnir. Late in the evening he slipped into Thrudvanger, Thor's lofty hall on the plains of strength. Creeping to where the son of Odin lay in deep sleep, he lifted Mjollnir from its place beside the bed.

Loki fled the hall—a silent shadow flitting through doors and darting along the courtyard walls—not wishing to face Thor's wrath should he be caught with the hammer in his hand. He sped on winged feet across the plains of strength, north into the cold lands of Jotunheim, eager to discharge his pledge to the ogre and rid himself of an unwanted burden. There, with shaking hands, he delivered the prize to the waiting etin.

As the eastern sky lightened with the arrival of Day, Thor stretched himself awake, rubbed his face with both hands, and rolled from the bed to greet the arrival of Sol. He pulled his sturdy vest over broad shoulders, then reached out for Mjollnir. He groped about his bedstead, fingers flexing for the handle of his hammer, but grasping only empty space.

The longer he searched, the greater grew his ire until his beard bristled with sparks, and thunder roared overhead to shake the hall.

Suspecting himself the victim of trickery, he summoned Loki to Bilskirnir.

The sun had barely climbed into the morning sky when Loki strolled through the main door. "I came as soon as I received your summons. To what do I owe—"

"I know you Loki," Thor interrupted.

"And I know you," Loki mimicked, then quickly dropped the smirking attitude as he observed Thor struggle to relax his clenching hands. "What is it you want of me?"

"You are the wiliest of gods. As such, you are familiar with thieves." Thor lifted his fists clenched tight before Loki's face. "My hammer has been stolen. Do you know anything of its whereabouts or who might be the culprit?

With perfect guile Loki stood before the son of Odin and unflinchingly claimed no knowledge of the weapon's whereabouts. "You must have mislaid it. For I doubt anyone could steal it unscathed from the person of the god's strong guarder."

Thor grimaced at the wall. "And yet it must have been taken while I slept, for I have searched everywhere and not found it." His heavy brows knit together. "Only a clever thief could have done it. Only a bold thief would have dared."

Turning about, Loki strode briskly across the room, waving his arms about his head lest Thor see the panic that flashed across his face. "Then we must call on everyone to help find it, the Æsir, the dwarves, the elves... why, we may even need to call on the aide of men. This is no time for pride. It is with this weapon you keep us safe from the ravages of our enemies."

Thor snatched the son of Laufey from his feet and held him close before his face. The force of his anger sent tremors rushing through Loki's body. "Listen carefully to my words Trickster. I know the freedom with which your tongue wags; you spread lies and truths with equal ease. But know that the story of this loss will not pass beyond the walls of Asgard. Only kin can know my hammer has been stolen."

Thor set the trembling Loki back on the ground. When his limbs were able to suffer his full weight, the son of Laufey wobbled across the floor and collapsed onto a bench near the wall. He swallowed, tried to speak, swallowed again before managing a squawk. "We must search quickly. There is no way faster than by air. We must borrow Freyja's wings."

———————

In Freyja's court, they recounted Thor's plight. "I need your help." Thor's voice edged with panic as his hands strayed to the empty spaces in his vest. "I would borrow your falcon cloak to scan the land for my hammer! For having stolen it during the night, the thief cannot have traveled far."

Freyja turned her sharp gaze on the figure standing nonchalant beside the son of Odin. She lightly tapped her fingers against Brisingamen draped about her neck as she studied the son of Farbauti. "You are certain this thief has traveled far?"

Thor wrung his hands. "The thief has had a night's journey," he replied anxiously to Freyja's ear, "no more. The longer we tarry in speech, the greater the distance grows and the more difficult the search will be!"

Freyja waved at a chest resting near the hall door. "In there you will find my feather cloak. For your great need, I would freely lend it to you were it crusted with jewels. But it will not fit one of your size." She jerked her chin at Loki. "Your clever companion has borrowed my cloak before, often without consent, so I know it fits his frame. Let him search for your unknown culprit. He is an apt student of Althjof, the learned thief among wizards, and will know the best places to look."

Under the pressure of Freyja's severe gaze, Loki hurriedly donned the cloak and flew off. Wind whistled over the feathers as he made several passes over the land. Once he was well beyond the courts of the Æsir, a mere speck in the blue sky, he turned his aerial path north and headed straight into the cold lands of Jotunheim.

Loki landed at Thrym's hall where he found the Jotun hard at work trimming the manes of his many steeds. "So," Thrym smiled as Loki strode forward, "you've given up the ways of a sneak and now plainly announce your presence. I've been expecting one of the Æsir. I am not surprised it is you. What news do you bring of the arrogant gods?"

Bracing himself before the mighty Jotun, Loki thrust out his chin. "I have come for Thor's hammer," he shouted, hoping the quiver in his voice might be concealed by volume, "that which I delivered to you as ransom for my life. Return it, else the news I bear turns from bad to worse."

Thrym tipped back his head and roared. His laughter echoed off the surrounding hills, filling the air with its raucous sound. "You deliver threats as an old man shouting into a gale. Weak words snatched away by the wind long before they deliver any meaning." The Jotun chuckled to himself, then turned back to trimming his horse's mane. "The hammer you gave as fair payment for your life lies buried eight leagues beneath the earth. None but I can ever retrieve it."

Puffing out his chest, Loki raised himself tall before Thrym. He spoke loudly in the hope that the Jotun would heed the threat of his words. "The Æsir demand the hammer back! Do not doubt that they will have it. What is your price for its return?"

Thrym paused his busy work, shifted the shears between his hands, and then looked directly into Loki's eyes. "You say the Æsir demand the hammer's return. That is well, for it is of no use to me, save as a bargaining tool for that which I desire. My price is simple. There is no hidden agenda. I will return the deadly Mjollnir to Thor if Freyja is brought to me as wife."

Loki vehemently shook his head. "The Æsir will never give up their beloved daughter, the glittering jewel of their eyes." He waved away the etin's request. "Name another price."

Thrym glared directly into his visitor's eyes, then spoke slow and firm that there be no misunderstanding. "I have stated my price. There is no other. Deliver Freyja to me as wife or the hammer remains buried, forever. Then the Æsir can huddle in their halls with piss running down their legs as they quake in fear without its protection."

Even with Thrym's final reply, Loki still tried to wheedle concessions from the Jotun. "There must be something else you would take for the hammer. Livestock, silver, gold name it. At least tell me where you put the hammer, so I can return with evidence of your good faith." Thrym's hostile silence indicated attempts at further deliberation were useless.

"No. Nothing? Alright then." Loki made a show of drawing his mantle tight about his shoulders, hoping the Jotun would reconsider at the last moment. But Thrym watched, sullen and silent, as Loki spread his arms to catch the breeze and flew off. Wind whistled over the feathers as he made his way back to the Æsir court.

Thor paced in the center of the courtyard. He beckoned to Loki when he appeared overhead, eager to learn what his aerial search had discovered. "Have your efforts been successful? Tell me before you land what you have found! Now, while it stands fresh in your mind!"

Loki replied from between beats as he hovered over Thor's head. "Though the journey was long, and the search difficult, even dangerous, I found your hammer. The thief escaped into the lands of Jotunheim, there passing it into the hands of Thrym, a powerful ogre lord. The clever etin buried it deep in the earth, hidden from all eyes. He vows that no one will ever retrieve it unless Freyja is brought to his hall, there to take her seat as his wife."

"Then get down here." Thor snatched at Loki's leg, dragging him from the air. Loki squawked as he hit the ground with a dull thud. "We must see Freyja... Now!"

Loki climbed to his feet rubbing his backsides. "I could have flown..."

"We go together." Thor yanked the cloak from Loki's shoulders. He shook the feathers straight then bundled the cape carefully under his arm. "You will not need this."

Rushing to Folkvang, the pair beat on the door of Sessrumnir, the great hall of Freyja, shoving it wide open in their urgency. The son of Odin shouted out to the goddess. "Freyja, dress yourself in finery and don the headdress of a bride! We ride immediately to Jotunheim, where you will greet a new husband!"

Freyja tossed her head as she strode to the door. "I already have a husband who holds the highest regard in my eyes." She withered the two with her gaze. "I have no need of another."

Thor wrung his hands together, took a firm stance before the sister of Freyr, and again stated his demand. "Mjollnir is held by a Jotun of bold standing who demands you as wife in exchange! For the return of my hammer, I will make this deal!" He tried to look her in the eyes but could only stare at her feet. "We ride at once to Jotunheim, where you will greet a new husband!"

Fire flashed in Freyja's eyes, her voice a venom sting, as the halls of Asgard echoed with her rage. "Here stands the god's Strong Guarder.

Ha! More is expected of you, Thor than, this!" Her anger was so great Brisingamen started from her breast, clattering unnoticed with each rapid breath. "It is not my problem you cannot safeguard your own weapons. I'm surprised your precious manhood remains intact between your legs. Were you as careless with it as you were with your hammer, it would have been snatched away long ago."

"What is more," she sneered, flipping her hand in his face so he had to step back to keep from being swatted, "you would dare give me away without my consent, and to a scheming etin no less! While I do not stint on my bed partners, know that I have had my fill of Ymir's children."

Loki stepped into the tension, cringing between the angry glares. "Perhaps it would be prudent to hold a council. We can call on the guidance of all the Æsir."

———·———

Gladsheim echoed with the grumble of many voices as the Æsir gathered to debate on how best to retrieve Thor's hammer. Odin rose, waving his hand for silence. "Whatever action is decided must fall on Thor to carry out, for it was his property that was stolen. And let Loki assist in the deed. He is crafty and well experienced in dealing with giants."

Heimdall stood before the council, banging his cup on the table for attention. "Let us build on the giant's demand, the delivery of a veiled jewel of the Æsir ready for a wedding feast." He jabbed a finger into his palm. "For only when Thrym has a bride at his side will he bring the hammer from hiding. Only then will we have hope of its recovery."

Freyja's icy voice sliced through the gathered clan. "It will not be me delivered to the sons of Thrudgelmer! I made that clear to Hlodyn's son and the devious Loki when they first demanded it of me!"

Heimdall grinned wide, his golden teeth shining bright as the midday sun. "I would never suggest that we risk our most precious jewel. Though your necklace, the lovely Brisingamen, will be needed for the plan. The bride we offer up to Thrym must embody the strength of the earth but be perceived by the dull Jotun as the very spoil he demands."

He pointed to Thor, waving his fingers as he pantomimed a long, flowing cloak. "Thor will wear the garland headdress of a bride. Its long veil will conceal his rugged features; otherwise his bristling beard would quickly give him away. A long, blue gown covering his rough knees will soften the angles of his sturdy frame. A cord strung with keys will jangle about his waist, the symbol of a woman's role in the home. And Brisingamen will drape about his neck, for even those who dwell in the cold reaches of Jotunheim know who owns this greatest of chest ornaments. When such a bride is delivered to the ogre's hall, the hammer will be brought forth to consecrate the union. After the hammer is placed in Thor's hands, then the bride's true nature can be revealed."

Thor bristled at the words. Jumping to his feet, he waved them away with both hands as if trying to scatter a swarm of bees. "Everyone would call me perverted were I to parade about the lands dressed as a woman. I am not a disciple of Freyja, though I hold her in high regard. Never will I don a woman's clothes."

Loki lifted a cup to his lips to conceal his teeth clenched against laughter. "This morning you cared little what others thought of your garb when the manhood of your hammer first went missing. The white god presents a plan of small inconvenience to you and of such a blatant design it is bound to deceive an overeager ogre like Thrym."

Edging close, he clumped a hand on Thor's shoulder, ready to dart back should the storm god become wrathful. "Set aside your pride. Don the outfit. I will accompany you to protect your virtue from any indignities we may encounter along the way."

"Let's face it," he coughed lightly, slipping his hand away as Thor continued to stare stonily straight ahead. "Unless you retrieve Mjollnir, we will have giants knocking at our gate, while Trolls and Ogres lounge about our courtyards. Even the lands of men will be overrun with their kind. Then all our grand oaths of protection will have become meaningless."

Thor grumbled, nodding acceptance at Loki's words. None dared laugh outright, though many mouths were covered as he struggled into the dress. With the help of the goddesses and their handmaidens, Thor cinched a cord of keys tight about his waist.

"Every bride," Frigg grunted helping her son with the belt, "must carry the keys of home."

Freyja draped Brisingamen about his neck. "I expect this back," she muttered, hooking the clasp. "You," she pointed to a handmaiden, "set broaches about his breast. Let me have pins for his shoulders. They may just be able to keep this gown from falling off."

Frigg offered precious rings from her jewelry box. "They will never fit me again," she sighed as the rings were broken and stretched open to accommodate Thor's thick fingers.

Finally, they secured a bride's headdress upon his brow. The wreath of delicate white flowers woven together with sprigs of greenery sat high on his thatch of thick golden hair. From it drooped a gauzy veil that reached to his collar and concealed his face from ear to ear.

Freyja examined him carefully, tugging here and there at the gown to straighten its lines as she adjusted the fit. "We've had to let out the laces in back; there's barely room to tie them off." She stepped back, hands on her hips. "He looks like a beached whale at low tide, but I am certain to an etin he will seem a delicate blossom, full-flowered, and ready for plucking."

Thor glared straight ahead while muffled chuckles sounded about the gathering. Grinning openly now at Thor's discomfort, Loki shifted his form to the greater feminine, then draped himself in woman's attire. "Together we will present ourselves at Thrym's rocky hall." He set a veil about his face, dragging it around to conceal all but his eyes. "As your personal handmaiden, I will protect you from unwanted questioning, as is proper for a bride to be."

Thor's goats were promptly harnessed. Tanngniost and Tanngrisnir danced in their traces, eager for the journey. After loading the wain with bridal gifts to complete the ruse, the son of Odin shouted for his goats to pull.

Dark clouds roiled in the sky, and mountains tore themselves apart as Thor sped his wain from Asgard. The wheels sparked fire whenever they touched the ground. As the pair raced along the rough road, Loki looked up and burst into laughter at the fierce eyes burning from beneath the headdress. Thor was so eager to arrive at the hall of Thrym that he paid little attention to the mirth of his companion.

Thrym, pacing the length his hall, heard the booming sounds from Asgard. Rushing outside, he saw bright flashes arcing across the heavens, felt the dull rumblings that shook the air a few moments later. From the strength of these portents, he knew the Æsir had acceded to his demands. A cool breeze rippled his hair, while the distant lights twinkled in his eyes, bringing a smile of satisfaction to his lips. The prize would soon be his.

The Jotun gruffly ordered his household to tidy the hall, stamping here, gesturing there to encourage the flurry of activity. "Wipe down the sills. Don't miss the shelves. Brush clean those seats! I want this hall to shine for my bride to be! Bring in fresh rushes for the floor; spread the benches with golden straw. Use the rake to clean up the area around the eldskáli. I plan to marry tonight, not threaten my hall with the danger of fire."

He snapped his fingers as a servant rushed by with a tray laden with victuals precariously balanced over her head. "Load the boards with roasted meats. Arrange plates of dainties such as women desire. Set the table with clean bowls. Ready the cups for ale. I will not have us appear uncultured oafs."

Thrym watched the preparations, smiling with delight at the clatter. "The fates have treated me well. I am the luckiest of my line, greater than my father as he was greater than his." Servants scuttled out of his way, busy with preparations, as he paced in thought through his hall. "By the strength of my own hand I have gathered great wealth: iron-banded chests brimming with jewels, pallets stacked with bars of precious metals. Herds of golden-horned cows and snow-white horses graze in the fields surrounding my yard, while black oxen roam my far pastures. My pack of well-trained hounds wards the grounds, keeping intruders at bay. All I lacked was Freyja by my side."

In the early evening, when Sol had just returned to her hall and Mani was yet to climb the sky, when Day was ready to take his rest, but before Night fully embraced the land, Thor and Loki arrived at the hall of Thrym. As they stepped from the wain Thrym himself rushed from the gate to greet them. "This way into the hall," he blurted, bowing deeply. "In my family, the groom is always first to welcome the bride on her wedding day."

Wading through the wedding revelers as a heavily laden barge plows through the cresting waves, he guided the pair to seats of prominence at the table. The pair demurred as they took their seats, fluffing their robes for comfort so the gold embroidery and silver stitching along the hem winked in the firelight, dazzling the eyes of every etin maiden. Glowing from the bride's chest, Brisingamen outshone all the lights in the hall. Thrym took it in as a hungry wolf stalks a sick hart, delighted with his good fortune, the obvious envy of others.

Famished from the long journey, without a word Thor helped himself to the splendid wedding feast laid before them. Alone, he drank three casks of ale, consumed an entire roasted ox ready for carving, and gobbled eight smoked salmon heaped on a nearby platter. Loosing a loud burp, he reached across the board, gathering to himself all the dainties within arm's reach. Bowl after bowl disappeared beneath his veil, only to be tossed aside, empty.

Thrym rocked back in his seat, marveling at what he saw. "Never have I seen any woman, even those of my clan known for their voracious appetites, eat or drink with such abandon."

The shrewd handmaiden seated alongside the bride raised a hand to her lips. "Nine nights Freyja fasted, so eager was she to consummate this union. Now with everything ready she is released to assuage her hunger."

Thrym's laughter filled the room and he slapped his knee. Those nearest glanced uncertainly among themselves, joining in with halting chuckles as Thrym placed a possessive hand on the bride's forearm. "She hungers no more than I for this union. Let me give her a taste of what lies ahead."

Leaning forward the lord of the hall twitched up the bride's veil to deliver a kiss. He glanced into her eyes as he puckered his lips, only to find himself halfway down the hall, so swiftly he sprang away. He cried out to the gathering, his voice edged with alarm. "Her eyes burn with a black fire that would consume everything I hold dear, leaving only ash. Never have I seen such a terrifying gaze."

The shrewd handmaiden seated alongside the bride raised a hand to her eyes. "Nine nights Freyja lay awake so eager was she to consummate this union. She burns with the heat of desire now that the event is near."

Then the sister of Thrym sidled up to the table. "Give me the red-gold rings set upon your fingers," she insisted, thrusting out an eager hand to the bride. "For these bridal gifts and no others, I will grant my blessing to this union!"

At the brazen demand the bride snorted to puff her veil and began to rise from her seat, stopped only by the firm grip of her companion. The shrewd handmaiden seated alongside the bride raised a finger to her head. "Odin gave clear instructions that no gifts be exchanged, nor this union consummated until Thor's hammer is placed in the bride's hands to consecrate the event."

"But my rights," the matron whined, scuttling back into the crowd. "My rights."

The handmaiden noticed the displeasure creeping across Thrym's face as he watched his sister retreat to her seat. "Odin insisted," she shrugged.

"Then let us waste no more time." Thrym clapped his hands. "Bring me the hammer of Thor, the mighty Mjollnir, which I retrieved from the bowels of the earth this day! You," he shouted to a young, heavyset etin with long, stringy black hair. The etin twitched at the command, groaned to his feet, and puffed from the hall.

Thrym smiled to his bride-to-be. "It will be a moment, then we can continue."

A round of applause rang from the walls as the retainer staggered back into the hall, wheezing for breath, the hammer clutched protectively to his chest. Thrym gestured at his guests. "Place it in my bride's lap, careful not to snag her dress, so that Var, the goddess of pledges, might sanctify our union."

Holding the hammer aloft, the retainer slowly turned in a circle, showing it to the cheering crowd, then set it in Thor's lap. Joy burst in Thor's breast as his hand clasped the solid haft of the hammer and his fingers tingled with its power. Jumping to his feet, he tumbled the table forward into the gathering, and tore the veil from his face so all could see who stood before them.

The son of Odin's voice boomed over the din issuing from the terrified throng milling about in panic. "Let it be Veor's hand that consecrates this union!"

Thrym, frozen in his seat, was the first to fall as a crushing blow from Mjollnir shattered his skull. Then Thor swept his hammer through the crowd, battering the guests about the room until blood soaked the rushes on the floor and bodies piled up to fill the hall.

Last, the son of Odin towered over the sister of Thrym, the matron who had demanded payment for her blessing of the forced union. "Never let it be said that I am stingy in meting out just payments. Here is my bridal gift for your favor, delivered by my own bejeweled hand." With that, she who out of greed had demanded gold rings from the bride, instead, received death from the hammer of Thor.

The Wanderings of Freyja

Brightly shown Brisingamen—the envy of women—hanging grandly about the neck of Freyja. When the goddess wed a mortal man called Svipdag—a hero of uncommon valor who dared achieve that at which the gods had failed—she continued to wear the necklace, delighting in the beauty of a well-appointed wife. When to them were born Hnoss and Gersemi—Freyja's precious jewels, still she wore Brisingamen, proud of her beauty in motherhood.

And when her husband, angered at the slaying of his father by the sons of Halfdan, defied Odin's command that he end his feud with the house of his enemy, she stood by his side against the host of Asgard, the necklace flickering her defiance.

And when, for disobedience, Odin banished him to the realm of sea creatures, changed into the guise of a serpent, she sought for him across the nine worlds, the brilliance of Brisingamen lighting her way.

South across the lands of men she traveled, her lynx tugging at their traces, skimming over earth with swift, noiseless steps. Her heart ached with sorrow as she searched the breadth of Midgard, roamed hills, traversed plains, forded rivers, circled lakes, enquiring of all she met along the way over the fate of her lost husband. She stopped at each town, at each city, at every farm. Interrupted travelers on their journeys. Called field workers in from their duties. Among the splendor of the rich, amid the squalor of the poor, she ceaselessly asked after Svipdag.

Was he living among them? Had they heard of him and his terrible plight? Could they tell her anything at all: whom else she might ask, where else she might look?

Always the answer was the same. "He is not here. The one you describe would certainly stand out. We have never heard of such a person."

Some, taking pity on the maiden, offered her what comfort they could. She stayed with them a while to collect her thoughts. Blessings she gave to these kind hearts.

Others brusquely pushed her off. She turned away from these, leaving misfortune at their doorstep and continued her search.

Having discovered nothing in the lands of men, Freyja turned her wain eastward to Jarnvid, the Iron Wood that bordered the frigid lands of Jotunheim, whose tall black trees claw the sky with their branches. She drew her wain to a sudden stop beside the gnarled bole of a massive fir. Bending forward, she whispered to her cats as they hissed at a hunched form rocking back and forth amid the shadows. Between the humped roots sat an ancient ogress, howling to her furtive children as they slipped through the wood behind her.

Veiling her hatred for the race of etins, Freyja tightened the reins in her hands. "You there," she shouted to the huddled form squawking in the shadows, "squatting amid the tangled roots, I seek my husband cast out from Asgard. He wears the guise of a serpent. Can you tell me if he has passed this way?"

The ancient made no response to her call but continued to screech at her children. The horrible din was so deafening, Freyja feared her entreaties had not been heard. Climbing down from her wain, she inched close to the old woman. Her nose wrinkled from the thick smell of decay as she bent near the aged face.

"Can you tell me, old mother," she shouted into the twisted knobs that were the matron's ears, "if you have seen my husband? He was cast out from Asgard into the lands of men wrapped in the breath of a dragon. I have been searching for him for a long time. Have you seen him pass this way?"

The shadows twitched, and a bright, icy eye turned abruptly on the maiden. The movement was so quick, the glare so harsh, that Freyja jerked back drawing a sharp breath. The unsympathetic gaze made Freyja quiver inside. Still she held her ground, refusing to retreat or bow her head.

The ogress made a deep gurgling from her throat then spit a large wad of phlegm near Freyja's left foot. "You are an Asa, so prattle and moan like all your kind. Should the fly bite and you swat it dead, do you care what its kin feel at its passing? Loss is something shared by everyone and everything. Accept it or die!"

The ogress' words struck like a dagger into Freyja's heart. It burned, bringing the pressure of tears. Her hands fluttered to her face, then fell weakly to her chest. "Your words are harsh, old woman, as is typical of all your kind."

"As hard as the trees of this forest." The ogress slapped the tree root beside her leg. "As sharp as the three corners of Hrungnir's heart." She sneered, thumping her chest. "Now get away, girl. Go mourn your loss elsewhere!"

Freyja teetered from the near physical blow of the rejection. Hands gripping a low-hanging limb for support, she bowed her head, lips quivering, tears spattering the thirsty forest loam. Absently, she worried a fragment of bark free from the limb and crumbled it to dust in her fist.

The ogress grunted. "There is no use standing there blubbering like a child." She turned her head aside. "Your tears are meaningless to me. I, too, have lost someone close, many in fact, but do you see me whining about it?"

Drawing herself erect, Freyja struggled to sniff back tears that continued to flow unchecked, and dabbed a sleeve at cheeks chafed raw from constant attention. Mustering her small reserve of dignity, she gathered her long bright hair behind her head, then tied it off with a loose cord.

The ancient glanced up at the weeping maiden, letting her gaze linger a moment on the exhausted features, the deep lines that etched a once-smooth and happy face, the sunken eyes swollen red from endless tears. "Go!" She snorted, waving Freyja away "Leave me alone! I have no more time to waste on foolish questions. You will find nothing to your liking if you continue on your present course."

The shadows exploded with a quavering yell that was cut off in mid screech. Freyja blanched, her breath catching in her throat, while her lynx crouched, ears flat, hissing back at the darkness. "Were I you," the ancient continued unperturbed, "I would turn my back on these cold reaches. You'll have more luck seeking your husband among the warm waves of the sea."

Freyja hugged her traveling cloak about her shoulders, the air suddenly grown cold. Stumbling into her wain, she turned it about until the black forest was behind her. She hissed a sharp command to her cats, then flicked the reins, sending the cart jolting back along the path.

After days of jarring travel that brought deep aching pains to tired limbs, Freyja heard waves crashing in the distance. A weight lifted, then settled again; she was approaching the shore of the southern sea. At length, she came to a wide beach where great waves tumbled across hard, gray sand in a long, steady line of snowy foam. A constant breeze blowing over the water pushed back her hair and she drew her robe closed to ward off its chill.

Along one side a cliff jutted out into the sea. Its towering formation broke the savagery of the waves and stalled the chill ocean breeze. Its lee formed a shallow cove where seabirds strutted along layers of muddy, fine gray sand that marked the beach. Green shrubs climbed the rock face, softening its sharp angles. Lush grasses matted a narrow space along the base of the cliff. Nestled in repose on this verdant carpet a wave-tossed timber overgrown with barnacles jutted from the sand, its free end wrapped with fine strands of dried seaweed.

She lightly twitched the reins to pass it by as nothing more than a spar lost from some doomed ship when the wood shifted position and waved an arm in greeting. "Welcome, stranger. Come join me in this pleasant spot if you can take time from your travels. The sun is warm, the ground soft, and this cliff blunts the sharpness of the sea breeze."

Drawing her wain to a halt in the protection of the cliff, Freyja stared a moment at the figure tottering to its feet in the sand. That which she thought to be a piece of flotsam washed ashore was instead an ancient man with long gray hair flecked green. A grizzled beard matted with bits of dried seaweed reached to his waist.

About his shoulders hung a tattered, nut-brown robe of rough weave splotched with clumps of mud the color of the sand. The remains of a soiled kirtle wrapped his waist. A black mire caked his bare legs, from foot to mid-calf, and dried into gray streaks the higher it climbed. While his appearance was unsavory, his broad smile bracketed by deep, long-familiar lines bubbled with welcoming laughter. His bright eyes flashing with warm good nature won her trust.

Freyja nodded as she climbed down from her wain, glad to be free, if only for a moment, of its rough jostling. "It has been a long while since I have stopped, and a longer while since I have heard words of welcome. I can only rest a moment. I fear any delay that keeps me from my search."

"I welcome most the moments," the old man smiled, letting his gaze wander from beach, to cliff, to sea, then back to Freyja, "for they make up the day." He spread wide his arms. "Come take a brief rest. No journey is so urgent that a moment's respite won't ease its toil. It clears the mind and soothes the aches of a tired body."

"You need not stay long in my company." Skipping up to her wain, he held out his hand. "Surely, we can pass a short time in pleasant conversation. I've little to offer save a warm spot in the sun on soft ground. If you're hungry, I've gathered some seaweed, the sweet nutty kind. Should it be too salty for your taste, a clear stream trickles down from the cliff." He pointed at narrow rill streaming from a cleft in the rocks. "The cool water will slake the greatest thirst."

Freyja courteously accepted the hospitality, allowing the old man to take her arm as he guided her to a seat in the warm grass. "Now," the old man settled himself beside her, "tell me of your journey. I am famished for the sound of another's voice. Tell me of your travels. I would delight in hearing of other places."

The smell of the sea, the gentle rhythm of the waves, and the lonesome call of sea birds wheeling overhead worked the tension from Freyja's limbs. She soon found herself relating her woes to the kindly ear of the ancient beachcomber, who nodded his head at her every word. As she spoke fondly of her husband, Freyja noticed a single tear coursing down the cheek of the old man. When she sought to ask, he waved her question aside.

"It is nothing," he smiled sadly, staring a moment over the sea as if what he recalled rested somewhere beyond the waves, "just a memory best forgotten." Shaking the pain from his eyes, the old man turned back to Freyja. "Please," he gently touched her hand, "continue with your story."

On reaching the point in her tale where she had mistaken him for a piece of driftwood, the old man laughed and slapped his leg. "It is a good thing your cart woke me as it passed, or I would not have called out. Then we would not have spent this wonderful time together." He grinned, gripping his ankles, while rocking side to side. "Surely the fates sent you to cheer up an old man's morning. For while this is a favorite spot of mine I do not often rest here this early in the day, but when Sol stands lower in the sky. It is only because the warmth of Sol's rays lulled me to sleep as I took a moment's rest from my search for food that you found me here at all."

A faint smile lifted Freyja's lips, then just as quickly faded. "I am glad our talk brought you some pleasure. As for me, a friendly face and an understanding ear have been most welcome. Now, having rested, I must be on my way." She climbed to her feet, brushing sand from her robe. "I wish you the continued blessings of good fortune and health. But before I take leave of your kind hospitality, can you tell me if you have seen my husband. He was cast down from Asgard wrapped in the breath of a dragon. I have been searching for him for a long time. Have you heard anything that may help me find him?"

The old man frowned and scratched his head, releasing a shower of sand to dust his shoulders. "All my life I have lived by the sea learning the language of the rolling waves and the birds that ride the winds circling about the headlands. They tell me where best to catch fish or spear eels, where best to harvest the bounty of the sea that washes ashore. They tell me of wonders that lie farther along the seashore than I can roam."

Closing his eyes, he turned his face to the sun, content in its shining warmth. "I have learned to trust what they tell me, for in my youth I was skeptical of such grand stories. Many is the time that I wore my feet sore along the headland paths only to discover the truth of their tales."

The ancient beachcomber smiled sadly upon the maiden. "I have heard of something such as you described. Though I feel I do you no favors in telling what I know."

Freyja leaned forward, her eyes burning bright with eagerness, barely able to restrain the hope that welled up within her breast. She spoke slowly, keeping her words calm, fighting back the urge to shout, so as not to scare the old man into silence. "Tell me. Tell me all that you know."

The old man coughed, tugging at his beard, as his eyes scanned the sky, tracking a white bird that screamed as it made a low pass at a small, dark object floating in the water, then turned to gaze out across the rolling surface of the sea sparkling silver and gold from Sol's rays. He muttered softly to himself, his head bobbing with the rhythm of the waves.

"What is it... some seasons back now, I think, the birds told me of... some said a man... some said a dragon who appeared suddenly on the seashore in a wreath of smoke. The waves told me he made his home on a rocky island far up the coast. The island is a stone's throw from the shoreline. It was once a place of seals. Now all avoid its edge for fear of the one who lives there." He shrugged. "I do not know if it is your husband they told of, for as I said, some said it was a man, others a dragon. He lives alone on the island, never leaving its shores, but broods day on day as he sits gazing out across the waters."

Freyja started at the old man's words and would have snatched him from the ground had he not danced back at her sudden charge. "Tell me where I can find this island," she shouted. "You must tell me!"

"There!" The ancient pointed in near panic west along the shoreline. "Follow the course of Sol's wain as she returns to her home. It is a long way, many days, many nights. At the point where Sol dips below the waters there you will find an island just off shore."

With tears rolling down her cheeks and a broad smile stretching her lips, Freyja shouted thanks to the old man as she leapt into her wain. Sharply urging her cats to speed, she turned their course along the shoreline in the direction of Sol's path.

The old man called out as she dashed off, his words carried away by the breeze. "I warn you. Do not be overeager to accost him; he is terrible to behold! None see him but must run away in fright. His glance... it is said his glance is as sharp as the north wind that tears the clouds, breaks the sea, and shakes the mountain pines."

———————

Freyja drove nonstop, pushing her lynx and herself beyond the point of exhaustion. From sunrise to sunset, even under the bright gaze of Mani they rattled along the coast. Finally, she arrived at the shore of the western sea where the terrible dragon was said to roam. There, where the sun dipped below the horizon, she found Svipdag on Vágasker, a rocky isle off the mainland coast. He was horrible to behold, with the haggard profile of a serpent, his brow wearied with long-held grief. He crouched on the rocky shore, his head hanging low, eyes misted as he gazed out across the endless expanse of gray sea.

When Svipdag saw who approached, he hunched his shoulders and made to retreat to his lair. Well he would have slinked away had she not called out to him, her voice choked with loving words. When he stopped and turned his horrid gaze upon her whom he loved with all his heart, neither was she repulsed nor did her love turn cold, for the eyes glinting from the dragon's brows were not those of a serpent, but those of Svipdag, shining without change or loss of beauty.

In a cavern hollowed out beneath a gray rock, lulled by waves that crashed overhead, Freyja comforted him in his sorrow, seeking to soothe his misery with her faithful love. Each day she donned her necklace, diffusing a glimmering across the sea, to remind them both that true beauty remains unchanged.

Slowly the gloom that wrapped the island began to lift as sea fog melted beneath a dazzling sun. The serpent who had haunted the shoreline no longer stalked the edge of the sea. Instead, with a keen, fearsome gaze, he protected Freyja and guarded all her precious ornaments. As long as the serpent lived, Brisingamen had a faithful watcher, for it is the nature of dragons to brood over treasure that falls under their charge.

On the day Hadding, the celebrated son of Halfdan, raised a war camp on the mainland shore, Brisingamen lost its stalwart guardian. Incensed with blood anger at the sight of his old adversary, the serpent writhed from the cavern, churning the ocean to white foam in his eager charge to shore. Spotting the approaching beast, Hadding drew his blade. With a battle cry on his lips, he dove for the serpent.

They fought a furious battle amid white breakers now frosted pink with blood. Sharp teeth flashed with bright sword as they raged along the shoreline, both attacking, neither retreating. Hadding's blade skittered along the serpent's protective scales while the dragon's teeth scored the bright links of the warrior's byrnie. Whipping its head around, the dragon lunged for his foe. Hadding leapt aside, avoiding the attack. Struggling to his feet in the watery sand, he brought the full power of his shoulders into a swift arcing cut. The dragon fell, partially decapitated from the savage blow of Hadding's sharp-edged blade.

Too late to intervene, Freyja could only watch from a boulder perched on the isle edge as the victor dragged the serpent's body ashore, crowing loudly in triumph over his conquest. Svipdag's body twitched then lay still as his blood poured out into the sea. The goddess stared a moment at the gray waves, their white caps now stained red, before returning to the cave. There she divested herself of finery, removed all her jewelry, and loosed her tresses from their bindings to fall limp about her shoulders. She took a final look around, recalling the poignant solitude before leaving the cavern hall.

Hadding stood in silent awe of the great beauty that strode toward him across the surf, the surface of the rolling waters a firm path for her feet. A steady sea breeze swept back her golden hair. The startling blueness of her eyes shown bright and liquid in the sunlight.

Reaching the dragon, she placed a hand on the limp head and lovingly caressed its brow. Then, bending to one knee, the lady placed a kiss on each scaly eye. "Here on the rocky shoreline of our prison home," she whispered, closing the lids in rest, "the faded glory of Sol staining the horizon red, the low sigh of ocean waves echoing my loss, I let fall tears in your memory."

Bitter tears of pure amber coursed down her cheeks as she rose to confront the victor. Eyes flaring with fire, she stood before him, fists clenched at her sides. A torrent of sharp invective poured from her lips. "You are a fool! You know not whom you have struck down! This one who lays lifeless at your feet was once a dweller in Asgard, enchanted in a form that was not his own."

Hadding fell trembling to his knee. He made to speak, but Freyja's fury cut him off. "For his death, you will suffer my vengeance, the vengeance of the Æsir! On the battlefield, you will know the agony of loss. On sea, tempests will hinder your travels. Bitter cold will plague your home; its hearth fire will bring no comfort. In your lands, farmer's flocks will perish in the fields. Throughout the world men will shun you as a foul disease. In vain you will find the ocean waves and sea breezes have been squandered on you, in vain the warmth of the sun. Sorrow will consume your remaining years. Such is the wrath that will pour against you, cursed wherever you go, in whatever you do, until you honor him who has fallen here with prayers and sacrifice to the kin of Summer's son."

A great column of fire arced through the sky and a bank of black storm clouds stole away the light as Freyja ended her speech. Giving herself fully over to sorrow, she wept without ceasing, great gulping breaths that swelled with the waves. Her amber tears fell in a steady rain, finding their way to all the shores edging the wide seas.

Terrified, Hadding did as directed. On the shore of the battle site, he wasted no time in organizing a great festival in honor of the one he had slain in the surf. Sacrifices were made, with choice selections burned on mounded alters. While all feasted, a pledge horn passed from mouth to mouth, asking favor of the kin of Summer's son, and ending the ages-old vendetta between the House of Orvandel and the House of Halfdan.

When the gods saw Freyja's tears shed on the earth for the sake of pure love, and the tribute of men offered up to the one slain by his very slayer, they acknowledged the loss of one of their own. Their will bent before the power of Freyja's sorrow, they raised up her husband, healed his body, restored his litr, and accepted him once more into their clan. Lifted back to the halls of Asgard, the bold son of Orvandel rejoined his faithful wife as he took his place among the Æsir.

The Theft of Brisingamen

While Freyja chastised her husband's killer, Loki, ever eager for mischief, spied Brisingamen unprotected in the cavern nestled amid the scattering of Freyja's jewels that she had cast aside in her grief. Since the night he had first plucked it from her neck at Odin's command, he had desired to regain its beauty.

In the guise of a seal, Loki visited Vágasker. His seal-self lumbered up the rocky shore, pausing to bask in the sunshine while remaining watchful for any movement. After making certain the cavern remained vacant, he shifted back to his normal form before ducking into its depths to steal the necklace from the unguarded hoard. Delighted with himself, Loki climbed onto the rocky beach to examine the treasure he had taken. Before a line of boulders that faced out to sea, he hunkered down out of sight of Freyja, who stood in full view on the mainland shore delivering her curse to a quivering Hadding.

From his post on the bridgehead of Bifrost the white god, charged long ago by Odin to keep a watchful eye on the actions of Farbauti's son, watched the passing events. When Heimdall saw what Loki had done, he left his post to intervene. Loki, ever vigilant when in action, caught the brilliant flash of the sentry's approach. Tumbling forward, he ducked as the warden of the gods struck a wide blow with his gleaming sword.

Drawing into himself, Loki borrowed from the nature of his father. He glowed brightly, then burst into a column of fire that snaked its way up into the sky. Ever quick at responding to attacks, Heimdall drew in a bank of thick, dark clouds that burst open, loosing a blinding downpour. The column sputtered as the sudden deluge threatened to quench its blaze.

A sharp curse slipped from Loki's lips as he shifted into the form of a bear. Growling low, he made menacing swipes with his clawed paws. Heimdall grinned wide, angled his blade at the beast's heart, and charged, a bloodthirsty howl bursting from his throat.

Loki dropped his guise and fled to the seashore. Hastily, he turned himself into a seal and dove into the surf, the necklace gripped in his teeth. Donning his own seal skin, Heimdall followed the frantically swimming Loki. He chased his prey through cresting waves onto the rocky shore of Singastein where rested a herd of seals.

The white god scanned the crowded beach, gazing into the eyes of each seal for the telltale sign of Loki, for a person in disguise can change all but their eyes. Recognition flashed between them, a glint of hate fresh as a ray of sunshine breaking through the clouds. With loud bellows, they charged one another across the rocks. Crashing together, the huge beasts slashed at each other's throats, with long tusks drew blood, screamed, and crashed together again.

They fought all along the shore, slamming into other seals that barked trying to get out of their way, until the brave son of nine mothers forced Loki to retire into the sea, bellowing in anger and frustration without his stolen prize. As Loki disappeared into the foaming surf, Heimdall removed his seal skin and gathered up the necklace dropped during the fight. He turned it over in his hands, so it seemed liquid fire dripped from his fingers. He stood a moment considering its beauty, then smiled thoughtfully. This was not theft from kin, but goods recovered from a hard fight. As victor, the spoils were his to do with as he pleased.

———— · ————

Fair light angled through the doorway of Gladsheim as Heimdall knelt before Frigg, Brisingamen dripping from his outstretched hands. "A gift I offer to the wife of Odin, a great treasure won in a hard-struggle fought far at sea on the ornament rock. I freely place into your hands, the most wondrous ornament under heaven that it may brightly adorn your breast in the years to come."

Frigg smiled, delighted with the gift, and donned the necklace. The gold glowed against her skin with the inviting appearance of a warm summer's day.

Cycle 4: Premonitions

The Devouring Bond

At the word of the Alfodur the Fenris Wolf, the son of Loki was adopted into the Æsir clan. He lived many years among the Æsir, learning the ways of Asgard. With each passing of Mani, he grew larger, his temper shorter. It was not long before his combative nature unnerved his new kin.

As his size and irritability increased, so did the Æsir's fear of him, until only Tyr dared be his companion. They came together in secret, the fearful gods, to decide what to do with this terrible force that dwelled unbridled among them. After days of whispered conference, they decided on a dangerous strategy, to use his own arrogance to constrain him.

Often the son of Loki boasted of his strength, claiming no foe could detain him nor bond hold him now that he had grown into his full stature. To this, the gods offered challenges that he might readily prove his brag.

First, they challenged him with Laeding, a fetter woven of raw sinew and cured leather, the strands knotted over themselves in an intricate pattern of strength. He laughed as they wrapped it about his limbs. When they were certain it was secure, he winked at his audience and broke it with a light flex of his muscles.

Next, they challenged him with Dromi, a fetter of iron skillfully forged in their own smithies, each double-folded link hardened in ice water. Fenris grinned broadly as they locked it about his limbs. Before they were fully out of the way, he took a deep breath and manfully snapped the chain. Its links shattered into pieces, the fragments scattering to the far horizons.

Worried that their strategy might fail, the Æsir sought help from the sons of Andvari, those smiths most skillful at forging bindings. Odin himself traveled the dark road to Nidaveller to commission them to create an unbreakable fetter.

Beside the rumbling maw of their cavern forge the brothers

Andvari huddled together in deep discussion. Their voices blended with the low grumble of the furnace fire as they debated what must be done. The eldest brother stepped forward as his brothers fanned out behind him.

"The task the Æsir set is fraught with countless impediments." He shook his tongs in the Alfodur's face. "These can be overcome, but it will take time. We will need to think about it. Come back when the Shiner has reached its highest point in the night sky. We will let you know then when it can be done."

Odin crossed his arms before his chest. "Time is a luxury we cannot afford. Our need is urgent as the danger grows with every passage of Sol." Glaring down at the dwarves, he held their defiant stare until they grew nervous and looked away. "We will not wait until it is convenient for you to start. You will begin today and work on nothing else until it is finished! We need the fetter now!"

The eldest brother's eyes grew large at Odin's demand and a ribbon of spittle trickled from the corner of his mouth. The sons of Andvari again huddled together, this time stomping their feet and gnashing their teeth, their shouts drowning out the roar of the furnace. Still bickering, the group turned to face the Alfodur.

The eldest brother stepped forward, his lips set in a deep frown that nearly reached his chin. "It can be done, but we have no time to waste. A full cycle of the Shiner will see it completed. Return the next time Mani shows his full face in the night sky to claim the work. Now go! We have much to do!"

———————

With patient method, they laid out the tools needed for the task ahead, stationed them around the forge, each to their purpose, each to their time of need. After skillfully gathering uncommon elements from across the nine worlds, they distilled each to a waning phase of the Shiner.

Stoking their furnace to a high heat, they forged the elements together, binding each, layer on layer, according the waxing phase of the Shiner. When at last its length was drawn out and its width set, they draped the fetter across the benches to cool. Dark eyes gleaming, heads bobbing in satisfaction, each brother leaned close to examine the completed work.

When Mani's face filled the night sky, Odin sent Hermod along the dark road to retrieve the fetter, giving him the use of his swiftest mount to navigate the way to Nidaveller. On Sleipnir, the warrior rode through dim grottos where narrow fissures in the rock showed yellow light glowing from deep within. Turning at a wide gap in the trail, he guided his mount down a rocky path. The sure-footed horse slipped along the winding route to where the bright yellow glow that lit their course became the blistering heat of a smithy furnace.

The sons of Andvari clustered before the open maw of a rumbling forge that filled the center of the cavern. They bowed deeply as their visitor dismounted. "You know why I am here?" The brothers glanced furtively among themselves then stared back at the rider. "I am sent by the Alfodur of the Æsir," his stern voice echoed through the cavern, "to retrieve a fetter of uncommon strength. Is the commission ready or do I return to tell him my trip was in vain?"

The sons of Andvari nodded as one at the words of the courageous host. Silently, they passed into his hands the work commanded by the Æsir. Hermod pinched the fetter between two fingers, blew on it so its ends floated in the breeze. He shook it in disbelief before his eyes. The silken cord was light as air and when he cast it down it made no noise.

"This is what you have made," the warrior grumbled to the smiths, "to bind the great wolf? The cord is so light I doubt its strength. Why his breath alone will snap it."

Andvari's sons laughed at his words. The eldest brother picked up the fetter, shook it free of dust, then folded its length over his forearm. "Do not let its appearance or its weight fool you. You will find no stronger binding anywhere. Of six elements, it is crafted: the roots of a mountain, the sound of a cat's footsteps, the growth of a woman's beard, the strength of a bear's sinews, the breath of a fish, and the lightness of a bird's spittle. It is the unique nature of these things that gives the fetter its uncommon strength."

Hermod gave a sour look. "Still..." he shook his head.

The smith glanced over his shoulder at his brothers, each vigorously nodding encouragement. "A mountain stands solid and unmoving," blackened fingers gently stroked the fetter, "its base firmly planted on the ground, yet it has no roots. Cats are lithe, quick to catch their prey, yet make no noise when they run. The hair on a woman's head grows as long and thick as does a man's, yet they have no beard on their chin while men have trouble keeping their lips free of hair."

A light shudder raced up Hermod's spine. As he stared at the furnace light flickering in the smith's eyes, confronted by the power of a mystery so easily mastered, the warrior reached up to smooth the hairs that had suddenly raised up on the back of his neck.

The dwarf continued, unconcerned with the emissary's apparent discomfort. "The embrace of a bear can crush the bone cage of the mightiest, best-armored warrior, yet with gentle swipes of its powerful limbs it sports with its young. Fish live in the water and are seen to gulp air at the surface, yet they do not breathe as we do. Birds have mouths and tongues; some even speak the language of men, yet they do not drool."

The smith lifted the fetter over his head, three times lifting it high, before placing it back in Hermod's hands. "It may appear fragile to the eye and weightless to the hand, but no strength of limb can break it. The more it is strained, the stronger it becomes. Gleipnir we have named it, the devouring bond."

Hermod snorted. "The proof is in the deed." He tucked the fetter into his vest. "We will soon know the truth of your words." Leaping onto his mount he raced back to Asgard where he placed the marvel in Odin's hand.

Fenris Bound

On the island Lyngvi where sweet broom grows amid the rocks, the Æsir staged a challenge to Fenris' strength beside the pitch-black waters of Amsvartnir lake. When the fearsome wolf was shown the silky ribbon, he noted its tenuous length and ethereal nature. His gaze turned dark, deep furrows creased his brow, and he instantly suspected deceit.

"Little do I fear my ability to snap this nothing. Little honor will I gain from the effort. Yet I am curious that you present me a challenge that appears weaker than those before. I suspect there is more here than meets the eye." He looked out over he gathered gods, noting the shifting gazes that avoided his stare. "You wouldn't be planning some trickery, would you?"

Odin stepped forward from the crowd of onlookers, his hands raised for silence. "There is no trickery." He spoke evenly to the wolf. "The silky bond you see before you we offer to challenge your much-touted strength. Prove your oft spoken boast to break all bonds by donning the fetter. We defy you to snap it as you have done others in the past."

The great wolf glared at the Alfodur. "Sath you have been called, but I've learned caution when presented with only words. What assurance, what pledge will you give, that should I fail to break this bond you will release me from its hold?"

When no one spoke, Fenris grinned. "Don't all rush to promise at once. Because you do not readily offer a pledge, let me suggest one. As guarantee of my release should I fail, let one from the ranks of you mighty gods freely place a hand in my mouth while I test my strength against this... this thing."

The gods huddled together to mutter among themselves. Sharp words flowed from their clique, low grumbles, frantic gestures, and raised fists shaken overhead. They nervously glanced back at the wolf whose smile grew wider the longer they deliberated.

With a loud expletive, the god of war shoved all aside. Muttering darkly to himself, he stomped forth to stand before the great wolf. "You know me, Fenris," Tyr looked up into the baleful glare of deep amber eyes. "When all others of your adopted kin shied away from your size and manner, only I remained to stand boldly by your side. You know my bravery," he proudly thumped his chest, "and that my word is bond. I pledge to you my good right hand to ensure the honesty of the Æsir." With this vow, Tyr thrust his hand into the mouth of the Fenris Wolf.

Satisfied, Fenris donned the silky ribbon. After it was fitted to his limbs, the wolf strained hard to burst the bond. The band grew stronger, tighter with his every exertion. He fought harder, until sweat beaded his brow and his muscles shook with the effort.

The Æsir smirked at his struggles, chuckling with delight at each fruitless effort. "Look at him, wrestling against such a pitiful little thing. Here we were concerned. He is not as powerful as he thought."

At last Fenris gave up and with a low growl acknowledged defeat. "It is so small. I am ashamed to admit that the fetter is too strong for me to break." He turned his eyes to the ground. "Now honor your promise. Release me from this bond that pins my limbs."

The Æsir continued to laugh. "Why would we do that? Now, when at last we are certain you are subdued."

Lost then Tyr his hand, bit off at the wrist joint—ûlfliðr it is called—as the wolf gnashed down hard with his teeth. His jaws set against the agony, the god of war clutched the bloody stump tight beneath his left arm. "I pledged my hand," he shouted, voice strained with pain. "I pledged our reputation! I demand you honor my oath and free the wolf!"

Turning deaf ears to the war god's plaint, the Æsir dragged the defenseless son of Loki across the field to the enormous stone Thviti, whose upper half angled up from the ground; the rest lay buried deep in the earth. Three times they wound Geliga—the tenuous remnant of the fetter that dangled unused from the wolf's leg—about the stone to secure it in place.

With snapping jaws Fenris tried to bite. The clash of his sharp white teeth nearly clipped the hairs on the Alfodur's head. To still his attacks the fearful Æsir gagged him with a long sword wedged roof to jaw. The wolf growled menacingly, unable to move as the laughing troop of Æsir marched away. Drool pouring from his dewlaps formed the river Van, a placid stream whose hope flows until Ragnarök.

The Abduction of Idun

Often the gods traveled the lands to experience the world they had created. Their journeys took them far afield, over fir-wrapped mountains, through deserts dusted with scrub brush, across snowy plains swept by icy winds. Returning home from one such journey, Odin, Loki, and Hoenir passed across barren lands where food was scarce, their every step dogged by the hunger of rumbling bellies.

Turning their feet north, they took a winding path through the cold domain of the Wolfdales in hope of finding game that could be easily caught. In a valley protected from chill winds they spotted a herd of black oxen grazing in a grove of stunted oak trees. The powerful beasts pawed through the autumn leaves carpeting the ground to feast on the acorns scattered beneath.

They cut a bull from the herd, a large one with thick, meaty thighs. While Odin and Hoenir slaughtered it, Loki dug a pit and built a fire to roast the meat. After flaying the flesh from the carcass, they placed it in the oven-hot pit, covered it with green boughs cut from nearby shrubs, then piled a layer of dirt on top. When they considered the meat cooked, they broke open the pit, eager to begin eating, but to their dismay found the flesh dripping fresh blood. They covered the pit a second time, this time waiting longer for the meat to bake. On uncovering the pit, they found the meat still raw.

The three Æsir gods conferred together in hushed tones of what they should do. They interspersed their conversation with quick glances over their shoulders, hoping to catch some sight, some glimpse, of what could cause such a strange occurrence. Each started when a voice sounded from above. "I am the cause of your raw meat. It is my doing that it remains untouched by the fire."

Looking up they spotted a golden eagle, a male draped in the full plumage of its kind, perched on a high limb of the oak tree under which they were standing. Its massive talons gripped the branch that bent low under its weight.

Loki squinted up into the tree, his hand raised to shade his eyes. "That is a big bird."

Odin grunted agreement. "It is far larger than any eagle I've ever seen. You?" He nudged Hoenir, who silently shook his head.

"I, too, am hungry," the eagle called from his perch. "If you are willing to share your meal and let me eat my fill of the ox, I will let the pit cook the meat."

"I've heard them screech, but this one," Loki scratched the side of his head, "this one talks."

Odin stepped forward. "All birds do," he muttered from the corner of his mouth.

He planted a fist on his hip and shouted back to the eagle. "A one-sided offer to be sure, though if we were willing to eat raw flesh you would be out of luck."

The eagle shifted from foot to foot as it replied from its high perch. "That is true enough. But you built the cooking pit, even kindled a hot fire. Twice you have attempted to roast the meat. Twice you have failed. With all this effort, it seems to me you are not that hungry for the taste of fresh blood."

Odin laughed. "Then it seems if we want cooked meat we have no choice in this matter." He spread his arms wide in welcome. "Come join us."

The eagle wafted down from the limb, kicking up a cloud of leaves as it landed beside the fire pit. It glanced side to side, noting the three Æsir who stepped back to give him room. "On the other hand," the eagle bobbed its head once, twice, a third time, "I like raw meat." Striking deep into the hot oven, the eagle gobbled up the thighs and both shoulders, leaving the ribs and neck untouched.

"Why you deceitful..." Snatching up a stout branch from the ground, Loki struck the eagle a ringing blow across the back. As he made to strike again the eagle pivoted about and grasped the stick with an enormous talon. Alarmed, Loki found his hands stuck fast to the wood. The eagle launched into the sky, pleased with its second catch of the day.

Loki screamed curses, then just screamed as the eagle swung along a course intended to bring discomfort to its squalling burden. Flying low, he dragged Loki across thorny thickets and bounced him against tree limbs until the son of Laufey dangled from the branch bruised, bleeding, his clothing shredded. The beating was so constant that

Loki could not catch his breath to beg for mercy until the golden eagle alighted on a boulder, exhausted from carrying its now limp burden. When his feet touched the ground, Loki cried out in a voice shrill with pain, promising to do anything, to say anything, if only the torment were stopped.

The eagle turned to face the son of Laufey, cocking his head from one side to the other as he considered his captive. "Know that I am Thjasse cloaked in eagle shape. We have had dealings in the past, so you know my mind. I tell you the torment will continue unless you do as I demand. You will swear to me an unbreakable oath to entice Idun from the protective confines of Asgard. You will do this when the Hastener next reaches its full face. Bring her outside in the full light of day."

Loki grimaced in agony as he worked his shoulders; it felt as if his arms had been pulled from their sockets. When he spoke, his voice was the squeak of a mouse. "Is that all?"

Thjasse bobbed his great eagle head. "That is all I require of you for your freedom."

Loki swallowed past a sudden dryness in his throat. "Yes." A painful shudder wracked his frame. "Yes, of course."

When Loki gave an unbreakable oath, he found his hands free of the branch. Climbing shakily to his feet, he gingerly touched his shoulders. "Where..." he staggered a few steps, squinting at the unfamiliar surroundings. "How far..?"

"I brought you in a great circle." The eagle raised a wing at the hillcrest. "You will find your companions just over that rise. I will leave you now to return to your friends. Remember your oath. Speak of it to no one." With those words the eagle spread wide its golden wings, caught the breeze that swept up the hill face and spiraled up into the sky until disappearing into the distance.

Rubbing his shoulders, Loki limped back to his companions. As he topped the rise, they leapt to their feet crying out at the ragged state of his once-tidy clothes. Trudging into the camp, Loki flopped onto the ground, grumbling of a harrowing flight, of finally wrenching free from the eagle's grip, only to fall from a great height into thick underbrush. From the welling cuts and dark bruises that marred his flesh, Odin and Hoenir readily believed his words.

On their return to Asgard, the story spread of Loki's encounter with a great golden eagle. All in Asgard found it astounding he had lived to tell the tale. Many laughed at his expense.

———————.———————

On the day of the first full moon, Loki approached Idun as she tended her garden. He stood admiring her form, bent over working the soil. His tongue moved slowly over his lips and he looked to the sky, shaking his head. "Your skill in growing plants is great. You tease such wonders from the soil that only Hlodyn herself can challenge your ability."

Rocking back on her heels, Idun glanced at the son of Laufey leaning against a nearby tree. Slouched amid the shadows, he appeared a lonesome snag shorn of its limbs. "My skill with plants is great, that is true. But I only work with what is needful for our use. Hlodyn is the very earth itself. Her hand falls across all that grows. My skill would be naught without her strength."

Loki nodded while idly scratching an arc with his toe in the dirt at his feet. "I agree Hlodyn is the power with all growing things. But," he casually waved toward the garden wall, "in the nearby forest I have found fruit hanging from the limbs of an amber tree. It is golden yellow, smooth skinned and the size of my fist. In any sacred wood or hallowed glade there could not grow better fruit on bough. I feel these would be more than a match for the golden delicacies you grow."

Idun stood, wiping her hands on her apron, curiosity sparkling in her eyes. "Is this true? My harvest is potent. I have never encountered in the wild the equal of that which I husband by hand. I must see such fruit for myself."

"Follow me." Loki headed toward the gate. "Oh," he snapped his fingers, "bring along several of the golden orbs you grow that we might better compare the two."

Leading the way, Loki called over his shoulder as they stepped past the walls of Asgard. "The route is through these woods," he pointed to a path that meandered through the surrounding forest.

They had barely entered the forest when a rush of wings thundered overhead. Swooping down from the sky, Thjasse grabbed Idun with his powerful claws, drew her in close to his chest to muffle her screams, and headed back to his hall, Thrymheim, nestled deep in the Wolfdales.

Loki watched Thjasse disappear over the horizon before slinking back to the halls of Asgard. No one else had seen the giant eagle swoop down and fly away clutching its heavy burden.

———————

All Æsir were alarmed when they found Idun had disappeared. The halls were searched, the forest hunted for any sign, but turned up nothing. Emissaries were sent across the nine worlds with queries regarding the fate of their sister. Months passed in expectation, but they received silence in reply. Without the golden apples prepared by Idun's skilled hands, age soon began to creep upon them. Their features grew winkled, their hands gnarled with popping veins, and gray hair sprouted where once the color of youth had held fast.

Odin convened an emergency council of the gods to discuss the disappearance of Idun, who had seen her last, and where she might have gone. He stood before the gathering taking in the anxious gaze of age-ravaged faces. "The hand of Eli is laid upon every one of us, that which the grace of Idun's apples had long held at bay. Just look about to see the truth of my words in the deepening lines that mark each face, the once-youthful hair now streaked with swatches of gray." Light wheezing coughs sounded from the crowd. Here and there a frail hand shook to cover eyes that feared to see. "And I, who cultivated the image of age-old wisdom, suddenly feel aches where once strength flowed. It is a disagreeable sensation shared by many of you."

The trembling stare of the gathering held his gaze until he bowed his head. "We must face the unpleasant truth that without Idun we are all lost. Only she knows how to prepare the golden apples that restore youth. Already her grove withers from the lack of her care. The grasses brown and the leaves, which have always been green, flutter to the ground spent of life. She must be found at all costs or we, too, will follow the inevitable course of the leaves."

A great moan rose from the crowd. Voices cried out from all corners. "Missives have been sent everywhere to no avail! No one has reported seeing her! Our searchers have found nothing; it is as if she vanished into thin air, snatched away from us by the winds!"

Amid the anxious chorus of the gathering Bragi set down his mug and stood wringing his hands. A fresh tear trickled from his eye as he cleared his throat. "I spoke with her the morning of the day she disappeared. She was working in her garden while I prepared to leave for Sokkvabekk. As I drove through the high arch of Valgrind, I thought I spied her leaving Asgard, headed out along the forest path in the company of Loki."

Odin swung around, blasting his voice across the gathering. "Why didn't you speak of this earlier? You know Loki's penchant for mischief!"

The skald cringed back into his seat. With quivering hands, he grabbed his mug from the board and held it protectively before his chest. "I was not certain it was Loki. I held my tongue rather than unfairly accuse another."

Odin ground his teeth, glaring at the skald. His hands clenched and unclenched as he turned his attention to the white god. "Heimdall! You were tasked with keeping a watchful eye on Loki. Did you see anything?"

The Warder of the gods pursed his lips. "I saw him return to Asgard that day, traveling alone from the forest. I cannot speak to anything else," he sadly shook his head. "I remain vigilant but cannot watch him all the time."

Frigg squinted her eyes, deepening the lines that webbed out from their corners. She tapped a ringed finger against her lips. "Bragi's vision was not muddled. Loki was the last to see Idun. Heimdall's words confirm it."

Fire burned up Odin's neck to flush his cheeks with anger. "Loki! Come forward!"

The gathering milled about, necks craning to look over shoulders, whispers snaking among the throng. Finally, Thor stood and glanced around the hall. "He is not among us."

Leaping from his seat, Odin jabbed a finger at the crowd. "Then find him!" The rafters shook with the force of his command. "Bring him here! He will freely tell us what he knows, or it will be wrested from him bit by bloody bit!"

Search parties fanned out across the lands, scouring every mountain valley, every peak, hunting across the hills, exploring the depths of every forest. After an extensive hunt that left no nook unsearched, they found the son of Laufey in a grove of ancient oaks, cradled in the arms of his mother.

Squawking loudly in protest, he was dragged before the assembly. Shaking off the hands that held his arms, Loki sneered at the fierce glares of the gathering. "What a sorry sight: gray heads, wrinkled faces, dull eyes. Are these the same great Æsir that direct the worlds? You seem to be fading before my eyes, blown away as spent leaves driven by an autumn wind."

"And you," Loki bowed to Odin seated in his high seat, "lord and master of all this withered flesh. At least you now appear more natural seated next to your wife and no longer look like a spring winter paring."

Odin ignored the taunt. Leaning forward from his seat, he fixed the burning glare of his one eye on Loki, who studiously examined the walls, anything but face the fierce gaze of the Alfodur. "You received the summons to attend this gathering. We are in great peril. Why did you not come?"

Loki lifted his nose to the roof beams. "I am not blind to what is before my face, though many here would turn away their eyes." He gave a slight, dismissive wave of his hand. "I simply did not want to spend my time among this aged rabble listening to their laments of aching joints and stopped up bowels."

A low, menacing grumble rose from the crowd as it shifted forward drawing a tight circle about the dark son. Loki's eyes darted side to side as he fought to hold his sneer firm. Odin's lips crinkled at Loki's obvious discomfort. He waited a moment to let the pressure grow.

Well he knew Loki's mind and that only the direct approach could hope to elicit a truthful response. "Idun has gone missing. We have searched, but she is nowhere to be found. It is certain that you were the last to see her; Bragi saw you walk with her into the forest; Heimdall saw you return alone. Tell us all you know."

The son of Laufey snickered, shaking his head. "You dragged me here because you lost a sparrow and with all your vaunted skills cannot find her. Now that I call pitiful."

Bragi shouted from across the room. "I swear, if you had anything to do with my wife's disappearance, I'll see you pinned beneath the waters of a bog, held fast by a lattice of hazel branches!"

Loki spun around and Bragi stumbled back into the crowd, concealing himself behind a screen of neighboring cloaks. "Bold threats backed by the power of ale. Of what am I accused?"

Freyja stepped forward, her lips gathered into a scowl of deep wrinkles as she spat words filled with venom sting. "You were the last to see Idun. Tell us what you have done with her or so help me you will suffer our wrath."

Loki pressed a hand to his chest. "Me?" He peered about with exaggerated shock. "You accuse me of her disappearance? You have no proof. It is just as likely she became bored and left, rather than endure another day of your scintillating wit."

Freyja hugged her cloak tight about her shoulders to ward off a sudden chill. "I'll not contend with a fool. You will tell us the truth," she snorted, stepping back into the crowd. "One way or another you will talk."

Sneering over his shoulder, Loki circled to the far side of the open space, careful to keep Freyja in sight. "Save your threats for the swine when you are mucking about with their swill. Your words are tedious, little more than the blustering of fear, though you seek to disguise them with menace."

Thor called out from his seat. "We need Idun for her skills in preparing the apples that keep us young. That her disappearance puts us all in danger is something of a grand jest that carries the hallmarks of your doing. Tell us, if you know, where we can find her."

"What is the matter, Thor?" Loki laughed, crossing his arms before his chest. "You have had the fortune of encountering Eli before when you wrestled her in the hall of Utgarda-Loki. Do you fear the slow, languid bending of the knee again?"

Thor surged to his feet, his fingers snatching at the back of Loki's cape as the son of Farbauti danced away laughing. "Bold you have become in your newfound age, bold as the kitten of a cat."

The son of Odin gathered himself for another lunge, but was blocked by Heimdall's broad shoulders, while the strong arm of Tyr grappled his waist. The god of oaths leaned close, whispering words into Thor's ear that carried clearly through the hall. "Not yet. We need him to tell what he knows."

Holding an outward smirk, Loki sauntered stiffly back and forth, his eyes taking on the glint of a trapped animal. With each turn the living circle narrowed until the hot breath of the Æsir steamed his face, their hostility forming an inescapable cage.

The white god grunted through his teeth as he struggled to block the angry Thor from his goal. "Listen to me Loki, we have no time for your banter. Another evasion and our next questions will be asked with sharp edges and red-hot coals. Death will be a blessing long in coming."

"Now choose," Odin's voice suddenly boomed through the hall, "Speak or remain silent!" Loki flinched as Odin leaned down from his high seat. "Come Loptr, you can make up your own mind; all harms are measured out. Freely tell us what you know of Idun's disappearance or face the brave persuasions of Heimdall!"

Cringing before the savage glares bearing in from all sides, Loki felt the terrible certainty of their intent in the chills racing up his spine. Shaking the fear from his robes, the son of Farbauti turned to brave the threatening faces of the crowd. "It is said toward kin be slow to avenge though they do harm... still," he dragged a shaking palm across his brow, "I suppose that only benefits the dead. As I have no desire to perish at your hands or from the advance of decrepit age, I will speak what I know."

Loki made a show of tugging his robe straight while the rumbles of the crowd continued unabated. Taking a deep breath, he lifted his chin and let his gaze sweep across the angry faces. "It was a wonderful day, the sky clear with bright sunshine warming the air. A pleasant breeze carried the fragrance of the forest. I desired company and asked Idun to join me for a walk outside the walls of Asgard where we could enjoy nature unfettered. We walked along a winding path chatting, admiring the bright foliage of the forest, not paying attention to much, simply enjoying the day and each other's company.

We had just entered a clearing when, without warning, an eagle, a massive bronze male, swooped down from the sky." He swept an arm over his head, then suddenly dove his hand down. "We heard nothing until he was upon us. A rush of wings knocked me to the ground. I heard Idun scream as she was snatched from the path. I scrambled to my feet as soon as I could, but by then the eagle was winging over the treetops with Idun gripped in his talons as easily as he might seize a hare to feast on. I swear I could do nothing to save her."

The heavy breathing of the crowd whispered through the hall as Loki looked up, first at the unflinching glare of Odin, then at the sharp unsympathetic faces hemming him in. "I know I should have spoken of this sooner, but I feared you would blame me for her disappearance." He smiled uneasily. "You might have demanded my life for her loss."

Thor leaned forward in his seat, grumbling into his cup. "In that you may be right!" With his words came a round of nodded heads and muttered agreement.

Surrounded, afraid the Æsir would carry out their threat, Loki blurted into the silence, "I suspected then as I suspect now that it was a giant cloaked in eagle shape. For I know of no natural eagle capable of such a feat. If my suspicions are correct, she is alive somewhere in the eastern lands." He swallowed hard, then beckoned with his fingers. "If Freyja will lend me her falcon cape, I will scour Jotunheim and find Idun! You have my oath that if she lives, I will bring her safely home!"

With no other recourse before them, the Æsir agreed to Loki's scheme. Freyja's cloak was brought from her hall. The golden maiden's face flushed with bitterness as she handed it over to the son of Laufey.

"Watch for my return," Loki's voice quavered as he straightened the cloak's feathers for flight. "I may be followed. Be ready should I need assistance." The Æsir nodded gravely as they listened to his words. "A giant able to take flight will not give up his catch without offering deadly pursuit."

Loki hurriedly donned the cloak and flew off. Wind whistled over the feathers as he turned north, heading straight into the cold lands of Jotunheim. He landed at Thrymheim on a clear, windless day when Thjasse had left the hall to fish a nearby lake. Swooping down over the threshold, Loki found Idun sitting alone in the hall.

Idun jumped at the sudden appearance of a falcon. When the son of Laufey removed his cloak and stood undisguised before her, she laughed, pressing a hand to her breast. "You startled me. From the thundering of your wings," she swallowed hard, "for a moment I thought I was back in the wood being abducted. Now that I see it is you, I count myself among the most fortunate. I am glad to see my kin have not abandon me."

"Are we alone?" Loki craned his neck, attempting to peer in all directions at once, fearful of enemies lurking in the shadows. "We're alone. Let us go," he motioned frantically with his hands. "Quickly, before the giant finds me here!"

Idun laughed, tears rolling down her cheeks. "Thjasse is large. Far larger than you. Cloaked in his eagle shape, he tired as he carried me here." She shook her head at Loki's slim build. "You arrived as a small falcon. How will you carry me?"

Darting quick looks about the room; Loki inched forward. "Know that I have skills," he whispered, "acquired at great cost. I will shift you into the size and shape of a nut. Then you will be light enough for me to carry from this place."

Idun leaned forward smiling. "There is no need to whisper," she whispered back. "Thjasse is not here. He has left to catch fish for tonight's table."

She turned about, drinking in the sights of the hall. "Loathe am I to leave this place. I have been well treated. My wants fulfilled. My every need met. To be this doted on is an entrancing thing. In confinement, I have come to understand my captor. In this place, he is shut off from the world and oh, so lonely for company. Well learned in many things, he aches for someone to share it with. We have often talked late into the night, our conversations drifting as an unmoored ship that bobs about the sea, touching here and there along the headland until finally making landfall. So, too, I have grown fond of his daughter. She is called Skadi. Brave and fierce-minded like her father, even now she is out hunting meat for the larder."

Loki ushered impatiently with his hands. "All the better time to leave. Now, while there is no one to hinder our passage. Come seat yourself before me so I can shift your shape. I am eager to be away before Thjasse returns. He is clever, and I have experienced for myself his power. I do not hold high our hopes for escape should he catch us in the act."

Idun sat down before Loki while with mumbled tones and arcane gestures he stretched his skill to turn her into an acorn. Wasting no time, he jerked Freyja's falcon cloak over his shoulders, gathered up the nut—nearly dropping it in his haste—then dove out the doorway. The rush of his beating wings faded as he climbed into the sky.

Cold and tired from a full day of fishing, Thjasse stumped into the hall, eager to warm himself by the hearth fire. He shouted out as he lay his catch beside the door. "It was a long day, but I had great success. You will enjoy tonight's dinner. The fish in my lake are the best anywhere. Why, I have a recipe that you are bound to like." He hesitated when there was no response.

"Idun? I'm back!" He called out again to announce his arrival but received silence in reply. "Idun, where are you?" An ancient agony lanced his breast as his calls remained unanswered.

Frantically, he searched the hall, bellowing out Idun's name as he hobbled through the rooms. On finding her gone, he scanned all approaches to his hall, first the forest, then the sky. Far in the distance, silhouetted against the clouds, he spotted a falcon shape beating its way toward Asgard. "My swan," he whispered. He knew then the Æsir had invaded his home and reclaimed their stolen sister.

"No! You'll not take her from me!" Bellowing like a bull, he donned his eagle shape—a great cloak of golden feathers cleverly crafted by his own hand—and leapt to the chase. The air booming with the sound of his wings, he roared through the sky, exerting himself to his utmost as he fought to close the distance between them.

When Loki heard the booming and saw the eagle shape rapidly approaching from the rear, he beat his wings harder, faster, working the air until his limbs ached, fearful lest Thjasse intercept him before he reached Asgard.

From the courts of Asgard the Æsir kept watch, looking ever north in the direction Loki had flown. When they saw a falcon closely pursued by a large eagle, they sprang into action. With savage intent, they stirred up the moat of black clouds that surrounded the walls of their stronghold until its surface raged with ashen foam that glittered with fiery embers.

From high above Loki saw the proceedings and dove into the courtyard as the wise vaferflames targeted his arrival. Thjasse swooped in behind, just missing the falcon's back, his talons snagging tail feathers. As the roiling, black clouds exploded, he banked hard, trying to turn aside, but the vaferflames kindled around Asgard struck him full in the chest.

The great eagle screamed in agony as the flame enveloped his form. He tumbled into the courtyard below, his feathers melted, unable to fly. When he crashed to earth, the gods fell on him as a group. Raising wicked lances high over their heads, with strong thrusts they speared him to death.

Thor plucked the eyes from Thjasse's charred skull. "This," he held them aloft for all to see, "is how we treat with enemies of our clan."

Taking the orbs from his son, Odin gazed sadly into their depths. "Once you were a trusted friend. But now..." He sighed. "As you crafted the eyes of Nidud's sons into glittering ornaments to grace the evening cloak of Sinmara, so will your eyes decorate the night sky." With a mighty heave, he tossed them into the eastern heavens. "Let them always gaze upon that which you tried to destroy."

Njord's Marriage to Skadi

When Skadi learned of her father's death at the hands of the Æsir, the war-minded maiden set her resolve. She carefully dressed herself for combat. Around her chest, she snugged a byrnie of closely welded rings. She twisted her long, black hair into a knot behind her neck and tied it off with a cord of woven sinew. On her head, she set a sturdy helmet adorned with the tusks of a boar brought down by her own hand. She strapped a sharp-edged sword at her side—a finely crafted gift from her father—took a short thrusting spear and a longbow from their racks, then slung a quiver of arrows over her shoulder. From the wall, she lifted a banded shield to fit her arm. Storming from the hall, she headed to Asgard to avenge herself against the arrogant gods.

When the formidable daughter of Thjasse stood outside their

gate loudly challenging everyone within, the gods sought to appease her whose battle prowess was known to equal that of their greatest warriors. Waving all others aside, Odin himself braved her challenge.

Opening the gate, he approached alone to boldly face her burning glare. "I am the Alfodur, so speak for all the Æsir. Over the years, grievous events have harmed both our houses; the latest is the death of your father. No good can come from continued conflict. Æsir everywhere are eager to reconcile with the line of Thjasse. That you will know the truth of my words, we offer marriage into our clan. As kin, you will know the full protection of our house."

The daughter of Thjasse rapped her blade against her shield. The metal bands clinked ting... ting... ting with each blow, as she considered Odin's offer. Finally, she stopped and sheathed her blade. "While my breast burns for vengeance, still I must face the truth of life alone. It is a prospect I do not desire. I accept your proposal." She slipped the shield from her arm and leaned it against her leg, ready to snatch it back should the need arise. "But it is a poor bargainer who accepts a bull from a herd without examining it first. Trot out your eligible males. Let me see what you have to offer."

Odin shook his head, indignant. "They are all Æsir," he snorted. "And any are the finest match you will find anywhere. I will select the best for you."

Skadi's eyes flared with the uncompromising fire of her father. "You deny me even a cursory choice of temperament. This seems a dubious offer, full of hidden conditions. These are the very things my father warned me about in dealing with your clan." Jaw jutted forward, arms crossed before her chest; the warrior maiden spread her feet in a defiant stance. "If I am to accept this proposed paring, you must at least allow me to examine some aspect of their form. If you deny my request, then be ready for battle. You will find no sterner foe."

Odin turned an approving eye on the daughter of Thjasse. A light twitch curved the corners of his lips before disappearing behind the cloak of his mustache. "Fine! If you wish to choose by form, then let your choice be made from the feet alone. Their face and hands will not be your guide."

Skadi brightened, her smile confident. She relaxed her arms and set her hands on her hips. "Hunting is my life. I can tell a great deal from the tracks left by my quarry. Line up the eligible males of your clan that I might choose my husband. Their feet will be my guide."

As Odin started to agree, she shifted her stance, bringing her blade arm to the fore. "And since you are fond of imposing conditions, then hear mine." The warrior maiden lifted her chin. "Comforts I had in my father's hall, but the fates had not treated him well. He was ill-given to humor. While growing up, my only enjoyments were the clash of battle and the thrill of the hunt. I expect more from newfound kin. Much more." Skadi spat into her palm then extended her hand. "So, for this reconciliation between houses to conclude, you must also make me laugh."

Odin stared at her outstretched hand while Skadi's eyes began to narrow. Before she could withdraw and reach for her blade, he spat into his palm. "Agreed." He clasped her hand in friendship. "Let us begin."

At a brusque command from Odin, all eligible males of the Æsir gathered in the courtyard. Hoods placed over their heads concealed their features. They tucked their hands inside the cloaks to give no clue to their owner. They arranged themselves in a silent line, unshod before the daughter of Thjasse.

Skadi paced along the line of men bending to examine their feet for telltale signs of wear that might give away their age and demeanor. Unhurriedly, she moved down the line, passing some by and bending low for a closer look at others. She had her mind set on the beautiful Baldur as her mate.

Odin began slowly tapping his toes on the ground, creating small divots before his feet. He held his breath when Skadi stopped, then started rapping his fingers in a steady tat-tat-tat against his byrnie as she continued to another hooded candidate. "You are taking a long time. Come now, choose and be done."

Skadi paid no attention to Odin's demand, but bent closer and ran her finger tips lightly along the feet of a candidate so the would-be suitor struggled to remain still, choking back a giggle that might give him away.

"Wait!" Odin bustled up to the line. "No touching! You are to look only."

Skadi flashed a black look over her shoulder, freezing Odin's advance. "The agreement was that my choice was to be made from the feet alone. Nothing was said as to how I might inspect the feet. "Why," Skadi drew a dagger concealed at her waist, twisting it before her face, "if I choose to prick or slice the skin as part of my examination, it would be permissible under our agreement."

The line of candidates shifted uneasily at her words but remained silent. Odin stared at the slim blade, its wicked tip glinting in the sun. "Of course." He swallowed hard, silently cursing himself for underestimating the young woman, for forgetting, if only for a moment, from whose loins she had sprung, under whose tutelage she had grown up. "The means of examination are up to you."

Skadi smirked at the Alfodur's obvious discomfort. "But you need not worry." She snapped the knife back into its sheath. "I am here to choose a husband, not to maim."

After passing along the line, first from the front then the back, one pair of feet stood out from the rest. Their smooth skin unblemished by time was lovely to look upon. Their youthful ankles and slim toes, unscored by firm character, were a definite sign of innocence. Skadi pointed to the owner of the feet. "I choose this one. Of all those presented before me only these carry the look of beauty." She smirked, well satisfied with her decision. "It is well known there is no ugliness on Baldur."

When the hood was removed from her choice, she was shocked to see the kindly, aged face of Njord. "Wait! Wait, this is the wrong one! I did not mean to choose an ancient from the stable of youth!"

Odin stepped forward, pitching his voice to the gathering. "You chose fairly by the means agreed. There were no tricks. The choice cannot be undone. Njord is your husband now."

Njord took Skadi's hand in his. "Do not fret about my age." He smiled gently into the confused eyes of his bride. "I am not so old that I cannot keep up with you. I have learned many things in my long life that will greatly benefit us both." He winked as a sudden flush colored Skadi's cheeks. "Too, there are advantages in an older husband. I am not an impetuous youth always seeking the soft limbs of another but am delighted to remain loyal to one. As well, I understand the cycle of storms and, like the learned mariner, can navigate their course.

I do not fear dark clouds or turbulent weather, for I know they are followed by clear skies and calm winds. We can find concord only if we try."

Skadi stared hard-eyed at her groom then let her harsh gaze track around the gathering until it settled—the bitter sting of a barbed dart—on Odin. She slumped down on the nearest bench, crossing her arms, and locking her ankles. "Now make me laugh."

Heimdall tried music. Hoenir beguiled with riddles, those he had learned from Mimir. Gefjon, worldly and wise, related bawdy tales of her adventures among men. One by one the gods and goddesses tried their hand at eliciting some response other than gloomy silence from the would-be bride.

The gathering dutifully laughed at each quip, at each jest, while Skadi's scowl deepened and her fingers flexed on the pommel of her bright blade. At each attempt her lips grew thinner, the set of her teeth a barred gate.

Odin dragged Loki to the back of the gathering as Bragi began a humorous story. Huddling beside the entryway, Odin whispered urgently into Loki's ear while the great skald's voice faltered beneath Skadi's harsh glare. "She is stern-minded like her father and like him is little given to compromise. See, even Bragi is unable to move her. You know the verities of people. Use your cleverness. If anyone can make her laugh, it is you."

Loki craned his neck, peering over the crowd to where Skadi sat hunched in on herself, angry, ready to burst. "She is a warrior and a hunter, familiar with the demands of harsh elements. Such people rarely smile, let alone laugh." He shook his head. "And, too, you stuck her with a nag when she wanted a stallion. Know that any humor she might possess is well shielded. It will be difficult to reach."

Odin leaned close until his breath washed over Loki's face. "But you can do it. You must. We cannot risk the failure of this reconciliation. Raised by one who thrice harmed our clan—his cunning nearly bringing us to our knees each time—the danger she poses is too great."

Loki tapped a finger against his chin as he studied the maiden now enduring a long story from Frigg. "Yes, I think I can." He winked at Odin. "But I will need a moment. Occupy her while I prepare." Loki began untying his vest as he slipped from the room, a mischievous grin flickering his lips.

Odin approached the warrior maiden, touching two fingers to his brow as she speared him with an icy glance. "You have the patience of a hardened hunter given to silence in pursuit of your prey. But here among kin you can relax. There are many things..." he began to turn when a loud squawk interrupted his speech and an outrageous sight greeted his eyes. Loki, naked, his testicles bound by a string to a Billy goat's beard, tottered squealing, arms flailing, into the room.

The goat brayed, tugging its helpless victim back and forth before the gathering. First the goat pulled one way; Loki shouting, his face twisted in agony, followed the directions of the goat. Then Loki would set his heels and drag the goat back across the room, his teeth set, his testicles stretched out into a bright red knot. Bleating, the goat would try to brace its feet, but the taught string pulling his beard set him tiptoeing forward.

Skadi sat open mouthed, her eyes wide and staring, as the pair enacted their brutal tug-of-war. Thor broke the silence first, his booming laughter joined by Odin, then by the entire gathering. Finally, even Skadi was holding her sides, squealing at the spectacle.

Tugging his way over to Skadi, Loki snatched at a blade proffered by Odin and cut the string, releasing himself from the goat. He collapsed, breathless into the warrior maiden's lap while the goat bolted away through the crowd. Grinning up into her eyes, he winked before climbing painfully to his feet. Still laughing, Thor lent a supporting shoulder as Loki hobbled from the room.

Odin's grin lit up the room as he raised his hands. "Come everyone," he shouted. "We have a wedding to celebrate." The gathering cheered as drinks were quickly refilled. Odin lifted his cup to a forest or raised mugs. "Let us rejoice in the peace between houses."

———·———

First, the new couple moved to Noatun, the hall Njord built for himself by the sea—a place of ships, mariners, and gray ocean waves. The ocean god's smile lit the clouds in warm welcome as he led Skadi beneath the arched doorway. He did all he could to make his new wife comfortable in her new home, but Skadi quickly wearied of the insistent cry of sea birds, the dank ocean air, and the crash of breakers on the strand. She longed for the howl of the wolf pack, the bright sheen of snowfields, the still surface of mountain lakes, the seclusion of wooded mountain dales, and the hiss of wind through the firs.

Her mind decided, she stomped up the walkway where Njord stood gazing placidly out over the sea. "Come husband. We must talk."

Taking him by the hand, she led him away from his perch to a spot inside the hall well away from the doorway. Sitting him down by the hearth, she took the seat opposite and looked him frankly in the eyes.

"You have decided something." He smiled kindly. When he tried to take her hand, she drew it away from his grasp. "Your face shows the determination I remember when you challenged the Æsir gate. Tell me, what is it you would have me know?"

Skadi took a deep breath. "I have been unhappy for some time." Njord's lips twitched as a slight pain flashed in his eyes. "Not with you," she added. "You have more than lived up to your role as husband."

Njord relaxed as Skadi let her gaze rove about the hall, shying away from the open doorway. "But this place..." She shook her head. "The incessant rush of the waves annoys me as I walk along the shore seeking solitude. All day the doleful cry of sea birds offends my ears. At night, their constant chatter keeps me awake. And the stink of the wind..." Skadi grimaced. "I cannot abide it here any longer. Now you must come live with me in Thrymheim, the mountain hall nestled deep in the Wolfdales, mine since my father's death. There we will make a home or none."

Heading inland from the seashore, they climbed arduous paths to Thrymheim. Skadi was relieved to be in the mountains. She grew calm, her happiness growing as they traveled through dark forests, dipped into the chill air of shadowed glades, and trekked across the blinding expanse of snowfields.

When the snow-crusted roof of Thrymheim came into view, Skadi rushed forward and threw open the doors of her hall. It was only an afterthought that she turned and beckoned Njord to follow. "Come in. This is our new home."

The daughter of Thjasse took up her old pursuits, abandoning her husband to his own devices as she trekked the forest paths on extended hunting forays. Left alone to ramble about the empty rooms, Njord wearied of his new home, the long, drawn-out silences of the hills, the lingering scent of fir trees that tickled his nose, the sharp white-blue hue of meadows blanketed with snow, and the harsh caress of dry air whispering among the trees.

He longed for the wide vista of the sea with the fire of Ægir reflecting from its rippling surface. He missed the sting of salt spray blown by fierce wet winds. Each day he stepped from the mountain hall, straining his ears in the forlorn silences for the call of sea birds and the rhythmic rush of waves; each night they haunted his dreams.

His mind decided, Njord greeted Skadi at the hall entry as she returned joyous from the hunt. "I was successful," she waved an arm at the carcass of a stag laying outside the door, the dragline still wrapped about its horns. "I took it with a single arrow through the neck." Shucking off her robe, she hung it on a knob protruding from the wall. "It will feed us until Mani begins to cover his face. Now help me hoist it up and skin it." She tossed the line over a protruding beam and began to pull. "We'll have fresh roast tonight."

Njord placed his hand on hers, pressing lightly until she looked around. "It can wait. There is something we must discuss."

"But..." Skadi looked at him then back to the stag.

"It can wait." Taking her by the hand, he guided Skadi into the hall to a seat by the hearth. He took the seat opposite, tried to speak, once, twice, three times, then smiled sadly at his feet.

"What is wrong? Has something happened?" When Njord shook his head, she firmed her lip and looked him directly in the eyes. "You have decided something."

"Yes." He took a deep breath. "Yes, I have."

His lips twitched with a slight smile. "I know I was not the choice of husband you wanted, but I am glad I was chosen. I have been happy and cannot imagine my life without you." Skadi's eyes became confused. She looked away to the glowing embers in the hearth. Colors of red and black rippled in waves across their surface while the chimney rumbled with drawn air.

Njord sighed, letting his gaze rove about the hall. "But this place..." He shook his head. "This place I cannot abide. The constant howl of the wolf pack disturbs my sleep. The relentless sluicing of wind through the trees annoys me until I must make fists of my ears. The unbroken expanse of snow burns my eyes. The unmoving ground brings pain to my legs." Njord looked out across the mountains. "We are as unalike as Ran and Ægir, that lofty pair who rule mountain winds and churn the sea. We are as dissimilar as they in nature. Yet where they live in harmony, we cannot reconcile."

Skadi turned away to stare over the mountain peaks that spread out around her hall. "Then we will live in separate halls. You to the rolling sea that calls you and me to the mountain forests that are my home. But we will remain united in marriage to keep the peace between our families. All gatherings we will attend together as joined couples must."

The next day as Njord prepared to leave, they embraced before the doorway.

"You're sure you have all that you need," Skadi fussed checking his provision sack. "It is a long way to the sea."

Njord nodded, bundling his fur robe beneath his chin. "I am familiar with mountain travel. I will be fine."

"Well then," she stared at his feet.

"Well then," Njord hoisted his walking staff and set off along the rutted trail they had taken on coming to Thrymheim.

Skadi watched until he reached the point where the trail angled around the hill. "Until the next gathering," she shouted then turned back into her hall.

"Until then," Njord muttered, looking back to watch as Skadi disappeared behind the door.

Baldur's Dreams

They gathered together those glorious gods in the great hall of Gladsheim, filled their cups and leaned close over the bench to chat among themselves. Gentle chuckles answered low murmurs, followed by explosions of barking laughter that echoed through the hall.

Bragi shouted out to those nearby. "Who has called this meeting of kin? Is there a critical issue we need to discuss or are we celebrating the close of another glorious day?"

The Alfodur raised his cup, taking a long swallow before wiping the back of his hand across his lips. "Baldur asked that everyone be gathered. He did not say why, but from his sallow expression it must be something important."

Frigg wrung her hands, always her gaze strayed to the empty doorway through which Baldur must pass to join them. "Perhaps we will learn why he mopes so." She began absently twisting the rings on her fingers.

The skald peered into his mug, frowning at the level. "That would be a relief for everyone." He sloshed the contents about before taking a drink. "The way he drags himself about the halls has us all on edge. It is terrible to see one we love in such pain. Everyone is sick with concern." Bragi craned his neck to look around at the gathered host. "Do we wait on anyone or is everyone here?

The Alfodur shook his head. Those seated closest leaned in to better hear his words over the din of surrounding conversation. "Only Heimdall." He tapped the edge of his wine cup against the arm of his seat, signaling the nearest servant for a refill. "The white god holds to his duty at the bridgehead so cannot be present. His ears will tell him everything that passes here today."

Bragi laughed. "Then all the more for me," and drained his mug. He snapped his fingers at a young maiden carrying a heavy pitcher, who immediately headed his way. "Let me have another cup of that fine mead."

As they continued to talk among themselves, a shadow angled through the doorway followed by a haggard figure that shuffled silently into the room. Frigg drew a sharp breath at the sunken eyes and hollow cheeks of her son. All conversation stopped as Baldur's listless gaze ranged about the room, settled for a moment on his mother's face, then fell to rest on the dust at his feet.

None spoke. Mouths hung open. Many drinks remained half lifted to suddenly parched lips. All gazes stayed horribly fixed on the gaunt figure swaying before them, unable to reconcile the bright light that had been Baldur with this ghastly apparition. As one their voices cried out in concern. Some rose from their seats with thoughts of offering comfort, but none dared approach his side, fearful of being infected with whatever malady gripped the innocent son.

Frigg raised a shaking hand for silence. "At your request," she choked back tears, leaning forward in her seat, "we have all gathered here, your family who cares deeply about your well-being. Tell us my most precious son, what is it that troubles you."

Baldur lifted his head, letting his dull, weary gaze slide about the room. His lips moved but made no sound. His hands fluttered a moment, as a bird trapped in cage, then dropped limply to his sides. His body trembled as he took a deep breath and tried again. "My tongue, listless with misery, will not stir to song. I have little breath. Colors flee from my gaze. And my life, which was once filled with delight, now lies wrecked before me, a great ship dashed to pieces against headland rocks."

Silence gripped the hall, a breath held waiting to expel at the next sound. "Such fear, such hopelessness! All my thoughts turn to despair. How can I breed joy, how can I bring light from such blackness? How can I raise my mug in good cheer when rain floods my heart stone and gray clouds obscure my vision? This dull storm of depression drives all before it, as the tempest that drives a lone ship far out to sea away from home, family, and good friends."

He stretched out a trembling arm and many hands automatically raised, ready to grasp his fingers. "I search for speech, those words I might use to convey my story to my family, wise in the ways of the world, in the faint hope you can provide succor from the imaginings that plague me or at least divine the meaning of their terror."

Baldur dragged a hand across his face, rubbed wearily at his eyes, then drew his hand across the top of his head and down to squeeze the back of his neck. "In ominous dreams my life is threatened. Night after night they chase the elf disk across the sky; their rude awakenings drive me screaming from sleep. While Mani has cycled from dark to full light to dark, I have endured their ceaseless torment as they drain the very life from my being."

A shudder wracked Baldur's frame. A groan sighed through the gathered company as he swallowed hard, struggling to continue.

"Apprehension hovers within me as a quivering veil. Like a cloud, it mists my eyes, turning joy into dread."

He stared at the far wall, lost in a vision only he could see. "Through the darkness of my mind's night wanderings, I am pursued by a forbidding presence of gray shadows, a relentless foe bent on my destruction." His fingers traced images in the air, curving, flowing, outlining an invisible foe. "Always the stranger's face is shrouded, but there is something familiar about him—I am sure it is a he—so that I feel, somehow, he is known to me. Each night I fall asleep to find him lurking amid the shadows ready to pounce and rend me into pieces. His bloody talons flash through my flesh, sending me screaming into wakefulness as his voice echoes in my ears: "Woe! Woe to all! Baldur the beautiful is dead!"

Tremors ran through the gathering and many cups were emptied followed by immediate calls for refills. Frigg buried her face in her hands while Odin reached across from his seat to place a comforting hand on her arm. "In forest, in field, or at sea, armed for battle or not, no matter how hard I struggle my life seems lost. I have come to fear sleep. Each night I fight to stay awake, bedding knotted in my fists, my body bathed in sweat, desperately waiting for Sol's warm rays to caress the lands."

Baldur stared out the open doorway where a shaft of sunlight spilled into the room, its beam forming a clear pool near his feet. He stepped back from its edge as if afraid to touch its warmth. "And now the bright light of the risen sun, which once shielded me from the night terrors, has lost its ability to protect me from the torment. On waking, if I close my eyes, he looms up before me, reaching out with bloodstained claws. I who have never known fear or distrust of anyone, stand before you terrified of every shadow, startled by every sound, shaken by every sudden movement, flighty and exhausted as a stag hunted by hounds."

The god of innocence shuffled to his seat then collapsed on the bench. He buried his face in his hands. "I thought to keep this to myself," his words came muffled as a voice lost deep in a cave, "to show a strong face, but it has plagued me for so long that is has worn my resolve to dust. I can no longer bear the burden alone." Dry tongues rasped over drier lips. Somewhere a cough sounded from the gathering, its sharpness quickly smothered by the still air that pressed in from all sides. None dared interrupt as Baldur lifted his face, tears streaming down his cheeks. "So, I have called you, my family and closest friends, to this hall of wise counsel, baring my weakness, seeking your help."

When Baldur finished speaking, Frigg rose from her seat, letting her pleading gaze mark each upturned face. "My son is suffering, tormented by sinister dreams. He comes to us, his kin, seeking aide. Among us there is much wisdom. Let each offer what insight they can. Let none hold back."

Then each spoke, those powerful gods and goddesses, of why these ominous dreams plagued Baldur. Together they shared their knowledge, each offering an interpretation of what meaning the images held.

Alone, Odin rose from his seat. As the throng debated, he slipped to the back of the crowd and away from the great hall. Calling Sleipnir from the pasture, he saddled the cloud-gray steed. "We travel," he whispered cinching the saddle tight, "a road we have traveled before. We must do it quickly. My son's life depends on it." The great horse nudged his shoulder in understanding.

Together they raced down the dark roads to Mist-hell. Along the east wall of Eljudnir, Hel's dark hall, he followed a familiar path to where the snow lay thinnest and sharp breezes stirred white moats across the ground.

There, with corpse-reviving spells, he called the wise woman from her grave. Three times he shouted his demand to the chill winds that snatched away the words as they puffed from his lips. "Arise you who know the future. Arise to my summons. Arise and heed my demands."

On his third call a misty form uncoiled from the frozen earth. With sharp commands the Alfodur exerted his will over the tenuous figure that swayed before him. "I, Odin, Alfodur of the Æsir, call on your sight. I demand a clear, unvarnished view of what lies in store for my son Baldur. I command you relate everything you see of his fate and that of my clan. By the power that is mine, I swear you will get no rest until you accede to my demands."

The seeress spoke from brittle lips cracked with cold, her words lifted on the circling winds that whipped snow across her mound.

"Again, Harbard, you use your magic to force my tongue to tell you what I know. Very well. I hope your ears are accustomed to the pain of fore knowledge, the agonies of the nine worlds, and the sound of tears wept by gods."

Raising up skeletal arms swathed in tatters of dried skin, she turned her empty sockets to the dark clouds. "In Eljudnir stands mead brewed for the innocent god; the gleaming liquid chilling in mugs. A bench is draped with ring byrnies coated in frost. The long table of death is set with ice; the serving dishes laden with hunger. Hung behind the bench an age-worn warrior waits on the wall tapestry. His sword dangles from stooped shoulders. His kirtle hangs loose on a bent and withered frame. His bowed legs are unable to bear him into battle. Never again will he go gold-rich to glory.

From a beam stretching high above hangs a burnished shield glowing bright with images of boars racing across its surface. The flashing, the war-minded boars peer through the foggy gloom of despair that shrouds the halls of the Æsir.

Hodd dispatches the light of innocence to Niflheim, in an act of darkness to match his own dimmed sight. Tricked by Loki with an arrow crafted of mistletoe—deadly forged by an ancient enemy of your clan—he steals the life from Frigg's son.

Now the daughter of Loki stands on the Ness. Across the Gjoll Bridge, across the pitfall of Fallandaford, Hel waits to interrupt his journey to the Thingstead of Urd. With grand gestures, she welcomes the fallen hero to her shadowy hall."

Odin slumped against Sleipnir, his face buried in the horse's mane. The black pits of the seeress bore into his back, her frigid voice carrying on, relentless and uncaring. "In a blatant act of dishonor that colors his position among his clan, Odin fathers a vengeful son with Rind, the daughter of a Ruthian king, who births Vali in the western halls. Impatient to avenge his brother's death, Vali liberates himself early from his mother's womb. Unwashed and uncombed, fighting from his first breath, he brings Baldur's killer to the pyre.

As the beginning of a story augurs its end, so these events will come to pass, the first omens of the twilight of the gods. Reluctantly, I shared my vision. I will share no more sight. You must discover the remaining truths for yourself. Now I will be silent."

Bowing her head, the seeress faded into the ground. Wordlessly, Odin watched the tendrils of her litr soak back into the frozen earth. When the last wisps disappeared amid the swirling snow, he banged his fists three times against his thighs and turned back to his waiting mount.

Teeth clenched, the Alfodur raced Sleipnir across the nine worlds to Asgard, a rush of cold wind that chilled the white sentry as the pair charged over Bifrost and though Valgrind. In Gladsheim, he interrupted the still raging debate to relate the seeress' warning of Baldur's death—and no more. He kept to himself the details of the first premonition of Ragnarök.

The Death of Baldur

When Frigg heard the dire warning of the long-dead seeress, she decided at once on how to save her son. With the urgency of a concerned mother, she sought a truce from all dangers imposed by all things across the nine worlds, exacting solemn oaths not to harm Baldur from earth, stone, fire, water, ice and snow, wind and sun, metal, and wood, all the animals, all insects, every tree, all the plants. Only mistletoe she omitted. High on its oaken perch in the deep wood, she felt it too young to give an oath. Certainly, it was much too weak to do harm.

In the company of his family, Baldur tested the oaths of life. The Æsir were astonished. Whatever was done, regardless the source, the innocent god suffered no injury. Spears did not pierce, nor did rocks crush. Fire did not burn, nor did waters drown. The sharp edge did not bite, even the blunt mace failed to mar the white skin of Frigg's beloved son.

From his high seat, Odin observed the amusements being played out in the courtyard below. His one eye glazed with sadness as the seeress' stark words echoed through his thoughts about the inevitable fate of innocence.

———————·———————

Loki slumped on a bench along the courtyard wall, sullenly watching the assembly sport with Baldur, growing jealous of the attention lavished on the glorious son. With each deflected blow, he became angry that Baldur remained uninjured, affronted that all things had given an oath not to harm him, that there should be one being in the worlds that could not die. As an arrow thumped against Baldur's chest, only to uselessly fall way, Loki's eyes twinkled with a plan.

Shifting himself into the guise of a handmaiden, the son of Farbauti sidled up to Frigg as she dressed. He carefully questioned her, listening closely to her every response in hope of discovering a key to Baldur's weakness.

The handmaiden chatted with Frigg as she helped the goddess don her robe. "I would never have thought to ask such a promise from all things across the nine worlds. It was the shrewdest of ideas."

Frigg laughed a light breeze of merriment as she slipped her arms into the sleeves of her cloak and drew it snug about her shoulders. "It was not easy to convince all of the need. But none can deny me what I want when my mind is set, for I would do anything to keep my son safe."

"Indeed." The handmaiden drew a heavy chain necklace from an ash wood box.

Frigg waved her hand. "Not that one. Something light and gay to match my mood."

"As you desire." The handmaiden dug back into the box. Extracting a delicate bauble that dangled from a light chain of woven silver, she held it up for approval. Frigg nodded. "But there are so many things in the world," the handmaiden settled the thin wire weave over Frigg's head to drape about her chest, "how can you be certain you asked all? Is there none that were missed?"

"None of any importance." Frigg flipped her hair from under the necklace and straightened her robe, so the luxurious locks settled about her shoulders in a bright cascade. "I passed by a solitary green shoot perched high amid the limbs of an ancient oak. It was young in the ways of the world, too young to understand the need or give a binding oath. I deemed it too weak to do any harm, so there was no need to ask."

The toilet done, the handmaiden backed from the room, whispering to herself as she left. "You are the cleverest of goddesses to have thought of everything."

Avoiding the crowd gathered about Baldur, Loki raced from the Asgard courts and flew into the wilderness to find the green sprig Frigg had considered too young to give a binding oath. There, perched high amid the oaken boughs, in clumps bursting from the limbs, clung the evergreen mistletoe. The slender shoot, tender and frail, seemed hardly fit for use as a weapon. But in the bitter cold while all others lay dormant, then its strength became apparent; it stood bare to the weather, unaffected by the cold.

Loki took the green shrub to the Regin of the Wolfdales. There, spurred by his hatred for the Æsir, the skilled craftsman forged its length into an unnatural hardness and concentrated the poison from its white berries at the tip. Into Loki's hand, he placed the dangerous arrow of pain, a Gambanteinn of harm to fool the watchful eye of Frigg.

With the treacherous arrow held close to his side, Loki approached the blind god who stood quiet and alone outside the laughing circle that hurled weapons at the now invincible Baldur. The son of Farbauti whispered clever words into the ear hands of Hodd, cajoled the one-time warrior into joining the amusement. "Why do you mope here far away from the crowd while your kin enjoy rough play with Baldur? Are you indifferent to the great gift he has received that nothing across the nine worlds may harm him, or are you too proud to take part in the amusements?"

Shaking his head, Hodd turned his sightless gaze to the voice that spoke softly in his ear. "Pride has nothing to do with my reluctance to join the hard sport that plays out before me. Nor am I envious over Baldur's gift of promised safety from all things. His well-being is my greatest desire. Rather, it is my blindness that keeps me from honoring my brother. Since I cannot see to gauge a target, I would certainly miss my aim." The blind warrior turned his face back to the sounds of merriment. "Imagine an arrow sailing over everyone's head, or worse, striking an unintended victim." He shivered. "Such an affront would shame us both."

"Have no fear," Loki laughed, clapping a hand on Hodd's shoulder, "of missing the mark. I will help direct your aim." With gentle pressure, he guided him to the circle of celebrants.

"Here is an arrow expertly fletched with white goose feathers to fly straight. I have with me a sturdy bow, such as you wielded when steadfastly holding the battle line against stalwart enemies of our kin." Loki placed the bow in Hodd's hand, slipped the deadly shaft into his fingers, then helped him knock the arrow and bend full the yew. With a light touch he guided Hodd's gloomy aim. "Use these now," his honey voice whispered into Hodd's ear, "and show everyone how you honor your brother."

A twang of gut, a whisper in flight, the dull thud of a target struck. A feathered shaft sprouting from his breast, Baldur uttered a soft groan; his radiance fading as his knees buckled and he sank to the ground. Silence fell among the Æsir, as a drawn breath held at a sudden, impossible sight. From everywhere and everything a voice cried out: "Woe! Woe to all! Baldur the beautiful is dead!"

A wave of sorrow rushed across the nine worlds. All the mighty Æsir wept. Earth, stone, and wood were beset with tears. Tidal flats shuddered with Baldur's passing. Shorebirds wheeled overhead with raven and hawk—blood enemies mingling without feud. Whales cried amid the breakers, seals rushed the beaches, and fish leapt straight from the sea.

Frigg rushed to the side of her stricken son. Cradling his head in her lap, tears streaming down her cheeks, she cried out to the assembled gods. "Who among the Æsir would gain all my love and favor? Who would ride the dark road to ransom back Baldur? Forseti, you are his son. It is your responsibility."

The domar shook his head. Long folds of sorrow creased his brow as he turned aside his face. "Death is a decision that is not mine to dispute."

The mother of Baldur flapped her arms in exasperation. "Is there no one brave enough among our clan to dare the gloom of Niflheim and bring back Baldur?"

Hermod the Bold pushed himself to the front of the crowd. "I agree to undertake the mission!" He thumped his fist against his chest. "I will need the swiftest horse in our stables."

The Alfodur pointed to the pasture where his mount stood saddled and ready. "Take Sleipnir. I had meant to take him on a journey of my own, but your need is greater. He is the fastest of all living beings and knows well the route you must travel."

The fearless warrior leapt onto the greatest of horses. With a sharp kick from his heels he urged the eight legs to swift motion. All heads turned to follow as they galloped off across the Quivering Way.

The Burial of Baldur

Everyone throughout the nine worlds remembered Baldur well. Many came to honor his cremation, all the Æsir, contingents of elves, and troops of dwarves. Even etins of fire and frost solemnly looked on in respect, though Thor, angered at their presence, would have crushed their heads had not all the gods demanded they be left in peace.

His closest kin gathered together to prepare his body in the traditional way. With tufts of wool they stopped his nose and silenced his ears. They looped a dark scarf edged with silver thread under his chin then bound it atop his head to keep closed his mouth. Sharp blades carefully cleaned and trimmed his nails, denying Naglfar planking for its hull. Using a boar bristle brush, they worked his hair until it glistened gold as the setting sun. The finest livery wrapped his body. On his feet were bound Hel-shoes of sturdy leather, protective wards for his journey.

His body stretched on a litter of ash, the Æsir carried Baldur to his ship, Ringhorn the greatest of all sea stallions. Beached on rollers of stately fir, the mighty ship sat tall and proud, its mast rimed with ice, sails plumped in the wind, eager to set out.

Odin approached the body of Baldur, staring a moment at the peaceful face, then lifted his arms. "It is difficult for a parent," he shouted so all could hear his words, "to bear the loss of any child. But when the loss is this great all the worlds cry out their grief. Here lies Baldur the Good, my second son, the best, and most merciful of the Æsir. He flourished under the heavens, built his hall in Breidablik, found comfort in Nanna, Nepp's daughter. With her, he sired Forseti, a son skillful in law to honor a father."

Thin clouds scudded across the sky, shrouding Sol with their white gauze. Mournful cries filled the air as seabirds dipped low over the ocean waves in respect. For a moment, the breeze picked up, whipping Odin's hair into a tangled frenzy before dying down. "In innocence, he spread his light across the nine worlds. He alone among our clan never fought or raised a fist in anger, but always sought reconciliation, his thoughts always turned to peace. By exerting the strength of his nature, he won the good will of kin and enemies alike. He earned great honors by freely giving gifts, no greater breaker of rings ever lived. Through such deeds, he prospered among all things, living and dead."

Odin placed a hand on Baldur's chest, his single eye smoldering as he fought down the urge to weep. "When called on for judgment, he decided for the betterment of all. All he knew, everything he did was for the betterment of others. But how to secure the safety of his own life, this he did not know."

A low groan sounded from the crowd and many heads bowed with tears as Odin knelt close to his son. "I gently slip Draupnir onto your arm and whisper softly into your ear before you mount the pyre. No man will know the words I speak, a secret message between father and son."

Frigg approached her son, head bowed to conceal the depth of her grief. "Had I not thought you, my son, would live forever, I would have reared you in my wool basket, safe from the worries of life, protected from the dangers of the world. But what is and will be, not where or who you are, shapes lifetimes."

Tears ran from her eyes to drop in a steady rain on Baldur's chest. She reached out to stroke his hair, then brushed her fingers along his brow. "Alive you shone among us bright as the noon-day sun, a brilliant light erasing shadows, revealing all within the reach of its glow. Now in death, gleaming like the full face of Mani, you throw darkness into stark relief, a great whirling wheel illuminating the land of the dead."

She placed an apple bough on his breast, fresh cut so the sap still ran. "You will drink of the rune-etched cup with the serpent of eternity coiled around the bowl filled with water from the three fountains. Bliss will be yours and great will your litr grow."

They nestled Baldur in the bosom of his ship stretched out on a bed of fir boughs piled next to the mast. His horse they slew with a quick knife stroke below the right ear, then placed him at Baldur's feet, along with all his riding gear. Around the deck were set treasures from all lands. Never was a ship more splendidly laden with gifts.

Nanna, loose hair waving in the breeze, cheeks streaked with the tears of loss, clutched her hands to her breast and sang out in grief as they placed the shining god—luminous even in death—on the great ship, Ringhorn. "Through all time, I worshipped him. Eager am I ever, though the fire's rage grows close, to feel his cheek beneath my caress, to gaze into his bright beaming eyes and revel again as a bride wrapped in his strong embrace. He who outshone the sun, his love was life to me.

Remember when we sat among the reeds. Sun-radiant, the world waited on our desires. Games we played. Pleasures of the body we shared. Sunlit, glorious days spread out before us with an endless string of delights that would always be ours.

Restless now, I awaken each morning in misery, my heart aching, as the one I miss departs with the arrival of the sun. But time has passed, and rather would rivers run uphill. I see that which the heart denies but dare not. I laugh, sick at my very core when rather I should weep."

With that Nanna, struck her hands together, three times she clapped her hands. A great moan escaped her lips as she fell to the ground, her heart burst. Tears streaming, the Æsir gathered up her lifeless form and laid her in the ship beside Baldur, her head resting on his shoulder.

Then each of the mourners approached the ship. About the couple, they piled dry branches ready to kindle. With each log, they built a pyre of their memories, their lost aspirations and wrestling for the truth; all gone now that the light of innocence had faded from the nine worlds.

When everything was ready, Thor raised Mjollnir over his head. With powerfully sung words, he consecrated the ship and its passengers while the mourners stood side by side, heads bowed, tears dampening the earth at their feet.

Putting his shoulder to the prow of the great ship, Thor shoved hard, so the mast shuddered. His feet dug deep furrows in the ground, but the ship would not budge from its rollers. Then Magni joined his father's efforts. Setting their shoulders to the prow, together they exerted their greatest strength. Timbers groaned, and still Ringhorn would not move. Other gods joined the effort, shouted among themselves as to the best approach, but despite their most vigorous attempts the ship still refused to move.

Frustrated that the combined effort of the Æsir could not move the ship, Odin sent word through the attending Jotun to enlist the aid of a powerful enemy, the giantess Hyrrokkin.

She thundered across the frozen, windswept landscape of Utgard astride the back of a wolf, adders coiled about her wrists for reins. On reaching the pyre of Baldur, the Smokey one dismounted, leaving her mount to the graces of Odin's retainers. When she strode away, her mount became unruly, tossing the men about as it strove to return to Hyrrokkin's side. Fearful it might break free to maim mourners clustered along the beach, they drew their blades and slew the beast.

Hyrrokkin approached the ship. She walked around the prow, knelt beside the rollers, and ran a hand along the slick surface of the hull. With a shrewd eye, she spied out the situation, noted how the great ship rested on the log rollers and that a layer of ice coated everything. Placing her shoulder against the prow, the giantess shoved first to one side then the other, until the gentle cough of cracking ice sounded, its softness nearly lost in the din of the crowd.

A mighty groan rumbled through the air, for a moment hushing the waves rushing against the shore, as Hyrrokkin brought her full strength to bear. She shoved hard against the prow, her feet digging deep furrows in the sandy beach. Then, as the ship slid back, she began to run, pushing so hard that great plumes of earth spouted behind her churning heels, and the log rollers beneath the keel burst into flame. When the ship struck the sea, it lifted a great wave that crashed down to shake the entire beach.

Njord cried out, raising his arms to the sky, his chanted words guiding the winds and rushing waves to lift the ship clear of the sands. A blazing shower of thorn-wrapped firebrands heaved by the mourners sent the couple on their way into the flow of the sea.

Thor stormed about the shore, angered that Hyrrokkin—a giantess, no less—had accomplished that at which he had failed. When Lit, an emissary of the dwarves, stumbled into his path, tripping his feet, Thor roared out, loosing a swift kick that sent him screaming through the air into the inferno that engulfed the great ship.

The funeral fire raged upward in a storm of flames that wound their way to the heavens, rumbling from the wind-driven ship as the greedy spirit of Eymyrja, daughter of Logi, consumed all.

Hermod's Ride to Niflhel

Hermod charged down from Asgard, racing his way through the nine worlds. Nine nights he rode without pause or rest on his urgent mission.

In the misty world of Alfheim, the light elves dodged Sleipnir's drumming hooves, a scattered cloud of twinkling lights, as the pair raced across the wide blue.

In the lands of Vanaheim, the Vanir stood solemn on watery paths, heads bowed, hands clasped before them, acknowledging their purpose.

In the green lands of Midgard, men cringed from peals of rolling thunder that shook the air and ran in fright from the fleeting shadows that marked their passage across the sky.

In Utgard, giants stepped aside to let them pass unmolested as they charged across the cold frosty lands, kicking up plumes of snow, and bursting through heavy drifts that barred the way.

The dim caverns of Svartalfaheim echoed with the clatter of their passing. The dark elves remained silent, withdrawing into stony recesses as the pair sped along shadowed paths.

Hermod nudged Sleipnir to greater speed as they raced through the deep valleys of Nidaveller where the elf ray never penetrates. Forges silent, fires banked in mourning, no dwarf emerged to hinder their journey.

Beneath the flush of Surt's smoldering gaze, the pair dodged raking thorns from scrub brush crowding the trail. Heads bent, they plowed ahead, eager to be free of the embers that choked the air of Muspellsheim. The fire giants stayed their hand and did nothing to impede the rider's progress.

Passing into the dark cold of Niflheim, they encountered the warden of the first gate, a massive hound, breast smeared with blood, with feet braced wide to bar the way. Straining at its tether, the hound drew back his lips to bare sharp white teeth and snarled in perilous warning. At Hermod's nudge, Sleipnir leapt Helgrind, his eight hooves easily clearing the top of the high gate. The great hound snapped at the flashing hooves, his deep baying chasing the pair as they rode onward.

At the river Gjoll, he clattered onto a bridge roofed with shining gold that spanned the rushing waters. Modgud stood in the center of the span, her hand raised to halt their advance. "Who is this that makes the Gjoll Bridge tremble? You have neither the color nor weight of the dead. Yesterday three fylki of fallen oaks passed this way, yet the bridge echoes more under your single tread."

Hermod called out from atop his steed. "I ride under order of Frigg in search of Baldur. Have you any news of his passing?"

"Two passed this way," the stark maiden pointed along the bridge, "a pair united in death; the shade of Baldur and his wife, Nanna. Their journey to the Thing of Urd was interrupted. On the far side of this bridge they met a crippled figure wrapped in a gray frosted robe, who took them north to her hall in Mist-Hel."

"Then I seek Hel," Hermod gritted his teeth, "and not Urd." Modgud silently nodded her head.

Raising two fingers to his brow, he thanked the maiden, then cantered off along the north road. The route twisted into the mountains to become a steep, rugged trail that wound its way to a massive iron gate. At Hermod's command the great Na-Gates squalled open. The ground resounded with the clop... clop... clop of Sleipnir's hooves as they angled through Nagrind into the frozen wastes of Niflhel.

Through the sharp sting of sleet Hermod approached the snow-drifted hall of Eljudnir. In a sheltered alcove, the rider dismounted, draped a heavy woolen blanket over Sleipnir. "You are to wait here for my return." He tugged the blanket until it fully covered the horse from chest to flank, then cinched it loosely so it wouldn't fall off. "If I am not back within three days, return to Asgard alone. Frigg will know then that I have failed." Snorting a cloud of steam, the great horse nuzzled Hermod's shoulder, letting him know his command was understood.

Hermod clapped a hand along Sleipnir's neck, scruffled his ears with fingers stiffened from holding the reins, then gently stroked his muzzle. "But with fortune on our side, I will soon return, accompanied by a pair of riders. Then we can leave this frigid place together, our task completed."

Cinching his byrnie tight, Hermod climbed the icy steps of Eljudnir, crossed the dizzying height of Fallandaford, and shouldered through the ice-rimed doors into the hall. A glow at the far end of the room pushed back shadows that crowded in from all sides. Squinting his eyes, Hermod moved toward the light, his breath puffing white clouds with each step.

The shining god sat in a seat of prominence at the famished board of Loki's daughter, as brilliant in death as he was in life. Nanna slumped silent and forlorn beside him. At the head of the table sat Hel, threatening and imperious in her gray robes.

Hermod called out to the son of Frigg. "What is this? You seem alive, untouched by the dimming hand of death." He leaned closer. "No," he shook his head. "No, I am mistaken. It is not life that blushes your cheeks, but more like the frenzied colors cold weather paints on the autumn leaf." The bright shade frowned at Hermod's query and, without uttering a word, turned his face aside.

Hel smiled with amusement at their conversation. "Here the dead cannot speak unless I permit it. But that is not the condition of Baldur; his tongue is free to wag as he pleases. He does not speak for the shame of his present circumstance. He finds it difficult spending time in my company."

Her dagger-sharp gaze turned on Hermod and he felt a chill race up his spine. He set his jaw that his sudden unease not show. "But you rider, I know you. You have come from the land of the Æsir along a road few living have ever traveled. I am delighted to have a guest from your hall. I recall the hospitality my brothers and I received on our one visit to Asgard. Know that I am happy to return the courtesy."

Hel clapped her hands, the sharp report snapping in the still air of the hall. A figure that Hermod had thought to be a sculpture broke free of the rime that caked the walls and shambled forward to stand beside his mistress. "You arrive late, exhaustion shows keenly on your face, but dinner is done, the table long cleared. Now my mind turns to thoughts of sleep." The room sang with a brittle ring as she clapped her hands. "Rest the night from your long journey. You will find the furnishings of my hall suitable, if somewhat uncomfortable. We will speak tomorrow."

The silent shade, wrapped in the frozen robes of his death, conducted Hermod to a room in the frigid hall. The door opened to dull stone walls and a dirt-packed floor barren of furnishings, save for a worn straw mattress lumped in the far corner. The bed was hard, its tick infested with vermin. The thin blanket provided as an afterthought proved inadequate to ward off the cold.

The bold warrior got little sleep. The silence of the dead unnerved his rest, amplified and given voice by the low call of winter winds that moaned and sobbed about the hall. Chinks between the stones allowed tiny drifts of snow to spread across the walls, the bone white fingers seeming to reach for his bed with each breath of wind.

He snapped out of a doze that was half nightmare to see an ashen figure hunched in the doorway mutely regarding him. There was nothing threatening about the shape, it merely looked at him with a great wistfulness that he somehow knew to be the hunger for his heat and form.

Gritting his teeth, Hermod raised himself up grabbing at his blade. "Who..?" But as the challenge barked from his lips, as his fingers closed on the sword handle, the image faded silently back into the darkness. He relaxed, slowly stretching himself out on the mattress, keeping his face turned to the door.

Another came, then another, and still another. All night they visited, the dull gray shades drawn to his spark as those deprived of heat are drawn to fire, afraid its presence may vanish at any moment. They never entered the room, just lurked in the doorway watching, yearning.

The next morning found Hermod haggard from lack of sleep. Bleary-eyed, he rushed to audience with Hel, eager to not spend another night in her grace. Still chilled from the night's unrest, he waved away the offer of a cold meal though the sharp pangs of hunger gnawed his gut. "I thank you for the offer of food," he bowed to the half-gray maiden, "but I do not desire to impose on your gracious hospitality any longer than is necessary for me to carry out my duty." Hermod struggled against the brutal cold that bid him huddle into himself. "I am sent here to ask for Baldur. All the gods call for him to ride home with me. All the worlds mourn his passing. The Æsir dwell in constant sorrow. They cannot stop wailing for his loss. We are powerless to bring him back without the consent of a ward of the dead."

Hel gazed down from her seat, frowning at the messenger of the gods. "I hardly lament your loss. He has dwelled in your lands for many years, gladdening your hearts with his brightness. It is a rare opportunity for me to honor innocence at my own hearth. For me to release such beauty from my home demands I receive just compensation."

Hermod chaffed at her words. Thumping his chest, he grit his teeth and forced himself to stand proudly erect, every bit the undefeated warrior of a thousand, thousand battles. "I do not believe Baldur would be judged twice-dead and so find his final respite in your hall! He is known across the nine worlds as a peace bringer. Everything laments his loss. He belongs among those destined for the glittering plains of Niflheim. Perhaps I should speak with Urd, she who judges the fates of the dead? You answer to her. I am certain she would agree with me."

Rising stiffly from her seat, Hel hobbled forward on crooked legs. "He died from a treacherous blow, not in battle!" She shook a bony finger at Hermod. "His fate is not one for the Æsir to decide. On his way to judgment he came into my hands and under my power."

Hel flicked her robe, kicking up a dusting of ice crystals, and tottered back to her bench. With a loud groan, she relaxed back into her seat. Hermod stood unflinching beneath the angry brittleness of her gaze as she idly massaged her knees. "This is my hall, my land. Here none may challenge my rule! You will deal with me or no one at all! So, hear my conditions. Love professed by the tears of the Æsir is hardly enough. If all things in the world, alive or dead, weep for Baldur, then he can return to the Æsir. But if anyone or anything speaks against him or refuses to cry, then he remains with me."

Baldur shouted suddenly from his seat. "At least let Nanna return with him! Such a bright and beautiful creature belongs among the warmth of the living, not here surrounded by frozen shades of the dead!"

Hel's eyes sprang wide as a crooked smile crossed her lips. "He speaks... and asks for a boon. Here I feared the ice had seeped in to freeze his voice." The daughter of Loki leaned forward, a deep hunger burned in her gaze, pinning the quivering light to his seat. "What will you offer for her release?"

Before Baldur could respond, Nanna dug her nails into the cold flesh of his arm. "In life, we were as one," she declared firmly. "In death, we will remain together. Nothing could tear me from his side. He will give you nothing!"

Hel clapped her hands. "So," she narrowed her eyes at Nanna. The icy black slits bore down, stripping away the maiden's cloak of self, laying her bare for all to see, all that she was, all that she might have been, all that she yet may be again, if... if. Baldur wrapped an arm protectively around Nanna's shoulders but continued to stare straight ahead as Hel made her pronouncement. "It will be as the good woman says. If all cry for Baldur, then she too can return."

The mistress of Niflhel returned her icy glare to Hermod. "Now leave!" She waved him away. "Scuttle back to the Æsir. Let them know my terms. Be quick about it. Light fades quickly in this land. Wait too long and your precious Baldur will become a permanent fixture in my hall, just another frozen husk that once walked and talked beneath the Everglow."

Baldur followed Hermod to the gate. With a voice of shadows, he spoke: "It is good you came to remind me of life. Here in the dark lands what I miss most is sunlight, after that the stars, a full moon, and my kinsmen—mother foremost."

Hermod jerked his chin at the cold hall. "She remains angry at the Æsir for her fate." He reached Sleipnir, who tossed his head, delighted to be leaving. With practiced skill, the warrior began checking the riding gear still strapped on the horse's back. "She seeks to cause us pain by keeping you from us, for surely Urd would have honored our request."

Baldur shook his head. He bent close, keeping his voice low that it not carry to prying ears. "Leikin—she calls herself Hel now—is crafty like her father. She brought me here before I could reach the Judgment Thing. Until released from her control, I am trapped between life and death. But soon Urd will tip the scales; Hel cannot deny her mistress forever. Then I will face judgment unfettered. When I drink from the cup of fate the blend will send me on a journey to the glittering plains or, if the fates decree, return me here."

Hermod arranged his gear and leapt onto the back of the eagerly prancing Sleipnir. "If the Æsir can deliver her ransom, you will soon be secure among us. If we are unable to win your release from Hel, then it will be as you say. I am certain Urd will not give you up. For our attempt at ransom having failed, she will not permit fate to be twice thwarted."

"Wait." Baldur drew the ring Draupnir from off his arm. Turned it over in his hand so the metal winked in the faint light that shown through Eljudnir's doorway. "Give this token to my father as proof you have accomplished your task. You have always been brave; I would have no one doubt the dangerous journey you made."

Nanna stepped forward from Baldur's shadow carrying a small, tightly wrapped bundle. "Take these to those I hold dearest among the Æsir." She held it out to the gruff warrior, who accepted the charge with a silent nod. "They were precious to me in life. I would have them return to the light. In death, I've no need for them." Hermod tucked the bundle into his vest so the left side of his chest bulged awkwardly. "To Frigg present the linen robe edged with silver thread, its spread embroidered with scenes of life. To Fulla give the gold ring inscribed with runes to protect; it is folded snugly within the robe. Let them know that even in death we hold them in the highest honor."

Hermod touched two fingers to his forehead, turned his mount to face the direction of the sun, and bolted from the shadows of Niflhel. For nine days, the bold messenger of the gods rode nonstop, retracing his journey through the nine worlds. Charging over the misty bridgehead he raced across the Rainbow Bridge into Asgard. Once safely through the courtyard gate, he made his way to the council of gods.

A wall of faces etched with worry hedged the rider as he braced himself on shaky legs. With a weary voice, he recounted his adventure, all that had happened, all he had seen, all he had heard. Nanna's gifts he delivered to Frigg and Fulla, who burst into tears as they accepted his charge. Draupnir, he placed in the hand of a somber Odin. The Alfodur slowly closed his fist around the ring as a hot mist clouded his one eye.

The Æsir gathered in council to discuss how best to respond to Hel's ransom demand. Frigg stood, tears flowing down her cheeks, the distaff of motherhood gripped tight in her hands. "Send emissaries to every corner, every nook across the nine worlds asking all things to weep for Baldur's return. Leave now." None disputed her order; even Odin bowed his head to her command.

They fanned out in a wave flowing over the lands, across the seas, beseeching all they encountered to weep Baldur out of Niflhel: fire, water, earth, and air, the sun, the moon, stone, metal, wood of every kind, all the furred animals, birds, lizards, snakes, all the fish, all the insects, every tree, every plant. They received agreement from men, giants, dwarves, and elves. Tears flowed, the sky wept; the nine worlds swam in salty rain.

Everyone and everything cried, save Thokk, the giantess huddled alone in her cave at World's End, crouched amid the crusted bowls and tattered weavings of her everyday life. The Æsir emissaries wrinkled their noses at the stench of her warren while their eyes roved over the scene of a meager life, bare as the rocks amid which she lived. They glanced at each other but made no comment as with hands outstretched they bent their knees. Once, twice, three times the emissaries entreated her to cry for Baldur.

Thokk cackled as with two fingers she fished a morsel from one bowl and dipped it in the rancid oil of another, before plopping it into her mouth. She chewed noisily, smacking her lips while the emissaries fought to suppress uneasy rumblings in their stomachs and the rising gorge that burned their throats. "Dry tears I wept at Baldur's funeral pyre. Alive or dead he gave me no joy. I say accept his fate, not deny it. No one is ever grateful for innocence. Only when it has gone is there remorse."

One of the emissaries cursed, drawing on himself the angry glare of the giantess. "Bold men used to having your own way, who are you to barge into my home making demands of me?"

Bowing their heads in apology, the visitors again pleaded, but Thokk only sneered, the oil thick on her lips. Slowly, luxuriantly, she licked her fingers. "Return to the Asgard. Tell Frigg. Tell them all that I will not weep for their dead. Do not think you will change my mind. Go now! Leave me to my solitude!"

Surf broke hollowly along the pebble beach below the cave as the emissaries scrambled back onto their ship and shoved off into the receding tide. In the brooding twilight, the sun smoldered low on the southern horizon, vague and troubled, shrouded in a blood-red mist. The keen, offshore wind plumped their sail as they angled along the coast, keeping a wary eye on the black mass of clouds piling up along the horizon, the promise of bitter weather soon to come.

The Masks of Odin

Distraught, caught up in the threads of his own fate, Odin sought solace in the western hills. For months he wailed where none could see over the death of his cherished son. A desire for vengeance grew hot in his breast, a fire that threatened to consume his heart in the embers of impotent rage, for the gods were forbidden to avenge a base deed of one of their own or bring them to death by their own hand.

He could do little alone. Often the vengeance of a father is incomplete and cannot be realized without a son to bear the burden for him. Then Odin recalled the words of the faded seeress, of a son born to him by Rind, daughter of a Ruthinian king, a son whose impatient hand would avenge the death of Baldur. Determination set the line of his jaw as he muffled his face with a scarf. A thick leather cap scuffed from weapon blows was pulled down to conceal his eye. Hugging a gray woolen travel cloak about his shoulders, he sped his journey along westward paths to the isle of Samsey, where the Ruthinians raised up their fortress hall.

———————

The guard captain looked over the new recruit, walked around him examining him from head to toe, noted the worn, neatly-patched livery, the ring byrnie scarred in front, the serviceable blade strapped at his waist in a scuffed, well-oiled scabbard. "Your demeanor and garb mark a seasoned warrior. We can make use of such experience. In service to the king your pay is food, lodging with the other warriors alongside the great hall, a warm cloak, and four pieces of silver at each turning of Mani's face. The king is generous; he only asks a tenth part of all you capture. What is your name, if you have one?"

The warrior smiled, baring a solid gate of yellowed teeth. "Call me Herteit, for the battlefield is my home. Nowhere else have I found such joy as amid the clash of arms."

The captain laughed, pleased with the warrior's reply. "Welcome, Herteit." He clapped a hand on his shoulder. "You will find much delight amid our ranks."

From the first, Herteit distinguished himself in combat: his raging cry and flashing blade sent the enemy cringing from the field. In the melee of battle, his bold voice gave heart to his comrades. When the field leaders failed to halt an enemy attack, he took command, quickly shifting tactics on the field to blunt their advance, then routing them into full retreat.

His prowess in battle won him the respect of his peers and accolades among the nobles of that land. With each victory greater than the one before, he rose swiftly through the ranks until the king, impressed with his achievements, called him to approach his seat. "Herteit come forward. Many have praised your prowess on the field of valor, that under your guidance my warriors have expanded our authority over those who give tribute. For all you have done, I extend my hand in friendship. Come," he waved at an empty space on the bench near the head of the table, "I bid you enjoy a seat of honor by my side."

As his victories mounted, his position in court increased. A member of the council now, at each dinner, at each assembly the king sought his advice. He was often called forward to receive some token, some gift from the grateful king.

Confident he held a respected position that had the sovereign's ear, Odin boldly advanced his plan. One night, when the dinner had been cleared from the table, and all mugs topped off, he lifted his cup in salute to the king. "You have shown me great honor. My arms weigh heavy with the gift of rings that mark my success on the field of battle. I owe my seat in this hall to the magnanimity of your favor. All this proves you to be a great king among men."

The king smiled, pleased with the praise. "I believe in recognizing," he raised his cup, "that which is deserved."

Encouraged by the approving murmurs that rounded the table, Herteit stood up and thumped his chest, three times thumped his chest. "I would approach your seat that I may speak directly with you."

The king arched an eyebrow, surprised at the bold request. But certain of his champion, he beckoned him forward with two fingers. "You may approach."

Climbing free of the bench Herteit circled the tables until he stood before the king. Bending a knee, he rested a hand on the pommel of his blade and bowed his head. "By your command, I hold a position of honor at your side from which I continue to expand your greatness. To show everyone the esteem that I hold for you, I ask a boon that I might pledge myself fully to your house."

The king raised a hand, silencing the rumbles that sprang from about the board. "All know that I hold you in high regard and implicitly trust your wisdom. By the palm of war hard pressed by your hand you have secured our borders until none dare attack us. Little enough I have given in position and rings to honor such achievements. Name your boon."

Herteit stood tall before the king, so he appeared as a leek among shoots. Twisting his shield arm forward, with a bold voice he filled the hall. "I ask for the favor of your daughter's hand in marriage. Rind I would have as wife."

The king rocked back in his seat at the directness of the request. He stroked his beard, weighing the benefits of attaching such a great warrior to his house against the dangers of slighting the errant appeal of a warrior who commanded the allegiance of his army. Steepling his fingers, the king sagely nodded his head. "I agree to this union, provided my daughter accepts, for to Rind falls the right of final acceptance or refusal. Such is the custom of our land."

Herteit slapped a palm flat against his chest. "Then, with your permission, I will ask her."

The king smiled slightly and lifted his goblet, followed in unison by the rest of the court. "It has been spoken. Let it be so."

Armed with her father's concord, Herteit sought out the young maiden's company. He found her in the courtyard attended by her handmaiden, enjoying the warmth of the afternoon sun. Ignoring the handmaiden's squawks of protest, Herteit pulled Rind aside and set forth his demand for her hand. "Your father has already agreed to this union. It is your duty as a daughter of this house to follow his lead by accepting my command that you submit. Come, let us kiss to seal the bargain."

As he leaned forward, lips pursed, eager to taste another victory, he missed the flames raging in Rind's eyes and the line of determination stiffening her lips. Instead of a yielding kiss, he received a solid cuff to the ear that jarred his back teeth. Rind's voice was edged with brittle cold as she drew back her hand, ready to deliver another blow. "Go back to the bloody fields where your aged desire is backed by the edge of your sword. I will never accept a union with one who demands my allegiance as he would a saddled mare."

Affronted by the maiden's denial, Herteit stormed off through the gates, his bright red features twisted with rage, his ear still ringing from the blow.

Later, none could tell the king in which direction he had left. Only the ravens saw, and no one thought to ask them.

————————

The next month Odin returned to the hall disguised in the soiled clothes of a foreigner. His ancient features were well masked beneath layers of grime and matted hair. Claiming great abilities with the forging of metal, the traveler was presented to the court. The king sat in regal audience, his daughter seated beside him. He sniffed, looking down his nose at the dirty, unkempt figure that huddled before him. "Who are you that clutter my court?"

The traveler scuttled close to the king's seat, his gaze flickered to the young woman, then back to the silver inlaid hem of the king's robe. "Men call me Roster. I am an accomplished smith, skilled in the creation of wondrous objects. Few can surpass my abilities with the working of metals."

The king grunted. "You claim great accomplishment, but by sight and smell," he waved a hand before his nose, "have not had much success at your profession."

"Do not let the ravages of a hard journey cloud your view." Roster shook his rags with an apologetic frown. "Few could travel as I have, beset by thieves who stole my livelihood, left to survive a rugged trail afoot with no food and only the robe on my back, without suffering wear along the way."

The king ground his teeth in disgust. "That may well be." He turned his face aside to look at anything, but the wretched, evil-smelling figure huddled before him. "What is it you want from me? And what do you offer me in return?"

The traveler bowed deeply, his face nearly touching the floor. "I seek a position in your hall where I can fulfill the designs of my fate through the practice of my skills. I offer to you all the fruits of my labor."

The maiden reached across from her seat to tug at her father's sleeve. He leaned close as she whispered into his ear. The king frowned and shook his head. Again, the young maiden whispered, this time squeezing his arm. The king took a deep breath and patted her hand. "You speak well of yourself Roster, but you do not persuade. Were I to follow my own counsel, I would have you removed at once from my presence. But my daughter advises compassion and reminds me of the duty of hospitality, especially to strangers in need."

The vagrant smith groveled lower while the king tucked his feet beneath his seat, well back from the dangers of being touched. "I accede to my daughter's wishes. She is always right in such matters; a gift she inherited from her long-passed mother. I agree to give you a chance, but the telling is in the deed. Room will be made for you at the forge in my hall that you might prove the boldness of your claim."

———————————

Roster made himself at home in the Ruthinian hall. With deft handiwork, he honored the promise of his profession. Using copper, gold, iron, tin, and silver, he struck out ornaments to gladden the eye. The king was delighted with Roster's work. As the pieces came into his hands, each more splendid than the last, he turned an ever-favorable eye on his new master smith. He was so impressed that he summoned the smith to join his table.

The king beamed down from his high seat as Roster sidled into the room. "You did not deceive when you claimed great skill at the forge. I am glad to see my kindness was not misplaced. The works you craft are magnificent. The entire hall lauds your ability. My daughter delights in the intricate ornaments. She is always asking what new creations you are working on. In honor of such superb work," he waved the smith to a place at the far end of the board, "tonight and every night hereafter you will join us at table."

Roster bowed before taking a seat at the bench. His benchmates grunted welcome as they shifted position to make room for the smith. "I am glad that I can repay, in some small measure, the kindness you have shown in allowing me a place in your hall. It is a blessing to share that which I produce."

Emboldened by his rise in status, Roster created a matched set of golden arm rings, their surface intricately etched with the pattern of a bird's wings fluttered on sand. Using a piece of soft leather, he polished the rings to such a high gloss that when held up to sunlight they pulsed with the low fire of the hearth. When he was ready and certain no one was looking, the smith brazenly approached the king's daughter in the courtyard.

"I see you wear many of my creations." Rind pursed her lips as Roster attempted a winning smile. "It is a delight to see the works of my hand adorning such a comely creature. It is little enough I can do for one who persuaded the king to give me a position in this hall."

Roster snatched off his cap and clutched it tightly to his chest. "There is a kindness I would ask," he appealed gently to her chin, "but I cannot ask it here. If you will grant me a private audience that I might present my request, I will place in your hands a wondrous gift, one to make all eyes turn to you in admiration."

The young maiden edged away from the smith until she had placed an arm's length of distance between them. "You say it is a wondrous gift. I have been looking for a new adornment to wear. I suppose it would do no harm to listen."

Roster raised a finger to catch the maiden's attention. "But it must be only you." He tapped the side of his nose. "I dare not speak of it before anyone else."

Rind shook her head, her eyes darting about the courtyard walls. "But such an impropriety..."

Roster slid closer, reaching out to touch her sleeve, his voice a husky whisper. "No one need know, save us. Be assured that I will say nothing... ever. This I swear."

A tangy mix of rancid sweat and forge smoke rolled from the smith in a thick, choking wave that wrinkled her nose. She drew back her arm, scowling at a black smudge that marked where his fingers had grazed her cuff. Disgust warred with desire as Rind bit her lip. "Tonight then, you can speak freely in my chamber. I will send away my companion."

Roster's eye twitched as he forced an urge to grin from his face. "It will be as you say." He bowed deeply before quickly backing away.

Clouds scudded across the moon deepening the shadows as a furtive figure made its way through the hall to Rind's chamber. A leather-capped head peeped around the corner, taking in the young woman who sat alone beside her bed sweeping her hair with a boar bristle brush. Flickering in the corner, a lone tallow candle sent a pungent stream of dark smoke curling into the air.

"You are alone?" The young woman started at the sound, then nodded as Roster slid around the corner, scurried across the floor, and knelt at her feet.

Rind glanced furtively at the doorway, then nudged the smith with her foot. "First show me the gift you bring. Then you can speak what you have to say."

Reaching into his apron Roster withdrew a fold of cloth. The maiden's face brightened with a delighted smile as he unwrapped the matched set of golden arm rings inscribed with intricate designs. "I see that you are a lover of ornaments. I know others that share such a passion, so much so, that they are willing to give anything to possess them."

Rind reached out a hand to caress a ring, ran a finger lovingly along its rim. Roster turned the arm rings, so they glowed warm and inviting in the candle light. "Beautiful, are they not? They are the greatest of my works, the best of my skill. I offer these for a night of your favor. Let the promise of a kiss seal our bargain."

The maiden's hand jumped back from the ring as if burned and a sneer twisted her lips into a distasteful grimace. Insulted by the audacity of the smith's proposal, she swung her fist, delivering a ringing cuff to his ear. Caught by surprise, the smith, lips still puckered, fell back on his heels clutching his ear. A soft grunt squeaked from his chest as heat raced up his neck to flush his face and brighten his eyes.

Rind pushed words through her teeth in a low, steady stream like the hissing of a log in the fire. "Though common, I had thought you a generous man, worthy of my compassion, but I see now the lust and guile concealed behind this gift and... and all your works."

She stabbed a finger at the chamber door. "Get out of here! Leave my presence and never seek it again or so help me I will bat your other ear!"

Stung with the shame of her rebuff, Roster drew his smithy apron from his neck. With a sharp stamp of his heel, he ground it into the earth before dashing from the king's hall.

Later, none could tell the king in which direction he had left. Only the ravens saw, and no one thought to ask them.

The following month a young warrior approached the gate of the Ruthinians. Three times his gauntleted first crashed against the gatepost, shaking the entire structure. "Is there a gatekeeper? Where is the gatekeeper? I have never seen such dereliction of duty."

A figure detached itself from the doorway of the nearby jakes. "Hold your shouting. I'm coming."

The young warrior looked down his nose as the guard teetered toward him buttoning his kjafal. He passed a scathing look that sent a flush of shame racing through the sentry, who quickly averted his eyes. "Never would I allow a guest to be kept waiting while the gatekeeper hikes up his kirtle. Were you under my command, I'd soon set you to rights."

The gatekeeper bobbed his head, but kept his eyes fastened on the feet of the mounted warrior who, from the splendor of his garb, was obvious nobility. "Welcome to our hall. What do you desire?"

The young warrior glared at the gatekeeper. "That is a pitiful greeting. Open the gate!"

The gatekeeper danced from foot to foot, keeping his eyes fixed on the rider's feet. He swallowed hard and raised his chin. "That I cannot do without knowing who you are."

Leaning down from his saddle, the young warrior shook a menacing finger as he shouted into the guard's face. "I demand you open the gate!" The sentry rocked back from the force of the command.

He glanced into the fiery eye of the rider, then looked away, but held his ground. "That I cannot do without knowing who you are and what it is you want."

The young warrior nodded his head, letting a slight smile twist his lips. "That is better. Never assume the goodwill of an unannounced guest. Always hold to your duty no matter how strong the demand." The gatekeeper plumped under the praise.

The young warrior jerked a chin at the hall inside the gate. "Now send a message to the one who rules this hall. Tell him a bold warrior of superior skills has arrived to offer his service."

With a loud shout, the gatekeeper called a sentry from a nearby guardhouse, whispered urgently into his ear, and sent him rushing off with a message to the king.

In the great hall of the Ruthinians, the sentry approached the seat of the king, knelt on one knee, waiting until the king beckoned him forward with a crook of his finger. "You are from the gate. It must be important if you have left your post. It will be a whipping if it is not. Now speak."

The sentry nodded, his eyes focused on the hem of the king's robe. "Outside the gate sits a single man draped in the mantle of a warrior. His robe carries the bright colors of the sky and the setting sun. The rings of his byrnie glisten in the light. The blade at his waist shines as if fresh from the forge. He sits astride a cloud-gray mount that seems to float rather than prance before the gate."

He dared a glance at the king's dark steady stare that silently demanded he continue. "Broad-shouldered and of regal bearing, his hair the color of spun straw, he commands at a glance. I have never seen a man like him, other than yourself. He claims great skill as a warrior and asks to offer his services to the master of this hall."

The king rose to his feet before the kneeling sentry. He stared at the shaft of sunlight angling through the open door at the far end of the hall. "Only a fool opens his eyes to be dazzled by the light. But only a greater fool would gaze directly into the light and then shut his eyes for fear of what he might see. If you came in walking, go out running. Bring this man before me... now!"

The sentry raced up to the gate, slamming to a stop against the gatepost. Between gulps for air, he blurted the king's order. As the gate opened, the young warrior dismounted with the smooth, unhurried effort of a trained horseman. Taking off his riding gloves, he slapped the dust from his robe before tucking them into his belt. He handed the reins of his mount to the gatekeeper. "See that my horse is rubbed down and well fed; give him a serving of oats and sweet hay along with a bucket of fresh water." He turned to the sentry now able to stand without gasping. "Lead me to your king."

The sentry's shaky introduction still ringing amid the rafters, the young warrior strode briskly into the hall, bowed to the king then waved his arm to encompass everyone seated at court. "Hail to the lord of this hall. Let my greeting apply to every seat under this roof. My name is Atríth. I have sought out your hall for the greatness it holds. It is well known that the surrounding regions pay tribute to your power. Such renown draws the best to your banner."

The king of the Ruthinians smiled, impressed by the young warrior's bearing. With a solemn nod of his head he returned the greeting. "Hail to you as well, Atríth. It is true my house has known success, but recently my ranks have been lessened by the loss of a great warrior—one who on the field of valor knew few equals."

Atríth flung back the edge of his robe to display the brilliance of his armor. "Then it seems my arrival is timely. I seek a position in your hall. By calling, I am a warrior trained in all aspects of soldiership. In the brief time I have been here, I have seen much that can benefit from the ready application of my skill."

The king snorted, looking over the warrior who stood before him. Noted the cut of his clothes, the proud stance, and the air of wisdom that seemed out of place in one so young. "You make bold claims, Atríth. "Tell me," he leaned back in his seat, "what benefit will you deliver should I accept you into my service?"

"Very well." Atríth raised his hand, thumb and forefinger extended. "That your men know how to fight is well known, but they must be trained to remain watchful, especially when there are no battles being fought. If you value your life and that of your family, I would first look to those who guard your walls." He folded his forefinger down. "A sharp eye and dedication to duty are needed, as these form the first defenses against attack."

Low mutterings sounded around the table, while the king sat frozen in his seat, his hard stare never wavering from the warrior's face. "Next, I would see to those who guard your household. In passing, I have seen unkempt weapons and slovenly behavior. Rather than guarding, they sport at games of dice. This should not, it cannot, be tolerated." He shook a clenched fist before his eyes. "Their appearance reflects not only their preparedness for battle, but also the outward impression of your power. Now all your enemies hold you in awe but were they to see what I have seen today, they would soon be making plans to breach your gate."

Silence filled the hall as the king drew a hand over his eyes. "I would be insulted had I not noticed the same. When Herteit left my ranks, the men became despondent, their confidence weakened, their discipline shaken."

Grinning confidently, Atríth spun in a slow circle to take in the entire hall. "I mean no insult. I speak truth, though it be uncomfortable, and hold only your safety at heart. I say your men are not so far gone that I cannot whip them into a fearsome force the likes of which few have ever reckoned."

The king gave a brisk wave to his court. Immediately, space was made on the bench for the young warrior. "Your words instill confidence. I find your bearing impressive. Join my table and I will set you over my hirð, the guard that protects this hall."

———————

The young warrior quickly assumed the mantle of captain. Each day, he paraded before the guards, sunlight glinting on his helmet, the rings of his golden byrnie gleaming. Booming commands astride his tall, cloud-gray mount, he inspired awe in everyone who saw him. Always he kept a lookout for Rind, readily flaunting his authority over the soldiers and displaying his warrior skills whenever he caught her watching.

One day when Sol had reached mid-sky, he spied her standing beside the gate as he made ready to take the guard on maneuvers. Shoulders set square, lips quirked in a confident smile, he boldly approached the golden-haired maiden. Her handmaiden squawked, flapping her arms, as he grandly swept Rind into his arms. Nuzzling her ear, he murmured wheedling words to gain her love. "I have often seen you watching me at my duties. My heart cheered to have you witness my mastery."

The young woman struggled to get away, but he laughed and strengthened his grip. "We are well suited, you and I, you the daughter of a king, myself in the bloodline of nobility. I know you agree that the fates would have us together. Give me the token of a kiss to seal the bond."

Outraged at such forwardness, Rind wrenched free of his embrace. With a powerful hook of her arm, she delivered a ringing cuff to his ear that knocked the warrior to the ground. "How dare you touch me without my permission! How dare you make assumptions of me without first speaking with my father! For all your flash and finery, you are nothing more than a coarse oaf."

From their earlier encounters, Odin knew the sternness of her mind. Eager to fulfill the prophecy of the seeress, he had designed a plan to gain access to the maiden, if this time she refused his advances. From his vest, he drew a slip of elm bark etched with runes—those Gullveig had used when she roamed the lands of men—the glyphs stained red with his blood. With a flick of his fingers, he touched the slip to her ankle. The innocent maiden staggered across the yard, hands pressed to her face, as a fire crept up her neck to blossom bright red on her cheeks.

Odin rose to his feet, his lips twisted with the ugly gloat of satisfaction, climbed onto his mount, and cantered through the gate.

Later, none could tell the king in which direction he had left. Only the ravens saw, and no one thought to ask them.

———— · ————

He had not been gone long when Rind broke into a frenzy. Her eyes started blindly from her face. Deep growls rolled from her throat as foam dribbled from her lips. She became wild and terrible—a berserker in female form—slamming herself repeatedly against the walls, striking out at anyone who crossed before her. The king could do little for his daughter except shut her away in her room. Attendants sat at her side to ensure the maiden brought no harm to herself or to others when a fit took hold. For many painful days, the king wrung his hands as the shrieks of his daughter rang from her room. Helpless, he wept through the nights, hoping each new day would see her well.

The Mead Ship cycled to full and he had nearly given up all hope of his daughter regaining her health when a stout matron came to his hall. Heavy robes concealed her crooked frame. A white scarf, yellowed with age, concealed her face. By voice, step, and action she seemed to the king an elderly woman wise in the teachings of Eir.

The matron waddled forward until she teetered before the king's seat. "My name is Wecha," she gave an awkward bow, "skilled in the healing arts, those passed down through the women of my line. These old legs carry me from place to place as the fates decree. Long

I have traveled across the lands, driven by duty, delivering healing to those in need. I have helped many in my travels. In doing so, I have learned much that is of use. The greatness of the Ruthinians is known far beyond the mountains. When I heard the dire stories of your daughter's sickness, I came to offer my services in hopes of effecting a cure."

The king listened with an interested ear to the recommendations of Wecha, his heart half hope, half agony that she could perform all she promised. Once Wecha finished speaking, the king tapped a finger against the side of his nose as he considered the healer. "If you can do all that you claim, a torrent of generosity will flow from my hand to sate your every need."

The old crone shook her head. "I am a disciple of the goddess Eir." With both hands, she waved away his offer of reward. "I will not dishonor her by accepting payment. I treat men as well as beasts. My skills I offer freely to noble and slave alike; it is knowledge I gladly share with those in need."

The king examined the ancient who stood before him. "Goods freely given between total strangers are suspect." He steepled his fingers before his face. "Either their workmanship is in question or there are hidden conditions on accepting them. Before I let you treat my daughter, I seek proof of your healing skills."

Wecha nodded to the king. "A great leader must always be prudent of action. It is the mark of wisdom to exercise caution."

"Caution," the king mused. "Yes, caution." He sat up in his seat and speared Wecha with a shrewd glance. "You claim great skill. The families of several trusted retainers are ill. Treat them first. Your worth will be gauged through their recovery."

The healer bowed her head. "It will be as you command. Direct me to them." To each Wecha ministered as their sickness required. Men, women, children, even their animals regained health with her aide.

Satisfied that she possessed the true healer's skill, the king led Wecha to his daughter's room. He paused, hand on the ring as a string of growling screams sounded from the behind the door. "She lies in here." Stepping aside, he let the healer enter to examine the young woman.

Many days Wecha spent with Rind, plied medications while she sat by the young woman's knees. Strongly she sang, powerfully she sang, bitter spells for the young woman's health. Each day she laid compresses on Rind's brow, applied poultices to her legs starting with the feet, then rising to the calves before finally stopping inside the upper thigh. Each morning the king found his daughter calmer, her mind clearer, but still subject to sudden fits of frenzy.

Wecha took the king aside away from the house retainers, so no one could overhear their conversation. "I have examined your daughter," she said bluntly, "noted all the symptoms of her trouble, and her response to normal treatments. I have been able to check her disease; as you can see she has grown calmer. To cure her requires a drugged draught, a bitter compound that will eject the malady from the innermost core of her being."

The king's eyes widened in alarm at the pointed words. "The shock to her body will be great. Though she is young and vigorous, the stress of the treatment will be difficult to endure. She may harm herself unless bound to her bed." The healer looked the king steadily in the eye as he nervously wrung his hands. "It is best if none but myself see her in this condition, for once I administer the draught you will want no one to witness what happens next."

The king had become so confident in Wecha's skills that he readily agreed to the treatment of his daughter. Clapping his hands, he gave orders for his retainers to follow the healer's every direction. Rind was bound to the bedposts of her bed, legs spread wide, arms stretched out from her sides.

The king patted the shoulder of his terrified daughter. "Be brave my child," he struggled to show a confident smile. "Tolerate the ministrations of Wecha. She means only your wellbeing."

Once the draught was mixed, all were ushered from the room. Wecha nodded to the anxious king as she shut and bolted the door. Without a word, Odin set the draught aside and removed the scarf from about his face. He leered as he hiked the young woman's robe high up about her waist. The business of healing abandoned, he finally had his way with Rind. The young woman did not complain as she kept faith with her father's request. Eyes shut, teeth clenched, she endured the attention.

When he had finished, Odin stood gazing at the young woman stretched out bound before him. "I have done as the fates required of me. You will bear a son, Vali he will be called. By his hand, I will have vengeance on the one who slew my golden child."

Rind's eyes sprang open. "You!" She twisted around shouting out in anger and fear, shocked at discovering the true nature of her healer. "Father! Help me! This is not a healer, it is Herteit and... and Roster! As you love me, bust through the door. Rescue me from the hands of this ancient lecher! Take off his head! Father, please! Save me!"

As the young woman struggled against her bonds, Odin pinched her cheeks until her lips puckered. With difficulty, he tipped some of the draught into her mouth and made her swallow. Immediately, Rind's eyes grew heavy, her struggles slowed, then stopped as she fell into a deep, dreamless sleep. After straightening the young woman's robe, he knelt beside her bed. "You have been blessed by me," he whispered into her ear, "and so will know my protection forever more."

Drawing the yellowed scarf about his face, Odin rearranged his robes until he was again a hunched old woman, then unbolted the door. Wecha stepped into the hall where the king paced before the door, his fingers flexing on the hilt of his blade. The healer spoke softly to the king as she knotted the travel scarf about her neck, keeping her voice gentle to calm the rage that burned in his eyes, stirred up by the cries from his daughter.

"She sleeps now. The outburst has stopped. Tomorrow she will awaken rested. Feed her wholesome food, nothing rich or overly fatty. Only give her fresh, clean spring water to drink. In seven days, accompanied by her attendants, she can begin to walk short distances. If you keep this up through the economical months, she will regain her health." With these words the crone bowed to the king. His glare followed her as she backed away from the maiden's room. He continued to stare even as the sound of her footsteps disappeared around a corner.

Guards ignored the healer as she hustled past their stations into the evening shadows gathering outside the hall.

Later, none could tell the king in which direction she had left. Only the ravens saw, and no one thought to ask them.

The Birth of Vali

The king's messenger banged on the door of the hut. Three times his fist rattled the door of the good woman's home, his urgent calls rousing the midwife from her sleep that the king's daughter was having terrible pains. With knowledgeable hands, the matron gathered together the tools of her profession, the salves, the ointments, the bitter herbs, and ash berries roasted slowly over a fire—the gift of Yggdrasil to help ease a difficult birth. These she wrapped in a travel pack. Drawing a heavy cloak about her shoulders, she glanced about the room should there be something forgotten before heading for the door.

On a bridled mount, she swept over smooth paths, dashed through the shadows of early eventide to the high hall of the Ruthinians. With all haste, she was ushered before the girl. Rind lay on damp blankets, her body bathed in sweat, her belly swollen with a child eager to be born. The midwife bent low over the girl. "Here lies Rind," she whispered gently in her ear, "overcome with labor pains. Do not fear, young lady. A steady hand is here to help."

With these words the midwife took charge: ordering out those not needed and putting to work those who remained. "I'll want two basins of hot water," she snapped, "and strips of clean cloth torn into ell lengths a double-hand wide."

She jabbed a poker into the fire then thrust it into the hands of a nearby attendant, who grasped at it, eager to be doing something other than staring at the pregnant woman moaning on the table. "Keep the fire roused for warmth. The young woman must be warded from chill."

The midwife stopped, hands on hips, to survey the room. "It is too dark in here," she muttered. "You," a maid who had been busy ripping lengths of cloth jumped at her voice, "set fresh candles about the bed. I need better light to clearly examine the young woman."

Muttering chants for aid from the disir, she marked birthing runes on the palms of her hands then circled the prostrate maiden, clasping her palms to the young woman's joints as she made her way around the bed. With gentle fingers, she spread wide Rind's legs to check the child's presentation. A light touch was enough.

Sighing deeply, the midwife wiped her hands on her apron, then stepped from the room to speak with the king. "The child presents feet first and seems far larger than the young woman can bear." She sadly shook her head. "There is one hope for life. I will need your sharpest knife to open another way for the babe. I have a needle but will need an awl with sturdy thread to close the wound after. Know that I have done this before. Oftentimes both have lived, sometimes only one. Do nothing and both will die."

The king placed a hand over his eyes and stood in silence. None dared speak while he called on his hamingje's counsel to rightly guide his decision. His hand slipped to his side to draw a knife from the sheath belted at his waist. Placing the blade in the hand of the midwife, he nodded his head as he turned his face aside.

The good woman entered the room, shrilly calling all those present to follow her directions. She mixed a draught to dull the pain and administered it to Rind. "Drink it all," she pressed the cup edge to Rind's lips. "It will help." Sputtering, coughing, the young woman managed to drain the cup.

While waiting for the draught to take effect, she washed the knife in the boiling water, a warrior's blade honed to Regin-sharpness, then heated its edge over an open flame. Helpers were set at each limb and instructed to take firm hold so the young woman could not move.

With a firm stroke she slit Rind's belly beside the navel to liberate the son from his mother's womb. The newborn, eager to draw breath, raised a loud, impatient wail to the world as he was dragged through the incision. She held the bloody, squalling child before his mother's eyes. "What lusty breath he has and such vigorous limbs too. He squirms with the strength of a one-year-old."

The young woman saw her son, the red wizened face of an old man swam before her mind. She spoke then to the child, her voice a coarse whisper. "Vali, you are named, arrived awkward from his mother's womb. Whetted with my blood, you are born into this world to take no rest for yourself and give none to others, a valiant bringer of strife to enemies of your kin." Lost then, Rind, the last shreds of herself.

Using strong twine, the midwife tied off the birth cord in two places before cutting it between. "Have to be certain," she mumbled, cauterizing the open ends. "Can't have you two bleeding to death now can we."

After making certain the umbilical had stopped bleeding, they placed the child, still dripping from his arrival, on a pile of wool arranged in one corner of the room. An old blind man was set as guardian to keep him safe.

The midwife went swiftly to work on the mother. With awl, needle, and thread well boiled, she stitched closed the incision, then bound the wound with an herb poultice to draw off bad blood and reduce the swelling. All night she fought to keep the new mother alive. Sitting by Rind's knees, strongly she sang, powerfully she sang for the young woman's life, bitter spells blessed by Eir.

The Death of Hodd

Huddled in the far corner of the room, away from the shouts of the midwife, the old man cooed to the child, gently running his fingers over the baby's face, and caressing the damp locks on his head. He leaned forward, letting his hair fall in a protective shroud about the boy.

"You are a lucky lad." His low raspy voice soothed the child's ears, even as it carried with it the pain of shattered dignity. "The fates smile upon you. Many months ago, I came to this hall, sent by a great power to await your arrival. I know your true father. It is he who sent me to watch over you. I am called Hodd by my kin, one of whom you are now."

Catching a curl of hair on his finger, the old man drew back his hand, feeling the hair slip across his skin. "Once I guided armies into battle. Many were the enemies who fell before my strong arm and the winged shafts launched from my deadly bow. I stood indomitable on the bloody field, war god among the Æsir. Then I suffered a chance blow to the back of my head, a battle strike delivered by a craven enemy that robbed me of my senses. When I awoke, my sight was gone.

I stand before you now, a blind god of war. Sightlessness cripples my judgment. No longer can I bestow triumph on one of my choosing but must deal out victory at random. And my enemies... my many enemies... lie in wait all about me, concealed in the shadows that cloud my vision.

It was because of this darkness that I fell prey to the trickery of Loki and was disgraced before all my kin. My brother whose brightness filled my days, I struck down with a poison arrow, the yew strongly bent by my own hand, its aim guided by the son of Farbauti.

Now none trust my judgment nor believe my story of fault. They speak little in my presence, turning my darkness into unbearable silence. They assign menial tasks to keep me out of the way.

They withhold the apples of Idun, though in truth were I not forced to consume the little allowed I would forego every taste and let the ages take me, my name faded into dust, forgotten. But such luxury is not mine; my penance disallows such an escape. Though nursemaid to a newborn is lowly to me, know it is a burden I gladly bear. There is much I have to atone for. If I can protect the life of one child, I may be forgiven for causing the death of another."

Hodd drew a calloused finger along the crest of the child's head, smiling at the thick, curly hair beneath his fingers. "Slowly grow the sons of men from the kernel placed in the matronly lap," he crooned softly to the young ears. "Long they take to reach their full size. But you... you are born of Æsir. Soon you will gain your full stature. Your strength will be that of a bull. From swaddling clothes, you will leap up to take your place at the feast table, make known your thoughts, and, unshorn, roam the nine worlds. Until that day my arm will protect you and my body will be your shield."

Hodd sat beside the child, resting his hand on a blade half drawn from its sheath. All night the ancient warrior stood guard, his ears turned to every footfall and every voice that passed near. As Day began to follow his mother into the world, Hodd's head nodded with sleep, his breath deepened, changing to a heavy snore that filled the air.

The child cried out at the sound, a loud throaty wail that startled the sleeping sentry. Half awake, the old warrior lurched to his feet, his hands flying to the blade at his waist. As he blindly fumbled it from its sheath, it slipped from his fingers hilt downward. Lunging to catch the weapon, his foot slid in bloody birth fluid that had formed a puddle on the floor beside the child. Falling forward, he landed on the blade. Its sharp point pierced his breast, slicing deep to still his aching heart, and set his weary feet along western paths.

The Seat of Power

As the beloved wife of Odin, Frigg held an exalted position in the ranks of the Æsir clan. Protector of children, benefactor of the home, she reigned in heron-plumed elegance, worshipped in the lands of men by lovers and tender parents alike.

Always careful of her appearance, whenever presenting herself, she enriched her attire with a veil of white clouds, or, if her mood was somber, a mantle of dark gray or deep purple. The golden girdle at her waist jangled with the keys of position. Her breast, arm, and finger jewels were chosen with taste. Her hair was always arranged in an attractive manner, at times braided or loose about the shoulders, at others drawn back into a severe knot behind her head.

Always she sought some new decoration to wear. Desiring to outshine all others, she called the master smith, Dvalin, to her hall. "You will make for me," she ordered, "a marvelous piece; one worthy of my status."

The shrewd dwarf smiled at her request then sadly shook his head. "My brothers and I are always eager to accommodate your desires, but we are hampered by a shortage in our smithy stores."

He shrugged lightly turning his face to examine the far wall. "We are well stocked in the base metals used in our everyday works: iron, lead, tin, and copper. But our supply of precious metals has not yet been replenished. Oh, silver we have in plenty, but gold, the prized yellow metal, we lack to craft the work. It is that metal, the warm light of the furnace, which should be used to adorn one such as yourself."

Frigg's lips twisted into a pout. "And when do you expect to have your precious stores replenished?"

Dvalin shrugged, then looked aside scuffing his feet before answering. "It is difficult to say. We have much work lined up. Two cycles of the Shiner should see our smithy restocked. Then we will readily craft that which you desire."

Frigg snorted at the dwarf's reply. "I cannot wait that long." She tossed her shimmering hair over her shoulders. "A gathering of our clan is planned for the next rising of Mani's full face. I must have a new necklace to wear for the occasion."

Frigg stared at her feet, leaving the dwarf to wait. She sat for long moments in silence, drumming her fingers against the arm of her seat. Uneasy, Dvalin shifted his position, dancing from foot-to-foot before her bench. He glanced over his shoulder at the open doorway behind him. His feet had begun to mark a quick path to the exit, when Frigg roused from her thoughts, leaned forward. "And what," she hissed in a hushed voice, "if I could procure the gold for you today? Would you then have the time to craft a wondrous ornament for me to wear?"

The dwarf swallowed hard and sharply nodded his head. "Were the gold in our hands this day, gladly would we devote ourselves to crafting your pleasure. The necklace would be in your hand well before the Shiner shows full in the sky."

Beaming a smile to brighten the day, Frigg rose to her full height before the master smith. "Meet me beside Valgrind, in the shadowed niche east of the gate, just before Sol disappears to her rest. There I will deliver into your hands, the gold necessary for my request."

With stealth to rival that of Vidar, the goddess of wedlock swept down to the world of men and stole into the sacred temple in Trondheim. Frigg stared hard at the wooden statue carved in the likeness of her husband that had just been set into an alcove along the wall; its hollow eyes stared out of the recess, taking in the actions of the entire hall.

Frigg frowned as she ran her fingers along the carved lines of its cheek. "Little honor you deserve for your treatment of Rind and the disrespect you have shown for our vows. By little strokes such as this, I show my displeasure."

She removed the headpiece of hammered gold that adorned its wooden brow. A satisfied smirk twisted her lips as she tucked the headpiece securely beneath her robe, "This will do nicely." Winding a cloud of milk-white gossamer about her throat to ward of the chill touch of the evening breeze, she wafted back to Asgard.

In the niche beside Valgrind, she entrusted the stolen metal to the dwarf pacing nervously amid the shadows. In hushed tones, she reviewed her instructions for the fashioning of a marvelous necklace. Dvalin placed two fingers to his forehead, then rushed back to his smithy. He tossed many glances over his shoulder as he sped on his way to Nidaveller. He dared not tarry long above ground lest the treasure be seen carried off in his hands. The shrewd dwarf had noted the symbols that wound the edges of the circlet, recognized the expertise of skilled men, and guessed the origin of the gold.

Gathering his brothers before him, he laid out the work to be accomplished in all haste. "Why the rush?" asked the first. "What is the urgency?" demanded the second. "We don't even have a design," complained the third.

Dragging the gold circlet from the bag, Dvalin shook it before their eyes. "This gold was given to me by Frigg. I do not trust its source. Look at the symbols winding its edge; divine the maker from the work. Can you not recognize the craftsmanship of men? Can you not read the name inscribed in runes on the band?"

Each of the brothers took the crown and ran it gently through their fingers. Their eyes widened in alarm as they accepted the truth of Dvalin's concern. They began shouting and waving their arms in panic.

Snatching up a hammer, Dvalin banged it on a workbench to get the attention of his brothers. When the three had quieted down, he leaned forward hissing through his teeth. "We must quickly transform it into something completely new. If it is found on us, we, not Frigg, will suffer the terrible wrath of Ygg. None of us need to be dragged into a squabble between the Æsir."

The dwarves were all elbows sorting tools along the benches, stoking the forge, and hurriedly forming the casts to use. They lost no time transforming the stolen gold into a delicate ornament. The furnace flared yellow, then blue, as they melted the metal in ironstone crucibles and drizzled it into the long, delicate molds of fine clay. When cool, they broke the rough strands from the molds, then shaped them into slender wires by drawing each strand through the sharpened edges of an iron eye.

Dvalin hung over the shoulders of his brothers, wringing his hands, and shouting directions into their ears. "Six wires. No. No. Wait." He cuffed his nearest brother. "Do it over. Make it eight. Yes, braid eight wires around the dowel, then draw out the ends until they meet. Finish the clasp with a silver link. The whole must be light, but still have presence."

Their fingers flew as they rushed the intricate work to completion. With a jeweler's eye, they set a polished moonstone to hang as a pendant; the final flourish. When finished, Dvalin snatched up the necklace, still warm from the smithy fires, and raced off to deliver it to Frigg.

Frigg was so delighted with the resplendent neck ornament, that she immediately slipped it over her head. When Odin spied the delicately braided chain and elegant pendant set with a pale moonstone that shown luminous from Frigg's neck, his love for her increased tenfold, so great did it enhance her charms.

From his high seat in Hlidskialf, Odin detected distress in the temple in Trondheim. On discovering the theft of the gold circlet from the brow of his likeness, he broke into a wild rage that roared down from Asgard and shook the foundations of the earth. The Alfodur fumed in silence as he pondered who would have hazarded such a theft. Some man, perhaps one of the priests. No. None would dare. Besides, he would have seen the culprit from Hlidskialf. "Loki," he mused, but dismissed the thought as Loki was far away in the Ironwood and Heimdall, who now always kept a sharp ear tuned to all movements of Farbauti's son, would have readily informed him if Loki's activities aroused suspicion.

His every thought dwelled on the gold. Each day his eye was drawn to the beautiful ornament that now graced the neck of his wife. His thoughts strayed wide seeking all possibilities, but they always returned to the dwarf-crafted necklace. He mulled over his thoughts, recalling how it had appeared so soon after the theft from the temple.

Odin chatted with his wife about the ornament, laying heavy praise on its splendor. "Such a bauble becomes you. Never have I seen another bring such radiance to your face. Which of the skilled craftsmen created its beauty? I would ask them to craft an arm ring of matching splendor to accompany the necklace."

Delighted with his compliments, Frigg told him of her request to Dvalin that he craft a marvelous piece for her to wear at the next Mead Ship gathering. The Alfodur smiled at the information. "Thank you my dear." He patted Frigg's arm and settled back into his seat. "I will speak with him right away."

An urgent command from Odin summoned the dwarf to his high hall. With fiery eye and a voice of thunder, he announced his intent to the quivering smith. "Not long ago someone dared to assault my statue, one newly raised up in the temple at Trondheim. A golden circlet was removed from its brow. I seek the audacious thief that they might know my displeasure at the brashness of their crime."

Dvalin stared hard at his feet, his hands twisting behind his back as the Alfodur continued. "I noticed a startling coincidence of events. Soon after the circlet's disappearance from the land of men, you presented a rich bauble in this hall, a work in woven gold requested by my wife." He leaned forward until he towered over the smith, a quivering lump that cringed at his feet. "Speak up! Tell me where you acquired the gold used to craft the necklace for Frigg!"

Dvalin replied to the command, his eyes darting side to side as he sought some avenue of escape. "Gold we have. Gold we use. It comes from the rocks and earth. Always we use the precious metal when crafting an ornament for the ásynja."

"But this gold," hissed the Alfodur. "Where did this gold come from?"

Reluctant to suffer punishment for a crime he did not commit, the smith hesitated, then spoke, stumbling over his carefully chosen words. "Gold we have. Gold we use. It comes from the rocks, a gift of the earth."

Odin nodded at the smith's words. "Ah-h, so it was a gift then. From whom?"

Dvalin paused, then raised himself tall before the chief of the Æsir. "I found a circlet of gold," he looked Odin full in the face, "alongside the path as I returned to my home from honoring the goddess Frigg's request that I attend her presence. It lay in the well-rutted earth, in a bag tightly bound with bast twine. No one was nearby. There was no sign of ownership. I could tell by its workmanship that it came from the forges of men, such are the limits of their skill, but I could tell nothing else."

The Alfodur leaned forward, casting a menacing shadow over the dwarf. "Was not the circlet signed as to its owner?" He growled through his beard. "Were there no runes to indicate its dedication?"

"The symbols of men," Dvalin shrugged, turning his face aside, "mean nothing to me or my brothers; just random etchings for decoration. I cannot say what or if any such markings were present. I thought it a pity to waste such treasure, one obviously discarded by its previous owner who held it in such low esteem as to leave it lying in the muck. Whereas I could raise it to a higher standing by using it to craft the necklace your wife now proudly wears."

Odin huffed at Dvalin's words. "Am I to believe," he glared down his nose at the dwarf, "that a thief bold enough to steal from my temple would casually discard such a valuable treasure, that he would walk away leaving the result of his daring laying in the mud of the road?"

Unwilling to betray the queen of the gods, Dvalin clenched his jaw. "It is as I say," he hissed through his teeth. "I found the gold in a bag alongside the path on my way home. I cannot say who left it there."

The Alfodur glowered at the dwarf, shook his head then leaned back in his seat. "You are crafty, but not brave. Never would you dare steal the gold yourself. Tell me if you know, who violated my temple?"

Red-faced, Dvalin squared himself before the Alfodur. "I hold to my words!" His voice peaked with an angry squeal. "I found the treasure abandon beside the road and used it to craft an ornament requested by one whose word is law! Perhaps you should ask the statue who stole the circlet!" The dwarf clapped a hand over his mouth. "I meant no disrespect. I... I meant only..."

Odin nodded his head as the dwarf fell silent under his steady glare. "You are quite crafty when under stress. Even now you seek to discourage me, to send me on a fruitless errand to gain information from a wooden tongue. Well know this son of a maggot, I who learned to loosen the tongue of the dead will contrive the means to make wood speak!

While I cannot fault your story, know that my anger is great. In respect for your many services past and your courage to stand unbowed before me today, I will let you live. Now leave this place. Do not tarry to converse or loiter about gawking at the halls. Fly back to your smoky cavern. Do not let me ever see you here again. My good favor you have used up!"

———·———

Odin commanded his retainers to retrieve the statue from the temple in Trondheim. With loops of rope they secured the wooden effigy above Valgrind, the fortress gate of Asgard. He stood below, fists on his hips. "By my hand," he shouted up to the wooden face, "I will make you talk! What you have seen, you will say!" With the harsh spirit of determination, Odin set to work devising runes that would endow splintered lips with the power of speech and enable the wooden figure to denounce the thief.

When Frigg heard of Odin's plan to impart speech to the statue, she collapsed to the floor, trembling with fear. Her trusted attendant, Fulla, found the goddess quivering in a corner, a dark shawl covering her head. Frigg wept bitterly on Fulla's shoulder as she poured out her story. Between sobs, she implored the handmaiden to use her abundant wiles and invent some means of protecting her from the Alfodur's wrath.

Fulla knelt beside her distraught mistress. She lightly stroked Frigg's hair until her sobbing subsided. "Always I am ready to stand beside you as a trusted confidant. Credit my words. Have faith in my discretion and confidence in my actions. I have a plan to shield you from Odin's anger."

Fulla swept from the hall, leaving Frigg to her thoughts of dread. She returned that evening in the company of a hideous dwarf. With a formal bow Fulla stepped aside and presented the pale, twisted creature to the distraught wife of Odin. "This is Nûr, a dwarf of Motsognir's Clan. He has given a solemn promise to prevent the statue from speaking if only you will smile graciously upon him."

Frigg wrinkled her nose at the dwarf's corpse-like appearance but being in no position to bargain—for already an ominous croaking could be heard issuing from the statue—she readily granted Nûr's request. As Frigg's smile shown down, the dwarf grinned widely, exposing an uncomfortably wide gate of snaggled teeth. His paleness held for a moment then gave way as his features lit with a warm healthy glow.

With a skip in his step, he hastened off to the gate. On reaching the statue, Nûr used his skills to cause a deep sleep to fall over the guards Odin had posted about the effigy. While they lay unconscious, he wrenched the figure from its moorings. With his bare hands, he tore its wooden body to pieces, strewing the fragments in all directions to ensure it would never betray Frigg's theft, despite Odin's efforts to bestow the power of speech.

When Sol drove her wain once more into the sky, Odin, encouraged by the responses he had elicited the day before, returned to the gate, eager to continue. But when he found his guards in charmed sleep and the statue scattered in pieces across the ground, a wave of flame coursed up his neck to blossom bright red on his cheeks.

His voice rolled like thunder across Asgard. "One of my own thwarts my efforts! Never did I expect to receive such dishonor from my own clan! If in my own land my likeness can be dashed to the ground, how can I command respect anywhere? If my visage is treated with disdain, how can I show it with honor?"

Sparks flashed in his eyes as he pounded his fists on his thighs. "If none can bear my likeness in wood, then they need not suffer my face in flesh. I leave, unwelcome in my own home." He glared blackly at his surroundings, grinding his teeth at the pain that gripped his heart.

"Too, I take with me all my gifts of protection and wisdom! Let them enjoy their world without my presence!" Odin stomped off through Valgrind. A cold breeze swept across Asgard as he disappeared into the mists.

Odin found refuge far to the north in the home of Skadi as an honored guest in the great hall she inherited from her father. Skadi kept her own counsel. The cunning daughter of Thjasse did not divulge Odin's whereabouts to anyone but enjoyed the blessings of good fortune the Alfodur's presence bestowed on her home.

In Thrymheim, Odin reflected on his anger, residing there in comfortable solitude until time softened his rage and he began to miss that which he had once loved. With a sharp eye, he tracked the goings on in Asgard, maintained his vigil over the lands of men, while keenly watching the Yurkul—the valley-bound sons of frost— for signs they were extending their icy embrace.

While brooding in self-imposed exile, Odin widely traveled the world of men, continuing to help those he favored. Some he carried to safety on his steed Sleipnir, bundled up in heavy robes as they sped across rough seas or charged over the high peaks of mountain ranges. He interceded on the behalf of others, offering shrewd counsel, planning battle tactics to win the day, in all ways bestowing success on their endeavors. But no matter how far he traveled or how great the longing that ached in his breast, Odin always returned to the solitude of Thjasse's snowcapped retreat.

———

Seven months passed while Odin wandered the earth. He was absent for so long that many in Asgard believed his anger would never abate and he would never return with the blessings of his guidance. Hands were wrung, there were many shouts, many curses, and each day anxious eyes scanned the horizon.

Ever keen is fire to consume, so, too, was Lodur for power. Encouraged by his brother's absence and eager to gather authority into his own hands, he took advantage of the unrest. Letting just enough anxiety creep into his voice to catch hold of the fear in others, he loudly called for a Husthing in Asgard to decide who should take leadership of the clan.

Distraught at Odin's long absence, the Æsir rushed to Gladsheim, impatient to discuss their future. The crowd jostled among the benches, their voices rising until everyone seemed to be talking at once. Lodur slammed his hands on the table, making the nearest jump while shocking silence across the gathering. "We have no head and without a head the body dies. When the body dies, disorder ensues. This I will not tolerate. There will be order. I demand you appoint me as head of the clan. By the strength of my hand I will enforce accord. I will ensure continuation of the peace and prosperity to which we are all accustomed."

He glared about the room, intimidating eyes that turned away at his bold stare. "Who will deny me? You, Heimdall, with your sour look? Thor? You frown as I call your name. Will you deny my right?"

He strode across the floor, haughty, proud. "Frigg turns her face aside. She knows the greatness that shines before her. There is none of you equal to me. None of you." Defiantly, he thumped his chest. "Only I am the equal of Odin. Son to the same father, it is by this right I claim leadership of the clan."

A soft cough sounded from the back of the room as Bragi raised his hand for attention. "You speak of greatness, of being equal to Odin by birth. You say there is none other who can make such a claim. I stand before this gathering and declare you are wrong. Hoenir is your equal. His claim is as valid as your own."

Many heads nodded in agreement at the statement and appreciative murmurs rounded the room. Lodur snorted. "My brother is too appeasing of the concerns of others." He turned his face away from the speaker to scowl at the wall beside his seat. "His is not the mind to rule."

The skald took a deep drink from his cup. "Still, he is even-handed in his dealings. There are many who trust his judgment. When fire consumes, it destroys and leaves only ash. His is the nature of growth."

With a roar Lodur stormed down the table until he reached the bench were Bragi sat. He leaned across the board and spit into the skald's face. "You are an outsider with no right to speak! You are tolerated here, no more. Leash your wagging tongue or I will have it ripped out."

Heimdall jumped to his feet, shaking his fist at Lodur. "Bragi is an adopted member of our clan." The gold of Heimdall's teeth flashed with his fury. "As such, he has the same right to speak as all gathered here do. What he dared to say is that which all feel."

The soft menacing tones of Freyja carried on the thought. "You fling sharp words about the hall, intimidating words meant to coerce others into supporting your claim. Few here appreciate such an appeal."

Hoenir turned to face Lodur from across the room, but when he spoke his words were for everyone. "My brother is impatient. He seeks to grasp with his fist the reins of power excluding all thoughts of anyone or anything else. A leader must be willing to consider the views of others, not run roughshod over their concerns."

Harsh glares focused on the fiery son of Bor as low grumbles of agreement rounded the room. A grin forced itself across Lodur's face. "I meant no harm or disrespect to the storyteller of our clan." He turned slowly about to take in the gathering. "I am concerned for the well-being of all. If my words seemed harsh, it is only the worry shining though. We have no idea when or if Odin will return. For all our sakes, we must have a new leader."

Thor stood, his hand raised for attention. Everyone fell silent as the rafters rang with the low growl of his voice. "My uncle is right; his concerns are valid. We need a leader to ensure the blessings of our life." His brow sank into a brooding shelf as he thumped back into his seat. Taking up his cup, he leaned forward on the bench. "But I say it should not be him."

Lodur sputtered, facing a wall of backs as new voices sought another from their ranks to fill the position Odin had vacated. By popular call, Hoenir was raised up as Odin's successor, for his views were most like those of his brother.

Lodur seethed in silence, teeth gritted in anger, as his brother mounted the throne.

Hoenir adopted the name of Odin. With the power of position, he inherited the trappings of rank. Frigg, too, he took as his consort. Always he sought a moderate road, one not to offend anyone in any way. He tried hard to hold all to task, to uphold every oath. But given his gentle, conciliatory nature, he failed to restore the blessings lost when Odin stormed from the hall.

With the skill of Loki, Lodur schemed for position by sowing seeds of dissent among the clan. The gods became dissatisfied with Hoenir's leadership, words were whispered behind the cover of drawn cloaks, then spoken boldly in open hall. "He is weak and given to appeasement in all matters. How can he lead when he never stands his ground? If he cannot hold the line with family and friends, how will he stand against our enemies?"

Lodur smiled inside his cheeks when he heard his words uttered freely from the lips of others. He moved quickly, eager to exploit the growing dissatisfaction with his brother. The controlling fire called for an assembly to address the mounting discord. Raising a hand for attention, Lodur sang out to all the Æsir. "We are eager for a strong leader, one who knows the meaning of discipline, one who can ensure our clan's survival through this difficult period. As I foretold, my brother bears none of these qualities and so his leadership fails. We need another."

Striking a proud stance, he gazed across the gathering, a look of serene confidence on his face. "Born of the original father, raised up in the primal dawn with the skills of Bur, I am that leader. I stand before you again ready to assume the mantle."

Hoenir snorted at the words of his brother. Those nearest the chosen Odin grew quiet as he emptied his cup. "I see your moves clearly through the eyes of time, though others may think you concerned only with their well-being today." He snapped his fingers at a servant girl to refill his drink. The maiden topped his cup from an ale pitcher then quickly scooted away. "You have always held an exalted view of your own worth and nurtured a need for strict control. The pursuit of power has always been your drive."

Lodur glared at his brother, twitched his lips then turned, waving his arm in a wide arc to encompass the gathering. "My brother tosses barbs to stir uncertainty in your hearts. Are these the words of a leader, confident in his decisions, certain of his direction, or are they the actions of a desperate oarsman clinging in fear to his foundering ship? I say he is unfit to rule. He should be deposed of his dignity as head of our clan!"

The hall erupted with a roar of voices, each demanding to be heard, each declaring their decision for the clan's future. Sharp discourse flowed among them as differing factions sought to shout each other down: harsh words, calm words, words of wisdom, and words of panic. After many days of constant bickering they grudgingly reached an agreement.

Lodur, eager for rule, adopted the name of Odin, inherited the power of position, acquired the trappings of rank. Frigg, too, he took as his consort. Lodur spoke sharply over his shoulder as Hoenir reluctantly stepped aside to let his brother ascend the throne. "I am honor-bound not to be the death of kin, so you retain your life." The new Odin flicked his fingers in dismissal. "I give you leave to resume your duties at the foot of the great tree, mucking about in the mud of the Saga pond and delivering gifts of ódr to the homes of men."

Strict of nature, Lodur grasped the reins of power with both hands. His edicts were ruthless, as with an iron fist he sought to dominate the lives of his subjects. Even with the strength of his arm, the severity of his mind, and the fear he inspired, Lodur failed to restore the blessings lost when Odin stormed from the hall.

The gods became angry at the increasing harshness of his rule. Many were the grumblings muttered behind the folds of a robe. Lodur sought to quell the discord by tightening his grip. But as water clutched with a fist, control ran through his fingers until the walls of Asgard rang with open hostility.

When the ice-giants heard of the upheaval in Asgard, the instability of its seat of power, they took advantage of the discord. With a steady march the sons of frost invaded the earth, binding land after land in fetters of icy cold. Merrily, they nipped the buds of new-grown plants, shriveling them up until they fell, unopened, to the ground. Trees were stripped bare of leaves. They shook a great white coverlet over the fields, crusting, freezing, digging their fingers of frost deep into the earth. Icy winds carried their laughter as they veiled the sky with heavy mists that dimmed the sun.

The Yurkul eagerly slipped down from their mountain valleys. The giant sons of winter spread their arms wide about the mountains and ground hills beneath their tread as they embraced the lands. With bright, icy winds, the sons of frost made their march on Asgard, seeking to douse the fires of Bifrost and scale their way to the Æsir courts.

When Odin saw that all he had worked to preserve—his home, his family, the lands of men—threatened with destruction, he set aside his anger and rushed back to Asgard. The Æsir were astonished at his return. Some stood slack jawed, unable to speak, while others filled the air with joyous cries of welcome. Lodur frowned when Odin strode into the great hall. He had little choice but to step down as all his supporters deserted his side to stand firmly behind the Alfodur.

Hoenir took up his stance beside Odin, a smug smile twisting his lips. "It is time, brother, for you to relinquish the position for which you are ill-suited. You have no supporters here, so do not tarry or think to hold on through stubborn harshness. Step down. Let our elder brother take back his rightful place."

Odin glided forward until he stood before the high seat. "I am glad you kept my seat warm in my absence. Now that I have returned there is no need for you to continue protecting that which is rightfully mine." With much grumbling Lodur rose from his chair, letting his hand linger a moment on the seat of power, before stepping aside to let his elder brother ascend to the seat of Most High.

Everyone was silent as Odin took his place at the head of the clan. When all had bent their knee to his presence, he clapped his hands sharply for attention. "The frost giants must be forced to relax their grip on the lands and release the worlds from their icy bonds! We have no time to lose, already the etin horde advance." He pointed at different faces as he rattled off his commands. "Let all prepare for battle, let none hold back. Gather the Einherjar; we have grave need of their services. Assemble at the bridgehead of Bifrost. We march today."

At the foot of Bifrost, their defiance grew out from the mist. The Einherjar formed into a hamalt fylking, the deadly wedge-shaped battle array. Chanting the song of Odin behind their shields, they drove deep into the enemy's heart, cleaving their ranks into disorder, and scattering their drifts to the winds.

Their icy grip broken, the sons of frost retreated to their cold, northern lands where they could recover from their wounds, leaving behind the earth strewn with their dead. Floating bodies clogged rivers, forming massive bridges of ice that damned the waters. On land the white humps of their corpses lay scattered about meadows and slumped along dark forest paths, sinking slowly into the ground as day on day Sol climbed high overhead.

When the Yurkul had withdrawn to the sheltering walls of their high mountain valleys, leaving the lower lands free of their frozen grip, Odin showered his blessings upon Asgard and Midgard, cheering the worlds with the light of his smile. Satisfied that all was again in order, the Alfodur led the Æsir in a renewal of their sacred oaths, those freely given in the early days to protect all they had created.

And the world, now free of its icy cloak, sprouted lush and green from the body of Ymir.

The Wooing of Gerd

In Hlidskialf, Freyr took the seat of Odin to gaze across the nine worlds and peer into the lives of others. He laughed at the antics of men. Sweated at the sight of dwarves laboring before their fiery furnaces. Smiled with delight at the glittering plains in Niflheim. Shivered with unease at the cold, blighted landscape of Niflhel. When he gazed into Jotunheim a black hate from the past filled his breast—for memories born early are rarely forgotten or forgiven—as his mind easily recalled the rough treatment he had received at the hands of etins when in his minority.

His gaze raked across the cold lands to the well-kept gard of Gymir perched high on a hillside. There, a maiden strolled across the courtyard, sunlight glinting from the dark river of hair flowing over her shoulders, thick as a winter cape. The fine lines of her form, captured by the snug-fitting robe that clung at her neck and waist, swayed with her every step; the word "beautiful" echoed in his mind. As she unbarred the storehouse door, her sleeves slipped back to bare, brilliant white arms that lit up the day like twin beams from the sun.

The son of Njord could not look away. Smitten, he noted her every movement, the way her hair fell about her shoulders with each swaying step, the enticing flash of her ankles beneath her robe as she sauntered across the ground. As he watched, a great longing swept up from his loins to wash away the black hate that burned in his breast. He watched until she returned to her hall. It was only then, with great reluctance, that he exited the watchtower.

Each day his mind returned to the hall in Jotunheim. Each night he tossed and turned, unable to sleep for thoughts of the woman who dwelled there. When no one was looking, he stole time in Hlidskialf to catch any glimpse of the maiden. Soon his eyes, circled by dark rings, had retreated deep into his skull. He walked listlessly among the Æsir, staring vacantly at some distant vision, his heart wrapped in an aching sickness.

The assembly watched with alarm as he shambled about, no few recalling the affliction of Baldur. Few dared speak with him lest they learn some horrible truth. Those who did attempt conversation received an icy rebuff to their queries. Finally, Njord and Skadi called Skirnir aside that they might speak privately with him.

The gentle god of ships pushed words through taught lips, his voice edged with concern for his son. "Skirnir, we call on you for help. Each day my son sits alone at table. None dare interrupt his brooding; he gives an angry glare whenever approached. You are one of his oldest friends and brother through marriage, well experienced in the trials of life. If any can discover what bothers the shining one, certainly that one is you."

Skadi leaned forward letting her dark eyes bore into Skirnir until his seat became uncomfortable. He shifted his weight from one ham to the other, attempting to rub a sudden itch that threatened to send him into a frenzy of scratching. "Odin and the rest of the Æsir agree we must do everything we can to discover what pains the wise fertile one. There is a great fear his troubles are the same as those that plagued Baldur. Go to him now. Do not be daunted by his anger but persist until you discover the truth of his terrible affliction."

Gently rasping his knuckles against the stubble on his chin, Skirnir settled his gaze first on Njord then on Skadi. "It is with great reluctance that I intrude on the privacy of Freyr." He paused to tap a thumb against his lips. "I expect sharp words for meddling in his personal affairs, but his obvious pain has also troubled me. The brother of Freyja is dear to me as are few others. His esteem I hold in high regard. His well-being is my greatest concern. I will do as you ask."

The son of Njord sat at bench hunched over a cup of ale. His once-bright eyes, now lusterless, stared straight ahead at things hidden from the vision of others. Sitting down across the table, Skirnir raised his drink in greeting.

When Freyr didn't respond, he took a long swallow then set the mug down, smacking his lips. "Why such a long face?" He smiled companionably at his sullen benchmate. "Certainly no one has defeated you, the war leader of the Æsir, in battle. Not with Nagelring strapped at your waist. Come speak to me, an old and faithful friend, one who always holds your best interests at heart. Tell me why you sit bowed over your ale, alone day after day in this long hall."

Freyr lifted his cup, glaring over the rim at the one who dared impose on his solitude. After taking a long swallow, he slammed the cup back onto the table, slopping ale across his white knuckles. Paying no attention to the spillage, he leaned close, flopping his forearm in the puddle spreading across the tabletop. "Why should I speak to anyone of the ache that burns in my breast," his voice, harsh through disuse, pulsed with resentment, "least of all you who live in the happiness of a blessed union? Sol's rays brighten your world each day while leaving my longing shrouded in darkness."

Skirnir stiffened at the rebuke, a smile frozen on his face. He kept his hands in plain sight on the table, well away from the weapons at his waist. His breath grew hot and it took him several deep breaths to cool it down. "Your longing cannot be that great if you refuse to confide in me. Come, we were young together in earlier days, fought side by side as trusting warriors must. Now we are joined through marriage, brothers through kinship. We ought well to trust one another in all things."

Sharpness faded from Freyr's eyes as he returned his gaze to his cup, swirling the liquid about as he spoke. "Your words cut through my ache, dragging me back from the brink of sorrow. I have wanted to speak of this to another, but my longing was too great. Heated words were all I could muster for others, but to a true friend I can speak."

A deep sigh escaped his breast as a mist of great yearning filled his eyes. "There is a maiden in the court of Gymir, a powerful Jotun whose guard lies opposite the high peaks that run along our northern border. The beautiful creature is pleasing to me. I spied her walking as I watched from Hlidskialf. Her hair is dark as a raven's wing. Her eyes are brilliant as jewels. Her arms fill the air with their radiance; their glow sets the sea aflame. She is called Gerd and is more pleasing to me than any woman desired by any man."

He thumped a fist on the table drawing furtive glances from faces around the room that strove to appear uninterested while seeking to overhear every word. "But long ago my kin made it very clear that such a union was not desired. Since my youth, I too felt this way, for my treatment at the hands of Howler's tainted my view. I saw them as misbegotten creatures, the ill spawn of Ymir's feet. Their nature horrid as the stench that wafts from their halls, bitter and blighted as the blizzard wind. But once I beheld her, where once I saw only ugliness, I now saw beauty. Where once cold hatred filled my breast, now roars the burning flames of passion."

Nodding at these words, Skirnir spun his mug several times as he collected his thoughts. Grinning wide, he slapped his palm on the table. The sharp report caused eyes about the hall to snap away from the pair to examine the depth of their own cups. "Then we must do all within our power to win this maid as a bride for you! Lend me a sturdy mount; one capable of swiftly traveling rough mountain paths. Let me again carry the undefeatable blade strapped at your side - bane of giants and protection of the Æsir. Provide me with a selection of lofty presents, fitting tribute for an honored bride. I will carry your pledge to the maiden in Gymir's court and win her acceptance for you."

Freyr clapped a hand on Skirnir's arm. "You have lifted my heart when I thought all hopeless." A forgotten brightness glowed from his cheeks, washing away the shadowy circles under his eyes. "The items you request I freely give to carry my pledge to the beautiful maiden. I endow you with full power to negotiate on my behalf. There is nothing in my possession I will not give to win her hand."

He dragged Skirnir close, his hands shaking with the gravity of his desire. "By my command use any gift, work any design to bring about the consummation of this union. Take Hamskerper as your mount to speed you along the way. Thick-skinned and tough on the trail, he will carry you safely over the rugged terrain between our halls."

Skirnir clasped Freyr's hand tight with determination. "It is best that I leave now," he rose, pushing away from the table, "while darkness cloaks my journey. Know that I will return to your hall in the wideblue with her acceptance or Gymir will have shattered my bones and you can find my litr stumbling along the western path."

———————

Mounting Hamskerper, Skirnir settled himself comfortably in the saddle. With a light nudge of his heels, the pair charged along the dark route to Jotunheim. White drifts of snow and the black shadows of tall firs marked the way as they thundered through mountain passes. Trotting along a forest fence, they descended into a valley ablaze with autumn foliage of bright reds and flaming yellows that seemed to leap from the grasses as a fire run wild.

They made their way from hilltop to hilltop until the gard of Gymir rose up, overlooking a line of rolling hills fringed with good forage for livestock. Halting on a rise beside the gard, Skirnir spied out the high timbered walls, frowned at a pack of massive hounds tethered along the wooden stockade surrounding the elegant hall.

On a nearby hillock a lone herdsman kept watch over his herd of goats. The soft strains from a harp he plucked, drifted on the winds. Skirnir turned Hamskerper away from the gard and trotted over to greet him. The herdsman watched his approach but did not rise in welcome as the warrior drew his mount to a halt before him. "I am called Skirnir. I have come as a supplicant for the hand of Gerd." The herdsman stared at him, amusement flickering in his eyes. Skirnir waited, but there was no response, save for the goats braying at his disruption of their feeding.

"I have found that those whose livelihood is watching often know things of great value." The herdsman still said nothing, just lightly fingered his harp, waiting as the warrior gazed across the expanse of rolling hills before returning his attention to the gard. "You sit here every day tending your charges, through sun, rain, warm winds, and bitter cold, observing all the approaches to this court. I ask the advice of such a sage watcher. How may I safely enter the compound to speak with the maiden?"

"I am called Eggther, a trusted servant of Gymir," the herdsman chuckled, strumming a chord, "and know that I will play this harp at your burial. You will never hold conversation with Gymir's daughter, so jealously he guards her honor."

Eggther pointed a crusted finger at the stockade. "The high walls surrounding her are topped with fire-hardened stakes. The heavily barred gate is impossible to pass through. Should you attempt stealth when approaching the gard, the dogs will alert the great Jotun to your presence long before you can speak with the maiden." He grinned, wriggling into a more comfortable position. "If by some chance, you do manage to breach the wall, know that her father is well schooled in the art of warcraft. It is with him you will hold strong-armed converse."

Calloused fingertips plucked lightly at the harp strings, filling the air with a mournful melody. Then he placed a palm against the strings, stilling their sound. "Better you should leave this place in one piece and seek the hand of another's daughter."

Skirnir nodded, peering back at the stockade. From the hilltop vantage, he noted its height, the open courtyard within, observed the dogs tied up in front, saw how the ground leveled out before them. The saddle creaked as he turned his mount to face down the hill. "I have never avoided the difficult path but have always advanced my cause regardless the obstacles barring the way."

Eggther's lips twitched in amusement as he hugged the harp to his chest and began to play. "I have freely given my advice; the choice is yours to heed it or not. If you wish to throw your life away, I will not lift a hand to stop you."

Skirnir raised two fingers to his brow as he began his charge. "I thank you for your candor," he shouted over his shoulder, "but I find no profit fearing that which is fated!"

The thunder of Hamskerper's hooves rattled the wooden stockade and the hounds raised a howling cry as the rider charged their line. Their baying rose to a snarl as Skirnir reached the flat ground before the wall. Barely a stride's length before the hounds, he spurred his mount into a mighty leap that carried them safely over the stockade into the open courtyard beyond.

In the hall, Gerd steadied herself on her seat as she beckoned her serving maid to come quickly. "What is the cause of the commotion outside? The hounds bay as if an army approaches. Even the walls of my father's court tremble before it."

The maid darted to the door and peered out. "A rider has arrived inside the walls. He has dismounted, leaving his horse unfettered to graze in the courtyard outside the hall. By the cut of his mantle, he is a warrior; tall, with pride showing in the angle of his chin."

Gerd wrung her hands. "Only one bold and brave would dare approach unannounced." She glanced uneasily at the doorway. "Be quick. Invite him in, though I fear death may be his companion."

The maid greeted Skirnir at the hall door. Muttering words of welcome beneath her breath, she ushered him before the daughter of Gymir. Gerd nodded her head in greeting. "Be welcome." She waved a hand toward the bench before her. "Please take a seat."

Skirnir bowed lightly but refused the seat. "Then have a cup of our finest mead. You must be parched from your long journey, having traveled alone over the wild fire hills to seek out our company." She filled a mug and pushed it across the table. "Since I am not in the habit of entertaining strangers, who is it that I welcome into my home? Are you an oversized dwarf braving the light, some unknown son of the Æsir, or perhaps one of the wise Vanir who lost his way?"

Skirnir smiled, dismissing her question with a wave. "I am none of those you mention, though I have known the company of all. I am called Skirnir. I come alone to visit your hall on an errand of love."

As Gerd started to protest, the warrior lifted his chin and looked directly into her eyes. "I speak for Freyr, the most splendid and noble of beings. As war leader of the Æsir he holds a lofty position within the clan. As a child of the wise Vanir, he shares the greatness of their line." Skirnir spread wide his arms, a tender smile on his face, his mellow voice inviting. "To know him is to know the warmth of summer, the freshness of its rain, the brightness of its shining sun. He is bounty, peace, and prosperity. All of this he asks to share with you in his great hall Upsala for as long as your lives last. Know that I do not spout empty promises. I have brought gifts to fit an honored maid; gifts gladly given by the Æsir to show his offer is serious."

Reaching inside his armored vest, Skirnir drew out a handful of golden orbs. "Nine apples from the trees of Idun, prepared by the very goddess herself; a promise of youth that you may see Freyr in a kindly light."

Gerd tossed her head, flipping her hair over her shoulder. "Fruit of any kind is a paltry gift and a poor mark of true love's desire. I will never settle down with one of such a cheap nature."

Reaching inside his armored vest, Skirnir withdrew a golden arm ring, holding it out before him so its polished edge caught the firelight that flickered from the hearth. "I hold before you the ring Draupnir, burnt with Odin's innocent son and retrieved at great risk from his shade in Eljudnir - Hel's dark hall. When suspended, every ninth night eight equally heavy rings drop from it."

Gerd wrinkled her nose. "I will not accept a gold ring," she sniffed, holding up her hand palm out, "though it holds a lofty pedigree. We do not lack for silver or gold in my father's court; all here share its bounty."

Skirnir tucked the ring back into his vest, grimacing at the stubborn maiden. "Because you deny all my gifts," he drew the sword buckled at his waist, "see this sword, the fire-forged waves of its edge, how it catches the light of the sun and brings its brilliance to earth. Do you recognize the bane of you kin in this slender inlaid blade?" He whipped the sword tip upward, pointed it menacingly at Gerd's face, then slapped the flat of the blade against his chest. "Know that with it, I will have your head from your shoulders if you continue to refuse my offer."

Gerd spat on the floor beside Skirnir's feet. "I do not fear the threats of a braggart," she sneered at her guest, "nor a bully!" The words hissed through her teeth as she stood rigid, fists clenched at her side, barely able to restrain her rage. "I will not be coerced into accepting any man's desires. Know, too, that my father and mother have no love for the Æsir or the Vanir. When you meet my sire—for Gymir is surely on his way—you will have a hard fight to get clear of this hall."

Fighting back a smile of admiration for the maiden, Skirnir instead pursed his lips and lovingly drew a fingertip along the inlaid

495

length of the shining blade. Heat pulsed from the metal as a low glow flared from its edge. "Were I to meet Gymir in battle, know that the old Jotun would fall as hay before a scythe. You would be chanting laments long into the night to mark his untimely passing." He whipped the sword about, sending a wave of heat through the air, before slipping it back into its sheath. "Since you refuse my proposal, know that it is also within my power to mete out actions much worse than death."

Reaching into his traveling cloak, he withdrew a length of wood from its folds. "I have in my hand an apple bough cut fresh this morning, so its sap still flows, a potent wand of living wood." Digging an awl from his pocket, Skirnir first etched runes into the bark, then drew the awl across his thumb. A slight sneer curled his lip as he smeared the welling blood into the marks cut on the wood. He tucked the awl back in his pocket before pointing the wood at Gerd. "With this wand, I will tame your haughtiness. On it I have carved runes to encompass the rest of your life: a deeply etched curse of wretchedness, and unbearable, unattainable desire stained red with my own blood to bind."

His voice sank to a low growl as the curse flowed over his lips, binding the maiden with its purpose. "If you continue to reject my offer, you will know the depths of endless anguish. Food will turn to ashes in your mouth, all drink bitter. Your mind will be driven mad with intolerable desire. Each long, weary day you will look out over the world hungering for the release of death."

He circled the wand in the air, capturing the maiden's attention as she followed each swinging curve of its tip. "Everyone will shun your presence. Your kin, the gods, even the sons of men will reject your company and point at you on your lonely perch, laughing in derision as they pass by."

Gerd staggered back, gripping the table edge to keep from falling. Entranced in the web he wove; her eyes followed the movement of Skirnir's lips as a trapped fly watches helplessly the spider approaching to feed. "Day after day you will weep without hope of choice, forever denied the pleasure of union, until like the dried shell of a thistle crushed at the end of harvest, you waste away, a barren, aged husk. Even death will not release you from this curse. For down below the

Na-Gates, in the frozen land where etins bury their dead, you will suffer cold emptiness and weep forever without hope of joy."

Skirnir shook the wand at the maiden, his tongue flicking raptor-quick across his lips. "This will be my curse for your rejection of Njord's bright son. But know that which I carved on this bough I can rub away if you agree to my proposal."

Passing a hand over her eyes, Gerd wiped away the perspiration that beaded her forehead, trying to quell the dread Skirnir's words and the etched wood had evoked. "Your words tear at my deepest fears, dragging them realized to the surface. Always my father has kept me isolated, scaring away any who might relieve my loneliness. It is not a life I ever desired for myself. And now your curse would make it permanent." A tear dripped down her cheek around her trembling lips. "Readily I would change this course, but it is not possible for me to marry one such as Freyr, an enemy of my kin."

A gentle smile softened Skirnir's features as he slowly lowered the apple bough. From outside a gust of wind pressed against the walls, creaking the rafters. "I have passed many years among men, even more among the Æsir. In that time, there is one thing I have learned: everything is possible over the long course of ages."

Rising to her full height, Gerd straightened her robes with light tugs along the folds. "Then I will accept your offer," she stared directly into Skirnir's eyes, "if only you will rub clean the wood."

Retrieving the awl from his vest pocket, Skirnir scraped along the length of the wood, smoothing out the etchings until no trace of cut or stain remained. His lips twitched with satisfaction as he tucked the branch and awl back into his vest. "Your acceptance fills my heart with gladness knowing the joy its news will bring."

Gerd lifted a crystal bowl brimming with mead. "Accept this drink to pledge my agreement. Though I had never thought to find love in the warm lands of Asgard, my heart leaps with joy at the prospect."

Tipping back the bowl, Skirnir took a long swallow then returned it to Gerd who emptied the last of the mead. The oath given and accepted, he rubbed his hands together, eager to conclude the bargaining. "To pledge an agreement, but not conclude its arrangement would mark me a poor emissary. Before I leave, I must know when you will meet with Freyr."

Gerd pointed out the doorway. "South of this hall lies a peaceful grove where mountain breezes whisper though a stand of pines; Barri it is called, a place of fallen needles. Nine nights from this day, when the Hastener climbs to its highest point in the sky, there I will meet Njord's bright son beneath the high-branched pines where the thwarted wind sluices like a river through the limbs and on a cushion of pine needles offer up my love."

The bellowing of an angry bull intruded on their private exchange as the hall door burst open wide. The hulking forms of Gymir and his spouse, Angrboda, stomped into the hall. "Who is the bold scoundrel that dares enter my hall uninvited?" Gymir's voice seemed to fill the space, leaving no room for anything else. "Speak quickly or know the might of my fist!"

Skirnir raised himself up before the towering etin. "I am called Skirnir," he rested a hand on the hilt of his blade, "kin by marriage to the Æsir. I've come as an emissary of Freyr, son of Njord, charged with asking for your daughter as bride. We discussed the proposition at length. She has accepted the overture and pledged her agreement with a drink. That this will happen is certain for what is agreed over a pledge cup must come true."

Gymir rounded on his daughter. "Is this true? Have you accepted union with a son of the Æsir?" He thrust his chin into her face. "And without my consent?"

"I have accepted his bridal gifts," Gerd whispered, lowering her head, "and pledged to meet the son of Njord nine nights from this day in Barri grove."

Gymir slammed a fist onto the table scattering utensils, some clattering to the floor. Gerd's handmaiden cried out as she dove to catch the crystal bowl rolling from the table top. "I do not favor this union or permit its consecration! I will never give it my blessing!"

Skirnir shouted over Gymir's rage. The etin sputtered to a stop, glaring at Freyr's emissary. "To keep peace and honor this pledge, I am authorized to offer generous gifts for your blessing of their union. Ask whatever you want. I will see it done."

Furious glances passed between Gymir and Angrboda. Their hands flexed as they grumbled to each other. Watching their anger build, Skirnir slowly drew from its scabbard the sure flickering flame at his waist. He spread wide his stance to ensure firm footing, balanced the good blade in his fist, and made ready should the etins choose to attack.

The glow of the metal drew the eyes of both etins. Gymir glanced at his wife, noted her hungry stare. He pointed at the sword. "That blade you hold, ready to strike, I recognize the markings embossed along its length, the deadly light that shines from its edge."

The Jotun's tongue flickered eagerly over his lips. He tentatively reached out a hand then drew it quickly back as Skirnir dipped the blade toward his fingers. "There is a story, much told, about our hearths of a man from the land of Midgard who once traveled the nine worlds. He retrieved a powerful blade from the hall of the Njara, where it lay in a chest sealed by nine locks. This great warrior fought many battles against warlords of men and armies of my kin. Why, he even overcame the forces of Asgard itself. With the blade in hand, he never suffered defeat. It is said the weapon was given over to the Æsir as payment for a wife. The blade was then passed to Freyr to wield as war chief of his clan."

Gymir coughed, pointed at Skirnir, then at the blade. "Are you that man? Is that the blade?"

Skirnir swept the blade aloft. Heat flashed through the hall as he let its edges catch the light and bring the brilliance of the sun to earth. "I am that man," he nodded. "This is that blade."

Gymir winked at his wife. "You ask what gift I will accept to give my blessing of this union. For that blade you hold in your hand and no other gift will I freely give my daughter to Freyr."

Skirnir slid the blade back into its sheath, quenching the flame in its house of leather. "Know that I have been instructed to bargain with any means at my disposal, to offer any gifts to achieve this union." He removed the supporting shoulder strap, then slowly unbuckled the weapon from his waist. "Were it otherwise, I would never offer up this blade into the hands of a known enemy."

He presented the sword to Gymir, who ran quivering fingers over its length, slid it partway from its sheath to bask in its brilliance. Passing the blade to Angrboda, he instructed her to place it in Eggther's safekeeping. "Give this to the sword bearer on the hill. He will know what to do with it."

Gymir turned back to face Skirnir, a deep frown on his lips, his stern eyes squinted, quenching the eagerness that had shown only moments before. "This arrangement is done. I give my blessing to this union that my daughter may honor her pledge nine nights hence."

At these words Skirnir bowed to Gerd, saluted the parents with two fingers lifted to his brow, then, spinning on his heel, briskly left the hall. With the skill of a trained horseman, he leapt onto his steed and raced back across the wildfire hills. He nudged Hamskerper to speed as they charged down the mountain paths to Upsala, Freyr's great hall raised up in the wideblue of Alfheim.

The son of Njord paced about the doorway of his hall, looking ever north to the direction of his pledge. He stopped, wringing his hands, when Skirnir crested the top of a nearby hill. As the rider clattered into the courtyard, Freyr rushed up and grabbed Hamskerper by the reins. "Before dismounting you must tell me the outcome of your journey. Did you obtain the object of my affections; the prize with which you were charged?"

Skirnir gazed down, brow deeply furrowed, from his seat atop Hamskerper. He spoke in a voice graveled from the weariness of a long ride. "I have obtained that with which I was charged. But the cost was far greater than expected." He slapped the empty space at his hip. "As you commanded I used everything I had to negotiate on your behalf. The maid agreed with some difficulty, but it was the good will of the parents that cost the most. Odin will not be pleased that Gambanteinn was the price of her family's blessing."

Freyr laughed and clapped a hand on Skirnir's thigh. "The blade of Volund was put in my charge. When I bestowed on you the duty to negotiate on my behalf, I chose to trade one object of great value for another that is of greater value to me. Let the others complain if they wish. It is of little matter to me. Now, while my heart brims with joy, tell me when the maiden will be mine."

Skirnir pointed north of the hall indicating a spot beyond the line of far-off hills. "In nine nights, you are to pledge with your bride in a peaceful grove of pine trees called Barri. It lies midway between your halls amid the wildfire hills. There, when Mani has climbed fully into the night sky and his light has chased the shadows from the land, she will grant you that which you desire."

Freyr let loose the reins allowing the rider to dismount. Legs shaking, the son of Njord staggered across the courtyard and slumped onto a bench beside the wall. He buried his faced in his hands. "This premarital wait is difficult," he groaned with a muffled voice. "One night is hard enough. How will I bear nine?"

The Bright Slayer of Beli

Freyr lounged in Upsala, his great hall in Alfheim, the land given to him as tooth gift before his majority. From outside the open doorway a messenger, clad in the mantle of a warrior, loudly announced himself. "I am an Einherjar of Odin's troop, ordered to work closely with the white god who keeps watch from the Rainbow Bridge. Each day I assist him with his duties. I am sent today with a message important to the war leader of the Æsir."

Freyr emerged from the darkness, tall, fair-haired, gleaming in the sunlight. He leaned against the doorpost, sipping from a mug of ale as he examined the messenger. Hard blue eyes peered from beneath a helmed brow. White scars hatched his cheeks and hands. His skin, weathered by years of sun and rain, shone deep brown where armor or cloth did not cover it. The front of his byrnie was laced with the scorings of sharp-edged blows, many old, some new.

"There is no need for you to deliver your message standing outside." He heartily waved the courier in. "Come rest yourself beside the fire." The messenger stomped up the walkway, following Freyr into the hall, but once inside he shook his head, refusing the proffered seat.

Freyr raised an eyebrow but said nothing. He understood the nature of such soldiers and knew the man would refuse the seat just as he knew the affront had he not offered.

The warrior slowly shifted his weight from foot to foot, the dance of a long-trained sentry, waiting until Freyr had poured himself

501

another drink, before beginning his report. "Heimdall sends notice that there is a giant prowling about the bridgehead of Bifrost, seeking some way to make entrance into Asgard. He beats his breast, claiming for his own the deeds of a great warrior, while hurling threats against all who live above." The courier let his eyes roam to the golden shield embossed with a tusked boar's head that hung over the mantle, then added, almost as an afterthought, "He calls himself Beli."

The mug stopped partway to Freyr's lips and his hand began to shake, slopping liquid over the rim. The sentry stared a moment, then turned his attention back to Freyr's eyes. All the goodwill had faded, leaving a brittle, icy glare. "Heimdall says this giant is good looking, unlike many kin of Thrudgelmer. His raven hair, plaited in the warrior locks of his clan, frame strong cheeks and a firm, hairless chin. His loud boasts and childish insults offer little danger to Asgard. The white god sends this message as a matter of course that the war leader always be apprised of any potential threat to our home."

Freyr had shown only mild interest in the actions of the boastful giant, but on hearing the name the giant declared for himself, he leapt to his feet. His eyes were black as he dashed about the hall shouting in rage. "A weapon!" His voice shook with frustration as he scrabbled about knocking aside furnishing in his desperate search. "I must have a weapon!"

In a dusty corner leaned a horn from the head of Eikthyrnir, the hart that wanders the limbs of Yggdrasil. Its lofty head had proudly borne this crown until shed in the spring rains. Thick and gnarled at the base, it twisted into a long, deadly sliver of bone. Snatching it up, Freyr hefted it for balance before tucking it into his belt.

Gerd stood beside the hearth fire wringing her hands as she watched Freyr's frantic scrambling. "What is the matter? Why do you root about for a weapon? What has aggravated you so?"

Freyr paused, his breathing rapid and heavy. He tried to speak, stopped, wiped the spittle from the corner of his mouth, then tried again. "I have the chance to repay an old debt, the redress delivered by my own hand for the honor stripped from me when I was a child." When Gerd began to ask, Freyr waved her off. "The past is done. I will not speak of it. But know that I will exact my full revenge for its course."

He stormed from the hall, shouting for the Einherjar to follow. "Take me to Heimdall!"

Driving their mounts to a lather, they raced along high arc of the Rainbow Bridge. Freyr stopped only long enough to query the white god about the location of the giant. Refusing all companions, he charged across the icy ground that spread out before the bridgehead.

The giant towered on the edge of the frost covered plain, his armored legs spread wide; a large, heavy figure thatched with thick black hair plaited in locks that dangled down his back. His broad shadow stretched across the field. Freyr charged close, stumbled his mount to a halt amid a cloud of frost, then leapt from his saddle eager to face the deadly foe.

Drawing the heavy horn from his belt, he stomped forward, shouting out his challenge. "Who is this ugly spawn of Thrudgelmer that yowls so and disturbs the peace? Speak now that I might know who I am about to kill!"

The giant reared up until his shadow cast itself across Freyr's path. He slapped a long, heavy blade defiantly against his chest. "I am one you will come to know with much regret. Beli, I am called, for the power of my voice, a Howler warrior of renown. My enemies cringe before my might. My battle cry sends cowards skittering for home. I have never lost a fight. A sterner foe you will never meet. Now tell me, if you hold the courage to answer, who is this arrogant warrior standing before me who demands my name?"

"I knew you when I was a boy," Freyr's gritted teeth filled the air with rasping, "and suffered much humiliation at your hands. I am Freyr, grown into my full power." He grinned widely at the giant. "Glad I am of this day. I have waited a long time to repay the favors you bestowed freely upon me in my youth."

Beli laughed and slapped a hand on his knee. "Is that my old mare who now confronts me? My how you have grown, large and good-looking. Rumor has it that you have become the war leader of the Æsir, a lofty position to be sure; one demanding skill with bright weapons. So why do you carry a bone in your hand? Where is the blade so many have spoken of, the one that fights of its own accord? Were you so afraid you might cut yourself with its edge that you preferred the blunt round of an antler and left the sharp metal behind?"

Freyr rapped the antler lightly against the iron rings of his byrnie. The sharp clack, clack, clack sounded across the frozen field. "I gave Gambanteinn for a bride of great worth, one who has healed the blackness in my heart and filled my empty longing with love."

The giant clucked softly. "It shows poor judgment for a war leader to willingly give away a weapon without one of equal or greater strength ready at hand." He shook his head, so his heavy braids slid about his shoulders. "And for such a miserable reason. You will find such lack of foresight a great handicap now that we have met again."

Ignoring Beli's taunts, the bright son of Njord advanced fearlessly through the frost, crunching frozen grasses beneath his feet. "It matters little if I had my sure flickering flame or were I empty-handed, bereft of all weapons. Know that I can kill you with my bare hands." His heart thundered in his ears the closer he approached the rock-boned thurs. "Your bold talk hides a coward while your good looks conceal a horrible, morally corrupt monster. I have much to pay you back for the blot of rubore you placed on my character."

Beli spat on the ground. "You talk of stain," his grin lit up the field, "but I recall pleasure. Your stepfather delivered to me a wonderful bride, marriage fodder to do with as I pleased. If you fall to me, dead or alive, know that I will have you again."

Sweeping his blade in a bright arc, Beli charged, his lips spread wide in a chilling howl. Freyr easily parried the wide swing as he slipped aside to avoid the attack. "Your yowl is a hollow mockery of earlier days when as a youth I cringed in fear before the animal noises barked by you and your kin."

Beli spun about, his blade held ready. "You were such a handsome lad when I made you drink my seed." He smacked his lips while the tip of his sword danced overhead. "And when I had you as Grani has a mare, often your howls were louder than mine."

Freyr frowned, rapping the horn lightly against his leg. "I well recall the liberties you took." He gripped the horn tighter as memories flashed through his mind, times of blind pain and humiliation. "It is for the indignities I suffered at your hands that I will spit you as a pig for roasting and let ravens feast on your corpse."

Beli stepped forward, feinted an attack, then skipped back out of Freyr's reach. "You talk like one unsure of himself, bandying useless words to build your courage. Do you want to keep talking or show you have the temperament for battle?"

"Come ahead." Freyr raised the horn, its tip pointed at Beli's breast. "Since my youth, I've been an enemy to your kin. My heart softened when I took an etin as wife, but to you my heart has ever remained full of malice." He canted his weapon ready to parry. "Though I've only this horn to wield against your needle of metal, know that my weapon will certainly find its way to your bitter acorn of a heart."

Raising his blade overhead, Beli attacked, eager to deliver a killing blow. A piercing howl issued from his lips to freeze the blood and turn guts to water. Freyr stood his ground, the black hate burning in his breast turned his eyes into a sure, flickering flame. He hefted his horn ready to parry, set his feet ready to dodge. He leapt aside as Beli's blade crashed into the ground, spraying frozen dirt into the air. Bringing his horn to bear, Freyr thrust it into the etin's side, feeling the satisfying quiver as it dug deep into the flesh. Beli cried out as blood gushed from the wound to drench the ground. He collapsed, rolling onto his back, moaning, and clutching at his side.

Freyr danced about the wounded giant, scuffing clumps of frozen dirt on his foe. "You boast of your prowess in battle," he laughed, "you even threaten to return me to a humble plaything. That will never happen." He swung the horn high over his head, its tip pointed at the giant's breast. "I end this now!"

Hunching his shoulders, he brought the hart's protection down with full force, driving through the etin's weak attempt to parry. Grinning savagely, Freyr twisted the horn deep into Beli's breast. "Feel the strength that is mine which you once thought to humble. Feel it sear, red hot, through your icy heart and know that it is my turn for pleasure!"

Quarrel of the Gods

From across the nine worlds the Æsir, Asynjor, and guests from among the dwarves gathered at Ægir's great hall to feast. Shining gold was raised in the fire's light, its brilliance dispelling the gloom that soured Ægir's normally placid features. Ale made the rounds, served by Ægir's capable servants, Fimafeng and Eldir, who slipped smoothly among the guests. Good-natured laughter reigned amid the gathering.

A loud knock reverberated through the rafters; thrice it sounded, then the hall doors swung open as a trembling Eldir announced a late arrival. The son of Laufey strode past a befuddled Syn. Head held high, he crunched across the rushes, a broad smile spreading his lips. As one, the gods fell silent about the tables when they saw who had entered the hall.

The dark son gazed about the gathering, his eyes lively as sparks leaping from a fire. "Far away, in the depths of the Ironwood, I spied a flock of ravens heading west. They were flying so low I could hear the rush of their wings," he opened his eyes wide in mock astonishment, spread his arms beneath his cloak and gently flapped them, "and every word that passed among them."

'Hurry,' they exclaimed, driving each other to greater speed. 'Hurry or we will miss it!'

"When I asked after their urgency they replied, shouting over each other, so it was difficult to understand at first. But when I did..." Loki rubbed his hands together.

'Hunger drives us onward. We cannot stop our flight to talk lest we be late for the great feast.'

"Now, I had not eaten for some time, so of course I was very interested," he glanced around patting his stomach. 'I am hungry as well,' I shouted to the flock winging high above. 'Tell me of this great feast!'"

Cupping a hand to his ear, Loki canted it toward the roof as if straining to hear some far-off voice. "The last of the flock shouted back, a youngster, frantically beating his wings to keep pace. 'It is held at Ægir's high mountain hall. All the Æsir gather to celebrate. There will be leavings in plenty to satisfy our flock.'

Head bobbing, he sauntered slowly across the rushes, thoughtfully stroking his chin. He stopped, chuckled lightly, then tapped a finger against his lips. "I was surprised at the news. Naturally, I assumed your invitation had not reached me in the Ironwood, for surely a call was sent to all Æsir kin. I immediately set out across the etin's home, forded rivers, navigated valley floors, and climbed the steep slope to this mountain retreat that I might celebrate with my adopted family. Now, thirsty from such a long journey, I have arrived for a drink of Ægir's famous mead."

The gods remained quiet, only the rhythmic tap... tap... tap of Odin's cup on the arm of his seat sounded in the hall. Loki turned in a circle looking each angry face in the eye. "Why so silent? Is it your delight in seeing me or has arrogance stilled your voices? Must I carve runes to loosen your lifeless tongues? Assign me a seat or turn me away!"

Bragi coughed into his mug, sending a spray of ale across the board. "Your presence is loathsome to us. You have caused much mischief, leaving behind a wake of damage. Many are the wounds that still weep from your actions. Cry as you might, we will never assign you a seat at this feast or any gathering where we have say. We have learned, much to our pain, the price of bestowing kinship too freely. A gambansumbl is all you deserve!"

Loki pressed a hand to his breast. "I entered to the sounds of laughter," he turned a hurt look upon the gathering, "but received no friendly word in greeting. And when I ask for a seat among my supposed kin this eloquent voice denies me a place."

Wiping a dry tear from his eye, he turned to the high bench at the far end of the board. "Must I remind Odin," his voice took on a sharp edge, "of his oath given freely in bygone days? When we mixed our blood in kinship rite, you promised never to drink ale unless it were served to both of us."

The Alfodur glared down from his seat. Hugin and Munin danced uneasily on his shoulders. "These days I drink only wine, but I know my oaths—all those given freely and those extracted by coercion." He snapped his fingers. "Vidar, make room at the bench for the wolf's father, lest his tongue spit sharp words to lash us all."

With much grumbling, Vidar slid himself up the bench. Grinning, Loki wedged himself in the empty space as his benchmates slid away to give him more room. Loki wriggled his elbows for comfort while one of Ægir's servants poured him a cup of ale. Hefting the cup, he glanced about the room. "I see many familiar faces; nearly all, in fact. But there is one I do not see. Where hails the mighty son of Odin, he whose furrowed brows bring thunder? Of all the great ale drinkers, I was certain he would be here."

Odin set his cup aside then wiped a hand across his lips. "Thor travels far eastern paths." His voice thundered over the crowd, silencing those nearest his seat. "A message was sent. He has yet to arrive."

"It is a pity." The dark curls shook sadly from side to side. "I should wish he were here. Of all in the great Æsir clan, it is the words of Hlodyn's celebrated son I know I can trust."

Winking at his benchmate, Loki lifted his cup in toast to the gathered clan. "Hail to the Æsir and all invited guests. Hail to the hall of Ægir. Let us have more of this delightful drink." A pleased murmur traveled round the table at his words.

As Ægir's servants made the rounds, filling each cup, bringing more food, praise was heaped upon their excellent service. Beaming at the compliments, the servants strutted about as they continued to serve refreshments.

Such overweening praise of another burned the ears of Farbauti's son. When Fimafeng bent to fill his cup, Loki slipped a knife from his belt. With a quick upward thrust, he buried the blade's length in the softness beneath the jaw, just behind the retainer's chin. As Fimafeng toppled backwards the hall erupted with fury at Loki's action. The rattle of fists knocking against shaken shields accompanied the deafening roar of curses coloring the air.

Loki quaffed deeply his drink then slammed the cup onto the board. "You glorious gods shower me with a torrent of wounding words for an action taken against a mere servant and dare hold yourselves superior!" The howling increased as more than one voice shouted disdain for his heritage.

Jerking the knife from Fimafeng's throat, Loki wiped it clean on the servant's blouse then snapped it back into its sheath. "As I did for this head swollen with praise now returned to its normal girth, I will do for you by throwing your failings into relief." The sneer of his lip reached around his head. "I'll bring you all down to proper size."

Bragi stretched out an arm to encompass the gathering. "We gather to celebrate the continued fortune of our clan. Now you have arrived bent on disrupting our peace. If..." Bragi swallowed to clear a suddenly dry throat. "If you do not exasperate those assembled here, I will give you this gold ring from my arm and," he patted his side, "the bright blade at my waist."

Loki rocked Bragi back in his seat by spitting on the floor. An expectant silence filled the room as the gathering waited, horrified and eager, for the sharp reply they knew must come. "I speak as my spirit urges, not as ordered, especially by one who wields a sharp tongue rather than a strong arm. I am not surprised your blade is clean and arm rings few. A valiant warrior has arm rings in plenty—ready to bestow on others—while his blade is constantly being sharpened from use." He took another swallow of ale then squinted at Bragi. "Now your blade is always sharp as its edge rarely encounters more than hot air. Of all those gathered in this hall you are the most comfortable holding down the rear in a fight."

Eyes bulging, Bragi sputtered, then shouted to the gathering. "I offer my best and receive insult! Were we outside, the two of us, you would feel the strength of my arm! For your lies, I'd spit your head on my blade!"

Loki waved him away. "Such strong words," he laughed, "from a bench ornament. They are no more a threat than the wood pressed against your ass. Before the challenge of a brave man you would don the bench as a helmet."

The skald surged to his feet, eyes clouded with drink. Benchmates scrambled to get out of the way as he fumbled with the long blade strapped at his waist, but gentle words stopped his arm as a firm hand guided him back to his seat.

Idun leaned close. "Bragi," she whispered softly to her husband, "you are a guest in a friend's home. For the sake of kinship, I ask you not to argue with Loki. Nothing good can come from harsh words spoken at table."

Loki shouted from his seat at the bench. "Idun, we are indebted to you. You have done us all a great service by silencing the bore."

Idun rounded on the son of Laufey, hissing words through clenched teeth. "I did not do it for you! I quieted Bragi to keep the peace in our family. I won't have you two fighting!"

Loki took another swallow from his cup, leaned forward, elbows on the table, chin cradled in his hands. "It is the sign of a faithful spouse to save her husband's honor. Though I find it difficult to speak your name and faithful in the same breath without laughing. For of all women, you are the easiest with men."

Idun pressed a hand to her breast, her face flushing at Loki's shaming words. "You utter harsh words for no other reason than to cause humiliation."

Loki leered across the table at Idun. "Willing you were—a nut split wide—when I carried you from Thjasse's stronghold. You embraced me then with arms washed bright." He slipped a hand under his vest to lightly massage his right side. "Nearly cracked my ribs too, with your knees."

"You dare!" Idun snatched a mug from the table. She cocked her arm, making ready to hurl it into Loki's face, but the gentle touch of Bragi's hand on her arm interrupted her throw.

"Why fight over drunken banter," Gefjon called out from her seat to the quarrelling pair. "Such words ought to be forgotten among kin. We should respect each other equally."

"Gefjon," Loki spun about in his seat, fixing her with his sharp gaze, "you interrupt with trite advice. So, I will mention how for a spit of land you laid your thigh over Gylfi, your heart seduced by the promise of real estate."

Gefjon's lips twisted into a thin, blade-sharp smile as her neighbors looked away at the walls, at the table top, into their cups, anywhere but at the sudden fury boiling behind her eyes.

Odin thumped the table with his fist. The gathering hushed at his words. "Loki, you are a fool to antagonize Gefjon!" His voice rolled as thunder across an empty sky. "Her knowledge of fate rivals my own," his eyes squinted, taking on a shrewd look. "She knows how to use that knowledge as well as I."

Loki raised his mug in mock salute to the highest seat in the hall. "The Alfodur offers up his wisdom to the masses that truth should remain unspoken, and only banal lies be shared among friends.

This guidance coming from one whom often gives victory to the fainthearted and defeat to the honorable. Tell me, would the brave have been so brave in battle had this truth been known to them beforehand?"

Odin leaned forward in his seat, thrusting out his chin. "You dare speak of truth, then let's state loudly, before all, that you mated with a stallion." His dagger-sharp words brought a gasp from the crowd. The sudden inrush of air momentarily flickered the hearth fire. "This corrupt union bore the colt which I ride. There could be no greater sign of depravity than this."

Loki's eyes shined bright at the Alfodur's words. "And when you practiced seid to the torment of Rind," he grinned, leaning eagerly forward, "just so you could have your way with the maid, that action I hold to be the sign of depravity."

Scowling, Odin sank back into his seat and snatched up his goblet of wine. "Spite like venom drips from your lips." The low grumble of his frustration echoed from the cup as he took a deep drink. "Lies trip one over another from your tongue, so eager are they to spill forth. You are a worker of terrible things. Of all those living, you are the vilest. A worker of great evil."

Loki burst out laughing. "You would assign me the reputation you have won for yourself in the halls of the etins?" Hands pressed to his breast, he rocked back in his seat. "I say it is only fitting that you call me the worst, since you have often declared me your equal."

Clapping her hands together in exasperation, Frigg shouted out from her seat beside Odin. "Enough of this! Whatever you two did in times past is fodder for gossips. Ancient matters should remain in the past. It is not only poor manners, but also a sign of poor breeding to mention such things before others."

Loki slapped his hand on the table. His benchmates jumped and scooted away. "Grand words from a grand lady who prefers to conceal her own past. When Odin stormed off in petulant anger at the defacing of a wooden statue, you wrapped his brothers up tight with your legs about their waists; all to keep your position within the clan."

Raising a hand to cover her eyes, Frigg replied coldly to the son of Farbauti. "Were my son Baldur among us, you would be wagging a bloody tongue for your daring insolence."

Leaning forward in his seat, Loki gazed levelly at the mother of lost innocence. All inched closer to hear what he would say. "Just for you, shall I recount more of my wickedness? Whispered tales of terrible deeds to titillate and delight?" A cruel grin quirked his lips. "Know that Hodd was an ignorant tool wielded by my hand," he tapped a finger against his chest. "It was through my craft you will never again see Baldur in the halls of Asgard."

Frigg's gaze turned black and fire burned up her neck to flower bright red on her cheeks. Freyja rose quickly to interrupt the outburst building in the wife of Odin. "Loki! It is sheer folly to anger Frigg by parading your terrible deeds before this gathering of kin. If you keep on with this malicious prattle, she will ensure you a bitter reckoning."

Loki's twinkling eyes focused dagger-sharp. "I have heard this counsel before," he jabbed a finger at the sister of Freyr, "to conceal truth behind platitudes. You think mine are the only deeds that should remain unspoken among kin. Know there is shame enough for all to go around." A leer spreading across his lips sent a quiver of nausea racing through Freyja's stomach. "You have always been free with sex, willing to give or barter as you please. The necklace that now hangs about Frigg's neck, that which once gaily adorned your chest, you purchased with four nights of moaning and groaning beneath four different dwarves."

Glaring down the stares directed at her, Freyja snatched up her drink then sat back sharply into her seat. "You reek of contempt, jealous that others revere me while seeing you for the vicious little creature that you are. Go ahead," she sneered over the rim of her cup. "Keep bragging about your wicked deeds. You will soon find yourself howling in pain."

Njord coughed for attention from his place near the head of the table, a wet phlegmy rattle as he cleared his throat. "It is of trivial for a woman to have lovers besides her husband or a husband besides his wife. The nature of pleasure is that it is found nearly everywhere." He raised a finger as his sweeping gaze stopped on Loki. "But I find it outrageous that a male god has born children. Such aberrance is detestable."

Loki turned his black stare on the god of waves, looking him over until the elder began to shift uneasily in his seat. "Now the old man of the sea speaks out in defense of his daughter, offering up homilies on correct conduct. Please spare us the lessons in morality. We all know the flexibility of the Vanir in choosing their bed partners. Why, you had no qualms welcoming your sisters into bed."

Njord turned his head away from the speaker. "My choice of bed partners is no concern of yours." He lifted his nose into the air. "What is of importance to everyone is my having fathered a son whom no one hates, and a courageous daughter of unsurpassed beauty."

Loki plucked a piece of straw from his vest, examined it for a moment before flicking it out across the table. "Oh, come on now. Tone down that famous arrogance. Show some humility. It was your sisters who birthed your children. With such close ties, I'm surprised they are not drooling idiots."

Loki's laughter filled the air as Njord sputtered, hands waving in front of his face, unable to reply.

Rising from his seat, Tyr drew the gathering's attention from Njord by lifting a goblet to Freyr. "Freyr is the boldest of our warriors. That is why he was appointed our war leader. No woman weeps from his actions. Captives he quickly frees from their bonds. His heart holds honor dear."

Loki choked on his drink, sputtering a moment before getting his tongue under control. When he finally spoke, it was a voice edged with venom. "You dare speak of honor? One need only glance at the stump where once your right hand used to be, to know how closely you hold honor. My son took it off at the wrist when he should have taken the entire arm for the treachery all of you showed him." He glared into his cup then slowly lifted his gaze to stare directly into Tyr's eyes. The god of war did not blink, but steadily returned the stare. "I can little help him now, bound on Lyngvi. But I have gotten some little recompense for his treatment. Know your seed is stale and withered; it is from my loins your son has sprung."

Tyr's face twisted with rage. He reached for the blade at his waist when Freyr shouted from across the room, his voice raw with barely checked anger. "You will find yourself bound like your son unless you silence that craven tongue!"

Shifting in his seat, Loki turned his attention to Freyr. The room hushed as he cast his words into the sudden silence. "So, chides the

Summer's son now given to bold threats in his newfound manhood. One would have thought the Howlers taught you humility in your youth. Certainly, you've not grown prudent in your actions. For the daughter of Gymir you gave away the mighty weapon that once hung at your side." He grabbed at his crotch, laughter spilling from his lips. "When the final battle comes, how will you fight without the guidance of the sure flickering flame? Will you draw your hair girt sword from your breeches, shake it about flaccid in the enemy's face, and hope your foes cringe before it?"

A voice piped up from beside Freyr's elbow, its words directed to Freyr, but spoken loud enough that all might hear. "If I had your bold lineage, I'd take that loudmouth out back, break every bone in his wicked body, and grind him to limb grist to feed the crows."

"Who said that?" Loki stood up, cupped a hand to his ear and mock searched the gathering for the speaker. "Were those words from the imp perched by Freyr's seat?"

The dwarf climbed up on the bench beside Freyr, stretched himself to his full height until his head and waist cleared the tabletop. "I am called Byggvir, known among the gods for my speed. It is my honor to have been invited to drink among the kinsmen of Odin."

Loki wagged a chiding finger at the dwarf then settled back onto the bench. "Ah! You are the one always gibbering before the grindstone of the World Mill. You claim great efforts at the mill, but despite all this diligent hard work you never share your meal equally among the hungry."

Byggvir's face turned crimson as he flapped his arms in impotent rage. Loki laughed while several snorts—quickly hushed—sounded from around the room.

"As for speed, know you are slack of foot compared to Hugi, the swiftest runner in Jotunheim. Even the great Thor can attest to this." Loki placed his hands palm down on either side of his cup. "And as for your bold threat to lame my every limb," he leaned forward, "here I sit unafraid of your menace. For whenever bold warriors go into battle, you can be found quivering beneath the straw, fearful of being made to fight."

Heimdall joined in from his seat beside Vidar, his gold teeth flashing as he rounded on Loki. "Too much drink has loosened your tongue, Loptr. Why don't you stop speaking? With silence, you may yet keep some self-respect."

Twisting round on the bench, Loki leaned far back in his seat to get a clear view of the white god. "You speak rightly Heimdall. Each should have a measure of self-respect, though you must chafe at your own words. Brave and bold you came to join the Æsir there in the early days of the worlds. For the worth with which you were perceived you were assigned a position of sentry whose duty often finds him in the mud, endlessly pacing cold pickets, while others languish in warm, brightly lit halls."

A sharp wind blew from across the table as Skadi called out from beside Njord. "Go ahead, keep on with your gay speech. You will see what it gets you, bound down on a bed of sharp rocks screaming your heart out."

Loki lightly tapped a finger against his chest. "Well and good," he grinned. "But if I am to be bound on sharp rocks, know that I was foremost at the killing of Thjasse along with my kinsmen gathered here. It was my cunning that drew him from his stronghold into the vaferflames of Asgard, burnt down to where the others could spear him to death as he lay helpless on the ground."

Leaning forward in her seat, Skadi rapped the table three times, bloodying her knuckles against the wood. "If you were responsible for my father's death," her eyes glittered like slivers of ice as she spoke, "then I will always be your enemy. Should you ever fall under my power, I will delight in making your days a painful misery."

Sif slipped up beside the son of Laufey, a heavy pitcher in hand. "Be welcome among us Loki," she smiled, filling his mug to the brim with mead. "Harsh words backed by strong drink are best forgotten."

Lifting the mug, Loki drained it in a single pass while Sif continued to speak softly into his ear. "You have heaped sharp invective on the children of the Æsir for guilty actions, but of them all you must agree that I am free of blame."

Setting down his mug, Loki turned slightly to smile amiably at Sif. She smiled back, laughing a little as he smacked his lips. "I would agree," he reached out a hand to cup her chin, "if you were fierce-minded toward men other than your husband. But I know who has lain with you besides Thor." He smiled, bowed his head, and tapped his breast. Raising a hand to her eyes, Sif fled from the table followed by Loki's hearty laughter.

The hall shook with low rumblings as the sky grew dark as soot. Beyla, the wife of Byggvir, set her hands on her hips. "I think Thor has arrived." She tossed her head at Loki. "He will certainly silence your loud mouth. Especially when I tell him what you said about his wife."

Loki yelled at Beyla as Thor stepped into the hall. "Be silent Beyla! You are an intruding, gossiping bore. You belong sweating at the millstone with your simpering gnat of a husband!"

Thor stepped through the doors, bristling at Loki's harsh words. "What is going on here?" His shout shook the rafters, startling a flock of ravens from their perch on the roof. "Loki, why such cruel words among family?"

Sif slid up next to the god's strong guarder, placed a hand on his shoulder and whispered into his ear. "He has offended everyone. Poison darts flicked by his loose tongue have wounded all who dared cross words with him."

Thor's expression grew dark at the news. His teeth clenched as he hissed at Loki. "Stop this now trickster or I will rip out your tongue!"

Loki clapped a hand to his mouth, laughter escaping from between his fingers. "The son of Odin has finally arrived, but why such rage? You didn't exhibit this assurance when you crouched shivering in the thumb of Skrymir's glove. I know. I was there."

Thor reached into his vest to finger Mjollnir. "Be silent, vicious creature, or I will silence you for good with my hammer!"

Loki stood at his seat, his mug raised in salute. "Of all the Æsir, I know your words to be truth. That you speak as you feel and will strike is certain. What I said in this hall was spoken as my spirit urged. I received many threats this day, but it is only before you, the son of Hlodyn, that I take leave of this gathering."

Eldir darted out of his way as Loki slipped along the bench, avoiding Thor, whose eyes tracked his every move. He shouted over his shoulder as he pushed though the heavy doors at the end of the hall. "We are kin and so share the fate of wolves who don't know they've eaten each other up until they come to the tail."

516

The Punishment of Loki

Loki flew from the feast. He knew the Æsir would give chase, eager to repay him for insults freely delivered—for words of rancor, when true doubly sting, especially when spoken for all to hear. He did not return to the Ironwood but retreated to the top of a high mountain. On the rocky knoll, he built a sturdy hall, a great domed circle of stone with doorways open to the four directions so he could watch all approaches.

During the day, he sought to obscure his shape from the sight of Odin and his watchers. At dawn, he snuck to a deep pool beneath Franang's Falls. Changing himself into a large salmon, all day he swam the cold waters, watching the play of light that filtered down from the rippling surface, taking refuge at the bottom of the pool when he sensed movement along the shore.

At night, he reverted to form and returned to the hall. Huddling before the hearth fire, he set his crafty wiles to conceive of how the angry gods might attempt to capture him. On land, few were faster; his winged shoes allowed him to skim over land, water, and through the air with equal swiftness. He held no concern there. Provided he had a sufficient head start, he could outdistance any pursuit. But life in water was new, submerged all day long in his hiding place, his movements restricted to the river course, so it was here he turned his thoughts.

Clumsy at first, then moving with ever greater precision, his dancing fingers created that which his mind conceived. Taking a length of tough bast twine, he fashioned a net of loose interlocking squares, strong enough to hold small prey while letting water easily pass through its weave.

From high on Hlidskialf, Odin scanned the nine worlds until he spied out Loki's high mountain warren. Over several days, he observed the son of Laufey move between the falls and his hall. Once certain of the pattern of Loki's movements, he sent the Æsir out to capture the dark son.

Odin stood before his blood-eager kin, still fuming from Loki's verbal humiliation. "The son of Laufey is not to die." A cry of boiling anger erupted from the group as voice after voice demanded his death. Odin let the uproar run its course before waving it to silence. "It is true his actions have caused us much grief. But it is not our way to strike down kin, be they blood or adopted into our clan."

"You will find Loki north of here," he pointed a finger at the distant horizon, "huddled in a mountaintop refuge. My Valkyrie will guide you. After you capture him, take him to Kettle Grove. I have given my directions to Heimdall. We will take our vengeance in a way he will long feel and never forget."

The company charged from the hall muttering threats against Farbauti's son. "And hunt down his sons Nari and Narfi," Odin shouted at their backs, "that we might make use of them. You will find them roaming the Ironwood. Take care as you seek to capture them. They are as crafty as their father and share his ability to shift their shape."

Night had begun to chase her son from the sky as Loki settled down before his hearth, still warm with coals, to shake off the cold of the river waters where he had spent his day in hiding. A nearby flash caught his attention, a glint of fading sunlight reflecting off the rim of a polished shield that marked the Æsir troop silently climbing the hill a short distance away. Jumping to his feet, Loki swung about as he sought to look out all four entrances. From three directions, he spied movement. The fourth that faced the river, remained clear.

They were too close to escape by land or air; their stealth had carried them too near. He tossed the net he had been working on into the fire—the flames eagerly consuming the twine—and dashed through the doorway to the river. A light splash disturbed the surface of the water. Churning currents quickly concealed any ripples as a salmon swam furiously away from the bank into the dark pool beneath the falls.

The Æsir troop burst into Loki's retreat, rushing through three of the four doorways, eager to surprise their elusive prey. They ransacked the empty hall, overturning furnishings, tearing down tapestries, scattering bedding, but found no trace of their quarry. Heimdall peered into the smoldering hearth, pondering where Loki may have hidden himself. There nestled amid the bright coals, he noticed the gray outline of the net, now ash.

The white god beckoned his companions to his side. "A hunted man often dwells on his means of capture." He pointed into the hearth. The warriors crowded around to look over his shoulder. "See here, draped as ash in the coals, the image of a clever device that Loki created, a web of woven string for snaring prey in the water. He would not have created such were he not..." Heimdall snapped his fingers. "Downhill from this hall—the one direction we did not block—near where the river empties into the sea, a deep pool lies beneath a towering waterfall. A swift runner could have reached the protection of its waters before we were aware he had escaped. I am certain we will find the son of Farbauti concealed beneath its surface." He grinned, rubbing his hands together. "We can use his own invention to catch him."

Immediately everyone set to work copying with hard, twined cord the woven loops they had seen in ash. They worked all night until satisfied they had recreated Loki's snare. As Sol began her climb over the edge of heaven, they trekked the short distance to the falls. After casting the net across the turbulent waters, the troop arranged themselves along both sides of the pool—Thor at one end, the rest at the other— "All together!" they cried and dragged the net up the foaming current.

When Loki saw what the Æsir intended, he dove deep into the churning waters, wedging his salmon form between two stones at the bottom of the pool. From the banks his movement was noticed. "There!" Heimdall pointed to the shadows in the deep water "I saw him dive deep! We need to fit the lower edge with stones, so it drags firmly along the bottom!"

Again, the Æsir cast the net. This time they weighted the bottom edge with rocks so that it dragged the pool bed allowing nothing to escape beneath. Driven ahead toward the unknown dangers of the sea, Loki turned to rush the net. Kicking hard with his tail, he leapt high over the top line then dove to the bottom of the pool.

"Catch him!" screamed Skadi. "Or let me hunt him down! I'll thrust a spear through his middle and pin him in the mud where he belongs! Let him try to leap then!"

Thor shifted the draglines in his hands as he roared to the haulers on the far bank. "Again! Let us start again! This time half of you take my place. I will wade up the center of the river to catch him should he again leap the top."

The Æsir cast the net across the waters, this time dragging it upstream while Thor waded up the center of the watercourse. Again, Loki sought to leap the net, but this time was snagged in mid-flight. He wriggled furiously and would have escaped, except for the crushing grip of Thor that squeezed his body near the tail.

Caught, Loki returned to his normal form. The dark son sneered at his captors as they bound his arms with strong cord before hauling him away, still dripping, from the river. They stopped in Kettle Grove amid steaming hot springs that spit scalding water and fumed a sulfurous stench. In a deep cavern, they shucked off their travel gear then hunted around until they found three large, flat stones. Standing the stones on edge, they arranged them side by side, chipped their ridges sharp to worry flesh, and then broke a ragged hole through the center of each.

The Æsir arrayed themselves about the son of Farbauti. Skadi stepped forward until she hovered, with fists clenched, over the bound captive. "Through cunning you brought down Baldur, the light of innocence in the nine worlds, and concealed your part by shaming the hand of Hodd. Through contrivance you arranged the death of my father, Thjasse, burned down by the vaferflames of Asgard."

A body was dragged into the cave and dumped in a bloody heap at Loki's feet. "We hunted down your sons that we might make use of them. We would have had Narfi, but he turned himself into a wolf and escaped; no doubt a skill learned from his father. Nari was not so nimble." Skadi nudged the lifeless body with her toe. "As punishment for your many misdeeds we will bind you with his ice-cold guts here in this stinking womb until the end of time."

A slight figure shouldered through the gathered gods. Dropping to her knees, Sigyn enfolded the body lying in the dust. A sharp keening escaped her lips; the ritual cries of a mother's loss. Three times she struck her hands, moaned once and was silent.

Loki glared at the familiar features of his son peeping out from his mother's embrace. Turning back to his captors, he spat into their face. "You seek to inflict pain upon me for truthful words and clever feats that throw your own contemptible actions into relief. Your conduct is that of children, angry at being caught in the act of their own misdeeds." Water bubbled in a nearby pool ejecting a spray of hot droplets. Loki twisted his shoulders to follow the crowd as it danced away from the rim. "I am delighted to chastise your arrogance. It offers some recompense for the suffering you inflicted on my children."

Heimdall's laughter roared through the cavern, its echo briefly drowning out the hissing from the hot spring pools. "Call out loudly, Slanderer, you who are the source of deceit among the gods. Let us hear you complain to deaf ears of the injustice perpetrated upon you. I am incredulous you dare speak of the arrogance of others, you who have always considered himself superior everyone!" He shook a fist in Loki's face as the spittle from his lips splattered across the captive's cheeks. "I have long stood watch on the bridgehead to Asgard, by command of the Alfodur. My eyes keen, my ears tuned sharp to your detestable acts. When I could, I intervened to thwart your bold actions, those that brought sorrow—deeds too numerous to count. Cunning in all matters, you have often placed us, your adopted kin, in difficulties that only ill dealings could resolve. We have suffered indignities by your hand long enough!"

The wife of Loki wailed from beside the body of her son. "Please let my husband go. He has done nothing to deserve this. My son did nothing to deserve this. How can you... Why," she cried. "Why?"

Skadi sneered down at the wife of Loki. "Quiet Sigyn! Your pleas are useless here. For far too long we have suffered a constant stream of torments from this vile creature. It is time we put an end to his mischief."

Loki struggled in their grasp, snapping his teeth at their hands as they bent him back onto the rocks. He howled in pain when the sharp edges bit into his flesh, a scream echoed by Sigyn kneeling in the dust, rocking back and forth, clutching her head.

Using a sharp knife, they slit wide Nari's belly. Sobbing loudly, Sigyn tried to stop the defilement of her son's body but was shoved rudely aside as the length of his intestines was drawn out. Loki cursed them all as the entrails were wrapped snugly over his shoulders, then looped firmly about his knees before being slipped though the holes in the rock and knotted tight beneath his feet.

The gods crowded around the bound captive. Pooling their knowledge, they carved runes into wands of living hazel wood then stained the symbols with Nari's blood. Chanting words of power infused with intent, they struck the gut strings with the wands, transforming the cold flesh into iron-hard bonds.

His back an agony of deep cuts with streams of blood running down the stones, Loki twisted his head to face his tormenters. "Though I suffer," he choked through gritted teeth, "remember how you treat your kin. It will reflect upon you and all your creations. It will be remembered... always!"

"If it is suffering you want," Skadi grinned, bending close to the captive, her hands squirming with vipers, "I will give you more than the ice-cold guts of your son to keep you company." Twisting the snakes into a loose knot, she suspended them over his head. "For the death of my father that you caused, I hang these serpents above your face that their poison will burn you drop by drop. It will remind you of the constant torment you casually inflicted on others and which burns forever in my heart."

Loki howled as the venom dripped onto his cheeks, writhing in pain as each drop seared a hole through his skin. Sigyn screamed while the others laughed. Scrabbling about, she dug a bowl from a nearby travel pack and held it over Loki's face to catch the poison as it fell.

Skadi patted Loki's shoulder, digging her fingernails deep into his flesh until blood flowed. "We leave you to the ministrations of your wife, what little she can do to ease your suffering. She refuses to leave your side. Little do you deserve such loyalty, you who have never shown it to others. Just remember that all bowls fill and must sometime be emptied. Though your wife may be attentive, she cannot always shield you from the poison."

With grim satisfaction, the mighty gods left Loki to endure his fate, with Sigyn in tears at his side. Together they trooped from the grotto, their vengeance appeased by the punishment meted out.

Cycle 5: Ragnarök

Enemies in Wait

They wait on the edge for twilight to arrive, the glorious enemies of the gods. Each wrapped in their own thoughts and dedicated to their own purpose. Mind alone knows the desire for revenge. Deliberating over carefully calculated plans, it gives no truce to its enemies. No sickness is worse for the bitter heart than the inability to act. Hatred spreads through the breast, a rage-kindled wildfire that consumes the spirit.

In silence, they wait for twilight to arrive.

The Fenris Wolf

On the island of Lyngvi, beside the pitch-black waters of Amsvartnir Lake, the son of Loki lies unable to move, his limbs bound with an unbreakable fetter. The Fenris wolf growls low around the sword wedged roof-to-jaw. A steady rumble issuing from his throat prepares the course of the river Van, whose waters flow freely from the corners of his lips.

Each hour of each day he flexes his limbs to test the strength of Gleipnir, the elf-made fetter of tenuous wisps that keeps him bound to the boulder Gjoll, ready to snap its bonds the moment any weakness is encountered.

Each day he broods on the fear of those who deceived him—the arrogant Æsir, puffed with pride at their ruse. How they circled him, laughing while he struggled bound and defenseless before them, crying out for them to honor their pledge.

Each day he recalls how they broke their oath to remove the fetter that entrapped his limbs. Instead, gloating, they bound him to the earth, anchored by the enormous stone Thviti. How his cries choked in his throat as they turned their backs, leaving him to pass the years alone through the waning ages until the twilight of the gods arrived.

In grim anger, his mind fills with black thoughts as he plans his revenge against the gods. The hand of trust he has already taken, the

524

bilious palm of Tyr, found its bitter flesh distasteful. It is the head he seeks in his dreams and as he contemplates each waking hour—the Alfodur of the Æsir. The gray-haired, one-eyed face swims before his mind, ancient lips burning his ears with kinship promises. Anger flaring through his breast, he cries out loudly for revenge.

The Midgard Serpent

From the ocean depths glowers the mighty, oar-struck, ocean-lasher. His water-washed eyes aflame with hate, recalling the judgment received at the hands of the Alfodur. Stolen from his foster home by the fearful Æsir, dragged with his siblings before the seat of judgment in the great hall of Gladsheim, where the one-eyed god deemed him unworthy and hideous to look upon. Cast by the son of that same airy god into the ocean that surrounds all lands, their intent that he would perish by the fall from such a great height. Instead he lived, made his home in the depths, grew large amid the codfish, increasing in size until he encircled the outer sea, a great wolf's fish biting his own tail.

Over the passage of years, he faced Fjorgyn's son. First in the hall of Utgarda-Loki, where, disguised as a cat by the crafty giant, he glared with limpid hate as the thurs-destroyer strove to lift him bodily from his bed. Again, he faced the son of Odin, when the god of Thunder snagged him from Hymir's skiff intent on taking his life. A swift knife stroke from Hymir, the fearful giant quaking beside the oarlock, freed him from the sturdy line and an early fate.

Circumscriber of the world, he moves restlessly, his thrashing coils roiling the ocean surface, the long rhythm of his dreams touched by nightmares of tumbling down, down, down from the sky. When he flexes his muscles, spindrift spatters the shores, while above the heavens burn like fire. For now, he waits, growing in strength, readying himself for the final battle.

Hel

Snared with her brothers in the Ironwood, she fared poorly at the judgment of the Æsir gods. Life she kept, but the cost was servitude to the goddess of life and death—she who along with her sisters weaves the fates of men. Cast down to Niflhel by Thor's mighty hands, she landed hard amid the frozen wastes, her body broken on the rocks of

Nidaveller. Now Hvedrung's kinswoman grudgingly aides the work of death.

Legs healed badly, back twisted, her ribcage crushed so each wheezing breath is misery, she hobbles about in constant pain. Half white, half gray, her countenance grim, she remembers the harsh treatment received at the hands of the Æsir. In her silent hall of frozen snow, the daughter of Loki bides her time. Her hate grows as a glacier creeping steadily down the mountain valley, its thickness built up layer on layer over the passage of years.

Loki

In kettle grove, amid fuming hot springs that spat scalding water, Loki lies bound with the enchanted entrails of his son Nari, punishment meted out by the Æsir for his scornful words at Ægir's feast, his many duplicities, and his hand in Baldur's death. The vengeance of Skadi hangs above his face, poisonous serpents whose venom drips to burn holes in his flesh. With each drop he curses the gods.

"With mistletoe driven by Hodd's arm, the shaft directed by my eye, I brought down the love of the Æsir. Baldur will never again stride the golden halls. Though the sky wept, dry-eyed counsel given by a ragged matron at world's end ensured that all who die, remain dead.

I will give account for every drop of poison.

They came near, fading back into the mists of time when I brought Idun to Thjasse. Gray grew all the godheads without her golden apples. Would that all the kin of Ingvifreyr, gaunt with old age, had dried to dust and blown away on the winds.

I will give account for every drop of poison.

They were choked with fear when Thrym acquired the weapon of the god's protector. For a bride, he would return it. Instead, the ogre received the son of earth wrapped in a linen gown with keys belted at his waist, and as dowry secured death for everyone in his hall. For kinship now cursed, I aided the return of Thor's hammer. Without its powerful protection, the gods would be hard-pressed to survive.

I will give account for every drop of poison.

In Ægir's hall, I contended with wounding words and offered rich replies to stony silence. The Æsir's sons cringed, their arrogance diminished, as I topped their drinks with the glare of blatant truths.

I will give account for every drop of poison.

When free of these bonds, I will erect a spite pole high atop a rocky knoll that faces Asgard—a staff of hazelwood wedged tight in a stony cleft, a horse's skull perched atop with jaws set agape, the shaft etched with curse runes. I will shout to the heavens, 'Here, I erect a spite pole. This spite, I turn against those hoary gods that infest Asgard, that they will know my revenge in their twilight.'

Never again will they gather beneath the shade of the great tree or feast in Hlesey, Ægir's island hall. All that they were, all that they are, all that they ever could be, I will rend from their hearts."

Garm

Once was born in the lands of Midgard, a hound greater than all hounds. First to teat, foremost in play, fearless he explored his world. Curious and clever, he learned to navigate its ways. He grew large with an immense head, thick muscular body, and massive feet with thick, horny nails. A wiry brindle coat with a blazing white chest marked the indomitable strength of his line. Quickly, he learned the language of men, learned the ways of the living.

Schooled in war from an early age, he knew no fear of the battle storm, feared neither the bite of steel, the sting of whispering dart, the lunge of bloody spear, nor the raging voice of men under siege. Hard-skilled in the field of battle, trained to combat and the taking of life, in countless battles he bested helmed foes as easily as taking down a stag in the forest. Quickly, he learned the language of war, learned the ways of the dead and dying.

Eyes that in youth knew wonder, grew fiercer with each battle. Silently, he raged against a fate that sought to sever the tie of his life with his body. In the blind fury of battle, a pointed shaft bit deep into his breast, the lucky thrust of a bold warrior who refused to turn. Life's blood splashed across his white chest, a crimson badge of honor. With an agonizing lurch of breath, the litr of the great hound lost its bonds with his flesh.

Passed then the greatest of hounds to directions west. With bloodied breast still dripping, he trotted along the primrose way. None dared contest his right. Every shade stepped aside as he passed, for few were braver or more valiant in life.

From the seat of Judgment, the gods turned a cold eye. The words of his hamingje were ignored. Only the honor of his actions in life remained to relate his character. Had he been a man, the Valkyrie would have chosen him first from the field of valor. Instead, the gods snubbed his warrior's heart.

Alone among the judges, the one-handed god cried out. With a booming voice, Tyr called for the recognition of honor, demanded those seated to reconsider their decision. Still they turned away their faces and made fists of their ears. They feared the mighty hound would stand as man's protector against the gods, so close was he aligned with men. That he would change allegiance if were he brought among the Æsir was unthinkable. And what of Geri and Freki, Odin's wolves, watchdogs of Asgard? Could they stand against an implacable foe trained to war from birth? This, the Alfodur was unwilling to test.

The cup of fate was held low so Garm could drink. Eagerly, he lapped at the mixture of three fountains. With each mouthful, the warmth of mang restored his litr. He shook his head, spraying the courtyard with the long ribbons of drool that streamed from his jowls. The low grumble of his voice filled his breast as his stave-like ribs flexed with a thunderous howl that shook the dais.

The gods rocked back in awe as Garm stared at them, unflinching, expectant. Still, they denied him a place in Valhalla and forbade him entry to the glittering plains of Niflheim. Instead they assigned the greatest of hounds a thankless task, warden for the dead, guardian to Niflheim.

Bound before Gnipa cave, he rages at the tether that holds him. Each day he menaces the passing dead to keep them moving while holding the living at bay. His deep growls warn of the perils of passing through Helgrind, the cold, golden gates of Niflheim. Every moment he strains against his chain, resentful of those who slighted his honor and bound his once-free spirit.

The Giants

From Ymir, we are descended: hill giants, frost giants, fire giants—even Hraesvelg, the wind giant from whose wings blow deadly tempests. All strong. All proud. All free. With power, we were born to freeze, to burn, to tear with wind, and crush with hard stones.

In Jotunheim our halls once were many. Wisdom warmed our hearths, while bright shields glittered on walls draped with thick, ornate tapestries. Now in despair we view the cold, empty spaces, listening to the hollow ring of footfalls past. The son of Odin has devastated our land. Many have faced his wild fury, fallen beneath the rain of heavy blows delivered by his hammer.

In our youth, we were quick to avenge treachery, dealing mortal wounds to thieves, hacking low our enemies. We guarded our wealth better then; few dared challenge our rights. But now we glean chaff from stubble fields and compete with starlings that gobble the grain. Never shall sorrow wane in this sullen fortress. If we do not act now, soon all we have left will be gone.

Those who brought us to this place listen closely to our curse. Soon the world will echo with its storm. It brings spite on those who hear it. Dreadful things are called to happen. Cliffs tremble, sending their walls crashing down. The heaving earth gapes wide with giant maws that swallow the living. Raging storms tear at shorelines, their heavy rains swelling rivers to flood the lands. Thunder fills the air as black clouds dim the sun. Flames spew from the earth while droplets of fire rain from the sky. With sorrow, you will look upon empty houses, desolate ale halls where moldering silence greets the ears. Your great warriors will embrace death. They will sleep where they fall without rites, their bleached bones scattered beneath an open sky.

The Hastener lights full the world above, chiding us to be ready for war. Soon we will close battle ranks, a living wall of terror to still your hearts. The thunder of our march will deafen your ears. At the sight, at the sound, your eyes will turn white, your limbs will freeze in panic, and your guts run free as water.

We are the instruments of fate, destroying what lies near its doom, our strong arms striking down that which cannot stand. Never will you escape our wrath. All your paths lead straight to death.

The Sons of Muspellsheim

Beyond the cool border of Mirkwood—the dark forest shelter of fir and oak—lies a land of fire, whose blistering red sand scorches the feet of unwary travelers. Sparks leap from fissures in the earth.

Caught on a breeze they whirl through the sky, rising up to adorn the heavens with stars. This is Muspellsheim, the home of Fire Giants. Here, Surt and the sons of Muspell tend their hearths, bide their time, even as a bright coal lurks beneath the ashes waiting to rekindle flames that with a breath renews from the unseen ember.

The kin of fire come together in council, jostling with each other for position. The heat of their assembled presence drives the flames to a mighty roar. From his high seat of prominence, Surt calls out to the eager warriors gathered before him. "Some long time ago the seeress with singing voice foretold that with fated footsteps the sons of Muspell would fare northward to win back that which was lost at the beginning of time. A high-blazing pyre of ravenous flame was her forecast. Though many will fall to fill the belly of the wolf, the embers of Muspellsheim are destined to ignite the world… So, she foretold."

The gathering moaned as one at his words, a low groan of barely checked excitement. Surt paused, nodding his head at the sound. "This day I stand before you," he planted his fists firmly on his on hips, "with my vision clear to the ends of the worlds and tell you that the time has come for us to fulfill our destiny. The portents line up, the events stacked one by one until none can deny their meaning. We march at once through the lands of Midgard. From there we ascend to Asgard. Carry only what you need for battle. The land of men will supply our route provisions."

War-eager cries swept the gathering. "On Vigrid plain our ranks will be buttressed by giants wielding weapons with vigor, while the numberless army of twice-dead from the frozen land of Niflhel lends their support. The Æsir will resist amid a storm of sharp-honed weapons that bite both ways." Licking back his excitement, Surt dragged the back of his hands across his lips. "Great death we will encounter. Greedy wolves will feast on the fallen while ravens sup at blood. And that which was ours past, will be ours again."

He struck a massive fist against his chest. "With fire, we will cleanse the nine worlds of those who would thwart our claim." Three times the heavy beat rolled across the field. "With hurtling flame, we will burn them from deepest root to smallest branch until none are left. All will know the heat of our march, a red-hot breath sweeping all before its deadly exhale, wrapping the worlds in its embrace." Sparks leapt from his breast as the crowd's roar trembled the air. "Alone we will be the victors and let the nine worlds perish!"

Cocks Crow

Perched amid the bare branches of the Gallows Wood, Fjalar, the bright red cockerel, gaily crows. At its call, Eggther, Gymir's herdsman, strikes his harp from his hilltop watch at the din of waking giants roused to battle. Retrieving the sword of victory from its niche deep in the crusty earth—the malicious brand of Volund entrusted to him by Angrboda—he passes it to the fire's servant to deliver into the hands of Surt.

In the worlds beneath a second cock of dark, soot-red hue crows lustily across the lands of Niflheim. Garm hears the call and bays loudly in reply from his tethered post before Gnipa-cave. On Corpse Strand, Eljudnir turns north its doors. In the darkness, horror stirs, awakened from its long slumber.

From his roost above the bright-shingled halls of Asgard, high amid the branches of Yggdrasil, Gullinkambi preens his gleaming feathers. Flaring his golden comb, he cheers loudly from the bright green foliage, calling the warriors of Asgard to rise, knuckle the sleep from their eyes, and make ready their weapons of war.

This day the great ash is sorely tested. Wracked with deep moans, its mighty branches tremble, its leaves quiver. Harts and squirrels cringe beneath the foliage. Unable to keep their purchase on the tossing limbs, pale hawks take flight, voices crying as they wing through the air.

Hills quake. Meadows ripple like a blanket shaken out over a mattress. Cliffs tumble into the sea. Dark elves, groaning in fear at the gateposts of their underground warrens, bar their doors, for they know what soon must be faced. Wise dwarves, staggering before bright forges, bank the fires of their smithies as etins, shaking the loam of ages from their limbs, rise up from the earth to do battle.

The Elivagar Rivers freeze in their course, sprouting rime-cold arrows of murder frost, the death-cold storm that kills men and animals. The world-tree, robbed of warm sap, shudders with the cold.

Asgard Awakes

Each night Odin climbs the winding steps of Hlidskialf, the watchtower whose silver roof gleams in the Mead Ship's light. From its high seat, he spies in all directions, ever watchful for the advance of Surt. The directions North, West, and East remain clear, their far horizons unblemished by disturbance. This day his gaze penetrates south past the Dovre Mountains, through the heavy line of Mirkwood, the dark forest that borders Muspellsheim. The vision that greets him turns his heart to sorrow.

Great spheres of light flash on the horizon, dull echoes boom from Midgard. Burning clouds mushroom into the sky. The heavens blaze with fiery lightning as hail lashes the lands of men. Billowing clouds of ash dim the sun. The terror of the linden dances across the heavens.

Furies scream in rage amid dark churning clouds that tumble across the sky. The air reeks with the breath of sulfur. Sunrise brings a bloody orb. Midday sees it nearly blotted out by clouds. At eventide, the sun runs red from the sky.

A dry fog clogs the ground; its thick, yellow mist swirling about the trunks of trees, creeping in under doors. Eyes and throats burn in its embrace; each breath becomes a searing agony. Men and animals die gasping in meadows, stanchioned in barns, huddling in homes, their lips flecked with blood. Grasses, shrouded in haze, wilt brown as the promise of harvest perishes in the fields.

Parched winds spill out of doorways. The homes of men stand

empty. The silent, desolate halls shattered by the winds of war seem like an ancient fear deprived of believers, its once-terrifying form become barren and left to crumble.

Still, great balls of white light wink along the horizon while echoes boom from the homeland of men. Relentlessly, the fiery lightning crawls ever closer to the bridgehead of Bifrost.

———————

"The days have settled into shadows. Twilight comes, and I can do no more to slow its progress. The sons of Muspellsheim have begun their relentless advance. Indomitable, they trample all before them as they make their way to Vigrid plain." The Alfodur pulled a long draught from the wine goblet stationed beside his seat. He turned it slowly side to side, studying the brilliant reflections that glinted from the intricately woven knots embossed along stem and bowl.

"You are certain of this?" Frigg's slim fingers stroked at an inky ringlet, pulled it straight out from her forehead, and then let it snap back into place among its sisters.

Odin spoke into his cup, watching the wine ripple with the breath of his words. "These things I say, I know well, and grieve the more for knowing. The living are driven from their homes as rats before a wildfire. The dead, whose bones earth bosomed long ago, are torn up from their rest and scattered across the plains."

He sighed heavily, pushed himself up straight, then slumped back again. "At the beginning of things," his voice sounded far away, "the end is often hidden, but, once the final path becomes clear, it is difficult to ignore the course. I bend my knee to fate, though it is hateful to know the end, but be powerless over the event."

Odin's gaze lingered on she who shared his life; she who had always stood beside him. His lips twitched with a faint smile as he wistfully recalled the ardency of earlier days, when the knowledge of what had been was much nearer than that of what was to be.

'We loved years ago, when our youth was all hot breath and sighs. I was eager then to chase wisdom and you—you seemed content with my passion. Remember how as you lay beside me, I would comb my fingers through your hair and loop precious trinkets around the swan-white ring of your neck.

Our love grew with each embrace, each success, and each painful loss. No holy place existed without us, no dance, no feast, no wedding, no battle, no birth. Even now, my blood still runs as does yours, the same pure, warm stream that coursed through our veins when we were young. We loved each other then with one heart, one breath, one intent, keen as a knife point. We hold that love today though the winds of maturity have blunted its edge.

With each remembrance of Mimir's draught, I prayed our timeless days together might be twice as long. But Skuld cannot be denied, though our hearts wish different. While our journey soon ends, someone, I tell you, will remember us, even in another time.'

"Aye." The grizzled gray head nods. "Frodi's peace is done. Grotti has nearly ground all the grist. Soon Fenia and Menia will have had their full stint of milling. Were you not wakened by Gullinkambi's call?"

Frigg wrung her hands, bound them up in her robe on her lap until her fingers ached. "Wasn't it Salgofnir who roused us from our dreams; the bright cockerel that crows each day from the wall to waken the victorious people of Valhalla?"

The gray head shook slowly side to side. "No. The cheer truly came from the splendid foliage high atop the ancient tree. The golden cock calls all to the final day."

Frigg's hands lay as dead in her lap. Staring up at the great beam that bore the weight of the hall roof, its surfaced darkened with the soot of ages, she felt the burden in the aching tension of her shoulders. "I suspected it was so. Wyrd goes ever as it must." A deep sigh escaped her lips. "Skuld will not let us avoid our fate."

She stared wistfully out the doorway at the green branches of the great tree that shook its leaves overhead. "Too often Salgofnir jarred me from sleep, the din of his ceaseless crowing with the mad clatter of his flapping wings rousing me to the early blue dawn light. Often, I wished some furry thief would steal through the night and sever his head below the cape, forever silencing his voice." A tear trickled down her cheek. "But now," she lifted a hand to wipe it away, "now I wish it had been his call I heard this morning and not the dread promise of Gullinkambi's cry cutting through the morning air."

Frigg reached across her lap to stroke the rugged hand of the Alfodur. "In a dream, just before the waking crow, you Farmatýr, I clasped tightly in my arms. Your features were scored with bloody gashes; terrible wounds that had carried off your life. For me, to remain alive was a heavy burden."

Odin gazed into his goblet, turned it slowly in his hands so the wine seemed to lay motionless, a red pool reflecting his thoughts. "Upon dark times the host has fallen. Only a few will live to see the days renewed. May they have Urd's protection when the flames are first quenched, for then the worlds lie open to view, their secrets exposed as when a boiling kettle is lifted from the fire." He tapped a fingernail against the edge of the goblet, watching ripples rush across the wine's surface to collapse in the center. "What terrible visions will they see?"

Frigg rustled her cloak about her shoulders. Her fingers fumbled with the pin as she clasped a brooch at her throat. "Then we must each to our destiny." Rising, she gazed wistfully one last time around the great hall raised up in dawn's glow, when the warm sun shone bright overhead and the final days lay hidden deep in the mists of future twilight. The hall stretched out before her, an image chased in gold declaring the glory of the gods before the breaking of the world.

Helmets, shields, and bright-edged weapons adorned the walls. Mail coats covered the benches. Groves of ash spears leaned in corners. Serpent-carved beams stretched high overhead layered with overlapping gold-rimmed shields. The floors glowed with a carpet of amber rushes laid fresh that morning. Fit furnishings for a grand warrior's home.

Munin called softly from the Alfodur's shoulder, his cry an echo of ancient revelries, of a hall filled with bright, laughing faces, glorious days now past. Then, carved food bowls filled to brim stood on the board. Ale cups topped with the amber brew waited nearby. The eldskáli crackled with cheerful warmth. On the wall, blood-stained victory banners gave notice that here, warriors celebrated.

Each day rank on rank of Einherjar gathered in the goodly hall. Joyful benchmates sat at table, some playing games of chance, others frowning over boards—engrossed in strategy, some drinking, laughing at jests, while others, still bloody from the field of blade sport, clinked mugs with their recent adversary.

The merry feasts when lively music was played, and everything not held onto—knives, plates, cups—began to move. Then, watching as guests leapt from their seats to dance wildly amid the rushes, as much gladness to the eyes as was the music to the ears.

On that bench, Thor cheered victorious over Hrungnir, though he still bled from where the stone shard had gouged his forehead, a near-fatal blow delivered by his stalwart foe. Along the far end, Bragi's melodious voice entertained with stories old and new. When the days were young, Slagfin enchanted all with his musical skill, a harp propped on knee, his head thrown back in verse. It was through those doors the gifts of talented craftsman made their way into Æsir hands.

On these benches the high council met, draped in court finery, gold shields aglow with the sun's rays. Great were the solemn judgments made among the gods. In this hall, the war with the Vanir was started by an arrogant outburst and settled after much bloodshed; in truce the reluctant decision made to share sacrifices from the land of men.

Her breast ached remembering difficult trials of personal loss. There, outside the door—Frigg's greatest grief and Nanna's loss—Baldur was struck down with an arrow of mistletoe, Hodd's dark aim directed by the son of Farbauti.

At the head of the table, Loki quarreled with everyone, fanning the enmity that peaked at Ægir's feast, sealing his fate when he boasted to the gathered clan of his hand in Baldur's untimely death and shamed everyone with his blatant truths.

Frigg gently caressed the Alfodur's brow. "Prosperity never continues steadfast in the same place but moves like the earthen bank eaten away by a river, its contents shifted downstream, deposited along the shore, building up before the waters tear it away again." She let her hand rest on his head. "It grows late." Light from the setting sun angled through the western doorway, casting everything with the red glow of a slumbering fire. For a moment, her hand seemed to lay on a glowing ember, consumed from within, ready to crumble beneath her touch. "There is naught to do but face that which all must face. I leave to prepare with those whose fate remains uncertain." In a swirl of dark cloud, she strode through the western door of the great hall. Syn stepped aside, bending a knee as she passed beneath the crouching wolf and hovering eagle.

Tears welled from a single dry eye as the Alfodur watched her leave. Wisdom gained at such a price feels the loss but accepts the known. He tipped back his goblet, taking a long swallow of wine, then slammed it down on the bench beside his seat. "The hardest works to release are those nurtured by one's own hand."

A deep smoldering fire blazed to life, drying the tears. A twitch of shoulders sends mind and thought to flight. Odin's voice rose as the winds on a gale, the hall rafters booming with his command. "Send the call... quickly! Let fly my Heror across the nine worlds! Three frost years have passed. Now a bloody moon fills the sky. The worlds echo with portents of great carnage: turbulent storms tear across the seas, shorelines are drowned beneath rising swells, while towering walls of flame ravage the world."

His shouts chase the black forms hurtling toward the door. "Tell those from the edges the time has come. Let the Vanir know of the portending storm, if they haven't the wit to know already! Tell Heimdall to gather up the Gjallarhorn! Tell Freyja to call her half of the battle chaff from their tasks at Sessrumnir! Tell Ran to send along her catch of upright horsemen of the field where ships race! Call all those of warrior blood to gather beneath the shining hall shingles of Valhalla!"

In a rush of wings Hugin and Munin streaked past Syn, who threw wide the entry doors. Swifter than Hugi, the victor over Thjalfi, they struck out over the worlds.

Alone, the one-eyed god peered into his cup, his thoughts floating on the surface of the wine. "How strange it is to find myself missing the anticipation of Gullinkambi's call. Now, having heard it sung through the leaves of Mimamirth, my brows deepen at the thought of what lies ahead. Oh, that this day had never dawned, and the golden cock had remained silent."

The Counsel of Mimir

Heaving himself up from his seat, Odin pulled on his thick-soled travel boots then gathered a heavy cloak about his shoulders. Brusquely, he commanded his retainers to saddle Sleipnir and pack a small bag of provisions. "I must visit a wise advisor—an old friend, a dead friend. Him whose head, a gift from the bloody Vanir in the early days of our truce, I bathed in waters from the three wells to keep fresh and with speech runes bestowed with a lively tongue. His prudent counsel may yet clear the air of an untimely holocaust."

Clasping the reins tightly in his fist, he mounted the great gray horse. "While the day allows me time, I ride Sleipnir into the underworlds. I take the shortest way to Mimir's well, a hard ride without delays north beyond the bridgehead where Heimdall stands watch, then swiftly across frost-covered fields that melt into the Dark-of-Moon plains."

With a light touch of his heels, he nudged Sleipnir to speed.

———— · ————

At the well of Mimir, where rushes grow tall along the water's edge and their slender lengths give voice to the wind, Odin wrestled a keg from its niche beneath the roots of the mighty ash. Prying the lid from the top, he peered in at the pickled head. "Wake old friend," his voice echoed in the hollow, "I have need of your counsel."

Features stirred. Eyelids flickered. From the depth of the keg a voice croaked out. "Once more I am awakened from deep slumber." Mimir struggled to focus his gaze through the circular brightness. "Once again light streams through these tired eyes and words dribble from the swollen tongue of a withered bag. There is only one who would dare disturb my solitude. Odin, Alfodur of the Æsir, what do you want?"

Odin lifted the head from the keg until it swung free. He spoke carefully to the wizened face, shaping his words to avoid misunderstanding. "Gray-haired with anguish, I seek your counsel—its insight clear and direct." His arm sagged, and he nearly slipped his grip on the wispy hair, but with a quick lunge he caught the head before it dropped into the mud at his feet.

"Wrecked is the world." He swung Mimir's head, its hair now firmly tangled in his fingers, in an arc to take in the nine worlds. "It stands blighted on a tortured root, like the ice-blasted pines of the Nidaveller Mountains, stripped of their needles, and nearly barkless from the frost-white caress of three years' winter. The portents line up one after another, settling on my shoulders like heavy weights bearing down, each an agony of trepidation; they foretell the approach of the final days.

You already know of Baldur. I related the story to your ears of how he fell in the Æsir courts, of how all wept strong tears for his safe return, save one, whose refusal condemned him to face Urd's judgment. Now, three endless winters have passed. The air draws life from every living thing that cannot protect its warmth. Even the summer sun travels a frozen path across the sky.

For weeks, from my high seat in Hlidskialf, I've watched a wall of burning smoke approaching from the south. The sounds of battles echo across the world. Chaos visits the homes of men. At dawn this morn the golden cock called from high in the foliage of Lorad. Now the ancient ash groans as if in pain, its branches tremble with fear. I must know; I must be certain that this is the day of twilight, the terrible doom of the victory gods."

"Patience," whispered Mimir, his voice soft as the breeze that stirred the grass.

Odin bristled at the word. Swinging the head aloft, he shook it mightily. "Patience! Patience is a word made for dead men and bodiless heads! Not for birds of prey with strength yet in their wings! I've lived always with talons outstretched! I will not be as one who, having thrice failed to kill, now waits in gloom without strength, to die even as food passes before his mouth!"

Mimir's lips moved with a soft breath. "Have patience, my old friend. Without it, you plan a vase, it dwindles to a pot."

Odin dangled the head before his face. "I need talk clear of riddles. I've no time for double meaning." He peered directly into Mimir's sunken eyes, hunting out the bright sparks hidden behind the slitted eyelids. "That which I have long sought to avoid takes form from my dreams to threaten the waking day. A mighty storm brews on the horizon. I need your advice on what can be done to avoid its terrible fury."

A weary smile spread across Mimir's face, lightly turning up the corners of his mouth. "Patience. We are the tools of time and terror. Epochs steal on us and steal from us, yet we persist. Though we have long held our own, we cannot hold our shape forever. We are like great crags of basalt lashed by the sea that crumble bit by bit until naught remains, but the memory of their once-powerful form.

Let me close my eyes that I might clearly see.

Darkness clouds my vision, though far off stands a faint light, the twilight of a cave mouth seen dimly from its depths.

Through closed eyes, much I see.

The homes of men stand empty. Parched bodies spill out of doorways. Paths wander without tenants, save for the slain. The shadow of death dances in the firelight cast by burning timbers. Thick clouds of gray smoke and ash clog the air, awaiting the breeze to carry them away when the day is done.

Through closed eyes, much I see.

Loki's ranks swelled with dark shades of the ages, angry spirits that lurk in narrow places whispering silent curses to the night. The feet of thurs shod in rout march sandals trample the green earth to dust. Hungry ravens circle a wide field hedged with hazel. A wall of flame with roaring voice challenges all who would oppose its advance. Bright is the light of the sun brought to earth that sweeps all before it.

Through closed eyes, much I see.

The sheen of spears flickers as stars on the sea when blue waves roll across the strand. On Vigrid plain, a valiant wall of heroes stands firm against the darkening light. None retreat.

Through closed eyes, much I see.

A storm of shrikes lifts into the air and the cries of ten thousand, thousand rise up to greet their flight. Lightning drawn from the sky kindles the earth. Firelight flickers across score on score of warriors fallen with their mounts, limbs tangled in the bracken of battle. Cloven byrnies and dented helmets litter a rusty plain. High climb the flames as parched lips cry out for a last drop of water to cool them for the grave. Amid the ashes of the passing fire four stalwart sons of the Æsir and one long-legged son of Bor remain standing."

The Alfodur shuddered. "I know the visions that play against your closed eyes." He raised a hand to rub his brow. "I have seen the same in fitful sleep raging through the dark currents of my dreams. Is there any way to avoid it?"

Mimir's voice, previously soft, now boomed across the waters of the well. The rushes quivered with excitement at his words. "With my eyes wide open, I say this can be no more avoided than the air you breathe or the final knot on the skein of fate be unraveled.

Many long years have passed, but they are nothing to the moment we face—yes, I include myself in the events now in motion. That on which our existence depends is clear. Your actions become our epoch. In this moment, our days draw together to become imperishable. Even should we survive through tomorrow, it is for this one moment, we will be remembered.

While fated to die, death does not mean defeat. They never fail, those who die with honor in a great cause. Though their sodden heads shrivel in the sun, still their litr walks abroad, proud and free.

The sun and moon continue to cycle across the heavens. Our actions augment sweeping thoughts that overpower all others, guiding a new green world born from the smoldering embers of the old.

Return to Asgard. Set all in readiness tonight. Delay doubles the danger. Arrive punctual at your point of battle. Hold true to oaths given long ago. Now is the time to fulfill them all."

Odin gently lowered the head back into the keg. "Your words chill my heart and steal away the very warmth of my blood: to strive for greatness or collapse forgotten, like dust blown away by a stiff breeze."

The muted voice of Mimir echoed back from the hollow depths. "Only those who admit defeat are defeated. Do not spend your final moments grieving over that which cannot and must not be avoided. You cannot defeat Surt and his followers, but you can meet them in battle just the same."

Closing the keg, Odin wedged back in its lodging among the roots. "I do not fear death, just the end of meaning, the loss of purpose. So, know that today will be a day long-remembered; a day when bold warriors denied an overwhelming foe."

Niflheim Rises

Beyond the Na-Gates, in the cold misty lands of Niflhel, Leikin governs the twice-dead of nine worlds. Established at the order of Odin, she shares food with the damned dead—those who received the namaeli: traitors, ranks of cowardly warriors, thieves, rapists, murderers, the disreputable who passed from sickness or age, the disaffected who fled into the embrace of death.

Called Hel for the domain she controls, she remains the daughter of Loki.

In Eljudnir she resides, the dark hall sprayed with sleet and wrapped with drifted snow. Its threshold is called Fallandaford, a pitfall where the unwary tumble to their peril. Hunger is her bare board, famine the knife with which she serves. Kor is her bed where sickness lays. Bed curtains shroud a moldy tick; disaster shines in their weave. Lazy is her slave who labors at chores. Slothful is her handmaiden who waits her pleasure.

Half ashen, half dark, she stands on the Ness offering welcome to a weary traveler who stumbles over her threshold, the frosted hem of his ragged cloak brushing the ground at each step. His harsh expression is fearful to look upon. Sunken, pockmarked cheeks house a gate of gritted, yellow teeth. Eyes aflame beneath heavy, unkempt brows glare inward with barely restrained fury. The hollow echoes of his footsteps on the Gjoll Bridge have long been snatched from the air by a bitter wind.

Hel called out to the weary traveler, beckoning to him with outstretched arms. "Welcome father. It has been a long time since last you visited. I heard of your encounter at Ægir's feast; I laughed thinking of the discomfort it must have caused." He flinched away as she lightly touched his scarred cheek. "You paid a hefty price for honesty."

Taking the sullen figure by the arm, she guided him to a seat beside the cold flames. "You must be tired from your long journey. The cold in this land is difficult for those whose form retains the ties of life. Come, seat yourself by my hearth. You'll need to lean close; fire kindles little heat in this home."

"Here," she placed a mug in hands that trembled, not from cold, but exhaustion and anger, "take ale charged with a red-hot poker to warm your insides."

She drew a finger lightly along his cheek. Jerking back from the touch, Loki barely stopped himself from snapping his teeth at the hand. "It will help," he mumbled settling back.

"Time has been rough on you, father. I see in faded light that your face is healing from the poison burns that pockmark your cheeks; grave payment for your last deeds. Your matted hair and ragged clothes give the appearance of a scruffy Ram, but when bound to a rock I suppose there is precious little one can do to spruce up for a visit. Or have you chosen to keep your hair uncut until the final day is resolved?"

Loki snorted, tugged at his grizzled hair, then dragged fingers through his matted beard. "Being bound in a dark cavern offers little light by which to groom. I used my strength to ponder vengeance. My hair I kept from lack of effort. Now it remains unshorn until those who chained me are paid back for my harsh treatment."

He took a long pull at the heated ale, dragged a tattered cuff across his lips, and stared into the flames that seemed to shiver in the cold. "When the etins roused themselves for battle, shook the loam of ages from their limbs, I was able to free myself from the ungainly fetters of Nari's entrails that I might have revenge on those who took away my liberty. I am here because the light of days now dims to terrible twilight." He glanced up at his daughter standing silently by his side. She turned away as he began to speak. "I need your aide, Leikin. Have no fear for yourself. The conflict to come will little touch your realm. For the let of battle chaff you will reap a mighty harvest."

As Hel seated herself before her father, her robes parted revealing bent, badly healed legs. Loki scowled at the damaged limbs, which once carried his daughter running amid the trees of the Ironwood. Hel drew a finger along a ragged scar, a purple blotch that wrapped her knee and ran up her thigh. She smiled as Loki's grimace deepened, then flipped her robes to cover her twisted limbs. "Call me Hel, for that is my title in these cold lands. It is true that I have no love for the Æsir, though I owe them my domain. It is by their hand I have this crooked body. It is by their decree that I am charged to perform an unsavory mission in an unwanted land. I take the dregs while they skim the cream. Only through your connivance did I once hold a wondrous prize whose loss brought them all to tears."

She reached over to pat Loki's arm. He twitched at her touch but gritted his teeth and forced himself to endure the contact. "Certainly, I will help you."

The whirling wheel spinning overhead illuminated her vengeance. From her seat of power, Hel's voice cried out over the bitter winds that howled about the walls of Eljudnir, reviving legion after legion of victory-hindering warriors, bestowing on them the power of speech long deprived.

Shaking their limbs free of crusted snow, they rose grumbling at her command. "We are the dead in Niflhel. Poor creatures of a passing day, a shadow's dream lost in the spray of snowstorms. In Hel's domain, we sell our shields for crusts, our bright battle flames for meat. Hunger is her dish—our constant companion. Famine is her knife that doles out scant leavings. Belts cleave to the backbone of those who withhold service. For sustenance, we fight."

Hel waved a pale arm over the ragged army formed up in lines too numerous to count, the dead of the ages drawn up before their cold mistress. "Here, father, is your revenge."

Jotunheim Prepares

Short day. Long night. In Jotunheim the mighty rock dwellers hunker about the eldskáli, warming themselves beside the fire. Sinister shadows slide withershins across the walls, a parade of mottled light marching contrary to the path of the sun. With muted voices, they prepare.

Whetstones sing along bright metal edges. Sharp points with wicked barbs are fitted to stout shafts of ash. Drawknives scrape the length of solid oak logs to shape clubs with thick heads and knurled handles. Hammers ring on the anvil raising sparks from the burning points of spearheads. They chant a song to pace their grim work, words muttered beneath their breath that puffs white in the air despite the fire's warmth.

> "A warrior must square himself to strike,
> weapon raised high overhead,
> back bent for the blow,
> to quicken the rush of air and blood.
>
> Grown strong from a stout oak,
> its head fire-singed to hardness,
> eager and ready in my hand
> I raise the shatterer of many skulls.
> The Einherjar's bane, the Æsir's foe,
> and the Jotun's wooden defense.
> While I live, helm crusher shall meet out death
> to the followers of Bölverkr.
>
> With a bright blade, I reap the harvest of battle.
> Hew the tall grasses from the field.
> Bust the over ripe grain from the stalk.
> Bathe the ground in wound dew.
>
> A desperate fight lies before us.
> The storm of war draws near.
> The host of Asgard shows a bold front,
> but we laugh and sharpen spears.
> They'll not see our backs today."

Hrym called out from his high seat at the head of the warrior's table. "There is one in this great hall whose mere presence fills me with joy. A dark-haired cousin who quickens springtime in my heart. She roams through my mind, giving me little rest night or day. There she strolls by in stately garb. Where wend you, Hlin of the forearm's fire? Never have you appeared in such splendor. To what occasion do you attend?"

"What occasion?" The maiden paused, twisting a long lock of her black hair around her fingers, as she considered Hrym. "Why, the final occasion, of course. With our lands desolated by the loss of kin, you rush off to join them, eager to lead our people into an orgy of death."

Hrym held out his hand palm up. "The hawk circles with the raven, leaving me no choice; fate drives me to its purpose. It is with a heavy heart that I turn from your light, for never again will I see such beauty."

The maiden lifted her gaze to the heavens. "This vow I make to those gathered here." The preparations for war stopped, as all turned in their seats to face the maiden that they might hear her words. "A high cairn I'll heave up for the haunters of this dark den. A restful howe that I may visit day or night to speak with those who leave tonight and do not return."

Hrym pressed a hand to his chest. "It is with much sorrow that I turn aside my face. Let the bones of Ymir keep you safe beneath the Everglow."

The maiden bowed her head to Hrym then turned away, tears streaking her cheeks as she continued her walk. "In death, you will forget those left behind, but we will always remember you."

Gathering of the Gods

All together the Æsir came in council, to meet beneath the great tree, twelve to decide, the rest to discuss, how to proceed into the twilight. All the heroes of the Æsir and Vanir shuffled beneath the crouching wolf and hovering eagle, leaning their bright shields in clear spaces against the walls, brushing past dangling tapestries as they sought out familiar faces. At this final Husthing there is a throng grown numerous from all time.

They crowded together in the great hall, the garth of Odin. In the center of the room the Most High arranged himself on the tallest seat. Just-as-High took his place beside. Next High sat opposite the two. On a bench below, eight of the twelve arranged themselves in a silent row. The remaining host filled benches that lined both sides of the central fire.

Odin glanced across the sea of faces jostling for position. The growl of their voices was as the lashing of a heavy rain whipped by the wind. "Are we all gathered? I see an empty seat on the council bench." He craned his neck looking over the restless waves of heads, some with helmets, some uncovered with heavy locks tied back, some completely shorn of hair. "Who is missing?"

The deep voice of Heimdall rolled from the crowd, briefly drowning out the rumble of nervous chatter. "We wait on the strong guarder. You sent your ravens. They should have reached him by now."

Odin relaxed back in his seat. "Then we will wait a while longer." He took up his cup of wine while others took the opportunity to snap their fingers for refills. "I know my son; he will waste little time once receiving my command." He whispered into his cup, his words silent save for the ripples on the wine surface. "But we cannot wait long."

———·———

Word reached Thor in the far hills where he often journeyed to battle trolls, the urgent call of Hugin and Munin to return to final council in Asgard. The son of Hlodyn splashed across the Ifing to Ull's hall. After harnessing his goats to his cart, he called Thjalfi to his side. "The appointed time has arrived. Hang on." With a snap of the reins, the cart jerked forward. "We travel with all haste to Valhalla."

With a snap of the reins the cart bucked along a perilous path. Thjalfi clung to Veor's wide belt as the storm god drove his goats to greater speed. The landscape became a blur as the cart streaked across the hills, its wheel barely touching the ground. "Hold tight," he shouted to his companion. "We approach Asgard. There will be a little bump."

Roaring thunder shook the Æsir halls as they lurched through Valgrind. Hauling back on the right rein, Thor banked the cart sharply, momentarily tipping it up on two wheels and eliciting a piercing wail from his passenger. It settled back with a hard thump as they drew to a halt before Valhalla.

Thjalfi stumbled from the cart, fighting to catch his breath, while Thor brushed past him, hurrying beneath the wolf and eagle that looked down from their perch in seeming disapproval of his tardiness.

Odin called out as his son burst into the hall: "You run late as you often do. Today is not a forgiving time. We ready ourselves to deliberate that which must be done that our days will be remembered."

Thor took his seat among the twelve, gulped down a mug of proffered ale, then gestured for a refill. "I came as swiftly as allowed. The rivers were unruly, the pull of their currents strong, but only the Kerlaugs offered danger. Why it was by the hair of—."

Odin waved a hand, interrupting the account. Thor's teeth snapped shut with an audible clack. "We have no time for tales of your journey." Odin ignored the dangerous flashing of his son's eyes as he made ready to address the gathering. "There is much of importance to discuss."

The Father of Armies turned to the gathered host. His voice swelled to fill the hall, a voice well used to command. The gathering fell silent at his words. "The withered fir tree that stands alone on a rocky hill, neither bark nor needles protect it as the winds of time wear it down. So, it is with forgotten gods. Why should we live? What do we purchase by existing past our time?"

Thor set down his mug then wiped the back of his hand across his mouth. "As kin—blood and adopted—we are duty-bound to constrain the enemies of the Æsir, to protect the lives of men and gods. When such a challenge arises, no matter the age or the coin already paid, what else is important, save our honor? I say it is better to die keeping our oaths with honor intact, bravely facing the fear that will take us, than cringing in some corner awaiting the same fate."

The Alfodur nodded, approval reflecting from his face. "As ever, my son speaks plainly, his words honed with the sharp edge of truth. Today, I follow his lead. I speak not as one who would entangle with words or incite others to strife, but as one who holds our honor dear. I stand before you, offering good counsel to benefit all."

All eyes followed him as he stepped down from the high seat. Legs were drawn back, feet tucked beneath the benches to clear a path as he paced before the gathering. "We come to a great point in our existence, the time to honor the sacred oaths given at Idavoll long ago. Always we have held our pledges close, even when we were struck from the temples in Trondheim, our great oaks felled across the lands, our followers slain, our rites purged from the homes of men to be forgotten in the dust of ages. Even when it seemed our entire world had turned against us, yes, even then we held them dear.

True, it is hard to remember or even care what happens next to the race of men—those who have forgotten us—or to the fate of the nine worlds. We have fought so long to clear the way, the why of our actions has dimmed, a faded memory of brighter days. All that remains is the purpose of Skuld to direct what we must do."

An expectant stillness filled the air, the hushed excitement of anticipation broken by the rustle of nervous feet and an occasional muffled cough. Odin raised his hand. All faces turned to follow, some the finger pointing to the carved beams high overhead, others the burning of his eye. "Now I speak words, those weightiest of all, but we descendants of Bor have always held insight into such things. Calm we were. Smoothly ran our realm. Each Æsir, each Vanir, each Einherjar untroubled. Now the haughty flame of Muspellsheim threatens us all. From Hlidskialf I have seen his relentless advance through Midgard. Even now his fires lick at the bridgehead of Bifrost."

Odin nodded his head, scanning the crowd as alarmed murmurs raced from lip to lip. "The day is sprung. The golden cock's clear voice calls from on high. Not for ale or the converse of an evening table, but for the hard clash of the shield storm, for the hard sport of Hild!"

He paused, letting his gaze rove over the gathering as the import of his words made their mark. Eyes sparkled, some with excitement, others in apprehension, but no one looked away or attempted to leave the hall. "I have held counsel with Mimir's head. His words cut cold. This is no time for peace or for delay. The final day is upon us. The relentless spiraling of fortune's course would have us take up hard-edged weapons to tame the wolf's hunger and sate the raven's thirst."

With a light shrug he stumped back to his seat. "There is nothing else to do. We have no other choice. Honor demands we protect that which we created. True enough our numbers grow; each day sees a new harvest from the fields of battle, but not enough for head-to-head victory. We must take our triumph elsewhere. Our honor will not be celebrated by success, but by how we face defeat. That we must see this through is well known to all. And if it is to be done," all eyes followed him as he swung about, "then it must be done with hardihood and daring!"

Odin thumped his chest with his fist, three times thumped his chest, rocking the crowd with each blow. "Pleased we are to bask in the Valkyrie's warm wind. Blood-spattered, their eyes turned forward, the brave eagerly deal out death with a strong arm. This day many foemen will howl amid the harsh storm of spears!"

The crowd grew restless at the direct speech. Mugs were drained of their contents, but few throats were cleared of dryness. Many looked about seeking refills. Bragi banged his mug on the table. "Where are the war maidens who wait on the Einherjar at table? Is there no one to pour ale? Odrerir's mead streams readily from my lips, but a parched throat dams the flow."

Vali sipped at his own drink, wetting his mustache in the liquid that lapped at the rim of his mug. "Have you forgotten how to serve yourself at bench? It is typical, this helplessness. The aged oftentimes wander in their thoughts as well as their abilities."

Bragi flipped his beard at Vali. "You are not so young yourself to scoff at others for being old. Without Idun's apples, we should all be withered to dust ages ago."

"My Valkyrie are in the field as their duty demands." Odin's voice carried across the crowd to reach Bragi's ears; irritation plain in its tone. "The days shorten, and conflicts increase. All their time is spent in the storm of battle choosing the honorable slain." He jerked his chin at the pitchers of ale making their rounds. "Serve yourself. They have no time to wait your table."

Bragi jerked back at the reprimand. Nodding at the Father of Armies, he raised his empty mug in salute. "Then tonight I'll take my ale from this earthenware cup filled to the brim by my own hand. Its taste on my lips will remind me of the clay from which I came and to which I will return. Know, I proudly face death as does a farmer returning to the embrace of tilled earth, calmly as if to his home."

Long locks plaited in a warrior's braid, tied back to keep them from the string of a drawn yew, rustled about wide shoulders as Vali leaned back, sipping his mead. "You drink overmuch for one who readies for battle. You'll need your wits to guide you tomorrow. Not a mind wrapped in the soft wings of the heron of forgetfulness. Perhaps you fear that which all must eventually face?"

The bard filled his mug from a pitcher passed down the board, topping it off so liquid dribbled over the rim to form a puddle on the table. He smacked his lips then took a long swallow. "Life for all the bitter-faced enemies of pleasure is not really life, but sorrow that steals life even as it is lived. To live such a half-life is what I dread, not the chill embrace of death." He tipped back his mug filling his mouth, then swished the contents around in his cheeks, savoring the flavor, before letting it roll down his throat. "Death is a debt we all must pay no matter how long its embrace is stayed. None can know if they will live to see Night's arrival. No amount of wisdom imparts that knowledge. So, I choose to be happy, drink hearty, and know each moment as my own. The rest I leave to Urd's good grace."

"Already you speak as one deep in his cups, his words braced with the boastful strength of ale." Vali sneered, pointing at the puddle forming under Bragi's mug. "See how you spill this excellent mead. A shaky hand often belies a fear-filled mind."

Bragi took another long draught, then sucked the residual from his mustache. He banged his mug down on the table. "Clear head or no," he leaned forward leading with his chin, "you'll not find me lagging behind afraid to face the full brunt of the storm. I do not dread the cresting wave that capsizes a ship nor the flame of Surt's embers, nearly as much as the man who sips his drink so that he can better remind all later exactly what everyone said."

Vali tapped a forefinger against his brow. "A clear head is not a hardship. A mind dulled by drink is more hindrance than help in a fight. It is often the refuge of doubtful courage."

Bristling at the words, Bragi jerked himself upright, grabbing at the bench edge to steady himself. "You accuse me of lacking courage! Were we outside just as we are now inside I'd have your head spit on my blade!"

Vali's hand slipped to the knife strapped at his waist. He stared evenly at the eloquent voice swaying in his seat across the table. "I recognize this retort. Perhaps Loki was not far off in his assessment.

Ever the Sanga svitiri, never the Sanga hroeriri. In a fight, you often lag to the rear, delivering timid strokes with weapons warily held. Fearful of attack from before and behind, hardly do you dare feed a crow."

With stern voice Odin called out from his high seat. The gathering hushed as he slammed his fist on the table. "Enough of this bickering! There is chastisement enough for all. We should all get along. Our breath is better spent on planning, rather than withering our ranks with infighting. Few get to choose their end, let alone sacrifice for a noble cause. What we face doesn't call for argument, but for celebration!"

Odin turned to the watchman of the gods, the white god Heimdall, seated nearby. "Have you retrieved the Gjallarhorn from its place among the roots of Yggdrasil?"

Heimdall shook his head, his golden teeth flashing in reply. "I received the order from your ravens but thought to assure myself the call was not garbled in the delivery. The horn is not something I retrieve on a whim. Its sound, full of dire threatening, is not one I desire to hear more than once in my life. Now having received the order directly from your own lips, I will spare no effort to further it. None need bring my kinsman's head to rouse my actions. At your urging, I take the forefront. It isn't always safest to be in the rear."

He stood, draining the last dregs from his mug. "I race now to Hoddmimir's wood, where I will retrieve the Horn Resounding from its niche beneath the showery falls of Fjolnir's pledge."

With a quick tug, he cinched his sword belt tight at his waist. "From its dew, what sacred wisdom will I gain, come at these final moments of calm, when my lips purse and the great horn swallows the wind puffed out from my breast to announce the final battle?"

Strategy Session

In council, they discussed strategies of who should lead different forces, of what standards to bear before the massed ranks. The formations to employ: when attacking the front, when worrying the flank, when regrouping. Free license was given to the Einherjar to arrange their lines as they saw fit, those hardy warriors who well knew the language of battle. The gods set themselves to lead.

"We know our enemies," Odin thundered. "Their arrival is foretold. The hordes from Niflhel are thieves and oath breakers, nothing more than a rabble of condemned cowards. Commanded by the scourge of our clan they are battle fodder; we need not fear their gormless stare.

We all know what to expect from the children of Loki: no quarter asked, and none given. There is no love lost between us." Thor brooded into the depths of his cup recalling his hand in their fate while Tyr shook the stump of his right wrist in the air.

"Now, truth be told, the etins have enjoyed some success. They have proven many times they have the temperament for wielding weapons to good effect. We will need to carefully watch their lines." A muttering of 'Ayes' circled the hall, the loudest from Thor who perked up at the naming of his old foes.

"I expect no good from Surt's followers. They have done much scathe in Midgard, devastating the lands and works of men. Of fire, we can be certain, of their resoluteness assured. Foreordained to sweep all before them, they will throw themselves recklessly into the fray. Overconfident of their triumph, they will not consider the cost."

Tyr raised his one good hand for attention, eager that his concerns be heard. "And where will the elves stand? Can we count on the dwarves? Sneaky and contrary creatures all, but are they with us or against us? The time is now when all must stand together or everything we hold dear is lost."

Odin glanced at his feet, then lifted his eye to take in the council. "It is true they have no love for us, but neither have they love for the etins. I fear we all have sorely abused their services far too long to warrant their affection. They know the dark offers little protection from the elemental burn of Surt's embrace. Their only hope is to help drain the host of Muspellsheim so that some portion of their folk will survive.

The dwarves have much on hand. Clever craftsmen well steeped in ancient Lore, and oh so nimble with the making of weapons, they have stockpiled for just this event. Over the march of years, they have become effective warriors, more than capable in the tight clinch of battle.

The sons of Mimir have slept these long ages but are bound to awaken at the call of the Gjallarhorn. Its sound will cut across the nine worlds, rousing all to fight or flight. They will take their place on the walls of Hvergelmir amid the ranks of their kin.

Be assured that the Varinian will protect their own. If Mundilfari's children can reach their fortress alive, they will find safety behind its walls. No enemy will pass the gates while the Varinian stand.

The Dark Elves can only fight in darkness, for in sunlight they turn to stone. In truth, they are an unknown, but I am certain they will join the dwarves in the shadowy lands of Nidaveller. The citadel of Hvergelmir can use their cunning. Courageous when the occasion calls, they well know the deep caverns, their stone warrens, their treacherous pitfalls. A rockslide here, a cave-in there, a fissure gaping wide to snare the foot or break the leg, even the small can be effective in battle.

Should the Light Elves join in the fray, friend and foe alike run the risk of blindness, so bright is their glow. They are of no use in the worlds below; their light would dazzle sunblind eyes accustomed to the dimness of caverns. Still, I am certain some few will insist on joining the fight above. Everyone must be prepared to shield their eyes against any unexpected flash."

Tyr slapped his one hand flat against his chest. "Then we fight unaided." He nodded, grinning to everyone around. "I would have it no other way."

Raising his open hand, Odin ticked off weapons on his fingers. "Of weapons, we have many. The mighty gifts of Sindri and Volund: Mjollnir welded by Thor, my own spear Gungnir, and all the remainder of our godly weapons. Sadly, we will miss Freyr's slender inlaid blade, the great weapon crafted by Volund. It was an unfortunate day for us all when you bartered the clever sword to satisfy the urges of your loins."

Gray eyes turned to the Summer light. Freyr glanced about the hall, his eyes darting from chin to chin, then stared hard at the goblet clutched in his hands as the Father of Armies continued. "Of Midgard weapons, we have the best. From the Regin-sharp edge of Gram to the enchanted metal of Skofnung. The fire-hardened lengths of Adder, Long, Skrymir, Hviting, and Ulfberh+T. The blood-hungry Dainslief, Maering, Vig, Skrep, Jokul's Gift, and all between. The blades wielded by famous warriors, the staunch fighters of the Einherjar."

Tyr stroked his chin, beaming a satisfied smile. "It is good we face this day as warriors should, shoulder to shoulder, shield locking shield, without the timorous whining of a clinging female."

The Alfodur turned a baleful eye to the grinning face of war. Tyr's lips faltered, then collapsed before the steady glare. "You speak of women as if they were weak. Only in the ignorance of my youth did I entertain such a notion. I have never encountered a woman incapable of strategy, heedless of honor, or unable to fight. Many are the Einherjar who boast breasts to suckle the young, their skill in warcraft the equal of any man."

Tyr stirred uneasily, his seat suddenly uncomfortable, as Odin's voice bore down. "My Valkyrie have been in every battle ever fought. Undaunted, unflinching, they have faced every foe. Many have fallen before their sure swift strike. Freyja would certainly take you to task for uttering such impudence, she whose robe has often been spattered with the red gore of battle." A light sneer flickered across Odin's lips, then was gone. "And Skadi would have already handed you your head."

Tyr stammered a reply to assuage the Alfodur's anger. "I-I-I only meant the enemy will think us weak for having women among our warriors."

Odin returned his gaze to the gathering, dismissing Tyr with a wave of his hand. "It does not matter what they think."

The Challenge

Raising Gungnir high above his head, the ancient one of the Æsir set his challenge before every member of the gathering. "The past is done. Today slips swiftly from our grasp. All that remains is tomorrow. It is a burden that weighs heavy on life. In youth, it opens eyes to endless possibilities. In middle age, it teaches the cautious need for preparation. In old age, it is an irksome friend, a constant visitor always at table whose departure is expected at any moment. But for we, age is a fancy and this knowledge is as nothing. It alights upon our shoulders like the spider's gossamer net, entangling us, drawing us into purpose."

As he shook his spear, light glinted from its wicked tip. The gathering swayed as all eyes followed the wavering light. "I call on all the valiant beings gathered here, you with ready skill in weapons for whom honor is your breath and courage your blood. What do you say? Will you fight?"

One by one they stepped forward, those never known to show their backs to an enemy, the merciless foes of hollow-hearted speech and faint action.

———·———

The son of Fjorgyn stepped forward, his fierce eyes glittered from beneath heavy knit brows. Thunder rumbled outside the hall, ringing the shingles, as he cleared his throat to speak. "I am called Asa-Thor, son of Odin and Hlodyn. My strength is that of earth and storm. My mind that of a trustworthy friend."

Taking a deep breath, he thumped his chest with a massive fist, the deep thuds echoing through the hall. Those closest flinched away as the air around Thor crackled with bright swirling sparks that seemed to shower from his head. "By the power of my own hand, I have protected our home and the homes of men throughout the ages. Flight-shy in battle, I hold the line against all the enemies of my clan, from ogres to trolls, even the bitter cold of frost giants. I have never been afraid to speak my mind. Long ago my tongue was forged on the harsh anvil of truth. When I speak, what flies up, even if it be a spark, carries weight.

Today we face the greatest of all challenges, the final strife between powerful foes, a battle storm from which we will not return. Its raging flood even now catches us in its grip. Though many would ignore the din of rising waters, we cannot escape their pull. Honor bids us face the bloody torrent. I stand before you, alone if fate decrees, head held high, ready to give challenge."

———·———

Freyr pushed himself to his feet, scraping back the bench until he stood with head bowed before the gathering. Everyone hushed to listen as he spoke to his feet. "I am sorry that the price of my love has disappointed everyone. It is true the smart blade would be most welcome on this of all days. Still my arm is strong. With another blade, I gladly face any foe, no matter how powerful they might be."

As he spoke, he lifted his chin until he gazed unflinching into the eyes of those who pressed close to hear him speak. With every breath, his voice grew in volume until none could doubt his words. "With enemies, I have traded blow for blow, given harsh words for insult, dealt a sharp edge for lies. Many have fallen by the strength of my hand. As war leader, I wielded my might for the benefit of all. When the rage of bloody action passed, I stood as calm as the dead about my feet."

Flipping open his robe, he stood bare chested before the crowd, fists planted on hips. "I stand before you ready as ever to lay down my life for those I swore to protect long ago. More than the oaths I've given, I stand eager to collect recompense from the thurs for harsh treatment at their hands when I was young. Their payment will be the bloody bodies of their kin laid out before me row on row. Though I know my fate, I will take the lives of many before I face Urd's grim justice."

———————

Tyr laughed and drew his blade. Holding it high with his one good hand, he turned slowly to take in the entire gathering. "Always I stand ready to fight in a just cause, my left hand eager to strike the moment it is called upon.

Boldly, I pledged my right hand in the mouth of the great wolf when none other of the Æsir dared. Great honor I won that day for my courage, while the wolf won a sour stomach.

Now we are asked to face a foe greater than any we have ever encountered. An honorable death awaits those brave enough to stand firm before the onslaught. Never, in all the nine worlds, would I dream of running from such a fight. For the oaths I freely gave when accepted as kin into this clan, and to the same honor that cost me my hand, I pledge my life."

His blade whistled as he whipped it in a circle over his head. "Eagerly, my hand grips this blade held to the fore whose sturdy edge has frustrated many foes. More yet will travel the red road from its swift fall guided by my strong arm."

———————

Magni and Modi rose together to stand brave and courageous before the assembled gods. With heavy, defiant brows like their father, their chins thrust forward, eyes eager for glory; none doubted their intent to be in the front lines.

Magni spoke first to the gathering, letting his voice ring out bravely before the assembled gods. "As a child, I lifted Hrungnir's limb from my father when none other among our kin could move it, such is the gift of my strength that I gladly offer to those in need."

Then Modi spoke from beside his brother, casting his daring gaze about the crowd, turning side to side as he declared his intent that all would know his voice. "Since the early days of my youth, I have faced giant and storm without flinching. Nothing, neither fire nor enemy arrayed, could be so terrible as to make me afraid."

Together the brothers spoke with united voice. "This challenge we gladly accept to assure our kin that nothing daunts our stout hearts nor weakens our strong arms by its opposition. This day we expose monsters to our blows. By pledges made on ancient battlefields we link sword, spear, and shield with the strong arms of stalwart comrades. Together we fight this greatest of all battles, wining honor by the palm of war hard pressed by our hands."

Ull rocked to his feet, shifted his quiver of arrows to one side and leaned heavily on his bow. "My father was Orvandel, known across the nine worlds as an archer of unsurpassed skill. A trusted comrade of Thor, when he died the Æsir adopted me as one of their own. From them I learned courage. From my stepfather, Fjorgyn's celebrated son, I learned honor. But from my true father, I learned integrity and inherited his skill with the bent yew.

Long ago I pledged my life to my new family, placing my mighty bow at their service. That pledge rings as true today as when the words first left my lips. This battle will see me eager, my weapons ready. I've stored sharp quills enough to last a full day. When my bow tires, my store of arrows exhausted, my blade will be ready in hand. I'll darken the plain with the bodies of our foes."

Stood the great arbiter, Forseti, son of Baldur. He gazed silently about the crowd, waiting calmly until all hushed to hear his words. "Many are those who attend only what is seemly and deafen their ears to that which embarrasses or bears anguish. But in times of crisis every truth is better unveiled, as a bride's face to her husband on their wedding night.

Once men constructed temples in our honor, sacred howes where the silver ring of pledges rested on the pedestal of honor beside the sacrificial bowl. Many offerings were made on those stones; goods, grains, animals, even at times, the lives of men. Blood flowed across the altar, while smoke carried their prayers aloft. We were honored then, held in high esteem across the nine worlds. Our advice was sought on all matters, our names invoked when pledges were freely given, and we received grateful sacrifices in tribute.

Now the stain of blood has long faded from the stone of the judgment circle. No longer are Laut bowls passed in our honor, no remembrance drinks taken. Little scot do we collect in these lean times.

We, who were young at the dawn of time, are reduced to shadows and, like shadows, have been cast out in the light of a new day. When men, done with the rights of the raven gods, changed their allegiance to the promises of others, they tossed us aside, reviled, forgotten."

Forseti glared unblinking about the gathering until the eyes of others looked away. He sneered and slammed his cup on the table. Many winced at the sound. "Protectors of men? Protect those who spurned us for other gods and now blame them for all their troubles just as they blamed us when we were in favor? Protect those ever eager to place blame on others, when it has always been themselves who, through overreaching arrogance, propagate their own woes?" He paused to let his case take hold. "Why not look out for our own and let the dross of Midgard perish in the coming fire?"

The hall filled with loud voices raised in reply. Some howled in objection, while others cheered back in support. Odin lifted his hand to silence the outcry. "It is true that many have turned to ill will, but such is the pressure of suffering. Even a loved house dog—injured and in pain—will snap with bared teeth at his master's helping hand."

Forseti raised his hand to make argument. "True, but even a house dog can turn wild. Scant few would extend a hand to help such an unpredictable animal lest they suffer the same fate as Tyr when he dared his hand in the jaws of the Fenris wolf. A wolf, I remind you, who was raised among us as kin."

Shifting in his seat, Odin lifted his cup. He turned it slowly, pondering its lip. "Men are not the Fenris wolf. They are born of the gifts we bestowed. Fenris was not. Each holds true to their nature." Forseti frowned as the eyes of the crowd danced between the two. "We can expect a greater fellowship from men. Many times, we have been welcomed as honored guests in homes that knew nothing of us. We visit them to this day, though not as often." Odin took a long drink then set his cup carefully to one side. "We have our original pledge," he eyed the arbiter, "freely given, if you recall. So, too, we owe a debt to those among men who still welcome us into their home."

Forseti sat down, tugging his robe around to be more comfortable. "Do not think you have convinced me," he shook his head, "of my duty to men. I am enraged at this call! But sooner would I cut out my own eyes than endure the dishonor of breaking a freely given oath. That is not the only reason I acquiesce. I still owe Loki for my father's fall. Honor as an avenging son requires that I join this battle.

Since coming of age, I've held the role of arbitrator, responsible for dispensing justice among disputing opponents. In so doing I learned a bitter truth; force and honor must rule the world, not opinion and fear. For without force and honor, justice, law, liberty, even rights are phantom notions, good only to dazzle gullible minds.

To back away from this challenge would diminish my existence and discredit all I have achieved in an instant. And though my blood boils at the dishonor shown us by men, I would never abandon my family to peril. I stand today, head held high, ready to lay down my life for my kin."

———————

Leaning forward, Skirnir banged his fist sharply on the table. Cups leapt from their places, spilling their contents onto the rushes scattered about the floor. The great warrior pushed himself to his feet, his hand raised to speak. "I call on all to hear my voice. Long I have held the courage of hosts in my heart. Honor has always held a place close to my breast, an invincible shield that no weapon could breach.

Many names I have held: Svipdag, Odd, Hermod, and now Skirnir. Named for those duties I've embraced, each fitting for that time in my life.

As a man, I braved stalwart foes—many are the battle lines broken by the strength of my arm. Alone, I faced the terrors of the nine worlds to single-handedly retrieve Freyja from her captivity in the Howler's hall. With a weapon of great power, one feared by the very gods, I defeated in single combat the guard of the Æsir, its bright edge leading me to victory over ranks of foemen across the nine worlds. For the right to a bride unsurpassed in beauty, superior to all in character, I gave over that very weapon into the hands of newfound kin.

In the halls of the Æsir, I have held the positions of warrior, messenger, and trusted confidant. Unflinching, I have performed many perilous tasks for the glory of my adopted kin. I have never shirked a bold challenge or backed away from a hazardous adventure. Eager always for the dangerous mission, I am willing before all others. When called, I retrieved the silken fetter, which has held the Fenris wolf these long years. For the sake of Baldur, I traveled dark roads through the nine worlds and faced the barren gaze of Hel in her grim, ice-choked hall. For Freyr, I braved alone the court of Gymir, stood firm before the Jotun's menace, and defied the hateful glare of Angrboda to win him a bride.

In war, no enemy has ever seen my back. Battle-scarred, my wounds are always in front. With my byrnie cinched tight, I am always first in the fray as I will be tomorrow."

He grinned and thumped his chest, the steady heartbeat of an undaunted warrior. "Freely, I agree to perish again in honorable struggle. None will stop me from taking my place among the ranks of valiant gods."

————·————

Leaping to his feet, Vali slapped the flat of his blade hard across his chest, rasping its edge along the iron rings of his byrnie. "I am the son of Rind by Odin. Conceived for vengeance, I brought down my brother's slayer when but an infant fresh from my mother's womb."

He swept his blade in a wide arc making those nearby, dodge back, cursing under their breath. "My words I keep brief. I hold to my birth purpose, to uphold the integrity of my family and make miserable the lives of our enemies. So, I dedicate myself to this battle.

Before all, I make this pledge. Not the sting of feathered darts driven by a strong bent yew, the harsh thrust of an iron tipped spear, or the crushing blow of a head-heavy mace will account for the rivers of blood destined to sweep across the wind-swept battle plain. It will be the sharp blows from my keen-edged blade wielded by my strong arm as I wade through the ranks of enemies, beating them down one after another, until the earth runs red and I stand in bold challenge gripping the wet hilt of my ready blade."

———————

Vidar the son of Gríd, tapped his boots, heel-toe, heel-toe, in a steady rhythm of pulsing blood. The silent god, hater of garrulous speech, tipped his head in assent. "We gain nothing reflecting on the past, save what service it might provide in facing the present. It is not right to let the scourge of wood consume unchallenged that which we have nurtured throughout time. We must brave what lies ahead with what is ours today, holding fast to the sacred honor we have carried across the long ages."

Shadows flit across the gathering, a rustling of dark wings. All eyes turned to follow their flight as Hugin and Munin fluttered to rest on Sigfodur's shoulders. He cocked an ear first to one then the other, nodding his head at the raven's speech, then turned his attention back to the crowd as Bragi stepped forward.

———————

Bragi stood before the gods, took a sip from his mug to clear his throat that his words would ring true, not garbled with the phlegm of age. "By calling, I decreed for myself years of hard labor laced with sorrow. With anguished tears streaming down my cheeks I've ripped clean, flawless verses from my breast. But for some time now I've found it difficult to compose new works. Thoughts are born, with verses forming tier on tier, only to disappear as a shallow puddle baked by the sun shrinks away, forgotten forever.

Once our stories cradled the essence of life. Passed down from generation to generation, they brought focus to the years; their telling gave direction to the lives of men. Now the meaning of our stories fade from memory as carvings on a rock are worn down by the constant press of elements, the stone face returned to a smooth unblemished surface, the graven images vanished as if they never were.

To know the end is to wish never to have been born, never to see the blood-red elf-disk rise above etin home or set beneath the white crests of ocean waves. But once born, why hurry to the grave's cold embrace? There is time enough for the severe table of death when the skein of our life ends.

Long ago I wed the Hlin of gossamer veils. We played in the headlands of the forearm's fire and later beneath her apple trees paired as swans in season. Our days were restless like mountain winds rushing through a stand of birch trees. Everyone lives by their desires; we were no different. Our kissed lips lost no savor, but like the moon were renewed each night, eager to find the other the next day. Together, we enjoyed the pulse-quickening arrival of spring, basked in the warm sunny days of summer, and delighted in the ripening harvests of fall. Gratefully, we donned the cold cloak of winter that draws friends and family near.

In our youth, we knew we would never die, that sickness and decrepit old age were mere phantasms easily warded off by Idun's golden apples. Fools we were. Fools we are.

Ours is the tragedy of birch leaves, long drained of spring's bloom, blown from their tenuous hold by the autumn wind, fluttering to the ground, forgotten beneath the debris of passing seasons.

But, too, like a leaf, wrapped in dreams of summer, that has steadfastly refused to fall at season's end, and now in winter's gale blindly clings to the tree limb, so, too, I have let my attention drift to fond memories of days long past and grown lax in attending to the final duties of existence.

Dead, I stand ready to renounce death, for never have I been so attached to life. My hand clenched tight on the hilt of my good blade throbs with each ragged beat of my heart.

Dead, my lips are quiet, but never have I talked so much about the future nor railed against the lost moments of the past. Never have I hated silence as I do now.

Dead, I stand immobile, but never have I been so in love with movement, the long low strides of lean limbs shifting from place-to-place, arms outstretched to embrace the world.

Dead, my breath is stilled, but never have I so savored the sharp delight of clean crisp air filling my chest, the fragrance of the earth, the trees, the heady aroma of men and beasts.

Dead, my ears grasp only silence, but never have I so enjoyed the laughter of my fellows, the sound of wind in the trees, the rush of waters flowing along their course, the call of birds as they wing through the sky.

Dead, I've no need for a skald's tongue, but hurriedly I create forms that collide to create wondrous new shapes, the words spilling from my lips without thought.

Dead, I am no longer hungry, but food and drink pass across my palette, their savory flavors, and intoxicating aromas so intense that I cannot image a second death.

Dead, I am so very busy, much busier than when life stretched its endless years before me, and I held no concern for the grave.

Dead, I yearn for love's warm embrace. Would that I could clasp my beloved; without her no full day under the vault of Ymir is easy.

Dead, I succumb to the inevitability of death. Unable to stop the flow of tragic events, I look forward to the end of this ache.

But enough lament. The time for poetry is past. I neither boast nor mourn with drooping head heartfelt companions and hated foes long since turned to dust. This day comes as no surprise. Only a blind fool would say it so. The portents have been building. Now the final signs have become clear.

If my beloved Idun enquires for me, tell her I boldly face that which we all must face, that which I have put off for eons in her embrace, and to seek me out on the glittering plains."

Assemble the Heroes

Wave upon wave of Einherjar heed the Alfodur's summons, swarming as bees to the hive of the great hall, wading in from the practice fields, staggering from wounds that heal as they walk, sheathing the fires of Odin at their waist before passing beneath the crouching wolf and hovering eagle.

Geri and Freki bay welcome as they take their accustomed places at bench. Tempered oaks of battle jostle about the table, their byrnies ringing out with the battle song of heroes. Shouts echo among the high beams. Veterans' laugh, relieved the time has arrived. New arrivals grumble, wishing it were yet far away. Ever the last to arrive, but always faithful, the Hjadnings rumble into the great hall, merging their stormy volume with the already raucous throng.

The shield-thatched hall soon glitters with armaments, its broad beams knotted with boar-tusked helmets, its benches draped with mail coats, its walls adorned with sturdy weapons. Painted shields, bosses gleaming, their thick broad wood rimmed with iron, are stacked in neat piles along the sides of the hall. Groves of ash sprout in corners, a sturdy forest of iron-tipped spears; the weapons of warriors. Along the walls hard-honed, inlaid swords forged by the smith's hammer, their battle-proven edges nicked from harsh blows, jostle with clusters of maces and sharp-edged axes. Grieves hang on wall pegs alongside shining metal breastplates, worn byrnies of studded leather, and vests of light, cleverly woven fiber that keeps sharp edges from biting.

War gear of all designs lean in neat pyramids about the floor. In Odin's name, not a scrap of equipment is untended. Cleaned, polished, all stand ready now that the final battle is near.

Hunched over, darting about the kitchen, Audhrimnir toils over this final feast; the fire-sooted cook curses with the effort to feed such a multitude. The arriving host stretches the limits of Eldhrimnir's providence, the black pot filled with Saehrímnir's eternal sacrifice. Savory smells fill the air. The anticipation of rumbling bellies challenges the volume of laughter and conversation.

Taking direction from the Alfodur, the cook of Valhalla blends the juice of Idun's apples with the bounty of Heidrun. Served up in a round of earthen mugs, the hungry crew eagerly quaffs the drink. The hydromel, now spiked with the vigor of youth, is as refreshing as ever; the strength conveyed will outlast the coming conflict.

Geri and Freki sit at attention beside the seat of Odin. With slavering jaws, they feast from the plate of the battle-skilled father of armies. Eyes bright, ears pricked to every sound, they follow the gathering with rapt attention, eager to share the Æsir fate, their long watch at an end.

Hugin and Munin bob about Odin's broad shoulders, their darting black eyes tracking the currents of boisterous warriors bustling among the benches. At dawn, they will rejoin their flock, their penetrating sight not needed to spy out the well-known terrain.

The great doors beneath the eagle and wolf swing wide. Into the hall march the Choosers of the Slain, those warrior maids sent by Odin to watch over every battle. Freshly returned from the field of valor, Brynhild leads a trailing troop into the hall, a culling of ten score from recent Midgard battles.

At a beckoning wave from the Father of Armies, the bright-helmed war maiden stepped forward, her corselet reflecting the fire of the linden in shimmering waves about the hall. When she stopped before his seat the Alfodur nodded for her to report. "We traveled the westerly road down through the green realms, then up across Bil's way to bring this fylki to Valhalla—a double count of fallen oaks. Freyja declined her choosing. Why bother when all are destined for greatness on the morrow."

Odin shifted his gaze over the troop noting the lines of weary determination that marked the nearest faces. "This tough bundle of battle rods is smaller than the last you selected from the wolf's feast."

Brynhild's shrug sent flame rippling across her golden byrnie. "It has been this way for the last centuries. As battles become less personal and warriors shun the eyes of their foe, the worthy become ever fewer. Until recently, armies were destroyed from afar without ever coming into contact. It was difficult to find the skirmishes that permit warriors to distinguish themselves on the field."

Odin dragged fingers through the tangles of his beard as he considered the fresh batch of warriors who stood rolling their eyes at the surroundings, many shaking their heads in disbelief. His one eye examined the ranks, squinted a moment at a face before moving on. Geri and Freki cast questioning looks at the Alfodur, ready to act at his slightest command. "Like chaff gleaned from a stubble field, the distance is great between stout shafts."

Brynhild nodded her head in agreement. "But now, as the end of days draws near, the battles have become more confined. With smaller bands confronting each other," she swept her arm toward the troop of recent recruits, "we have found many more to choose."

The Alfodur lifted his goblet to his lips and took a long, slow drink of wine. "Is this all you deemed worthy?" He jerked his chin at the ragtag host gazing bewildered around the gold-shingled hall. Liveries of olive drab, camouflage browns, desert tans, and winter grays, mingled with scarfed figures, some in dark robes, others in a ragtag assortment of brightly colored uniforms. The garments of commoners sprinkled through the troop attested to the informal nature of many battles.

"Yes," Brynhild glanced over her shoulder. "From those worthy, few accept." She jerked a chin at the milling crowd of new recruits. "Some, their battle done, outright refuse the honor of being chosen. They drag their feet, reluctant to follow, and instead turn their faces to the glittering plains of Niflheim. Others, even after their blessing is explained, continue battling with such personal wrath that it is difficult to determine if they are not actually followers of Surt. Then there are those who simply refuse to believe, hence are useless to our need. Many such we have left to find their own way along the red road."

The golden-haired Valkyrie smirked to herself. "Our only profit lies in their belligerence. Even Loki will find those who are twice damned to be difficult conscripts—unbelievers—impossible to manage."

Odin winced at the notion of leaving valiant warriors behind when the upcoming battle needed as many stalwart arms as possible. Still, he trusted the judgment of his Valkyrie. He shook the thought from his head. "And what of those who followed your lead?"

The lady of the helm waved her arm to encompass the troop. "Sturdy oaks all," her broad grin lit up the room, "very deadly with their own style of weapons. Though few are familiar with the ways of a long blade wielded by a strong arm, many are more than proficient with the stealthy use of a small blade. So, too, their combat training lends them to wielding, staff, spear, and mace to good effect."

The war father nodded as he took another swallow of wine. "Their own weapons will suffice while they hold. During the rage of battle, the dead gladly offer up their weapons to the need of those still standing. While they may encounter the unfamiliar, a warrior quickly learns to use what is at hand. When men match their strength in battle, it is often found that foremost is no one, and the weapon wielded means nothing."

Odin reached up, chucked the beak of Hugin then stroked the black head of Munin. The ravens turned their dark eyes on the bold Valkyrie who stood before them. "Have we enough?"

Brynhild glanced at the troop, some tentatively returning waves from familiar faces already seated, and shook her head. "No, but you knew that. We all knew it would be so. War father who charges foes in battle, we ride short of strong oaks."

Odin heaved a sigh. "It is too late in any case." He knuckled his one good eye while waving them toward the benches. "Let them take their place. You and your sisters are to remain here tonight. Tomorrow will see a different need of your services."

The warrior maiden started in disbelief. "But what of tonight's harvest of worthies?" She jerked a thumb at the throng gathered about the benches, laughing, making room for the new arrivals. "They shall know only their battle and naught else."

The wise head nodded. "Then in that they are blessed. The Norn's weave will decide their sorting. All they will know is the journey to judgment. Urd can handle that by herself. The blessed will see the glittering plains. Those deserving a second death will face Nidhogg on Corpse Strand."

The Warrior's Vow

"Einherjar be welcome!" The Alfodur's voice rang down from amid the rafters to boom over the gathered warriors. "Take ale and benches where you can. You will find only comrades here. Tonight, we feast as warriors should on the eve of the greatest battle."

Saehrímnir, the soot-black sacrificial boar, was presented on the board. The closest warriors placed a hand on the one whom daily offered his life for their repast. No greater courage or bravery could any man or god display.

The Alfodur lifted his goblet; reflections from the rim dazzling eyes with the fire of the Æsir. The mighty host raised their cups filled to the brim with amber mead, their bowls inscribed with loyalty. "By this oath cup," he shouted out to the warriors massed in the great hall, "we make pledge."

"Hail to the day! Hail to the sons of day! With gracious eyes, may you bestow honor on those gathered here! In hallowed stead, we stand in glorious company to chant this pledge on the sage's chair that none may doubt our intent to defy the embers of Muspellsheim.

This day there arrives on the threshold grievous actions to dam up the joy of etins and wring bitter tears from their eyes. The hour of wolves is upon us. Spears will be shaken. Shields splintered. The bright edges of eager blades will light the field. This is a warrior's day! A day of honor!"

The great hall rang from end-to-end with the shouts of valiant men and the barking of running dogs. When the cheers subsided, Odin continued. "We who sit here are fated to die far from this hall on Vigrid plain. No longer do we wait in anticipation for the challenge of our greatest foes. Already they descend upon us, destructive as the sea storm that crashes onto the rocky coast.

And though the waves of ocean ceaselessly lap at the headland, does the cliff fail to resist though it be worn away? I say, No! We who have endured through thousands of bloody afternoons, whose names are enough to set lances quivering, will not lay down our honor for fear of the flame.

Rise now from your seats! Send the goblets of warriors topped high with mead passing around the hall from hand to hand. Tonight, we give the oath of fraternity on the body of an honored foe, by the side of a mighty ship, the rim of a sturdy shield, the back of a powerful horse, and the keen edge of a strong blade.

Livestock dies, friends die, kinsmen die, the self also dies, but glory never dies for those able to achieve it. Let all who seek no truce with spears or old age be joyous in fighting. Heroes stand shoulder-to-shoulder, holding fast against any onslaught.

This battle ushers in a new world that the dust of man may survive. That this will happen, be assured, for what is pledged over ale must come true."

It began slowly; a soft tattoo of knuckles on board that grew to a rhythmic stamp... stamp... stamp of marching feet beneath the benches. Battle-roughened voices rose to call out their song.

"Warriors who shelter behind their shields
will never ride the Quivering way.
On fair paths tread heroes
unafraid to face the battle storm.

Bright helmed maidens ride the buffeting winds of war.
From the steaming slaughter fields
they choose only the bravest, only the best
to manage the halls of Asgard
and battle beside the airy gods
on Vigrid Plain at Ragnarök.

Call out Einherjar!
Shout out loudly to Heriar!
Let the Sigfodur hear your pledge!

Sitting alone, we grasp our strong sure blades,
we who in the flush of life
died defending our honor.
Gone are the spoils of Summer-lading.
Now we work to a higher cause.

Keen I am to wade into combat,
to face foes of no mean metal.
But until I fall or they,

torn down by the eagle's talon,
my heart will never cower,
my arm never fail in its trust.

So, sharpen the sword, grind the axe,
make ready the spear of war.
When a warrior of courage accepts the choice,
then what is there to regret.
Flesh quickly decays.
Deeds of honor live forever.

Better the Einherjar's promise
than to breathe one's last breath on a bed of straw,
faded away with old age,
manly pride shrunken like a lamb's tail,
useless as a dead man's ears.
Harsh are the lessons learned in the rage of the blood storm.
When you wield a sword, swing the sharpest.

When you draw a bow, pull the strongest.
When you use a spear, thrust the stoutest.
In battle stand among the foremost and never retreat.
Great warriors fight and die alone."

As the chant died away the Alfodur turned up his goblet onto the sacrifice, pouring red wine over the stripped carcass of Saehrímnir that lay spread across the table. "And now, with his last gift gratefully consumed, I give release to a long-honored foe."

With a roar the greatest of boars leapt to his feet, whole again in body and mind. His large soot-hued frame filled the board. Earthenware clattered to the floor as he spun about ready to ward off attack. Ragged, blood-caked ears fanned an immense, thick-jowled head supported by a massive neck and well-muscled shoulders. A scarred bristling back sloped into thick hind legs that shivered just beyond shadow. His nostrils quivered with each drawn breath. His black eyes glittering with firelight, darted warily, marking the surroundings.

Dagger-sharp tushes flashed side to side as all knelt to honor a great warrior. The great boar tilted back his head, loosing a bark that rings the golden hall shingles of Valhalla, loud as Himinbrjotr who bellowed against heaven.

Syn flung wide the doors. With a whooping bark the great boar charged from the hall. The open sky beckoned with a warm breeze. Crashing through a bramble hedge, Saehrímnir dove deep into the concealing shadows of the murky wood. Exulting, he threw back his mighty head toward the stars. A long, clear note sliced through the night, spearing the heart of Mani. The bravest of boars held no fear of Mundilfari's child.

Saehrímnir is denied by the host of Asgard and freed to rejoin his brethren foraging amid the foliage of Yggdrasil, rooting out the offspring of Nidhogg that gnaw at the roots of the great ash.

———— ∘ ————

Straight away the Æsir and Vanir dressed themselves for battle. Slipping off their shoes, they tugged on heavy leggings interwoven with colors to match their nature. With knotted cords, they bound on leather boots of sturdy make, a few adding gilded spurs that glinted in the firelight. Shaking off their coats, the mighty gods donned their strongest ringed byrnies, some choosing the sheen of polished silver, others the dull gray of hand-forged iron, while others preferred the fire of molten gold.

From the armory, they took up such weapons as their prowess dictated. At their waists, they girded swords, sharpened most skillfully as only Regin knew how, tempered as fitting their wearers. Over shoulders they hung bows of well-formed yew. In mailed fists, they grasped spear, mace, and scramasax for bloody tunneling.

Thor strapped Megingjard about his waist, the belt that doubled his strength. He pulled Jarngreipr on over his gnarled fist, the iron gauntlet useful in managing the power of Mjollnir. The mighty hammer, he strapped to his belt within easy reach.

On their heads, they set polished helmets adorned with boar's tusks—helms of terror to freeze the blood of foes. They left their helmet crowns uncovered, no hats to conceal their glow in battle, that all would know their rank. Together they stood, those mighty gods, draped in their resplendent garments of war, a daunting wall of might.

Adorned in death livery, the Father of Armies rapped his spear, Gungnir, on the ground three times to call attention to his words. "Today we face the greatest of all foes; Surt's fiery legions from

Muspellsheim, the etin horde of Jotunheim, and the scions of Loki. They do not count our life days of value. We will teach them the price of such arrogance!"

Grinning, Odin thumped his chest as the stalwart gathering roared back in support. When the cheering subsided, he waved Gungnir over the heads of the massed warriors. "Everyone fights, swords swinging, spears thrusting, hands grappling! No one quits!

Of good omens, we have three of the best: The company of ravens," he nodded to Hugin and Munin perched on his shoulders. "Men eager for glory," he waved his spear over the gathered host as the rafters rang with a burst of cheers. "And the howling of wolves to travel with us," he reached down to scratch between the ears of Geri and Freki.

"Tonight, we advance to Vigrid plain, where good tracks offer us the best footing. Let all be eager to face our foe. Put your gear in good order, have it ready at hand. It is bad to rush unprepared to one's fate. Remember to tie red bands on your arms as a sign to comrades. In the heat of combat to die battling an ally is a useless death.

We stand at dawn on the battle plain hedged with hazel, our lines in clear view of our foe that all will know our actions honorable. None will say that in fear we resorted to night killings; we are not murderers. In well-formed ranks, we will stand defiant that none can doubt our intent. None of us shall be buried in a howe but burst to ashes and scattered across the worlds."

As the cheering died down, Njord, who sings his songs by the sea, tottered forward on bandy legs. His long cloak dragged the ground, concealing his thin body in its dark folds. Odin stepped aside as the ancient mariner raised his hands to speak.

"Old I am. Older than the Behmer wold, and in my lifetime, have never seen such an assembly. So, I call on you gathered here, ready for war, to listen.

In the early days, when the sky was made, when the earth was made, when first my song echoed beneath the vault of Ymir, I carried myself tall and proud, a brash young warrior in the world. Then, I boldly faced each new day with eager confidence believing I knew all that was needed."

Drawing back his heavy hood before the assembled warriors, the sea god slowly turned in a circle. "Gaze upon my face wrinkled from life and time. See the many lines deeply etching my brow and scoring my weathered cheeks. Each mark is a care held close. Look at my gray head. Each hair is one day, one tear, one autumn, one spring, one summer, one winter. I have lived long and seen much."

He waved his hands before the gathering, turning them back to front and then back again. "Look at my hands in the faded light of this ancient hall, their wrinkled skin, the veins popping along their backs. I turn them over in amazement, gazing on them as I would a stranger. It is difficult to believe, let alone remember, the youthful strength these once held."

He raised his arms, letting the cloak sleeves fall back. "See these arms, the flesh shriveled from their full bloom of youth. Know that a woman has loved this face, held these hands, and has rested her head in the hollow of these arms. Years ago... Years ago...

Many things change in a lifetime. In our youth, it was unheard of to break an oath. Now we see bonds broken without thought or care, even by the noblest of men. Still, it is our duty to hold true to that which we are and to that which we represent.

Where once-placid seas washed steadily against the land, the sky now blackens while the ocean stirs up storms against the heavens. Towering waves surge over the headlands to submerge the shorelines, the inrushing waters drowning plains. The wailing winds yield snow and biting cold—three full years of biting cold. The All-Shining is dimmed in its wind weaver course. None can doubt the twilight of our days has arrived.

Good counsel, I give to those gathered here who embark on this final conflict, wise words offered without pretense or guile that you might better carry through your duty. Think before you attack, chance nothing. Everyone dies. It is just a matter of when. But few get a chance, let alone a second chance, to make their death count.

Do not sell your lives cheaply by rushing wildly into the fray, heedless of caution or careful thought, simply because you know your fate. You are seasoned warriors all! Each of you is easily worth twenty of the foe! Be certain to collect all that is your due, then take more. Be greedy!

Remember that each of you were chosen for your valor. It is right that every warrior exacts their full worth before they fall. Do not be overly hasty with foes. Mark your spot, then strike hard. Make every blow count.

Pace the field warily, strive always to keep your footing. Expect great misfortune if you stumble. Disir are always ready to challenge your balance by snagging at your feet with the limbs and weapons of those who fall before you.

The winds cut in all directions; Ran's domain rages with high-crested waves. You must go from here soon to confront the scourge of wood on the low-slung plain where once spears were splintered on the shields of Æsir and Vanir.

The land where I was born follows the edge of the sea. I return now to my people free of obligations, no longer a hostage for peace. Though I am too old for this fight, I will do all that I can to soothe the seas before the waves turn the rocks against the shore. There where ocean tides draw the winds across their surface, I command calm and war to gang together that your passage be safe from peril."

As the cheers for Njord ran down, Odin craned his neck around looking for the white god, finally spotting him emerging from the dusk, a large horn slung about his neck and shoulder. "You have arrived in time. We ready the troops. Heimdall blow the Gjallarhorn. Let it resound across the nine worlds. Let all know that tonight we ride. On Vigrid plain dawn will greet us in full battle array ready for the arrival of Surt."

Harsh blows Heimdall, cheeks swollen with the force of his breath, his back braced against the bulwark of Bifrost, the great spiral horn held aloft. Loud sounds the gleaming Gjallarhorn, three mournful tones, war blasts to announce the final battle. The call of the horn resounds across the nine worlds, notes intoned so deep and solemn, that for a moment all the worlds fall silent. At work beside the great tree, the Norns bow their heads and weep as the tones whisper through the branches.

Flanked by primaries, Odin stepped down from his high seat and marched to the exit of Valhalla. Drawing a package from his robe, he passed it to Freyr on his right. "Do you remember the instructions? Unfold it there before the great hall as a square of cloth is unfolded from a pouch."

As Freyr spread out the cloth, with each unfolding it plumped larger, grew wider until a massive ship floated just above the ground as a knorr bobbing in the sea waves. Many eyes stood wide at the sight, and the intake of breath from the warriors crowding the doorway was as a gale wind.

Odin spread his arms to the ship then turned to face the warriors standing slack jawed, staring up at the rigging that brushed the sky. "Now in the deepest shadows of night, we mount Skidbladnir, the foremost of ships, cunningly built by the master smith, Volund. Though smaller than Naglfar—the formidable vessel of Niflhel fashioned from the uncut nails of the dead—its sturdy hold is more than large enough to carry all assembled here and their war gear."

The father of Armies circled his spear overhead then pointed toward the ramp leading to the deck of the great ship. Jaws set, eyes steady, a column of warriors 800 wide passed beneath the crouching wolf and hovering eagle. In good order, they boarded the majestic sail horse, corselets studded, their shield rims gleaming in the waning light of a bloody moon already hunted by Hati Hrodvitnisson.

From the high deck, Odin shouted out his commands to the hardy sailors scrambling about the rigging. "Hoist the sails. A good wind will drive us to our destination. Together we ride the winds to the dusty battle plain, eager to face the flames of war. Scarce would cowards care to come where we go. Today spears will be shaken, shields splintered, helmets crushed, the ground stained red with blood, and the host of Surt slaughtered!"

On Vigrid Plain

The sun and moon pass overhead counting the years for mankind. They move swiftly this day as if to hasten the events that must pass. The Moon, sorely wounded by Hati, trails sorrow's dew among the clouds as he dodges beneath the edge of worlds. Close behind, Managarm follows the bloody spoor. Relentless, he hungrily nips at Mani's heels, eager to swallow the wounded prey.

Alfbeam ablush scoots above the eastern skyline, her backsides scored by the fangs of Skoll. Streaks of red mar the heavens as she climbs the sky closely pursued by the son of Fenris. She quickens her pace, hoping to live to see the close of day. Heavy grows the child-burden she carries. For its sake, she keeps a punishing pace.

Mundilfari's daughter drives her mighty steeds—Arvak and Alsvinn—to exhaustion, foam slathers their flanks while great streams drip from their mouths. The bellows, Isarnkol, mounted beneath their shoulders, fails to stem the overwhelming heat. Her chariot casts off sparks as lightning flares from its wheels. The heavens grow crimson with spattered gore.

As Svalin, the belly shield of Arvak and Alsvinn, glows white with the raging heat of their passage, the world exhales mist, wreathing the earth in smoke. Seas steam, their surface clogged with schools of dying fish. Mountaintops exchange their wreath of white for the gray of bare stone. Hoary mains of glaciers become screaming torrents clawing their way down the sides of mountains, gouging out valleys as they rush seaward. Rivers and streams dance among their banks, their volumes swelled by the sudden runoff.

Arrive the Æsir

Silent, each hunched into themselves, the glorious company of Asgard sit shoulder to shoulder as along the windheim road the great ship races to the fateful battle. On firth ways their hoisted sails hold secret converse with the wind. Rough gales buffet the ship, rocking the deck so it is impossible to stand. The screaming winds make speech impossible, but all eyes sparkle with anticipation.

Stars stream across the sky as Skidbladnir drives through the darkness. Near rise of Alfbeam's light, the great ship touches down on the edge of a wide, clear plain. The host of Valhalla disembark, stumbling from the rough ride. Row on row, legion upon legion, they assemble into fighting ranks alongside the ship.

Exhausted, Mani dips to the west as in the east the red hand of Mundilfari's daughter rises up to grip the horizon. Hearts and breaths quicken across the ranks as battle horns sound along the lines. Forming themselves into a broad column they advance onto the dusty plain. Blood-red rays of the Sun guide the formation as they maneuver into position.

Their byrnies flicker in the morning light, a moving sea of fire flowing across the land. As they move the bright iron rings linked hard by hand rattle with the song of war. The bright red banner of the Æsir is carried to the fore, on its weave an embroidered raven in flight. As the banner flutters in the breeze, the raven seems to fly ahead as herald for the force.

All march forward under the battle standard, eager for the clash of swords. The gilded head of Gungnir held high in Hnikar's hand flickers gold in the fresh rays of Sol, a living standard that outshines the stars.

It began as a song set in cadence to match their march, starting in the front ranks then rippling its way down the line to those bringing up the rear.

> "We who wield the blade of battle
> raise the roar of helm and shield.
> Warriors born to ply the sword
> and glut the wolf with manly gore.
>
> Bold in deeds we brandish arms.
> With brows shrouded in helms of war
> we advance ready to die
> sooner than yield an inch of ground.
>
> Shafts will splinter, and iron scream,
> the boar of helmets devours shields.
> The storm of spears we gladly face
> to see this day through to its end."

Above the moving body of fierce warriors flock the helmed ladies of Heriar, three times nine wound-giving Valkyries ever ready to charge into battle. Fair-skinned under shining helmets, corselets glittering, weapons held aloft, they straddle their airborne steeds. Their mounts tremble as they tread the sky, sprinkling dew from their manes onto the plain below while hail rattles against the shields of the Einherjar.

Brynhild sang out from atop her mount as she led the bright complement of her sisters across the sky.

> "Here, where the banners of bold warriors go forth,
> Valkyries decide who live or die.
> Here, where the froth of battle stains the earth dark red,
> the lands will learn of the loss of sturdy oaks.
> Here, we sing victory songs that those who listen
> may learn from the teachings of spear-women."

The mighty host draws up the width of Vigrid plain, 100 leagues in breadth and as many deep. They stand together, a clenched fist raised in defiance, the Æsir, the Vanir, and the Einherjar.

The Sons of Muspellsheim Take the Field

The mighty host of Surt advances from the heat of Muspellsheim, a rolling wave of fire crossing into the lands of Midgard. Furious battles are fought with those who deny his advance. Armies run screaming from the field as Surt decimates their ranks with his flaming sword. Their protectors routed, the raveners swoop down on defenseless cities and towns, predators glutting themselves on the soft bellies of the fallen, destroying all as they press forward.

Fire bells ring their clamorous warnings, even the stoutest hearts quail beneath the sound. Throngs, terrified by the attacks, dash before the relentless blaze, just as panicked sheep scurry before the pursuing wolf.

Flames play high into the heavens; their rage fueled by building timbers and dry forests. Great plumes of smoke spiral skyward, the exhaust of a dragon's breath. Animals, trees, men, and the homes of men are sheeted in roaring flame. The dying commune with the dead, as together their ashes float in the air, vainly seeking a place in the sky.

Too, men suffer from Surt's fearsome blade; the bright light of the sun brought to earth. The scorching heat of the summer day, a hundred times increased, sears the skin bright red. In-branded flames spread across the limbs. Fire, like the molten core of a dwarf's furnace, glows within the pit of the stomach, driving the sickened into frenzy. Scores fling themselves into streams, dive into rivers, and pitch headlong into open wells. Tumbling, mouths agape, their parched lips seeking the relief of cool water, eager to escape the flames raging within and without.

None are spared death. Corpses smolder amid the fires. Heads dangle from the saddles of victorious riders smeared with blood. City gates are braced from within and without by mounds of slumped, lifeless bodies.

Rivers clogged with innocent blood carry their burden of dead to the sea. Limbs entwined, they claim entire shorelines for their own. No shame now to be buried at tidemark.

Life-giving streams dry up with Surt's advance. Lakes retreat from their shores leaving behind beds of cracked, dry mud. The wide earth burns deep, even life in the soil perishes from the penetrating heat as the embers of Muspellsheim make their way to Asgard.

From the south, the sky splits open. Unchallenged, the sons of Muspell astride their coal-black mounts, thunder across the Quivering way. The great bridge of the Æsir, shudders beneath their weight. It sways, flickers, then shatters from the force of their clattering hooves.

Clouds pile fire-sharp along the horizon, built up as a wildfire raging across a dry plain that smolders first dull red in the bracken, then, driven by the winds of Hraesvelg, leaps high with bright, flickering flames. The dazzling orange bank advances, a wall of fire that sets the ground aglow. Wind-dried forests burst into flame as the host of Muspellsheim charge with weapons raised onto the battle-ready plain.

The Arrival of Loki and the Host of Niflhel

Over Fallandaford they tread a dreary path that winds through wind-cold wolf trees and skirts along sheer cliffs of the Nidaveller Mountains. At a pass blocked by a wall of webbed iron, frozen hinges squall in protest as the Na-Gates swing wide. Through the dim light the dark host lurches forward from Niflhel. Shuffling their way to the river Slid, they plod across the rough-hewn timbers of a moldering pier. Ancient pylons dank with rot quiver at their step.

Up mildewed ropes that dangle from its sides they scramble over the rails onto Naglfar, the dark ship born of dead men's nails. Its prow adorned with a plain carved skull. Its plumping sails striped black and white. Its dark hull swollen with bitter tears. One by one they take their seats.

From the arched crest of the Gjoll Bridge, the stark maid Modgud who guards the way, alerted by the sound of their passage, sadly marks their progress. Jaw set, face stern, she weeps for the world.

From his perch, high above Niflhel, nestled amid the branches of Yggdrasil, Ari, the dun-hued eagle, launches into the air, screaming in anticipation. Catching the buffeting winds roaring across the lands, he circles into the sky, climbing higher and higher until swallowed by low-hanging clouds.

Naglfar tears loose from its moorings. With creaking timbers, the dark-decked ocean mare drives down the river, now free of dangerous ice, into the stormy gales of a crashing sea. The black ship plunges into turbulent waters. Its musty timbers gripped by the white-tipped teeth of ocean. Its deck washed by towering waves.

Swiftly, the dark steed races along the swan's path, beyond the high headlands of deserted coastline and the rocky fingers of stark promontories that reach far out into the sea ready to snare the unwary. Bow lifted high to the vault of Ymir, the ancient vessel splits the clouds. With each breaker crash it carves a path to the moon.

No need for strong backs to work the oars, the shrieking wind strains tight the striped sails, driving the ship's prow through gray sea foam and onto the beach along the strand. The chaff of Niflhel alight from Naglfar as fleas from a water-soaked hound. Storm lashed foam licks their calves as they stomp ashore. His shrill commands carrying on the wind, Loki leads the army of Niflhel—the twice damned conscripted by death—into position on Vigrid plain.

Arrival of the Giants

As if a leak had grown up out of the tufted grass, so towered Hrym among the etin host. The war leader of the giants drives from the east drumming his shield song. The iron rim rings with his sharp rhythm, lockstep for the etin horde streaming behind.

In columns a league wide, the children of Ymir surge across the frozen plains of Jotunheim. At the bank of the Ifing the air fills with their shouts and hoots as they wade single file across Orvandel's ford, braving the treacherous waters to gather on the far side and continue their advance.

They do not pause. They do not stop. They cut a bloody swath of destruction across Midgard. What the forces of Surt fail to destroy, the giants crush with a savage vengeance. Forests topple, homes crumble, and green fields are trampled to barren soil, as their relentless march carries them to the appointed place.

The earth trembles as the fierce-minded descendants of Bergelmir stomp forward to battle across the dust-covered plain. At each step their lips keen the cadence of their stride, giving voice to their defiant steps. "Hah... Hah... Hah... Hah."

They advance as a wall, a towering range of mountain peaks too numerous to count. Hrym raises a clenched fist and the etin line stomps to a halt with a final, thunderous "Hah!"

The Sons of Loki Arrive

He whom the gods hate, the great circumscriber beneath all lands, Jormungand, releases his tail. Writhing mightily in rage, the Midgard serpent thrashes onto shore amid walls of crashing waves. His glassy eyes shine with a dull, cold hate as he carves a muddy trail across the plain.

The trembling ground tumbles boulders from their hillside perch as the Fenris wolf casts off Gleipnir. The fetter, like Laeding and Dromi before it, spins off into the distance. Ripping the sword from his jaws, he bounds from Lyngvi, eyes aflame with the memory of past deceptions. Hope dries up with the promise of revenge.

The sun races across the sky chilled at the sight of the loose wolf. For sport, he joins in her pursuit, racing, dodging across the sky. Nostrils whetted with the blood scent of Mundilfari's daughter, he leaves the hunt to Skoll and charges onto the battle plain.

The children of Loki bound amid the throng, jockeying for position as the multitude edge away to give them room.

Garm Freed

Garm bays loudly before Gnipa Cave. The mighty hound strains against his ancient tether drawn taught, lurching from side to side, excited by the tremors from the great ash and the fading echoes of the Gjallarhorn. With a savage howl of triumph, the great hound breaks free and charges back along the road of the dead who dodge away from his hurtling form. Passing through a swath of green fields, he cuts east along the westerly road. The slight incline does nothing to slow his speed as with drumming feet kicking up puffs of dust, he races along the red road.

He pauses on a ridge overlooking the battlefield, casting his nose side to side, evaluating the forces arrayed below. Tipping back his muzzle, Garm unleashes a deep-throated howl that rolls through the air, an ancient challenge of war. Heads jerk up, alarmed by the sound, as the greatest of hounds bounds down the slope and onto Vigrid plain

Battle Flyting

Odin swells to prominence on the field of valor, raised up before the ranks of warriors like a bright glowing ash beside a forest of stunted oaks. Swinging Gungnir over his head in a great circle, he directed his command to the nearest troops, confident it would be carried down the line. "As a thousand, thousands have done before us, we boldly greet the dawn! Glad we are of this day as are greedy hawks and jet-black ravens when they know of battle and the steaming flesh to come! We will not delay this meeting of swords!"

Surt strode forward from the massed throng opposite the Æsir formation. "Who are these scavengers of the fields," his voice boomed from the depths of his golden helmet, echoing across the battle lines, "that dare confront our might?"

The Father of Armies shook his spear, its deadly point glinting in the early morning light. "Who are the noisome rabble that screech from across the way?"

Surt thumped his chest, a deep hollow booming that rolled across the field. "Don't try to frighten us Báleyg," he shouted from the smoldering embers of his troops, "and don't bother to keep talking. We all know the outcome of this battle. Dragging out your words will only lengthen our miseries. Though you can ease the pain for all concerned. Stand down your line and I will make quick your passing. Why prolong your fate?"

Odin gestured to the sky with his spear, pointed at the orb racing across the heavens. Gungnir's wicked tip glinted with the red rays of Sol. "As long as the sun stays her windweaver's course, we will never bend our necks to your feet or stand docile to be butchered as cattle come the frost. Little does your fire impress us; it is as cold and insignificant as your words. Come," Odin beckoned with his fingers, "discover our strength. We face you unflinching in the light of a new day."

Surt spread wide his arms and laughed. "How proud you are of what you have done so early. You know what portends, unless your brains are muddled with ale and your ears stuffed with fresh dung." His lips curled into a sneer. "Your kin at home must be sad to have lost such an arrogant force."

Swelling up his chest, the Father of Armies thumped it three times with his fist. The lines of warriors rocked with the rhythm. "What you say now many would think great news," he thrust out his chin, "the outcome of this battle that all know. Yet still we stand before you undaunted."

Surt glanced along the ranks of eager warriors, noted similar taunts flying between the lines. "Who are you to display such boldness? Better you should wet your balls wading rivers in retreat than dare confront a superior force."

Odin slapped his spear against his chest, then waved a hand at the roaring throng behind him. "Who am I? Who are we? It must be your ears that are full of dung to miss the roaring waves that tower before you, ready to crash down and eat away your warrior lines."

Surt's glare grew sharp. "I notice you do not speak who it is I face." He lifted a hand to wipe the spittle from his chin. "Why conceal your name, unless you quarrel with someone you fear."

Odin spat onto the ground then kicked dirt over the phlegm with his toe. "Even had I no quarrel, even were I doomed to Niflhel, I would strive against one such as you. I have gone by as many names as lands I have visited and purposes I have lived. But today, here on this field of valor, you only need know my battle names.

Odin, I am called now. Ygg, the Terrible One, I was called before. In battle, I have cleared the field as Heriar for the General who leads, and Herian for the Warrior who fights. Grím and Grímnir recognize my battle mask. Fimblultyr evokes my undaunted might. Sigfodur acknowledges the hand I play in fathering wars. Herteit speaks to my merry delight in the clash of arms. Báleyg notes the fierce flame that lights my eye. Hialmberi marks me for the battle helmet I wear. Glapsvid recalls my madness when combat is joined. And, the most notable, Valfodur reminds all of my protection for those slain on the field of valor."

He nodded his head to one side then the other. "With me are those who would forever deny you. They will harvest your forces as a farmer harvests grain at threshing time. You will have a hard day getting clear of this fight."

"You speak well of yourselves," Surt flicked an ember from his shoulder, "though what I see does not tally with the boldness of your words. Ragged men all, you stand wearing beggar's gear. What have we to fear from this host of cream-faced loons?"

"And who are you," Odin's words hissed in a long, slow stream through gritted teeth, "who arrogantly raise yourselves above others, though you've only hot air to support your words?"

Surt placed a hand to his chest, turned to face his own line, then turned back to face the fire of Báleyg's single eye. "Never do I conceal my name. I am Surt, the black one, son of the first world; I am known by no other. I do not seek to confound with a multiplicity of titles. My land is Muspellsheim, impassible to any who cannot claim it as their native land.

Glowing embers from its hills brought warmth to Ginnungagap and breathed life into the worlds. I have waited long at the edge, defending what I had until I could—by right and authority—claim all that is justly mine."

A loud cheer shook the air as Surt planted his fists on his hips. "I do not come alone. This host of smoldering embers ranked to either side, eager to burst into flame, are the sons of Muspell. Already they have laid waste the lands of men. Expect your precious Asgard to know the same."

He turned slightly to sweep an arm back at the hungry faces crowding close behind him. "These others with me you know. Your dealings with them through the ages, your conceit at every turn, have brought them to my side. Here stands Loki, son of Farbauti—your once-brother—treated harshly by his adopted kin who bound him with the entrails of his son Nari. The Fenris wolf, son of Loki, first raised as a son among the Æsir, then, out of fear, tricked into eternal bondage."

Surt lifted his hand to point at the slender shape swaying above them. "And Jormungand, the Midgard Serpent, the older brother of Fenris, cast away by you into the well of ocean. He has grown large waiting for revenge."

He stepped into a looming shadow, nearly disappearing in its expanse. "Here stands Hrym of Jotunheim and his etin followers who blot out the sun, they who have known the baying of the earth hound ever at their heels.

At my side crouches Garm, the peerless war hound, spurned by you who denied him a rightful place among the valiant." Surt made to stroke the hound's head, but a sharp, sideways glare and sudden deep-throated growl stayed the gesture. Nonchalantly drawing back his hand, he fumbled his fingers a moment at his chest before perching them on his hip, all the while making certain they were out of immediate reach of Garm's teeth. "Long tethered before Gnipa Cave, he was forced to watch in frustration while those he once protected passed by. He now slavers for the mayhem of slaughter."

Regaining his sneer, Surt stretched his arms out to both sides. "And this dark, nearly endless sea behind me is the host of Niflhel— far more than your few puny warriors. No few passed over by your choosers of the slain. I spoke with a farmer who leapt the precipice on the expectation of plenty that came not in time. He held no good words for the promises of Farmatýr. He fights now with Loki's troops in hopes to avenge his burden."

Odin rocked back on his heels laughing. "You will find no farmers in my forces." He turned to face his own line, then turned back to confront the flame of Surt. "Did I not know that each of my Einherjar are worth fifty of your followers I might have been concerned. But together with Æsir and Vanir, you will receive better than you give."

He thumped the butt of his spear on the ground, three times he stated its claim. "Beside me stands the host of Asgard, ready since Ymir's bones were scattered to build mountains. Many your kin have encountered before, much to their detriment.

Thor, son of Earth, wielder of the mighty hammer Mjollnir, his is the strength of all the Æsir.

His sons Modi and Magni are equal to their father in strength and courage. In battle, you will never see their backs.

Bragi, the long-bearded. Eloquent with words, he is just as skilled with a battle needle. A ferocious adversary in war.

Vidar, the silent one. With the power of living wood, his strength is nearly the equal of Thor. You can rely on his strong arm to destroy many of your forces.

Vali, slayer of Hodd, is tenacious in battle. His deadly edge never misses its mark.

Heimdall, the white one. Tireless watchman of the gods, he can hear the vermin crawling on your skin. None can surprise him in battle nor avoid his strike.

Tyr, the one handed, honor is his second nature. Courageous in war, the battlefield is his natural home.

Freyr, son of Njord, the Bright Slayer of Beli. As war leader of the Æsir, the doughty blade wielder is undefeated in battle.

Ull the archer, he who makes the bowstring of guts quiver. His mastery of bow and single combat is unsurpassed. You had best keep your shield high lest a winged shaft pierce your tiny skull.

Hoenir, the long-legged. He is swift in a fight, but when pressed to yield before the battle storm, can be as unmoving as a boulder sunk in clay.

Lodur, the quickening flame. He kindles the blaze of war and by his own hand directs its carnage."

Gungnir's tip flickered above their heads. "Roaming the sky, brushing shoulders with ravenous hawks and shrieking ravens, flock my elite band of battle-hardened Valkyrie. War maidens all, they ride undaunted through the buffeting winds of the battle storm, lighting the air with their wound flames. Well skilled in the way of the blade, they are at home on any field of bloody combat."

He jerked a thumb over his shoulder. "And this great host pressing eagerly behind is my Einherjar, the greatest warriors of Midgard gleaned from thousands of battlefields across every land throughout the ages. They are all chosen by me, sturdy oaks, despisers of all blows, well-schooled in the ways or war, each with the strength of solid iron. The pebble hill of their count is a mountain that fills valleys and buries plains. Its peak rivals the height of the great ash."

The black one laughed. "Our legions are many," he spread wide his arms, "and yours, for all their grandeur, few. We will raze that which you have built. Unless you wish to withdraw from the field, for then I may leave you your home."

Odin gave out a battle cry. "It is too late to settle this any way other than blood!" He shook his spear at the enemy line. Light flared from its tip swaying high in the air. "With Gungnir I will loft your livers to the sky! A master smith crafted this shaft. Victory runes grace its lethal point. Together they speak death to enemies!"

Surt waved a hand to dismiss the threat. "You rattle your stick like a fearful shepherd trying to chase away a hungry wolf. You boast of your spear, but not of victory. That is well, for you will never walk away from this field."

With a voice of thunder Surt cried out to his troops. "I urge you to increase the grief of this redoubtable warrior! I want to see him lessened by loss as he sees his numbers reduced!"

Odin shouted out to his men, raising his voice to a loud boom that cut across the ranks. "My words to all, remember! On Vigrid plain now raise the storm! Gungnir, the brilliant shaft that never misses its mark, I cast over the enemy hoard to consecrate this battle! A hard blow against the fiery darkness!" The spear sailed in a bright arc through the dawn light. With a final flash, it came down, its golden tip nestled deep in the hard heart of a rock-born thurs. Softly, as a hill slides into the sea, the giant crumbled to the ground.

Drawing his sword, Odin pointed its tip at the advancing line. "Let each one's wounds be struck in front! Let none turn to escape this fate! Boldly, we enter this weapon-fray." He sprinted forward still shouting. "The ravens will not starve this day!"

Strongly they ran, powerfully they ran, the challenging horde of Surt, feet flying over the dew sprinkled dust of Vigrid plain, across the slope darkened by sheer numbers. The Valkyrie's airy sea trembled where they passed, and the ground rumbled with the fall of their feet.

Herteit called his warriors into line, an indomitable wall of the valiant. "Let all brace themselves! Let none linger behind! They are eager to advance and so are we. Let's offer resistance!"

There was a powerful crash as the battle ranks came together, competing storm clouds vying for room in the sky. Everything resounded with the fighting as the surrounding hills gave voice to trilling cries of war.

Deft, battle-seasoned hands clashed shield to shield, while bright, whistling brands sang the chorus of war. Hot blood dripped from well-thrust spear points. Shields shivered under the hardy blows of sword and mace. The soft song of death-dealing darts whispered through the air.

The struggle blossomed with bodies falling thick and fast. Wound dew spouted among the battle bearers; death swept through the ranks as many sank beneath the turbulent stream. Undaunted by the carnage, warriors stood with legs straddling mounds of corpses and continued to fight.

Wolf-coated warriors howled in delight as wound hail burst upon their byrnies. When the rain of battle paused, they raged forward en masse, white foam dribbling from their lips. Wild-eyed, slavering at their shield rims, the berserkers swung bloody, wound-giving blades to stem the wolf's hunger.

Loki's standard, the Land-Waster, swept forward. Close behind shambled the conscripts from Niflhel. Swearers of false oaths, murderers, traitors of benefactors, false witnesses, flatterers who seduced the close confidants of others, oath breakers spit out by Nidhogg, they raise their weapons and scream, a quavering ululation to freeze a warrior's limbs.

Charging ahead, the twice-dead of Loki's legions set about with weapons to hew through the lines. Wave after wave fall to the light touch of recent Einherjar brought from the latest battles in Midgard. With staccato bursts, Odin's youngest oaks mete out death while their munitions lasted, then quickly learned the value of a sharp edge wielded by a strong arm, a gruesome lesson as many fell shorter by a head.

Surt raged at the Father of Armies as he lashed about with his blade. "For eons, we've planned to take away your lives. You will not leave with them now!"

Laughing with delight at the carnage, Odin swept the field about him clear with the flicker of his own sure flame. "You appear not to have intended any such thing. You were not ready when we smashed back to the cold wastes of Niflhel a thousand, thousand score of your followers."

In fury, they responded at these words. Death brands glinted in the sun as they played hard the wound game, disdaining fortune with brandished steel. Javelins flew to their targets—uprooted forest groves that arced through the air—clanged when they struck stout shields, thudded dully when they bit flesh. Barbed darts darkened the sky so that no man saw another. Everywhere arrows rained to dim the sun.

The heat of battle increased. Stones and arrows poured down while swords shook off bright blood, for a second time taking the lives of great warriors. It became clear then to Surt that the stalwart Æsir host stoutly defied the close of his fiery fist.

Gore followed as ravens a bloody river. Warriors fell on both sides. Stiff iron was bathed in blood. Keen edges sheathed in flesh. Mountains of dead rose, toppled, then rose again. Over the cries of the wounded and dying sounded the screams of war-birds circling high above the plain.

Drawn to the gleaming gold of Odin's helmet, there clustered the primaries of both sides. The struggle grew fierce as the sons of Muspell pressed forward. High gleamed the shield wall around Sigfodur, and the Æsir line remained firm.

The dazzling arc of wound flames cut across the sky as bright helmed Valkyries circled the field amid flocks of shrieking ravens— white swans rubbing wings with the black birds of war. Disir dodged among the combatants, tripping up or giving secure balance to struggling warriors as their whim dictated. Wolves glutted themselves on the forest of fallen trees blown down by the harsh winds of battle, their twisted limbs strewn about the ground, fists still gripping their weapons.

Hrym's Flyting

Hrym, war leader of the etins pushed forward from amid the towering shadows of giants. Pointing a thick finger at the end of a thicker arm, he shook it menacingly at the Sigfodur while clearing the line of enemy that raged before him. "Bölverkr, your words are the blathering of a malicious, evil old fool! Broken pledges, lies, and deceit are all the Æsir have ever offered!"

Odin paused amid the slaughter, eying the speaker. "Giants have always been ugly, though in truth some of your women are pleasing to the eye." He chuckled to himself. "You make bold claims to impinge my honor. To what do you hold your assertions?"

Hrym smashed his club into the enemy line laying low a score of warriors. "I speak from my perch high on Ymir's cold bones, the truth that every etin knows in his heart. Often you have given ill for good, uneven in your dealings with friend and foe alike.

When you broke the ring-oath given in Suttung's Hall, you proved yourself unworthy of trust in any promise or vow you might give.

Helblindi, you repaid Hlebard's hospitality with evil by taking advantage of his diminished capacity. For the ancient's gift of a magic staff you charmed him out of his wits.

For fear of losing an honest wager—the rebuilding of battlements for a bride—you infused the air with treachery, sullied honorable pledges, and repaid the Master Builder with death.

When none could budge the funeral barge of Baldur, Hyrrokkin answered your call for help. While she shoved the barge to sea, your men killed her steed. Afterward, that mud-spawned son of yours threatened her life."

Hrym jerked his club around to point at Thor rampaging amid the enemy line. "And there stands that very spawn of your loins, Veor himself, Hlodyn's celebrated son, slayer of my kinsman though they did him no wrong. The son of Fjorgyn hunted us in our own lands, killing us without mercy. Now Jotunheim rings hollow with the sound of forgotten footsteps.

To brew mead in quantity enough to slake the mighty thirst of the Æsir, he stole a cauldron from Hymir's proud hall. Caught in the act, he sought to hide his shame by delivering death to the powerful Jotun and slaughtering the retainers of his house.

We see the craven butcher now by the light from Thjasse's eyes, plucked from the wonder worker's charred skull and tossed into the sky for all to witness, a trophy to your deceitful warrior might. I say that no more will the sky be a mount for your victories!"

Odin barked a laugh. "One man's ill is another's luck. In such dealings, it is each for himself. You complain to me of injustice. Yet your kin have always sought to destroy everything we created—that which, in the early days of the world, every Æsir gave oath to protect. The cold enduring hate of etins who would forever deny our rights is the savage truth I learned from the very Hlebard you claim I charmed out of his wits."

Odin turned back to swinging his blade, hacking down the faces that rose before him. "I have little patience to listen to your words. Take up your argument with my son. He has the ears to grasp your concerns. I leave it to him to answer your complaints!"

Thor tossed Mjollnir, striking down the giant that fought in line alongside Hrym. He raised his ironclad fist to catch the hammer as it swung through the air and returned to his grasp. "You speak loudly and ever full of yourself as do all giants; arrogant to the last!

I have fought many etins in mortal combat, malicious creatures who roamed the barren mountains and deep forest dales. Some have been honorable foes. Most have been craven, deceitful creatures. Had all lived their progeny would be great, as numerous as fleas on an unkempt dog. Midgard would be overwhelmed with your race. Men would have nowhere to live and be as nothing had I not stalled your arrogance.

It seems to me cause for endless laughter when you recount your injuries, you who have shown no compunction for destruction. You are all born of the poisons of Elivagar and the perverse joining of Ymir's feet."

Hrym bristled at Thor's words. His voice roared out across the field as a landslide thundering down a mountain. "Arrogant! You dare call us arrogant? Surely, your own arrogance exceeds any we may offer! Would that time permitted the fate you deserve, delivered back to your mother, trampled into the bosom of the earth, ground to dust beneath the slow march of my kin!"

Thor lay about with his hammer, shattering groves of stunted oaks sprouted from the frozen land of Niflhel. "I declare it is a small matter for me to play this word game with you, though it becomes tedious in the main. Why would anyone want to stand here listening to your endless screeching?"

Hrym watched as the son of Odin struck down a line of warriors. "You've strength enough of limb, but water for guts. In cowardice, you spent the night in a glove. You were not so tough then. In terror, you dared not sneeze or fart for fear that Skrymir might hear."

Thor waved his hammer in Hrym's direction, made as if to hurl it at his head. The great giant dodged aside at the movement. "You watch your mouth, you misbegotten son of an etin! You will howl louder than a wolf if you get a blow from my hammer!"

Hrym spread wide his arms. "Here I stand, Veor." He beckoned Thor with his fingers. "Do your best, I will not move. You have encountered no sterner foe since Hrungnir."

Thor muscled his way through the throng, a great ship parting the ocean of warriors as he strove to reach the etin leader. "That high-spirited giant with a head of stone and sharp-cornered heart to match fell before my might, as will you. Know that I will pay you back for your jeering words. Piss will run down your legs before I am through!"

Hrym leaned a moment on his club, then took a playful swipe at the battle line that spun a warrior through the air to land wet and hard on the ground. "Truthful words I give. Will you pay me back for such honesty, as you did the older sister of Thrym when she asked for the gift of gold rings from the hairy wrists of a swarthy bride; her life taken for petty rudeness?"

Savagely, Thor struck at any foe close enough to feel the brunt of his fury. A lake of blood spread out from beneath the teetering mounds of bodies that piled up about him. "I offered honest payment for blackmail; a blow from my hammer instead of red gold from an extorted bride. The same as you would offer for such dishonor."

Hrym snarled and began to lay about with a vengeance. The area quickly cleared before him as warriors backed away from the reach of his club. "My poor heart pounds for revenge. Patience, impatient heart. For each wound received, I will reward you with more than adequate recompense. Know Veor that before the day is done we will both be off to visit those ancients who dwell in the stone woods at home, the cairns raised for the honored dead!"

The mighty thurs bellowed to his rocky kin, "Avengers of Ymir to me! I call all to raise up your weapons! The time for banter has past! Eager we advance! Loud rings our cry of war!"

Garm and the Wolves of Odin

Garm bayed loudly, enraged by the scent of blood. The bold hound hurled himself upon the battle line in a snarling frenzy to destroy. Teeth bared, he sprang at the foremost warrior. Snapping jaws tore a ragged gash across his throat, stilling his voice. Hands tightly clutching his neck, blood spurting from between his fingers, the man gurgled, staggered a step then collapsed to the ground.

The greatest of hounds gave no pause to action, offered no mercy to his victims, but slashed from side to side in passing, a relentless whirlwind of destruction that defied the most skilled warrior to strike. The ravener was everywhere and all at once—tooth and claw flashing bright. To all he presented an unbroken front, as he rapidly whirled guarding his sides and flank.

Warriors packed close in line, panicked at the maelstrom swirling in their midst, struck out wildly, maiming and killing comrades in their terror. When they ran, Garm raged at their heels, pursuing them through the ranks, dragging them down as harts in the forest, leaving mattered bits shredded across the dusty plain.

The hound tore through the battling throng felling lines of warriors before his savage rage, his fierce onslaught forcing back a full square of battle-seasoned oaks.

Geri and Freki snarled in defiance from behind the warrior fence that surrounded Odin. Hair bristled along their backs and more than one hand reached down to smooth them flat. Pushing his scarred muzzle forward, Garm roared a deep howl of challenge, the song of battle learned from an early age. His challenge was answered as Odin's war-eager wolves, snarling in reply, burst through the line of protecting warriors and raced forward to attack the battle-wise foe.

Teeth flashed as Geri leapt straight for the bold hound. Like the lightning flash that splits an oak tree, Garm struck, breaking Geri's neck in flight. With a sharp shake of his head, he tossed aside the limp body of the greedy wolf.

Bounding over the fallen form of his brother, Freki dove for the throat of his adversary, missed, pivoted on his back legs, his snapping teeth drawing a thick red gash along the shoulder as the hound of war dodged past.

Without a pause the combat-skilled Garm spun about, saw an opening as Freki sought to turn around, darted in low and closed with his fangs. His teeth slashed deep to open the vein of the neck.

Freki stumbled, snarled, then broke into a ragged cough that shook his entire body. The grim wolf of Odin gathered his feet beneath him and sprang at his stalwart foe, missed in a tangle of legs, then lurched back to his feet. Freki quivered, the hair on his neck bristling, as he staggered side to side, growling with horrible menace, as though to frighten off impending death.

Bleeding, coughing, he fought while life remained. Each leap growing shorter, each lunge less powerful, until finally the strength in his legs faded and he collapsed against the body of a fallen warrior. Chest heaving, he gave two ragged breaths as the light of day dulled on his eyes.

Garm, weaned on war, tilted up his muzzle smeared with the blood of valiant foes. He loosed a deep howl of triumph, then charged back into the storm.

Odin and the Fenris Wolf

Odin strode forth to face the Fenris wolf, helmed in terrible gold, ring mail coat shimmering. In the shadow of his foe he drew Skofnung, an enchanted blade in temperament like its wielder, methodical of nature. Holding the mystic splinter before his lips, he misted its inscribed surface with his breath. A snake crawled from under its upper boss—the ward of the blade. He raised Skofnung and turned its edge to face his foe.

The son of Loki rose snarling before Sigfodur. On his head, he wore the skin of a wolf's forehead flayed off with the ears and the ruff, the ears set straight up, stiff and alert. About his waist was wrapped a strop of skin stripped from a wolf's back to its tail. Beneath it all he wore a light, nut-brown kirtle. In his right fist, he swung a sharp-edged sword, broad at the hilt, tapering to a long vicious fang. Leather straps adorned with disks of iron to ward off blows braced his weapon arm.

Fenris advanced into position. His leather arm brace creaked with each menacing step. His naked blade danced ready for battle, the wicked tip weaving a deadly pattern in the air. "We meet again

Hapta-god. But now I am free of your most powerful fetter, the silky Gleipnir. You will have no chance to trick me into donning such again. Come, attack me. I will send your head to your widow."

Odin circled to the right, keeping the wolf always to his front, waving the tip of his own blade before the eyes of his foe. "I that brave the battle-sleet know in truth that my Hild of the golden armlets does not care for such a gift. I hold my heavy-browed head untaken, but if the fates decree she should have my head delivered by the hand of another, then bring on this clash of spears."

No more words were lost on either side. Battle needles fanned the air. Neither could complain the other struck feebly. A quick stroke from Odin's blade slashed a deep furrow across Fenris' cheek. Blood dripped from beneath his fiery eye as he circled the Alfodur, keeping just out of reach of his blade.

Fenris slapped his blade against his chest. "You took me from my kin to raise as one of your own," the deadly tip whipped about to point at Odin's face, "assured me with encouraging words that I would not be loved less than any Æsir son! Large I grew under your tutelage. So, too, grew your fear. Though I had harmed no one, you feared my strength and my temper."

Sigfodur slid to the left, then danced right again. He struck at an opening quickly closed by the wolf. "Your future was known to me—who you were, what you would become. I sought to change it by fostering you among us. That which you bring on today you would have brought earlier had I not acted."

Fenris matched his steps to Odin's movements, keeping his blade always in line with the Alfodur's chest. "You are old Hapta God, your excuses feeble. Your head bobs like a bridled horse long in tooth. Your middle leg droops and drips. Even your ears are gnarled as oaken knots."

Odin shook his blade before him, letting the sunshine reflect from its polished surface, freeing the serpent to slid along its length. "White head pays no heed to a stout heart. Know that here you face a mighty antagonist, one who never flees when battle is joined and who has often fed the dun-colored eagles. While you, bound to a rock, only dreamed of such greatness."

Fenris feinted a slash at Odin's face and was nearly caught by a return thrust. He danced back out of range. "Once I considered you honorable. While still a youth, I learned that your true nature was one of deception. Know that things learned young last longest."

"One broken oath," Odin continued to circle, "does not destroy all others."

Fenris spat at Odin's feet. "An oath freely given cannot be broken, should not be broken, lest all oaths mean nothing."

With a sudden bark of laughter, Odin took three quick steps in. Harsh was the sound of metal on metal as blades met and struck fire. "Believe whatever suits you." Parrying a desperate thrust, he slipped aside, moving to the right. "But wisdom gained through many severe trials let me know you for what you are: a vicious beast who would destroy all before him. I saw this when first we met, yet I chose to give you a chance to prove my fears wrong. That you did not do!"

Odin lunged, his blade slipping past a hasty defense to bite flesh. Fenris retreated from the sudden attack, fingered the gash Skofnung's edge had opened in the cloth at his waist, felt the wetness that rose from the cut beneath. The wolf gritted his teeth and growled low. "The words that reach my ear hands are as addled as their speaker. They gush forth with little heed of mind or thought. Words from such a withered bag are little more than wasted breath."

Odin squinted at the movement of Fenris' blade, recognizing the defense taught him by Tyr when the wolf was an eager pup in the Æsir court. "I've seen every battle since before you were born. I bartered my eye for a draught from Mimir's well, so understand more and see farther than most. Idun's apples ensure you confront such wisdom in youthful vigor instead of decrepit age."

Fenris stamped his foot then made a wild swing that sent Sigfodur skittering back on his heels. "You will not walk from this fight away nor receive duel ransom. A cloven skull is all you shall have for this day's work."

"I've never been one to flinch from harsh words or bold actions." Odin gestured at Fenris' waist, now discolored with a bright crimson bloom. "Watch your wounds bleed. Though I am older, I've dodged all your blows while mine have struck and stained you red."

A snarl curled Fenris' lips. "You speak bravely for one so vulnerable. You no longer have your golden-tipped spear, the great death ash of the field, to protect you. Unwisely, you cast it across the host at battle's start. What else can one expect of an age-ravaged mind, but to toss aside a sure weapon for a toothpick?"

Odin swung his blade, so its polished length caught the sun. As the metal glowed red in the faded light, the embossed serpent seemed to rise ready to strike. "I do not need the sure tip of Gungnir, when I've a strong, keen blade in my fist. Though, if I still wielded my bright staff, your feet would already be on the thorny road."

Fenris stopped his movement, back arched, sword held at the ready. "Then let's see if your skill with a naked blade equals your luck with a dwarf-crafted spear."

Odin struck a sharp blow with the thin part of his blade. But the wolf's sharp edge parried the tip, then dipped to bite into the ancient warrior's thigh. Fenris laughed, shaking his bloodied blade as the wound dew ran down its length to gather at the hilt. "What is this? The once-mighty oak fails to strike, while I bite freely, and deep too, from the amount of blood that colors my edge. Now let us see that famous battle stance, the poised balance of a well-rooted tree."

The great wolf towered over the Father of Armies, grinning at the dauntless warrior who hobbled before him. "Your blade is sluggish like its wielder." Fenris whipped his blade in a high arc above his head. "And he who asks for doom I gladly send wandering."

Too late Odin returned his blade to the feast as Fenris' broadsword sped down, its heavy edge gnawing deep into the helm-of-terror, splitting wide his skull. Blood flowed in rivers over Odin's ears to drench his beard.

Straddling the crumpled body of Sigfodur, Fenris shook his blade over his head. "The goddess of shields was reddened this day. The famous leader fell beneath my hungry blade. I reckon it a start on revenge."

Freyr and Surt

Boldly advanced the bright light of summer—Freyr, war leader of the Æsir—to face the Fire of Muspellsheim. He missed his sure flickering flame—Gambanteinn the greatest of swords—etched with power over the sons of bitter frost, the bride price paid to Gymir for this daughter Gerd.

Surt turned to face the son of Njord. Bringing his sword to bear, he flashed it sideways so Freyr could plainly see the make of blade he carried. "So, Bright One, you come to battle dimmed in arm. No longer do you brandish your smart blade. Whose hand now wields its power?" Leering, he jerked his chin at Freyr's weapon. "All you grip in your sweaty fist is that pretty little cloak pin. A poor trade for a moment's pleasure. I see you even replaced deer horn with steel. A wise move, for you face an opponent greater in stature and skill than Beli."

Freyr strode grandly forward, weapon at the ready. His eyes lingered only a moment on the familiar blade, then turned back to gaze unflinching into the fiery eyes of Surt. "There may be some truth to your words, but my blade, as my arm, is stout enough to deal out sharp rebuke to the likes of you. Come see what I can do."

The Bright Slayer of Beli hefted his new blade, the sword of Sigarsholm, the evil one among battle needles: on its hilt balanced a ring of gold, the middle of the blade held courage, at its tip stood terror. In the light of a faded sun a blood-eyed snake coiled along its edge, while about its hilt a serpent chased its tail. There is no self-direction here; the cold steel is dumb to shrewd guidance. Still, his arm is wise in the ways of war and moves of its own command. The fire's blows were quickly repulsed.

Surt danced back out of range from Freyr's blade, flexing his arm from the shock of metal-on-metal. "Your skill is great," he glared at the war leader of the Æsir, "but you've gone the fool's wrong way in this fight. There will be only empty halls at your death. None will be left to hang gray wadmal. Perhaps you recognize my blade—the bane of the gods—retrieved from its earthy hideaway by Gymir's swordbearer. Once, your delicate hand guided its edge, now it is directed by my strong arm."

Freyr sneered at the black one. "Arrogance feeds your words. My ears are bored with its sound." He raised his menacing blade until its tip pointed at the hard acorn of Surt's heart. "Today I prefer the harsh clash of the battle storm to the haughty words of a pompous jay. Let us light the air with our wound flames."

Sparks flew from clashing blades. Metal screamed in protest as each delivered better than received. The ringing of their blows dimmed the sounds of the raging battle. A swiping cut split links of hardened mail, the blade tip drawing a thin red line across Freyr's chest.

"Your edge is soft," Surt grinned, gesturing with his blade, "and soon snaggletoothed. It is hardly a weapon to stand against mine. See how easily I slide past your guard."

Ignoring the pain, Freyr stepped over the bodies of fallen warriors until his footing was secure on firm ground. "You speak as if your words could wound. I think perhaps you lack a tail in front, as well as the gift for intimidating speech. Today is a good day for brave deeds, not the puffery of hot, blustery words."

Surt straightened up from a battle crouch until he towered over Njord's son. The tip of his blade dropped to point at Freyr's feet. "The ass receives what he gives at home, while the bold warrior takes what he wants in the field," he sneered. "None will hold back their praise of my skill when they see you fall beneath my flame."

Widening his stance, Freyr leaned forward, ready to attack or dodge. "You who make blades bound suppose my fate is held in your two strong fists. That is expected. But before you get to me craver-of-wound-strife there will be a victory cheer from me yet!" Freyr gave a battle yell and leapt forward, bringing his weapon in line. His blade tip narrowly missed the open throat of his foe as Surt twisted aside.

The Black one waved his sword, brighter than the sun. The glare blinded the child of the Vanir. The cry of the goddess of metal rang harsh as the blazing flame sang out greedy for blood. The son of Njord fell beneath Surt's burning blade. The foe of wood cheered loudly as the heart blood of the proud warrior mingled with the trampled dust of Vigrid plain.

Vidar and the Fenris Wolf

His appetite piqued on Heriar, Fenris turned to face the silent advance of a leather clad warrior. "You clump forward, Far Ruler, with the craven stealth I've come to expect from all Æsir. But it is your clownish footgear that tells who you are: Vidar, son of Gríd. Skinflint, you've built your boots from the castoffs of men, but in their largess, they held back the laces. I tell you misers never give a gift without a snag."

Sliding into position, Vidar placed a hand on the hilt of his sword, ready to draw and ward off any blow or to strike adder quick. "Laugh, if you will, at my footgear, for it is a collection of extra pieces that men have cut away from boot toe and heel. Armored with such spirit, you have no hope of defeating me."

Fenris chuckled, slid his blade across one arm to wipe it clean, then patted it in the palm of his free hand. "You were absent when the Æsir imprisoned me with their treachery. I have paid them back in full measure by splitting wide the head of your clan. Now, having defeated your mind, your thoughts are of no consequence. Beg that I spare you."

Vidar kept his eyes focused on the easy movements of the wolf, turned with his every step, careful to keep his sword side facing the foe. "I have more courage than most." He moved left as Fenris shifted his stance. "I hold high expectations of defeating a ravening wolf. Know that I am an avenger of the gods. Born to this role, I fear neither man nor beast. And I do not fear you."

"A tasty morsel after such a feast," the wolf crouched low, knees flexed, ready to spring, "you are little more than the just payment of a hand for years of painful bondage, hardly worth the effort to swallow."

Fenris glanced at the still-sheathed sword of his adversary. "Overconfident, you think to parry my attack by drawing your blade at the last moment. You will learn that on the field of battle the blade should always be carried in the fist or tied to your wrist, ready at an instant."

As Fenris launched himself across the space, Vidar swung about to block his leap. "Then, vile beast, start with my foot!" Kicking up his leg, the brother of Vali thrust his boot into the wolf's slavering jaws. Like the blade wedged in his jaws on the island Lyngvi, the wolf ground his teeth and growled menacingly against the leather impediment. Thick ropes of drool poured from the corners of his mouth, springing forth new courses of hope for the river Van.

His foot pinioning the lower jaw, Vidar dug his fingers into the eye sockets of Hvedrung's son. With a mighty heave, he wrenched the jaw free. The Fenris wolf choked, crying out in anguish as hope ran red with his blood. Vidar straddled the Beast of Slaughter, drew his long blade and, with a steady hand, thrust it deep into the heart of Loki's son.

A howl of rage faded to low gurgle as the lifeblood of Fenris rushed in a warm, crimson torrent over Vidar's hand. The death of his father avenged, Vidar stepped back, twisting free his blade. With a wide grin that bared his gate of white teeth, the son of Gríd, eyes alight, the red edge of his sword held high, laughed, and turned back to the field of slaughter.

Thor and the Midgard Serpent

With bold steps, Thor advanced to face the great circumciser of the world. Blue eye met red orb in the glare of battle hate. The terrible jaws of Jormungand gaped wide and a horrible squall split the air. A gate of yellow scythes hovered over the battlefield. From their tips burning venom fell like rain.

Thor stood tall before the serpent. His brow, graven with thunder scars, roiled with black clouds, as his dark brooding eyes flashed defiance. Megingjard girded tight about his waist, his mailed fist brandishing Mjollnir high overhead, the protector of the gods roared out his challenge to match the shrieking of his foe. "The air reeks with the stench of poison that drips from your fangs, while the very ground trembles with your scream. Few are the warriors willing to face such a fiend, but I do not flinch from this clash of foes. Twice before we met in contest. Each time you survived my challenges unscathed. This time, death fish, I will destroy you!"

The ocean lasher spat poison into the air. The son of earth dodged the gorge and wheeled in close. A powerful swipe from his hammer grazed Jormungand's head, tumbling the serpent back amid a writhing of coils.

With a mighty Yawp that deafened the storm, the tail biter lashed out with venomous teeth, tearing at the metal of Thor's mail coat, the gash baring his chest, but leaving his flesh untouched. The blow drove Thor backward over the killing field, his feet catching on tangled bodies that lay strewn about the ground. Cursing under his breath, he kicked free of the dead, stomping familiar faces from the mead bench, until his feet were planted firmly on bare earth.

A deafening roar ripped from his throat as Thor swung Mjollnir in a wide arc and struck the serpent a violent blow alongside the head. Jormungand reared back shrieking in pain, the ocean waves echoing his agony. The air shook as if all the ancient earth were collapsing. Blood spurting from his nostrils, the circumscriber beneath all lands gaped wide, stretching his jaws until his open maw seemed to fill the sky. A powerful spray of poison spewed forth, engulfing Fjorgyn's cherished child.

A shudder rippled the length of his body as, with a final breath, Jormungand sagged to the ground. His great coils unraveled in all directions, crushing warriors from both sides as they attempted to scurry out of the way. Choked with the deadly sputum of the serpent, Thor staggered backward nine paces before falling face down into his mother's embrace.

Modi and Magni rushed to the scene. Quickly, they gathered up Mjollnir from where it lay beside their father's body, stripped off his belt of strength and iron glove lest they fall into a foeman's hands. With a final salute for the fallen protector, terse battlefield death rights for a beloved father, the courageous and strong returned to the melee of battle.

Heimdall and Loki

Heimdall's silver helmet flashed bright white, ram horns shining, as rays from the sun crossed its brow. The field grew crowded with eager warriors as many bore their weapons against him. Like moths drawn to a burning flame, scorched by his fiery brand they fell in droves to flutter helplessly on the ground.

A dark warrior with pockmarked face, his features wrapped in a hoary mane of hair, jeered from the line of risen dead. "Who is that with the shiny helm hiding himself from creditable foes behind the shield wall of the Æsir? Why, it must be none other than the white god, the stalwart sentry of Bifrost, though yellow should be his color, since he is more used to watching than fighting!"

Heimdall yelled out in defiance, recognizing the barbed taunts and the one who delivered them. "Hold forth, if in your lust for victory you seek to face a worthy foe. I know you, son of Farbauti. Worthy is a word you do not comprehend. Unlike you, I have never borne two shields, but remained honor-bound to one."

Pushing through the throng of battling warriors, Loki made his way toward the shining helmet of Heimdall. "Brave words from the watch dog of the gods. Get up off your back! You'll need not wait over long to taste the edge of my blade!"

The two charged, eyes burning with fury, swinging their wound flames in the crowded field. Their bright edges took a heavy toll — the metal dyed with the blood of fallen warriors—as a ragged space cleared about them. Enemies of long standing, they circled as two curs on first meeting edge stiff-legged about each other, wary of a sudden attack.

Heimdall touched his blade to his helmet, then dipped it to point at Loki's face. "I see you've arranged your hair in a comical manner. Few would disagree you bear the likeness of a goat. Truly, it is an image more suited to your nature."

Loki slowly skirted the open space, cautiously planting each step between the twisted limbs of fallen warriors. "That my hair has grown in stiffness to resemble horns is only of concern to the effeminate. Your concern should be the sharp edge of my weapons."

Heimdall let his hate flow from his tongue and his scorn build through his words. "Bold words poorly backed, from what I see. You ride into battle as a stallion with a host of miserable geldings braying at your side."

Loki snapped back in reply, eager to wound in kind for the sharp rebuke.

"Harsh words from a lowly sentry tarnished with age. For you a hateful life was decreed, a muddy back and lonely outpost, while others reveled within the great halls. So much for the bringer of culture. Little honor you were shown for your deeds of goodwill to the race of men."

The white god rapped his blade against his shield. Three times the metal gave sharp report. "Long distances I can see, soft sounds I can hear, but I need look no farther than before my nose to see a black tongue and craven heart. While on watch, I could only warn, today I gladly finish that which should have been finished long ago on the rock of Singastein!"

Loki lifted his sword and scramasax, the single-edged battle knife of a bold warrior, feinted with one then lunged with the other. Heimdall deftly parried the blows. Loki danced back into a low crouch. "In the past, we've had our conflicts; you cheated me out of the Brising bauble and often stopped me from exercising my rights. Now you will get your fill of my hatred."

Heimdall shifted his sword in his hand, marked his spot, then struck out with a flurry of blows. "Your mouth runs as wild as ever. This time it is not mead that loosens your tongue, but arrogance that steals your wits. Today you'll do worse than being bound with your son's ice-cold guts."

Loki beat back the attack. "You threaten me? I, who sheared a slice from your clan shield. Bold was the act and, oh, what a howling I caused. Still it took all the Æsir to capture me, a salmon in the falls."

Heimdall turned the bright white of his shield to face Farbauti's son. "No matter what shape you take—gnat, fish, or hart—I can find you. Crawl as a worm, more fitting your temperament, or glide as an eagle, you will not escape me. My tuned ears will track you in whatever form you take."

The white god raised his blade of wave-marked iron. "Come Sanga svitiri, be bold in your attack, for I hold the keen-edged weapon of a dauntless warrior. In battle its stroke never fails, and its wounds do not heal."

Loki scuffed the dirt before him, kicking blood-soaked clods across the open ground onto Heimdall's feet. "It is you, mud turtle, who should come to me. For I hold in my right hand a wound wand, its hilt braided round with silver. In my left," he hefted a short blade, "this deadly, keen-tipped dagger well balanced for striking."

Heimdall stomped the ground, raising a splattering ring of bloody mud. "When you guided Hodd's blind aim you took away our innocence, forever dimming the nine worlds to harsh temperament."

"Your innocence had left you," Loki laughed, "long before Baldur's passing. And as for missing his light," he circled right seeking advantage, "as my actions ensured the death of a favored son, so, too, will I ensure you soon bask in his faded glow."

Heimdall stepped carefully over a fallen spear, a dismembered hand still gripping its shaft. "Whenever fighting, I am always in front, alone before all." He turned, keeping his shield facing his foe. "So, I will roar in this clash of shields while my life lasts, and my blade survives—the true iron that has stood steadfastly by me. Though I consider you a corruption, unworthy of its keen edge. Come, let us see if you have the courage to confront a valiant opponent who has never run from your challenge!"

The son of Farbauti teetered on the balls of his feet. "This warrior would sooner battle naked than falter in the fray before one such as you!"

Loki lunged, his sword and dagger poised as teeth to deliver death. The white god shot out his shield to ward off the sudden attack. A brutal blow crashed down, splitting Heimdall's shield to his arm. He staggered back, throwing the useless shield halves aside. Loki took advantage of the opening by savagely thrusting his long dagger deep into Heimdall's stomach. He stood close, glaring with delight as the sentry of the gods lurched aside, hunched over his wound.

Fumbling, staggering, Heimdall firmly gripped the braided handle of his sword in both hands. With a cry of defiance, he heaved it in a great arc. Too startled to dodge, the blow caught Loki square on the crest of his helmet, the blade splitting his head down to his shoulders, the edge stopping at his breastbone. The horns on Loki's head gaped wide and his brainpan sloshed down his chest. With a low groan both warriors collapsed into the dust.

Tyr and Garm

His face etched with a grin that nearly reached his ears, the one-handed god hewed lustily from side to side, splitting wide the corpse plains that sprang up before him, each blow spattering his ring byrnie with gore until none dared challenge his might.

Tyr stood before the enemy host, battle flame raised high over his head, shouting out abuse to egg them on. "Is the war fodder of Surt so fearful of a one-handed warrior that they are afraid to advance? Is there none that know themselves worthy to face me? I expected more from the followers of the wood's foe."

The enemy line burst wide with a sudden roar that drowned out the fury of the spear storm. The dim host of Loki cringed back, remembering their first encounter before Gnipa Cave. A thick-bodied hound stood before the dauntless Æsir, feet planted fore square, broad head dipped low, throat and muzzle stained red with the blood of fallen foes. Heavy lips curled back to bare yellowed fangs. A low rumble echoed from the massive chest. Garm of the bloody breast stood ready and defiant.

Flashing his own teeth in a wide grin, Tyr crouched low. "What is this menacing growl I hear? Could it be a puppy just pulled from the bitch's teat? Your daunting voice trembled the air when leashed before Gnipa Cave. Now it is barely a whisper in this storm of storms."

Garm advanced stiff-legged, lips fluttering with snarls, nose casting side to side as he sought out his foe's weakness. He slowly circled to the right. The battle-wary hound knew whom he faced.

Tyr beckoned Garm with the bloody blade held tight in his fist. "Come greatest of all hounds. Bare your teeth at one who will never flinch. I who dared my hand in the wolf's mouth will never cringe before a mere puppy."

He scraped his blade against his shield rim, sighting along its edge. "In truth, I am honored to finally face a noble warrior, one I know worthy of my challenge. I wearied of Hel's spawn that I cut down as chaff. Had the others heeded my counsel when first you stood before us at the Thing of Urd, you would be fighting on our side this day, but now as foes we must face each other."

With that, Tyr brought his blade about for a quick strike. A ferocious howl broke from Garm as he launched himself at the war god's throat.

The attack was relentless. With slash of tooth and hack of blade, both bit wherever they touched. Tyr swung wide at Garm, the sharp edge of his blade whistling as it sliced through the air, but the hound of Niflheim was quicker. Dodging aside, he lunged in beneath the blow to tear at areas unprotected by armor.

Tyr stumbled back, pressing with the stump of his right wrist to staunch the flow of blood that gushed from a ragged wound. He cursed softly, then laughed. "A lucky strike that caught me napping. You will not find me slow again. Your eyes are like those of a shining serpent. With the strength of my one good hand, I will soon dull their glow."

The one-handed god of war threw down his sword and shield. Ripping off his battle helm he cast it into the mud, then, with a deafening bellow, dove for Garm. The ever-eager hound rejoiced, roaring as he lunged. Tyr caught Garm's ear with one hand, wrenched the hound's head to one side and buried his teeth into the furry throat so blood gushed over his cheeks. Twisting around in Tyr's powerful grip, the hound sank his fangs deep into the neck of the warrior god. Locked in the embrace of battle lovers, they tumbled together onto the field.

Both fighters raged in fury as they fought for dominance. Each hated the other while both lived, the greatest of hounds against the most honorable of the Æsir. Clinched in death, bathed in mingled blood, they rolled across the ground. Blood pulsed from their bodies into the thirsty clay of Vigrid plain until the last of their life surged from their wounds and with a final shudder of breath, they lay still.

The Battle of Vali

In pockets now, the battle surged, bloody knots braided on a long rope that wavered as a serpent slithers across the plain. Each knot a cluster of warriors drawn to the shiny helmets of the Æsir gods. A huge warrior—easily 20 hands tall—stepped forward into Vali's path. Heavy thewed and broad-shouldered, his worn byrnie was sturdy, but of ancient make. In his fist, he gripped a bright blade dripping with the blood of fallen Einherjar. Lifeless, pale blue eyes shone from beneath a helmet dented from many blows. A sneer split his frostbitten lips as he looked down on the son of Rind.

> "Low do I behold a fiercely clad Æsir.
> Helmet burnished, ring-byrnie gleaming.
> Terror of the hearth stone,
> each morn he braves the oven fires for food.
> Boldly stands before me the bread destroyer,
> a distresser of loafs clutched warily in his fist."

Vali raised himself to his full height, a hand shy of his foe's ears, planted his feet squarely and did not move. "I emerged battling from my mother's womb; my purpose, to defeat my brother's killer. This onerous deed, I accomplished when I sent Hodd along the red road for casting a fatal sprig of mistletoe, though the real enemy was Loki."

"So, you are Vali, the avenger of Baldur." The foeman grinned, tapping his blade against his shoulder depositing a swatch of blood across his chest. "I have heard of your great accomplishment—the besting of an old blind man. An easy task for a wet-nursed infant, but it is hardly a triumph for a real warrior."

Vali thumped his blade against his chest, the dull thud of a stave rapped against a full barrel. "Who are you to toss such scorn, you who are already doomed? Dead twice, I'll soon send you lurching back along the dark road you traveled to get here!"

The foeman shifted his stance, so the rays of the sun fell into Vali's eyes. "My name is unimportant, Æsir scum. Know that I fought bravely in the army of Sigurd Fafnirsbani. We routed many enemies and defeated many valiant foes. But when my time came to fall on the field of valor, the bright helmed maidens denied my boldness and left me behind to face my judgment, alone." His lips curled into a deep frown as he sidestepped to the right. "The injustice still burns in my breast for what I endured. I have waited a long time for this moment, a chance to avenge myself against the boastful gods. You will not survive this battle, kin-destroyer, though the skalds may weave a different tale."

Vali settled in behind his shield and laughed at the threat. "You snivel like a child who failed to get his way. In life, I face my choices without wailing, for on one day the entire span of my life was laid out. In death, I do not fear the cup of fate, be it a draught of poison or the waters of the three wells. Though I can easily guess what was mixed in your drink."

"Many have fared badly at my hands." Blade gripped in both fists, the foeman advanced. "You will be no different." Impassive, relentless, he stomped across the corpses littering the ground. "When I am angry the very earth hides from me. If any living creature comes before my glance, straightaway it falls down dead. With my eyes, I can blunt any weapon. Show me what you've got!"

Vali lifted his blade to catch light along its length and reflected it back into the dead eyes of his foe. "Let your eye meet Skrymir, a strong blade, serviceable and worthy. My weapon is twice-etched with victory. Its edge is sharp and never dirty. Its balanced hilt well fits my hand. It is all I need to best the likes of you."

The foeman jerked his chin at Vali's sword. "I'm not afraid of that splinter. My own blade is as good or better. From the gore that wets the full length of its edge, it has certainly drunk more deeply than yours." He sneered and beckoned with a nod of his head. "Come, bold fighter, give me your best. I will spank you with the flat of my blade and send you weeping from war play."

Lowering the blade, Vali flexed his knees as he brought his shield to bear. "Your ridicule is lame. It may strike fear in the heart of a thrall or a farmer, but not in the heart of a brave warrior. Let us test our strength with reddened blades." He rapped his blade against the rim of his shield. Three times the challenging tones sang out. "I'll feed eagles your raw flesh!"

Bloody swords rang amid a shower of heavy blows. Sparks rained to mix with the fog of red mist that choked the air. With a ferocious blow, the foeman shattered Vali's shield; the pieces fell useless from his arm. He stepped forward, exposing his chest, unafraid of Vali's blade. "You need not wait over long for me to deliver a maiming blow from my gleaming wound snake. Come meet the warrior who swings his sword like a serpent inflicting wounds."

Then Vali struck back, a double-handed blow that split the foeman's breast, unleashing torrents of red gore from his chest. The avenger god smiled and held forth his weapon as the warrior toppled before him. "Your eye was blinded by arrogance. The victory runes etched on my blade's edge neatly warded off your gormless stare."

The Battle of Magni

Ferocious etins attacked, in murderous mood they went for blood. Mouths gaping wide, hard lips tipped with yellowed teeth, they dashed about with oaken clubs to burst wide the skulls of valiant warriors. Magni stood firm in their path, fearlessly waiting on their approach.

He felt his strength double as he cinched Megingjard tight about his waist. Slipping Jarngreipr, the iron gauntlet of this father, onto his right hand, he grabbed the handle of Mjollnir, felt its power crackle up his arm.

Raising the hammer over his head, with a bold voice he called out to the line of thurs. "I am Magni, son of Thor! My strength is equal that of my father! With my father's hammer in hand, I am the scourge of etins!"

The lofty behemoths advanced toward his position, the ground shaking with their steps as they stomped forward to meet his challenge. A hill giant called out from the front of the throng, his head higher than the fells, an oaken club stained red clutched in his hand. "I see you have retrieved your father's fallen weapon, his belt of strength and iron glove too. Pity the serpent wasn't able to swallow him whole and spare you the anguish of attempting their use. Inherited burdens are hardest for children to carry." He pointed his club at Mjollnir and snickered. "Lethal in your father's hands, it is little more than a cumbersome weight in yours. You had best put it aside and arm yourself with a more familiar weapon. Perhaps a rattle would better fit your temperament."

Magni's face flushed red in anger at the taunt. The etin chuckled, lifted his club, and sighted down its length. "I had hoped to crush the son of Odin myself and so gain vengeance for his slaughter of my people, though the Norns had decreed otherwise. Know child of my greatest enemy that you face Hrym, war leader of the etin. Come forward, little god, and fight me if you are eager to die, though I do not imagine I will grow in stature by taking your life."

Magni shifted the hammer in his hand, swung it lightly as he tested its weight. "Have no thought that I will refuse your request. I am eager to sport with a son of the Frost. Prepare for a fight! I offer no hope of mercy!"

Hrym tossed back his head and split the air with laughter. "Your skull is thick like that of your father. Such a dome would not be easy for weak men to break nor a clever thought to breach." He shook his club at the sky. "In my hand, I wield this bludgeon spiked with jagged scraps of iron and shards of bone. Over my shoulder, I carry this whetstone. Either will easily crush your brainpan. Have a taste of what comes next!"

A harsh blow glanced across Magni's helmet so sharply the metal rang as a bell, sending the son of Thor stumbling back to firmer ground. Hrym opened his eyes wide in mock surprise. "What is this?" He shook a chiding finger. "The self-proclaimed wielder of Mjollnir retreats from my force. From the strength of your loud boasts, I would never have thought it possible."

"For your scornful remarks," Magni grimaced, resetting his dented helmet, "you'll kiss the blunt head of my sledge. I have never retreated in battle nor did I now before your strength. I did not cringe from the blow, though it rattled my helmet, but merely sought to set my feet to a better stance."

Hrym waved his club, fanning the air, loosing a shower of blood-laden wind that spattered against Magni's face. "I hear the yapping of a new-born pup; brave words from such a small creature. Grab your hair girt sword and run before I rip it off. You may be brave, but you cannot defeat me in this test of strength." Reaching back with his free hand, the etin flipped a large flat stone over his shoulder.

The flinty whetstone spun through the air to graze the forehead of the son of Jarnsaxa. The stone wedged fast to the edge of his shield to jut, stained with blood, from the iron rim. Wound dew dripped into Magni's eyes, blinding him to the etin's advance. "You stand bewildered as a child before the raging waves of a gale-wrought storm before it crashes down to carry him away. Brace yourself, little god, for this storm comes now!"

As Hrym stepped in to deliver a final blow, Magni leapt aside. The etin's club crashed harmlessly onto the ground where he had stood. Spinning about, the son of Thor brought his father's hammer down with a clang onto Hrym's head. The sound of his gauntlet rattled above the battle storm while the crashing blow of Mjollnir echoed among the clouds. Mortally wounded, Hrym groaned as he crumpled to the ground.

Smirking to himself, Magni dragged his hammer from the bloody brow of the fallen thurs; flecks of gray matter clung to its iron head. "Many are those who know themselves strong that believe others are weak." He tore a rag from Hrym's battle shirt to wipe the hammer clean. "Often, when battling an unknown foe, such fools find it is they who are defeated."

The Battle of Modi

The battle lines spread wide across the flinty plain, weaving like snakes in the shimmering air. On the bloody field stood an ogress, her wide spread feet rooted to the ground—a mountain washed by the rising tide of war. Her shoulder crag was balanced on a thick neck and sprouted a dense forest of wolf-gray hair. An ungainly nose spread itself across the swarthy plain of her face. Dark gleaming eyes beaded from beneath a bushy ridge.

Her features were harsh with a fierceness to shrivel flesh as she laid about with fists like oaken clubs shattering helmet-clad skulls and rending limbs from their moorings. The red blood of valiant warriors dripping from her fingers, she snatched a fighter from the line, clutched him close as a spider its prey, then, with a ragged fingernail, slit him wide from throat to crotch. Blood flowed in thick ropy streams down her breast, and his screams lasted only a moment before she tossed him aside.

Modi approached the ogress, gliding across the ground made slick with blood to stand unflinching in her shadow. Shield held high, he raised his sturdy blade and rang it three times against the shield's iron rim in challenge.

The ogress turned at the sound. A leer twisted the corners of her lips as she spotted the brother of Magni in a defiant crouch nearby. "You act boldly for one so small and play a merry tune with your weapons. I don't think you are afraid of much. What is your name tiny warrior? What do your comrades call you?"

The young warrior shifted to a better position, brought his blade in behind his shield ready to ward off attack. "Modi, I am called, son of Thor, atrocious to you. Like my father, I am most hostile to giants and ogresses. For sport, I stand atop dew-washed peaks to torment night-riding spirits. I fear neither man nor beast and I do not fear you!"

He lowered his shield and jerked his chin at the ogress before bringing it back so only his eyes showed over the rim. "What is your name, corpse-greedy troll? Name your father! I would know who I hack down before I return you nine leagues beneath the earth, so fir trees can once more take root in your breast."

The ogress laughed at his words—a sharp grating sound that jarred the ears. "Hrymgard, the winds call me." Her gate of yellow teeth split into a wide grin. "Harrati is my father, the worst of the lava-dwelling ogres. He drives our battle line south from here. Already, he has cut a bloody swath through your forces."

Modi sneered. "Yet here you stand," he barked. "Barely have our lines moved. Blame the clay in your feet for your poor progress. You do Mokkurkalfi proud. Soon, too, the piss will run down your legs."

The ogress calmly flicked blood from her fingers. "You bray like a gelding, tiny Æsir. Come," she playfully patted her rump, "Hrymgard's raising her tail. I think your heart is in your ass, though you challenge me with a stallion's voice."

Modi shifted his stance, careful to keep his shield raised high. "A stallion I'd be if you wanted to try! Were we to couple on this bloody plain, you would be lame in every part. You would drop your tail and cry 'Enough!' I would see to that!"

Hrymgard barred her gate of snaggled teeth, great yellow plates flecked with the flesh of warriors tasted during battle. "Big boasts, little man. Advance now if you trust your strength. Know that I will straighten your ribs when I get my hands on you." She pointed a crooked finger at the red mounds of flesh clotting the ground about her position. "See strewn as rushes about my feet the bodies of your great warriors fallen in battle, foes of great strength crushed by my battle grip, their bone houses collapsed, their beating hearts stilled."

Modi lifted his blade to flash in the sun. "My sword was forged by Regin. Its keen edge can split a tuft of wool pushed against it by a burbling brook. Just as its brother split Regin's anvil and pierced Fafnir's heart, so, too, my blade will open your breast!"

Eyes flaming, the ogress reached out a bloody talon, eager to tear life from limb. A ribbon of drool ran from the corner of her mouth, and she licked her lips in anticipation. The strong son of Thor parried the scaled fist. Her claws raked divots across his shield, tearing bosses from its face. He bit back with his wound flame, slicing deep into her forearm, so she howled with pain.

At once Hrymgard struck out again, filled with rage, greedy for blood. Snatching Modi from the ground, she clutched him tightly to her chest, yet her terrible embrace did no harm. The gold-ringed byrnie that wrapped his chest protected from her claws. His father's blood coursing through his frame protected from her crushing embrace.

He repaid her fierce attack with his bloody blade. Drawing back his arm until the blade swung free, he tipped it round then thrust it forward. The battle flasher tunneled deep into her breast, its hilt standing flush against her leathery skin. A horrid wail escaped the ogress' lips as she found her wound fatal. Her body convulsed, blood bubbled from her lips, and Hrymgard fell dead to the ground.

Thick black gore gushed from the wound as Modi wrenched his sword from its fleshy embrace. The blade sweat blood while the warrior rejoiced. Shield held high, Modi rapped his wound flame against its iron rim. Three times, he struck with his blade. Three times, he rang his victory.

The Long Arm of Ull

The skilled archer stationed himself behind the front line to better offer cover for the Einherjar, his fletched shafts shielding them from rock-boned cliff dwellers, while they clashed with Loki's minions. The heated thurs were greeted by flocks of feathered darts, an arrow storm that struck deep the advancing line of formidable giants, piercing breastplates, and felling many. The bright points flit through the air, an endless flight of whispering goslings launched from his bow, to stitch crimson plumes across etin chests.

The noise of spears grew loud as a raw-boned rock dweller crashed its way through the battle line, scattering warriors as chaff before a strong wind, eager to seek revenge for kinsmen taken by the archer. "I am Hergaut, son of Hrymir, the mighty thurs fallen in battle to Hlodyn's son those years past when the Everglow graced the border of Utgarda. Who is the coward that withers our ranks with his volleys of fearsome darts?"

"I am Ull," the archer shouted as he nocked another shaft and sent the quill shrieking through the air to split the eye of an etin warrior, sending him toppling backwards into his own ranks, "stepson of the self-same god who struck down your father in fair combat. I've more than enough temperament for wielding swords, though my arm prefers the bow. You will never find me cringing before strong words or a boldly brandished fist!"

Hergaut stomped forward now that his enemy stood plainly visible before him. "You hide as all craven Æsir hide, crouched behind a wall of fallen heroes. Now that the wall's been breached, bodies and blood steaming in the cleft, let us see how you, who easily send death from a distance, fare when a foe looks you full in the eye."

The son of Orvandel leapt to one side as an oaken club crashed where he had stood, spraying clods of earth into the air. The ground trembled with the blow and the wind of its passing whipped Ull's byrnie. The giant spun about to follow Ull's swift movement. "You are fast Æsir, quick as a mouse scuttling before a hungry wolf, eager to conceal itself in the grass, but you are no match for me."

The giant took several shambling steps in pursuit. "Many are the foes I've defeated, crushed with my bare hands until their bones and bloody flesh sprang out from between my fingers. With a keen edge, I've split them wide, the two halves falling as one. With stout arm brandishing an oaken club, I've battered them into a red stain on the ground."

Ull nocked another arrow and made ready to draw his bow. When an opening appeared in Hergaut's guard, the archer called out from his new position that his foe would know where to look. "I am deadly with the bent yew as was my father before me, a star hero with tributes arranged in the heavens, his grandeur for all to see. I am skilled in the art of hand-to-hand combat and once knew the joy of warriors calling on me for aide in battle. Though few enough remember me now, still I am game enough to meet you."

Sighting down the shaft of his arrow, he waited on Hergaut's advance until he was looking directly into his eyes. "Many are the etin I've defeated. While not eager for this battle, I happily launch arrows from my good yew to pierce the corpse plains of my foes. I'll not stop until all of your kinsmen are lying on the ground, food for the gray stud horse of the troll woman, or I've fallen beneath the judgment of swords. Come feel the strength of my long arm."

Ull drew taught the quivering gut string until the yew bent deep. Straight flew the death dart loosed from its moorings to split the distance between the dark eyes of the rock-boned cliff dweller. The barb punched through his brainpan, the arrow penetrating as far as its bands. A second arrow followed before the first had touched, burrowing its head deep into the etin's neck so that the barbed tip protruded from the other side.

Then, like an Iceland poppy worn by the heat of summer that droops forward to lose it petals, the proud etin bowed his head and slumped to the ground. A crimson river meandered from his wounds to mix with the dust of Vigrid plain.

The Death of Bragi

Along the battle line rode a great Troll woman, a mother of etin's born to defy, astride a large grizzled wolf, a bridle of adders coiled around her wrists. Her white shield glowed in the bright light of battle as she swung a roped brick to jar the flesh of brave warriors. Bodies lay under the claws of her gray steed. Madly, she dyed inside the wolf's mouth with blood.

The fount of Odrerir shouted out, as he pushed his way to the front of the lines. "I see you, Hyrrokkin! You, who once aided the gods by putting to sea the funeral pyre of Baldur, the Ring ship that the gods themselves could not move!"

Hyrrokkin drew her mount to a halt, dismounted and sauntered through the mayhem to where Bragi waited uneasy in his armor. "And I see you, the loud mouth of the Æsir. One for whom sharp words are weapons, but who quakes in fear at a sturdy arm and sharp edge."

Bragi scanned her mount, noting the wolf in the harness. "I see you have acquired a new steed. The old one, no longer suited for riding, you left behind in the ash of the pyre."

Hyrrokkin swiped her brick to clear a space about them. "No thanks to the Æsir lackeys who struck down my mount. Cold payment for lending my strength in honor of pure innocence."

Bragi flinched at the wind of the brick that threatened to turn him back, but, taking a deep breath, kept his feet facing the enemy. "This mount appears ill suited to you," he shouted. "Your flabby thighs drape heavily across its sides, and its back bows beneath your weight. Show mercy to the poor creature and walk instead of ride?"

Leaning forward Hyrrokkin jabbed a scaly finger at the ancient skald. The power of her breath flowed over Bragi, choking him with the tang of fresh blood mixed with the stink of putrid flesh. With effort, he held back the gorge building in his throat. "Strong words from a quivering wretch. They barely warm my ears with their fire. Little do I fear the hare in rage. Even from here I can see your knees quivering. Come taste the clay of my hearth-fired brick."

She swung her roped brick, sending Bragi dancing back out of the way. "You have quick feet for such a loud mouth. Next time you won't be so fast."

"I'm swift enough for the likes of a clumsy, bloated creature such as you," Bragi wiped a shaking hand across his face.

"Oh, such sharpness," Hyrrokkin hissed, her fingers dancing eagerly as she dragged the brick back for another swing. "Of you I'll carve an eagle; hew your ribs from your backbone down to the loins then pull your breath sacks out through the cuts. From there your lofty words can take flight."

Thrusting out his chest, Bragi rapped his blade against shield edge. The sound was scarcely noticeable in the battle storm that raged about them. "For such harsh words, I offer hard tribute! Here, amid this grim din of shields, I will fall dead under the claws of your mount or, I'll toss my bright shield aside and with both hands have your head!"

The giantess swung her roped brick, striking the middle of Bragi's shield and splitting the iron-rimmed target into two parts. "Now," she jeered, coiling the rope of her brick, "you'll not need to toss it aside."

With bold steps Bragi advanced, a poem coming to mind of a proud minstrel who fell defiant beneath a foeman's chain. With the song on his lips he raised his blade and charged into the flash of tooth, claw, and whistling brick.

The Sending of Brynhild

Vali called Brynhild from the air, where the helmeted maidens of war whirled in a haze of raining blood, their blades slashing through the ranks of the enemy below. "A last duty, loyal daughter of the battle helm. Carry a message to Frigg. She waits with the others at Fensalir. Tell them what you have witnessed here on the field of valor."

Hild scowled at Vali. "Who are you to direct my actions?" She stepped forward, rapping the flat of her blade against her chest, menace shining from her eyes. "I answer only to Heriar and he lies dead, his skull cleaved in two."

"This order does not come from me." Vali gazed steadily into pale blue eyes that glared back in deadly challenge. "I would rather your strong arm remain to hew down the foe from your lofty perch. But I act in the name of Odin. It is from his lips this order came. Last night, before we disembarked for battle, he drew me aside. Under solemn oath he directed me to send you back with this message when the scourge of wood threatened to consume our line. By then, he said, the primaries of the Æsir will have fallen. The future, our future, will fall on the shoulders of those remaining. Our story must be told. It must be known."

Hild began to weep. "But I cannot leave!" Anger stamped her features as tears of frustration coursed down her cheeks "I have a right to be here! This is my fate as well as yours!"

Vali swept his sword in an arc to encompass the battlefield. "My fate perhaps. See there, not 200 paces ahead towers the bright flames of Surt. Already he advances as our numbers diminish. You must leave now to perform this last duty commanded by your general. Quickly, before the black one brings his flame fully to earth."

"Here," he passed her the golden reins, "Sigfodur has little need of his stallion now. Take Sleipnir as a sign of the truth of your words." The great horse stamped his eight hooves with impatience. "Bifrost lies in shards. Sleipnir is the only mount swift enough to cross the distance."

Eyes aflame, teeth gritted in anger, Brynhild leapt from her mount onto the honorable child of Loki and charged from the field.

Vali called out as the War Lady of the Helm dwindled into the distance. "Be comforted Hild! The Æsir cannot struggle against fate, or the giants, or even Surt himself. Even the screams of Egdir circling high above cannot turn us from our chosen destiny. For each of us, this is a good day!"

The Final Advance

The bright flame of Muspellsheim boomed with a voice that cut across the martial din. Eyes flickered to catch a glimpse of the speaker, but the deadly blows from stout arms never slacked. "Your gods are dead! Your great leaders fallen to kindred foe! Those few of you who remain will crumble before my strength!"

"Einherjar to me!" cried out Sigurd, he of the serpent's bane, circling his blade three times over his head to close the ranks of those warriors who remained alive. "Here I raise the sword Gram, crafted by Regin, the death of Fafnir. Its length well glutted on the flesh of enemies!" Still fighting, warding their backs, fighters collapsed toward his voice. The great hero stalked to the fore, waiting until the bulk of the men had gathered behind. "Today we show the nine worlds of what we are made! Today we earn honor greater than any reward! Today we show what mere men can do against the reckless hate that consumes gods! We can die as we have always lived, on our feet with weapons ready, the foeman faced with fearless gaze, our heads unbowed, and our honor intact!"

They fell together into lines, those stalwart warriors still firm enough of limb; the walking wounded, the near dead refusing to be left behind—propped against the shoulders of comrades. Together they formed a hamalt fylking, the terrible column with wedge head that can cleave the stoutest line; the formation of the famous and the brave, stained red with intent, with a sharp tip to pierce the breast of flame.

At the signal call to advance they raised their shields level with their upper lips, a sounding board for their warrior's song—the promise of Odin.

> "Under shields we chant.
> Safely to the battle.
> Safely from the battle.
> Safely we come everywhere."

It started low, a chant subdued in tone and color. With each grinding step, it increased in volume until it resembled the roar of breakers on the sea. And amid the roar sounded the voice of Odin.

> "I gladly lead into battle
> those whom I've long held in friendship.
> I sing with them under their shields,
> so there is no room for despair."

As one the bold warriors drove forward, spear against spear, shield locked with shield. The formation so tight their ring byrnies rattled as shoulders rubbed together. Its jagged point aimed at the flaming fence that drew up about Surt. They speared the line, driving deep into the wall of flame, while Surt waved his arms, screaming at his warriors to hold fast. The fence buckled. The sharp tip blunted, then rounded as the flames whittled away at the threatening shaft.

The fire of Muspellsheim winked as a candle guttering in its final throes dances before its fuel is spent. Raging at the formation that advanced step by bloody step, until he could feel the breath of their blades, Surt lifted Gambanteinn to the sky. Focusing its power, he drew the final rays of Sol to earth, rekindling the spent blaze of his forces. The world inhaled, gathering the furious breath of Volund into a storm that surpassed all others. The world exhaled, spreading a wave of wind-blown fire over the plain that toppled friend and foe alike.

Amid the rolling gate of thunder, slaughter chaff fouled fields. Swollen rivers thickened with blood wept with the runoff of battle. The piled bodies of slain, grown into tall mounds, collapsed from their own weight. All the Einherjar lay scattered across the plain, their corpses drenched with blood. None had fled the field but fought until their weapons fell from lifeless fingers. The once-raging horde of giants now huddled in silent mounds that trickled gurgling red streams. They were joined in the raven's feast by scores of Hel's minions, now thrice dead. The black humps of bodies clotted the plain, an otter's ransom in blood extracted by the Æsir.

Of the sons of the Æsir, only Vidar, Vali, Modi, and Magni remained upright. Of the children of Bor, only Hoenir watched as Surt rallied his remaining troops and drove the surviving sons of Muspellsheim onward, his wild blade bringing the brightness of the sun to earth, its deadly flame returning the world to its original embers. Red sparks winged into the purple smoke, flushing the faces of the dead with the blush of health.

The Return of Bryhild

Brynhild they called her in Hlymdale, War-lady in the helmet. Forgiven by Odin for the loss of Helmet-Gunner and the victory won by the brother of Audia. Long released from Skata-grove by Sigurd, immolated on a pyre of love, and reborn to serve again.

Her duty discharged at Fensalir, the maiden flew arrow-swift across the Mirkwood, the strange young creature to fulfill her fate. Astride Sleipnir she arrived too late, the battle storm had engulfed the entire field in flame.

Together they faced the raging tempest. The wall of flame reminds her of Skata-grove where enclosed by shields and bracketed by the fire of the linden, she rested in charmed sleep awaiting her fate. Here, awake, she faces the same unknown, save that this time the decision is hers.

With a terrible cry, she unsheathed her bright striker, the dread blade that heralded an eternity of battles. The son of Loki screamed his defiance as he reared up to challenge the flames. Brynhild, the last of Odin's chosen war maidens, and Sleipnir, the noblest of all horses, charged together into battle. The living flames roared in delight as they reached out to embrace the valiant pair.

From world's end Hraesvelg beat his powerful eagle wings. The blasts of wind spread across the world like a massive flood that drives all before its rush. Bodies tumbled through the air, joined by toppled masonry, ponderous stone, fragments of wooden beams, and the scarred trunks of massive trees. The mass seized in the arms of a mighty whirlwind scoured the ground with renewed assault. Then Corpse Gulper took flight, whipping the terrible storm to new heights. Embers flared to life as the wind blew across the nine worlds, fanning a great swirling fire that fed upon itself.

In the sky the sun turned black, fully consumed by the son of Fenris. The bright eyes of Thjasse winked from heaven, then tumbled into the sea. The earth sank as the ocean waves crashed over the land. Great gouts of steam swirled into the sky along with the life-feeding flame until the heavens danced with fire.

Then all became darkness.

Battle for Nidaveller

Now must be told of Mimir's seven sons, the dwarves, the elves, and the battle in Nidaveller—the engagement fought deep in the nine worlds that a new world might be born above.

The Seven Sleepers

Preparations were begun eons before when word arrived of Mimir's head returned by the Vanir in a keg of brine. In Nidaveller, Mimir's seven sons called a Husthing among the ásmegir, the dwarves, and all the elves, to carefully consider the last counsels of their father before he left as hostage to the Æsir's good conduct: what he related of events yet to come, what he expected of them, what they all must do.

Wary troops of dark elves brushed shoulders with dwarves as they gathered in the citadel of Hvergelmir. Bead-black eyes accustomed to the dimness of caverns and the stinging glow of smithy fires roved to take in the opulence as they shuffled across the courtyard into the golden hall to join with the kin of Mimir.

When all had taken seats, mead was passed until each guest clutched a brimming mug. Mimir's sixth son stood, both hands raised over his head. Low mutterings fell to silence as all turned their attention to Kornskurdarmánudr. Tall like his father, with well-proportioned limbs, hair the color of ash leaves in late fall; he spread his arms wide in greeting. "I give welcome to all the ásmegir, all the elves, to the clans of Motsognir, Durin, and Lofar. Those who have traveled far will find refreshment at our board. Welcome everyone to our hall. It is a sad event that sparks this occasion, the death of our beloved father, Mimir. So, I call on all to lift their mugs in honor of his memory."

Once remembrance drinks were taken and solemn murmurs of respect made their rounds, he paused, brooding into his cup, his breath rippling the surface as he considered his next words. "My father's counsels foretold this gathering. It is by his direct command that I share his burden of knowledge. There are actions he expected from each of us."

Grumbles rolled through the gathering, soft as a whispering breeze rustling the leaves of a birch stand. A well-muscled, stocky dwarf slowly rose from the throng. He tapped his chest with a fire-blackened finger as his gravelly voice called out for attention. "You all know me. I am Sindri. My brother Brok and I sweat at the forge as do many of you. Those who do not share in the great work often enjoy the products of our skill.

Mimir was always a good friend to us. Many times, he interceded on our behalf with those who placed heavy demands on our time and unreasonable burdens on our skill. Out of respect for this ancient friendship, gladly we would hear the message he meant for all." Choruses of agreements were shouted out while grumbling pockets of dissent continued to make themselves heard.

Kornskurdarmánudr cocked his head, his lips a thin, hard line slashed across his face. "I am glad you are willing to listen. These are not words I wish to repeat, but I am bound by oath, as are my brothers, to the last commands of our father." He took a deep breath to calm the sudden thudding in his chest. "Before Mimir left our home as an honored hostage to reconcile a war that was not ours, he spoke plainly to us of what is to come. My father was wise beyond years; his foresight rivaled that of the long dead etin seeress. He knew he would not return from his mission among the Vanir, so wasted no time on talk of what was or what is but looked down the eons to what must come."

Hands clasped behind his back, he began pacing before his seat. He paused to glance at his audience before returning to his pacing. "There will come a time of peril for everyone across the worlds. Ancient enemies will rise in a final effort to destroy us all. A wall of flame will blanket the nine worlds, consuming friend and foe alike."

Cries of alarm sprang from the crowd as gabbling voices tumbled between benchmates. Kornskurdarmánudr raised his hands for quiet. "There is no need for alarm. The events to occur are far in the future. This means there is hope for those gathered here, if we begin preparing now! Many weapons must be stored away for the time of great need. If we are successful, some few of us will survive to see a new world born from the ashes of the old. Those who are skillful at the forge must craft..."

Alarm turned to venom as shouts of anger raced about the room, drowning out the speaker. Dvalin banged his cup repeatedly on the board, demanding a turn to speak. "We have feasted the alfar in Mimir's honor! We have shown proper respect for the greatness he was his!" He leapt to his feet, shaking a fist. "But now we are asked to take on an obligation that may see us dead long before its conclusion!"

The dusky dwarf glared around at those seated, taking courage from the many nodding heads. "I say it is just another weight set upon our shoulders by those who have always taken us for granted and who again demand we bow to their will." He stabbed a finger at the seven brothers seated along the head table. "I say obligations imposed by the dead are ones we are free to refuse!"

Among the benches shouts of agreement raged against curses of dissent. Kornskurdarmánudr tried to speak, but the quarrelling guests shouted down each attempt. Throwing up his hands in disgust, he slumped down in his seat, snatched up his mug and drained it at a gulp. Grabbing a pitcher from the board, he topped it off. Liquid slopped over his white knuckles as he took a long pull.

Frermánudr glanced at the bright red anger burning in his brother's face before rising from his bench. Well-built, with frank, smiling features, the seventh son of Mimir waited patiently until the uproar died down, then three times he clapped his hands for attention. The sharp reports snapping loudly from the dais startled the visiting host, interrupting their intense bickering.

Bird eyes flickered sharp and bright as the gathering quieted to hear the new speaker. "I have no heart for words. A brave man knows nothing save the challenge ahead. And each of us have a mighty challenge to face."

His gaze passed over the sea of bead-black eyes. Their distrust was a palpable wave, their barely restrained voices ready to shout him down if he did not recapture their attention. "You each know the wisdom that was my father's. Too, you know that he would never urge such an action were he not certain of its need. It is true you can deny his vision. But if you do, know this, those who do not prepare will certainly die in the coming fire, and their line will perish along with them."

He spread his arms, waving at the solid beams high overhead. "Our only hope lies in resistance, here behind the protection of Hvergelmir. Its walls are built into the mountains that share its name. It survived the great deluge of Ymir's blood; it will protect us against any foe. In this citadel resides our best chance for survival and the hope of a world reborn. For if this wall falls, so, too, does Hoddmimir's wood, the great forest of life that lies behind us. That seed must be protected at all costs for anything to regrow from the blight of flame."

A hush fell over the gathering as each elf, each dwarf, and each ásmegir drew into himself to consider the import of Frermánudr's words. Sindri coughed then stood again among the now-silent gathering. "You ask us to take on a warrior's duty. None of us are trained to combat."

Chuckling, as if at some private joke, Frermánudr took a drink from his mug to clear his throat. "My father saw far ahead to what must be. His vision gives us warning eons before the event. For you there is much time yet for such training, as there is time to build up an armory."

Sindri scanned the eager faces that all seemed to have turned to focus on him, a rocky point standing tall in a suddenly clam sea. "I, as many of my kin, little relish the prospect of such a battle. But more, I dislike the idea of our lines ending. To have everything we have done, everything we will do, amount to nothing but ash galls me to no end. I speak, I think, for all here when I say this is an obligation we undertake with great reluctance."

Murmurs of agreement rolled across the crowd. The sharp bright gazes remained focused on Sindri, urging him to continue. The dwarf's eyes narrowed as he scanned the seven brothers seated before him. "But who will lead us in this great resistance? Other than the ones above, you and your brothers are the only ones we know trained in the arts of war. How will you pass on this knowledge? How will you—"

Frermánudr raised a hand, interrupting the dwarf in mid speech. Sindri snapped his teeth shut while those around him grumbled at the intrusion. "The ásmegir are long lived. Many of you will endure the passage of time to see these final days arrive. My brothers and I are not that fortunate. Ours is a shorter life that would end long before the time of greatest need unless drastic action is taken, a great gamble with eternity.

But even so, we will man the walls alongside you, for by our father's command we are destined, or cursed, to sleep until the world echoes with the terrible sound of the Gjallarhorn. The rest of you are to keep this purpose alive by bending your skills to its end. Remember to hold its confidence close to your breast, none but us can know. When the call sounds, gather behind these walls. From here we will make our stand!"

Sindri snorted then jerked his chin at the brothers. "That is all very well for you. But who will train us?"

Frermánudr glanced at his brothers, caught the slight nods from each head. "My father had a great friend, one well-schooled in soldiery. He understands the need for circumspection. Expect him to contact you within the next cycle of the Shiner. On him you can rely for covert help." He turned then swung back with a finger raised. "And, too, there are the Varinian, those who protect Mundilfari's children. They have agreed to share their expertise."

After the last of the mead was drunk and all the guests had reeled from the hall, the brothers gathered close around the board. Leaning heavily on their elbows they held forth their assessments.

Gormánudr coughed, a wet rattling sound, into his cupped hand. "The ásmegir are behind us. They have sworn an oath to keep the words of Mimir close." He absently wiped his palm on his robe. "But what of the dwarves and elves?"

Hrútmánudr scratched vigorously at his chin. "The dwarves are uneasy," his hand strayed to protectively cup an ear, "but they will follow." He leaned in, bracing his elbow on the table to support the weight. "They carry implicit trust in the words of our father." A round of nodding circled the bench. "But I am unsure of the dark elves," he whispered, staring glumly into his drink.

Enmánudr sighed, staring into the distance. "Dark elves have always been difficult to interpret." Absently, he rubbed a calloused finger alongside his nose. The spot, irritated from frequent attention, began to glow red with each stroke. "They sat the whole-time gibbering among themselves. It was difficult to tell if our counsel persuaded them. They trust the dwarves, not so much us or the Æsir, and certainly not the etin. I think that if the dwarves hold, the elves will follow their lead."

Sólmánudr's brow furrowed with a worried look as he fidgeted with his mug. Three times he lifted the mug to his lips. Three times he set it down without taking a drink. "Counsel has no value without trust. We need the support of both. A swift steed is useless, if but one leg is broken. If two are broken, then it will surely die. As well the security of this plan lies in secrecy. Will they keep confidence?"

"True," Selmánudr chuckled, taking a long pull at his drink, "this is not word we want passed around, especially among the etin. Since dwarves and elves carry no love for giants, nor the Æsir for that matter, I think we have nothing to worry about. Besides, the dwarves are well used to keeping secrets. Just try getting one to share the mysteries of their smithy."

Kornskurdarmánudr jabbed a finger at his brother. "And have you ever known a dark elf to willingly share anything?" A drunken leer twisted his lips as he fumbled words past his teeth. "Even threatened with the rays of the sun, they would rather turn to stone than share the most joyous news."

Frermánudr slapped his palms on the tabletop and pushed himself to his feet. "Then we have done all we can." He swung his mug in a wide arc, beckoning the others to do the same. "Now it is our time to prepare."

The brothers nodded over the rims as together they drained the last of their drinks. Their eyes locked in agreement, as they shook their robes free of the bench. No words were spoken, for each knew what lie in the other's heart.

They packed away many items in storage, hoarded against the day of great need. Sturdy armor, frightful weapons, thick shields rimmed with metal, all carefully protected against the ravages of time. Along the walls, they hung seven long swords, dwarf-crafted and Regin-sharp, which none save themselves could wield.

Care of the great tree they placed on the shoulders of the Norns, bid them use their every skill to hold fast its life until the twilight of the gods had passed. They left the remainder of Mimir's kin to their already appointed tasks: Day to follow Night, Sol to follow Mani, Byggvir to keep the World Mill turning so the seasons would continue to flow without interruption.

When all was in readiness they stretched out on cool slabs of polished stone, arranged their clothing for comfort, and placed sleep thorns in their ears. They set wards about themselves, fields of harsh withering protection, that they might remain undisturbed until the blare of the Gjallarhorn called them to arms.

Near the lands of the Skritobinians, they abide in deep repose, waiting in silence until the end of days. During their long slumber, the hiss of falling waters is ignored, raging storms pass unnoticed, and the World Mill grinds on unheeded.

Preparing for War

Slow is the passage of days, longer still the nights. The years stretch out until the past dwindles to a point on the horizon and the once-distant future rises up, an insurmountable wall that cannot be denied.

Odin confers with the head of Mimir. Together they speak of events to come: those near at hand, those yet far ahead, and the need— always the need. Wise in the ways of the worlds, the Alfodur, works the knots of fate to his own ends. Happily, he offers his experience to the ásmegir, but not as Odin, for he knows their distrust. Rather, the battle-scarred Grímnir visits their dark halls, covertly supporting their efforts with shrewd guidance in the ways of war.

In spacious caverns shielded from prying eyes, they practice at the art of war. Grímnir's commands echo from the walls, relentless, always demanding. It is not enough to craft the weapons; they must learn to wield them as well. The blade, the bow, the spear, the sling, even the shield become as familiar to their hand as the hammer is to the smith. It is not enough to know the land, they must learn the tactics of the battlefield. The driving force of necessity backs strategies for defense, retreat, and attack.

"Our lands, our people. Our honor, our future."

The chant echoes through the caverns reaching into the dark places awaking defiance in even the mildest heart.

In secrecy, the dwarves stock their armories with death-dealing weapons, while the dark elves brood in silence, scoping the land and making their own plans.

The Call of the Gjallarhorn

The last of the mournful tones from the Gjallarhorn, a solemn cry for the final battle breathed by Heimdall, cut across the nine worlds, waking all to war. Far below in the dark lands of Nidaveller, in a golden hall built into the mountain rock north of the raging fountain that bears its name, the seven sons of Mimir shook sleepthorns from their ears as they sprang up from their ageless rest, awakened now the fate of the World is called.

On wall pegs about the room hung their battle gear, readied since before time for just this moment. Shaking off the dust of ages, they hurriedly slipped ring byrnies of cleverly woven metals over their heads then hooked them snug about their chests. From wall pegs, they took down heavy blades crafted when the world was young, their fullers inlaid with the strength of dragons. Slinging the scabbards across their shoulders, they belted them tight at their waists. On their heads, they placed edge-repelling helmets embossed with boars and twining serpents that shone like stars in the darkened lands, fearsome helms to spark fear in the hearts of enemies.

They tried themselves in their armor, swinging their arms and squatting with their legs to ensure the heavy garments fit close, but not too snug. Ready hands caught up heavy bossed shields from shelves and lifted deadly spears from their racks. They gazed silently among themselves. Some frowned, others sported pinched, dour looks, a few grinned fiercely, but all nodded as one. Satisfied, they clumped out of the hall.

In the land beneath they gathered for battle, the dwarves, the sons of Mimir, the kin of Delling, bold warriors to defy the children of the frost. Rank on rank of sun-shy warriors troop through the gate to fulfill pledges made ages before when Mimir's sons first whispered among them the fate of the worlds.

From deep hollow caverns drift the kin of Durun. Tongues silent, eyes calm, they move as shadows amid the ranks, their whispered footfalls echoing off the fortress walls as they take their place in the front line.

From deep crevasses slide Motsognir's kin. Protected by rugged war garb crafted of stone and adorned with precious metals, they edge in among the host to fill gaps in the pickets.

From the dank pebble plains of Joruvellir march the resolute kin of Lofar. Faces stern, jaws set with determination, bodies streaked with the gray-green mud of Aurvangar, they stand with deadly slings at their sides.

Ready, too, are Sindri and his brother smiths, glinting in their polished armor, brandishing weapons forged by their own great skill. On armored mounts, they prance into the citadel, all eyes turn in admiration as they ride by.

From the ranks of the Njara and the Varinian march column after column of dark warriors, all ready for war. Their robes black as night, their byrnies the dull gray of iron, they seem an endless river streaming in to fill up the shadows within the walls.

Together they gird the wall rock of Hvergelmir, armed with weapons made ages before. With galdrar and seid they fortified the walls to hold against the blood squall. With thick beams of fire-hardened oak they barricaded the gates to withstand heavy blows.

Svarte elves call out from their dark caverns, silent domes formed of endless jags where shadows flow amid the rocks. Not eager for this battle, refusing to join the ranks behind the citadel's thick walls, they nonetheless ready themselves for war. They settled themselves along the edges of cliffs to wait, gibbering bats of despair. With grim purpose, they perch boulders along ledges, ready to tumble onto the advancing etin scourge.

High above the final battle had begun. The force of its storm reached across the worlds to shake the ground. Low rumbles echoed through the air, itching the teeth of nervous sentries. Dry, buffeting winds swept over the walls to prickle skin and sting eyes. Behind the wall rock of Mt. Hvergelmir, near the navel of the world, the valiant foes of frost girded themselves for the assault of an ancient enemy.

They stood silently on the battlements watching the bank of frost muster across the plain. The seventh son of Mimir rapped his shield. "That which my father foretold before his untimely death at the hands of the Vanir has come to pass. Today," he shouted over the ranks of defenders, "this very day, is Ragnarök. The twilight of the gods has arrived!

In the world above the battle has already begun. We feel the force of its rage shaking the ground; feel its breath on our face, the weight of its moment on our shoulders. Soon our foe of ice will begin their attack. It will take all our courage, every bit of our strength, it will take the very best from each of us to ward off their advance.

All of you know that we must hold. We are the last line of hope for a new world. Should the children of frost pass these walls, all we are, all we might ever be will be ground into dust and forgotten. And without our protection, the hope concealed within the wood beyond these hills will be forever stilled.

So, make yourselves ready for battle. Throw off your cloaks. Remove all loose clothing. Strap a blade to your wrist. Keep another at your side. Face the enemy's bleak gaze unafraid. Harden your hearts against mercy, for they will show none. For the safety of our homes, for the survival of our people, for the certainty of our future, the time is now to fulfill all your pledges!"

The Death of Hate

The wounded Moon dodged beneath the edge of worlds leaving a scarlet trail across the heavens—streaks of bright red wound dew that lit the sky. Hati charges close behind, on his heels trails Managarm. Together they follow the bloody spoor. Eager to catch their wounded prey, the pair race over the edge of worlds. There the Varinian warriors lay in wait—the bold protectors of Mundilfari's children.

As Mani collapsed through Billing's western gate, the Varinian guard surged forward from their posts. A thicket of iron-tipped ash sprouted up to surround the pursuers, cutting them off from their goal. Denied their prey the wolves tossed their shaggy manes, howling in frustration. Thumping their breasts, they tried forcing their way through the swarm of long-tipped spears, but the staunch guard fiercely repulsed each attempt.

Crouched back to back, the snarling wolves lashed about with horny claws, raking bloody swaths through the crowding warriors. Laughing, the pair ripped side to side, laying low warriors. As each fell, fresh sets of bright-edged blades wielded by ready hands sprouted to fill the gap in the iron-tipped hedge.

Hati showered them with the hoarse rasp of his threats as he tried and failed to get inside their reach. "Come maggots! Though you have us surrounded, you have no chance against us. Your weapon sting is little more than an insect bite, of no matter and easily swatted away!"

The guard captain roared out as a bear calls to the wild: "He speaks truth. Our spears do not penetrate nor do our blade edges bite. They have protection against such weapons. Let us call on Fjorgyn for aide. Stone them!"

Together the Varinians surrounded the pursuers. Eyes wide, shrieks torn from their lips, they let fly a rain of heavy stones. Hati and Managarm screamed as the rocks struck with a dull thud, shattering limbs raised to ward off the deadly blows. When the pair had collapsed beneath the weight of stones, the warriors rushed in, thrusting repeatedly with their spears until the fallen wolves stopped moving, their blood spreading across the ground.

Scrambling atop the bodies, the Varinian captain gazed up at the bloodied orb racing across the sky. "We have done all we can for Mundilfari's children. Mani is safe, but we can give no aide to

Alfbeam. Already she crests the northern skyline, her backsides deeply scored by the fangs of Skoll. She attempts to evade pursuit and will soon draw near.

Let us raise up a thicket of thorns, ready to protect should she succeed in reaching our line, though I fear it will be to no avail. After the Norns have given their verdict, none outlast the day."

The Attack of Frost

Now rise the rime thurs, those who trace their lineage to the feet of Ymir, an ice-cold front to challenge the wall rock of Hvergelmir. Blades beating a steady rhythm against shield edges, they advance in the slow glide of attack. The deft cunning of dark elves lessens their numbers as sudden rock falls tear through their ranks, and cleverly concealed crevasses snare unwary warriors, breaking legs expecting solid footing. Still the relentless advance continues. Wounded warriors are left to steel themselves against the pain of their injuries and continue or be trampled by those pressing from behind.

Their raging storm breaks against the fortress, a heavy rain of pitched rocks lofted high by strongly muscled thurs. Missiles fall short to skitter along the wall, tearing stone blocks from their moorings, while others arc over the embattlements. Roofs shatter amid a rain of splintering timbers. The defenders brace themselves against the storm, shields raised to ward off the hail of battle. Grim faces flinch at each ringing blow. Warriors driven to their knees scramble back to their feet to stand defiant at their posts. Warriors badly struck by the shower of stones crumple behind the wall.

Frermánudr shouted out to the warriors stationed along the fortress wall, putting the full force of his breath behind his words to carry over the din of battle. "Hold firm," he screeched. "Long we have lived under the shadow of etin threat. We have always endured, always survived. Today the fates would have us face them head on. I say it is good; they will face no sterner foe. Our will is as strong as our wall. Neither has ever been breached, and they will not be breached now!"

A cloud of hail cast from slings—the furious rain of Lofar—chip at the face of the etin line, denting helmets, cracking skulls, and putting out eyes. Arrows streak from deeply bent bows, flocks of feathered eider in flight to pierce high held shields, seeking their nest in ice-cold hearts. Spears, hard as files, fly from hands, the well-made javelins resound with a dull thud as they find their mark. With each repulse walls of ice slough off from the enemy line, large calves of winter warriors that crumble sighing to the ground.

The rush of battle is fierce, a song of weapons that echoes off mountain cliffs and booms through hollow caverns. The storm, raging across the dimly lit plain, swept up against the mountain wall, the wind of its passage choked with the sounds of clashing metal. Brave warriors on both sides topple in the onslaught. Their comrades charge in to fill the gaps.

Savagely, the children of frost attack the citadel walls. Prying fingers of ice work their way into crevices, expanding the gaps and forcing loose stone. Defenders are frozen in place as lethal arrows of murder frost reach through fissures opened in the walls.

The menace of ice is denied with molten tongues of fire, brew from the smithy forge turned into a weapon, poured over the wall edge down onto the enemy. But the relentless press of frost continued to threaten as hard white drifts angled up the walls offering an avenue for the attackers to the top of the battlements.

The Charge of Sindri

Fermánudr grabbed at Sindri's arm as the smith cinched armor on the head of his steed. "This is madness! The deluder runs red, nearly swallowed by Skoll. The battle above must be near its end. We have only to hold until its close. Though hard pressed, our wall remains unbreached, so why do you seek this rash charge?"

Sindri spun around. "Hold," he hissed, the fury of his words scarcely held in check by his gate of yellow teeth. "Barely! We have used every weapon in our stores, yet still they come! Even now fingers of frost pry at the gate and scrabble at the top of our walls! Do nothing and we will fall before this day is through."

He turned back to his horse and continued cinching on the battle armor. "They will not expect a daring charge. Its surprise may provide us the advantage we need. It will certainly buy us more time." Grumbling low to himself, he hooked the faceplate into place beneath the bridle. "Little enough I've done at the smithy fires of bold deeds. While I've trained in their use, always others have wielded the weapons I've made. Now on this, the end of our last day, rather than endure under the constant siege of an ancient foe, I choose to display the boldness of my heart. I am not alone in this desire. My brothers agree, as do a host of others. Together we must try."

Sindri mounted his great horse, working his armor into a comfortable position as he settled himself in the saddle. He pranced about on horseback while ranks of riders gathered behind him. "Today we set the stage for what we will become."

The gate groaned open crushing back a company of rime thurs, who had struggled to pry loose its edges. Sindri astride his great horse Modinn, his brothers astride their own mounts, charged out into the fray with helmets gleaming, keen-edged blades raised high over their heads, their voices raised in a full-throated, defiant roar.

Together they plunged through the massed ranks of etins as fire sweeps in fury up steep canyons of a dry, wooded mountainside, the bright flames lashed on by a driving wind to savage the depth of timber. Etins fall before their flashing blades, driven back as melting snow before the summer sun. A heavy toll is taken amid the enemy host. The frost line wavers, then collapses. The thirsty earth runs dark with their blood.

A rout now, the defenders harass the giant horde, slashing with impunity at their retreating backs, trampling the living and dead beneath the iron shoes of their mounts. Tripping, falling, the sons of Frost are crushed as barley on the threshing room floor by the steady plodding of a farmer's broad-headed oxen.

A low rumble calls them from their fierce swordplay as the wind sighs with heavy heat. The blinding light of an advancing inferno fills the sky, its blazing fire courses across the nine worlds, a dazzling whirlwind of crimson flames tinged orange, leaping high against the heavens, choking the air with thick smoke. Unprotected, the etin ranks collapse before the flames, frozen drifts that wilt beneath the terrible heat. The roar of the fire drowns anguished cries torn from their blistering lips.

Chests and arms spattered with gore, their legs and the fetlocks of their horses dripping with blood kicked up by flying hooves grinding through the bodies of the fallen, the bold defenders race back across the field. Diving through the wall rock of Hvergelmir, the massive gates slam shut behind and heavy beams rammed into place. Tumbling from their mounts, the warriors join the host crouched down behind the rock wall, braced for the impact of the coming inferno.

The flames break upon the Hvergelmir walls in a flash of lethal steam and heat, just as waves crash against cliffs that border the sea. Thunder roars from the collision, sending tremors rolling through the ground, tearing stones from the rock face, and bowing the gate. The wall shudders with the impact but holds firm.

Sindri scrambled atop the parapet, ignoring the heat that sucked breath from his chest. Silhouetted against the raging inferno, he raised a bloody blade high above his head. "We have fought well," he shouted to those crouched before him. "We stand on the crumbled bodies of fallen thurs, those who thought to drive us all from our homes, the last effort of an ancient adversary. Let all know, let the worlds know that we bask in the glorious light of victory, our honor upheld."

The flames raging beyond the wall reflected bright crimson along the length of his blade as he waved it toward the sky. "Above, the Æsir have found the truth of their fate, that which was known from the first days. The Einherjar—each one—gathered great honor to themselves once more. The guttering fire of mankind has been snuffed, save for two lights protected in the wood beyond this wall, while Surt has consumed himself on a pyre of victory. The terrible blade of Volund has finally accomplished the designs of its creator. It has struck down the gods and those who would supplant them, reducing all to the ignominy of dust."

He stumbled, nearly falling, as hands reached up to help him down from the height. Still shouting, he fumbled his blade into its sheath. "Now we wait, hunkered here amid ashes of the old world, for the renewal destined to take place."

Drawing off his gore-spattered helmet, Sindri slumped against the wall. Those nearest could hear the low mutter of his words. "For many it will seem fairer, for some much better, but for children," he rubbed soot and blood from his face with his hands, "for them it will be the same."

Hoddmimir's Wood

Now must be told of Líf and Leifthrasir as they endured the Fimbulvetr cold and struggled to conceal themselves beneath the protective canopy of Hoddmimir's wood.

Líf and Leifthrasir

The pleasant contentment of Svasud was gone, summer days a hazy memory of warmth. The world lay in the grip of Vindsval whose breeze increases the cold, and his father, Vasad, whose aching damp creeps into the bones, bringing stiffness. With biting cold, they nip at nose, freeze the tips of ears. With a sharp breath, they blow open cloaks, their icy fingers reaching in to strip away carefully hoarded warmth.

A small holding stood defiant atop a hill, its rugged walls braced with drifts, its thatch roof blanketed with snow. Smoke wafted from the mud wattle chimney, a tenuous white vapor snatched away by a steady wind as it curled into the air and spread down the valley. Inside a couple huddled close to the open hearth, their robes smudged with ash.

Líf poked gently at the fire before tossing another pine knot onto the embers. "This winter's rage freezes my blood." The flames danced with brightness as the resin-soaked wood kindled to life. "This makes how many now?"

Leifthrasir stared hard into the guttering flames, raised her hand, thumb and two fingers extended. "Three. This is the third."

Líf raked the coals side to side as he worked the knot deeper into the glowing embers. "Are you sure?"

Leifthrasir nodded, tugging her robe close about her shoulders. "Three summers have passed to snow with no sign of change in the seasons." She pointed toward the invisible horizon, her finger describing a shallow arc from east to west. "Sol travels her windweaver path but gives no warmth to mark her presence. Each morn we must melt the snow before we eat. It is certain we ride the edge of Fimbulvetr."

A gust of howling wind rushed against the walls with a hiss of drifted snow. Líf lifted his head to listen as the timbers creaked from the pressure. "There is something else?"

Leifthrasir stared hard into the flames. Images in black and red flowed across the coals, forming then disappearing before her eye could grasp their shape. "Yes. I worry about this between dusk and dawn, the time when the fabric between the worlds is thinnest, when hidden knowledge can be passed and things can be seen more clearly."

A shiver ran through her body. "Last night I had a dream." She wriggled closer to the flames, leaning in to soak up the warmth. "Rivers flowed across a bloody plain. Raging torrents crashed over boulders, swamping benches, as warm blood poured with the water out to the sea. Along shores clotted with red gore raven and wolf fought for marrow.

I saw flocks of starlings darkening the sky; nothing could stop their relentless flight. In fields of barley they gobbled grain, their raging hunger wreaking devastation. Within the ravaged fields raven and wolf fought for marrow.

As I looked across the land the wolf's maw gaped wide, its inside reddened with gore, the raven's beak dripped with fresh blood, while blistering flames played across the heavens. When I gazed at the clouds the bright sun turned black and the great bowl of Ymir shattered. The earth sank into churning waters. Mountaintops gasped once before dipping beneath storm-lashed seas."

Líf stared hard at his hands, the dark lines that edged his knuckles, the thick calluses that cushioned his palms. "You know what this means?"

Along the fire's margin a coal winked yellow with the drawn air. Leifthrasir watched shapes flowing one into another across the ember's surface. "I fear what it means."

Líf nodded. "But you know." Leifthrasir hunched her shoulders, saying nothing. "You know," he pressed. "Soon Surt's fire will make it more than warm enough for all."

He slapped his hands against his thighs. "Pack what can be easily carried. We'll head for the protection of Hoddmimir's Wood."

Leifthrasir started, her gaze darting about in panic. "Which way?" From all directions, she could hear moaning winds buffeting the walls. "Which way do we go?"

Líf stood, felt the bones of his back and shoulders pop as he stretched himself to his full height. "We go beyond the icy peaks," he pointed northward, "to where the land lies in darkness. Where the low growl of the Maelstrom can be heard among the breakers of the sea is a point of egress into the other worlds. From there we will find our way to safety."

"Of etins we need not fear." He snatched a pack from where it hung beside the door and began stuffing it with travel gear. "All their able warriors will stand on Vigrid plain or advance on the citadel of Hvergelmir in Nidaveller. The rest will hunker down at Brimir's hall with tankards clutched fearfully to their chests. Those few who remain in their halls will not travel far from the security of their homes; they we can easily avoid. Now we travel the reindeer's way. May the lords of the peaks pane watch over our journey."

———————

Along the treacherous high etin road Líf and Leifthrasir worked their way through dense thickets that snatched hungrily at their clothes. They stumbled along rugged paths bordered by towering firs whose shadows increased the cold. Crested bare mountain peaks. Slid along the rim of frost-filled basins where sharp winds raced unimpeded.

On wet ways, they traveled straight, no shelter here. Their pace quickened across the snowfields of the high timbered halls, passable now because the ground was frozen. Skirting the edge of dense forests, they trudged onward until their feet grew blistered though the wind blew cold.

That night they made camp on a windswept ledge; the rocky slope above free of snow and ice. Behind a bearskin windbreak propped with ash poles, they ate a cold meal then wrapped up together, huddling close for warmth beneath the blankets they carried. Exhaustion brought swift sleep.

The pair woke to gray twilight, stiff with blue-white fingers of frost clawing for purchase beneath their robes. Using flint and iron Leifthrasir struck a fire in a nest of fir branches she stripped from a nearby tree. As the fire crackled to brightness, she pulled a small pot from their kit, scooped it full of snow, and then set it beside the flames to melt.

"Little rest we received from hard travel." She paused to chafe her hands over the flames, working her fingers until the joints no longer ached. "You moaned all night. I could scarce sleep for all the noise."

Líf stepped away from the warmth of the fire, hoisted his kirtle above his waist and relieved himself over the ledge. Leifthrasir followed his lead, but squatted closer to the cliff face, well back from the edge.

When they returned to the shelter Líf wrung his hands over the fire, squeezing the chill from his knuckles. "Dark dreams marred my sleep, terrible wanderings of my mind. The truth of them I fear. Let me tell you..."

He stared moodily into the distance, the memory of the dream still fresh in his mind. "We climbed over steep cliffs where purchase was scarce and waded through deep snow that hampered our progress. My mind grew dull. Sleep tugged at my eyes. Weariness dragged at me, weighing down my limbs, and it seemed each step took longer to reach the ground.

In my dream, we traveled along open paths. The bones of bleached skeletons littered the ground, their white edges jutting up through a hard crust of snow. Unburied, scattered widely across the ground, they knew not to whom they belonged. Desolation swathed the entire land in a blanket of gray hoarfrost.

On our way, we passed starving women. They hugged their children then left them beside the trail. Turning their backs to the crying, the outstretched arms pleading for comfort, they wiped their tears. Their laments were all the same as they stumbled away. 'I don't know where I will die. How can I care for us both?'

We pushed past them, unable to help.

Amid the blocks of fallen walls knelt men in ragged clothes smudged with the soot of fires. They swayed slowly side to side, moaning softly to themselves, passing their hands along the barren ground as if a luxuriant carpet of heather still grew there. About them a light mist of swirling snow chased its tail, curled into frozen drifts that imprisoned their legs tight amid the blackened ruins.

We pushed past them unable to help.

Long we traveled a frozen path of snow. Icy mists obscured our view, until, parting at last, the green limbs of Hoddmimir's wood rustled before us. Our spirits soared at the sight."

Líf sucked a deep breath slowly through his lips. "I fear our journey will be difficult." He reached out to grip Leifthrasir's arm. "We will succeed, though hardships dull us to the misery of the world."

———————

Leifthrasir drew some black bread and a brick of fat from their provisions. Worrying a knife through the fat, she placed the slice on a chunk of black bread broken from the dense loaf and handed it to Líf. Rocking the blade through the brick, she cut another slice for herself. "We travel close to the edge," she mumbled around a mouthful of bread. "The curtains between the worlds part to our sleep vision allowing us glimpses of what lies ahead. When my eyes finally closed with sleep I, too, rode a wave as fitful as yours.

I dreamed a white bear lumbered through our camp, teeth bared, shaking his head side to side, growling all the while. Great swipes from his massive paws shredded the walls of our shelter, splintering the support poles, and scattering our provisions across the snowfield. We tried to run, but it was useless. He caught us up in his mouth. Our cries were lost beneath the thunder of his voice as his white teeth ground into our ribs, and his saliva froze in a white rime on our clothes."

Líf nodded. "Dreaming of a white bear means a blizzard is on its way. We must move swiftly."

He gathered their possessions into the travel pack, while Leifthrasir rolled their covers into a bundle and strapped it across her back. They checked the bindings of each other's load, then Líf pointed to the east where a soft glow edged the horizon. "Soon it will be dawn. Let us move while the weather holds. We are certainly fated to arrive, but the difficulties of the journey remain unknown."

———————

A sharp gale howled from the north carrying with it the roar of bears. Scouring snow whipped across the ground, blinding the travelers. It was a storm to freeze tears and keep wolves at home. With steady gate, they trudged the frozen wastes, fought the growing wind that pressed them back, took turns breaking trail through wide drifts that barred their way.

Snow began to fall, a dusting at first that quickly grew to obscure the nearby trees. They tied a bast cord about their waists to ensure they not get separated, then pressed on while their strength endured. The snow rapidly thickened into a heavy curtain that dimmed their faces to a hazy gray smudge in a field of white.

Líf lifted a hand to signal stop. "This wind is a lazy wind." Dragging frozen breaths through his scarf, he peered into the white wall. "It blows through rather than around. We can scarce continue without freezing. Pull out the bearskin we use for the shelter," he shouted into Leifthrasir's ear. "No need to set it up. We will climb under it and let the snow drift over us. I will thrust my spear up through the crust to keep a passage open for air. Wrapped together in our robes we will stay warm, protected from this life-draining wind."

All night the howling wind scrabbled at the edge of their cover until the blanket of snow grew too heavy to move. The growing weight felt comforting as the heat of their bodies warmed the space beneath. They slept in fits throughout the night, taking turns holding the shaft upright. A light jiggle of the spear kept the passage clear, the air easy to breathe. The muffled moaning of blizzard winds whispered through the air hole, while above the whipping currents of snow hunted out any who dared brave the open meadows.

In the late hours, the storm cleared, the winds calmed, and the sky opened to stars shivering in the bitter cold air. A crystal silence settled across the land, interrupted by the occasional hiss of snow falling from weighted branches in the distant forest fence. Líf and Leifthrasir clung together in the darkness beneath the shelter cover, tucked in a knot, sharing the warmth of their breath.

Dull morning light angled across a blank landscape of white, unbroken snow. A single spear shaft poked up through the crust. The surface heaved then fractured as a hand slid up the shaft to pull a body after. Líf stood to gulp a deep breath of fresh air, coughing as the chill burned his chest. He glanced around, then shouted down to his feet. "The storm has passed. We can continue our journey."

The shelter cover rustled, and the snow crust fell back as Leifthrasir poked her head out from beneath the bearskin. Ice clung to the tips of her hair, frozen droplets that glistened in the faint sun, brilliant as the bristles on Gullinbursti's hide. Líf helped her to her feet. Tugging at the corners, they dragged their shelter from the icy grip of the snow, rolled it up, and made ready to strike out.

The Odur, unruly as all Hvergelmir's children, boiled along banks laced with clumps of rowan trees that trailed their branches out into the current. Snagged within their limbs bobbed the shattered hulks of fallen trees.

"Is there no other way to cross?" Leifthrasir hugged her robe tighter, shivering as she looked out across the muddy water, its slow roll reflecting a thickening from the incessant cold.

"This is the narrowest point on the river that affords us any hope of success." With a heavy sigh Líf pointed his staff along the riverbank. "See how the ice blocks dam the upstream waters, slowing the current and the dropping the water level. From here the opposite bank is a half stone throw away. See how the rowen reach their arms well out from the shore; they will give us something to grab on to."

He spoke firmly against the uneasiness that quivered his insides. "But we must be quick in our crossing or the icy water will dull our strength and we will be unable to swim. The waters would have us then, just more refuse carried downstream."

Leifthrasir glanced nervously upstream. "And what happens if the ice blocks give way?"

Líf shrugged, pointing again to the far bank. "It is our only choice."

The pair stripped to their skin that their clothing not slow their movements in the icy waters. With shivering hands, they stuffed the dry clothes deep into their travel packs, then lashed the packs tight with a bast cord to the skeletal arms of an ash log.

Cupping Leifthrasir's cheeks in his hands, Líf spoke hurriedly to quell the fear that shone in her eyes. "We will make it; of that you can be certain. It is fated. Just remember to keep your gaze focused on the nearest point of the far bank. That is where we will land. Whatever you do, do not stop kicking, even should you lose feeling in your limbs."

Gritting their teeth, the couple stepped into the frigid waters, gasping at the violent contraction of their bodies to the icy cold. After carefully working their way through the tangle of root clumps jutting out from the shore, they took a deep breath and shoved off into the horse-brown current. Fiercely, they clung to the driftwood back of man as the slow current drew them into the channel. Kicking furiously, they angled their sluggish skiff, directing its course to the far shore while the chill waters leached the strength from their limbs.

After an eternity of effort that numbed mind and body alike, they crawled up the frozen bank of the opposite shore where they flopped breathless onto their backs, exhausted from the ordeal. They lay for only a moment, willing their ragged breaths to calm, then wordlessly dragged themselves to their feet, with fumbling fingers unlashed their packs, and pulled out scarves to blot themselves dry.

Tears ran down their cheeks as they tugged dry clothes over stiff limbs chilled a deep painful blue, then helped each other struggle into their boots. Clothed, they swung their arms, jumped, squatted, pounded fists against their legs, in all ways chafed their extremities until the ache of the cold subsided. When feeling had returned to their limbs, they loaded up their packs and struck out for the fortress walls.

Sanctuary

"We're close," Líf mumbled, staring up into an opaque sky where thick smoke from Midgard fires concealed the light from once-coursing stars. "We must be. But our guides are gone."

Leifthrasir gripped his arm. "You took directions when first we started. Last night you sighted while the world spike remained visible overhead and the toe winked faintly on the horizon. We were on course then. We will make it," she pressed heavily against his shoulder.

In deep twilight, they lurched around boulders that blocked the way. Líf stumbled, pitching forward onto his face. With main strength, Leifthrasir helped him to his feet. Unwinding a scarf from around her throat, she blotted the scratches that marred his cheeks and forehead, then stemmed the flow of blood trickling from his nose with pressure from the woolen garment.

Leaning into each other, they continued, traveling along desolate wolf-slopes where mountain streams gushed from beneath rock walls, their volume fed by melting glaciers, their exits shrouded in mists. Near the base of the slopes water gathered in deep pools, still and dark as dreams.

Sliding through a world wrapped in heavy fog, the dense mist concealing all but their feet, they moved slowly forward, each step a cautious test for purchase. On cresting a hill, the chill mists thinned then disappeared, vanquished by a bright light that promised a forgotten warmth. Before them spread a glittering plain, bright as sunshine, where clumps of brilliantly colored flowers grew despite the winter that reigned above. Passage across this wide way was without hindrance.

They stopped at the bank of a roaring river. In swirling eddies, the limbs of bodies twisted amid shattered beams scorched black. A sturdy, thick-timbered bridge spanned the torrent. On the far side grew the dense stand of immense trees that leaned out over masses of ancient gray stone, their drooping branches fringed with frost. The gnarled trunks were held fast by roots that dug deep for purchase.

Weary from the seeming endless paths, they pitched camp in a grove of ancient ash and oak, beside a mighty root of Mimamirth, deep within the embrace of Hoddmimir's Wood.

———·———

Night drew darkness over the earth, vapors boiled along the horizon, shapes scudded across the sky, their outlines lit bright from below as spirits glimpsed at dawn below a waterfall. A shard of red sliced through the mist, first an edge, then the whole of its bloody rim emerged. The Mead Ship trembled, struggling to pull itself away from the wolfish haze that sought to envelope it. Mists slipped their tenuous hold on its lower rim as the moon sprang free.

Great explosions rocked the earth. Branches dislodged from their wooden moorings crashed down about their makeshift shelter. Líf and Leifthrasir clung together, heads buried in each other's shoulder.

The sky burned. Flames began to play amid the clouds. A shimmering of linden fire faintly tipped with rose wavered across the sky, then disappeared. As swiftly as it had gone, the fire returned as an explosion of color. Several drifting curtains shaking across the sky converged into a single swirling mass overhead.

Neither dared raise their head or uncover their eyes, but kept them tucked beneath covers unless, under light from the naked sky, they witness the death of the world above.

Leifthrasir murmured from the darkness, her voice hushed beneath the tempest that played itself out high above. "I dozed just now and in that wandering my mind exploded with a vision. I stood in a garden all green with fresh buds and flowers; cool grasses lined my path, caressing my feet. Patches of brambles along the track spread thorny fingers to tug at a white shift wrapped around my shoulders.

From its hem, I plucked a long red thorn. As I held it the thorn swelled in my hand, lengthening until it reached to the ground. It had become a tree. One end burrowed deep into the earth, rooting itself in the soil. The other end grew high to brush Ymir's skull.

The canopy grew thick, shading all beneath, and I could no longer see the top. The trunk near the root was red as blood, fading to light green as it climbed the trunk. The branches stood brilliant white against a blue, cloudless sky. Bristling with twigs of uneven length, some long and stout, some short and thin, the living branches spread out over the land, casting their shade wide over the world."

Líf drew her close, gripping on to her as to a raft in a storm. He buried his face in her hair, filling his nostrils with its fragrance. "You saw far ahead to the future of our line, but I, too, saw with Glam's vision into the unknown of my night's thoughts. What I saw lies nearer.

Gales raged as the sea rose to drown the land. Clouds of mist tossed up by the rushing waves wafted into the sky. The world swirled about, then sank beneath the surface. The ocean waves grew calm and the winds turned soft. The currents slowed with nothing to impede their flow. For a timeless time, only the gentle sigh of wind coursing across the gently rippling surface could be heard.

Then the surface of the sea began to froth. Thunder filled the air as in a torrent of spray a lush, green land heaved from the sea. Streams tumbled down the mountainsides, while white waterfalls cascaded from craggy cliffs. Trees cloaked the hills, their trunks draped with twining vines. Dark shrubs filled the spaces between. In grass-filled valleys woolly flocks joined with herds of broad-horned cattle, horses, and wild harts. They grazed together beneath a clear blue sky, quenched their thirst from the same stream. Once more men walked the land, wolves circled in hunt for food, and ravens called to tell of leavings."

The Wait at Fensalir

Now must be told of those left behind the fortress wall of Asgard as they faced the terrible embrace of Surt's elemental fire.

The Gathering of Goddesses

They came together, there in the early morn, at Fensalir, the great hall of Frigg, those left behind, the few not needed in battle, resigned to face the final day unarmed. There in the light of a dimmed sun, Syn stood at the posts of the open doors greeting all who arrived, refusing none.

They came alone or in groups, the goddesses with their handmaidens, their brows deeply scored from worry.

A gentle smile made them welcome.

Sif and Idun came together, chuckling and touching foreheads, their forced laughter betraying heart stones gripped tight with the fear of wives whose husbands have gone off to war.

Eir, the most skillful in the healing arts, slipped through the doors, her head bowed, cloak hood drawn close to shroud her face. Of what use her skills with death assured.

Gefjon arrived surrounded by an entourage of virgin handmaidens. They would little need her protection at close of day.

Saga came, eyes dry for history past, tears held back for the memories of Sokkvabekk.

Sjofin staggered through the door arm in arm with Lofn, eyes brimming with tears that coursed down their cheeks, sharing the woe of a world turned against love.

Var and Vor stepped silently over the threshold, eyes downcast, lips set in a frown, their counsels of love and commitment no longer sought.

Hlin stalked alone into the hall, shoulders set, face a stern mask, her duty of protection done.

Snotra, always courtly and wise, nodded graciously to Syn as she glided stiffly across the entryway.

Hnoss and Gersemi arrived—Freyja's precious things. They huddled together along a bench corner, holding hands, afraid of what was to be.

Gna arrived astride Hofvarpnir, the one Hamskerper got with Gardrofa. Removing saddle and bridle from the airborne steed, she slapped his flank, freeing him to stay or go as he pleased.

Fulla greeted each as they entered the hall. "Straight lies the path to a friend's home. Blessed are we for the gift of guests. Be welcome."

She gestured at the benches. "Please take a seat. Our board is full for those who hunger. We've drink enough to quench the thirst of the driest throat. Solace and genial conversation are available to all who visit."

At her kind words, they raised fretful eyes, relaxing the lines that trenched their foreheads. Murky clouds had dulled their thoughts, but as each stepped through the carved archway their minds cleared as night before the dawn.

Inside tapestries glowed on the walls, their bright threads cleverly woven to tell the glorious deeds of the gods. Fresh cut rushes crunched underfoot, and the benches were draped with precious cloths. The board was spread for a feast. Down the center ranged bowls filled with sumptuous victuals. At each place goblets brimming with the precious mead sat beside earthenware bowls.

Fulla bowed to the guests. All heads bowed back. "Everyone, please make yourselves comfortable while I attend my mistress, who readies herself in her chambers."

The wife of Odin gazed out from her chamber window, searching the horizon to glimpse that which lay hidden in the distance. A thick cloud of brown dust hung in the air over the battle plain, occluding the feats of warriors. As Fulla approached, Frigg spoke without turning, keeping her eyes fixed on the dusty haze billowing from the far-off plain. "Have all arrived?"

Setting down her ashen box, the handmaiden swallowed twice before chancing a reply. "Several seats are empty at your table; they still wait for their occupants. Those reserved for expected regrets remain vacant."

Fulla nervously pleated a fold in her robe between her fingers. Frigg turned an ear toward her while keeping her attention focused beyond the window.

"Freyja is on her way. She has left behind her cats, instead choosing to ride in on her falcon cape. I spied her feathered form circling the hall.

Skadi declined the invitation, preferring to wait in her father's hall amid the snowcapped mountains, which Thjasse long made his home. She remains angry at being left out of the battle."

Frigg snorted. "Odin's ears were red from the blistering she gave him."

Fulla bowed her head in agreement, recalling Skadi's furious shouting and the scene she made stomping from the hall.

Frigg spoke over her shoulder. "The rest?"

"Gríd will not leave her home." Fulla waved a hand in the general direction of Gríd's hall. "She insists on standing vigil, keeping the hearth fire burning until the Far Ruler's return.

The Norns begged off. Unlike us, there is much yet for them to do. Urd and Verdandi work feverishly at plastering soothing loam on the trembling ash. Skuld did not ride with the other Valkyrie, but at Odin's command remained with her sisters to support Lorad in its time of greatest need.

Rind refuses to leave her chambers, the shock of the Alfodur's heated runes still burden her mind. The stress of today's events has breached her composure. Her reply was a plea for solitude.

Your mother sends her regards. She prefers to remain among kin in the fortress citadel of Hvergelmir.

And Ran sees no reason to be among us. She prefers the watery tempest that now rages over her home to the wildfire that will soon roar over ours. It is her belief that the white-capped ocean waves will protect her from the inferno's heat."

Nodding without turning, Frigg raised a hand to touch the far-off image of dust that swirled up in a dense knot before her. A heavy sigh escaped her lips. "Then let us greet our guests." Her hand fell limply to her side as she turned her attention back to the hall. "Fulla, open your box of ash. Give me Brisingamen. It is well to wear one's best on this day. No need to stint now that the end is near."

Withdrawing the necklace from her box, Fulla draped it about Frigg's neck. The finery lay heavy across the goddess' chest, its inset jewels and intricate gold weavings immediately brightening the room. Frigg lightly stroked the necklace then lifted its edge to catch the light. A sad smile dimmed her face as she admired the twinkling. "It is a shame that I have not the matching arm ring. That is still held by the sister of Freyr, the set bought by her with the lustrous hair, radiant as beaten gold."

Fulla tucked the ash box away while Frigg gave a last check of her robe. "Let's not keep our guests waiting."

Frigg glided into the chamber, Brisingamen glowing bright as the sun on her breast, diffusing a warm radiance through the room. "Welcome." She smiled, spreading wide her arms. "Welcome all. Your presence cheers my heart on this day of days. Please, let everyone be seated. There is no need to stand on ceremony. Not today. Everyone help yourselves to food and drink."

The goddess of hearth and home had just taken her seat when the amber form of Freyja swayed into the hall. The goddess casually tossed her cape to one side, forming a bronze pool of feathers on the floor.

The wife of Odin sniffed at the familiarity. "You expend great effort to travel in this manner, disregarding other ways that would have saved the exertion. Your arms must be tired."

Freyja paused in the entryway, a brilliant light amid shadows. "I wore my feather cloak today that I might ride in falcon shape and experience one last time the buffeting of winds, feel the rush of warm breezes tossing my hair, their caress on my face."

She examined her fingernails, running a finger along the edges to check for chips. "My cats I released in the field of Idavoll—Thor did the same for his goats, I could do no less—to face fate unfettered to my wain. I expect several geese will travel the westward path long before the end of this day." She pouted as a rough edge snagged her fingertip, then shrugged and turned her attention back to Frigg. "Gullinbursti was not mine to ride, the excellent mount created for my brother by the master craftsman Sindri. Freyr's has ever been the greater need. It remains ready at his hall should, in this dim sunlight, he need its golden bristles to clear the gloom."

"You dress well for this occasion." Freyja gestured at the necklace about Frigg's neck. "I see you wear that which once was mine."

"Possessions, like gifts, should frequently change hands. And prized gifts like this," Frigg tapped a finger against the necklace, "should be displayed often." Lips pursed in a taught smile, she crossed her arms before her chest. Fulla shifted uneasily behind her. "If you do not like what you see, why come to my hall? Why not go to Sindri?"

Freyja spread wide her arms, turned in a circle to take in the entire hall. "Where else should I be? Odin denied me the honor of participating in the battle storm; some nonsense about my place in the greater need that lay ahead. My warriors were taken—the half yielded to me. They fight in my stead on Vigrid plain. Now my hall echoes with the memory of footfalls so that I cannot stand to hear my own thoughts." A sour chuckle tipped her lips. "You say I should go to Sindri. I am not that virtuous, none of us are. And I do not seek to cower in Nidafjoll. Those dark mountains have never been to my liking. Too, they obscure the sight of Vigrid plain."

"Now Brimir?" Putting put a finger to pouting lips, she cocked her head to one side as if in thought. "While I enjoy good drink, can I not find its equal here? Besides, I do not abide the company of etins. While Fensalir is not as warm as Okolnir, my heart is warmest among those whose kin-bond is strongest."

Stepping aside, Frigg gestured toward the hearth. Several of her visitors shifted from their seats to make room on the bench for the last arrival. "You are welcome to join this gathering. It is a pleasure to have you as guest in my home."

Freyja glanced at the bench just cleared, smiled lightly, then with a sigh settled herself at equal high–the seat across from Frigg. Illuminated by the feeble light of a dulled sun, her face pale in the waning light, she seemed a faded image of past brilliance when the sun shone clear and lit her features in glory.

Freyja lifted a goblet from the table, sniffed at the aroma, then took a sip. She slowly swirled the amber drink, then took another draught. "The necklace looks divine on your chest, though the glow of youthful skin is essential to bring out the true luster of the ornament." She glanced at the golden circlet adorning her own arm. "You see that I wear the matching arm ring. Truly, I would rather have the set, this ring and the necklace stolen from me when its protector was slain—the mighty dragon for whose passing I wept amber tears."

She sighed deeply, letting her gaze rove about the room, a moth flitting amid the decorations, before settling on Frigg's arched brow. "One who holds should be ready to give. As a generous king gives an honored visitor that of his possessions which the visitor desires, surely in the godhead we share, a visitor, such as I, would be freely given a prized gift like the Brising necklace if it were so desired. It is, after all, only proper hospitality and good manners."

Knuckles white on the arms of her seat, Frigg worked her mouth with silent words that finally spit from between clenched teeth. "At such a time as this, you dare demand...!" Her voice choked. "Go away from this hall! Little respect have I ever received from you, let alone a freely given gift from your own hall! Go away, Heithrún. Dance in heat among the he goats! Be forgotten!"

The sister of Freyr laughed, a musical tinkle that filled the hall. "Let me remind you," she took another sip of the excellent mead, "that the nature of repartee is such that it should nip like the goat, not snap like the wolf. If a retort bites like the wolf, it is not a retort, but an insult."

A hard grin spread across Frigg's face. "As many have thrust themselves up the front of your skirt as have visited from behind. Go away Heithrún. Frisk in heat among the he goats."

Freyja arched a single golden eyebrow, her lips frozen in a thin smile that bared a narrow crescent of white teeth. Gersemi nudged Hnoss then jerked a chin at their mother. "Wretched and of evil disposition, your words cut to draw blood. You forget the one thing you ought to remember that you yourself are not free of fault."

The room hushed as Frigg leaned forward. "Your words gush forth without heed of mind or thought. Such counsel is little more than wasted breath, to be accepted with grave caution."

Freyja pressed a hand to her chest, her eyes wide and innocent. "I offer my counsel freely, without guile or pretense. Can you say the same? Often you charge the listener for the use of their ears. It is a price some painters may pay, but few men can afford."

Frigg tossed her head, flicking her long, luxurious hair over her shoulder. "You prattle senseless words. Can you never be silent? In time of grief few are given to ignoring insults." She shook a menacing finger, flames from the hearth fire flickering in her eyes. "You had best watch your mouth or your quick tongue will talk itself into trouble."

With a short bark of laughter, Freyja rocked back in her seat. "You give prize counsel, though in truth the rejoinders of others can reveal much of their character. Many seem wise if not challenged to reply, while a fool in company does best to remain silent less words betray an empty head."

A murmur rustled through the hall. Frigg raised a hand and the voices fell silent. "I am no fool and will not contend with one. For in the heat of barbed words parties often permit themselves to say worse than they mean."

The two stared in cold silence across the narrow divide between their seats. A grin quirked the corner of Freyja's mouth. Frigg struggled to resist as her lips pursed into a tiny smile. Freyja retrieved her goblet from the table, swirled it a moment in her hands then took a drink. "Many are devoted to one another, yet they quarrel. Among us there has always been strife. We have often traded barbs for the pure sport. Let us remember that on this day we choose to be together."

A sigh ran through the hall at Freyja's words. The mood of everyone lightened and the guests began to chat among themselves. Taking their cue, Frigg raised her own cup in salute. "Then let there be respite among us here at the end. Can we not admit that all manner of actions—good and bad—have passed between us, that now this bickering can end, and we can meet fate as we were when we gamed in the fields of our youth?

Things ill done and long past are often more easily blamed than forgotten. Yet what reasons remain for antagonism? There is no victory to be won when all share the same fate. What use is there in holding ancient grudges or spending time sniping among ourselves, tallying up our misdeeds until the fire consumes us? I call it a foolish course of action for those who seek companionship in the passing of their final hours. So, let our kinship bonds turn to the better and, forgiving-minded, find us happy while we wait."

A Message from the Front

Frigg rapped her knuckles on the board, three times she knocked for attention. Once all eyes were on her, she let her tongue utter that which they all dreaded. "This morning as I gazed out from my doorway, dim light marking the start of day, a trio of ravens flew over the shield roof of Fensalir. High shrilled the ravens, calling out to one another as they winged along that they were ready to feast.

Loud croaked the first, its voice young. 'I know something. Last night the glorious gods along with their retainers, all girded in the shiny rings of war, climbed aboard their high-prowed ship of the air.'

The second passed shrieking a matronly call. 'I scent something. From the world of men comes the smell of carrion to make the belly rumble.'

The third screeched terribly with the wise tone of age. 'I hear something. Many friends of wolves gather on the dusty plain to greet the dawn. Let us be cheerful for soon our hunger will pass.'

"As I listened to their talk, I thought to myself, 'The year old speaks, but knows little, the two-year-old chats, but I believe her not, and the three-year-old says what seems unthinkable.'"

Before any could reply, the wife of Odin held up her hand at a rough sound issuing from outside the hall that interrupted her speech. She gestured for silence as she strained her ears to hear. "What is that noise I hear in our dwelling? The earth trembles, shaking the entire court. My ears cannot deceive me. I know the pace of the mightiest of stallions. And did I not know what bodes today, I would imagine he whom I love best has come visiting."

She peered out the window. "My eyes agree with what my ears heard," she dropped her head. "The horse grazing amid the rushes is Sleipnir, but they are saddened that the rider is she of the golden helmet, the war-bent maiden of the general. Syn, ask her to join us in drink, though I fear she carries a message that I do not want to hear, for why else would she come alone from the wildfire of battle to seek our company."

The bright helmed lady of the general stalked into the hall. Whispers of steam rose from her byrnie and bright red stains marred its golden surface as she paused inside the doorway to scan the room. "Warmly I greet the wise one who dwells in this elegant hall. I arrived at your gate, uncertain if I would be greeted as friend or foe, invited in or driven away as a beast bent on harm—for messengers are often treated as the cause of their news."

The wife of Odin beckoned the Valkyrie to approach. "You are welcomed as a trusted friend. Tell me your message while you still stand, for news often escapes the sitting, and the one who speaks while lying down spreads lies."

Brynhild slid along the table of seated guests who drew away as she passed lest they be soiled with the stains of battle. The Valkyrie paid them no attention, but kept her march, helmet tucked firmly beneath one arm, until she stood before Frigg. "I come with a message sent at Heriar's order and Vidar's determined request. That I should leave this of all battles, sent on such an errand, chafes hard my honor. Unwillingly, I left my comrades to deliver this account."

She raised her chin and stared straight into Frigg's eyes. "Volupsa has come to pass, the battle ensues as the long dead seeress foretold. At dawn on Vigrid plain, we faced the horde of Muspellsheim, undaunted by their raging heat. The broad shoulders of towering etins blocked the sun. In spite and anger, the son of Farbauti roused the minions of Niflhel to fill the plain. Loki's savage spawn were true to their nature.

With sorrow, I bear grim tidings of our warriors' fall. Their passing makes my head droop in sadness where once it rode proud and high. On Vigrid plain fell Valfodur's forest of sturdy oaks, hewed down by the scythe of flame, but not before they exacted high payment for their lives. That the flames do not yet tower above this hall is a tribute to their dauntless courage and warrior skill."

Frigg asked: "And what of Odin?"

"Fimblultyr waged a glorious fight against the Fenris Wolf. With a broadsword, he parried savage blows while inflicting many wounds to the front. Both warriors struck great blows, but the ancient oak was toppled by his bitter enemy. First in death as ever he was in battle. So, passed Odin.

But the son of Loki did not long enjoy his victory. He met his end stabbed through the heart while gagging on Vidar's shoe."

Frigg asked: "What can you tell of Thor?"

"The Earth Girdler of whom scorn is never spoken faced the father of Magni. The serpent's coils stretched across the plain, his venom spew taking comrade and foe alike. Hlodyn's child approached, unafraid of the enemy, undaunted by his size. A mortal blow from the hammer of the god's strong guarder sent the great Circumciser screeching across the plain. Before he fell, he spat a final poisonous breath. Drenched head to foot in venom, the son of the Earth stumbled backward before crumpling to the ground. So, passed Asa-Thor."

Freyja asked: "What news do you have of my brother?"

"The Bright Slayer of Beli squared off with Surt. He gave a good account of himself, but without his wise distresser of shields, the son of Njord was as chaff harvested before the farmer's scythe. With a broad swipe of his fiery blade, Surt cut down the bright light of summer. So, passed Freyr."

Freyja blinked back tears and cleared her throat. "What can you tell of my husband?"

"Your husband showed the bravery we have all come to expect. He stood undaunted before the enemy, a sturdy oak firmly rooted before the flood. With lusty blows from his keen battle edge, again and again he drove back the line of foes. Never once did he turn aside. As I left the field, I saw a towering wave of mighty etins crash down on his position. I did not see him rise."

Frigg said: "Speak what you have seen of Heimdall."

"I saw the Warden of the Gods face Loki, the eternal bane of the Æsir. Many savage blows were struck. Both warriors received many wounds. Slaughter dew covered both, but neither retreated. Heimdall was struck a fatal blow, a wild thrust that set the white god along the red road. In falling, he drove his blade with both hands to split wide the shoulder crag of Farbauti's son, separating the strings of life from his body. So, passed Heimdall."

Then Frigg said: "Speak to us of Tyr."

"Of the one-handed god of oaths, I witnessed the bloodiest and noblest end. A savage struggle between honorable foes, Garm the greatest of hounds against the boldest of the Æsir. Hard they clashed, one against the other, with only the strength of their own bodies to press the hand of battle. Neither retreated while the other stood. Corpse plains shredded, limbs clinched together, teeth sunk deep in each other's flesh. Wound rivers poured from their bodies to nourish the baked clay of Vigrid plain. They lie as they fell, wrapped in death's embrace on the plain. So, passed Tyr."

Then Idun asked: "And what of my husband, Bragi?"

"The eloquent tongue faced the giantess Hyrrokkin, she who aided the gods at the funeral of Baldur. Unflinching, he faced her wrath, but brave words proved a poor shield against the shattering blows of a rope-wrapped brick. So, passed Bragi."

Sore were their hearts as news of the battle as the fate of their loved ones was made known. Tears coursed down cheeks drenching sleeves lifted to staunch their flow. Then others chimed in: "What of Vali and Vidar? Speak of Modi and Magni? Tell us of Ull. What happened to Forseti?"

The bright helmed victory maiden raised her hand. "Enough!" The voices quieted at her command. "I was sent on Sleipnir to deliver this account. That I have done. Of the others, I can only say that when I left, they were busy with slaughter. I have passed enough time in this delivery. I greatly desire to rejoin the battle, to face my fate as I have lived, always at the front, boldly confronting that which comes my way!"

Then Frigg reached out her hand palm up. "I know Herfodur. He held a soft heart for his chosen. He would not have sent his favorite back without the intent that you should remain here."

Brynhild jammed her helmet back on her head, turned on her heel to leave, but stopped short of the entry. "He may have meant to save me from the battle," she growled over her shoulder, "but to accept such an act goes against my very nature. It would dishonor not only myself but be an outrage against my sisters as well."

She made to spit her displeasure, thought better of it, and swallowed hard. "To sit squeezed tight with knees tucked beneath my chin, barricaded in a room waiting for death is not a path I choose to follow. I have always lived where shields are shattered, wounds bleed, and sturdy oaks fall. I choose to return to the harsh song of spears before Skoll completely consumes the light. For myself, it is better to die in the open than to have my trussed body dragged through a break in the wall. I rather my litr remain free to roam than ever try to re-enter this hall."

Frigg's Lament

Weeping, I went to Sleipnir. The great horse hid his head in the rushes. He knew his master was no longer living. I clapped my hands together so loudly that the goblets in the hall echoed my pain and the geese in the meadow cackled in reply.

I stand here bereft of happiness, stripped as a fir of its branches when a cutting girl comes gathering on a warm day. I, who once was the highest of Æsir ladies, am now as little as a leaf among the lindens at this our twilight.

How the Fates claw my heart! I miss in his seat and in my bed my friend to talk to. The child of Loki has brought me terrible grief.

I would that someone might bring me the cool, bitter draught of Gudrun. A drink to forget the past, in a horn risted with runes stained red: a sheaf of grain etched on its side, the serpent of fate wrapped about stem and bowl, its rim encircled with gripping beasts that watch the entrances to the lower worlds. A numbing drink augmented with fateful power brewed from sea water, sacrificial blood, worts of the wood, charred acorns, dew scraped from the hearth stone, sacred entrails, and a boiled pig's liver, all mixed to blunt memories of the past. Then would be forgotten the things that are known, and I could face each moment as a child greets a new day, uncaring of fate, enjoying the sun, the caress of wind, and cool drops of rain on the face.

But joy is for those who know little of woes I have suffered. The bliss of life is gone and with it my reason for being. I do not shun death; rather I welcome its cold forgetfulness.

Many pains I have endured over the long years. I've seen saplings fallen in the meadow, those which I had wanted to grow tall, hacked bloody from their roots. I have rarely known happiness since I cradled Baldur, he of purest thought. My son's life cut short through desperate cunning by the ill-conceived son of Farbauti.

Now the one I loved above all is gone. Would that I could perform the final service for my life's love, prepare his body for the journey west. But already Herfodur is washed in the water of life and shrouded in the finery of battle—the sacraments he would have chosen.

My heart is empty. I can weep no longer, nor strike my now numb hands together, nor continue to lament my loss. Wyrd goes ever as it must.

Freyja's Lament

Gone are the days when drums beat a steady rhythm and men danced in gauzy kerchiefs, women in kjafals, 'round the fire' and 'round the drummer', steps weaved for Freyja.

At many fires, I have warmed myself, but there are only two hearths I have ever called home: the halls of the Æsir and Vanir. My father was brought to this house as battle hostage to ensure peace. I was born into this life, a free loving child. I have endured in prominence, a woman of power. Only I alone know which was better for me.

When Od died, a more painful wound I have not felt. Jibes from forced family, even the biting words of Loki could not have devastated me more. And when he strode through my hall alive, redeemed in the eyes of my kin, he shone like a golden ray of from sun. He now resides alongside Baldur, safe in death.

I am not one to return to my bed, distraught at news of my lover's death. Long ago my tears dried up, leaving amber stains to mar the shores of men, though it burns still in my breast as a grievous wrong.

Now, even though I've chosen to fade with kin, my ire rises with the approaching flame. We were fools, as were they who left us behind, to think us safe while they sallied forth to final battle. Safe from what? We face the same fire, the same known end, though no glory attends our deeds! Harsh it is to view the mighty strife of armies embattled on that far-off plain, consigned to the side, no sharers of the peril.

Damn Skuld for our fate! I would rather take my stand on the bloody plain alongside the warriors who attended my hall, my sharp blade ringing defiance against the edge of my shield, than sit passively at table while the enemy's blade hacks me down.

Sif's Lament

My drink, I drink with sorrow—though we both knew our fates. My head droops in sadness with no spirit left to clap my hands, but only tears wept in payment for love departed.

We knew the happenings inside each other. Fierce as wolves, we coiled about one another, our embrace growing into an ancient tapestry of plaited green and silver threads, a noble hart in the foliage of a great tree.

When you held me tight one last time, oh, what sweet scents clung to your cheek. Difficult it was for my arms to release you, clasped like an iron ring about your neck. Harsh were my words then: 'Now go die, my best beloved, in the clash of fierce-minded men. Leave me here alone to shed cold tears.'

Your hands, so used to the heft of a hammer, rested lightly on my arm, squeezed gently, then slipped away. I watched as you walked down the path to the golden hall, until the mists swallowed your heavy shoulders and distance silenced your footsteps.

Though slain in his cold arms, I would risk my life to reach him now. For my fair-haired man, I know love unending.

Idun's Lament

Flowers blossom behind the breast. Worlds ripen like fruit on a mystic tree. There is the smell of apples and eternity. Gladly, I grew the golden crop that we should always live in youth never knowing the burden of failing health, the low burn of aching joints, and the heavy weight of passing time.

My heart longs with my breath as I recall our laughter when we would meet after a long day. For us our love was everything. The pains of the past disappeared before a brilliant future where our love would not, could not cease. Thus, our dreams fade in this hour, vanished back to the darkness whence they issued. Oh, that it was not so.

"And is he gone?" Three times Idun struck her hands together, then clutched them to her breast. "It seems but an instant past he stood beside me. Scruffy cheeked and wind-tousled hair, words of farewell tripping from his tongue."

Head bent, her lover's last words still sound, his gentle voice echoing in her ears: "All good, all light of the sun has come to me only from you. When you had been lost to Thjasse, my grief was boundless not knowing if you would return. My grief now is even more endless knowing that this day we forever part."

"And now," she stood before the fire pit, bright tears of memory trickling down her cheeks, "he's gone. We had both known after our final embrace there was nothing left to do but die. From the very beginning death was enfolded in our love."

Idun buried her face in her hands. "What is left now, but to lie here, face turned to the ashes piled about the hearth, all thought of food and drink dismissed, melting my last hours with tears." A low moan escaped her lips as she slumped onto the hearthstone before the flickering flames.

Gefjon's Song

Why pine away, lost in sorrow, at these last moments of our lives? Why be unhappy? True the fire approaches our home and there is nowhere we can escape it. At least, reconciled to our fate, we can share the burden among us. After all, a burden shared is no burden. Happily, I face this end, though I would rather its burning hand be stayed for an eternity to come.

I lived my life by my own design. Used my wits to get what I wanted. Overcame the lust of others to achieve my ends. Built up my store of wisdom to rival that of the Alfodur.

Proud I have been to protect virgins—women (and no few men) of all ages—my help freely given to those in need, for through all time they have ever been victims.

Munin alone knows what lies near the heart; mind alone knows the spirit. Worry will not crease my brow nor purse my lips. Well I know that all must die. Let us hoist a drink to all that was. I have much enjoyed the journey.

Facing the End

In somber joy, the gems of the Æsir sat together, their once-brilliant facets dimmed with grief. Frigg rapped her knuckles on the board. "Difficult is the time," her voice carried over the assembly speaking that which all felt, "tears dry before their birth. Hard it is to draw from my breast the words I feel burning within.

We have no arval feast to hold that respect may be shown for those who held the integrity of our clan close—maintained for each of us our rights by the might of their arms. Now with the head and limbs gone, none are left to guard our honor and see us safely into old age. True the fruit of Idun can keep we few young and full of health. But to what purpose? What remains to strive against when even our most dedicated foes are gone?

The firestorm has torn a grim gap from the depths of our heart's cage, a gaping break blasted wide by the terrible events of today. Sorely, have these twilight hours struck, left us bereft of our lover's embrace, frayed our kinsman's tight links, and ripped strong bands from our ranks. If our suit in battle we could press, rather than wait in this great hall for the flame's deadly caress, the fire's kinsman we would gladly meet as foe.

It is difficult to muster strength enough to endure so that all will know how we, the last of the Æsir line, bravely faced our kinsman's slayers. The sons of Muspellsheim have taken much from us while the son of Farbauti was never a true friend. Cruel it is to tally our kinsman's loss. Gone are our protector's strong shields.

Nothing in our life becomes us as the leaving of it. We die—we who have studied life's passing—discarding our greatest treasure as if it were a careless trifle, a shiny bauble worn for the newness, then tossed aside when its glitter dims.

And what will come after us? Something must endure. Mountains to hold things solid, fir trees, silver grasses, and heather on the heath. All the tiny creatures, field mice with glittering eyes ever watchful from behind blades of grass, crawling ants that work all day long, bees laboring among the meadow blooms, snails, centipedes, fish in the sea, even the great ocean itself.

While our future is certain, why hasten its arrival? Our loss is but once. We will not face another. Let us grasp hands here while the fire breaks. Merry, we leap together from the brink of the family cliff. This day let us drink to gladness soon gone forever.

To all warriors yet to come, may your lots be better. To all women, and men too, who survive the embers of Muspellsheim, may your heavy hearts grow light. To all children born of ash and elm, may happiness be your lot."

The World Reborn

Now is told of the world reborn and the surviving gods and goddesses who see its new light.

The Good Earth

Wide swings Delling's gate as Night takes her rest and Day begins his long march across the land chanting a joyful song of blissful awakening to a new world cleansed of war.

Elf-disk bore a daughter before consumed by Skoll, thrown free at the last moment by her dying mother, a daughter now protected by the Varinian. With the powers departed, she rides her mother's path. Alfbeam's daughter, clothed in light, reins in hand, guides the wain of the Sun.

The wounded moon paused to watch her arrival—dawn breaking across the wide Wind-Home—then sank, limping to his bed, eager for rest. From the south Alfbeam's daughter heaves her hand over heaven's rim. All the waters catch fire. From their depths fountains spew forth a rainbow of droplets to burst forth upon the shores of light.

The newborn Earth rises upward from the sea, mountains wrapped with clouds, fields full grained, pastures sprouting with growing grasses. Rain falls to water the newborn world in the dew of life's dawn. Sunlight scatters across broad plains fringed with thick stands of birch and oak. Wide meadows overflow with wildflowers rippling in wind-lapped pools.

In gladsome bends along riverbanks, winged throngs flit from tree to tree. Their liquid notes fill the air while their whistling wings cleave the sky. Amid shallow pools the swan's trumpeting voice rings clear against the clamor of cranes and the wild call of loons.

The great ash, worn with time, leafs out with lush new life. Squirrels and harts rejoice in its foliage. Perched amid the high branches, the great eagle ruffles his feathers in satisfaction. Saehrímnir barks with pleasure rooting amid its roots, while Heidrun brays back in delight.

The sea gentles to steadily rolling waves as storm winds lighten to a soft breeze, their massed banks of clouds giving way to flickering thought. Brine splashes from the gray-green waves to crust white the tidemarks on stony beaches. Swift currents shear rocks and sand from shorelines as the World Mill begins to turn.

In wooded glades, dawn glints on melting frost, the scattered light wrapping the dark fir trees in rainbow colors. Eyes open to a newborn morning. Elf rays tint the sky like daydreams with a bright glow that spreads across the land. Up springs shining grain from fields showered fresh with rain. Green boughs leaf out amid trees that wax tall, their bowed branches laden with fruit.

Sandy beaches washed clean by soft waves of the sea and verdant woodland pastures know footfalls two and four. Calls fill the leafy lanes and echo across hills matted with dew-quenched grass. Parents stretch their drowsy bulks along pasture tracks while their young scamper about on shivering joints, dashing among the tender herbs, their fresh hearts frisking with the new day.

Many longings are reawakened for life and the yearning for life. Joyous it is to stroll among the flowers opened to catch the early rays of the sun. Dew veils clinging to spider-spindle weavings cloud the meadow grasses. The heavens spill out in all directions while the songs of wolves fade from their mountain retreat.

The sky beams with the springtime face of day. Hollows glow with the diffused light. Lulled to timely rest are the savage works of war. Fruitful again is the Earth for all living things.

The Final Gathering
From the shade of Niflheim, two figures slipped away while the hoard of damned marched to their third death. Hodd and Baldur, strengthened by the mead of the ásmegir, set aside man-killing thoughts. In clear-eyed friendship, they return, footsore across the nine worlds, to the land of the living.

From the seared dust of Vigrid plain those of the Æsir who remain alive turn their weary faces home. Modi and Magni, hair singed, skin smudged gray by the now spent fire, gather up their weapons as they shuffle through the charred remains cluttering the ground. Vali and Vidar sheath their tools of war. With a tired wave, they accompany the sons of Thor on the long trek home. Hoenir scans the flame-ravaged plain, scuffs the soil now sterile of life, heaves a weary sigh, and trails behind.

Through the defile of snow-fed falls they come together, the living and reborn, onto the actively renewing field of Idavoll. From the blackened halls of Asgard trail those few of the goddesses and their handmaidens who survived the fire's blight, join the ranks of exhausted survivors.

Together, they gather in Gimle, a hall fairer than the sun, its high roof thatched with yellow gold—now dimmed by a layer of soot from Surt's fire. Idavoll, the unsown field, sprouts into fullness. In the tangled growth of ever-becoming, nestled amid the twining herbs, lay golden playing pieces they had possessed in ancient times.

Their hearts brim over with gladness. Merry, they play board games in the meadow, tell stories, run footraces, brighten their lives with contests of strength. With song and dance the party rejoices in good company. Lute strings sound, keeping time as tales are told of the mighty gods.

On the velvet-green meadow, they set forth a table to honor the new sun, boiled flesh from all four-footed creatures, fresh fruits, grains, wild herbs—all carefully arranged. Joyously, they feasted on the province produced by the earth.

To Hoenir—the last of the sons of Bor—falls the sacred duty of selecting cuttings taken from the bark of a living fruit tree. With a sharp blade freshly cleaned from battle, he carved runes of prophecy on the wooden slips, then stained them with his own blood mixed with the green juice of plants. After they dried, he placed them in a tall edged bowl.

"I am the last of three brothers whose feet began this journey and once held in our hands power over the heavens. It is right that I perform this final duty."

With solemn purpose, Hoenir drew slips randomly from the bowl. One by one he arranged them in a pattern of divination. Everyone leaned forward with anticipation as he raised his hands. "The patterns are clear. That for which we have sacrificed will come to pass. The offspring of Líf and Leifthrasir will spread to inhabit the newborn world that mankind might prosper once more."

Each started as a great mournful cry echoed across the sky. A thick form swirled up from the Dark-of-Moon Hills, a shining serpent laboring in flight. Nidhogg's shadow swept over the plain, his talons empty of corpses. The surviving gods clustered together, watching in silence as the serpent wheeled overhead, webbed wings spread wide to catch the air. The low, mournful wail sounded again as Nidhogg faded away over the horizon.

Then Hoenir spoke to the gathered few; his voice, though soft, clearly reaching the ears of all. "Gone are the simple days when a beast could have its life taken for the good of the community. Its blood sprinkled over the fields to make a plentiful harvest, to calm the tides, or to bring fortune in battle. We were more cheerful in those past seasons, though we have much now to welcome us here. The living sacrifice of others has shown us how to live joyfully and face death with hope.

Today, we set our eyes on the road ahead, waiting for that which time brings with it. Along with the funereal, we celebrate life, for the rowan trees are in leaf and fledgling starlings call from their limbs. The air resounds with the bewildered wail of infants newly arrived at the shores of light.

The pathways of purpose are hard to find. Truths of the ages wear thin, show gaps, and are tossed aside. Stripped of our beliefs we discover that what has meaning only for each one alone, has no real meaning at all. We are left to find anew what we often miss, that what is of any importance in us is what we share and permanently unites us with all others. It does not change, any more than does the growing tree that thrusts its branches toward the sun for warmth, while sending its roots deep into the earth for nourishment.

Before we part, let us commemorate our past by leaving our mark in small places across the lands for those who know how to look. Let us raise batua stones for those who have gone, their deeds inscribed in runes around their edge, so those who come after will know that others who passed this way held true to their honor and kept sacred their pledges.

It is important they be remembered, and their fate recognized. Those finding themselves in similar situations must know that they, too, can perform heroic deeds, for such deeds have been done by others."

Cycle 6: Of Gods and Men

*Now are told the stories of direct interaction between the Æsir gods and mankind,
those that contrast the price of human folly and morality...*

Lay of the Survivor

Sad to remember, sick with years, I tramp along with measured tread, like one who comes from so far away he does not expect to arrive at his destination. Eyes misted as the dove-gray edge of the sea, my mind is weighed with the memory of a blood-soaked plain.

War-death swept away my people, a firestorm that consumed those who had once known the joys of kinship and cherished bench companions. No longer is there pleasure in the lute's voice. The minstrel's ballad and skald's tales, which once held the company in thrall, issue now from silent lips to fall on deaf ears. No longer does the swift steed race along good paths. Nor does the great hound bound through the hall, claws scrabbling across the floor, as with joyous barks he greets his master's return.

Now silence cloaks the land, muffles the mind with thoughts of dust and ash, and grips the heart with pangs of grief. The drinking goblet for feasting stands empty, inlaid with silver, and plated with leafed gold, tarnished with no one to polish the precious vessel now that comrades and kin are gone. So, too, the ring-byrnie - which protected its wearer through fierce battle storms and biting swordplay - rusts with age and crumbles to dust like the warrior fallen alone on an empty plain.

Pale as ashes, I pass from where kin in wide-fields played rough games of war. Lost is my taste for the sport once loved. My breast now dwells in sorrow. What comes after for the sole surviving warrior, a solitary watchman mourning dead comrades and desiring the same fate, but to return to the halls of his people?

Shoulders slumped, head hung low, I tread a winding path to those empty, far-off halls, where once laughter and play were the only concerns. Each step wrings my heart with a memory that catches my breath: a smile, a wink, a whispered word, the embrace of soft arms about my neck, and the scent of tresses woven with summer flowers.

My mind floods with sights and sounds: the family hearth aglow with warmth, laughter from children at play amid the ashes, the smell of a good meal ready after a hard day, a close conversation across mugs topped with mellow ale.

Sorrow eats the heart when there is none to share your thoughts. To the trodden dust I loudly recall a world now past, a shouted memory to fill the emptiness. The wind carries my words, the cliffs echo and the waters ripple with my speech. Such sharing eases the burden. My feet grow lighter, the bonds on my heart loosened, the terrain less treacherous.

Alone, I plunge onward, buffeted by sharp winds, until the high cliffs of home rise into view. Sunlight flares across the crests of long familiar hills and the gleam of high roofed halls top the horizon. My steps quicken as I pass through familiar gates into a land long thought lost.

Mind alone recalls the world anew: where the sun knows her home, the moon feels his might, and the stars hold their familiar stations. A fresh world where spring rules the lands and the halls are filled with feasting and song.

The Lay of Gefjon

In the early days of the world, Gefjon traveled the land, walked its headlands and wide plains, crossed the high mountain paths of the etin's home. She often visited the halls of men as she kept watch over the fate of virgins. For women and young girls who die as virgins, and no few young men as well, find refuge in her hall as handmaidens and servants to their goddess protector. As a brood hen defends her chicks or a wolf bitch guards her pups against harm, the goddess was known to take vengeance on those who thought little of a woman's worth and willingly sullied their honor.

In Midgard, there lived a great king among men, called Gylfi, who ruled over lands that bordered the sea. His appetites were great, especially those piqued by the beauty of women. He had many, regardless their desire or consent, such was the urgency of his hunger. With trinkets, he paid for honor - given freely or taken by force - and he always sought more.

On one of her journeys into the lands of men, Gefjon entered the kingdom of Gylfi. She heard many tales of the king's actions, hushed stories muttered from averted faces shrouded in thick dark scarves, or boldly laughed to the world from heavily whiskered jowls. The accounts of his forays were so graphic, that she decided to instruct him in the worth of a woman.

———— · ————

Along a headland road, two paths crossed. Sol's wain had climbed into the sky, warming the lands, and stirring the winds while breakers sounded below the cliffs. A young maiden, clad in white linen, faced the sea, her arms spread wide to embrace the breeze that rushed along the rocky shore. The gown pressing against her body outlined a clean form beneath. Her golden hair was drawn back and tied off behind with a red ribbon. Aided by the steady breeze, errant locks had burst their bonds to fall alongside her high cheeks, framing the clear blue of her eyes.

Gylfi approached from downwind. He frequented the headland trail alone, enjoying the glittering sunlight scattered across the sea waves. Immediately the maiden came into view, her features aglow with Sol's warmth, his heart throbbed with her beauty and set his passion aflame.

Approaching the woman, he wasted no time on pleasantries, but launched into impassioned speech that she would know his urgent desire. "I neither know nor care who you are, your lineage or your station in life. I must have you! Your form is wonderful... The way the sun... the wind caresses... The way your hair... I grow hard and tall like a mighty fir!"

The maiden stared silently at the man, let his speech run down until it stopped, and he stood before her slack jawed, unable to say more. She sniffed once, tucked a loose lock of hair behind her ear, and looked down her nose at the man. "You babble as a fool or one too eager to speak straight. I see you wear an expensive cloak of fine wool dyed blue, so you must be someone of worth. That hardly means you are not a fool. Who are you, old man, that you accost me with such words?"

The great king swallowed hard, not used to chiding speech directed at him. He thought to be angry, but her beauty diffused his anger and turned his resentment into a stronger desire. "My name is Gylfi. I am king of this land, and I am no fool. Though the first sight of your beauty overwhelmed me and hastened words through my lips before I could gauge their worth, know that my request was in earnest."

The young woman paused, lazily curling a lock of hair about her finger as she considered his words. "That which you ask, many have requested before, but few have ever obtained. It is not something I bestow readily. As a king, you must possess great wealth. What will you offer in return for its promise?"

Gylfi, eager that his goal be acquired, fumbled a gold band set with a large red stone from his finger. "I offer you this signet, plucked warm from my hand. Its carbuncle is carved with the seal of three wolves; wolves so plainly glutted on the carrion of battle you can almost feel they will skulk off to sleep now that they have had their fill. And they would have, had the engraver not fenced them within a picket of golden wire.

In gem and gold, its worth is great. Greater still is the honor to be had of telling others from whom it was obtained."

The maiden glanced at the ring, then returned her gaze to the open ocean. "I have no need of trinkets. Such possessions weigh one down and are difficult to manage on the road. Easily lost or misplaced, they provide a false sense of worth and security."

Gylfi, keen that the prize not slip away, rushed his desire with blurted words. "Then name your price. I must have you!"

The maiden's voice carried by the wind came softly to Gylfi's ear. "I have wandered long and far, my only baggage a store of common sense that has served me well in my travels. Now my feet have grown weary of the endless road and I would have land to farm, a place where I might build a homestead of my own."

Gylfi laughed heartily, relieved at the inconsequence of her price. "If it is land you desire, then know I have that in plenty, as far as you can see and farther. From the breadth of my kingdom you may choose any piece of plough land, as much as four oxen can till in a day and a night."

The maiden smiled at Gylfi's offer. "Then today you may have your desire. Tomorrow, I will select my price."

The next day she rolled Gylfi aside, the man drained of fire from the night's exertions. Crisscrossing the room, she retrieved her clothes from where they lay scattered about the floor. Gylfi propped himself on one elbow and, with an appreciative eye, watched her dress. "Where do you go? Certainly, there is time enough for a morning meal. The night's enjoyment has left me quite famished."

The maiden belted her gown about the waist, and then pulled her travel boots onto her feet. "I am eager to secure my payment for last night's entertainment, but I need capable beasts to mark my claim. The oxen you have in this land are scrawny creatures, barely able to draw a harrow. I travel north to a land I know. I will return to your kingdom in four days with oxen fit to handle a plow."

"As you will," Gylfi laughed and rolled onto his back, tucking an arm beneath his head, "my lands go nowhere."

On the fourth day, Gefjon returned leading four large oxen, massive beasts with horns bent forward to nearly touch the ground. Their horns were so curved that when they lowered their heads to crop the succulent pasture grass, they walked backward to keep them from digging into the earth.

Their hide was thick and firm to the touch, stretched taut over rippling muscles and broad, powerful shoulders. They stood solid and implacable beside the maiden, bodies of great strength capable of great deeds.

As payment, she chose a spit of land in the southern reaches of the Gylfi's domain; a hilly point surrounded by the sea. Watered by fresh springs and abundant rainfall, the land was ideal for growing grain and hay. Its soil was so rich, when it bore, it produced a hundredfold.

The oxen were sons of a high-browed giant who found it amusing to assist the goddess. She yoked them to a plough and bid them draw. They pulled hard and steady in the traces until sweat dripped from their brows and clouds of steam rose from their backs.

The sharp plow dug a deep, wide furrow in the earth, and the oxen were so powerful that it cut the land free from the main. Gylfi could only stare in disbelief as they dragged the land out to sea, westward, far beyond the shadow of his control. At Gefjon's command they stopped in a channel where she fastened the land in place. She called it Sjaelland and gave it over to the Danes to hold. Water rushed in to fill the gap where the land had been gouged free of the main. This body of water is called Logrinn, a lake with inlets to match the headlands of Sjaelland.

So Gefjon carved away a piece of Gylfi's pride and left him with a harsh reminder of the price of avarice and unbridled lust.

The Fall of Gerriod

King Hrauding ruled in a northern land long favored by Odin. His high timbered hall set back from a rocky fjord, its shores washed by the gentle lapping of a gray sea that roared and heaved beyond the white foam of breakers protecting the inlet and its ship-ready beaches. Two sons graced his hall, sturdy reeds sprouting in fertile soil: Gerriod, the younger was eight, brash and precocious. Agnar, the eldest was ten, gentle and kind to all, thin and fair-haired, where his brother was dark and coarse.

Hrauding doted on his sons and gave them all that was in his power to give. As sons of a king, they were permitted freedom of action far in advance of their majority. The boys strutted about the court taking ownership of everything they saw; all that would be theirs in the due course of time.

One day the boys awoke to the golden light of new dawn. They crawled from bed, rubbing sleep from their eyes, as birds are nudged from their evening roosts when the warm rays of Sol strike the cold shadows from the trees. In the clear morning light, the sons of Hrauding called to each other as they sprang out of their beds, rustling like young partridge.

Gerriod shouted a plan as he bound boots on his feet. "Let's go fishing today!"

Agnar drew a tunic over his head and barked eager agreement. "We can take a boat from the dock!"

With the intent of youth, they set out to accomplish their will. From the docks Gerriod selected a small low-edged boat with oars of a size they could manage together. Agnar tied a line with baited hook to the stern, so their hands would be free for steering the boat. Grinning and laughing, they pushed out to sea, each working an oar to keep the course straight as they trolled the line through calm waters to catch small fish.

Sweat beaded their brows and trailed in rivulets down their cheeks. "You're pulling too hard!" Agnar complained to his younger brother. "You make us go in circles." Gerriod frowned and slowed his efforts to keep from tiring his older brother.

They had worked their way out to deeper water where the breaking waves gouged a rough channel, when a hard strike from a monster of the deep wrenched the stern of their boat about so it pointed out to sea. Excited at first, then alarmed, the boys looked on in helpless panic as the currents dragged their boat out past the breakers. Once they saw the hump of an ocean Ox break the surface, a shiny black back that rolled up from the depths, before their boat lurched over the foaming boarder and the line snapped, the sharp crack lost amid the crashing of waves.

Agnar squawked as the boat slapped down on the water's surface, the oar jumped from his grip and disappeared into the white froth. Gerriod lifted his oar still clutched in his hands and shook it before his brother's shocked face. "Now what will we do? We are free of the beast but have only one oar between us!" Agnar attempted to reply, but only a light croaking escaped his quivering lips.

Gerriod drew in the oar and slammed it to the bottom of the boat. He glared at the far-off beach as a stiff breeze rustled his hair. A low growl from the side of his mouth caught Agnar's frozen ears. "And now the wind rises."

The wind blew all day and into the night, a storm-wrought wind carrying them across the sea, far from the lamentations keened from Hrauding's hall when his children failed to return home. In the black of night, the two boys huddled together for warmth, clothes soaked through by splashing waves, as their boat heaved and rocked through the rough sea.

Teeth chattering, heads bent into each other shoulders, the boys gripped each other with one arm while they held tight to their seat. Gerriod started when he heard the unmistakable sound of waves breaking on an invisible shore. He placed chapped lips to his brother's frozen ear and shouted. "Do you hear that!"

"Hear what?" Agnar's voice was nearly snatched away by the roaring wind and deafening waves.

Gerriod nudged close and jerked a thumb over his shoulder. "The crash of waves has changed. It sounds like they do at home when they fall on the shore during a storm."

Agnar wiped water from his eyes and tuned his ears. He listened hard for the telltale hiss of water on rock. "You are right. We must be close to land."

The boys poked their heads over the rail attempting to pierce the surrounding blackness. Agnar pointed at a dark mass that towered before them. The boat's prow was pointed into a line of white foam that edged the dark mound, the waves guiding its wrenching movement directly into the heart of the darkness.

Agnar grimaced and pulled Gerriod down beside him. "Our boat will strike the beach soon. We must be ready to jump free or we will be dragged back out to sea." Gerriod scowled and gravely nodded his head.

The sound of the crashing waves grew louder, their boat shivered in the rough waves, taking on water until it wrecked itself on a rocky beach.

They leapt ashore, Agnar catching his brother's hand as they struggled from the hungry embrace of the sea. Gasping and clawing their way across the rocks, Gerriod climbed to his feet and pointed up the hill.

Through a heavy curtain of salt spray and mist, the dim flicker of a light on a nearby hill drew them stumbling up the rocky beach onto a tilled field. Cold, shivering, their clothes soaked through from the autumn sea, the boys approached the rough-built home of a crofter that edged close to the white hairs of the ocean.

Hands white and numb with the cold, the boys beat on the rough boards of a heavy door, the wood grains raised and splintered from constant exposure to the salt spray and winds. The door creaked open, so a sliver of light slashed their faces and, a breath of promised warmth caressed their cheeks. As one, the pair crowded through the doorway, shoving aside the old man who held the door.

An old woman dressed in a white kirtle and gray apron smudged with the remains of the day's labor glanced up from beside the welcoming hearth as the boys rushed into the room and hunched over the fire. "Come in and make yourselves comfortable," the old man muttered softly to the doorjamb as he quickly scanned the darkness for more visitors. Satisfied the boys had arrived alone, he shouldered the door closed against the howling wind.

A sharp glance passed between the couple as they waited for their unexpected visitors to quit shivering and settle themselves beside the hearth. Gerriod was the first to rouse himself from the fire. He spun about and glared at the silent couple. "We have been at the mercy of the sea all day and have had nothing to eat. I'm hungry! What do you have to offer!"

The old man snorted, and the woman smiled. "The unexpected guest should never demand. Before we share our home and food, tell us who you are."

Agnar frowned at his brother then rose and spoke to the couple. "I am Agnar, son of King Hrauding, and you have already heard from my brother Gerriod." Gerriod scuffed his feet and nodded his head. "Our boat was captured by the wind as we set out to fish. We could not fight the strength of the wind nor the pull of the currents as they dragged us out to sea. All night we were driven across the wave-tossed ocean until we were blown onto your shore. You can find the ribs of our skiff dashed on the rocks below, if the waves haven't carried them away."

The old man nodded, and the woman sighed. "It is indeed a terrible tale, but did you not bring oars to drive your boat in such need?"

Gerriod threw his brother a vicious glare. "They were lost when first we struck the breaker line. We could do naught but trust the mercy of the wind."

Agnar turned his face aside as the old man nodded and twitched his gaze back and forth between the boys. "Then you are lucky to be alive and fortunate the fates have driven you to our shore. Call me Farmatýr and my wife Esther. I have heard of your father and the lands he controls. You are not far as the raven flies from your home, for the sea course is straight, but the journey by land is many weeks.

Fortune is yours for having arrived before Gormánudr released his control. We are come on Frermánudr, and with his freeze travel will be impossible. So here is my suggestion. It is useful if you learn it, do you good if you take it. Stay with us. Do not be hasty to leave. Deep snows and sheet ice are expected within the week and any journey far too dangerous to undertake, especially by two young boys.

It has been a good year for us. We have food stored in plenty, and our home is sturdy and warm. Winter here with my wife and me. We can always use the help and would be delighted with your company. Remain with us through the economical months of winter, until Sólmánudr begins his reign and the seas are freed of ice. Then I will get you a boat, and you can return home."

Agnar and Gerriod turned away from the elderly couple and bent their heads together in conference. Their voice rose and fell, Gerriod stamped his feet, and Agnar's voice shrilled but once. When they had come to accord, the boys turned back to their hosts. Agnar nodded his head and spoke. "We agree to stay." Gerriod scowled, his lower lip thrust forward, and nodded sullen agreement.

Farmatýr and Esther smiled and spread their arms in welcome. Esther rose to her feet and busied herself at a large pot. "Now let us get these boys fed. They look famished."

Throughout the winter the boys helped about the farm doing chores they never had to do at home. Each day they hauled wood for the fire, cleared snow from the paths between shed and hut, melted ice and snow for drinking and cooking, learned to feed and milk the farmer's goats.

As the days shortened and the nights grew longer the boys gravitated as their nature willed: Agnar to the soft counsels of Esther, Gerriod to the rumbled teachings of Farmatýr. Many hours they spent in the company of their favorites learning from the wisdom of the elderly couple. Esther shared the understanding of home and hearth. Farmatýr coached with skills more martial in nature.

When spring arrived, and ice released its grip on the shore, Farmatýr gathered up a travel sack and left the farm along a deep mud track that snaked across the low hills. The boys remained behind in the good keeping of Esther. Three days later he returned by sea riding the swells in a small boat stocked well with provisions and fresh water.

The next morning, the sky was blue and the sea calm. Farmatýr and Esther made much of their charges as they bundled the boys in warm robes to fend off the cold and accompanied them to the shore to see them off on their journey home.

While Agnar hugged Esther good-by, Farmatýr took Gerriod aside to speak privately. "Today you begin your journey home. It is a short distance by sea, but one you should give great thought."

He placed a hand on the boy's shoulder and drew him close that his words not carry. "We have spent much time together, you and I, and I have come to hold your character in high esteem. Through word and deed, I have come to understand that the hardship which brought you to us was not one of your making.

Before you go I will give you a piece of advice. It will do you well if you learn it. Do you good if you accept it. The son who means to inherit his father's hall should act quickly and decisively. Bold actions carry the day. The timid never win victory.

Now go. Journey safely. Arrive safely."

The boys climbed into the rocking sea goat, gave a final wave to their kind protectors, then, setting their back to the oars, drove their boat through the waves, a fair breeze aiding their passage across the sound.

Agnar was chatty and throughout the day carried on a one-sided conversation heedless of Gerriod's silence and steady glare that grew sullen as they approached the green line of the far shore. The boat nudged a rocky headland where deep water kept them from beaching. Swiftly, Gerriod tossed his oar into the foaming currents and leapt from the prow onto a large rock that jutted out into the dashing waves.

Agnar braced himself with a hand on a bench while he tossed a rope for Gerriod to draw the boat close. "Here, take this and hold it fast. The waves make it difficult to stand and the wind is shifting. It will blow me out to sea if you don't brace the line."

Gerriod held the rope limp in his fist. His lips twisted into an ugly grin as he threw the rope back into his brother's astonished face, and viciously kicked the boat far back into the water. "Let the wind have you! Make your bed with the sea trolls!"

Agnar screamed for his brother's help as a large swell caught the boat and dragged it back out to sea. Gerriod laughed as his brother frantically waved his arms and nearly capsized the boat with his desperate antics. He hollered over his shoulder as he turned away and began traversing the rocky cliff face. "This time I lost my oar and you have held onto yours! Now we are even!"

———————

Hrauding was overjoyed with the return of a son long thought lost, but bitter tears streamed down his cheeks when Gerriod told of the wreck on the headland that claimed the life of his brother, a monstrous swell that lifted and smashed their boat against the rocks just as Agnar was about to leap to safety. He could do nothing but watch as the hull shattered into kindling and his brother was dragged screaming beneath the waves.

With one son lost to him, taken by the sea, Hrauding placed all his attention on his remaining son. Gerriod grew to know neither want nor limit; he had but to ask and it was given.

In time, Hrauding passed and Gerriod succeeded his father upon the throne, then all power fell to him and he ruled his lands with a wary eye. Always he was watchful of others and closely scrutinized each unknown visitor for fear he might somehow herald his brother's return from Ran's embrace.

In the company of known friends, he was a generous breaker of rings, though tight with food and drink should he feel too many crowded his table. But among visiting strangers he was a skinflint, stingy and suspicious of everyone. Only when he felt certain of a person's intentions did he relax his guard and allow generosity to flow.

His fears grew to such an extent that when he had a son, he named him Agnar, for in looks and, as he grew older, in actions he reminded him of his brother.

———————

From Hlidskialf, Odin looked out across the nine worlds. What he saw so delighted him, he called Frigg to join him at his watch. When Frigg wafted through the doorway, Odin stood and beckoned her to take his seat that she might have the best view.

Frigg arranged her cloud-white robe as she made herself comfortable. "Now what is it that you are so eager for me to see that you summon me from my duties?"

Odin grinned wide and gestured out across the lands, directing her gaze to a cave recessed along the edge of a rocky headland that jutted far out into the sea. "Look there, moving from the cave mouth, isn't that Agnar, your foster child from years ago, raising children of his own with a giantess among the flotsam and jetsam of the sea?

Frigg squinted her eyes for a better look, wrinkling her nose at the vision that rose before her. "Apparently, it is, and I had such high hopes for the boy. It was all I could do fending off the greedy fingers of Ran to keep him from being swallowed by the sea when somehow he and his brother became separated on their return."

Chuckling, Odin gestured to a well-appointed hall. "Now look here. There sits Gerriod, ruler over a wealthy land. He has certainly done me proud."

Frigg sniffed as she leaned forward the better to see. "In action and character." She nodded her head at the distant sight. "It is said that he is wealthy and lacks for nothing yet is begrudging of basic hospitality. Word has it, he is so stingy with food that guests arriving unannounced at his hall or who arrive in too great a number see an empty bowl delivered with the back of his hand."

Odin puffed his chest and stomped about the tower. His eyes bulged as he sputtered words though his heavy beard. "That is the greatest of lies! His generosity has been evident since he was a young lad come to us from the sea. You speak from jealousy and spite, your heart poisoned with venom."

Frigg chuckled as she drew her wrap down onto her shoulder exposing the fine swan-like curve of her neck. "No. I only repeat what I have heard, and it tallies well with the boy I remember. Are you so fond of a memory that you dare not challenge it? I say prove me wrong."

Odin glared at his wife, letting his lips purse in and out as his reply built up as water cresting an earthen dam, ready to burst free of its banks. "I will do more than prove you wrong. I will prove that I am right! You say he is stingy and hard hearted to the uninvited, well I will present myself at his hall and you will see how wrong you are!"

Frigg folded her hands in her lap as she shook her head. "That is hardly a test or even proof of his generosity. Were you to show up at his door as yourself, of course you could expect gracious service. Your glory would betray who you are in a moment, and he would never dare insult you."

Odin pounded a fist in his hand as his gaze darted back and forth along the horizon. "Alright! I will present myself as a weary traveler seeking shelter. Then you will see how well he treats unexpected guests and witness the true extent of his hospitality!"

As the Alfodur stormed from the watchtower, Frigg gently gathered her robes about her shoulders and with a faint smile on her lips began her descent from Hlidskialf.

In Fensalir, the hall of mists, Frigg drew Fulla aside and, with a brusque command, sent her handmaiden with a private message for Gerriod's ears alone. She instructed it was to be delivered in all haste.

Swiftly, Fulla dove through the air to Midgard and sought out the sleeping ear hands of Gerriod. Amid the early morning hours when the king lay between sleep and wakefulness three times she whispered his name and left her message. "Gerriod, attention. Gerriod, a message I bring. Gerriod, it is an important warning from the lips of an ancient protector."

Fulla smiled as the king stirred uneasily in his sleep. "Beware," she continued, "lest a powerful wizard bewitch you. He will visit your hall; a stranger to your lands. You will know him by these signs; with a pilgrim staff gripped tight in his hand, a slouch hat drawn over one eye, and the blue mantle of a traveling cloak about his shoulders, he will walk freely through your courtyard. No dog, no matter how fierce will attack, bark, or in any way molest him."

She paused, letting her words settle in and nest deep their barbs. "Listen to these words of warning and hold them close to your breast. They will do you good if you heed them."

Fulla touched a finger to Gerriod's forehead to seal the words in his waking mind. Her message delivered, she swept from the bedside as the king fought himself awake, gasping and trembling at the words echoing through his mind.

He immediately leapt from bed and called his húskarlar to his side. In a rage, he ordered ferocious hounds tethered at all entrances to the hall. Sharply pounding his fist in hand, he instructed his guards what to watch for.

———————

Slavering jaws menaced all known and unknown visitors, backed by snarling teeth, savage barking, and vicious growls. All visitors shuddered in fear at the peril, save one; an old man wearing a heavy blue cloak and a broad-brimmed hat. As the old man approached the front gate of Gerriod's hall, firmly planting his staff in the rock of the courtyard as he tottered along on weary legs, the hounds fell silent and cringed away.

Alerted by the actions of the hounds, the guards grabbed the surprised visitor and dragged him before the king.

Gerriod scowled at the elderly visitor braced between his guards, rose slowly from his seat, and stepped down. Waving the guards aside, he circled the stranger, lifting his cloak to examine its frayed hem, touched the rim of the hat that capped a nest of gray hair, snatched the gnarled staff from an elderly fist and hefted it in his own hand, in all ways tallying his dress and the response of the hounds with his waking memory of the warning.

Muttering to himself, "Pilgrim indeed." Gerriod turned back to his throne, satisfied that the one who stood silently before him was the wizard the gods had cautioned him about. Without warning, he spun about and barked into the old man's face. "Who are you and what do you want in my lands!"

The old man roused himself at Gerriod's shout, smiled slightly and bobbed his head. "Gangleri the world calls me and Sanngetal, a far wanderer seeking truth. My feet have beaten a path across the back of the earth. I've traveled through lands as Thekk and have been welcomed into homes as an honored guest. In your hall, you may call me Grímnir."

Gerriod snorted and flicked his fingers in the old man's face. "That you wear a mask, of that I am certain. But a pilgrim seeking truth, I think not! I think it more likely that you are a wizard bent on the destruction of me and my kingdom!"

Gerriod stood rubbing his hands together, grinding his teeth, pacing back and forth, before once again spinning about and shouting into the old man's face. "Tell me who are you and what you want in my lands!"

Before the old man could respond, Gerriod leaned close and whispered low so that only the ancient could hear his words. "Does my brother yet live? Are you sent by him to do me harm?"

The old man glowered at the king, sniffed once then turned his face aside in reply. Gerriod stared at the old man, sputtered once or twice, then stamped his feet and stormed back to his high seat, fuming at the stranger who stood silent before him.

He let his eyes slowly rove over the ancient, taking in the cut and ragged hem of the blue cloak, the battered hat dipped over one eye. He examined the weathered features swathed with a gray beard and the locks of coarse gray hair that sprouted from beneath the hat.

Gerriod sniffed his disgust and rocked back in his seat. He drew a finger idly along the hair of his upper lip as he watched the calm expression on the visitor's face. He began speaking as if to himself. "The dogs fear you. They are my best war-trained hounds. All others they have backed against a wall and, at my hound master's command, ripped into shreds. But on seeing you, they cower behind the legs of my sentries."

Gerriod nodded as he mulled over the words, then burst out from his seat. "Tell me who are you and what you want in my lands!"

The stranger dragged his tongue across his lips and smiled through his teeth. "For you I go by the name Grímnir and I ask for what any good host would offer a weary traveler; food, drink, and a place to rest the night. Now I have told you all a guest ever need tell his host. I will say no more."

Gerriod's lips twitched as he glared back at the stranger. "So, you say, but my ears remain skeptical. I ask again. What do you want in my lands?"

At this the stranger's face became as stone and his mouth set in firm line, and he remained silent. The one eye visible from beneath his hat flashed with a cold fire.

"Answer me! I am the king! Answer me!" Gerriod stamped his feet and beat his fists against the arms of his chair. Still the stranger refused to reply, and his lips twisted into a disapproving frown at the furious tantrum of the king. "So, your tongue has frozen and you seek a place to rest. Well, let us see if we cannot afford you a spot and help you thaw it out. Guards!"

With terse commands, Gerriod ordered the stranger bound in heavy iron chains, the ends fastened to bolts set securely in the floor. When the guest was firmly bond in place, he ordered fires be built, one on each side of the silent visitor.

As his retainers approached with burning brands, ready to set the wood piles aflame, Gerriod called out to his captive. "You know my intent. Have you anything to say now! Tell me true, what do you want in my lands? I know you have designs on me."

Still Grímnir remained silent and glared directly into the king's face. With a sharp wave, Gerriod ordered his retainers to set alight the bonfires. He watched in anger and some unease as the flames leapt high, lighting Grímnir's features with a lurid play of flame.

———·———

For eight days and eight nights the fire was kept burning. Each day the fires were nudged closer to the victim while Gerriod sat in his high seat exasperated at Grímnir's stony silence.

For the eight long days Gerriod's ten-year-old son had watched his father's actions and each day had grown more disgusted. He took pity on the old man being baked alive by the flames and on the eighth night Agnar stepped forward with a horn full of cool water.

The startled king made to rebuke his son for interfering. The young man ignored his father's protest and boldly marched between the fires to the bound captive. As he passed the horn into Grímnir's trembling hands, he spoke loudly that all might hear his voice above the crackling flames. "Our king is wrong to treat you thus, a weary visitor come knocking at our gate. When he should have extended the rule of hospitality, instead he wrongly tortures an innocent man. I cannot release you from the bonds, nor save you from the flames, but I can extend my heartfelt apology for the cruel actions of my family."

At his son's words the king raged for the stranger to speak. Grímnir only smiled and drained the horn before handing it back to Agnar with a nod.

Furious, Gerriod ordered the fires pushed closer until Grímnir's cloak began to smoke and its edges spark with eager flames. As the smoke from his cloak began to sting the nostrils of those gathered about the fire, he began to sing, softly at first, then louder and louder, until the hall re-echoed with triumphant notes of prophecy that brought a chill to the hall.

"The flames are hot and scorch my cloak though I stamp out the embers that burn its edge. I gaze with sorrow at the blackened mantle, which has sheltered me on my long journeys. A true and trusted friend, it always gave without asking whose shoulders it covered. I shed a single tear for the faces of old protectors lost to time and memory. And to bridges which once stood firm and proud that now crumble to ash before the consuming flame.

I have rested here for eight nights, a weary traveler shown the true warmth of a mighty king's hospitality. None offered me food or drink save Agnar, the son of Gerriod. Let Odin bless you Agnar. For the true gift of hospitality, you will never know a better reward. The fires burn near and singe my cloak, the only solace offered by the son, for a drink he wins a kingdom and the blessings of Odin on his line.

But it is to the father I now sing. Come, step down from your lofty seat, and you will learn who it is that fumes and burns before the hospitality of your hearth. I will sing of my people that you will know the one you treat with such disdain.

High above I see a sacred land of gushing rivers and verdant plains, the hills cloaked with thick mantles of firs, the valley's wooded with well-formed Yew. A land pristine since the dawn of time, filled with my people, grown to a large and powerful clan, and so it will remain until the powers are torn asunder.

But for all endings there is a beginning. And so, it is with my line.

When our days were young, and our song first carried across the lands, the stars shone clear and bright about the moon. Orvandel's toe perched high on the horizon, a twinkling guide for weary travelers. The air stood still and free of Ymir's thoughts.

The sun drove her cart through Delling's gate, threw her hand over the edge of heaven. Alsvinn and Arvak neighed and tossed their heads, the brilliant steeds that strain in the traces of Alfbeam's wain.

Day ushered Night from the sky, with gentle care sent his mother to her rest. Shafts of light pierced the twilight haze hounding shadows from the land. The ground grew damp with silver dew.

In that golden dawn, we played amid open fields without care or knowing our fate. Laughter was our voice, sunny days our mantle, nighttime our cloak.

We rested in shady groves of tall linden and beech, where gentle breezes cooled the grass; peaceful places filled with summer sounds. Stretched out among the tall grasses, we played board games with golden pieces, gambled over games of chance, boasted of prowess with sharp-edged weapons, and recounted tales of bold conquests for the enjoyment of all.

Heroes came from far and wide to gather beneath our banner, drawn as bees to the freshly blossomed flower, sturdy oaks to safeguard our honor. Mighty were our warriors then, esteemed throughout the nine worlds, showered with honors and wealth for brave deeds and daring exploits.

Gladly we quaffed the heady brew of Heidrun, gathered together in halls of gold and silver where the general's war-helmed maidens served droughts between the benches.

Mead we consumed, that honey-sweet drink made from drops the bee in her work distills, mixed well with clear cool spring water, and fermented into a potent elixir. And Ale brewed in pots, wide and deep, from a mash of rich grains freshly harvested, more than enough to quench the greatest thirst, topped off mugs and wetted grinning lips.

Pleasure never lacked in our joyous halls. Each made their bench-mate happy, entertained them with clever conversation, and the raucous laughter of ravens.

Joy was it in that season to live."

The old man stared at the floor then turned his head slightly to peer into the flames dancing from the bonfire beside. The crossed ricks of seasoned wood blazed orange and red, producing thin streams of smoke that gathered near the ceiling. His eyes followed the gray swirls as they climbed to pool amid the rafters.

"Many roofs were raised in the dawn of time; great buttressed halls erected across our domain, each built to the purpose of its master. In Asgard was raised gold-bright Valhalla, with a roof so high one can hardly see over it. Staunchly built of rock and earth, its clay brick walls will endure the long pressure of years.

The hall has massive spear shafts for rafters, tightly thatched with bright-rimmed shields. Massive beams support the thick walls; their wooden lengths carved with crashing waves of the sea, twined with fantastic serpents and beasts gripping hands.

Five hundred doors are set along its sides, each sill etched with runes of protection. Each lintel capped with wolf and eagle. Through these doors, each 800 men wide, pass the mighty warriors of Odin.

Silver roofed Valaskialf was also raised, and Hlidskialf too – the mountain watchtower from which Odin sees into the lives of men.

A sanctuary for the goddesses was built, Vingolf it is called, the abode of friends. A fair and stately structure, its doors are an open invitation to warmth and companionship.

In Thrudvanger stands Veor's lofty hall, there on the plains of strength. In Bilskirnir, the son of Odin makes his home. Five hundred and forty doors line its walls. It boasts more than even the Alfodur's home. Of all halls across the nine worlds, it is the greatest.

Breidablik gleams far and wide in a land where perils are few and evil is rarely known. Here Baldur makes his home and no impurity of thought or action is allowed. In pure innocence, he decides for the best, but few heed his ingenuous judgment.

Beneath the dazzle of Glitner's shingles, the hall built in the land of his father; Forseti holds court and dispenses justice. There he occupies the role of arbitrator, settles legal disputes, determines restitution, and decides the rule between warring factions.

In Yewdale, Ull makes his home in a fletched hall called Ydalir, nestled amid the supple trees the mighty archer uses to form his bows.

In Vithi, the wide land where Vidar raised his hall, here Baldur's avenger dwells on a mountain range grown thick with trees that brush the sky, and where grasses grow tall to carpet the forest floor.

Fensalir, built by Odin for his beloved, stands tall, broad, and splendid in all ways. Frigg calls this Ocean hall her own.

Saga lives in Sokkvabekk, a mansion ringed by cool rippling waters, where the one-eyed god comes to delight in conversation. Precious memories well up in a stream of golden words that grows wider and deeper as they speak, refreshing their minds with the glories of the past.

At the northern-most end of Bifrost, from whose bridgehead the white god keeps watch, stands the lofty hall called Himinbjorg. Here Heimdall rests from his duty, puts up his feet before the fire and relaxes with a mug of heady mead.

At Noatun dwells Njord in the hall built to his design—an ocean-born place of ships. Raised up in the fashion of his clan, it stands on deep sunk pylons surrounded by water. A restful abode for the lonely god of the Vanir.

In the bright, clear spaces of Alfheim, a land given as a tooth gift to the son of Njord, stands Freyr's hall, Upsala it is called; a building tall and brilliant to touch the summer sky.

On Folkvang - the Warriors' Fields - in her hall, Sessrumnir, Freyja decides the choice of seats. Half of the chosen fallen in battle belong to her. Many warriors crowd its benches."

The court shuddered at the old man's words and many drew far back from the fires. Only Gerriod leaned forward, his face a grim mask of anger, his hand clenching and unclenching on the hilt of his blade. "You sing lies to frighten children, making claims to a heritage you are unworthy to speak! Keep it up and you will soon make you bed in coals."

Then the old man climbed to his feet, the chains dangling from his wrists until he towered amid the raging flames, indomitable as the stone cliff worried by a wildfire. Spreading wide his arms, he continued to shout out his song.

"Many deeds I have accomplished. Some you may have heard told on the wind. Others that I relate may be new to your ears. Rest assured that all are true.

I often wander the long weary ways eager to seek out understanding. Many are those I have questioned, set my mind to test the strength and breadth of theirs. Boldly, I challenged Vathrudnir, the all-wise giant, the one well versed in knowledge and ancient lore, there in the high-timbered hall which Im's father owned. Under his examination, I held my own, kept my responses sharp and quick. Then the challenge fell to him. That I turned out the wiser one is why I am here.

Hot burns the fire in the smithy forge, hotter still burned the fire of my ambition, the desire for wisdom expanded. In Suttung's hall, I used craft and guile to acquire his hoard of precious mead. Many words I spoke to my advantage, shrewd, clever, and eloquent. A kiss I got from his daughter, a goblet well filled with song mead, and warm limbs wrapped tight in bed. Wisdom called for quick escape, an auger hole, earlier gnawed through stone between the paths of giants above and below allowed me to evade capture, my life and winnings held dear.

I was outwitted once, by Billing's daughter - the sun-radiant Hlin of bed sheets, when with honeyed wiles, I plied her to capture her heart and win her love play. Called to return in early evening, I met a brace of swarthy men with smoke-smudged cheeks gathered round her hall to protect her honor. In early morning, I returned to find her gone with her guard, but she had left a bitch tied to her bedpost. In this way, she deflected my attentions. But dressed in a handmaid's clothes I worked my skills, enticed her along intimate paths, and so obtained by devious cunning what was denied by upfront action.

Twice, I traveled the length of the nine worlds, deep into the darkness of death's domain, to query the long-dead seeress. Wisdom gathered from many challenges allowed me to call her from her grave, to ask her questions and hear her replies. I learned much in the blackness of Niflhel – the course of events from dawn's first light and the final days of twilight. But even in death, the wise woman was sharp and came to know with whom she spoke. Dead, she could not die again. She sank into the ground before all was revealed. And so, I returned home wiser. Though not as wise as I had hoped.

Wise, I felt myself the day Baldur fell beneath the hateful flash of Hodd's winged shaft, and bold enough to try my hand at Gullveig's skill. Rind, I caressed with dark runes to overcome her reserve and father the avenger of Frigg's son. Costly was the seid I practiced that day. A shattered mind it gave the young maiden, and a loss of status it won for me among my kin. Such is the perilous price of vengeance.

I placed my trust in a young boy fallen into my care, gave him wise counsel and direction, did all I could to set him securely on his way, all the while priding myself on the keenness of my insight, and the honorable prospects of the boy grown to manhood. When others spoke against him, challenging my trust, I sought to prove them wrong and placed myself in his power. Too late, I learned the truth of his nature and the flinty harshness of his heart.

Now Gerriod, listen carefully to my words. By the sword, your life is now run out and the disir, angered by the contempt you have shown, offer harsh payment for cruelty shown to visitors."

On hearing the ominous prophecy, Gerriod roared out in anger, leapt from his seat, and hastily drew his sword, intending to slay the insolent singer. But as the last notes of the old man's song died away, the shackles fell from off his hands, the terrible flames flickered and went out, and Odin stood tall and proud in the midst of the hall, raised up in all the power and beauty of a god.

All the hall was silenced with the intake of a single breath and Gerriod, startled by the sudden transformation, croaked out in surprise, tripped, and fell upon the blade, the tip slicing up beneath his ribcage and piercing deep into his heart.

As Gerriod's final breath slipped past his lips, Odin turned to Agnar and with a gesture bade him ascend the throne in reward for the timely draught of water. As everyone in the hall knelt before the vision, Odin placed his hand on Agnar's head, blessing him and his line with wisdom and prosperity.

Tale of the Longbeards

The setting sun found Odin and Frigg enjoying each other's company perched in the high seats of Hlidskialf, gazing with interest upon the Winilers and Vandals. Many long years the clans had fought for supremacy, and now they had assembled their armies for a final contest to decide which people should hold control over the lands.

The Alfodur gestured at open plain beyond the camps. "See there, that is where the battle will take place. The Vandals will approach with their flanks to the sea; the Winilers will face the rising sun. It is a bold strategy that takes a skilled army to execute."

Odin gazed with satisfaction upon the Vandals, who were gathered around their fires and chanting strongly behind their shields as they called on him for victory, but Frigg focused her attention on the calm, deliberate actions of the Winilers, because they had burned many offerings in her honor, calling for her aid.

Determined that her followers should prevail in the contest, she turned to Odin. "You are the Valfodur and so determine fate on the battlefield. I see you have taken an interest in the events playing out below. Who will you favor on the field tomorrow?"

Odin glanced at his wife from the corner of his eye and the apparent nonchalance of her profile. He coughed and returned his gaze to the field, watching as the camps arranged themselves in preparation for the coming battle. "You have never taken an interest in the game of war. Why do you ask now?"

Frigg fluffed her robe, letting the translucent mist become a thick, opaque white. "We are here enjoying the evening. I see that you are interested, so I thought I would ask."

The Alfodur squinted down from his seat, mulling over in his mind how to evade her question, for he had learned to be cautious around the keen mind of his wife; her casual interest could easily jeopardize the plans of others. Finally, he slapped his hands on his thighs and pushed himself to his feet. "It grows late, and I will not decide tonight." He smiled and gave Frigg a peck on the cheek. "Come let us return to our hall." He paused and jerked a thumb over his shoulder at the bustling war camps. "Likely I will leave it to chance and will bestow victory in those whom I first see in the morning. I will make an announcement when I take my seat tomorrow."

Frigg smiled and took his hand. A violet color tinged her robe as he led her down the winding steps of Hlidskialf. She looked always at her feet to hide the anger that flashed across her face. "But of course," she kept her voice calm and light. "It is only fair to let chance determine the winner." She knew her husband's answer was shrewdly calculated and that his bed was already positioned so that upon waking he would face the direction of the Vandal's approach, and that he intended looking out from his bed, instead of waiting to decide until he had mounted his high seat.

———————

Determined that the Winilers should know the victory, Frigg contrived a plan to frustrate Odin's goal. They lay down in their separate beds, and she waited until his breathing slowed in the sign of deep sleep. Flipping back her coverlet, she barefooted over to Odin's bed and noiselessly wrestled it around to face her favorites.

Several times her heart jumped when he gave a snort and rolled onto his side. Each time she waited until his breathing had slowed, before continuing moving the bed. When she had finished, and the bed faced in the direction of the Winiler camp, she slipped from the chamber and called Gna to her side.

"Go at once to the war leader of the Winiler forces; he is a man short of speech and swift of action. Whisper into his sleeping ear my instructions that they are to dress their women in armor and send them out in battle array at dawn, with their long hair braided and carefully combed down over their cheeks and breasts."

Swiftly, Gna dove through the air to Midgard and sought out the sleeping ear hands of the war leader of the Winiler army. In the early morning hours before the sun rises, when the chieftain lay between sleep and wakefulness, three times she whispered his name and left her message. "Many times, you have called on Frigg for assistance. She has heard you and sends this message that you might prevail in the coming battle. Take your women, maidens and wives, over their ankles and legs gird the leather windings of war."

Gna grinned as the chieftain stirred uneasily in his sleep and continued. "Over their chests cinch ring byrnies and leather vests. Plait their long tresses over their lips and beneath their chins so full-bearded Odin will deem them war beasts when at sunrise you meet his gaze over the gray sea-beach."

She paused, letting her message settle in and nest deep its barbs. "Listen to these words and hold them close to your breast. They will do you good if you heed them."

Gna brushed a finger along the chieftain's forehead to seal the words in his waking thoughts. Her message delivered, she swept from his side as the chieftain fought himself awake, gasping and trembling at the words echoing through his mind.

He immediately leapt from bed and called his commanders to his side. Urgently he ordered the women brought forward. "Quickly. Quickly. This must be done before Sol's hand crests the waves." Sharply pounding his fist in hand, he instructed everyone what to do that the instructions of Frigg be carried out with scrupulous exactness.

When Day led his mother Night from the land, and as Sol tossed her hand over the edge of the heavens, Odin awoke, and his first glance fell upon an armed host arranging themselves for battle. He laughed and exclaimed loudly to waken the hall, "What long beards are those? They must be some new warriors arrived in the night. See how the winds play merrily in the braided locks waving beneath their chins."

Frigg, upon hearing his shout of surprise, called out from her bed. "They are not a new group, but the Winiler's facing the dawn, ready for war. You have given them a new name; it is a proud name that shames neither you nor them; Lombards, the long beards. And as you have greeted them first, by your own command give them victory in today's battle."

Odin started and looked closer at the army arranged in bold ranks on the field. He glanced once at Frigg, then back out at the army. His leg bumped the bed and when he looked down his laughter boomed from the rafters and filled the hall. "Clever. That wife of mine is clever."

Rising to his feet, the Alfodur spread his arms wide to embrace the day. "Let the Winiler's know victory vouchsafed by my own command and let them ever retain the new name given to them by me: Lombards. And as I have named them so will I always watch over them. They will know my blessings and have won themselves a home."

Skrymsli

A blazing summer sun shimmered through a thick haze that nearly obscured the forest line on the far side of the field. Trees, those that could be seen, danced and quivered in the rising waves of heat. The farmer wiped sweat from his brow as he reached out and slid a game piece across the board. "My word its hot. Looks like Loki is sowing his wild oats. Only last week he was drinking, now he's burning things up. Your move."

The giant leaned down, his thick fingers tapping his lips as he examined the board. The farmer's piece threatened his king, but by doing so had left the way open for a winning stroke. "A bold move you make, perhaps too bold." Skrymsli grinned inside his cheeks and casually slid a game piece down the length of the board. "I believe that wins me the game."

"Now hold on. Hold on." The farmer stared in alarm, twisting the sides of his jerkin as he examined the board. His lips trembled and sweat beaded his cheeks as he traced out every chance, every alternate move before slumping back in his seat. Silently, he nodded his head, admitting defeat.

The giant grinned and rubbed his hands together. "Now bring him out. I would see my winnings."

The farmer dropped to his knees and pleaded. "Please he is my only son. Take my livestock but leave him with me."

Skrymsli sneered and spit off to one side. He shook a thick finger at the farmer. "It was a fare wager. We played for stakes that you set. You lost." He reared back his head. "Now trot him out."

The farmer stumbled to his feet and shuffled around the corner of his hut beside the field. He grumbled a few words to his son who was chopping wood for the house fire and returned leading a young boy of seven. As they neared the giant, the farmer pushed the boy ahead. Thick flaxen hair hung down over his face concealing blue eyes that danced in fear as the approached the shadow of the giant. Skrymsli leaned forward licking his lips as he pinched the boy's belly between thick fingers. "What a fine pig, and hefty too. You feed him well."

He let his eyes rest a moment on the quivering child, then abruptly slapped his hands on his thighs. "I will collect my winnings tomorrow. But since you whine that he is your only son, I will give you a sporting chance to redeem your loss. If the boy can be hidden so cleverly that I cannot find him within a day, he will remain with you. But if I find him, then everything you have, your son, your wife, your stock, your farm, even you are mine to do with as I please. Otherwise, he comes with me now. Do you agree?"

The farmer hesitated, let his gaze rove over the fields he had plowed with the help of his son, the sheds and animals he tended with the help of his son, at the cord of wood behind the house and the ax leaning against the block awaiting the chopper's return, at his wife wringing her hands in the doorway of their home, and finally settled on the upturned, tear-stained face of his son. He released a deep breath he didn't know he was holding. "Agreed."

"Very good." The giant rocked to his feet and turned to leave. He called over his shoulder as he stalked away across the field. "See that you feed him tonight. I don't want to listen to him whine like his father as I carry him away tomorrow."

All night the couple fretted and clung to their child. The good woman of the home berated her husband, letting him feel the brunt of her fear and anger. "Stupid! How could you be so stupid as to gamble with a giant, and with your own son! What could you have possibly won that was worth the risk?"

The farmer cringed at her words and clutched his head. "I know. I know. But, you know, I am good at board games and thought I could easily defeat the lumbering oaf, or so he appeared on our other encounters. It was not until we had sat down to play that I realized his deception; he is clever and good at strategy. Had I won, he would have left off challenging our rights to the farm and worked our holding for us for free. Imagine what we could have done with his strength, the wealth we would have gathered."

His eyes swam with tears as he stared into the hearth flames. "We would not have had to slave as we do, to break our backs each day. Your shoulders would not be rounded from having to carry water, my back might have time to heal, and our son might have been able to grow up straight and tall."

He clutched his head again and rocked back and forth moaning. "But it was for naught. All is lost."

The woman paced back and forth, casting quick glances first at her son, then at her husband. "Is there any chance we could hide him so that the giant cannot find him? We have the niche beneath the animal shed," she nodded hopefully, "and then there is the cave at the far side of the glen that few know exist."

The farmer sadly shook his head. "Skrymsli is too clever for us. He would route out the boy in a moment from wherever we might hide him."

The good woman planted her hands on her hips. "Then let us pray for help. Perhaps Odin will look favorably upon us and deliver us through his great wisdom."

Snatching up a burning piece of kindling, she marched over to the family shrine, a darkened niche beside the hearth, and lit a tallow candle already melted into a glacier of fat. The farmer followed and bent to his knees. He beckoned his son from beside the fire and reached up to help his wife kneel. "Come. Let each of us pray and let our worries and desires cry out so that Odin above will hear us and give aid."

All night they fervently prayed, first one, then another, then all three crying out for the wisdom of Odin to answer their need. Day had begun to lead his mother from the land, when a sharp knock sounded at their door. The farmer started, and his wife squeaked. They were certain Skrymsli had arrived to collect his winnings. Silently, the farmer gestured to his son and sent him sneaking out the back way to hide beneath the straw in the goat shed.

Again, a knock rattled the door, but this time it was accompanied by a deep shout that was not the giant's voice. "Ho, the house and the good folk who dwell beneath its roof. A new day dawns and I have traveled far. I can hear you rustling about. I know you are awake as any farmer worth his weight should be."

Rising shakily to his feet, the farmer hobbled across the room and opened the door. There stood a heavily cloaked figure with a broad brimmed hat dawn down over one eye. His wide grin was nearly as bright as the promised day.

The farmer sighed deeply and scanned the still dark fields. "You have arrived at a bad time. Travelers and strangers are always welcome in our home. You may come in and rest a moment by our hearth, but today you must be gone before Sol crests the treetops." Stepping aside, he ushered their guest into the hut. The woman of the home rustled about gathering a small bowl of food as the visitor took a seat beside the hearth.

"Men call me Sidhott." He tapped the brim of his hat.

The farmer stared wide-eyed, and his wife clutched his shoulders from behind. "That is a name often given to Odin."

"So, it is. So, it is." The traveler poked a stick into the coals and a bright fire blossomed to life. He stirred it around drawing shapes in the ashes. "Winds carry the prayers of the faithful to the doors of Asgard. Your cries were heard." The farmer and his wife dropped to the floor and gripped Odin's knees, crying into the hem of his cloak.

Odin rose and shook the couple off. "Enough. I say enough. Time is short. Get up and call the boy from the goat shed, quickly, before the giant returns to claim his prize. Already the fingers of Sol can be seen on the horizon."

The farmer rushed from the hut and whispered the boy from his hiding place. Odin leaned out from the back entry and gestured them into the hut. "Bring him here." He shook his head, nose wrinkled, as he looked the boy over. "It is difficult dealing with giants. I have some experience with the deviousness of their mind. We need a better place for you, lad, than concealed beneath goat dung."

Drawing on his wisdom, Odin, made several turns, and with the charred end of the stick that he still held, he scraped a circle of runes around the trembling lad. A cloud of smoke encircled the boy then sank with the child into the floor.

The parents looked on in alarm and turned as one to Odin. "What have you done with him?" cried the father. "Where has he gone?" screamed the mother.

Odin grinned at the parents. "I've changed him into a tiny seed of flax and hid it in a stalk amid the field beyond the sheds. Let's see the giant find him there. Now be quiet. I hear someone coming... someone large."

The clump...clump...clump... of lumbering footsteps shook the ground and stopped outside the hut. As the farmer moved to open the door, Odin placed a hand on his shoulder, "Let me handle this." and stepped out to greet the giant.

Skrymsli bent low, a dark shadow backed by the rising sun, and looked over the stranger who stood before him. "You are not the farmer I wagered with yesterday."

Odin's laughter echoed through the dawn light. "You are perceptive for your kind, quick to notice the obvious."

Skrymsli hawked and spit to one side. "It does not matter. I've come to collect my winnings. Bring out the boy or I will find where he is hidden and take him anyway."

Odin crossed his arms before his chest, a smug grin on his face. "Do your best. The child is hidden where you will never find him."

Skrymsli sneered and immediately made for the goat shed. He dug through the straw sniffing deeply. "Not here," he muttered, then turned, and followed the path to the back entry of the hut. Grunting low he peered into the house taking deep sniffs all the while. His eyes squinted hard when he spied the circle of runes etched on the floor.

"So." Nodding to himself, he snatched up a scythe hung on the back wall of the hut and strode off to the field. With great heaves of his shoulders, all day he mowed the flax, until evening when he reached the stalk where the boy was hidden. Counting over the stalks of flax he reached out to grab the right one when Odin, hearing the child's cry of distress, snatched away the seed as the giant's hand closed around the stalk, and whisked the boy back to his parents.

Skrymsli's voice boomed over the field and the air shook with his anger as he stomped back towards the hut. "I have been cheated. Just as my hand closed on the prize it was taken away."

Odin intercepted the giant as he approached the farmer's hut. "No further. The sun is setting, and you did not find the boy. He stays with his parents."

Skrymsli stomped his feet until the ground shook. A flock or ravens that had settled in for the night rose crying and calling from a nearby tree as they winged away seeking a quieter place to roost. "I was cheated. The sun had not left the horizon when he was spirited from my grasp."

Odin remained calm, but his hand slipped beneath his cloak to finger the sword strapped at his waist. Knowing the trick that he had played, Odin did not dispute the giant's claim. "You will still not have him tonight. What do you propose?"

Skrymsli ground his teeth and glared down at Odin. "I say the wager is not done. The stakes remain the same. I will return tomorrow morning to claim my winnings, unless the boy can be hidden so I cannot find him." With that the giant spun on his heel and stomped off over the fields, grumbling, cursing, and kicking his feet.

Odin guided the family back into the house and closed the door. "This giant possesses wisdom far beyond what I imagined. I have done all in my power to help you. The giant is kept away for tonight, but you will need the aide of another. I am sorry."

Bowing his head, Odin turned away. He called over his shoulder as he closed the door. "You need grace to help with this giant." When they opened the door, he was nowhere to be seen.

The farmer frowned as he stared out into the night. "His wisdom failed us. Odin's wisdom failed us."

His wife came up behind and took him by the arm. "He saved our son and told us to seek grace." She brightened, "We can call on Hoenir. He looks after the children of men; it is by his grace we have our son. Come, I will light the candle."

All night they fervently prayed, first one, then another, then all three crying out for Hoenir to answer their need. Day had begun to lead his mother from the land, when a quiet knock sounded at their door. The farmer started, and his wife squeaked. With a sharp gesture, he sent his son to hide, this time in the root cellar. They were certain Skrymsli had arrived to collect his winnings.

Again, a light knock tapped the door, this time accompanied by a gentle call that was not the giant's voice. "Hello, the good folk who dwell in this house. A new day dawns, and I have traveled far. I hear you moving about inside, so I know you are awake."

Tottering to his feet, the farmer hobbled across the room and opened the door. There stood a white-robed figure, tall and thin, with a black crested cap balanced on his brow. His placid smile calmed the fast beating in the farmer's breast. "My brother tells me you have a great need. Though I did not need him to relate your woes; your cries echo through the halls of Asgard."

The farmer stared wide-eyed and his wife eased up from behind to peer over his shoulder. "You are Hoenir. Are you here to help us?"

The god laughed, removed his cap, and winked at the couple. "I knew your son from the fruit I delivered to this very home. Certainly, I will help you."

The farmer stepped aside and ushered their visitor into the hut. Bowing deeply, he led him to the warmest seat beside the hearth. The woman of the home, bustled about gathering a small bowl of food and, her hands shaking, held it out to their guest. Hoenir waved away the offering. "We have little time. Already Sol peeps her head over the treetops." He glanced around. "Do you have a stick?" Hoenir smiled as the farmer handed him a long piece of kindling. "Thank you. Let's get started."

He poked the stick into the coals, stirring it around while drawing shapes in the ashes. "Get the boy from the root cellar." When the farmer didn't move, he glanced up, fire dancing in his eyes. "Now! Before the giant returns to claim his prize."

The farmer rushed from the hut and whispered the boy from his hiding place. Hoenir called from his seat by the hearth. "Bring him here." He cupped the boy's chin in his hand, looked him over appraisingly, and then gently brushed his hair back from his forehead. "You have grown into a fine, strong lad. Let's hide you somewhere other than a dank hole in the ground."

Drawing on his experience, Hoenir made several turns, and with the charred end of the stick that he still held, scraped a circle of runes around the shivering lad. A cloud of smoke wreathed the boy, then together smoke and child sank into the floor. The parents, familiar now with the spell, glanced nervously at Hoenir. The good woman wrung her hands and muttered low, "Where did you send him?"

Hoenir chuckled gently to the parents and fluttered his fingers in the air. "I changed him into a fluff of down and hid it in the breast of a swan swimming in a pond across the way. I doubt the giant will find him there. Now be quiet. Day has sprung, and I believe I hear his footsteps approaching."

The clump...clump...clump... of lumbering footsteps shook the ground and stopped outside the hut. As the farmer moved to open the door, Hoenir paced a hand on his shoulder. "I hid the boy. I will handle this." and stepped out to greet the giant.

Skrymsli bent low, a dark shadow backed by the rising sun, and looked over the stranger who stood before him. "What is this, another outsider to give aide? I should have known the farmer would not dare his wits against mine."

Hoenir bowed graciously. "The wager was for the boy to be hidden. It did not specify by whom."

Skrymsli ground his teeth and pushed words through his teeth. "It does not matter. I've come to collect my winnings. Bring out the boy or I will find where you hid him and take him anyway."

Hoenir laughed and waved his hand. "Go ahead and try. The child is hidden where you will never find him."

Skrymsli snorted and immediately made for the root cellar. He shoved his head through the door sniffing deeply at the cold dry air. "Not here," he muttered, then turned, and stomped for the goat shed, rooting through the straw and dung, sniffing deeply. "Not here," he muttered, and stalked off, spending the rest of the day crisscrossing the fields. Finally, as the sun touched the horizon, he stopped and glared about. "Not here," he muttered, and followed the path to the back entry of the hut. Grunting low he peered into the house taking deep sniffs all the while. His eyes squinted hard when he saw the circle of runes etched on the floor.

"So." Nodding to himself, he dashed off to the pond. Snatching up the swan he bit off its neck and would have swallowed the down, but on hearing the child cry out in fear, Hoenir wafted the down away from the giant's lips and spirited the boy safe and sound back to his parents.

Skrymsli's shout shook the air with his anger as he stomped back towards the hut. "I have been cheated. Just as my lips closed on the prize it was taken away."

Hoenir greeted the giant as he approached the farmer's hut. "That is far enough. The sun has set and you did not find the boy. He stays here."

Skrymsli stomped his feet until the ground shook. "I was cheated again. You farmer helpers are the worst deceivers. The sun was still above the horizon, and I could nearly taste him on my lips when he was snatched away."

Hoenir's gentle smile remained frozen on his face, and his hand slipped to the ready blade strapped at his waist. But uncomfortable with the trick played, he jerked his chin at the giant. "You will not have him tonight. What do you propose?"

Skrymsli ground his teeth and glared down at the gracile god. "This wager is not done. The stakes remain the same. I will return tomorrow morning to claim my winnings, unless the boy can be hidden so I cannot find him." With that the giant spun on his heel and stomped off over the fields, grumbling, cursing, and kicking his feet. Every few lengths he would turn and shout back at the house, "And this time no tricks!"

Hoenir guided the family back into the house and closed the door. "This giant is shrewder than any I have met before. I have kept the giant away for a second night, but you will need the aide of another for tomorrow. I am sorry."

Hoenir bowed his head and started to turn away, then glanced over his shoulder. "You need help from someone who is craftier than any giant." He left, closing the door softly behind him. When they opened the door, he was nowhere to be seen.

The farmer nearly collapsed weeping as he stared out into the night. "His grace failed us. Hoenir's grace failed us."

His wife came up behind and took him by the arm. "He saved our son and told us to call on cunning." She brightened, "We can call on Loki. He is known for cleverness above all others. Come I will light the candle."

All night they fervently prayed, first one, then another, then all three crying out for the cunning of Loki to answer their need. Day had begun to lead his mother from the land, when a series of sharp knocks rattled their door. The farmer jumped, his wife squeaked, and his son, exhausted from the long night and the trials of the last two days, stared dull-eyed and resigned at the door. They were certain Skrymsli had arrived to collect his winnings.

Again, an impatient knocking rattled the door, this time accompanied by a nasal shout that was not the giant's voice. "Open up. Day has begun to chase his mother from the land, and my feet are sore from traveling. Come on. I can hear you breathing in there. Open up."

Rising warily to his feet, the farmer crept across the room and jerked open the door. There stood a wiry figure lightly cloaked in dark gray, topped with a shock of tousled, black hair. His sharp gaze and insolent smirk sent a chill racing up the farmer's spine. "You... are you Loki?"

A wicked smile flickered across the stranger's face and was gone. When there was no further response, the farmer swallowed hard. "Are you here to help us?"

Loki sneered and shook his head. "Why should I help the likes of you? You build no temples in my honor; offer no sacrifices in my name. The only time I hear my name spoken is in fear or to designate some noxious weed."

The farmer swallowed again and stumbled back into his wife and son who had crept up behind. The woman caught her husband and the boy slipped under one arm to lend support. "Then why have you come?"

Loki examined his fingernails, first one, then another, and finally looked up at the family silhouetted in the doorway. "Curiosity mostly. I have heard your annoying wails echoing among the halls of

Asgard. They were disturbing my rest, so I came to see why no one had answered. Usually when cries get that far someone rushes to aid."

The farmer and his wife shook with great heaving sobs and clutched their child between them. "We have been heard. Odin and Hoenir have tried to help, but both have failed. Only you are clever enough to help."

Loki's eyes brightened. "Odin and Hoenir have failed you say. And now you come to me." His laughter echoed through the sky. "Oh, this is good. They will hear no end of it. I'll make certain of it." He rubbed his hands together. "Tell me everything they have tried."

Loki stared at his feet, listening intently, as the farmer related the attempts of Odin and Hoenir, and Skrymsli's routing out of each device. When he finished, Loki continued staring at the ground, a frown playing over his face. "This giant is wise and very perceptive. I must be more so."

He glanced over his shoulder at the still dark sky just beginning to lighten beyond the tree tops. "Come, pass over the boy."

The farmer hesitated before dragging his son around. "Do you want a stick to mark runes? The others did."

Loki laughed and cinched his belt tight at his waist. "And they failed. They stayed close to home. My plans are different." He jerked his chin at the far horizon. "The strand lies beyond the forest ridge where the hills slope down to a sandy beach. Let's see how your giant friend fares with the salt winds. I will carry the child out to sea and conceal him as a tiny egg in the roe of a flounder. I would like to see any son of frost find him there.

He grabbed the boy and hoisted him onto his shoulders. "Up you go, and hang on. If you fall, your parents will not want back what is left, and I doubt even Skrymsli will want the pieces."

———————

Breakers bent their white heads to the shoreline as sunlight crested the hills, turning the water into a shimmer plain of fire. Loki wafted in on the sea breeze and lightly touched down on the beach. In a cove, where a narrow cliff jutting out into the waves stalled the rushing sea, he spied the large shape of a giant busily preparing an angle hook and a length of stout line.

Sauntering up he called out in friendly greeting. "Hello fellow of Jotunheim, the sun breaks on a glorious day. Call me Loptr. I see you plan for a fishing excursion."

He was surprised when the giant glanced up, looked him over carefully and thoroughly – gave no sign of recognition, then turned back to his line. "My name is Skrymsli, and, yea, I am bound to cast my hook into the sea. I've winnings to collect and my nose tells me I can find them here."

Loki pursed his lips and fought back a sharp spasm of alarm. To ensure he did not fail, as had Odin and Hoenir before him, he decided it would be prudent to remain on the spot in case of need. He flashed a winning smile and strode briskly to the giant's side. "It is a wondrous morning for a fishing trip. Do you mind if I join you? I have always enjoyed the taste of fresh caught fish."

The giant shrugged and continued trying his line. "Twice I was thwarted in my attempts to collect on a wager. This morning, ere the sun rose, I arrived early at the gambler's farm to watch; he has enlisted the aid of others in his attempts to renege on our bet. Today, I spied a shadowed stranger carry the boy out to sea, but before he left I heard him speak of flounder roe, so I know his plan. I will fish all day if I have to and you can have all the fish I catch, but their eggs are mine." With that he cast his hook far out into the sea.

All morning Skrymsli hauled in fish after fish while Loki, true to his word, consumed each as they were landed, rubbing his belly, and groaning in satisfaction. "Never have I had such a feast. You can keep at this all day."

The giant paid him no mind, but continued angling, when he suddenly drew up the flounder in which Loki had concealed the child. Tearing open the fish on his knee, the giant proceeded to minutely examine the roe, sniffing deeply, until he located the egg. He held the egg up to the sun, rolling it slowly between his fingers. "Yes, this is the one."

Grinning widely, Skrymsli winked at his companion and closed his eyes as he made to lick the roe from his fingertips. Seeing his chance, Loki snatched the egg out of the giant's grasp and dashed up the beach. As he ran, he transformed the egg back into the boy.

When Skrymsli's lips closed on air, his scream of frustration rolled over the waves. He stomped his feet until the beach shook, and it seemed the waves retreated from his anger. "I am cheated for a third time. There will not be a fourth. I see you there running up the beach. You have no hope of escaping from me." With those words Skrymsli ducked his head and charged blindly like a bull.

Loki glanced over his shoulder and, on seeing the giant closing, hugged the child close and whispered between gasps into his ear. "Run. When I put you down, run as fast as you can for your home." He jerked his head to direct the boy's gaze forward. "Pass through that boathouse just ahead and be sure to close the door behind you. Do as I say, exactly as I say, and you will be safe."

When his feet touched the ground, the terrified boy did as he was told and darted through the boathouse slamming the door shut behind. Skrymsli saw the boy's flight and dashed after him into the boathouse. Bursting through the door, he had only time to grunt as he slammed full force into a spike cleverly positioned at his head level.

As the giant sank groaning to the ground, Loki raced up, whipped a long blade from the sheath at his waist, and cut off one of Skrymsli's legs. Loki laughed and danced around the fallen giant, but his delight quickly turned to dismay when he saw the pieces join and immediately knit together.

A sly grin spread across his face. "You are very clever, but not to one prepared for your tricks. Let's try that again." His blade flashed, and the giant's other leg fell loose to the side. "You will not heal yourself this time. Here taste the bite of flint and iron." Loki jammed a piece of flint and iron between the severed limb and trunk. This time the limb remained separated and Skrymsli's blood flowed unchecked from the wound, drenching the boathouse floor, and running into the water. A dark red plume swept into the sea as the giant's body shuddered and a final gasp escaped his lips.

Laughing to himself, Loki chased down the boy who had just reached the forest fence that bordered the shore. "You are safe now. The giant is dead. Let's get you home." Hoisting the boy up on his shoulders, he shook a moment to settle his load. "You really must learn to run faster. The giant nearly had you before he sprung my trap. Now hold on."

Using the power of Loki's shoes, they reached the hut in a moment. When the boy was set down before the front door, the farmer and his wife rushed out and hugged their child, stroking his head, brushing the tears and sand from his cheeks, cooing and clucking over his return. As Loki turned to leave, the couple dropped to the ground and grasped him about the knees. "You are truly the mightiest of all the Asgard council, for you have permanently returned us our son and struck down the giant, while the other gods had lent only temporary aid."

They climbed to their feet and gathered their son between them. "For your great deed, we will add you to our shrine and at blött will always give you the first choice of our offerings. You will always find welcome in our home, the homes of our children, and their children."

Loki nodded and polished his fingernails against his vest. "As it should be."

The parents grinned down at their son. The boy laughed as his father tousled his hair. When they looked back, Loki was gone.

The Three Stones

Often the gods traveled the lands to experience the world they had created. Their journeys took them over fir wrapped mountains, through deserts dusted with scrub brush, across snowy plains swept by icy winds, and into the fertile farmlands of Midgard. On one such journey, Odin, Loki, and Hoenir toured the plowed fields of a crofting township that they might see firsthand how mankind comported themselves.

It was a golden day, a glorious day of sunshine and fluffy, fair weather clouds as they approached the rough-built homes of the crofter community that edged close to the white hairs of the sea. Hoenir waited, placidly scanning the horizon, and Loki, ever-eager to be on the move, impatiently tapped his toes while Odin meandered amid the farms.

He stopped at a barn to inspect workers thatching its roof, nodding appreciatively as rushes were woven into bundles, then passed hand over hand up the ladder to the men on the roof who swiftly overlapped the bundles and bound them into place. Stepping out of the barn's shadow he muttered, "It is well done," then continued through the community, leaving behind a single straw on the haymow floor.

He peered in at a smithy door, tapping his foot along with the rhythmic clang...clang...clang of hammer on metal. A grin spread across his face as a sharp bark of orders to the bellows boy brought the wheezing breath of the pump and a sudden blast of heat, while the smith drove the metal back into the glowing coals. Working praise around his chuckling, "It is well done," he turned away to resume his trek, leaving behind a fragment of old iron beside the forge.

In an open field, he knelt in the turned earth and sighted along a furrow to see if the farmer guided his plough evenly through the soil. Far ahead at the end of the field the farmer wrestled the plough around and lined up for his next pass. Odin climbed to his feet, brushing dirt from his knees, and stepped back uttering "It is well done," then turned away, leaving behind a single grain in the furrow.

The praise seemed insignificant, the gifts innocuous, but ever after the barn remained full, the forge fire never went out, and the field yielded a bountiful harvest.

When Sol had reached midway through her journey, the three Æsir found themselves miles beyond the township in a shady valley where they decided to rest and eat. Odin stretched himself beneath a tree, tucked his hands behind his head, and smacked his lips.

Loki and Hoenir stood waiting while Odin grunted, wiggling his shoulders into a more comfortable position, and closed his eyes. Loki's face twitched, and he nudged Odin's boot. "Is that all you are going to do, just lay there? I for one would like to eat something rather than sleep."

Odin's eyes cracked opened to a slit and he smiled calmly at his companions. "I have not seen either of you doing anything along the way, save walk. I am tired; inspecting is hard work. I am leaving the gathering of food to the two of you. See that you do not disappoint." With that he closed his eyes.

A dark cloud swept across Loki's brow and his eyes flashed with ill humor. Stomping off to a nearby tree, he slumped down against its trunk, grumbling to himself. Hoenir smirked and tugged his jerkin straight. "You have made him angry."

Odin breathed a deep sigh and ran is tongue along dry lips. "He gets that way when he is hungry. He'll get over it once he eats."

The long-legged god nodded and looked around, lifting his nose to sniff the air, and cocking his head to one side to listen. "I will undertake gathering food for our afternoon meal. There is a creek flowing beyond the trees, you can just hear it. I think fish roasted on hot coals would be nice. I'll try my hand to see what I can catch."

Yawning hugely Odin stretched, climbed to his feet, and nodded. "That does sound good. Tell you what; I will start a fire while you fish." He glanced over at the tree where Loki sat brooding. "And you. Snap out of your temper and forage about to see what you can find to add to our fare."

Loki shoved himself away from the trunk, brushing leaves and dirt from the seat of his cloak. He stalked off, calling over his shoulder as he kicked his way down the valley. "Oh, I will forage all right. Don't expect me to trust my stomach to the vagaries of Hoenir's skill. I expect to be back with food enough for three before bird legs catches his first fish."

As he swung through the brush, Loki scanned the ground to ensure he was on the same track they had followed coming into the valley. Earlier in the day his nose had caught the smell of cooking as they passed a cluster of farms, and he meant to investigate to see what his resourcefulness might yield.

Slipping through the underbrush, he approached a small holding where the enticing scent of roasting meat drifted from an open shed built around a large fire pit and stone oven. In the heat of the fire, a busty farmwife labored at baking bread and roasting several geese. Along the harvest table six meat pies fresh from the oven were arranged for cooling. With a devious smile, Loki assumed the shape of a large black fox, slunk up to the outer wall of the shed, and waited for his opportunity.

When the woman turned her back to take a loaf of bread from the oven, he snaked out a paw and whisked away a pie. Three loaves of bread she pulled from the oven; three pies Loki slipped from the table.

As she set the last loaf down, she blinked at the empty space once occupied by the three pies. A deep frown settled around the corners of her mouth. "There were six, now there are three." The woman planted her fists on her hips and glared about the hut, looking under the table and all about the shed. "Who is the thief that is stealing my pies? Come on. Out with you. Let me see your face."

When she turned back to the table, she spied the thick bushy tail of a dark form slipping around the far wall. "Could it be? No. It is not possible, not during the day, but…" Picking up a stone, she edged near the wall, arm cocked ready to throw, and peered around the corner in time to see an old raven, with three young ones take wing and fly away calling like laughter as they sped away over the fields.

The small flock of ravens circled back along the hills to the valley where Odin and Hoenir waited. When they landed in the glade the large raven's shape shimmered in the afternoon sunlight into Loki standing with a gloating smile and three pies arranged about his feet where once the young birds had ruffled their feathers.

"I'm back." Loki pointed a toe at the pies. "As you can see, I have had some luck with my foraging. Now I see a fire but smell no cooking fish."

A glum-looking Hoenir scuffed a boot through the grass. "I had no luck. In the heat of the day few will bite and those I sought to grab by hand wriggled out of my grasp."

Loki snorted and rustled his cloak. "I expected as much. I had no such trouble with these. Once I laid my hands on them they were mine."

Odin reached down and picked up a pie. He held it under his nose savoring its smell, his belly rumbling in response. "These are wonderful. I expect you left a fair price."

Loki sneered and reached down to pick up a pie for himself. "Why should I? You had already left enough blessings on the farm. It is only our right that they feed us."

Hoenir kneeled and took up a pie. He thumped its top with a finger, three sharp raps that gave a satisfying solid sound. "These appear fresh made. There is heat yet in the crust, as if snatched straight from the oven. How willing was the farmer to part with his dinner?"

Loki chuckled and took a large bite. He spoke around the mouthful as he gleefully told of his theft. "You should have seen her, edging around the corner with a rock in hand. I had only just time to shift into bird shape and take off, else she would have pegged me with the stone."

When he finished, Loki was surprised at the looks of disapproval on Odin and Hoenir's face. "What is the matter? Here I have used my wits to provide us with a meal and you both frown as if I had stolen the last bit of food from their mouths. They are only pies; the farm had plenty to make more."

Odin sadly shook his head, muttering under his breath. He swallowed hard, glanced at Hoenir who stood alongside grinding his teeth, and then turned to Loki. "It is true that many would delight in furnishing all we require - they understand obligation, but it should always be done knowingly."

Loki growled and began to speak, but Odin raised his hand for silence. "Since you seem incapable of generosity and freely bestowing blessings, my brother and I will help you redeem yourself."

Hoenir reached into his pocket and withdrew three flat stones he had picked up during his failed fishing expedition; small, black, and polished smooth by the running waters. He placed them in Odin's hand. Odin juggled them a moment, mumbling words low and soft, then passed them to Loki. "Return to the farmhouse and place these three stones on the table from where you stole the pies."

Mouth open, crust crumbs rolling down his chest, Loki stared unbelieving, first at Odin and then at Hoenir. "Why? They are just pies. I'll bet the farm wife has already replaced them."

Odin sighed and placed a hand to his face, slowly rubbing his eyes. "Just do as I say."

Grumbling, cursing, and flicking an occasional nasty glance at the two, Loki shifted his shape to that of white owl. Gripping the stones tightly in his talons, he silently winged his way back to the farm. Dipping low over the cooking shed, he dropped the stones; they struck the table with a sharp crack. Sinking deep into the wood, their tops lay even with the surface of the table and looked like nothing more than three black stains.

The farmer's wife, still busy at the oven, jumped at the harsh sound. Spinning around, she glared about the shed, but saw nothing. Her gaze passed over the three stones, but their presence went unnoticed with all the other nicks and dents that marred the table surface.

Loki returned to the valley full of good spirits. Odin and Hoenir were pleased when they heard the stones were delivered. They sat down and returned to eating; feeling better knowing the pies had been paid for. Odin smiled at Loki's merry laughter. "I see your mood has much improved. Always the benefits of generosity spill over to the giver."

A sly grin spread across Loki's face. "Yes, that must be it."

———————————

From that time on the farmer's wife led an easy life; there was no need for her to grind grain, mix dough, or prepare meat. Let her enter the cooking shed, no matter the time of day, and food stood ready and hot on the table.

She kept her own counsel on this miraculous blessing, only approaching the shed when she was alone that she might keep it secret. Soon the economies of a smartly run household became apparent, and her reputation of being an efficient housekeeper spread across the countryside. Since she was not taking from the family stores, there was always extra that could be pointed to whenever visitors came or boasted of when others complained of having little. Then with much display, she would lend out some trifling amount saying it might pinch her family, but she was glad to share with those in need.

Pride swelled as she became the envy and wonder of the neighboring wives. She basked in the attention and carried her nose high wherever she went. And though all went well, one thing constantly nagged at her mind. As she had no cooking to do, she spent the greater part of her time cleaning, and from the first she was vexed that scrubbing would not remove the three black stains from the harvest table. It got so she couldn't pass the table without her eyes being drawn to the spots. The three stones would stare back, silently accusing her of being a poor housekeeper. Then her ire would build, and she would bend, huffing, and puffing, scrubbing vigorously until her fingers bled and her arms grew tired and sore. "If I can only get rid of these spots, I could enjoy life. What would others think if I cannot rub stains off my own table?"

The Discovery of Flax

It was the time of Selmánudr, pasture month, when farmers drive their herds of cattle and goats from the lower fields into the high mountain pastures to graze on the lush meadow grasses. One farmer, too poor to own slaves to do the work, hiked up his kirtle, bound his jerkin tight at the waist, pecked his wife on the cheek, scuffled his children's hair, and made ready to drive his herd up the mountain valley to the high meadows that were his to graze. "Keep the fire burning and send the older boy to relieve me once Mani has waxed to half his face. Keep the other children busy. We ride close to the edge now, and I'll not have us fall to ruin."

Reaching out, he gathered his children into a big hug. "You kids see you mind your mother while I'm gone."

As he slung a quiver over his shoulder, he drew his wife aside and spoke to her in low tones. "I'll not take rations with me." The good woman made to protest, but the farmer cupped her cheek in his rough palm. "I'm leaving what food we have for you and the children. I have my bow and, when the opportunity presents itself, will use it to bring down a hart or a goat. It will feed me and there will be enough to pack back for our larder. The boy is as accomplished as me with the bow. Between the two of us we will be able to gather enough meat to last us well into the winter months without seriously depleting our herd."

———————————

A shepherd's duty is constant diligence to the herd, but when it also includes the responsibility of feeding oneself and others, hunting becomes a necessity and sometimes the herd must care for itself.

Hunched low, arrow knocked in his ready bow, the farmer skirted the edge of a sharp ridge where fingers of the Yurkul reached down the mountain valley. He had spotted a ram wandering the far side and meant to cut him off before he cleared the scrub and topped the rise. The open field would allow it to easily outdistance any pursuit he might muster.

Peeping around a boulder, he was surprised to see the ram biding its time beside the edge of a large doorway carved into the rock wall, the entrance nearly obscured by a curtain of ice that hung down from the glacier. The ram dashed up the draw as he boldly stepped across the crusted snow that marked the entrance's approach. Reaching the cave, he ran his fingers along the opening, tracing out the mason marks of joined blocks. "It is man-made and well hidden." His eyes brightened as he un-knocked the arrow from his bow and slipped it back into its quiver. "There may be more inside than just ice."

Passing through the entrance, he edged cautiously along the lane of sunshine that lanced in from the cave mouth, feeling his way using his bow as a staff. A soft light glowed ahead, and he followed its guide as a moth the lighted torch. With each step the light became more intense until he found himself in a wondrous cavern hung with stalactites, lit up bright as a meadow in the midday sun. In the center stood a beautiful woman with long dark hair, clad in misty robes – tinged now red, now violet, now opaque white; on her breast was pinned a small corsage of blue flowers. To each side, ready to attend her needs, stood a host of lovely maidens crowned with ashen tresses woven with alpine flowers.

The dark-haired woman looked up as the man stumbled into the light. She raised the blue flowers to her nose and sniffed lightly. "We have a visitor."

One of the handmaidens leaned close and whispered urgently into her ear. "He carries a weapon."

"He is a farmer out hunting for food, not a wanton killer." She smiled at the visitor and waved him forward. "Come closer that I might better see you."

The farmer blinked his eyes once, twice, then rubbed them with his fingers. He looked again, and the woman still stood before him smiling, her hand extended in greeting. "I did not mean to intrude..."

"Yes, you did." The woman pursed her lips and for a moment her white garments tinged a deep purple. As she took in the much-mended cape and the loving patchwork of the farmer's clothes, her gaze softened, and her robes returned to white. "You are a poor man with a large family. You left off hunting and the promise of food in hopes of finding something of greater value in this cave."

The farmer nodded slowly at the obvious knowledge the woman held. He spied the golden girdle at her waist and the keys of hearth and home hanging from her belt and suddenly knew who spoke to him. He swallowed hard. "You're... You're..." and sank to his knees.

"I am known by many names. In this place and time, you can call me Holda." As in a dream, he heard her step forward and felt a hand lightly touch his shoulder. Sudden warmth gushed through him like a lowland summer breeze, and he dared look up into the gentle eyes of his mother, his wife, the dark-haired goddess of the cave. She waved her hand and the cavern walls flared to life with glinting precious stones. "Your need is great, and there is much in this cavern that can ease your misery. Look around you and choose from anything you see. It will be yours to carry away."

The dazzling glow of the precious stones filled the air and the temptation was great to stuff his pockets with the gems and rush from the cave, but he knew his neighbors and the townsmen would never believe his story. He was uncertain he could find the cave again, and unable to show them the trove, they would insist he stole the gems. Then what could he expect? A public beating, or worse, his rank of freeman revoked, his family left to fend for themselves, and confiscation of what little he owned.

A frown twisted his lips. His neighbor Aarn was particularly keen on acquiring his grazing rights. He sighed and looked longingly around, it had been a fool's errand this impulse to enter the cave in search of some unknown treasure. And having found riches beyond even his dreams, he could not, dared not, spend them.

Still the gem's promise glittered from the walls, and his eyes danced about the room until they were drawn to the little nosegay of plain blue flowers which the adorned the robe of the gracious apparition. "You offer many things that would ease the life of a poor man. But they are shadows to the sight of you."

He stood up straight and raised his voice a notch so that he might project greater strength than he felt in his shaking legs. "You ask what

I would have to take with me. I would have the bunch of flowers you wear. Never have I seen lovelier. It will be a gift to my wife, a reminder of the day I met a goddess."

Smiling with pleasure, Holda, unpinned the spray from her robe and gave it to him. "Your means are small, but you are prudent and your judgment sound. You have chosen wisely and will live as long as the flowers do not droop and fade."

She beckoned a handmaiden forward, a small sack in her hands. "Take this measure of seed and sow it in your field." The farmer took the sack and bowed, thanks tripping off this tongue. "Now, return to your herd before they scatter."

The air reverberated with sounds of thunder, and the earth shook until the poor man was certain the cavern would collapse and bury them all. He scrunched his eyes and braced himself for the pain of the rock fall he knew must come. But the sound stopped, and a cool wind caressed his cheek. Popping open one eye, he found himself standing on the mountainside just above the pasture where his herd grazed placidly in the summer sun. Beside his feet sat the bag of seeds and his hand clutched a small bouquet of blue flowers.

Far below, he spotted a figure struggling up the grade. From his shape and the color of his clothes, he knew it was his son come to relieve him of his duties.

———————

Slowly the farmer wended his way home to his wife, pondering his encounter, hefting the sack of seeds, and juggling his empty pockets. When he arrived home, he regaled his family with the tale of his adventure and, on reaching the end, flourished the bouquet of lovely blue flowers and the measure of seed.

His wife stared at the flowers and seeds, then back at him. She shook her head and collapsed against the wall. "Foolish man. You could have taken a ram whose meat would have been very welcome. Leaving that, you had the choice between precious stones and flowers... and you chose flowers." She stumbled to a bench and would have fallen had her husband not caught her and helped her to sit. "With the stones, we could have traded for more seed than we could plant. We would have had plenty for several seasons."

The farmer looked at his feet. "I deemed the wealth too dangerous." He shoved his hands in his pockets, pulled them out, and shoved them back in again. "Besides, the goddess said I made a wise choice."

The woman fixed her husband with a weary gaze, the dark smudges and deep lines drawing him down beside her. "She would. She doesn't have to eat." And she buried her face in her hands.

Resigned and with nothing to lose, the farmer proceeded to sow the seed across his barren fields, and to his surprise found that the sack supplied seed enough for several acres. Each day he visited the fields eager to see what would grow. Each night he kneeled at the field edge and prayed for the promise of Holda.

Soon the little green shoots began to appear, and one moonlight night as he called out to the sky, he watched the fog coalesce into a misty form above the field, with arms outstretched in blessing. The next day the field blossomed, and countless little blue flowers opened their petals to greet the morning sun.

The farmer shouted to his wife and children. "Come see! Come see the gift of Holda. They look just like the ones one the hearth, the ones she gave me." Together they stepped into the field and it was as if they treaded the sky.

His wife leaned her head on his shoulder. "They are beautiful, but we need the fields for crops - those we need for the winter and those we need for trade."

The farmer looked out over the field, and then glanced down at his youngest who clung to his leg, eyes wide, laughter bubbling from her lips. "I trust the goddess." And as he spoke the promise of the goddess echoed in his mind: 'You will live as long as the flowers do not droop and fade.' He shook himself and drew his wife closer to his side. "She gave me these for as long as they bloom. I feel certain they will somehow benefit our family. They stay for now."

For two passings of Mani's face the flowers bloomed, and their seeds ripened. But as the summer sun grew stronger, the bright blue of the flowers began to fade. Then one day a dry wind blew over the hills and the next morning found them withered and dry.

As the farmer stared in sorrow across the field, he heard the footsteps of his wife approach from behind and felt her hand slip into the crook of his arm. "You have held to the goddess, but now it is time to see to the needs of your family. The flowers are gone. Now will you listen to me and at least plant something that will help tide us through winter?"

The farmer's head drooped, and his feet dragged as if the weight of the world had suddenly settled on his shoulders. "Aye," he muttered to his wife. "You are right. Beauty doesn't feed hungry bellies. I'll start this morning. Call the boys we have much work ahead."

He stood ready with the scythe, his sons positioned at staggered intervals before and behind waiting on his call to begin. As he lifted the scythe to make the first swipe, he whispered a silent prayer to Holda. "Goddess, you have given me the pleasure of seeing your face, and the delight of your beautiful gift. For all this I thank you. But now the flowers have withered and faded and the promise of my life with them. I ask only that you look after my family when the day is done."

"Do you think my gift stops with the dried stalks of once pretty flowers?" The farmer jumped at the words and spun around to see the goddess and her entourage sweeping down from the sky, their robes billowing white as the clouds.

The farmer's sons gathered behind him, their scythes raised to ward off the unknown. He waved them down and dropped to one knee. His sons stared a moment at one another then slowly followed their father's lead. "You honor us with your presence. Please be welcome in our home."

The goddess glanced at the farm, lean with no room for extra, the few buildings – like the farmer's clothes –patched with loving care. "You have done well with my gift. The crop is generous, and I see you prepare to harvest. Well and good. Harvest it all, stalks and seeds, and put it in your storage shed."

Her fingers flicked, and the hand maidens fanned out to either side. "It is time you learned what to do with this bounty." She glanced at the kitchen shed where oven smoke curled lazily into the air. "Call out the good woman of this home and all your children. This will take your entire family."

She set the farmer and his sons the task of harvesting the flax. Once it had been gathered and bundled, they were instructed in how to process the stalks into fiber and the seeds into oil. They followed the stern guidance of the maidens in preserving seeds and setting a quarter-part aside for sowing the following year.

The wife stood open-mouthed with her daughters clustered behind her as Holda set her handmaidens to instruct the women of the household in spinning the fibers into a yarn thinner and stronger than the animal hair they were used to spinning, weaving it into a sturdy cloth, and bleaching the linen.

As the promise of their crop became known, the people of the neighborhood visited the farm to purchase both linen and flax-seed, and to learn the ways of the new crop. Wealth poured in, steady and sure like the spring rains and the farmer expanded his land to grow more flax, and while he and their sons ploughed, sowed, and harvested, his wife and their daughters spun, wove, and bleached the linen.

Each morning they gathered before the family shrine where the farmer led prayers of thanks to the gods, Holda above all. And each night during the month of Selmánudr, after checking his slaves had properly tended the needs of his herds, the farmer would step into the center of the field that had known the first sowing and whisper his private thanks to the goddess of the cave.

Seasons came and went, with today's plenty carrying the promise for harvests yet to come. The farmer lived to see his grandchildren and great-grandchildren grow up around him. They each had their own farms and kept a portion turned to growing flax, so that the flowers might always bloom and never fade from the land.

The Story of Heligoland (Forseti's Sacred Isle)

"What is the cost to a man who cannot rely on justice? What is the worth of justice when it is inconsistent?" The Frisian chieftain looked around, taking in the stoic faces of the other chieftains seated about his board. He rose from his high seat and strode slowly back and forth until he was certain all eyes followed his pacing.

"A killing in this village means death to the killer, but elsewhere is only a fine. Robbery and assault are causes to hang the criminal, while two valleys away the villain is only beaten and then let go. A theft loses a man his right hand, but beyond the mountain the stolen objects are returned, and a cash penalty paid with no maiming of the criminal. Here a wife can divorce her husband and keep her property, yet across the river only the husband can decide to divorce, and if he does, he keeps everything. And so, fall the judgments." The chieftain nodded his head as uneasy mutters sounded about the room.

He stopped at his seat, picked up a mug and took a deep draught. Around the table others hoisted their cups and called the serving girl for more. "Our people grow weary of each tribe dispensing justice as they see fit and their ire increases, especially among our merchants who must travel, of the unequal judgments raised between clans. We have called this council of tribes to beard the issue. Everyone has left their weapons at the door. There will be no fighting until we come to terms."

A thick hand raised high, called attention to a mound of wolf skins that guzzled down a cup of mead then snapped fingers to the serving girl for more. As the girl topped of his mug, hard blue eyes peered from above a grizzled gray beard, and he rocked back and forth, swaying the fur skins draped across his shoulders so they brushed his knees. "You speak truly. Once my merchants' ferried goods up and down the coast, sometimes they took on passengers. Now they refrain from docking in many places, fearful of being harshly taxed in trade, or being accused of offering transport to a criminal and punished by a levied fine, or worse, losing their cargo and ship." He grumbled staring into his cup. "The scot I collect has greatly diminished, as I am certain it has for others."

A tall, thin man, his face sharp as an eagle crested with thick black hair, stood, and banged his cup onto the table. He threw back his cape and his hand fumbled in the empty air at his waist for the long blade that usually hung from his belt. He snarled and tucked his wandering hand into a fold of his cloak. "Before arriving as this gathering, I received word that my youngest son was hung for killing another man. He had been traveling across the lands eager to learn of others and to make his mark in the world. Had it happened in my land, I would have paid weregild to the dead man's family and resolved the issue. Now there is a hole in my shield, and it is all I can do to not seek vengeance. But I checked my anger at the door knowing that when he left home, he placed himself in the hands of fate. We must have agreement, or I swear there will be war."

Wary, watchful, each certain their laws the best, the chieftains spoke their mind. For many days that stretched into weeks they quarreled over whose rules should be the law of the land. Unable to resolve the issue among themselves, but all agreeing that something must be done, they called on twelve of their wisest men, elders chosen from the different clans that inhabited their lands, to gather the laws of the various tribes and compile from them a common code that could be applied to all and to which every clan would abide.

The twelve arrived as commanded: some by cart, a few astraddle horses, others from further away followed the coastline in low-sided færings. Each were old, their faces etched with deep lines of concern, some proud with chins held high, others bent with the weight of years, but all stalked with determined tread to the meeting place. In a well-thatched hut erected on a hill overlooking the breakers of the sea, they huddled in council around the eldskáli to collect and record the different laws and rules of each clan.

Mindful of the importance of the task, a goat was slaughtered, and a torch-led procession, chanting devotions to the gods, circled the hut sprinkling its blood as a ward, while inside the elders raised up their voices, first one then another until all chanted the same prayer. "Forseti, son of Baldur, god of justice and eternal law, you who preside over every judicial assembly and who have never failed to help the deserving, your followers raise up this appeal. We, who are about to undertake the difficult task of unifying our people's laws, call on your wisdom and guidance in this most difficult charge. Direct our course that our decisions will be just and for the benefit of all."

They discussed long into the nights, sometimes with loud argument and gnashing of teeth. Always some clan leader sent a messenger to determine the status, their scratches at the doorway interrupting the debate as a representative was called outside and encouraged to push the laws of their clan to the fore.

Finally, the eldest of the twelve tottered to his feet and shook his robes free of his legs. "We have gathered all the laws, we have recorded and compared, yet still we get nowhere. The constant interruptions and pressures from without keep us bickering and from accomplishing our duty. I say that we remove ourselves from this place that we may confer in privacy."

A gruff voice sounded from beside the fire as a somber-faced elder jammed a stick into the flames and vigorously stirred the coals. "I wholly agree. I for one, do not want to spend the last of my days hunkered in this hut staring at your faces, watching them shrivel and die along with me. I have sons and daughters, and grandchildren too, who I would like to see again."

As a round of grumbled "yeas" circled the group, a wizened hand crept into the air and waved for attention. "Let us take a small vessel and seek out a secluded spot where we can conduct our deliberations in peace. There is a likely mount moored on the beach below us, a knorr that can easily carry us all. It can get us well away before we can be hindered."

Another voice chimed in from near the entry where an ancient held the flap closed from prying eyes and listening ears. "Let us tell no one where we go; otherwise we can be certain the interruptions will continue." Sage heads nodded agreement.

Eager to be away, they turned a blind eye to the ominous bank of clouds that piled thick and gray along the horizon. No sooner had they sculled their craft away from shore than the winds rose from a low moan and began to scream. Their sail billowed and popped with the ragged breath of a tempest which drove their vessel far out to sea. White-haired waves crashed over the sides drenching whiter heads, while hands, once firm at the rudder, struggled with frail strength to keep the craft from being swamped.

The prow rose and fell between the darkened sky and the rough peaks of Ægir's daughters. The screaming gale showered the deck with hail and drenched the ancient mariners with stinging pellets of bitter cold rain. Straight winds rolled up the murky waters until they loomed high, filling the sky, and the ship clove the narrow valleys between. All gripped tight their benches, bracing themselves against fear, should the towering peaks crash down busting the ship to timbers and burying all beneath their weight.

Shouts and groans escaped lips, defiant voices raised to challenge the storm, yet none cursed the decision to embark. The ship, wildly tossed by waves, which now towered above the mast, now raised the ship high above a dark plain of churning, gale-tossed waters that merged into the black clouds, creaked, and moaned from the assault.

All night they dashed over the waste waters, flung, and tumbled about until their limbs grew numb from the cold, and their weary purchase threatened to give way. Gathering on the deck, they crowded into a close circle, hands gripped tight that none would be swept away. Heads bowed into the center, they shouted back and forth of what could be done. Ear hands struggled to grasp words unchained from their source.

"We are not young," agonized a shaking voice from near the stern. "Even now our strength fails us, leaving the rudder to steer at the whim of the storm. We cannot direct nor hope to keep the ship afloat."

"Ran seems determined to have us," a thin voice wailed as a wave broke over the side and swamped the deck. "Let us call on Ægir to calm her fury."

"I doubt Ægir can sway her intent," shouted a gruff voice from somewhere beside the mast. "I say we call on Forseti. It is his work that sparked this journey and which we are bound to uphold. If there are any among the gods who can intercede on our behalf, it will be him."

A chorus of agreements sounded, barely heard over the shrieking winds.

All the judges raised their voices, shouting as loud as their aged throats allowed, begging Forseti to help them reach land once again. Once, twice they called out, each time their prayers nearly drown by the shrieking winds. On the third round, as the winds snatched the words from their lips, they perceived, to their utter surprise, that the vessel contained a thirteenth passenger.

Lurching across the pitching deck, the newcomer seized the tiller and silently wrestled the vessel round, steering it into the darkness where the waves dashed highest. The ship rocked side-to-side, nearly standing on edge as it ploughed through the waves. Ancient muscles found forgotten strength as the twelve fought to remain in a knot clustered tight around the mast. Hearts thundered with hope as they continued to shout out Forseti's name.

Time means nothing in a storm. How long they were battered and beaten by the waves, their ears deafened by the shrill crying winds, none could later say. It could have been days, but it seemed only moments after the steersman took charge of the rudder that they came to an island. Grinning, unbowed before the storm, he directed the ship past the breaker line into a narrow bay protected by a headland ridge that curved its sheltering arm out into the sea.

His voice rang out sharp and clear over the winds. "Drop the sail so it doesn't shred and bend your backs to the oars." Ears heard the command and hands fumbled to lower the sail and bind it tight. The oars slid out and dipped into the sea, sweeping back the waves in the elderly crew's eagerness to reach the steady calm of land. As the ship grounded on the gray sands of the beach, he motioned them to disembark.

In all haste the twelve men obeyed, clambering over the gunnels, and wading through the foaming surf to fall prostrate on the unshifting sands, their voices lifted in praise of their savior. The stranger followed, carefully tethering the ship by a heavy rope to the stout trunk of an ash tree that angled out from the overhanging bank.

He smiled at the old men heaped here and there along the beach, gasping for breath, and staring at him in awe. Each marveled, for it seemed his face held the familiar, resembling some aspect of themselves, yet differing from each. Striding along the shore he turned inland, beckoning with his arm for them to follow.

Scrambling to their feet, they shook sand from their damp robes and chased after into the greensward, eager to keep him in sight. They caught up with him on the edge of an open glade, watching excitedly as he untied a battle-axe from his waist belt and flung it into the air. Its edge flashed, a bright, spinning sickle of light, as it arced to the ground. Where its curved edge struck, a limpid spring gushed forth.

The stranger glanced over his shoulder and winked. "Seafaring and the law are both thirsty work." Bending low, he took a deep drink, then stretched himself upright, hands pressed against the small of his back. He stepped over to a dry space above the spring and sat down waiting for them to join him.

Imitating the stranger, the twelve silently lined up, each taking their turn at drinking from the spring, before stumbling up the hill to join in a council circle. When all were seated, the stranger tipped his head to each.

"You have done well collecting the laws of your peoples. Your goal to combine them into a single code is noble and worthy of high praise. But the laws of men are oftentimes born of greed, and it is difficult to separate selfishness from that which benefits all. As with a farmer's harvest, it is necessary to sort through the chaff, winnowing out the seeds of self-interest to find the kernels from which true justice may grow."

His beaming smile brightened the circle and all hearts lifted in anticipation. "Let's work with your harvest." The stranger began speaking in low tones, which grew firmer and louder as he expounded a code that combined all the good points of the various laws.

Sage heads nodded in unison at each statement. None disagreed with his direct reasoning and clear judgment. And a thrill of surprise, and delight, ran through the gathering at knowing such laws came from them.

When the stranger finished, the twelve leaned their heads together and collectively agreed to adopt the unified code of law. Looking up to give thanks, a single gasp sounded from the group as they realized their benefactor had vanished as suddenly and mysteriously as he had appeared on the ship.

Eyes still scanned the surroundings when a gentle cough alerted them to a frail hand waving slowly as a dried reed in the breeze. When he had their attention, the elder hunched his shoulders and stared at his feet. "I don't mean to raise concerns, but – while this code is good and just - how will we approach our chieftains? Though we have decided to adopt this ruling, it will be difficult for each of us to deliver and retain our lives."

Deep rumbles of agreement rolled around the circle. Many fingers ran nervously through gray beards until one spoke. "Your words are wise and ring with an unpleasant truth. None will believe we accomplished our task in such short order. There will be many who feel that through compromise we each, somehow, betrayed the rightful legacy of our clans. Indeed, our lives are on the line."

Another squirmed, lifting first one butt cheek, and then the other. "We must have a way to present this that all will accept and none will dare challenge."

The eldest tottered to his feet and lifted his arms to the sky. "I tell you it was Forseti himself who saved us from the storm and delivered the code by which all will henceforth be judged."

A soft chuckle sounded from across the circle as another groaned to his feet. "And who else but Forseti could have made sense of our laws and resolved our charge so quickly."

They all stood, wild grins spreading across their lips. "Each of us must hold to the truth of this story, we must speak with one voice that the code was decided by Forseti himself. How could we hope to challenge the divine ruling of the arbiter of the gods? And having delivered the charge of our chieftains, how can any find fault with the results?"

Laughing, delighted with their decision, they marched to the beach and the knorr floating unperturbed, still tethered to the tree. A careful examination found the ship undamaged and in good order, ready to set sail now that the storm had passed. With joyous hearts, they climbed aboard; clear skies and a steady breeze called them to return home.

As they cleared the breaker line, the eldest climbed up on the prow and turned to face those gathered in the ship. "When we accepted the commission to unify our people's laws we called on Forseti that he might guide us. That he has done and more. We owe him a debt greater than any man can repay."

He turned back to the island. "Let us commemorate Forseti's appearance and guidance by declaring this island a holy place, Heligoland, forever sacred to Forseti."

A throaty voice shouted out from the crowd. "And let there be a curse on any who dare to desecrate its sanctity by quarrel or bloodshed."

Another shouldered forward through the group. "Let them be cursed before their family, their clan, and the gods."

A soft voice called out, adding to the curse. "Let them know as punishment only misfortune in their endeavors, all judgments will fall in favor of their opponents, and they will suffer shipwreck or meet a shameful death."

The elder balanced on the prow raised up his hands. "So, it will be."

———————

The codes were delivered to the conclave of chieftains and, though some grumbled into their sleeve, none dared challenge outright the judgment of Forseti, for after hearing the exact same story recounted by each of the twelve elders, those known as the wisest and most honorable in the clans, none questioned its truth. All doubts were abolished when the twelve guided the chieftains to the isle and showed them the spring, still gushing clear and sweet from the gash Forseti's axe had made when it struck the ground.

From then on, judicial Things were frequently held upon the sacred isle, the domars always drawing water and drinking in solemn silence, in memory of Forseti's visit. The waters of his spring were considered so holy that all who drank of them were held sacred during the assembly.

And as Forseti was said to hold his judgments in spring, summer, and autumn, but never in winter, it became customary in all the Northern lands to dispense justice in those seasons. It is only when the sun shines brightly that right is apparent to all, for in winter's darkness it impossible to render an impartial verdict. Always twelve were called from the people to judge –in honor of the first twelve, and to honor Forseti, a thirteenth – the Law Speaker- was assigned from those most knowledgeable of the law.

Pedigree

It was Sólmánudr, sun month, when the call went out across the land for all freemen and nobles to gather at Thing. Those who had legal issues were to present their cases, local concerns were to be addressed, and the long-term welfare of the district discussed.

The day was set and freemen trudged from the far corners of the district to gather in a wide clearing bordered by a river whose shallow banks offered easy access and water. A forest crowded up on two sides, its center filled with wide stretches of impassible brushwood and scrub, and the occasional open glade.

Tents and temporary huts crowded the open space, dwellings for those and their supporters who had traveled to have their cases heard. The court was convened on a level plain amid a circle of hazel poles linked by ropes. Inside the circle of these sanctuary ropes sat twelve judges appointed from the district. In the center of the circle lay a large flat pledge stone – the Law Rock - where each claimant would stand and make his case.

Alone, a hooded figure stood on the stone, a birch staff gripped tightly in his right hand—the Law Speaker chosen by the judges to interpret the law and announce the decisions. Three times the staff was raised and struck against the stone calling for attention. "It has long been declared that only when light shines clearly in the heavens does right becomes apparent to all and equitable verdicts can be rendered. We are gathered here when Sol rides highest through the sky to render judgments that will keep the peace within our community. Those that submit cases for hearing are bound by the law to uphold the outcome, be it for or against."

He turned slowly looking everyone in the eye that they would know the seriousness of his words. "Now, let those who have issues come forward and state their case that all may be ordered."

They came in procession to the Law Rock, wearing what finery was theirs, to state their cases, in the evening the courts would be open for the lawsuits. The line of petitioners was short, for it had been a plentiful season and few were of a mind for disputes. Still, there were several land disputes, a demand of weregild for the slaying of a slave, and a call for dissolution of a union. All cases were heard, the lists of witnesses and supporters noted, and their places in the hearing assigned.

The Law Speaker stamped his staff three times, the sharp knock of wood against stone drawing everyone's attention to his voice. "The cases have been stated and the roster filled." He nodded to the judges and they solemnly nodded back to begin.

"The first case is that of the Óttar the Young, son of Innstein, and Angantýr, son of Arngrím. These men have been disputing for some time concerning rights to a piece of property that borders both their known lands. They have agreed to lay their quarrel before the Thing and abide by its judgment."

The plaintiffs stepped forward to state their case. By law the one who brought the case spoke first. Óttar nodded once to the judges and, as by custom, looked past the Law Speaker into the crowd beyond. He swallowed hard and tried to speak. A sharp squeak escaped his throat and the crowd chuckled at his discomfort. Gathering his composure, the young man turned to face the twelve judges.

His reedy voice cut across the Thing making some wince and sending others grinning into their sleeves. "You all know me. My family has lived here for generations. Before their passing many of you had fair dealings with my father and his father before him, so you know my words to be reasoned and honest."

The judges sat impassive in their high seats, while to his right Angantýr folded his arms across his chest and nodded his head. Óttar swallowed hard and pressed on. "South of my farm lies a wide strip of land, a fen called Stakksmyr. The stream, Hafsloek, borders its south edge. In winter the fen is flooded with water and dangerous to cross, but come springtime, when the sun has chased the ice back to the mountaintops, the water recedes with the snow, and its open meadow offers excellent grazing for cattle. Many count its lush grass equal to a stack of the finest hay.

The channel of Hafsloek has always set the boundary there, but now spring often finds Angantýr's cattle grazing the meadow before I have a chance to drive my own to pasture. For three years running I have complained directly to Angantýr that I own the land and he has grazing south of the fen, but he has done nothing save to make the absurd claim that the land is his to graze. In our last confrontation, he threatened me with the axe he carries at his waist should I accost him again."

Óttar paused and stared out across the gathering, his gangly youth giving him a bug-eyed appearance. "I am a peaceable man rarely given to violence. So, before I strike this man dead, I have come to the Thing and ask that my community decide in my favor."

The Law Speaker stamped his staff three times and looked at Óttar. "Have you finished?" The young man nervously shoved a lock of hair back from his forehead and nodded. "Then step back and let Angantýr come forward and state his side."

Angantýr strode forward. He was older than Óttar, heavy muscled with broad square shoulders, sharp chiseled features - as if the mason had just set down his tools, satisfied with the final work, all topped with a shock of thick flaming red hair drawn back into a warrior's braid. His deep, booming voice rolled across the assembly calling all to attention. "I am well known to every one of you. My family has lived in these parts for as far back as any can remember. Many of you have dealt with me and know my word to be bond."

He spread his arms wide, turning first to the judges and then to the gathering. "My neighbor speaks truth. South of his farm lies a wide strip of land, a fen called Stakksmyr. It is bordered by the stream Hafsloek. As it was set in the old days, Hafsloek defines the boundary between our farms. To all this I agree. The land, the boundary determined by the stream, and that side of the stream which is mine to graze."

Murmurs rolled across the gathering and even the judges leaned their heads close to whisper words. Angantýr strode back and forth before the high seats but directed his words to the crowd. "Three years ago, Hafsloek changed its course. Stakksmyr is still bordered by the stream, but now it cuts the fen along its northern edge."

He nodded his head as he turned to the judges. "By the word of law, I graze only that which is mine to graze; the meadows south of the Hafsloek. For three years, I followed the law, and each season of Óttar's complaints, I listened graciously to his words, but steadfastly maintained that which I hold to be mine. This last year, he drew the blade at his waist and would have struck me dead, had I not reached for my axe and cowed him down."

Óttar stomped his feet and shouted over Angantýr's speech. "That's not true! That isn't what happened! He threatened me!"

The judges frowned at the interruption, and the Law Speaker rapped his staff. "You will be silent while it is Angantýr's turn to speak. As you are young and not familiar with speaking before the judges, I give this warning, be foolish enough to interrupt again before it is time for rebuttal and this judgment will go against you."

Óttar grimaced and stared at the ground to hide the sudden flush that brightened his cheeks. Glancing from the corner of his eyes, he saw many faces turned into their robes, shoulders shaking in laughter at his discomfort.

A smirk twisted the corner of Angantýr's lips. "It is true Óttar called for resolution before this Thing. Well I would have preferred to decide this between us as men should, but given his youth, I am willing this time to bow to this judgment."

The Law Speaker stamped his staff three times and looked at Angantýr. "Have you finished?"

"No, I have one thing left to say." Angantýr turned and spoke directly to Óttar. "Let us be frank in all our dealings and clearly state all the reasons for this case. If my actions were such an affront, why did you not seek resolution at the Thing beforehand? There have been many before today that would have gladly heard your case and which I would have happily attended. I say you bring this case now in the hope that through winning you will impress a certain recently widowed highborn woman and so legitimize your pursuit of her hand in the eyes of her family. I say plan on remaining unwed and childless. You have no more hope of winning her affections than you do of winning this case."

Óttar's eyes bulged and fire blossomed scarlet up his neck until his entire face flared red. Laughing at the young man's discomfort, Angantýr turned back to the Law Speaker. "Now I am finished."

The Law Speaker stamped his staff again three times. "Each side has spoken their truth. It is opened for each to respond."

Óttar waved an arm taking in the surrounding hills and stands of birch that clung as moss to its sides. He clenched his teeth and struggled to keep his words focused on the case. "All of Stakksmyr belongs to my family, so said my father and uncles, now dead. These are my rights, and I would seek them even were I condemned to a life alone."

Angantýr crossed his arms and shook his head. "Dead sows don't count for farrowing. Your words mean nothing, nor do those of dead men. I can make the same claim by my kin long gone that all south of the Hafsloek is mine."

The judges whispered among themselves, some passive, some pounding their fists, all wary of setting a dangerous precedent on shifting natural boundaries. They beckoned the Law Speaker to attend and called on his knowledge. He listened carefully to their reasoning, then in soft whispers offered his counsel. When an agreement was reached, the Law Speaker stamped his staff, the sharps raps especially strident to the ears, and raised his voice for attention.

"From your own lips come the means of judgment, and I do not have to cover my head to decide the winner. Let the dead determine ownership of Stakksmyr. You each claim a long line of kin tied to the land. The man who can state the longest line of noble ancestors will be declared the winner." A general murmur of consent rippled through the gathering and many gray heads winked knowingly across the field.

Angantýr smiled and nodded his great mane of red hair, letting the locks sway into his eyes. "I agree to pit my memory of honorable kin against the line of foolish Óttar."

Óttar, his brow twisted with concern, could do nothing save consent to the general decree. "I agree to these terms but let us each have the cycle of Mani to ensure the truth of our words. I would not want it said that I rushed Angantýr to state his line and so falsely claim kin where no kin lay. I am no thief to pray on the weak mind of another."

Angantýr growled and brandished his fist at the young man. "I am not so feeble of mind that I cannot recount, right now, my line. But yours are the thin words of a pathetic fool unwilling to resolve the dispute by might of arms."

Óttar bristled at the words and thrust out his chest. "I trust in the fates and take my hand in their weaving. If you want…"

The stamp of the Law Speaker's staff interrupted Óttar before he could fully respond to the provocation. The Law Speaker had been chosen for his wisdom and his practical concern for the entire community. For while it was each man's right to challenge another, it was not something he would allow at Thing. Both sides of the claim had many followers and such a duel would be bound to throw the countryside into a mayhem of small skirmishes that would deplete the youth from too many households.

"Since Angantýr set the means for the judgment, the time of the contest will take place as Óttar asks. We will convene a special assembly here when Mani's face is once more full of light and each of you will take your stance on the pledge rock to recite the depth of your family line. He who can recount farthest back in unbroken line shall have the land."

Once more the Law Speaker's staff clacked its imperative against the stone. "Each of you arrived with a troop of companions, your numbers equal in strength. By the laws set down by our ancestors, there will be no violence while the Thing is convened. It is on each of you to keep your men under control or forfeit your case."

He waved them back, pointing with his staff. "Now step away from the circle and let the next plaintiff come forth."

The Thing lasted four more days, hearing the remaining cases and deciding general rules for the district. During that time Óttar and Angantýr kept to opposite sides of the encampment. Though tensions ran high, each kept to the judgment and managed to cool the high spirits of their followers.

When camp broke, each returned to their own farm, by unspoken agreement taking different routes. Both parties kept on guard, on approaching every bend, at passing beneath every hill, expecting ambush from every direction now that the binding of the assembled camp was lifted.

———————

Back on his farm Óttar worked his memory of the family line that his father had once tried to instill in him. He cursed himself for not paying more attention, choosing instead the games of youth, than the practicality of family history. For a week Óttar tortured his memory, but, beyond his father and grandfather, was unable to remember the names of more than a few of his progenitors. Frustrated, fearful of losing his case and being made to look more foolish than many already considered him, he turned himself over to his faith in the Asynja, Freyja.

To dedicate his offerings, he built a special altar with large black stones rounded smooth by the stream, Hafsloek, and piled high on a mound outside his home. He placed flat, smooth, firestone in the center of the altar. When all was ready, he built a fire and slaughtered a ram, spilling its blood across the stones. All this he offered to Freyja, entreating her assistance.

"Freyja hear me. A devoted follower calls on you for aid. After many generations, those who faithfully prayed and sacrificed to the Æsir, I Óttar, son of Innstein, the last of my line, find myself fighting for my rights and compelled by challenge to recount my line in a contest of memory. I can recall few of my forebears. Back to my grandparents yes, but beyond that, that ghostly line who ply in my body their features, habits, and attitudes, their names are lost to me. I need your aide to unlock the vault of memory that I may clearly state the line of my people."

Night and day, he kept he fire burning, his every moment spent on his knees before the stone altar chanting the same prayer over and over. The bleating from his pens rapidly diminished, until only three days remained before he was to appear before the judges and conclude his challenge with Angantýr.

Though he continued to pray as fervently as ever, a thought had begun creeping into his mind demanding attention as the challenge date drew near. "Since I have no hope of defeating him it is better to face him in combat and die by the blade than to bear the shame of loss."

He tossed another pine fagot into the fire. The greedy flames reached out and leapt to life. The black stones glowed from the steady heat and the coating of fat melted from the daily offerings.

Moved by Óttar's constant stream of prayer, Freyja swept from her seat on Hyfiaberg, a golden spark drifting down from the sky, to take form and step lightly from the altar flames. She smiled on the weary, soot–smudged face of the young man who knelt before her. "You have been heard. I am here to help."

Óttar choked, tried to rise to his feet then collapsed, tears streaming down his cheeks, while he stammered blessings and greetings. Freyja pressed a silencing finger against his lips. "You have asked for knowledge of your ancestors, your line back to the beginning. I do not have this knowledge." Óttar started and began to speak when Freyja shushed him again. "But I know who does. And to enlist her aid will take cunning for she is an untrusting creature, not given to helping others."

With crooked finger, she beckoned him to a wide, clear space away from the altar. "We must trick her. I will need to disguise you, so you can hear her words, but not be seen. She dwells a long way distant, and I cannot carry you, but…" her eyes twinkled, "you can carry me." With those words, she pulled a burning branch from the flames and snuffed it in the dirt. "Stay where you are. This will not hurt." Quickly she drew symbols in a circle around the kneeling Óttar, then jammed the stick back into the flames until the fire roared.

The young man's shoulders hunched, and he fell forward. He felt his ears lengthen and his nose stretch into a snout. His fingers merged into cloven toes and yellow bristles sprouted along his arms. He tried to shout, but only a sharp barking noise came from his lips. On his back, he felt a leather saddle behind his shoulders and strapped under his chest. He watched as Freyja stepped to one side, hands on her hips, a satisfied smile filling her face. "There! Now you look just like Gullinbursti, my brother's battle boar. But more than just looks, you have his abilities. We have to travel, and swiftly, to be back in time for your challenge."

Straddling the boar's broad back, she directed his head towards the north. "We travel to the cave of Hyndla. She is an etin, old beyond years, and nearly as wise as the ancient seeress herself." She tapped her heels against his ribs and the boar launched himself into the air, his golden bristles lighting the way.

Travel was swift as they crossed broad forests and wide expanses of water. Óttar barked his pleasure as they swept through the sky, but he let out a low squeal as the land shifted from lush green to snow swept rocky ridges where frost still held sway. At Freyja's command, they landed outside the dark mouth of a rocky cave. The glow from his bristles illuminated a narrow circle of barren earth and barely penetrated the shadow that marked the cave's entrance.

Freyja sat up straight in the saddle and called out. "Hyndla! Awake sister from your rest. I journey to Valhalla. The way is long and dark, and I would have a friend accompany me to pass the time."

A sharp voice grumbled from the cave depths. "I know you, daughter of Njord. We are not sisters nor are we friends. Go away."

Freyja pouted and crossed her arms. "Why do you say that, of course we are friends?" She shook her head. "Is it that you fear for your safety? Have no fear. I will that pray Thor keeps watch over you. Though he has no love for etins, he will hear my words and promise never to do you ill in any way nor let ill befall you from others."

Hyndla shuffled from the cave, a hand raised to shield her eyes from the boar's light.

"You ride a boar. What happened to your cats?"

Freyja grinned and thumped the boar on its side, a soft grunt of pleasure at the attention echoed through the air. "The way is dark. I borrowed Gullinbursti from my brother that I might ride through the gloom unimpeded." She beamed a welcoming smile. "Come join me. Take a wolf mount from your pen and let us be off."

Frowning, Hyndla stepped forward and bent to examine the boar's face. For long moments, she peered into the boar's oddly pale blue eyes, then snorted, and pushed herself straight. "It is said that Freyr's boar is the swiftest of mounts. I'll not tire my wolves trying to keep pace on the road to Valhalla."

Freyja patted the open saddle space behind her. "Then let us both ride the boar. Come. Climb atop. There is plenty of room and my mount is sturdy. The boar blinked his eyes at the giantess, noting her size, then twisted his head so he could just see Freyja perched atop his back.

The goddess gave him a reassuring thump on his shoulder and waved Hyndla to join her. The boar grunted with the added weight as Hyndla climbed the slope of his back and settled herself behind Freyja.

When they were air born, the giantess glanced to the sides, watching the passage of land below. "Why do you befriend me now? What is it you want from me?"

Freyja directed the boar to turn west with a nudge of her knee. "Why I only ask for your companionship as I ride to Valhalla. I am bound to aid a hero and devotee, Óttar the Young. He built an altar of piled stones dedicated to me and burned it to glass with constant offerings. He has entered into a contest, and I intend to see he does not fail."

Hyndla leaned back and harrumphed. "You are a poor liar Freyja. Though his form is changed to a boar, the eyes do not lie. They are the pale blue of Óttar the Young. It is your erstwhile charge that you lead on this, his final journey."

Freyja laughed and called over her shoulder. "You are quite mistaken. This is battle-boar, my brother's mount fashioned by the great smith Sindri."

They rode on in silence save for the grinding of Hyndla's teeth. "I know," chirped Freyja, "let's play a game of wits to pass the time. We will recount in order the line of Skjoldungs, Skilfings, Othlings, and Ylfing, from landholder to lord and lady. You can start."

"Your deception is weak. You want to know the lineage of young Óttar here." Hyndla plucked a bristle from the boar's back, eliciting a sharp grunt. "Aye, I will play. But know that my price for winning will be great."

———————

Hyndla screwed up her face, lips pursed, brows peaking as she arranged her thoughts. "You are Óttar, son of Innstein, son of Álf the Old. Álf knew life from Úlf, son of Sæfari, son of Svan the Red. Your father's mother was Hlédís, a priestess of the old ways, sprung from Fróthi, a noble man and Fríaut, a noble woman; both from lines of highest rank.

Authì was their ancestor, a great king born of Halfdan—himself a great king and noble warrior—and Álmveig, daughter of Eymund, king of the Roos and Hildigunn, daughter of Sváva—the Suabian and Sækonung. Their eighteen sons set out to dominate their world. From them sprung the Skjoldungs, Skilfings, Othlings, and Ylfing. All these, Óttar, mark your line.

Dag, son of Halfdan, married Thora. Their sons were: Frathmar, Gyrth, Ám, Jofurmar, the Freki brothers, and Álf the Old – your father's father. On the spindle side was Ketil, son of Klypp, your mother's grandsire. On the spear side was Fróthi – your mother's father and Kári were born to Alf the hero and Hlid. Then Nanna was born, Nokkvi's daughter whose son your father's sister married.

Isolf and Asolf were born to Olmoth and Skurhild, Skekkil's daughter. From them sprung a host of heroes: Gunnar Midwall, Grim the Hardy, Thorir Iron-Shield, Úlf the Gaping, and Brodd and Horvir who recklessly followed Hrolf the Old. Also, there are Hervarth, Hjorvarth, Hrani, Bui, Brami, Barri, Reifnir, Tind, Tyrfing, and two Haddings. Angantýr—the very one with whom you contest—is their sibling and your kin. In Bolm in Eastland twelve Haddings were born, sons of Arngrim and Eyfura. Berserks all and of your blood, you stupid little man.

Brodd and Horvir were kin to King Jormunrekk, brother through marriage to Sigurd, son of Volsung. Svanhild was the daughter of Sigurd, and his mother was Hjordís daughter of King Hraudung and Eylimi. To Gjuki were born Gunnar, Hogni, and their sister Gudrun who married Sigurd. Gudhorm was stepbrother to all. These too are your kin.

Randver was born to Radbard. Harald Battletooth to Hroerek and Aud, the deep-minded was the daughter of Ivar. All these reckon up your kin among men, for all the good it will do you."

While Hyndla was preoccupied with reciting her knowledge, the boar guided by the pressure of Freyja's knees had made a wide circle and now came to ground before her cave.

The giantess started and glared about, slowly slipping from the boar's back as she took in the scene. "What is going on here? Why have we returned to my home?"

Freyja smiled and patted the boar. "Our mount grew thirsty. I thought to return for a drink. Bring him a cup of memory ale, I'm certain you have a vat in your cave, so he can hold all the words you have spoken and be able to repeat them on the third morning when he must state the line of his kin."

Hyndla's lips drew down about her chin. "I knew this was a trick. Leave me now. I'm tired. You will get nothing more from me." She stomped off, then turned, and shook a finger at Freyja. "And you, my shameless friend, as many have stolen up the front of your dress as have visited from behind. Go away and waste yourself among the he goats."

Freyja's eyes burned, and a dark cloud misted her brown. "You are a vile creature given to vicious attacks. Then know mine. Do as I ask, or I will strike a fire about you and bind you to this place. You will never be able to leave."

Knowing the power Freyja wielded, Hyndla ground her teeth and nodded her head. "I must go to my cave to retrieve the draught. Do not hedge me with flames. I will return."

Grumbling, the giantess disappeared into the darkness, then in a moment reappeared cup in hand, a malicious smile on her lips. "A fire burns, the earth blazes. He who loves life will gladly seek release. Take this cup to Óttar and bid him drink. I've mixed the mead with venom that he will know only an ill life."

Freyja sneered and took the cup. "Though you cast a wicked spell, it will work no harm. By my blessing, he shall know only delicious draughts and the favor of all the gods."

Back before the altar, his form restored, Óttar tipped back the cup and emptied its contents. With a shy smile of thanks, he returned the cup back to Freyja. "Your quest is complete, to learn the line of your family down through the labyrinth of generations. For three days and no more you will be able to recall all that the giantess said. Be assured, she spoke the truth."

Óttar turned to look at his farm, happy to be home. "And what…" he turned around and Freyja was gone. A bright mote spiraled into the sky and disappeared among the clouds.

On the third day people gathered for the special Thing. Many were eager to see the outcome and jibe the looser. Óttar and Angantýr each took their turn climbing through the sanctuary ropes and approaching the judges.

The Law Speaker stepped onto the pledge rock and stamped his staff three times, the sharp clack… clack… clack calling all to silence. "We are gathered here at this special assembly to conclude only one case, that of the land dispute between Óttar the Young, son of Innstein and Angantýr, son of Arngrím. Are both present?"

Both men stepped forward and gave a resounding "Aye."

"As agreed you will each take your place on the pledge rock and state the line of your kin as far back as you can recall. The one who can state their line furthest back without error will win the case. Since it was Óttar who set the time, it will be Angantýr who goes first."

Angantýr shuffled forward and stepped onto the rock as the Law Speaker made way. He looked about at the impassive faces of the judges and the eager grins of the crowd. His tongue rasped over dried lips, and he shoved a loose lock of red hair back from his damp forehead. Three times he cleared his throat.

Angantýr began with his father and brothers, his grandfather and his before him. His grandmothers he recited two generations back. He stated the line of his mother back to her mother's mother before faltering and stumbling to a stop.

When he said no more, the Law Speaker stamped his staff three times and looked at Angantýr. "Have you finished?" The man nervously shoved the lock of hair back from his forehead and nodded. "Then step back and let Óttar come forward."

Óttar strode forward and took his place on the pledge rock. He looked straight into the impassive faces of the judges and ignored the eager grins of the crowd. Taking a deep breath, he glibly recited his pedigree as Hyndla had stated it for him. He missed no one, easily naming many more ancestors than Angantýr could recollect.

A low murmur rose from the crowd as he finished and stepped down. The judges conferred, and none could find fault with the recitation of either plaintiff. But, it was obvious to all that Óttar had overwhelmingly won his case.

The Law Speaker stamped his staff three times against the pledge rock. The sharp clack... clack... clack echoing across the grounds. "We are each obliged to cultivate the oak under which we live. Let this judgment stand and be an end to your contest of pride."

Divergence

The earth smoldered while the sunset turned the hilltops a molten red. The silhouette of a lone figure of a man topped the rise and began a slow, ponderous descent down the rocky hillside, picking his way across the rubble slope to the hard-scrabble farm below. The jangle of warrior's gear sounded in the creeping twilight as he angled towards an elderly farmer leaning on his hoe. The old man wiped sweat from his eyes as he watched the armored figure approach.

The stranger raised a gloved hand and called out as he skipped over the cobbles and flat stones jumbled across the ground. "This holding is small, the ground hard and rocky –hardly worth planting, and its grand hall is nothing but a rickety patchwork of sod and stone. How is it, old man, that you live here?"

The elderly farmer sighed and pushed back the ragged weave binding his forehead. His pale gray eyes scanned the stranger, taking in his worn boots, the ring byrnie scored with slashes but still serviceable, the leather helmet clapped over a nest of graying hair that sprouted from under the edges, the ragged cloak- its hem festering with thistles and grass seed. A small sliver hammer hung at the man's neck, its bright surface worn smooth and shiny from constant fingering. He sighed, his hand sliding up and down the hoe handle, then wandering to the sacred token hanging around his own neck. "It is a gift bestowed on me by good king Olaf for services rendered during the battles of Trondheim. I distinguished myself on the field, driving a back full line of heathens and helping secure the victory for our king. In honor of my service I was gifted this small holding."

"So, you were a follower of Olaf." The warrior ground his teeth and his fingers flexed a moment on the pommel of his sword before falling loosely at his side. "And why were you not with him at Sliklesbad?"

The farmer sniffed and blotted a tear that ran down his cheek. "I caught a great sickness and was too weak to effectively wield a weapon. By the time I had regained my strength, it was too late. Canute had won."

The stranger dragged a toe of his boot across the dry clay, sniffed and passed his gaze to the hills and sky before turning it back to the farmer. "I am surprised you were allowed to keep this farm. Did you bend a knee to Canute and ask his indulgence?"

The farmer frowned and rapidly shook his head. "Never! But it is as you say. I had feared with Olaf's death that it would be taken from me, but my faith in Olaf never faltered, and while I expected it every day, no one ever came to reclaim this land. Now he is called a saint and I need never fear losing his gift."

The stranger slowly crushed a dry clod of clay beneath his boot. The clod crumbled into powder as he slowly ground it beneath his heel. "It is poor land, little given to drinking water. No wonder it was not taken back. A pitiful giver this saintly king, if this land is any indication of his wealth. And to bestow such land on a warrior..." He grunted and tossed his cape over one shoulder baring the long sword strapped at his side. "Better he had chopped up his gold arm rings and passed them out to the men, then all would have known his true beneficence and the honor he held for your service."

The farmer snorted and lifted his chin. The late sun set his features aglow, shifting the lines of weariness into deep black fissures that seemed to resolve his cheeks and jaw into flat, determined plains. "It is better than begging. A farm of your own is better, even if it is small, than owning nothing. I labored for years in the service of kings with nothing of my own save my blade. I was no one, with no place save where I might sleep for the night. Now this place is my home, and everyone is someone at home."

A short chuckle hiccupped the warrior's chest and he turned his gazed away from the farmer. They stood a moment in silence listening to the wind whistle over the field and the low babble of a nearby spring winding down the hillside. The stranger shifted his stance and rolled his shoulders. "My trek has been long. I could do with a rest and something to drink. Has it been so long that you have forgotten the ancient rules of hospitality?"

The old man jerked his chin towards the sound of water gurgling in the shadows. "If you thirst, there is water over there. If it is rest you seek," he gestured with his hoe towards a large flat rock angling from the ground nearby, "then sit down on that rock."

The warrior sauntered over and propped his foot against the slab. "Generous and brave men live the best and seldom harbor anxiety, but the coward is afraid of everything. You turn me away from your door. Are you afraid of me farmer?"

The old man shook his head and fingered the sacred token hanging around his neck. "Afraid? No. My larder is bare, and I can offer you no better refreshment. My hut is ill-thatched. There is little difference between sitting inside and sitting under the sky. I offer nothing because I have nothing."

The warrior folded his arms across his chest and spat to one side. "Yet you live. And by the looks of things have done so for some time."

The farmer turned his hoe over, listlessly dragging its edge back and forth through the dirt. "In Spring, I harrow the thirsty field, working the manure of winter deep into the soil that it may drink up new life. In Summer, I clear back the weeds and hope for rain. In Fall, I harvest what little has grown and store all that I can. In Winter, I huddle in my hut and try to stay warm."

He dragged a hand across his face, over his head, and squeezed the back of his neck. "These days my wants are few. Each day I eat a little, I work a little, and I sleep when the need comes. With the passing of each year, my hair grows thinner, and it seems I lean a more heavily on my hoe."

The warrior scratched his chin, dragging his fingers through a beard long flecked with gray. "To that I will agree, you are grown old, your ear pressed to the ground, eagerly awaiting the footsteps of an unseen visitor. You are not like you were in your younger days when we fought for the joy of each waking breath and the quiet rest of a day well lived." He planted a fist on his hip and beckoned with the finger of his free hand. "Come now, don't you recognize your old comrade?

In the fading light, the farmer squinted hard at the face lined with the ravages of years. Searching the brow, the eyes, the lips for any recognition, he shook his head slowly from side to side.

The warrior thumped a fist to his chest. "Remember the battle of two hills? How the first rains of summer poured down on our position nearly flooding us out of our shelter? And we, trembling from the icy waters, hunkered together while streaks of fire scored the sky, and the air rumbled as bright vafer flickered across the heavens and flared among the trees?"

The farmer started, then seemed to wither into himself as his eyes turned away to search the ground at his feet. "Aye. I know you now."

A broad smile lit the warrior's face. "As well you should. To ward ourselves against the cold, we shared the tales of our lives, the truths stretched no farther than they could go. Talking and laughing, we tossed damp fagots on the fire to gutter and sputter in the ring before us. Oh, to be back again on that field of battle well-won, hunkered 'round the fire while the rain poured down, trusting comrades in arms."

The old man nodded, his eyes misting with the memory. "Aye. It would be grand."

"Grand!" A sneer slashed across the warrior's face, then quickly faded as he turned his eyes to the setting sun. "Once I found a lance lying in the dirt of an ancient field, shaft broken, tip bent, the stains of war crusted along its edge, and I wept remembering how we had stood side-by-side before the endless tide of foes, trusted companions to each other's right hand.

But now sea waves gently raise their head and murmur, 'Unjust,' when I recall your back as you turned away to follow another, leaving me behind to battle on my own. Fickle is man's love, so, too, his friendship, as purpose drifts and dies with the passage of years.

I searched long and hard to find you, across many lands, following a thread here, a passing conversation there. And when I do find you, what have I found, but a husk of what used to be.

So, I leave you here to fend for yourself until decrepit age finds you crouched before the hearth of a son, a brother, a friend, or a stranger, trying to stir the lingering coals to a blaze. Your welcome over-stayed and the days, grown desolate and weary with the aches of time, linger and sigh to each other.

With each rasping stroke at the embers, a roaring storm rattles the chimney, and you bend close to the fire trembling with cold. And while your heart dreams of battles once broken by your hands and the remembered embrace of love, a straw death grips fast your limbs and the moon like a flower, fades and withers away.

Your eyes half open, dulled with the smoke of dreams, peer in anguish at the loss of what you once held dear. And like the hare grown old playing in the sun, you lift your gaze from the ground and gaze about to find the swift things once dreamed of undone and aged whiteness your companion on the trail."

Tears streaming down his cheeks, the old man reached out to tug the warrior's cloak. "Will you pass this way again?"

The soldier jerked his cloak from the farmer's feeble grip and turned away. As he climbed the hill, he called back over his shoulder. "You ask if I intend to return. Not for some time for duty and honor call me elsewhere."

Glossary

Ægir / Œgir / AEgir: Personification of the deep sea. The god who presides over winds and the stormy sea. He is the husband of Ran. (See also Hlér.)

Ægir's daughters: The nine daughters who are the personification of the ocean waves. Also considered the nine mothers of Heimdall and the nine giant maidens that turn the mondul of the World Mill.

Æsir / AEsir: (Sing) The gods of Asgard. The family clan name of Odin.

Ai: (Great Grandfather) 1) A dwarf of Motsognir's clan. 2) A dwarf of Lofar's clan. 3) A river.

Alething: King, Leader, Ruler.

Alf: (Elf) A dwarf of Lofar's clan.

Alfar: (alfari – to go far away) Sacrificial feast dedicated to those who had gone away. The alfablöt took place on a certain day in the late fall. The feast may have been a kind of ancestor worship; the alfar the souls of the departed.

Alfheim: (Elf home, Elf Land) The third world. World/country of the Light Elves (See Nine Worlds.)

Alfodur / Alfather / Aldafodur: (Father of Men, Father of All) A name for Odin. (See also Odin Men Names, Odin God Names, and Odin Battle Names.)

Alsvinn: (All Swift) A steed of the Sun. Together with the steed Arvak, they pull the wain of the sun. (See also Arvak.)

Althiôf: (Master-thief, All thief, An accomplished rascal.) A dwarf of Motsognir's clan. (See also Wizards.)

Alsviss: (The all wise.) A dwarf who joins in a contest of wisdom with Thor. Thor defeats him by keeping him talking until the sun rises and turns him to stone.

Alvit: A Valkyrie. (See Hervor.)

Always Young: Idun's grove beneath the protecting canopy of Yggdrasil. Here she grows and prepares the apples of immortal youth.

Amsvartnir: The dark lake surrounding the rocky island of Lyngvi where the Fenris wolf lies chained until Ragnarok.

An: (Now, Then, Still.) A dwarf of Motsognir's clan.

Anar: (Rushing river.) A dwarf of Motsognir's clan.

Andhrímnir: (Sooty in the face.) The cook of Valhalla. (See also Eldhrímnir and Saehrímnir.)

Andlang: (Long and Wide.) A dimension of Alfheim, it is the length and breadth of the land of the light elves. (See also Vidblain.)

Angrboda / Angrbotha: (Boder of Ill. Anguish Creating.) 1) Mother of the Fenris wolf, Hel/Leikin, and Jormungand (the Midgard Serpent) – Loki is their father. She later becomes the wife of Gymir. 2) A giantess. (See also Aurboda and Hyrokkin.) 3) Some sources consider Aurboda, Angrboda and Hyrokkin to be alternate names of the same being, the thrice burnt and thrice reborn giantess known as Gullveig-Heid in Voluspa.

Animals of Yggdrasil:

- **Are:** (?) A great eagle perched high amid the limbs of Yggdrasil.

- **Dain** (Sleep.), **Dvalin** (Delayer.), **Duneyr** (To resound/snore.), **Durathror** (To nap.): Stags that browse on the leaves of Yggdrasil.

- **Eikthyrnir:** (Oak Antlers.) The hart that lives among the branches of Yggdrasil. Dew collects on his horns and flows off in mighty rivers to the Hvergelmir fountain.

- **Gullinkambi:** (Golden Comb.) He perches on the top limbs of Yggdrasil. His call announces Ragnarok to the Æsir.

- **Heidrun:** (Heath runner, Bright-running.) The goat that stands over Valhalla, from whose udder flows endless mead.

- **Ratatosk:** (Drill Tooth, Rat Tusk.) The squirrel that carries messages and antagonizing gossip between the eagle above and the serpent below.

- **Vedrfolnir:** (Wind Bleached.) The hawk that sits between the eyes of the great eagle perched high amid the limbs of Yggdrasil.

Annar / Onarr: (Water, Next, Second.) 1) The second husband of Nott (Night) and the father of Fjorgyn – the earth. 2) A giant.

Are / Ari: (Charge, invasion.) 1) The great eagle perched high amid the limbs of Yggdrasil. 2) The dun-hued eagle whose perch is high in mountains in Niflhel. From his perch the glittering plains of Niflheim and the frozen lands of Niflhel can be seen. His scream announces the launch of Naglfar – the ship of the dead. 3) Ar: a mote in a sunbeam.

Arvak: (Early awake.) Together with the steed Alsvinn, they pull the wain of the sun. (See also Alsvinn.)

Arval: Spirits of the past.

As / Ás / Ass: God, Gods.

Asa: Æsir

Asbrau: The Rainbow Bridge of the Æsir that stretches between Asgard and Midgard. (See also Bifrost.)

Asgard: The first world. Garth/fortress home of the Asas/Æsir. (See Nine Worlds.)

Ask / Askr: (Ash.) The first man created by the gods from an ash tree; he is supple and strong. (See also Embla.)

Asynja / Ásynja / Asynjor: Goddess, Goddesses.

asmegir / ásmegir: 1) Sons of Asas who dwell in the lower world (i.e., in and about Mimir's grove). 2) A reference to Dwarves.

Atrith: (Attacker by Horse?) A name for Odin. (See also Odin Men Names, Odin God Names, and Odin Battle Names.)

Audhumla: (Void, Vacuity, darkness, tenebrosity—a state of darkness or gloom.) The primal cow whose milk feeds Ymir. She licks Bur out of the ice. From her udders flow the milk/seed of life.

Aud: (Wealth.) The son of Nott (Night) and Naglfari (the jagged nail).

Aurgelmir: (Mud Bellower.) The name given to the primal giant, Ymir, by his decedents the Frost giants. (See also Ymir.)

Aurboda: (Mud Creating, Snow, Rain, Storm. To announce.) Wife of the giant Gymir and mother of Gerd – Freyr's lover. Some sources consider Aurboda, Angrboda and Hyrokkin to be alternate names of the same being, the thrice burnt and thrice reborn giantess known as Gullveig-Heid in Voluspa.

Aurvang: (Loamfield.) A dwarf and member of Durun's Clan.

Austri: (The East.) 1) The eastern pillar that supports the skull of Ymir – the sky. 2) A dwarf of Motsognir's clan. (See also Nordi, Sudri, Vestri.)

Baldur: (The Glorious.) Son of Odin and Frigg. He is the personification of innocence and the god of summer. He is killed by an arrow of mistletoe shot by Hodd.

Báleyg / Baleygr: (Bale-eyed, Flame-eyed, Fiery-Eyed.) Endowed with clear piercing vision. A name for Odin. (See also Odin Men Names, Odin God Names, and Odin Battle Names.)

Bana ord: A subterranean judgment delivered at the Thing of Urd. (See also dauda ord, feigdar ord, urdar ord, and namaeli.)

Barri: (The needles of pine.) The sheltered pine grove where Gerd and Freyr consummate their marriage.

Battleboar / Battleswine: The golden mount of Freyr. Crafted by Sindri, its bristles light the murkiest gloom. (See also Gullinburtsi.)

Battle Strike: A blow inflicted to the back of the head.

Batua stones: Stones raised in commemoration of others living or dead. The stones are often edged with carved runes telling the story of the event or person.

Bavör: A dwarf of Motsognir's clan.

Behmer Wold: (German) A tract of open rolling country (especially upland) in Bohemia (home of the Boii).

Beli: (The Bellower.) The Howler giant slain by Freyr with a horn from the great hart Eikthyrnir.

Bergelmir: (The Mountain old.) The old man of the Mountain. A frost giant. The only frost giant who with his family survive the flood of Ymir's blood. From him the race of Frost giants continues.

Bestla / Beistla: Born out of Ymir's armpit with her brother Mimir, she is the mother of Odin, Vili/Villi (Haenir/Hoenir), and Ve (Lodur). From them rises the clan of the Æsir.

Beyla: She is Freyr's attendant and the wife of Bygver who directs the World Mill.

Beylist / Beyleipt / Beyleiptr: (Flame of the Dwelling.) The brother of Loki.

Biflindi / Blindi: (Blind One.) A name for Odin. (See also Odin Men Names, Odin God Names, and Odin Battle Names.)

Bifrost: (The rainbow.) The great bridge of the Æsir that stretches between Asgard and Midgard. Also called Asbrau, Bilrost, Rainbow Bridge, Windheim bridge, Trembling Way, Quivering Way, Bil's Way, and the Primrose path.

Bil: (The waning moon.) The daughter of Vidfinn/Ivalde, who, along with her brother Hiuki, Mani, the moon, abducted to aide him in his nightly work. (See also Hiuki.)

Bild: (Bright, Twinkle, Reflection.) A dwarf and member of Durun's Clan.

Bileyg: (Weak-eyed, One-Eyed.) A name for Odin. (See also Odin Men Names, Odin God Names, and Odin Battle Names.)

Billing: (Twilight.) 1) He guards the gate of the setting sun that lies in the west in the forest of the Varinians. 2) A dwarf and member of Durun's Clan.

billow swine: Net.

Bilskirnir: (Wide and Bright. Storm-Stilling.) Imparting serenity to the tempest. The hall of Thor, built in Thrudvanger (the plains of strength).

Bivör: (The Tremulous.) A dwarf of Motsognir's clan.

Blikjandabol: (Gleaming Disaster.) The bed curtains of Leikin/Hel.

Blöt: 1) Sacrifice. 2) A sacrificial feast or banquet.

Bodn: (Altar, obligation.) One of the three vats or casks that hold the precious mead. (See also Son and Odrerir.)

Bolthor: Bestla's father and Odin's maternal grandfather. (For the interpretation used in this work, Bolthor is another name for Ymir and the famous son of Bolthor is Mimir.)

Bolthorn: (Calamitous/Evil thorn or wood.) A frost giant.

Bölverkr: (The evil doer, Working terrible things.) The giant's name for Odin.

Bolverk: (Bale-Worker.) A name for Odin. This is not a name from men, but a name given to Odin by the etins/giants. In some sources, it is translated to refer to evil worker (Bölverkr). However, since it initially occurs in reference to Odin taking on the duties of a farmhand for Suttung's brother, bale worker seems more consistent. (See also Odin Men Names, Odin God Names, and Odin Battle Names.)

Bömbur: (Swollen, Born.) A dwarf of Motsognir's clan.

Bor / Borr: (Born, to bear.) He is the son of Burr and father of Odin, Vili/Villi (Haenir/Hoenir), and Ve (Lodur). From them came the race of the Æsir.

Braggi / Bragi / Brage / Bragr: (The Eloquent.) God of music and poetry. The skald of the gods, he is considered the best/foremost; the most eloquent.

Bragarœdur: The speeches of Bragi. The stories of the gods.

Breidablik: (To gleam or twinkle.) The hall of Baldur.

Brising / Brisingamen: (Flaming.) The chest and neck ornament of Freyja. Crafted by Dvalin and his brother smiths, it is the greatest of all necklaces.

Brow Moons: Eyes.

Brynhilda / Brynhild / Hild: (Battle Helmet, Helmet, Lady of the Battle Helmet.) Chief among the Valkyrie, she is Odin's favorite.

Bûri: (Born, To bear.) A dwarf and member of Durun's Clan.

Burr / Burl: (Son.) The primal ancestor of the Æsir, he was licked clear of the Elivagar ice by the great cow Adhumla. He is the father of Bor.

Beyla: Wife of the dwarf Byggvir who runs the World Mill.

Byrgir: (The Hidden.) The spring of song mead found by Vidfinn/Ivalde. Mani, the moon, took Vidfinn's son and daughter (Hiuki and Bil) as they gathered the mead for their father.

Byggvir / Bygver: The dwarf who runs the World Mill. His wife is called Beyla.

Byleistr: (Whirlwind from the east.) A giant.

Byrnie: A vest or coat made of or covered with metal rings. It is the warrior's protection in battle. (Also, mailcoat.)

Calve / Calving: To release or throw off from itself, as in the process of a glacier throwing off blocks of ice (calves).

Carve an eagle: (See Ristaörn).

Cranog: A man-made island constructed of a base of closely set pylons bound together and surfaced with dirt. Homes were then built on these "islands".

Dagr: (Day.) Son of Delling and Nott (Night).

Dain: (Sleep, The Sleepy.) 1) One of the stags that browse on the leaves of Yggdrasil. (See also Dvalin, Duneyr, and Durathror.) 2) A dwarf of Motsognir's clan.

Dauda ord: The judgment of death delivered at the Thing of Urd. Capital punishment. (See also bana ord, feigdar ord, urdar ord, and namaeli.)

Deluder / Dvalin's Deluder: The dwarf's name for the sun.

Delling: (Daybreak, Dayspring, Sunrise.) 1) He guards the gates of the morning sun. 2) A dwarf and member of Durun's Clan.

Disir: Spirits that accompany people. Good spirits help. Evil spirits plague men, especially during battle.

Dolgthraisir: (The Contentious.) A dwarf of Lofar's clan.

Domar: Judge.

Drápa: A form of skaldic poetry, Drápa refers to a long series of stanzas (usually dróttkvætt), with a refrain at intervals. The dróttkvætt (or lordly verse) stanza had eight lines, each having usually three lifts and almost invariably six syllables.

Draupnir: (The Dropper, the dripper.) 1) The wealth-giving arm ring of Odin. It drops eight rings of equal weight every ninth night. It is a remnant of Andvari's hoard that was taken from the dwarf by Loki to pay the God's ransom for the death of Otter. This sets off a chain of events that comprise the Sigurd/Gudrun/Rhine Gold myth. 2) A dwarf of Lofar's clan.

Dromi: (The strongly binding.) The second shackle the Æsir attempt to use to bind the Fenris wolf. He snapped it with a flex of his limbs. (See also Laeding and Gleipnir.)

Duneyr / Duneyrr: (A hollow sound, to resound, to snore.) One of the stags that browse on the leaves of Yggdrasil. (See also Dain, Dvalin, and Durathror.)

Durathror: (To nap.) One of the stags that browse on the leaves of Yggdrasil. (See also Dain, Dvalin, and Duneyr.)

Dvalin: (Delayer, Sleep.) 1) One of the stags that browse on the leaves of Yggdrasil. (See also Dain, Duneyr, and Durathror.) 2) A dwarf of Motsognir's clan.

Dwarves: *Durun's Clan.*

- **Aurvang:** (Loamfield).
- **Bild:** (Bright, Twinkle, Reflection).
- **Billing:** (Twilight).
- **Bûri:** (Born).
- **Delling:** (Dayspring, Sunrise).
- **Eikinskiald:** (Oakenshield, Scarlet oak).
- **Fili:** (The thin).
- **Frâr:** (Swift, Lightfooted).
- **Fræg:** (Good, Famous).
- **Fundin:** (Foundling).
- **Hanar:** (Himself a river).
- **Hepti:** (Haft).
- **Hornbori:** (Hornborer).
- **Iari / Jari:** (The Shield).
- **Lôni:** (Sea-pool).
- **Kili:** (The fondling, The spoiled).
- **Nali:** (The Needle).
- **Sviur / Svíarr:** (Smith, Forger).
- **Svigdur:** (The Champion Drinker).
- **Vili:** (The Chooser).

Dwarves: *Motsognir's Clan.*

- **Ai:** (Great Grandfather).
- **Althiôf / Althjof:** (Master-thief, All thief.) (See also Wizards.)
- **An:** (Now, Then, Still).
- **Anar:** (Rushing river).
- **Austri:** (The East).

Glossary

- **Bivör:** (The Tremulous).
- **Bavör / Bavor / Bávǫrr:** A dwarf.
- **Bömbur:** (Swollen, Born).
- **Dain:** (The Sleepy).
- **Dvalin:** (Delayer, Sleep).
- **Gandâlf:** (Staff elf, enchanter.) (See also Wizards.)
- **Litr:** (Wise).
- **Miodvitnir:** (Mead Wolf).
- **Nâr:** (Corpse).
- **Náin / Nâin:** (kinsman) Near.
- **Nidi:** (Dark-of-Moon).
- **Niping / Nipingur:** (Handsome).
- **Nordi:** (The North).
- **Nóri:** (The Inlet) sea loch.
- **Nûr:** (Corpse).
- **Nýi:** (New-moon).
- **Nýrâd:** (New advice).
- **Râdsvid:** (Sharp Counsel).
- **Regin:** (The broad sea).
- **Sudri:** (The South).
- **Thekk:** (Known).
- **Thorin:** (Brave, Daring One).
- **Thrain:** (The Pertinacious).
- **Thrôr:** (Inciter to Strife).
- **Veig:** (Liquor).
- **Vestri:** (The West).
- **Vindâlf:** (Wind elf.) (See also Wizards.)
- **Vitr:** (Color).

Dwarves: *Lofar's Clan.*

- **Ai:** (Great-grandfather.) Also, a river.

- **Alf:** (Elf).
- **Dolgthraisir:** (The Contentious).
- **Draupnir:** (The dripper).
- **Eikinskiald:** (Oakenshield, Scarlet oak).
- **Fialar / Fjalar:** (Multiscent, Multiform, many).
- **Finn:** (Found/Finder, discovered/discoverer).
- **Frosti:** (Frosty).
- **Ginnar:** (Betrayer).
- **Glôi:** (Glow).
- **Hâr:** (Greyhair).
- **Hlævang:** (Lee-plain).
- **Haugspori:** (Mound-river).
- **Heri:** (The Leader).
- **Hliôdôlf / Hljodalfr:** (The Genius).
- **Höggstari:** (Striking Light).
- **Moin:** (Moor dweller).
- **Skafid:** (The Scraper/Shaver).
- **Skirnir / Skirvir:** (The Pure, The Bright, Clear, to become clear).
- **Virvir / Vírvír:** (Alive).
- **Yngvi:** (We all young).

Ear hands: A kenning for the Ears. To catch sounds.

Economical Months: 1) The seven changes of weather which make up the economical year. 2) The seven sons of Mimir.

- **Gormánudr:** The first winter month (October – November).
- **Frermánudr:** Frost Month. (December).
- **Hrútmánudr:** The third month of winter (December – January).
- **Enmánudr:** The last month of winter. (Feb – March).
- **Sólmánudr:** Sun Month. (April – May).

- **Selmánudr:** Pasture Month. (June – July)
- **Kornskurdarmánudr:** Harvest Month. (August – September)

Egdir / Egder: An eagle that appears at Ragnarök. The howling winds from his wings increase the terrors of the final battle.

Eggther: (Sword bearer.) The giant herdsman of Gymir and Angrboda, he watches over the Sword of Victory, and plays his harp when the giants rise up at Ragnarök.

Eikin: (Raging, Wild.) A river that flows into the sea from the land of men (Midgard). (See Rivers.)

Eikinskiald: (Oakenshield, Scarlet oak.) 1) A dwarf of Durun's clan. 2) A dwarf of Lofar's clan.

Einherjar: (The lone warrior, hero.) The warriors selected/chosen from the field of battle dead who have displayed bravery in battle. They are brought to Asgard and split between Odin and Freyja. Half dwell in Odin's hall, Valhalla and half dwell in Freyja's hall, Sessrumnir.

Eir / Eira: (Peace/clemency.) A goddess of the Æsir. She is an attendant of Freyja, and the most skillful in the healing arts. Considered the best of doctors, she gathers simples from all over the earth to cure both wounds and diseases, and it is her province to teach the science of medicine.

Eldhrímnir: (Sooty from the fire.) The kettle used for cooking at Valhalla. (See also Andhrímnir and Saehrímnir.)

Eldskáli: (The fire hall/room.) The fire pit that runs down the center of a hall.

Elivagar: (Ice waves, Storm waves, Stormy rivers.) Primal Chaos. The collective name for the venom cold rivers flowing out of Niflheim. (See also Rivers.)

Elli: (Eld, Old Age.) She wrestles Thor in the Hall of Utgarda-Loki and nearly defeats him until Utgarda-Loki intervenes and stops the match.

Eljudnir: (Sprayed with Snowstorms.) 1) The great hall of the dead. 2) The hall of Leikin/Hel in Niflhel.

Embla: (Vine.) The first woman created by the gods from a vine; she is fruitful and tenacious. (See also Ask.)

Enmánudr: The last month of winter (February – March). One of the seven changes of weather, which make up the economical year. One of the seven sons of Mimir. (See also Gormánudr, Frermánudr, Hrútmánudr, Sólmánudr, Selmánudr, Kornskurdarmánudr.)

Erna: (Brisk, Vigorous.) The wife of Lord—one of the three human sons of Rigg/Heimdall (Lord, Farmer, and Thrall) as he brought culture to the lands of men.

Erinnye: Heipter armed with scourges of thorns. They lead the dead condemned to a second death from the seat of judgment in the lower world to and through the Na-Gates into Niflhel. (See also Heipter.)

Etin: Another name for a giant. (See also Jotun.)

Eylúdr: (Island flour bin, the sea.) Along with Lúdr, they are the millstones of the World Mill that are set in Mt. Hvergelmir. (See also Lúdr.)

Eymyrja: Daughter of the wild fire (Logi).

Færing: A small four-oared boat.

Fal's rain: The fall of javelins and arrows under which Baldur was standing when struck down by Hodd's arrow of mistletoe.

Falhofnir / Falhofner: (Hollow-hoof.) A horse of the Æsir.

Fallandaford: (Falling to Peril.) The threshold of Eljudnir, Leikin/Hel's hall.

Fánn: 1) The name for a mythical serpent / dragon that is painted or engraved. 2) The serpent of eternity/fate.

Farbauti: (Beater of Ships, Ship destroyer, Oak destroyer, The lightning bolt.) The father of Loki. (See also Laufey.)

Farmatýr: (Burden God.) A name for Odin. (See also Odin Men Names, Odin God Names, and Odin Battle Names.)

Fates: (See Nornir/Norns.)

Feigdar ord: (Death judgment.) A judgment determining death at the Thing of Urd. (See also bana ord, dauda ord, urdar ord, and namaeli.)

Fenia: (Gain.) The giantess who along with her sister Menia, is forced to grind out wealth and peace for King Frodi on the millstone Grotti. They ground out everything until the peace was done and war came. Captured by King Mysing from King Frodi, they ground out salt on his ship until the ship sank, and so salted the Ocean. (See also Frodi's peace, Grotti, and Menia.)

Fenrir / Fenris / Fenrisúlfr / Fenriswolf: (Bog Dweller/Bog wolf.) The wolf. Son of Loki and Angerboda. Bound by the gods, he escapes to kill Odin at Ragnarok.

Fensalir: (The Ocean Hall, The Hall of Mists.) Frigg's splendid hall in Asgard.

Fialar / Fjalar: (Multiscent, Multiform, many.) 1) The red cock that awakens the giants at Ragnarok. 2) The giant who retrieves the Sword of Victory from Eggther and delivers it to Surt. 3) The dwarf who, along with Galar, slew Kvasir. 4) A dwarf of Lofar's clan.

Fili: (The thin.) A dwarf and member of Durun's Clan.

Fimbulthul: (Steadily Loud.) A river of Niflheim. One of the eleven venom cold rivers called Elivagar that emptied into the void: Ginnungagap. (See Rivers.)

Fimbulvetr: (Chief of Winters, Extreme Winter, Mighty Winter.) The final portent of Ragnarok, it consists of three harsh winters with no summer in between.

Fimblultyr: (Mighty One.) A name for Odin. (See also Odin Men Names, Odin God Names, and Odin Battle Names.)

Fimkaldr: (Very-Cold.) A frost giant. Father of Vinkaldr and grandfather to Vákaldr.

Finn: (Found/Finder, discovered/discoverer.) A dwarf of Lofar's clan.

Fiolnir / Fjolnir: (The Concealer.) A name for Odin. (See also Odin Men Names, Odin God Names, and Odin Battle Names.)

Fiolsvith / Fjolsvith: (The Very Wise, Much-Wise.) A name for Odin. (See also Odin Men Names, Odin God Names, and Odin Battle Names.)

Fiorgyn / Fjorgyn: (Earth, Mother Earth.) The personification of earth. Frigg's mother or– in some interpretations– another name for Frigg. She is also referred to as Hlodyn, Thor's mother.

Fiorm / Fjorm: (Hurrying.) A river of Niflheim. One of the eleven venom cold rivers called Elivagar that emptied into the void: Ginnungagap. (See Rivers.)

Fletta: Plaited/braided hair.

Folkvang: (The Warriors' Fields.) The place where stands Freyja's hall, Sessrumnir.

Fornjótr: (Old Giant, Old Jute.) A frost giant.

Forseti: (The Fore-seated, He Who Sits Foremost, The Presiding One.) The great arbiter of the gods. He is the son of Baldur and Nanna.

Frâr: (Swift, Lightfooted.) A dwarf and member of Durun's Clan.

Fræg: (Good, Famous) A dwarf and member of Durun's Clan.

Freki: (Grim one.) One of Odin's wolves. Geri is the other.

Frermánudr: Frost Month. (December.) One of the seven changes of weather that make up the economical year. One of the seven sons of Mimir. (See also Gormánudr, Hrútmánudr, Enmánudr, Sólmánudr, Selmánudr, Kornskurdarmánudr.)

Freyr: (Lord.) The god of summer, fertility and prosperity. The Seminator. The Fructifier. He is the son of Njord and brother to Freyja. He is the war leader of the Æsir. His mount is Gullinbursti.

Freyja: (Lady.) The Æsir goddess of love, fertility, and war. She can also be considered a goddess of war as she splits the Einherjar with Odin. She is the daughter of Njord and sister to Freyr. She is the equal of Frigg in nobility. She rides into battle on her wain pulled by two cats/Lynxes. Other names she is known by include: Menglad, Mardoll, Horn, Gefn, Syr, and Goddess of the Vanir.

Frigg / Frigga: (Love, The Beloved, The Free, The Beauteous, The Windsome.) She is the wife of Odin and foremost among the Æsir goddesses. Patroness of Housewives. The goddess of the hearth, conjugal and motherly love, motherhood, childbirth, and protector of children. Typically represented as a tall, beautiful, and stately woman, crowned with heron plumes, the symbol of silence or forgetfulness, she is frequently portrayed as wrapped with clouds, either snow-white or dark garments—as per her mood, secured at the waist by a golden belt, from which hung a bunch of keys—the distinctive sign of the Northern housewife.

Frodi's Peace: On a smaller version of the Grotte-Mill the giant sisters Fenia and Menia, slaves captured in battle, ground out gold and safety for Frodi, and good will among men from his kingdom. The peace ended when Frodi, egged on by greed and avarice, refused Fenia and Menia rest from their toil. Angered by this, they ground out fire and death upon him and his kingdom. So, ended Frodi's peace. (See also Fenia and Menia, and Grotti.)

Frosti: (Frosty.) A dwarf of Lofar's clan.

Fulla: (Fullness, Abundance.) A goddess of the Æsir. The handmaiden of Frigg, confidante of, and advisor to her mistress, she is represented with long, hair flowing over her shoulders restrained only by a golden circlet or snood. Because her hair symbolized the golden grain, this circlet represented the binding of the sheaf. Often considered the symbol of the fullness of the earth, she was also known in Germany by the names: Abundia or Abundantia.

Fundin: (Foundling.) A dwarf and member of Durun's Clan.

Fylki: A division of an army.

Gagnráth: (Giving Good Counsel.) A name for Odin. (See also Odin Men Names, Odin God Names, and Odin Battle Names.)

Galar: The dwarf who, along with Fjalar, slew Kvasir.

Galdrar: Enchantment. (See also Gand and Seid.)

Gambansumbl: A banquet of revenge or a drink of revenge.

Gambanteinn / gambanteinn: (Sprout/Twig of Revenge.) 1) Any sword or arrow weapon created by Volund/Thjasse. 2) A standard reference name for any sword. 3) The arrow crafted from mistletoe that felled Baldur.

Gand: Wizardry, Craftsmanship.

Gandâlf: (Staff elf, enchanter.) A dwarf of Motsognir's clan. (See also Wizards.)

Gangleri: (Wanderer, The Way-Weary, The tired wanderer.) A name for Odin. (See also Odin Men Names, Odin God Names, and Odin Battle Names.)

Gannet's bath: A kenning for sea. The gannet is a large water bird.

Garm / Garmr: (Voracious, Devourer, Ravener, to gorge.) The greatest of all hounds, he is bound before Gnipa Cave there to worry the dead until Ragnarok. He and the god Tyr slay each other at Ragnarok.

Gard / Garth: A stockade. A fortification. A home.

Gardrofa: (Fence Breaker.) A horse of the Æsir. The dam of Hofvarpner.

Gastrofnir: (The one refusing admittance to uninvited guests.) The wall surrounding Asgard. It is built of rock, earth, and hard fired clay brick.

Gaut: (God of Goths, God of Men.) A name for Odin. (See also Odin Men Names, Odin God Names, and Odin Battle Names.)

Gefion / Gefjon / Gefjun: (She Who Gives, the earth.) She is the Æsir goddess served by those who die as virgins. She receives all those who die unwedded and makes them happy forever.

Geironul / Geirolul: (Spear feeder.) A Valkyrie.

Geirahod: (The Spear warrior.) A Valkyrie.

Geirskogul: (Spear point/promontory.) A Valkyrie.

Geitir: (The Goat.) A frost giant.

Gerd: (To gird.) A giantess. Wife of Freyr. Daughter of Gymir and Angrboda.

Gerrion: Landslide.

Geri: (Greedy one.) One of Odin's wolves. Freki is the other.

Gervimul: (Spear Teaming.) A river that flows past the home of the gods. (See Rivers.)

Giants / Etin / Jotun / Thurs:

- **Annar:** (Water.) A giant.
- **Angrboda / Angurboda:** (Anguish creating.) A giantess.
- **Aurgelmir:** (Mud Bellower.) The first giant. (See also Ymir.)
- **Aurboda:** (Mud creating, Snow, Rain, Storm. To announce.) A giantess.
- **Beli:** (The Bellower.) A frost giant.
- **Bergelmir:** (The Mountain old.) A frost giant.
- **Bolthorn:** (Calamitous/Evil thorn or wood.) A frost giant.
- **Byleistr:** (Whirlwind from the east.) A giant.
- **Elli:** (Eld, Old Age.) A giantess.
- **Farbauti:** (Beater of Ships.) A giant.
- **Fenia:** (Gain.) A giantess.
- **Fimkaldr:** (Very-Cold.) A frost giant.
- **Fornjótr:** (Old Giant, Old Jute.) A frost giant.
- **Geirrod:** A giant who challenged Thor.
- **Gilling:** (Gil/Gill- ravine/gully.) A giant.
- **Geitir:** (The Goat.) A frost giant.
- **Gerd:** (To gird.) A giantess.
- **Grep:** (Hand, The space between the thumb and other fingers on the hand.) The collective name for three etin brothers who guarded the Skerry of Syr.

- **Greip:** (Grip.)
- **Groa:** (Grow.) A giantess.
- **Gunnlod:** (Inviter of War.) A giantess.
- **Gymir:** (The Lamb, The Concealer.) A frost giant.
- **Hlér:** (The Sea, Door, Eavesdropper/Listener.) A frost giant.
- **Hlora:** (Heat.) A giantess.
- **Hraesvelg:** (Corpse Swallower.) A wind giant.
- **Hrimgrimner:** (The Rime Mask/Helmet.) A frost giant.
- **Hrimner:** (The Frost.) A frost giant.
- **Hrungnir:** (Heaped-up.) A stone giant.
- **Hugi:** (The Thought.) A frost giant.
- **Hymir:** (The Dog Headed.) A giant.
- **Hyrrokkin:** (Smoking fire, Shrunk in Fire, The Smokey one shrunk in fire.) A giantess.
- **Jarnsaxa:** (Iron Chopper.) A giantess.
- **Jökull:** (Ice sickle.) A frost giant. (See also Yurkul.)
- **Kári:** (The Wind.) A frost giant.
- **Logi:** (The Wild Fire/Blaze.) A frost giant.
- **Menia:** (Growth.) A giantess.
- **Mokkurkalfi:** (A Dense Cloud.) A clay giant.
- **Naglfari:** (The fingernail.) a giant.
- **Nari / Narvi / Norvi:** (The Binder.) A giant.
- **Rimgrimner:** (The Rime or Frost Mask/Helmet.) A frost giant.
- **Rimner:** (The Rime.) A frost giant.
- **Skrymer:** (Proud One.) A giant.
- **Snær:** (Snow.) A frost giant.
- **Sokkmimir:** (Deep Thinker.) A frost giant.
- **Surt / Surtur:** (The Swart, The Black, Obscure, Invisible, Unintelligible.) A fire giant.
- **Suttung:** (The mead wolf.) A giant.

- **Thjasse / Thjazi:** A giant.
- **Thokk:** (Gratitude or Thanks.) A giantess.
- **Thrudgelmer:** The strange-headed. (Thrud=fortitude.) A frost giant.
- **Thrym:** (Thunderer.) A giant.
- **Thrymheimr:** (The Loud/Noisy One, Noisy Home.) A frost giant.
- **Utgarda-Loki:** A frost giant.
- **Vafthrudner:** (Way Strong, Strong Weave.) A frost giant.
- **Vasad:** (Damp Cold, Sleety.) A frost giant.
- **Vingnir:** (The Winged.) A giant.
- **Vindsvaler:** (Winter Wind.) A frost giant.
- **Vindloni:** (Chill Wind.) A frost giant.
- **Vindsval:** (Deadly Wind.) A frost giant.
- **Vákaldr:** (Spring-Cold.) A frost giant.
- **Vinkaldr:** (Wind-Cold.) A frost giant.
- **Ymir:** (The Roarer.) The first giant.

Gilling: (Gil/Gill—ravine/gully.) A frost giant. Father of Suttung. Son of Surt.

Gillingr: (Gyllingr.) The gilded key to Helgrind (Hel gate), the gate to Niflheim.

Gimlè: (Gem Roof, Fire Shelter, Protected From Fire, heaven.) The shining heaven. The hall of the blessed during and after Ragnarok. Here the righteous dwell after death.

Ginnar: (Betrayer.) A dwarf of Lofar's clan.

Ginnungagap: (The gap of gaps, The great chasm, The Vast, The Beginning.) The great void at the beginning of all things.

Gipta / Gipte: (To give away.) A norn of lower rank (gafe – giver of marriage, audne – giver of wealth, heille – luck/enchantment) that carried out the Goddess of Fate's (Urd's) resolves under which a person received unexpected, almost accidental, good fortune.

Gipul: A river flowing from Hvergelmir that flows past the home of the gods. (See Rivers.)

Gisl: (Sunbeam.) A horse of the Æsir.

Gjallarhorn: (The Loud Horn, The Horn Resounding.) The horn blown by Heimdall to announce the final battle – Ragnarok.

Gjoll: (Noisy, Dazzling Sound.) A river of Niflheim. One of the eleven venom cold rivers collectively called Elivagar that emptied into the void: Ginnungagap. (See Rivers.)

Gladr: (Clear/Bright.) A horse of the Æsir.

Gladsheim: (Glad home.) The abode of joy and bliss. Odin's dwelling and council hall of the Æsir gods.

Glapsvid / Glapsvith: (Seducer, Maddener.) A name for Odin. (See also Odin Men Names, Odin God Names, and Odin Battle Names.)

Glaur: (Glow.) The first spouse of Sol.

Gleipnir: (The Devouring.) The third shackle the Æsir attempt to use to bind the Fenris wolf. He is unable to break this bond and with it is bound on the island of Lyngvi (the sweet broom). (See also Laeding and Dromi.)

Gler: (The glassy.) A horse of the Æsir.

Glitner: (Radiant Place, The glittering.) Forseti's Hall where he dispenses justice.

Glôi: (Glow.) A dwarf of Lofar's clan.

Gna / Gnaa: (Messenger/grumble/mutter.) As the messenger of Frigg, she is sent to different worlds on errands. She rides the horse Hofvarpnir through the air and sees all that happens upon earth; information that she relates back to her mistress. Because she travels with such rapidity through the air, and over land and sea, she is considered the personification of the refreshing breeze.

Gódr tirr: A good reputation. (See also lofs tirr and ords tirr.)

Gods of the Æsir:

- **Baldur:** (The Glorious).
- **Bragi / Bragr:** (The Eloquent).
- **Forseti:** (The Presiding One).
- **Haenir / Hoenir:** (The long legged.) (See Vili/Villi.)
- **Heimdall / Gullintanni:** (Golden Toothed, The one shining above the world).
- **Hermod:** (Warrior / Man of War, Courage of Hosts).
- **Hod / Hodd / Hodder:** (Warrior).
- **Lodur:** (To Flame.) (See Ve.)
- **Loki:** (The Ender.) Also called Loptr (The Arial) and Hvethrungr.
- **Njord:** (Humid).
- **Magni:** (The Strong).
- **Modi / Móthi:** (The Courageous).
- **Od/Odd:** (Point, First, Leader, One).
- **Odin:** (To wade through).
- **Skirnir:** (The bright one. The pure/serene/clear).
- **Thor:** (Thunderer).
- **Tyr:** (God).
- **Ull:** (Wool).
- **Vali /Ali:** (Chooser).
- **Ve:** (Temple, Holy).
- **Vidar / Vithar:** (Far Ruler, The Silent God).
- **Vili / Villi:** (Will).

Goddesses of the Æsir:

- **Eir / Eira:** (Peace/clemency).
- **Freyja:** (Lady).
- **Frigg / Frigga:** (Love, The Beloved, The Free, The Beauteous, The Windsome).
- **Fulla:** (Fullness, Abundance).

- **Gefjon / Gefjun / Gefion:** (She Who Gives, the earth).
- **Gna / Gnaa:** (Messenger, grumble/mutter).
- **Grid:** (A home, a truce/peace/pardon).
- **Hlin:** (Protector).
- **Lofn:** (Love, Loving, Praise).
- **Nanna:** (Bud, as in a tree or flower bud).
- **Saga:** (To foretell, History).
- **Rind:** (The crust of the earth).
- **Sif:** (Affinity).
- **Sigyn / Signý:** (Rising Moon).
- **Sjofn / Sjofin / Sjofna:** (To See).
- **Snotra:** (Neat, To make wise).
- **Syn:** (Refusal, Equity, Truth).
- **Thrud:** (Strength).
- **Var / Vara:** (Beloved, Troth).
- **Vor:** (Careful).

Göll / Goll: (Shriek.) A Valkyrie.

Góinn / Goin: Son of Grafvitnir. A serpent that lives beneath Yggdrasil. (See Serpents.)

Gomul: (Old.) A river that flows past the home of the gods. (See Rivers.)

Gondlir: (Bearer of the Wand.) A name for Odin. (See also Odin Men Names, Odin God Names, and Odin Battle Names.)

Göndul: (Clue, Entangler.) A Valkyrie.

Gopul: (Gaper, Forward Rushing.) A river that flows past the home of the gods. (See Rivers.)

Gormánudr: The first winter month (October – November). One of the seven changes of weather that make up the economical year. One of the seven sons of Mimir. (See also Frermánudr, Hrútmánudr, Enmánudr, Sólmánudr, Selmánudr, Kornskurdarmánudr.)

gormless stare: Dead stare. (For details read "*Grettir's Saga*.")

Gosling bright: Golden.

Grabakr / Graabak: (Gray Back.) A serpent that lives beneath Yggdrasil. (See Serpents.)

Grad: (Greedy.) A river that flows past the home of the gods. (See Rivers.)

Grafvitnir / Grafvitner: (Grave Wolf.) A serpent that lives beneath Yggdrasil. (See Serpents.)

Grafvolludr / Grafvollud: (Field Burrower.) A serpent that lives beneath Yggdrasil. (See Serpents.)

Grep: (Hand, The space between the thumb and other fingers on the hand.) The collective name for the three etin brothers who guard the skerry of Syr where Menglad / Freyja is found.

Greip: (Grip.) 1) One of Heimdall's nine mothers. 2) The first spouse of Ivalde.

Gretta: (To frown, make a wry face).

Grettir: (A frowner, a dragon.) (See Grettir's Saga.)

Grid / Gríd: (A home, a truce/peace/pardon.) A giantess, she is the mother of Vidar.

Grídarvol / Grídarvöll: (Gríd's staff.) The staff Gríd loaned to Thor to aid him in his confrontation with the Jotun, Geirrod. She also loaned Thor her belt of strength and her iron gloves, so he could truthfully assert that he had not brought his own godly weapons with him to the confrontation.

Grím: (Mask, Helmet.) A name for Odin. (See also Odin Men Names, Odin God Names, and Odin Battle Names.)

Grímnir: (Masked one, Helmeted one.) A name for Odin. (See also Odin Men Names, Odin God Names, and Odin Battle Names.)

Groa: (Grow, To grow together, become joined.) 1) Wife of Orvandel. 2) A giantess.

Grjottungard: (Courtyards of rock fields, stone fortress.) The place Thor dueled the giants: Hrungnir and Mokkurkalfi.

Grotti: (Millstones.) The major Grotti refers to the millstones that comprise the World Mill. The lesser Grotti refers to the magic millstones that ground out Frodi's peace. (See also World Mill, Fenia and Menia, and Frodi's peace.)

Gullfaxi: (Golden Mane.) The giant Hrungner's horse. Taken by Thor as duel payment when he killed Hrungner. Thor gave the horse to his son Magi for lifting Hrungner's limb from his neck.

Gullinbursti: (Golden Bristles.) Also called Battle Boar (Hlidigöltr) and Battle Pig/Swine (Hlidisvín). The golden mount of Freyr built by Sindri. He can traverse land, water, and air. His bristles glow to light the way through the darkest gloom.

Gullinkambi: (Golden Comb.) Also called Vidofnir. The golden cock that roosts in the top branches of Yggdrasil/Mimmamirth/Lorad. Its call wakens the Æsir and Einherjar on the day of Ragnarok.

Gulltoppi / Gulltoppr: (Gold Top. Golden Tuft.) Heimdall's horse.

Gullveig: (Gold Thirst, Bright Gold, Mighty Gold.) 1) A daughter of the Vanir, she is burned three times by the Æsir for practicing seid (witchcraft) among men. Each time she was reborn. Her punishment instigates the first war of the world between the Æsir and Vanir. (She is also referred to as Heith—a name frequently borne by witches.) 2) Some sources consider Aurboda, Angrboda and Hyrokkin to be alternate names of the same being, the thrice burnt and thrice reborn giantess known as Gullveig-Heid in Voluspa.

Gun: (Battle.) A Valkyrie.

Gungnir: (Swaying One.) The spear crafted by Volund for Odin. Its tip etched with victory runes can pierce any armor. When thrown it always strikes it mark. When withdrawn it never hangs or catches.

Gunnlod: (Inviter of War.) A giantess. Daughter of Suttung. Odin tricks her into giving up the poetic mead.

Gunnthra / Gunnthro / Gunnthorin: (Battle, Tremble.) A river of Niflheim. One of the eleven venom-cold rivers called Elivagar that emptied into the void: Ginnungagap. (See Rivers.)

Gylfi: A King of Sweden. 1) The king chastised by the goddess, Gefjon. 2) In "The Prose Edda," by Snorri Sturlson, he is presented as a seeker of wisdom.

Gyllir: (Golden.) A horse of the Æsir.

Gymir: (The Lamb, The Concealer.) A frost giant. The father of Gerd, Freyr's wife.

Haenir / Hoenir: (The long legged.) A brother of Odin. (See also Vili/Villi.)

Halls of the Æsir:

- **Bilskirnir:** (Wide and Bright. Storm-Stilling.) The hall of Thor.
- **Breidablik:** (To gleam or twinkle.) The hall of Baldur.
- **Fensalir:** (The Ocean Hall, The Hall of Mists.) The hall of Frigg.
- **Gimli:** (Gem, heaven.) The shining heaven.
- **Gladsheim:** (Glad home.) The abode of joy and council hall of the Æsir gods.
- **Glitner:** (Radiant Place, The glittering.) The hall of Forseti.
- **Himinbjorg:** (Heavenly Protection, The Heavenly Mountains, The All Embracing.) The hall of Heimdall.
- **Hlesey:** (Hler's Island, Sea Island.) The hall of Ægir.
- **Hlidskialf / Hlidskjalf:** (Mountain Watchtower.) Odin's watchtower.
- **Landvidi:** The hall of Vidar.
- **Noatun:** (Place of ships.) The hall of Njord.
- **Ran's Hall:** Built beneath the sea. It is an underwater Valhalla.
- **Sessrumnir:** (Seat-roomy, Hall with many benches and rooms.) The hall of Freyja.
- **Sindri:** (Sparkling).

- **Sokkvabekk:** (Sinking brook, Sunken Bank/Bench.) The hall of Saga.
- **Upsala / Uppsala / Uppsalir:** (Up/High.) The hall of Freyr.
- **Valaskialf / Valaskjalf:** (Silver roofed.) A hall of Odin.
- **Valhalla:** (Hall of the Slain.) Odin's hall for heroes.
- **Vingolf:** (Abode/Hall of Friends, Hall of Bliss.) The sanctuary for the goddesses.
- **Ydalir:** (Dales of the bows.) The hall of Ull.

Hamalt fylking: (Wedge-shaped battle array.) A battle column with wedge head (shaped like a boar's head) that can cleave the stoutest line. (Hamalt fylka: To draw up a wedge-shaped column.)

Hamingje / Fylgjes: A norn of lower rank assigned to each human at birth. The hamingje stays with the person through their entire life, offering counsel and higher moral direction. At the person's death, the hamingje separates and is the chief witness at their final judgment. A hamingje could separate from a person before their death if the person becomes a hideous and bad person. Such a person is bereft of their protection, and at death this is a telling reason for their condemnation.

Hamskerper / Hamskerpir: (Hide-hardener.) A horse of the Æsir. The sire of Hofvarpner.

Hanar: (Himself a river.) A dwarf and member of Durun's Clan.

Hanga-God: (Gallows Lord, God of the hanged.) Name for Odin. (See also Odin Men Names, Odin God Names, and Odin Battle Names.)

Hâr: (Greyhair.) 1) A name of Odin. (See also Odin Men Names, Odin God Names, and Odin Battle Names.) 2) A dwarf of Lofar's clan.

Har / Hár: (The High One, One Eye, The One-eyed.) A name for Odin. (See also Odin Men Names, Odin God Names, and Odin Battle Names.)

Harbard / Hárbarth: (Graybeard.) A name for Odin. (See also Odin Men Names, Odin God Names, and Odin Battle Names.)

Hati Hrodvitnisson: (Hate.) The wolf Hate. Son of Hrodvitni. Companion of Sköll and Managarm, he pursues Mani (the moon). At Ragnarok he is slain by the Varinians, the moon's protectors.

Haugspori: (Mound-river.) A dwarf of Lofar's clan.

Havi: (High One.) A name for Odin. (See also Odin Men Names, Odin God Names, and Odin Battle Names.)

Heart: Thought stone, acorn.

Heidrun / Heidrunr: (Bright-running/runner.) The goat that stands over Valhalla, from whose udder flow endless mead. (See hydromel.)

Heimdall / Gullintanni: (Golden Toothed, The one shining above the world.) The White god. Sentry/Warder of the gods, all white with golden teeth, he stands watch on Bifrost.

Heipter: (Spite.) Erinnyes armed with scourges of thorns, which drive the doomed dead to Niflhel. They lead the dead condemned to a second death from the seat of judgment in the lower world to and through the Na-Gates. (See also Erinnye.)

Heithrún: (Ardent/hot friend.) 1) A goat. 2) A lascivious person.

Hel: (The Concealer, Death, the goddess of death.) Also called Leikin, the daughter of Loki, she rules over the twice-dead in Niflhel.

Helblindi: (Hellblind.) A name for Odin. (See also Odin Men Names, Odin God Names, and Odin Battle Names.)

Helgrind: The gates to Hel's domain, Niflhel. (See also Na-Gates.)

Hepti: (Haft) To take/seize by force. A dwarf and member of Durun's Clan.

Herfjotur: (Fetterer of an Army, War Fetter.) A Valkyrie.

Herfodur: (Father of Hosts.) A name for Odin. (See also Odin Men Names, Odin God Names, and Odin Battle Names.)

Heri: (The Leader.) A dwarf of Lofar's clan.

Herian: (Warrior.) A name for Odin. (See also Odin Men Names, Odin God Names, and Odin Battle Names.)

Heriar: (General.) A name for Odin. (See also Odin Men Names, Odin God Names, and Odin Battle Names.)

Hermod: (Warrior / Man of War, Courage of Hosts.) He rides to Niflhel to ask for Baldur's return. He retrieves the fetter Gleipnir from the dwarves. (See also Od, Skirnir and Svipdag.)

Heror: This arrow (crafted of iron or wood) was sent around the countryside to spread the news of the arrival of an enemy force. Passed from homestead to homestead like a relay, it was a summons for all able-bodied men to take up their arms and join the war levy. Failure to obey the summons was punishable by being outlawed.

Herteit: (War Merry, Glad in Battle.) A name for Odin. (See also Odin Men Names, Odin God Names, and Odin Battle Names.)

Hervor/Alvit: (The strange creature.) A Valkyrie. She is captured by Volund and his brothers but escapes after nine years. (See also Hervor, Hladgud, and Ölrún.)

Hialmberi / Hjálmberi: (Helm-wearer, Helm-bearer.) A name for Odin. (See also Odin Men Names, Odin God Names, and Odin Battle Names.)

Hild: Another name for Brynhilda/Brynhild, she is the foremost among the Valkyrie.

Hild's Sport: Hild is a Valkyrie and her sport is fighting.

Himinbjorg: (Heavenly Protection, The Heavenly Mountains, The all Embracing.) Heimdall's hall built at the northern-most end of Bifrost/Bilrost.

Himinbrjotr / Himinhrjot: (Heaven Breaker. He who bellows against heaven.) The largest ox in Hymir's herd. He is killed by Thor and his head used as bait for the Midgard Serpent.

Hirð: Bodyguard.

Hiuki / Hjuki / Hyuki: (The waxing moon.) The son of Vidfinn/ Ivalde, who along with his sister Bil, were taken by Mani, the moon, to aide him in his nightly work. (See also Bil.)

Hladgud / Hlodver: (The Swan White.) A Valkyrie. She is captured by Volund and his brothers but escapes after nine years. (See also Hervor, Hladgud, and Ölrún.)

Hlævang: (Lee-plain.) A dwarf of Lofar's clan.

Hlér: (The Sea, Door, Eavesdropper/Listener.) 1) Another name of Ægir. 2) A frost giant.

Hlesey: (Hler's Island, Sea Island.) The island hall of AEgir.

Hlidigöltr / Hlidisvín: (Battleboar/Battleswine.) The golden mount of Freyr. (See Gullinbursti.)

Hlidskialf: (Mountain Watchtower. To waver or tremble.) 1) The silver-roofed watch tower of the gods from which Odin can see into all aspects of Midgard and into the lives of men. 2) A slope or declivity.

Hlin: (Protector.) A goddess of the Æsir. She is sent by Frigg to those she wishes protected from danger.

Hliôdôlf / Hljodalfr: (The Genius, Elf of Sound.) A dwarf of Lofar's clan.

Hlodyn: (Earth.) The personification of Earth. Thor's mother. She is also referred to as Fiorgyn/Fjorgyn.

Hlokk: (Noise, Battle sound.) A Valkyrie.

Hlora: (Heat.) Foster parent of Thor. The personification of sheet lightning. (See also Vingnir.)

Hnikar / Hnikuth: (Thruster/Spear Thruster, Victor, Conqueror.) A name for Odin. (See also Odin Men Names, Odin God Names, and Odin Battle Names.)

Hnitborg / Hnitbjorg: (The clinched crags.) The mythological name of the crags where Suttung set his daughter Gunnlod to watch over his hoard of poetical mead.

Hod / Hodd / Hodder / Hoth: (Warrior, War.) The blind god of war. He is the brother of Baldur and is tricked by Loki into killing him with an arrow of mistletoe.

Hofvarpner: (Hoof Kicker.) A horse of the Æsir. The horse of the goddess Gnaa, he can run through the air.

Höggstari: (Striking Light.) A dwarf of Lofar's clan.

Holl: A river that flows into Niflheim from the land of men (Midgard). (See Rivers.)

Holm: A site used for single combat consisting of a circular space marked out by stones.

Hornbori: (Hornborer) A dwarf and member of Durun's Clan.

Horses of the Æsir:

- **Hamskerper / Hamskerpir:** (Hide-hardener).
- **Hofvarpner:** (Hoof Kicker).
- **Falhofnir / Falhofner:** (Hollow-hoof).
- **Gardrofa:** (Fence Breaker).
- **Gisl:** (Sunbeam).
- **Gladr:** (Clear/Bright).
- **Gler:** (The glassy).
- **Gullfaxi:** (Golden Mane).
- **Gulltoppi / Gulltoppr:** (Gold Top. Golden Tuft).
- **Gyllir:** (Golden).
- **Lettfeti:** (Light foot).
- **Silfrintoppr:** (Silver Top).
- **Sinir:** (Thick sinewed).
- **Skiedbrimir:** (Race Runner).
- **Sleipnir:** (The Slippery).

Howe: A burial mound.

Hrafngud / Rafnagud: (The raven god.) A name for Odin. (See also Odin Men Names, Odin God Names, and Odin Battle Names.)

Hraesvelg / Hraesvelgr: (Corpse Swallower.) A giant in eagle shape who sits at the world's end. When he beats his wings, the winds blow over the waves.

Hrid: (Snow Storm.) A river of Niflheim. One of the eleven venom cold rivers called Elivagar that emptied into the void: Ginnungagap. (See Rivers.)

Hrimfaxi: (Frost-maned.) The steed that pulls the wain of Night. Foam from his bitted-mouth sprinkles the land and leaves frost. (See also Skinfaxi.)

Hrimgrimner: (The Rime Mask/Helmet, Frost-Odin.) A frost giant. 1) Hrimgrimner and Rimgrimer may reflect the same name. Many translations drop the H so Hrim- becomes Rim-, Hrungnir becomes Rungnir etc. 2) Possibly another name for Thrudgelmir, the 3 headed (or 6 headed) giant produced from Ymir's feet

Hrimner: (The Frost.) A frost giant.

Hronn: (Wave.) A river that flows into Niflheim from the land of men (Midgard). (See Rivers.)

Hroptatyr / Hroptatýr: (God of Gods.) A name for Odin. (See also Odin Men Names, Odin God Names, and Odin Battle Names.)

Hrungnir: (Heaped-up.) The stone-hearted mountain giant, who challenges Thor to a duel, and loses.

Hrútmánudr: The third month of winter (December – January.) One of the seven changes of weather, which make up the economical year. One of the seven sons of Mimir. (See also Gormánudr, Frermánudr, Enmánudr, Sólmánudr, Selmánudr, Kornskurdarmánudr.)

Hugi: (The Thought.) A frost giant. He defeats Thjalfi, Thor's servant, in a foot race at the hall of Utgarda-Loki.

Hugin and Munin: (Thought and Mind/Remembrance.) The ravens of Odin. They fly across the wide world each day and bring him intelligence on all they have observed.

Húskarlar: The household retinue/servants.

Hvergelmir: (Seething cauldron, Old cauldron, Navel of the world.) Located in Niflheim, this maelstrom is the source of all the rivers of the world.

hydromel: The Asgard mead of the Einherjar, daily furnished by the she-goat Heidrun, who browses continually on the tender leaves and twigs in Yggdrasil's top most branches.

Hyfiaberg: The mountain of healing. It is the seat of Freyja/Menglad.

Hymir: (The Dog Headed.) A Jotun. Father/Stepfather of Tyr.

Hyrrokkin: (Smoking fire, Shrunk in Fire, The Smokey one shrunk in fire.) 1) A giantess. She pushes Baldur's funeral barge out to sea. 2) Some sources consider Aurboda, Angrboda and Hyrokkin to be alternate names of the same being, the thrice burnt and thrice reborn giantess known as Gullveig-Heid in Voluspa.

Iafnhar / Jafnhár: (Equal High.) A name for Odin. (See also Odin Men Names, Odin God Names, and Odin Battle Names.)

Ialk / Jálk: (Lord of Boatloads.) A name for Odin. (See also Odin Men Names, Odin God Names, and Odin Battle Names.)

Iari / Jari: (The Shield.) A dwarf and member of Durun's Clan.

Iarngreiper / Jarngreiper / Jarngreipr: (Iron gripper.) The iron gauntlet of Thor, which allows him to firmly grip and wield the hammer Mjollnir without injuring himself. (See also Megingjard and Mjollnir.)

Idavoll: Eternally Renewing Field, Field of great activity.

Ifing: The wide river that runs between Midgard and Utgard. This formidable barrier protects the land of men from giants. (See Rivers.)

Ingvifreyr, Kin of: The Æsir gods.

Isarnkol: The bellows beneath the shoulders of the Sun's horses, Arvak and Alsvinn, that keeps them cool. The belly shield, Svalin, protects them from the heat.

Itha Plain: The Shining Plain.

Jarnsaxa: (Iron Chopper.) A giantess. She is also the mother of Thor's sons: Magni and Modi.

Jarnvidjur / Jarnvidiur: Dwellers in the Ironwood.

Jökull: (Ice sickle, Glacier.) 1) A frost giant. 2) The giant sons of winter. (See also Yurkul.)

Jormungand: (Great Serpent, Enormous Monster.) The name of the Midgard Serpent, a son of Loki.

Jormungrund: The great ground or foundation.

Jotun: Another name for giant/etin. A dweller in Jotunheim.

Jotunheim: The fifth world. Also called Utgard—the Outer Ward. The land of the Giants. (See, Nine Worlds.)

Kári: (The Wind.) A frost giant.

Kerlaugs: Two rivers along with Kormpt and Ormpt that Thor wades each day. (See Rivers.)

Kettle-grove: The grove around hot springs. Loki is bound by the Æsir in such a grove.

Kialar / Kjalar: (The Keel.) Guider of ships. A name for Odin. (See also Odin Men Names, Odin God Names, and Odin Battle Names.)

Kili: (The fondling, The spoiled.) A dwarf and member of Durun's Clan.

Kirtle: 1) A long gown or dress worn by women. 2) A short tunic worn by men.

Kjafal: A garment with hood at the top, but no sleeves. Open at the sides, it was fastened between the legs with a button.

Knorr: Norse trading ship.

Kor: Sick bed. Leikin/Hel's bed.

Kormpt: (River Bed.) A river along with Ormpt and the two Kerlaugs that Thor wades each day. (See Rivers.)

Kornskurdarmánudr: Harvest Month. (August – September) Grain reaping/cutting/shearing/slaughtering month. One of the seven changes of weather that make up the economical year. One of the seven sons of Mimir. (See also Gormánudr, Frermánudr, Hrútmánudr, Enmánudr, Sólmánudr, Selmánudr.)

Lá: (Blood.) One of the gifts given by Ve to Ask and Embla—the first man and woman. He gave them lá (blood), laeti (the power of conscious movement), and litr goda (an inner body made in the image of the gods).

Laeding: (Fetter.) The first shackle the Æsir attempt to use to bind the Fenris wolf. He snapped it with an easy flex of his limbs. (See also Dromi and Gleipnir.)

Laeti: (Conscious movement.) One of the gifts given by Ve to Ask and Embla—the first man and woman. He gave them lá (blood), laeti (the power of conscious movement), and litr goda (an inner body made in the image of the gods).

Landvidi: Vidar's Hall. Built in Landvide (the primeval forest).

Laufey: (Leafy Island.) Loki's mother. Also called Nal (needle).

Laut: Sacrificial blood that flows from cattle and horses.

Laut bowls: Bowls for holding the sacrificial blood.

Laut-teinar: Bowls made like a sprinkler for showering laut on the stalls and temple walls.

Leifthrasir: (Life Yearner, Life Persister.) The spouse of Líf. Together they are the two of mankind that survive Ragnarok in Hoddmimir's Wood.

Leikin: (The Concealer.) The daughter of Loki. (See also Hel.)

Leiptr: (Flashing Bright.) A river of Niflheim. One of the eleven venom cold rivers called Elivagar that emptied into the void: Ginnungagap. (See Rivers.)

Lettfeti: (Light foot.) A horse of the Æsir.

Líf: (Life.) The spouse of Leifthrasir. Together they are the two of mankind that survive Ragnarok in Hoddmimir's Wood.

Limar: Staff, Scourges of thorns, rods of thorns wielded by heipter.

Lit / Lítt: (Glance, Little.) The dwarf Thor kicked into Baldur's funeral pyre.

Litr: (Wise.) A dwarf of Motsognir's clan.

Litr-goda / Litr: (Color.) Man's inner body made in the image of the gods. It brings a healthy glow to the features. One of the three gifts given by Ve to Ask and Embla, the first man and woman. He gave them lá (blood), laeti (the power of conscious movement), and litr goda (an inner body made in the image of the gods).

Ljóna: Peacemaker.

Ljónar: Those whose business it is to settle disputes and bring peace among conflicting parties. (Among the Æsir these are typically: Baldur, Forseti, and Hodd (Hodder), but may be any of the gods called into service.)

Lodur / Lodurr: (To Flame.) (See Ve.)

Lofn: (Love, Loving, Praise.) A goddess of the Æsir. A mild and gracious maiden, it is her duty to remove all obstacles from the path of lovers and arrange unions between men and women. She inclines obdurate hearts to love, maintains peace and concord among mankind, and reconciles quarrelling husbands and wives.

lofs tirr: A laudatory reputation. (See also gódr tirr and ords tirr.)

Logi: (The Wild Fire/Blaze.) A giant. He defeats Loki in an eating contest that takes place in Udgarda-Loki's hall.

Loki: (The Ender, Hvethrung, Loptr, Ariel.) The god of mischief. Son of Farbauti and Laufey. Father of the Fenris wolf, Hel/Leikin, and Jormungand (the Midgard Serpent). Angrboda is their mother.

Lôni: (Sea-pool.) A dwarf and member of Durun's Clan.

Loptr: (The Aerial.) Another name for Loki. Loki had a pair of shoes that allowed him to fly.

Lúdr: (A trumpet, a flour bin.) Along with Eylúdr, they are the millstones of the World Mill, set in Mt. Hvergelmir. (See also Eylúdr.)

Magni: (The Strong.) A son of Thor and Jarnsaxa. The brother of Modi.

Magn: The liquid from Urd's well. It gives strength (magnar). Also supernatural strength by magical or superhuman means (magna).

Managarm: (Moon Dog, Moon Wolf, Moon devourer.) Brother of Skoll, he wounds and almost swallows the moon at Ragnarok.

mana mjötudr: (The little fruits of man.) The fruit that falls from the great tree Yggdrasil into the saga pond at its roots. Vili/Villi (Haenir/Hoenir), the brother of Odin, carries this fruit to the maternal laps of women, and so confers the gifts on Ask and Embla on newly conceived life.

Mang: Trade, barter.

Master Builder: The giant who bets with the Æsir that he can rebuild the walls of Asgard within the cycle of one season. His price if he wins is the Sun, the Moon, and Freyja. He is tricked into losing by Loki and is slain by Thor.

Menia: (Growth.) The giantess who, along with her sister Fenia, is forced to grind out wealth and peace for King Frodi on the millstone Grotti. They ground out everything until the peace was done and war came. Captured by King Mysing from King Frodi, they ground out salt on his ship until the ship sank. (See also Frodi's peace, Grotti, and Fenia.)

Modi / Móthi: (The Courageous.) A son of Thor and Jarnsaxa. The brother of Magni.

Megingjard / Megingiörd: Thor's belt of strength. When he dons the belt his strength is doubled. (See also Iarngreiper and Mjollnir.)

Midgard: The fourth world. The home of men. (Middle earth/world, The Enclosure, Verland). (See, Nine Worlds.)

Mikligardr: Great City.

Mimer / Mimir: (Mindful, To keep in memory.) He who thinks. He guards the well of knowledge. Given as truce hostage to the Vanir at the end of the first war, they beheaded him for his incisive wit. They send his pickled head back to Odin. Odin revives the head and consults its wisdom in times of need.

Miodvitnir: (Mead Wolf.) A dwarf of Motsognir's clan.

Mjollnir / Miollnir: (The Crusher.) 1) A hammer that breaks or grinds into tiny pieces. 2) The hammer of Thor, crafted by the dwarf Sindri. Because this hammer, the emblem of the thunder bolts, was generally hot, the god had an iron gauntlet (Iarngreiper), which enabled him to grasp it firmly. He could hurl Mjollnir a great distance, and his remarkable strength was doubled when he wore his belt of strength (Megingjard). In Norse culture Thor's hammer (as a symbol) was used to consecrate weddings, events, and even grounds/locations. (See also Iarngreiper and Megingjard.)

Modgud: (Courage, Graceful.) She guards the Gjoll Bridge to ensure only the dead may pass.

Mokkurkalfi: (A dense cloud.) The clay giant created as a comrade in arms for Hrungner in his duel with Thor. He crumbles to pieces before the onslaught of Thor.

Moin / Móinn: (Moor dweller.) 1) A dwarf of Lofar's clan. 2) Son of Grafvitnir. A serpent that lives beneath Yggdrasil. (See Serpents.)

Mondul: Mill sweep.

Moon: 1) Called Mani and "fiery one" by the Æsir. 2) Called the Whirling Wheel in Niflheim 3) Called the Hastener by giants 4) Called the Shiner by dwarves 5) Called "counter of years" by elves.

Most High: A name for Odin referring to his status in council. (See also Odin Men Names, Odin God Names, and Odin Battle Names.)

Mundilfari: The creator of fire (by friction). Once who mechanically creates fire. Some sources consider him to be Lodur, the brother of Odin.

Munin and Hugin: (Mind/Remembrance and Thought.) The ravens of Odin, they fly across the wide world each day and bring him intelligence of all they observed.

Muspellsheim: The sixth world. Home of Surt and the Fire Giants. (See Nine Worlds.)

Na-Gates: The great dark gates that open into the domain of Niflhel.

Nagaikas: Rawhide leather thongs twined with bits of lead. They are wielded by heipter who drive the damned dead to Niflhel.

Naglfar: (Fingernail.) The black ship of the dead constructed from the fingernails of dead men. It will set sail at Ragnarok and bring the host of Niflhel to battle on Vigrid plain.

Naglfari: (The fingernail.) He is the first husband of Nott (Night).

Náin / Nâin: (Kinsman, Near.) A dwarf of Motsognir's clan.

Ná Strand: The Strand of the Dead.

Nal: (Needle.) Loki's mother. Also called Laufey (Leafy Island).

Nali: (The Needle.) A dwarf and member of Durun's Clan.

Namaeli: At the Thing of Urd, this is the judgment in death that sends a person through the Na-Gates to Niflhel. This is a second death and is an opposite judgment from ords tirr. (See also bana ord, dauda ord, feigdar ord, urdar ord, and ords tirr.)

Nanna: (Bud, as in a tree or flower bud.) A goddess of the Æsir. Nepp/Nokkvi's daughter, she is the wife of Baldur. Considered a growth goddess, she is often associated with spring/summer and blossoming/ripening.

Nâr: (Corpse.) A dwarf of Motsognir's clan.

Nari / Narvi / Narfe / Norvi: (The Binder. He who binds.) 1) The father of Nott. 2) The son of Loki who was killed and whose entrails were used to bind his father.

Nidaveller / Nidavellir: The eighth world. Domain of the Dwarves. (See Nine Worlds).

Niddhogg / Nithhogg: (The Dastardly Striking.) The serpent that lives beneath Yggdrasil and gnaws at the roots of the great ash. On the Nastrands in Niflhel he gnaws on corpses. (See Serpents.)

Nidi: (Dark-of-Moon.) A dwarf of Motsognir's clan.

Nidud: King of the Njara. After capturing Volund, he takes his sword and arm ring.

Niflgódur: (Foggy/Corrupted morals.) The damned dead who suffer in Niflhel. They are the dead who, because of their conduct in life, in death received the death judgment: Namaeli.

Niflheim: The ninth world. Dark World/Nebulous home. Here lie the Glittering Plains and Niflhel. The joyous dead reside on the Glittering Plains. Leikin and the doomed (twice-dead) reside in Niflhel. Here too are found the frost giants and their dead. (See: Nine Worlds.)

Nine Mothers of Heimdall:

- **Angeyja:** (Fragrant island).
- **Atla:** (Intend, Purpose).
- **Eistla:** (The Stone).
- **Eyrgjafa:** (Sand Giver, ore/gravel gift).
- **Gjálp:** (Yelper).
- **Greip:** (Grip).
- **Ímd:** (Dust, Ash, Ember).
- **Jarnsaxa:** (Iron Chopper).
- **Ulfrun / Úlfrún:** (Woolen mistress?)

Nine Worlds

- **Asgard:** The first world. The land/home of the Æsir.
- **Vanaheim:** The second world. The land/home of the Vanir
- **Alfheim:** The third world. Elf Land. The country of the Light Elves.
- **Midgard:** The fourth world. The home of men. (Middle earth/world, The Enclosure, Verland.)

- **Jotunheim:** The fifth world. The land/home of the Jotun/Etin/Giants. Also called Utgard—the Outer Ward.
- **Muspellsheim / Muspellsheim:** The sixth world. Home of Surt and the Fire Giants.
- **Svartalfaheim:** The seventh world. Land of the Dark Elves.
- **Nidaveller:** The eighth world. Domain of the Dwarves.
- **Niflheim:** The ninth world. Dark World/Nebulous home. Here lie the Glittering Plains and Niflhel. The joyous dead reside on the Glittering Plains. Leikin and the doomed (twice-dead) reside in Niflhel. Here too are found the frost giants and their dead.

Niping / Nipingur: (Handsome.) A dwarf of Motsognir's clan.

Nitha Fells: Dark Fells.

Njard-locks: Binding locks.

Njord: (Humid.) 1) God of the seas. 2) The Vanir god given as truce hostage to the Æsir after the first war. 3) A man of water and charmed judgment.

Noatun: (Place of ships.) Njord's hall.

Nonn: (Strong.) A river that flows into Niflheim from the land of men. (See Rivers.)

Nordi: (The North.) 1) The northern pillar that supports the skull of Ymir, the sky. 2) A dwarf of Motsognir's clan. (See also Austri, Sudri, Vestri.)

Nóri: (The Inlet, sea loch.) A dwarf of Motsognir's clan.

Nornir / Norns: The three Norns/Fates. Urd/Urdur (Becoming, The past, Fate), Verdandi/Verthandi (Being, The present, To become), Skuld (Shall be, The future, Have become).

Not: (Dark.) A river that flows into Niflheim from the land of men (Midgard). (See Rivers.)

Nott: (Night.) Wife of Annar/Onarr. Daughter of Norve.

Nûr: (Corpse.) A dwarf of Motsognir's clan.

Nýi: (New-moon.) A dwarf of Motsognir's clan.

Nýrâd: (New advice.) A dwarf of Motsognir's clan.

Nyt: (Milk.) A river that flows into Niflheim from the land of men (Midgard). (See Rivers.)

Od / Odd / Oddr: (Point, First, Leader, One.) Husband of Freyja. (See also Svipdag, Hermod, and Skirnir.)

Odin: (To wade through.) Chief among the gods he permeates all things. God of wit and wisdom. (See also Odin Men Names, Odin God Names, and Odin Battle Names.)

Odin Men Names:

- **Aldafodur / Alfather:** (Father of Men, Father of All).
- **Bileyg:** (Weak-eyed, One-Eyed).
- **Bölverkr:** (Evil Worker).
- **Bolverk:** (Bale-Worker).
- **Farmatýr:** (Burden God).
- **Fiolnir / Fjolnir:** (The Concealer).
- **Fiolsvith / Fjolsvith:** (The Very Wise, Much-Wise).
- **The Giver of Victory**
- **Gagnráth:** (Giving Good Counsel).
- **Gangleri:** (Wanderer, The Way-Weary, The tired wanderer).
- **Glapsvid:** (Seducer).
- **Hanga-God:** Gallows Lord, God of the hanged.
- **Har:** (One Eye).
- **Helblindi:** (Hellblind).
- **Hrafngud / Rafnagud:** (The raven god).
- **Kialar / Kjalar:** (The Keel.) Guider of ships.
- **Odin:** (To wade through.) Head of the Æsir clan. Chief of the Æsir gods.
- **Ofnir:** (The Entangler, i.e., entangler with words).
- **Sanngetal:** (Truthfinder).

- **Sath:** (The Truthful).
- **Sidhott / Síthhott:** (Broadhat, Long-Hood).
- **Sidskegg / Síthskegg:** (Broadbeard, Long-Beard).
- **Skilfing / Skilfingr / Skilfung:** (Shaker, Shatterer).
- **Svafnir / Svafinir:** (He Who Lulls to Sleep or Dreams, Put to death).
- **Svipal:** (The Changeable).
- **Thekk:** (Known, The Welcome One).
- **Vegtam:** (Way-tame).
- **Vidrir:** (Ruler/Moderator of Weather).
- **Ygg:** (The Terrible, The Terrifier).

Odin God Names:

- **Alfodur:** (Father of All).
- **Biflindi / Blindi:** (Blind One).
- **Gaut:** (God of Goths, God of Men).
- **Gondlir:** (Bearer of the Wand).
- **Har:** (The High One, One Eye).
- **Harbard / Hárbarth:** (Graybeard).
- **Havi:** (High One).
- **Herfodur:** (Father of Hosts).
- **Hroptatyr / Hroptatýr:** (God of Gods).
- **Ialk / Jálk:** (Lord of Boatloads).
- **Iafnhar / Jafnhár:** (Equal High).
- **Most High:** The highest position in council.
- **Odin:** (To wade through.) Head of the Æsir clan. Chief of the Æsir gods.
- **Omi:** (A sound, a crash).
- **Oski:** (Wish).
- **Skilfing / Skilfingr / Skilfung:** (Shaker, Shatterer).
- **Svidur / Svithur / Svidrir / Svithrir:** (The Wise).

- **Thridi / Thrithi:** (Third, The Third).
- **Thund / Thuth:** (Second?).
- **Thror / Thrór:** (Inciter to Strife).
- **Ud / Uth:** (One?).
- **Vak:** (Wakeful/Alert or Vigilant One).
- **Vifud / Vafud / Váfuth:** (Wayfarer).
- **Ygg:** (Terrible One).

Odin Battle Names:

- **Atríth:** (Attacker by Horse?)
- **Báleyg / Baleygr:** (Bale-eyed, Flame-eyed, Fiery-Eyed.) Endowed with clear piercing vision.
- **Fimblultyr:** (Mighty One).
- **Glapsvid / Glapsvith:** (Maddener).
- **Grím:** (Mask, Helmet).
- **Grímnir:** (Masked one, Helmeted one).
- **Hnikar / Hnikuth:** (Thruster/Spear Thruster, Victor, Conqueror).
- **Heriar:** (General).
- **Herian:** (Warrior).
- **Herteit:** (War Merry, Glad in Battle).
- **Hialmberi / Hjálmberi:** (Helm-wearer, Helm-bearer).
- **Sigfodur / Sigfather:** (War Father, Victory Father).
- **Valfodur / Valfather:** (Father of the Slain, Father of the Battle Slain).
- **Vidur / Vithur:** (Wood, Tree of Battle).

ódr: (Intelligence, personality, and ego) The gifts given by Vili to Ask and Embla—the first man and woman. From these gifts grew understanding, memory, imagination, and resolve.

Odrerir / Óthrœrir: (Mind Exciting.) One of the three vats that hold the precious mead of Skald-ship/poetry. (See also Bodn and Son.)

Odur: The river crossed by Líf and Leifthrasir on their way to Hoddmimir's wood. (See Rivers.)

Ofeig: (Not fated to die.) A name.

Ofnir: (The Entangler.) 1) A name for Odin indicating his ability to entangle others with words. (See also Odin Men Names, Odin God Names, and Odin Battle Names.) 2) A serpent that lives beneath Yggdrasil. (See Serpents.)

Ókólnir / Okólnir: (Ever Cold.) The mountain/field on which stands Brimir, the etin's beer hall.

Ölrún: (Swan, She who is ready for battle.) A Valkyrie. She is captured by Volund and his brothers but escapes after nine years. (See also Hervor, Hladgud, and Ölrún.)

Omi: (A sound, a crash.) A name for Odin. (See also Odin Men Names, Odin God Names, and Odin Battle Names.)

önd: (Spirit) The gift given by Odin to Ask and Embla—the first man and woman. He gave them önd (spirit), breath, and conscious life.

ords tirr: An honorable reputation. Also, an imperishable judgment delivered at the Thing of Urd, which gives the dead fair renown. This is an opposite judgment from namaeli. (See also lofs tirr, gódr tirr, ords tirr, and namaeli.)

Ormpt: (Snaking, Winding?) A river along with Kormpt and the two Kerlaugs/Kerlaugar that Thor wades each day. (See Rivers.)

Orvandel: (Germ.) A great archer, brother of Volund and Slagfin. He is a friend of Thor. He is the husband of Groa and their son is Svipdag. When Groa dies, he marries Sif and has a son named Ull.

Oski: (Wish.) A name for Odin. (See also Odin Men Names, Odin God Names, and Odin Battle Names.)

Peace Weaver: A woman given as a wife to an enemy as a sign of peace. An action typically taken out of political necessity. (Does it work? A statement from the poem, Beowulf, describes its efficacy: "*Seldom does it happen that a spear stays at rest, for even a short while, after a man has been slain, though the bride be splendid.*")

pebble hill: When a gathered host is numerous, and counting is difficult, as each warrior passes they put a pebble on a pile. The size of the pile denotes the size of the troop.

Radgrid: (Counseling Truce.) A Valkyrie.

Rådsvid: (Sharp Counsel.) 1) A dwarf of Motsognir's clan. 2) A Valkyrie.

Ragnarök / Ragnarok: The final battle of Norse Mythology in which the world is destroyed by fire and sinks beneath the sea. Afterward, the world resurfaces fresh and fertile from the sea.

Ran: The goddess of the sea. She is the wife of AEgir.

Randgrid / Randgrith / Ráthgrith: (Shield Truce.) A Valkyrie.

Rauch-Else: (Rough Alice.) From the tale of Wolfdeterich, she was the queen enchanted into a bear.

Ratatosk: (Drill Tooth.) The squirrel who lives on Yggdrasil. He races ceaselessly up and down the trunk carrying messages and gossip between the eagle above and the serpents below.

Red-short: Brittle when red-hot. Said of iron or steel that contains too much sulfur.

Ref-guild: Payment for a slaying that brings a peaceful resolution between two parties.

Regin: (The broad sea.) 1) A dwarf of Motsognir's clan. 2) A shaper or workman. A craftsman. (As in "Regin of the motion of the feather leaf", i.e., a wing or a bird's wing.)

Reginlief: (Dear to the Gods, Vast Life.) A Valkyrie.

Rennandi: (Running, The one Course.) A river that flows past the home of the gods. (See Rivers.)

Rig: The name Heimdall took when creating the classes of human society: Thrall, Farmer, Lord. He was known as Sceaf when bestowing the gifts of civilization. (See also Sceaf of the Scani.)

Rimethurs: Frost Giants

Rimgrimner: (The Rime or Frost Mask/Helmet.) The three-headed clan chief of the frost giants. Hrimgrimner and Rimgrimer may reflect the same name. Many translations drop the H so Hrim- becomes Rim-, Hrungnir becomes Rungnir etc.

Rimner: (The Rime.) A frost giant.

Rin: A river that flows past the home of the gods. (See Rivers.)

Rind: (The crust of the earth.) Mother of Vali. She is driven mad by Odin's use of seid to twist her mind so that he might gain access and impregnate her.

rist: To carve.

Ristaörn: (To Carve an eagle.) An especially bloody dismemberment done to foes—alive or dead—on the field of battle. The sword is stuck into the body by the backbone. The ribs on both sides are cut free down to the loins, then the lungs are pulled out through the incisions.

Rivers:

- **Eikin:** (Raging, Wild.) Flows into the sea from the land of men (Midgard).
- **Elivagar:** (Storm Waves.) The collective name for the primal rivers of Niflheim.
- **Fimbulthul:** (Steadily Loud.) A river of Niflheim. One of the eleven venom cold rivers called Elivagar that emptied into the void: Ginnungagap.
- **Fjorm / Fiorm:** (Hurrying.) A river of Niflheim. One of the eleven venom-cold rivers called Elivagar that emptied into the void: Ginnungagap.
- **Gervimul:** (Spear Teaming.) A river that flows past the home of the gods.
- **Gipul:** A river flowing from Hvergelmir that flows past the home of the gods.
- **Gjoll:** (Noisy, Dazzling Sound.) A river of Niflheim. One of the eleven venom cold rivers called Elivagar that emptied into the void: Ginnungagap.

- **Gunnthra / Gunnthro / Gunnthorin:** (Battle, Tremble.) A river of Niflheim. One of the eleven venom cold rivers called Elivagar that emptied into the void: Ginnungagap.

- **Gomul:** (Old.) A river that flows past the home of the gods.

- **Gopul:** (Gaper, Forward Rushing.) A river that flows past the home of the gods.

- **Grad:** (Greedy.) A river that flows past the home of the gods.

- **Holl:** A river that flows into Niflheim from the land of men (Midgard).

- **Hronn:** (Wave.) A river that flows into Niflheim from the land of men (Midgard).

- **Hrid:** (Snow Storm.) A river of Niflheim. One of the eleven venom-cold rivers called Elivagar that emptied into the void: Ginnungagap.

- **Ifing:** The wide river that runs between Midgard and Utgard. It is a formidable barrier to giants that protects the land of men.

- **Kerlaugs:** Two rivers along with Kormpt and Ormpt that Thor wades each day.

- **Kormpt:** (River Bed.) A river along with Ormpt and the two Kerlaugs/Kerlaugar that Thor wades each day.

- **Leiptr:** (Flashing Bright.) A river of Niflheim. One of the eleven venom-cold rivers called Elivagar that emptied into the void: Ginnungagap.

- **Odur:** The river crossed by Líf and Leifthrasir on their way to Hoddmimir's wood.

- **Ormpt:** (Snaking, Winding?) A river along with Kormpt and the two Kerlaugs/Kerlaugar that Thor wades each day.

- **Nonn:** (Strong.) A river that flows into Niflheim from the land of men.

- **Not:** (Dark.) A river that flows into Niflheim from the land of men (Midgard).

- **Nyt:** (Milk.) A river that flows into Niflheim from the land of men (Midgard).

- **Rin:** A river that flows past the home of the gods.

- **Rennandi:** (Running, The One Course.) A river that flows past the home of the gods.

- **Sekin / Saekin:** (Advancer.) Flows into the sea from the land of men (Midgard).

- **Sid:** (Broad, Slow Moving.) Tending to flow downward.

- **Síth:** (Long.) Flows into the sea from the land of men (Midgard).

- **Slid / Slíth:** (Dangerous, Fearsome, The Frightful.) Often referred to as Cutting. A river of Niflheim. One of the eleven venom-cold rivers called Elivagar that emptied into the void: Ginnungagap.

- **Strond:** A river that flows into Niflheim from the land of men (Midgard).

- **Svol:** (Cool.) A river that empties into the Hvergelmir fountain.

- **Sylg:** (Swallower.) A river of Niflheim. One of the eleven venom cold rivers called Elivagar that emptied into the void: Ginnungagap.

- **Tholl:** A river that flows into Niflheim from the land of men (Midgard).

- **Thund:** (The Noisy.) A river that flows into Niflheim from the land of men (Midgard).

- **Thyn:** (Frothing, to thunder.) A river that flows into Niflheim from the land of men (Midgard).

- **Vadgelmir:** (A wading place, a ford.) The river of pestilence through which the twice-dead must wade.

- **Van:** (Hope, Expectation.) The river that flows from the jaws of the Fenris Wolf while he is bound on Lyngvi.

- **Vegsvinn:** (Road Knowing, Way Swift.) A river that flows into Niflheim from the land of men (Midgard).

- **Vid:** (Broad.) A river of Niflheim. One of the eleven venom-cold rivers called Elivagar that emptied into the void: Ginnungagap.
- **Vimur:** A river forded by Thor. Its strong currents can make the wader stumble and appear giddy in the crossing. (Vim: giddiness, wavering.)
- **Vina:** (A Friend, Feast of Friends.) A river that flows into Niflheim from the land of men (Midgard).
- **Vith:** (Wise.) A river that flows past the home of the gods.
- **Vond / Vönd:** (Bundle/Confluence.) A river that flows into Niflheim from the land of men (Midgard).
- **Ylg:** (Swelling.) A river of Niflheim. One of the eleven venom-cold rivers called Elivagar that emptied into the void: Ginnungagap.

Rogner: Smith, creator, singer of magic songs. (See also thingskil.) A great dwarf smith of antiquity renowned for his splendid craftsmanship and art. (Typical reference for Volund/Thjasse.)

Roskva / Roska: (Quick, Lively, Active.) Daughter of Orvandel, sister of Thjalfi, and a servant of Thor. She symbolizes the ripe fields of harvest. She marries Forseti.

Rota: (Stung, Sting, Stinger.) A Valkyrie.

Rubore: Latin for Redness, blush, modesty. In reference to Freyr's situation among the Holwers: shame, humiliation, disgrace.

Saehrímnir: (Sooty black, Rime-producer.) The great boar that battles the Einherjar by day and is eaten by the Einherjar each night. The boar is cooked for the Einherjar each evening by Andhrímnir in the kettle Eldhrímnir.

Saevarstadir: The hall of the Njara.

Saga: (To foretell, history.) A goddess of the Æsir. The goddess of history, she calls Sokkvabekk her home.

Salgofnir: The red cock that wakens the Einherjar each day.

Sanga svitiri: Leader of the warrior's back.

Sanga hroeriri: Leader of the warrior's forward.

Sanngetal: (Truthfinder.) A name for Odin. (See also Odin Men Names, Odin God Names, and Odin Battle Names.)

Sath: (The Truthful.) A name for Odin. (See also Odin Men Names, Odin God Names, and Odin Battle Names.)

Saxboard: The gunwale of a boat.

Scot: Tax. Hence, getting off scot free is getting off tax free/ punishment free.

Sceaf: Sheath, as in sheath of grain.

Sceaf of the Scani: The name Heimdall took when bestowing the gifts of civilization on human society. (See also Rig.)

Scyld Skefing: The son of Sceaf of the Scani.

Sea: 1) Called Endless-lier by the Æsir. 2) Called "Rolling One" by Vanir. 2) Called "home of the eel" by giants. 3) Called "the deep ocean" by dwarves. 4) Called Lagastaf by elves.

Seat of Quarrels: A person's chest or mouth.

Sekin / Saekin: (Advancer.) A river that flows into the sea from the land of men (Midgard). (See Rivers.)

Selmánudr: Pasture Month. (June – July.) The month in which milk cattle are removed to the Sel—shed on a pasture. One of the seven changes of weather, which make up the economical year. One of the seven sons of Mimir. (See also Gormánudr, Frermánudr, Hrútmánudr, Enmánudr, Sólmánudr, Kornskurdarmánudr.)

Serpents: They live beneath Yggdrasil gnawing at the roots of the great tree.

- **Niddhogg / Nithhogg:** (The Dastardly Striking).
- **Góinn / Goin:** Son of Grafvitnir.
- **Móinn / Moin:** (Moor dweller.) Son of Grafvitnir.
- **Grabakr / Graabak:** (Gray Back).
- **Grafvitnir / Grafvitner:** (Grave Wolf).

- **Grafvolludr / Grafvollud:** (Field Burrower).
- **Ófnir / Ofnir / Ofner:** (The entangler).
- **Svafnir:** (Put to sleep/death).

Sessrumnir: (Seat-roomy, Hall with many benches and rooms.) Freyja's hall built in Folkvang (Warrior's Fields/folk's field).

Shield (Red): A red shield signifies peace.

Shield (White): A white shield signifies war/death.

Sid: (Broad, Slow Moving.) A river tending to flow downward. (See Rivers.)

Sidhott / Síthhott: (Broadhat, Long-Hood) A name for Odin. (See also Odin Men Names, Odin God Names, and Odin Battle Names.)

Sidskegg / Síthskegg: (Broadbeard, Long-Beard.) A name for Odin. (See also Odin Men Names, Odin God Names, and Odin Battle Names.)

Seid / Seiðr: 1) Witchcraft. 2) A form of magic regarded with awe and distaste. The one performing it falls into a trance, freeing his/her spirit to discern the future or to do good or evil to another person.

Sif: (Affinity.) The Æsir goddess of the sanctity of family and wedlock. She is the wife of Thor.

Sigyn / Signý: (Rising Moon.) A goddess of the Æsir. The wife of Loki. From Sig (a rope which is let down, victory) and ný (the new of the moon, the waxing moon or full moon).

Sigfodur / Sigfather: (War Father, Victory Father.) A name for Odin. (See also Odin Men Names, Odin God Names, and Odin Battle Names.)

Silfrintoppr: (Silver Top.) A horse of the Æsir.

Simul / Sumul: (Ever.) The pole on which the pale Soeg/Sægr was carried by Ivalde/Vidfinn's daughter and son. As they carried the pale along a hillside path, Mani (Moon) took them to aid him on his nightly journey.

Síth: (Long.) A river that flows into the sea from the land of men (Midgard). (See Rivers.)

Sindri: (Sparkling, Scintillating, Sparkling, producing dross, Worker at the Forge, Forger.) 1) A master smith and brother of Brokk. He is the maker of Gullinbursti, Mjollnir, and the great arm ring Draupnir. 2) A great hall.

Sinir: (Thick sinewed.) A horse of the Æsir.

Sinmara: (The one who maims by doing violence to the sinews.) The ashes colored giantess, queen of the Njara who along with her husband Nidud take the Sword of Vengeance from Volund.

Sjaelland: Zealand.

Sjofn / Sjofin / Sjofna: (To See.) A goddess of the Æsir. She turns the thoughts of men and women to love.

Sköll: (To strike, to smite, to repulse.) Brother of Managarm, he chases the sun across the sky and will catch it at Ragnarok.

Skadi: (Harm, Damage.) Daughter of Thjasse. A ski-runner and a great warrior, she marries Njord.

Skafid: (The Scraper/Shaver.) A dwarf of Lofar's clan.

Skeggjold: (Axe Age.) A Valkyrie.

Skidbladnir: (Lath, Shingle, billet of wood, a Sheath.) The collapsible ship build by Volund for the gods.

Skiedbrimir: (Race Runner.) A horse of the Æsir.

Skilfing / Skilfingr / Skilfung: (Shaker, Shatterer.) A name for Odin. (See also Odin Men Names, Odin God Names, and Odin Battle Names.)

Skinfaxi: (Shining mane.) The steed that pulls the wain of Day. His shining mane illuminates the sky. (See also Hrimfaxi.)

Skirnir / Skirvir: (The bright one. The pure/serene/clear, to become clear.) 1) He is Freyr's messenger and the husband of Freyja. (See also Hermod, Od, and Svipdag.) 2) A dwarf of Lofar's clan.

Skogul: (Point/Promontory.) A Valkyrie.

Skrymer: (Proud One.) A giant. He directs Thor and his companions to Utgarda, the great hall of Utgarda-Loki.

Skuld: (Shall, The future, Have become, Obligation, Necessity,) 1) Oldest of the three Norns who weave the skein of life for each person. They succor the great tree Yggdrasil. (See also Nornir, Skuld, Urd, and Verdandi.) 2) A Valkyrie, she is also the oldest of the three Norns.

Sky: 1) Called "home of planets" by the Æsir. 2) Called Everglow by giants. 3) Called Deluder by dwarves. 4) Called "the lively wheel" by elves.

Slagfin: A skilled bard and warrior, he is the younger brother of Volund and Orvandel.

Sleipnir / Sleipnir: (The Slippery, Fast Traveler.) Odin's eight-footed horse, he is the swiftest of all horses. He was born of Loki by Svadilfari, the great workhorse of the Master Builder.

Slid / Slíth: (Dangerous, Fearsome, The Frightful.) Often referred to as Cutting. A river of Niflheim. One of the eleven venom cold rivers called Elivagar that emptied into the void: Ginnungagap. (See Rivers.)

Snær: (Snow.) A frost giant.

Snotra / Snót / Snotr: (Neat, Gentlewoman, Wise, To make wise.) Courtly and wise, Snotra is the Æsir goddess of clever women and men.

Soeg / Sœgr / Sægr: (A large vessel, "the one seething over its brinks".) The pale suspended from the pole Simul carried by Ivalde/Vidfinn's daughter and son. As they carried the pale along a hillside path, Mani (Moon) took them to aid him on his nightly journey.

Sokkmimir: (Deep Thinker.) A frost giant.

Sokkvabekk: (Sinking brook, Sunken Bank/Bench.) Saga's hall.

Sólmánudr: Sun Month (April – May). One of the seven changes of weather that make up the economical year. One of the seven sons of Mimir. (See also Gormánudr, Frermánudr, Hrútmánudr, Enmánudr, Selmánudr, Kornskurdarmánudr.)

Son: (Sound, song.) 1) One of the three vats holding the precious mead of poetry that Odin steals from Suttung. 2) A cauldron that holds liquid from Mimir's well. (See also Bodn and Odrerir.)

Stag of billows: Kenning for a ship.

Straw Death: Death by old age or sickness. To die on a straw bed.

Strond: A river that flows into Niflheim from the land of men (Midgard). (See Rivers.)

Sudri: (The South.) 1) The southern pillar that supports the skull of Ymir—the sky. 2) A dwarf of Motsognir's clan. (See also Austri, Nordi, Vestri.)

Summer-lading: Viking raiding during the summer months.

Sun: 1) Called All-shining by the Æsir. 2) Called "the wind-weaver" by Vanir. 3) Called "the world above" by giants. 4) Called "the dripping hall" by dwarves. 5) Called "the lively roof" by elves.

Surt / Surtur: (The Swart, The Black, Obscure, Invisible, Unintelligible, The great First Cause least understood.) A fire giant. The leader of the sons of Muspellsheim. He will defeat the gods at Ragnarok.

Suttung: (The mead wolf.) A giant. Son of Gilling. Odin steals the mead of poetry from his home.

Svadilfare / Svadilfari: (Lubricity, Slippery ice, Slippery traveler.) The great workhorse of the Master Builder. With Loki, he sires Odin's eight-footed horse, Sleipnir.

Svalin: The belly shield that protects of the Sun's horses, Arvak and Alsvinn, from the heat of the sun. The bellows, Isarnkol, beneath their shoulders keeps them cool.

Svartalfaheim: The seventh world. Land of the Dark Elves. (See Nine Worlds.)

Svásuth: (The Mild One.) 1) A winter giant. The brother of Vindsval.

Svásudr: (The delightful.) Some sources refer to him as father of the sun.

Sváva: A Troll woman. Her mount is the gray wolf, her bridles adders that coil about her wrists. (Svá: so.)

Svafnir / Svafinir: (He Who Lulls to Sleep or Dreams, Put to sleep/ death.) 1) A name for Odin. (See also Odin Men Names, Odin God Names, and Odin Battle Names.) 2) A serpent that lives beneath Yggdrasil. (See Serpents.)

Svidur / Svithur / Svidrir / Svithrir: (The Wise.) A name for Odin. (See also Odin Men Names, Odin God Names, and Odin Battle Names.)

Svipal: (The Changeable.) A name for Odin. (See also Odin Men Names, Odin God Names, and Odin Battle Names.)

Svipdag: (Bright day.) The son of Orvandel. He retrieves Volund's sword from the Njara and with it defeats Thor in battle, rescues Menglad (Freyja) from the giants, and for the gift of the mighty sword marries Freyja. As a member of the Æsir clan he takes on the names: Hermod, Od, and Skirnir (depending on his role).

Sviur / Svíarr: (Smith, Forger.) A dwarf and member of Durun's Clan.

Svigdur: (The Champion Drinker.) 1) A dwarf and member of Durun's Clan. 2) The name given to Ivalde by Suttung for his capacity to drink large amounts.

Svol / Svöl: (Cool.) A river that empties into the Hvergelmir fountain. (See Rivers.)

Swans road / Swans way: The sea. A ship is said to travel the swan's road/way.

Sygne: (Blessed, The Blessed.) 1) Daughter of Sumbl, King of the Finns. 2) Wife of Halfdan. 3) Second wife of Orvandel.

Sylg: (Swallower.) A river of Niflheim. One of the eleven venom-cold rivers called Elivagar that emptied into the void: Ginnungagap. (See Rivers.)

Syn: (Refusal, Equity, Truth.) A goddess of the Æsir. She guards doors and shuts out those who are not to enter. Once she shuts the door, no appeal will change her decision. She presides over all tribunals and trials and protects those in judicial cases.

Tanngniost (Tooth Gnasher) and **Tanngrisnir** (Snarl Tooth): The goats that pull Thor's chariot/wain.

Terror of the Linden: The northern lights.

Thekk: (Known, The Welcome One.) 1) A name for Odin. (See also Odin Men Names, Odin God Names, and Odin Battle Names.) 2) A dwarf of Motsognir's clan.

Thing / Thingstead: A gathering of all people from a district, for the purpose of presenting, and deciding lawsuits, determining and passing laws, and deciding direction for the community. (For example, Thingstead of Urd, Husthing of the gods, the Althing of Iceland, the Gulathing of Norway, etc.)

Thing-bod: A legal summons to appear at a thing before the seat of judgment.

Thing of Urd: The judgment thing of the dead where a person's final fate is decided.

Thingskil: A smith. An artist.

Thjalfi / Thialfi: (Digger, Delver.) Son of Orvandel, brother of Roskva, and a servant of Thor.

Thjasse / Thjazi / Thjatsi: (Fadir mörna: the father of swords.) 1) The giant who kidnaps Idun who is later rescued by Loki. Struck from the sky by the vaferflame as he chases Loki over Asgard seeking to recapture Idun, he is speared to death by the Æsir when he falls into their court. 2) The second name of Volund, taken after he escaped from the Njara. He is the father of Skadi. (See also Volund.)

Tholl: A river that flows into Niflheim from the land of men (Midgard). (See Rivers.)

Thokk: (Gratitude or Thanks) A giantess. She is the only thing in the world that refuses to weep for Baldur's return.

Thor: (Thunderer.) God of thunder. The strongest of the gods. He is the son of Odin and earth (Hlodyn/Fiorgyn/Fjorgyn) and the protector of gods and men. While honorable and generally good-tempered, he occasionally flies into a terrible rage and is very dangerous at these times. The strongest of the gods, he is the son of earth (Hlodyn/Fiorgyn/Fjorgyn) and Odin. Other names for Thor include: Veor, Asa-Thor (Thor of the Æsir), Oku-Thor (Thor the Charioteer, Thor the Driver), Ving-Thor, Hlorridi, and Donar.

Thorin: A dwarf of Motsognir's clan.

Thorn: The emblem/symbol of sleep.

Thrain: (The Pertinacious, Stubborn.) A dwarf of Motsognir's clan.

Thridi / Thrithi: (Third, The Third.) A name for Odin. (See also Odin Men Names, Odin God Names, and Odin Battle Names.)

Thror / Thrór / Thrôr: (Inciter to Strife, To increase/amplify.) A name for Odin. (See also Odin Men Names, Odin God Names, and Odin Battle Names.)

Thrud / Thruth: (Strength.) A daughter of Thor, she takes her place among the Valkyrie.

Thrudgelmer: (The strange-headed.) (Thrud = fortitude.) 1) A frost giant. 2) Possibly another name for Hrimgrimner.

Thrudvanger: (The Plains of Strength, Region of Fortitude.) The location where Thor built his hall, Bilskirnir.

Thule: Sage, bard, spokesperson.

Thund: (The Noisy.) A river that flows into Niflheim from the land of men (Midgard). (See Rivers.)

Thurs: A giant. An etin. A Jotun.

Thuth: (Second?) A name for Odin. (See also Odin Men Names, Odin God Names, and Odin Battle Names.)

Thrym: (Thunderer.) A giant.

Thrymgjoll: (The Loud Grating.) The gate to Asgard. (see also Valgrind)

Thrymheim: (Noisy Home.) Thrymheim is the home of Skadi's father. Skadi's father is the elf-jotun hybrid known as Thjazi, also called Volund, and the main smith of Ivaldi's sons, who creates

Odin's spear Gungnir. Since Volundarhus (Volund's house) means a labyrinth, this is likely a well-fortified series of winding mountain-caverns in accessible to the gods.

Thrymheimr: (The Loud/Noisy One) A frost giant.

Thyn: (Frothing, to thunder) A river that flows into Niflheim from the land of men (Midgard). (See Rivers.)

Tyr: (God.) The one-handed God of War. He battles for just causes.

Twig of Revenge: Any weapon created by Volund/Thjasse. The name can refer to the arrow crafted from mistletoe that felled Baldur or Volund's Sword of Revenge. (See also Gambanteinn.)

Ud / Uth: (One?) A name for Odin. (See also Odin Men Names, Odin God Names, and Odin Battle Names.)

Udr: A son of Night.

Úlfliðr: (Wrist.) The stump of Tyr's right arm, all that remained after the Fenris wolf bit off his hand at the wrist joint.

Ull: (Wool.) Son of Orvandel the archer and stepson of Thor. Like his father, he is a highly skilled archer.

Upsala / Uppsala / Uppsalir: (Up/High.) Freyr's hall built in Alfheim.

Urd: (Being, The past, Becoming.) Youngest of the three Norns who weave the skein of life for each person. They succor the great tree Yggdrasil. (See also Nornir, Skuld, Urd, and Verdandi.)

Urdar ord: Urd's judgment. The judgment of fate, which must come to pass, no matter if it concerns life or death. (See also bana ord, dauda ord, feigdar ord, urdar ord, and namaeli.)

Utgard: (Outer Ward.) The land of the giants. Named by the Æsir gods in honor of Ymir's first settlement. It is also called Jotunheim. (See Nine Worlds.)

Utgarda: (The outer enclosure.) The first settlement of the great giant Ymir, in Ginnungagap.

Utgarda-Loki: A frost giant. The clan chief/king of the frost giants in the stronghold Utgarda in Jotunheim.

Vadgelmir: (A wading place, a ford.) The River of pestilence through which the twice-dead must wade. (See Rivers.)

Vafthrudner: (Way Strong, Strong Weave.) A frost giant.

Vákaldr: (Spring-Cold.) A frost giant, son to Vinkaldr and grandson to Fimkaldr.

Vak: (Wakeful/Alert or Vigilant One.) A name for Odin. (See also Odin Men Names, Odin God Names, and Odin Battle Names.)

Vala / Volva: (Seeress.) The dead seeress of the giants who Odin visits in Niflhel. From her he learns the history of the worlds, the fate of Baldur, and the fate of the Gods.

Valaskialf / Valaskjalf: (Silver roofed.) 1) Another of Odin's halls. 2) Choice or election

Valgrind: The gate to Valhalla. (See also Thrymgjoll.)

Valhalla: (Hall of the Slain.) Odin's hall for heroes, built in Gladsheim. Through its gate, Valgrind, only those may enter who know its secret.

Vali / Ali: (Chooser.) Son of Odin and Rind, he is the born avenger of Baldur. Fresh out of the womb he kills Hodd, the slayer of Baldur.

Valfodur / Valfather: (Father of the Slain, Father of the Battle Slain.) A name for Odin. (See also Odin Men Names, Odin God Names, and Odin Battle Names.)

Valkyrie: (Choosers of the slain.) To choose.

Valkyrie: (Choosers/Gatherers of the Slain.) Odin's warrior maidens who are sent into every battle to choose the bravest and best for the halls of Asgard, the heroes (einherjar) destined to fight alongside the gods at Ragnarok. Among the Valkyrie's other duties is to serve ale to the warriors in Valhalla.

- **Brynhilda / Brynhild / Hild:** (Battle Helmet, Helmet, Lady of the Battle Helmet).
- **Geironul / Geirolul:** (Spear feeder).
- **Geirahod:** (The Spear warrior).
- **Geirskogul:** (Spear point/promontory).

- **Göll / Goll:** (Shriek).
- **Göndul:** (Clue, Entangler).
- **Gun:** (Battle).
- **Herfjotur:** (Fetterer of an Army, War Fetter).
- **Hervor / Alvit:** (The strange creature).
- **Hladgud / Hlodver:** (The Swan White).
- **Hlokk:** (Noise, Battle sound).
- **Ölrún:** (Swan, She who is ready for battle).
- **Radgrid:** (Counseling Truce).
- **Randgrid / Randgrith / Ráthgrith:** (Shield Truce).
- **Reginlief:** (Dear to the Gods, Vast Life).
- **Rota:** (Stung, Sting, Stinger).
- **Skeggjold:** (Axe Age).
- **Skogul:** (Point/Promontory).
- **Skuld:** (Obligation, Necessity, Future).
- **Thruth / Thrud:** (Strength).

Van: (Hope, Expectation.) The river that flows from the jaws of the Fenris Wolf while he is bound on Lyngvi. (See Rivers.)

Vanaheim: The second world. Homeland of the Vanir. (See Nine Worlds.)

Vanir: (Beautiful.) Gods of wind and sea. They challenge the Æsir over the death of Gullveig and defeat them in the first war of the world. They eventually unite with the Æsir to form a single godhead.

Var / Vara: (Beloved, Troth.) A goddess of the Æsir. A handmaiden of Frigg, she listens to the oaths and private agreements made between men and women. She hears all oaths and punishes perjurers, while rewarding those who faithfully keep their word.

Vartari: (Thong, Strap.) The strand of leather that Brokk, brother of Sindri, used to sew shut Loki's lips after Loki lost the bet that the gods would consider the works of Volund greater than the works of Sindri.

Vasad: (Damp Cold, Sleety.) A frost giant whose damp creeps into the bones. Father of Vindloni and Vindsval.

Vásuth: (The Wet and Cold One.) A winter giant. The father of Vindsval and Svásuth.

Ve: (Temple, Holy.) A brother of Odin. Referred to as the producer of fire. Also called Lodur/ Lodurr (to Flame).

Vedrfolnir: (Wind Bleached.) The hawk who lives in the great ash tree, Yggdrasil. He sits between the eyes of the great eagle that is perched amid its branches.

Vegsvinn: (Road Knowing, Way Swift.) A river that flows into Niflheim from the land of men (Midgard). (See Rivers.)

Vegtam: (Way-tame.) A name for Odin. (See also Odin Men Names, Odin God Names, and Odin Battle Names.)

Veig: (Liquor.) A dwarf of Motsognir's clan.

Veor: Thor.

Veraidar Nagli: (The North Star, The Pole star.) The world spike that is the central star around which the World Mill forever turns.

Verdandi / Verthandi: (The present, To become, Fate.) Middle of the three Norns who weave the skein of life for each person. They succor the great tree Yggdrasil. (See also Nornir, Skuld, Urd, and Verdandi.)

Verland: The land of men. (See also The Nine Worlds: Midgard.)

Vestri: (The West.) 1) The western pillar that supports the skull of Ymir – the sky. 2) A dwarf of Motsognir's clan. (See also Austri, Nordi, Sudri.)

Vid: (Broad.) A river of Niflheim. One of the eleven venom cold rivers called Elivagar that emptied into the void: Ginnungagap. (See Rivers.)

Vidar / Vithar / Víthar: (Far Ruler, The Silent God.) Son of Odin and Grid. He lives in a grass and brush grown realm called Landvide (The primeval forest). He kills the Fenris wolf at Ragnarok.

Vidblain: (Wide Blue.) A dimension of Alfheim, the land of the light elves. (See also Andlang.)

Vidrir: (Ruler/Moderator of Weather.) A name for Odin. (See also Odin Men Names, Odin God Names, and Odin Battle Names.)

Vidofnir: The golden cock that wakens the Æsir and Einherjar on the day of Ragnarok. Also called Gullinkambi (Golden Comb).

Vidur / Vithur: (Wood, Tree of Battle.) A name for Odin. (See also Odin Men Names, Odin God Names, and Odin Battle Names.)

Vifud / Vafud / Váfuth: (Wayfarer.) A name for Odin. (See also Odin Men Names, Odin God Names, and Odin Battle Names.)

Vigfus: (Eager to slay.) A name.

Vigrid / Vigrith: (Field of battle, Spear field.) The plain where the final battle, Ragnarok, takes place.

Vili / Villi: (Will, The Chooser, wish, disposition of mind, delight, joy.) 1) A brother of Odin. Also called the Haenir/Hoenir (the long legged), the long legged one, the mire king, the white bird—a stork. 2) A dwarf and member of Durun's Clan.

Vimur: A river forded by Thor. Its strong, erratic currents can make the wader stumble and appear giddy in the crossing. (See Rivers.)

Vina: (A Friend, Feast of Friends.) A river that flows into Niflheim from the land of men (Midgard). (See Rivers.)

Vindâlf: (Wind elf.) A dwarf of Motsognir's clan. (See also Wizards.)

Vindsvaler: (Winter Wind.) A frost giant. The father of winter.

Vingnir / Vinginir: (The Winged.) A giantess. Foster parent of Thor. Personification of sheet lightning. (See also Hlora.)

Vingolf: (Abode/Hall of Friends, Hall of Bliss.) The sanctuary built for the goddesses.

Vindloni: (Chill Wind.) A frost giant whose breeze increases the cold. Vindsval is his brother and Vasad is his father.

Vindsval: (Wind Cold, Deadly Wind.) 1) The winter giant. The son of Vásuth. His brother is Svásuth. 2) A frost giant whose breeze increases the cold. Vindloni is his brother and Vasad is his father.

Vindsvaler: (Winter Wind.) A frost giant. The father of winter.

Vinkaldr: (Wind-Cold.) A frost giant. Father Vákaldr and son to Fimkaldr.

Virvir / Vírvír: (Alive) A dwarf of Lofar's clan.

Vith: (Wise.) A river that flows past the home of the gods. (See Rivers.)

Vitr: (Color.) A dwarf of Motsognir's clan.

Volund: A skillful artificer. Son of Ivalde, he is a master smith whose works are depreciated by the gods in favor of the works of Sindri, another master smith. He seeks revenge and crafts the ultimate weapon—the Sword of Vengeance: See Gambanteinn and Twig of Revenge. (See also Thjasse.)

Volupsa: The Seeress' Prophecy. The prophecy Odin received from the lips of the ancient seeress when he calls her from the dead. She can remember before the beginning of the world and see as far ahead as after Ragnarok.

Vond / Vönd: (Bundle/Confluence.) A river that flows into Niflheim from the land of men (Midgard). (See Rivers.)

Vor: (Careful.) A goddess of the Æsir. She is so knowledgeable and inquires so deeply into things that nothing is hidden from her.

Weapons of Myth and Saga:
- **Adder:** Sword wielded by Egil Skalla-Grimsson. Egil carried the blade "black Adder" all his life. He used it in all his battles and duels.
- **Atgeir:** A thrusting spear.
- **Dáinslief:** (Daines Life/Daines Legacy.) The great sword of the Daines. If drawn, it must be used to kill someone before it can be resheathed. Wielded by King Hogni in the Fight of the Hjadnings against King Hedin Hjarrandason.

- **Dragvadil:** Sword given to Egil Skalla-Grimsson by Arinbjorm Thorirson.
- **Fetbried:** Sword wielded by Toralv the Strong, son of Skolm during the battle between King Hacon of Norway and Harald Ericson at Fitjar in Stord (an island in Hordaland).
- **Gambanteinn, Nagelring, Lævantien:** (Vengeance of Volund, Twig of Revenge, Wand of Destruction): The smart blade that fights by itself. Crafted by Volund as a weapon greater than any possessed by the gods. It passes hand to hand from dwarf to king to man to god to giant. Captured from Volund by Nidud, king of the Njara. Retrieved by Svipdag, he used it to free Freyja from the giants and gain entrance to Asgard and Valhalla. It was given to Freyr. Through Skirnir, Freyr gave it to Gymir and Angerboda as marriage payment for their daughter, Gerd. Gymir gave it into Eggther's safe-keeping. On the eve of Ragnarok, Eggther gives it to Fjalar to pass on to Surt. The gods sorely miss its strength at Ragnarok.
- **Gram:** Sword crafted by Regin and wielded by Sigurd Fafnirbani. Sigurd used the blade to slay the "dragon" Fafnir on Gnita-heath.
- **Gungnir:** (To tremble violently.) The battle spear wielded by Odin. The spear crafted by Volund, its golden tip and edge are carved with victory runes. Its tip never misses its mark, and it never hangs up when withdrawn.
- **Hakon's Gift:** Axe carried by Kormak Ogmundsson and wielded in battle by Hallfred.
- **Heirloom of Hrethel:** The great sword of the Geats, adorned with gold, given to Beowulf by Hygelac.
- **Hmeiter:** Sword wielded by King Olav. Keen edged; its handle was bound with gold.
- **Hothing / Hodding:** Sword wielded by Agnar, son of Ingild. Shattered in battle on the helmet of Bjarke.
- **Hrunting:** Sword wielded by Beowulf when facing Grendel's mother. The man-made blade failed to bite.

- **Hviting:** Sword wielded by Bersi the Dueler. Undefeated in many duels, this sharp sword came with a healing stone. The warrior could use the stone to heal his own wounds or those of his adversary.

- **Hwíting:** Sword wielded by Ragnald of Norway.

- **Hwyting:** Sword wielded by Halfdan and named after the sheen of its well-whetted point.

- **Jokul's Gift:** Sword wielded by Grettir Asmundson (Grettir the Strong). This was the first sword carried by Gettir. His mother, Asdis, passed it down to him from his grandfather Jokul.

- **King's Gift:** 1) Sword wielded in battle by Hallfred. On his deathbed, he passed it onto his son Hallfred. 2) Sword wielded by Gunnlaug Serpent Tongue. A gift from King Ethelred, the son of Edgar. Gunnlaug used this sword to best the berserk, Thororm. He carried this sword his entire life and used it in his feud with Hrafan Onundarson over the love of Helga Thorsteinsdötter.

- **Kvernbit:** (Millstone-biter.) Sword wielded by Hacon the Good. It was given to Hacon, son of King Harald FairHair (Finehair) of Norway by King Athelstan in England—a gift to his foster son. Hacon later became king of Norway (Hacon the Good).

- **Lauf:** (Leaf.) Sword wielded by Bearce.

- **Lævantien:** (See Gambanteinn.)

- **Logthi:** Sword wielded by Ole Halfdansson. Ole used the sword to slay Hrale and Skate.

- **Lögthe:** Sword wielded by Ole Siwardson.

- **Long:** Sword wielded by Thorolf Skallagrimsson in his battles and raiding ventures. While under the employ of King Athelstan during his battles with King Olaf, and the Scottish Earl's Adils and Hring, he was killed in the battle of Wen Heath by Wen Forest and was buried with the sword.

- **Lövi:** A sword of "wonderful sharpness and unusual length," wielded by Bjarke.

- **Lyusing:** Sword wielded by Halfdan.
- **Lyvsing:** Sword wielded by Ragnald of Norway.
- **Maering:** Sword wielded by Bjorn Arngeirson. Bjorn was the Champion of the Hitardal People. He won the blade by killing its previous owner Kaldimar in a proxy dual for King Valdimar. He carried this sword his entire life and used it in his feud with Thord Kolbeinson over the love of Oddny Thorkelsdötter.
- **Mistelteinn:** Sword wielded by Samring, Thráinn, and Romunnd Greipson. A good sword and strong. (Note: In later poetry, this name was given to the sword wielded by Freyr.)
- **Mjollnir:** (The Crusher.) Hammer/mace crafted by the dwarf Sindri and wielded by the god, Thor. It reached its utmost power when Thor donned his belt of strength and iron gloves.
- **Nagelring:** 1) Beowulf's great blade of ancient iron, shattered in his final battle with the dragon. 2) Sword of Volund (See Gambanteinn.)
- **Ridill:** Sword wielded by Regin to cut out the heart of his brother, Fafnir, after Sigurd had killed him.
- **Rosen:** Sword wielded by King Ortnit and Wolfdieterich. Wolfdieterich used the sword of King Ornit to slay the Lind Worm. On its hilt was set a huge carbuncle that shone bright red.
- **Scramasax / Seax:** In the tenth century, this was a single-edged battle knife carried as an auxiliary weapon to the sword.
- **Screp / Skrep:** Sword wielded by Wermund and Uffe Wermundsson. The sword, though long buried and rust eaten, remained sharp and trusty. It is known by the whistling it makes when swung. The sword is of such great sharpness that with a single blow it can cut through any obstacle.
- **Sel's Avenger:** Spear wielded by Asmund Grankelson and Tore the Hound. Spear wielded by Asmund Grankelson (accompanied by Karli of Langöy) to kill Asbiorne Selsbane. Tore the Hound was given the spear by Asbiorne's mother, Sigrid, to avenge his death. Tore used it to kill Karli.

- **Skofnung:** Sword wielded by Kormak Ogmundsson. Kormac borrowed the sword from Skeggi of Midfjord for his dual with Bersi over the love of Steingard Thorkelsdötter. The blade was unlike Kormac in temperament; it was slow and methodical while he was headstrong and rash. The blade was enchanted. The sun was never to shine on the upper length of the blade. It was not to be wielded until the warrior was ready for combat; attempts to draw it any earlier resulted in howls of anguish from the blade. When on the battlefield, the warrior was to be alone, draw the blade, hold it out before him, and breathe on it. A snake would crawl from under the boss. Turning the sword sideways made it possible for the snake to crawl back under the boss.

- **Skirteinn:** A charmed sword that reflected the guilt or innocence of the one who touched it.

- **Skrymir:** Sword wielded by Steinar, the son of Onund Sjoni.

- **Snyrtir:** Sword wielded by Bearce and Bjarke. Bjarke used this blade to kill Agnar, son of Ingild.

- **Sword of Healfdane:** Sword given to Beowulf by King Hrothgar, son of Healfdane, for the slaying of Grendel.

- **Thorfin's Gift:** A short sword (possibly a seax) wielded by Grettir Asmundson (Grettir the Strong). Grettir recovered the blade from the grave mound of Kar the Old and returned it to Thorfin Karson. Thorfin gave it to Gettir for saving the lives of his family. Grettir carried it for the rest of his life. When he was killed, no one could remove the blade from his grip until they hacked off his hand. Grettir's brother used the blade in Byzantium to avenge his death, by splitting the skull of Gettir's slayer.

- **Twig of Revenge:** (Gambanteinn.) Arrow cast by Hodd that killed Baldur. Crafted by Thjasse/Volund as a weapon from the sprig of mistletoe that Loki retrieved from Hoddmimir's wood. (Mistletoe was the only thing in the world that had not given its oath not to harm Baldur.) Loki passed the arrow off as a normal arrow to Hodd who shot it at Baldur, killing him. (The name also used to refer to the sword crafted by Volund.)

- **Ulfber+T:** The inscription on a handful of legendary swords crafted of a superior quality steel from ~900AD to 1000AD. Scarce and valuable, only the wealthy could afford these weapons.
- **Vig:** Spear wielded by Kormak Ogmundsson while on campaign with King Harold in Permia.

Weregild: Payment for killing a person. This payment was to reconcile the act between offended parties and avoid a vendetta.

Wind-home: A kenning for the sky or the heavens.

Withershins: A direction contrary to the apparent direction of the sun. (i.e., passing from right to left.)

Wizards: They live in the land of Nidaveller and are members of Motsognir's clan.

- **Althiôf / Althjof:** (Master-thief, All thief.) An accomplished rascal and a learned thief.
- **Gandâlf / Gandolf:** (Staff elf, enchanter.) He teaches magic.
- **Vindâlf / Vidolf:** (Wind elf.) He rides the wind.

World Mill: (The mill of storms.) Created by the gods to balance the earth. It resides in Mt. Hvergelmir. Its millstones are called Eylúdr and Lúdr. Water drawn through the eye of the millstones is called the maelstrom—the navel of the world. Nine giant maidens turn the mondul of the World Mill. Turning beneath the north star, it rotates the heavens, causes the ebb and flood tide, and regulates the ocean currents.

Wound birds: Scavengers of the battlefield: Eagles, Hawks, Ravens.

Ydalir: (Dales of the bows.) Ull's hall built in Yewdale.

Ygg: (The Terrible, The Terrifier.) A name for Odin. (See also Odin Men Names, Odin God Names, and Odin Battle Names.)

Yggdrasil: (Mount/Horse of the Terrible One/Odin.) The great ash tree that grows at the center of the universe. It is also called Mimamirth and Lorad.

Ylg: (Swelling.) A river of Niflheim. One of the eleven venom cold rivers called Elivagar that emptied into the void: Ginnungagap. (See Rivers.)

Ymir: (The Roarer.) The first giant. The primordial giant. From him all giants are descended. Called Aurgelmir (Mud Bellower) by the Frost Giants, he is killed by Odin and his brothers (Vili and Ve) and his body used to create the earth. (See also Bolthor.)

Yngvi: (We all young.) 1) A dwarf of Lofar's clan. 2) One of the tribes/houses of man.

Yurkul / Jokull / Jökull: (Glacier, Ice sickle.) 1) The giant sons of winter, they spread their arms wide about mountains and hills to embrace the land. 2) A frost giant. (See also Jökull.)

References

The following references are for anyone who wants to delve deeper into the study of Norse myths. This bibliography is restricted to books published in or translated into English.

Source References

The following sources were referenced in the compilation of this work:

The Agricola and the Germainia. Tacitus, Publis Cornelius. Translated by H. Mattingly, revised S.A. Handford. Penguin Books. 1970. ISBN: 0-140-44241-3.

Anglo-Saxon and Norse Poems. Edited and Translated by N. Kershaw. Cambridge University Press, London: Fetter Lane, 1922.

Asgard & The Norse Heroes. Boult, Katharine F. Edited by Ernest Rhys. Everyman's Library. J.M. Dent & Sons, LTD. London. E.P. Dutton & Co. New York. 1910.

Beowulf. Translated by John McNamara. Barnes and Noble Books. New York, New York. 2005. ISBN-13: 978-1-59308-266-6. ISBN-10: 1-59308-266-5.

Bulfinch's Mythology. Bulfinch, Thomas. Abridgment, Edmund Fuller. Dell Publishing, A Division of Random House, Inc. New York, New York. 1959. ISBN: 0-440-30845-3.

Celtic Myths and Legends. Ellis, Peter Berresford. Running Press, Philadelphia, PA. 2008. ISBN: 978-0-7867-1107-9.

A Choice of Anglo-Saxon Verse. Editor: Richard Hamer. Faber and Faber. London, UK. 1970. ISBN: 0-571-22836-4.

The Complete Saga's of Icelanders – I. Editor: Vidar Hreinsson. Editorial Team: Robert Cook, Terry Gunnell, Keneva Kunz, Bernard Scudder. Leifur Eiriksson Publishing. Reykjavik, Iceland. 1997. ISBN: 9979-9293-1-6. Volume I.

The Complete Saga's of Icelanders – III. Editor: Vidar Hreinsson. Editorial Team: Robert Cook, Terry Gunnell, Keneva Kunz, Bernard Scudder. Leifur Eiriksson Publishing. Reykjavik, Iceland. 1997. ISBN: 9979-9293-3-2. Volume III.

A Concise Dictionary of Old Icelandic. Zoëga, Geir T., Oxford at the Clarendon Press. Oxford University Press, London, U.K. 1910.

The Danish History, Books 1 – 9. Saxo Grammaticus. Translated Oliver Elton, B.A. Norrcena- Anglo Saxon Classics: Vol. 1 – 2. Norrcena Society. London, Copenhagen, Stockholm, Berlin, New York, 1911.

De Rerum Natura: Of the Nature of Things. Titus Lucretius Carus. Translated by William Ellery Leonard. The Heritage Club, New York, New York. (Copyright 1957. The George Macy Companies, Inc.)

The Elder Edda of Saemund Sigfusson – Translated Benjamin Thorpe. Norrcena – Anglo Saxon Classics: Vol. 11. Norrcena Society. London, Copenhagen, Stockholm, Berlin, New York, 1911.

Eyrbyggja Saga. Translated by Paul Schach and Lee M. Hollander. University of Nebraska Press. 1959. Library of Congress Catalog Card No: 59-11221.

Gautrek's Saga and Other Medieval Tales. Translated by Hermann Pálsson and Paul Edwards. New York University Press. 1968. Library of Congress Catalog Card No: 68-16829.

Gods and Heroes of War. Burland, C.A. G.P. Putnam's Sons. New York, New York. 1974. SBN: GB-399-60873-7, SBN: TR-399-20383-4.

Greek Lyric Poetry. Santos, Sherod. W.W. Norton & Company. New York. London. 2005. ISBN-10 0-393-32915-1, ISBN-13 978-0-393-32915-5.

Grettir's Saga. Translated by Denton Fox and Hermann Pálsson. University of Toronto Press. 1974. ISBN: 0-8020-1925-0.

Hammer of Thor – Norse Mythology and Legends – Special Edition. H. A. Guerber and Shawn Conners. El Paso Norte Press, 2010. ISBN 1934255335. (Reprint circa "Myths of the Norsemen". Original Published 1909. George G. Harrap & Company.)

Arne Haegstad, "Har at-Tartushi besogt Hedeby (Slesvig)?" *Aarboger for Nordisk Oldkyndighed og historie.* 1964.

Ibrahim ibn Yaquib al-Tartushi (Abraham ben Jacob). A traveler and merchant from the Caliphate of Cordova. Translated extract from a surviving account of his visit to Slesvig (Hedeby) in 950 AD.

Heimskringla: The Lives of the Norse Kings. Snorre Sturlason. Edited and Translated by Erling Monsen with A.H. Smith. Dover Publications, Inc., Mineola, New York.1990. ISBN: 0-486-26366-5.

The Heimskringla: A History of the Norse Kings. Snorre Sturlason. Vol. 1–3 Translated by Samuel Laing, Esq. Norrcena Society, London, Copenhagen, Stockholm, Berlin, New York. 1907.

Hero Tales and Legends of the Rhine. Spence, Lewis. George C. Harrap & Company, London; New York. 1915. Dover Edition, Dover Publications, Inc. 1995. ISBN: 0-486-28870-6.

The Heroes of Asgard: Tales from Scandinavian Mythology. Keary, A. & E., The Macmillan Company, London: Macmillan & Co., Ltd., 1909.

Honor: A History. Bowman, James. Encounter Books. New York, New York. 2006. ISBN: 1-59403-198-3.

Ibn Fadlān and the Rūsiyyah. Montgomery, James E. Journal of Arabic and Islamic Studies 3. 2000. (Translation of the Rūsiyyah passage in Ibn Fadlān's account, the Kitāb, recording his journey from Baghdad to the King of the Volga Bulghārs— as part of the deputation sent by the Caliph al-Muqtadir in the year 921 AD.)

Ibn Fadlan's Journey to Russia: A Tenth-Century Traveler from Baghdad to the Volga River. Translated by Richard Frye. Markus Wiener Publishers. Princeton, New Jersey. 2005. ISBN-13: 978-1-55876-366-1. ISBN-10: 1-55876-366-X.

An Icelandic-English Dictionary, Second Edition. Initiated, Richard Cleasby. Enlarged and Completed, Gudbrand Vigfusson, MA. Oxford at the Clarendon Press, London, U.K. 1874, 1957, 1969.

The Junior Classics, Vol II: Folk Tales and Myths. P.J. Collier & Son Company, New York, NY. 1912, 1918.

Lukfus Poeticum Boreale: The Poetry of the Old Northern Tongue, From the Earliest Times to the Thirteenth Century. Vol. I: Eddic Poetry. Edited, Classified and Translated: Gudbrand Vigfusson, M.A. and F. York Powell, M.A., Clarendon Press. 1883.

The Mabinogion. (Eleven medieval Welsh prose tales.) Translated by JefFreyr Gantz. Penguin Books Ltd. 1976. ISBN-13: 978-0-140-44322-6. ISBN-10: 0-140-44322-3.

Myths of the Norsemen—From the Eddas and Sagas. Guerber, H.A. George G. Harrap & Company, London. 1909.

Norse Mythology: A Guide to the Gods, Heroes, Rituals, and Beliefs. Lindow, John. Oxford University Press, New York, NY. 2001. ISBN: 978-0-19-515382-8.

Norse Stories: Retold from the Eddas. Mabie, Hamilton Wright, Edited by Katharine Lee Bates. Rand McNally & Company. Chicago, New York, London. Copyright 1902.

Norse Mythology: Great Stories from the Eddas. Hamilton Wright Mabie. Dover Publications, 2002. ISBN 0486420825. (Apr. 10, 2002.) (Reprint. Originally Published: 1908. Dodd, Mead & Co.)

Norsk-Engelsk Ordbok. W.A. Kirkeby. H. Aschehoug & Co., A/S Gyldandal. Norsk Forlag, Oslo. 1986. ISBN: 82-573-0275-9.

Old Norse-Icelandic Literature: A Critical Guide. Ed. John Lindow and Carol Clover. Cornell Univ. Press, 1985. Rpt. University of Toronto Press, 2005.

Orkenyinga Saga: The History of the Earls of Orkeny. Translated by Hermann Pállsson and Paul Edwards, The Hogarth Press, London. 1978. ISBN 0-7012-0431-1.

The Poetic Edda. Translated by Carloyne Larrington. Oxford University Press Inc. New York, New York. 1996. ISBN: 0-19-283946-2.

The Poetic Edda. Second edition. Translated by Lee M. Hollander. University of Texas Press. Austin, Texas. 2004. ISBN: 0-292-76499-5.

Popular Epics of the Middle Ages of the Norse-German and Carlovingian Cycles – Vols. I and II. Translated by John Malcolm Ludlow. London and Cambridge: Macmillan and Co. 1865.

The Prose Edda: Norse Mythology by Snorri Sturluson. Translated by Rasmus B. Anderson. Digireads.com, 2010. ISBN: 1420934600. (Reprint. Original Published 1880.)

The Prose Edda – Norse Mythology – Snorri Sturlason. Translated by Jesse L. Byock. Penguin Classics – Penguin Group. 2005. ISBN: 0-1-140-44755-5.

The Prose Edda of Snorri Sturlason – Tales from Norse Mythology. Translated by Jean I. Young. University of California Press. Berkeley and Los Angeles, California. 1954. ISBN: 0-520-01232-1.

The Saga of the Jomsvikings. Translated by N.F. Blake. Thomas Nelson and Sons Ltd.: London, Edinburgh, Paris, Melbourne, Johannesburg, Toronto, and New York. 1962.

The Skalds. Hollander, Lee M. Princeton University Press. Princeton, New Jersey. 1945. Copyright: The American Scandinavian Foundation.

The Story of Burnt Njal. Translated by Sir George Webbe Dasent. London: J.M. Dent & Sons LTD., New York: E.P. Dutton & Co. reprint 1931.

"The Survivor" And Other Poems. Różewicz, Tadeusz. Translated by Magnus J. Krynski and Robert A. Maguire. Princeton University Press. Princeton, New Jersey. 1976.

Teutonic Myth and Legend – An introduction to the Eddas & Sagas, Beowulf, and the Nibelungenlied, etc. Mackenzie, Donald. William H. Wise & Company, New York. 1934.

Teutonic Mythology, Vols. 1-4. Grimm, Jacob. Translated from the Fourth Edition – James Steven Stallybrass. W. Swan Sonnenschein & Allen, London. 1880.

Teutonic Mythology – Gods and Goddesses of the Northland, Vols. 1–3. Rydberg, Victor, Ph.D. Translated Rasmus B. Anderson, LLD. Norrcena – Anglo Saxon Classics: Vols. 3, 4, 5. Norrcena Society. London, Copenhagen, Stockholm, Berlin, New York, 1911.

Three Northern Love Stories and Other Tales. Translated from the Icelandic by Eirikr Magnusson and William Morris. Longmans, Green, and Co. 1875. Reprinted: April 1901.

The Viking World. Graham-Campbell, James. Ticknor & Fields. New Haven and New York. 1980. ISBN: 0-89919-005-7.

Viking Women Dressed Provocatively. Posted by Jonathan Kantrowitz at 1:12 PM. Archaeology News Report, Blog Archive. Monday, February 25, 2008.

REFERENCES

The Younger Edda of Snorre Sturlason Translated I. A. Blackwell. Norrcena – Anglo Saxon Classics: Vol. 11. Norrcena Society. London, Copenhagen, Stockholm, Berlin, New York, 1911.

Additional Reading

The following resources provide insight into religious traditions and historical meanings behind Norse Mythology. These sources were not referenced when compiling this work:

Exploring the Northern Tradition: A Guide to the Gods, Lore, Rites and Celebrations from the Norse, German, and Anglo-Saxon Traditions (Exploring Series). Galina Krasskova and Swain Wodening. New Page Books / Career Pr Inc., 2005. ISBN 1564147916.

From Asgard to Valhalla: The Remarkable History of the Norse Myths. Heather O'Donoghue, I.B. Tauris Co Ltd, United Kingdom, 2008. ISBN 1845118294.

Gods and Myths of Northern Europe. Hilda Roderick Ellis Davidson. Penguin (Non-Classics), 1965. ISBN 0140136274.

Shamanism in Norse Myth and Magic: Volume One. Clive Tolley. Helsinki: Suomalainen Tiedeakatemia. 2009. ISBN 978-951-41-1028-3.

The Viking Way: Religion and War in Late Iron Age Scandinavia. Neil Price. Department of Archaeology and Ancient History at Uppsala University. 2002. Revised second edition. Oxbow Books. 2016. ISBN: 91-506-1626-9.

REFERENCES

Reference Website

The following website provided reference source materials used in this work.

http://www.archive.org/index.php

The Internet Archive, a 501(c)(3) non-profit, is a digital library of Internet sites and other cultural artifacts in digital form. Like a paper library, they provide free access to researchers, historians, scholars, and the public.

About the Author

Glenn Searfoss

Glenn Searfoss is an American author of fiction and non-fiction works in computer science, natural history, science fiction, and mythology. He lives in Colorado, USA with his wife and two boxer dogs.

NOTES